THE GROVE OF EAGLES

By Winston Graham

THE GROVE OF EAGLES

Winston Graham

———

GARDEN CITY, N.Y.

Doubleday & Company, Inc.

1964

c.2

Contents

The illegitimate son of a Cornish family is kidnapped for the Spanish and later returned with a message for his father who is to aid the Second Armada when it lands at Cornwall.

Book One

CHAPTER 1

I WAS born on the twenty-fifth of February, 1578. Later in the year my father married Dorothy Monck, an heiress, of Potheridge in Devon, and by her had fourteen children—nine sons and five daughters—of whom only four died in infancy.

I did not know my mother. I was brought up in my father's house, as his son, and bore his name of Killigrew, and was christened Maugan.

We came from St Erme, near Truro in the county of Cornwall where one Ralph Killigrew about 1240 was granted permission by Henry III to bear arms. Ralph's great-great-grandson was called Simon, and this Simon in 1385 married Joan, of Arwenack, which is at the mouth of the river Fal, and the family moved there and was enriched. Five generations later when the eighth Henry, at war with the French, thought to build a castle commanding the mouth of the river Fal, he chose as his site an old ruined fort on Killigrew land hard by Arwenack House; and the John Killigrew then living—my great-grandfather—was created first captain of the castle and knighted the same year.

This John Killigrew was a man then in middle life, stout and a little pock-marked; his portrait, which we had until it was burned, shows him to have the round face of the Killigrews, with the prominent eyes and cleft chin and fair hair that come to some of the men. He had married a rich woman, Elizabeth Trewinnard, and had gained much from the dissolution of the monasteries; so that his lands and properties extended from the river Fal to the Helford Passage, and he held the tithes of sixteen parishes and had an incoming of above six thousand pounds a year. No doubt it seemed to him that the house he lived in under the shadow of the castle was unworthy of his new wealth and status, for he decided to pull the old house down and to build in its place the biggest house in Cornwall.

So the new Arwenack in which I was born was built. It was not finished until 1567, and my great-grandfather lived only to see the last stone in place before he fell from his horse and died.

He was not a popular man, and there were not lacking people to whisper that this was an omen that overweening pride should bring no good in its wake. True the new Arwenack was seldom a happy house in my lifetime; but equally one can seek for a practical cause and see it in the simple fact that my great-grandfather overreached himself. Our family, for all its ancient lineage and good estate, lacked the solidity of great possessions such as could maintain without strain the extravagant way of life he set for it. From his time, therefore, there was a hint of the feverish and the insolvent in our lives. Each generation tried to re-establish itself; each generation failed in greater measure than the last. My grandfather and my father were much at court, spending heavily to gain royal favour and office. When they received office they could no longer afford to be scrupulous in their use of it.

But of all of this I knew nothing when I was young.

The Fal River, which is navigable as far as Tregony, broadens three miles from the sea and forms a great natural anchorage, one of the finest in the world. A mile inland from the mouth a narrow tongue of land splits its west bank, and the creek thus formed runs another mile or more off the main river to the town of Penryn, which is the main port of the river.

But at the very mouth of the river there juts out, again on its west side, a promontory of land shaped like the head of a guinea fowl. Imagine that in the head there is an eye: this is the Pendennis Castle of which my great-grandfather, my grandfather, and my father were captains; and like an eye it commands all ways of approach. Just below the neck of the guinea fowl is the house of Arwenack, and all the huge body of the bird was Killigrew land.

So Arwenack House, facing south, looks on the blue smile of the river mouth. But behind the house, behind a narrow hump of land, is the sea again, all the width of Falmouth Bay and the Channel.

I never knew if the house was built to any design. It was like a little town containing within its palisades all that was needed for life and sustenance. When I was born, there were upwards of fifty people living there. Additional to the ever growing family and near relatives there were thirty-five servants and retainers and a half-dozen hangers-on, people with some claim on my father's generosity or forbearance who lived and fed with us.

The buildings of the house enclosed a quadrangle on three sides, the fourth facing the harbour being open except for a castellated tower with low walls flanking it and a big gate under the tower. By this gate the house was approached by anyone landing from the sea, and over the gate, supported by cantilevers, was the Killigrew coat of arms, an eagle with two heads and spread wings. At the north corner of the house was another tower pierced with loopholes for bows or muskets, and tall enough to command the landward approaches. On all sides the house was protected by stockades and earthworks, for, situated as it was in so exposed and isolated a position, not even the castle near by could give it complete immunity from invasion by sea.

My own bedroom—which I shared with my half-brother John, who was by eighteen months the younger—was in the left wing of the house and looked over towards the harbour. It was eight feet broad by eleven feet long and it had a tall narrow window at one end with the bed beside the door at the other, and a second door leading into the bedrooms beyond. When the south-easterly gales blew, the wind would whistle into the room however tightly latched the window and suck its way out with such vehemence that our straw mat would float and quiver as if a snake were under it. The room was plainly but comfortably furnished, for besides the bedstead we had two stools, a window cushion of needlework, canvas to cover the window at night, a box of shelves, and on the wall an old map of the French Brittany coast drawn by Baptista Boazio.

All my childhood memories are of a dark room looking out on a bright scene, because the window for all its tallness seemed not so much to admit light as to stress the brightness without. The first memory ever I had was of John my half-brother being fed by his wet-nurse—he was breast fed until he was three—and myself tiring of the entertainment and trotting to the window and looking out of the darkness of the room and seeing a great blueness of still water like a blue dish, with a ship whose chocolate sails were just crumpling as she came to anchor, and behind that the green wooded hills of the east bank of the river.

All my early memories are of water, of sea and river and rain and wind and sky. Either I was looking down on it or was abroad on it with some older member of the family, or I was down at the lake where we bred our swans or I was climbing among the rocks below the castle while the waves showered me with spray. Before I was old enough to reason I came to love the sea, to know it as an element as natural as earth. As soon as I was old enough to reason I came to fear it—not as an element but for what it could bring.

For always we lived under the threat of Spain. There had been no peace as long as I could remember, and we never knew when the enemy galleons might appear off our coast. When the First Armada came and passed us by I was ten; and I remember on the thirtieth of July of that year, which was a Saturday, standing with my father and John and my great-uncle Peter and my uncle Thomas on the highest turret of the castle and screwing up our eyes to scan the horizon.

We got a sight of the ships in the late afternoon as the wind freshened and the haze over the sea cleared. The great fleet, of which we could see only a part, looked elevated above the sea like castles, like our Pendennis Castle, built on the horizon, the sun glinting on them and gilding them. As dusk fell Walter Powell of Penryn put in and told us that he had passed close by and that he had counted many more than a hundred ships and that they all had their flags and pennants streaming and that the bands on board were playing martial music. My great-uncle Peter, though by then above sixty years of age, had already put to sea in a coaster to follow the enemy up channel.

But even after the first danger was past, and even after the great rejoicings when it became known that the Armada was sunk and dispersed, we knew well that this was not the end of the war for us.

Nor was it only Spaniards that the sea brought. We suffered no menace from English pirates; but in the Channel there were other ships of foreign marque, from Turkey and Algiers and Tunis. When I was five John Michell of Truro lost two ships in the river, six miles up river from the mouth, boarded and seized; and the coast towns of St Ives and Penzance and Market Jew were seldom free from risk of raid and fire and abduction. Before I was born, before we were at war with Spain, French ships one day, being pursued by Spanish ships of war, took refuge in the river Fal. The Spaniards sailed past our castle, following the French ships in, which themselves retreated farther and farther up the river in a battle lasting three hours. At length the French ships were driven aground at Malpas near Truro, and then Sir John Arundell, our kinsman from Trerice, sent messages to the Spanish admiral to try to stop the fighting; but the Spaniards refused and bombarded the French for another two hours before being forced to withdraw by the falling tide.

All this my grandmother told me, for it had happened when she came to Arwenack as a young widow to marry my grandfather.

This was before my grandmother took against me.

I have many memories of youth. But over all there is the first memory, of being within four walls like in a dark cell, pressed down, and looking out on a world of vivid brightness, of being held down in darkness like a prisoner and wanting to get out, of a sense of confinement and constriction. And there is the second memory, the longer memory, of there being no peace in the world, of fear and danger outside and a limited safety within.

We were always in those days at the mercy of rumour, of the false alarm, the whisper behind the hand, of a change of atmosphere, of a growing tension without cause, of suspicion of treachery and betrayal. A calf would die for no reason, or the horses would be restless in their stables, or a cloud would form at sunset red-tipped and shaped like the Judgment Seat. Or Meg Levant, one of the serving maids, would come in with a story she had had of Harold Tregwin of Gluvias, who had heard that a Papist priest had been found in a secret cupboard in the house of the Roscarrocks at Pentire and they were all arrested.

When I was four I was put to study with horn-book and primer under Parson Merther, the chaplain of the house, and the following year my brother John joined me. Every year, almost, another came: Thomas, then Odelia, then Henry. Then there were no more for a while because Grace died at three months. With our group often was my cousin Paul Knyvett, a sulky boy older than I by a year, and another, more distant cousin Belemus Roscarrock who was a year older still but very lazy and mutinous.

By the time I was eleven I had been introduced to Lily's *Grammar* and Recorde's *Arithmetic* and the *Colloquies* of Erasmus, and had got by heart some Ovid and Juvenal. I had learned the first twenty propositions of Euclid and knew something of history and the stars.

Each morning the whole house would rise at sun-up for prayers, then we children would have to read a chapter of the Bible aloud before we broke our fast: we would have meal bread with porridge and sometimes a slice of cold mutton or a piece of Holland cheese. Parson Merther would watch over us, fussy as an old woman, his long yellow fingers picking at his doublet, his small, sword-point eyes ever on the move to find cause for reproof in our manners or our dress. John was caught blowing on his porridge to cool it, Odelia had forgotten to wipe her nose, Paul had left off his garters, we all bent too close over our food.

This was a special care of Parson Merther's: even at lessons we were made to work with head upright lest humours should fall into the forehead and cause injury to the eyes.

After dinner at noon we would have three hours of the afternoon free, when we could practise fencing with rapier or sword, or go hawking with one of the grooms, or take a boat and play on the river, or sit telling each other frightening stories in the dark aromatic shed in the herb garden where the herbs were dried. Or we would play with the dogs or help feed the horses or even ride a nag if Thomas Rosewarne, the steward, was in a good mood. Or we would climb the elm trees or play in the thick wood going down to the swan pool.

But we had to be in and dressed and properly clean to be at board for supper at six. Having supped, we had an hour with Parson Merther again and would have to repeat some paragraphs out of Cicero's *Epistles* or some other good author we had studied in the morning; and if we got them wrong we were beaten before going to bed.

I remember especially my fourteenth birthday. My father's sixth legitimate child, Walter, had been ill for three weeks of a quartan ague and had had many fits. My father's wife, Dorothy, was great again but there was to be a banquet that evening. Two ships were in the bay, and there were to be a dozen guests at table. So the day had flown, with hurryings and scurryings of servants and preparations of food.

With my step-mother so industrious in child-bearing, my grandmother often held the reins of the household—or perhaps, being how she was, she would have retained them in any case. When there were guests she always took charge, and I think although my grandfather had been dead seven years she had never really given way either to her son or her daughter-in-law. Certainly she was the only person in the house who did not stir uneasily at my father's footstep.

I had spent the afternoon with Belemus Roscarrock. We had played with a tennis ball on the archery lawn until driven off. Then we had tried stalking the crows which milled around the newly turned earth of the turnip field. When we tired of this, having killed only one, we mooched back in the fading light to the house and stood a few moments looking at the two vessels, both shallops, which lay close in to the shelter of the land.

"*Neptune* and *Dolphin*," said Belemus, scratching his black hair. "It's more than six months since they were here before."

"I don't remember 'em," I said.

"No, they were over at Helford. Did not show their faces here. The *Crane* was on the prowl. We'd best be going in. Old Ink-horn will be chewing on his gums with rage."

Although I did not always get on with Belemus, I found his company challenging and a stimulus. A heavy boy, already at sixteen a full man's size, with black eyes set deep in his face like cave dwellings overhung by rock, he talked cynically out of a wide full mouth. He seemed to have so much more knowledge of affairs than I had.

"You at least," I said, "should hardly fear Ink-horn, for although you'll not work you are his favourite."

"Ah, and do you know why I am his favourite? It's *because* I don't fear him, see?"

He turned to go in, but I stared a few minutes longer at the two low dark ships, their masts swaying slowly with the swell. Behind them, on the other side of the river's mouth, there was a light in St Mawes Castle, built at the same time and for the same purpose as Pendennis but indifferently sited. I had often wondered why Parson Merther treated Belemus with greater respect than the rest of us. Was I being incited to rebellion so that my cousin could sit back and be entertained by the result?

The evening was cold, and I remember the sense of warmth I felt as I came into the quadrangle under the tower and through the central gate and saw the lights of the house beginning to glimmer. In the south corner the lights were brightest where my grandmother's room was and where she would now be dressing. As I moved to go in a girl came hurrying across the grass, taking a short cut from one wing to the other; it was something the maids did not dare to do in the daylight. I drew back intending to jump out and frighten her but she had already seen me, and instead of darting away she came towards me.

"Walter is mortal sick, Master Maugan. He has just been taken with another tedious fit. Go quietly if you enter his room."

I said: "Meg, Meg, thin as a peg," but only from habit, and really thinking of what she had told me. Last night there had been comings and goings all the dark hours through our bedroom. I had never been ill in my life and the idea of illness interested me. We had been taken in to see Grace last year, and I had kissed her chubby dead little face and had found it soft and cold and smelling.

When I got in I rubbed my hands and face hurriedly and dressed before Parson Merther could come in and provoke that trial of strength that Belemus was inciting me to; but in fact Ink-horn was busy next door and saw me not at all that evening.

The banqueting hall held not above its normal fifty persons that night, for some ten of our servants who usually supped at the same time were needed extra in the kitchen and to wait at table. The hall took up most of the middle part of the house and was served by kitchens behind and separate from the rest of the house. A handsome room in the summer, it grew very damp in winter; the plaster walls would run with moisture and a chill spread over it that no arras could keep out. Tonight a big fire had been lighted early, and since there was little wind it was cosy enough.

The top table was full, and six of the lesser guests had been put on the end of our smaller table which was at the side of the hall. The trestle table and benches for the servants ran crosswise at the bottom. The beech-wood fire made dancing reflections on the oriel window opposite, and the latten candlesticks held twenty-four candles of fine wax, not the stinking tallow of ordinary evenings.

New rushes had been strewn on the floor and most of the dogs had been banished. My father had a weakness for dogs and would seldom bring himself to order one destroyed, so they bred and multiplied into all sizes and shapes of mongrel. There was seldom a time without puppies and seldom a time—except when guests were expected—when there were not pools on the floor and sometimes even on the chairs. Most rooms in the house had a smell of dog about them, but in the hall it was always strongest.

A child accepts its environment unthinking, unseeing for many years. Then comes a day when the mind unlinks itself and stands apart for the first time, looking around with a new eye. For the first time that night I wondered at the strange variety and quality of the guests who sat at my father's table. One day it would be our cousins the Arundells or the Godolphins, or the Bassets, distinguished and wealthier than ourselves; another it would be the captain of a naval pinnace sent to watch the coasts for pirates, together with Hannibal Vivian across from St Mawes Castle to complain about his ordnance. Then there were banquets given to people in small authority about the county, and all this did not take into account the occasional visits of the really great. Seldom a week passed without entertaining of some sort. But the strangest of all were these noisy feasts given to the captains and crews of the ships which quietly from time to time dropped anchor in our bay.

Captain Elliot of *Dolphin* was a man of sickly complexion, dark-bearded, raw-boned and thin. He had a nose which whistled when he breathed through it, and he spoke scarcely ever above a voice used for confidences. All his orders afloat, one felt, must go through his mate, William Love, who came from Weymouth, a red-faced jolly man with strange greedy eyes. They were both dressed for the banquet, but the others with them were all sixes and sevens, most in ill-fitting clothes which might have been made for someone else, rough spoken, long-haired and unshaven, coarse of manner. Captain Burley from *Neptune* was a big pale-haired shabby man who looked a rogue.

That my grandmother should choose to sit between him and Elliot I found hard to understand. For my grandmother was a great lady.

Others at this banquet were my father's unmarried sister, Mary Killigrew, and Henry Knyvett and Bethia Wolverstone. My grandmother was the daughter of Philip Wolverstone of Suffolk, and Mistress Wolverstone was her sister, a gaunt ailing woman well on in years. Henry Knyvett was my grandmother's son by her first marriage. This Henry Knyvett lived with his wife and four children at one of my father's manor houses, Rosemerryn, but he more often than not ate at Arwenack, for he did not agree with his wife, and his second son, Paul, lived with us all the time.

In the corner by the stairs three men played tunes, but as supper went on their music rose and fell like a raft in rough weather, half submerged in the sea of voices.

My father was always at his best when entertaining, and in those days he was a handsome man, still in his early forties, a trifle short of stature but fresh-complexioned, with a fine full head of blond hair, expressionless, rather prominent blue eyes, and a light brown moustache, silky and pampered above a firm but cleft chin. He drank and gambled and wenched much of his time away in a feckless carefree fashion, though his temper was a trifle unstable and his determination could be great if his own welfare was concerned.

On this noisy, fire-flickering, greasy company came suddenly Parson Merther, blinking at the noise and light, sidling round against the walls of the room like a cockroach until he came behind my father's chair, whence he ventured forward and whispered some words in my father's ear. It so happened that the players had come to the end of their piece, and talk too hesitated as guests and servants stared.

"What is it, John?" Lady Killigrew, my grandmother, said. "News of Walter?"

"Yes. Wat is dead." He turned unemotionally to the others. "It is my son. At the tender age of five. My chaplain will say a prayer or two."

Everyone stumbled to their feet while Parson Merther muttered a long prayer. He was about to start another but my father grunted and cut him short. After we had all settled in our chairs Captain Elliot asked some whispered question but my father said:

"No, God's eyes. It will give him no aid to break up now. His mother is with him. He died a Christian. What more is there to it?"

Yet there was more to it, for talk in the room would not get going again. My father sounded callous but I was not sure he was as callous as he seemed. He kept wiping his moustaches with a stained napkin, and he ate no more but blinked stonily across the room over the rim of his glass.

In another silence I heard Captain Burley say to my grandmother:

"We need the stuff bad, your ladyship. It is not to be found in every port, and we'll pay well; you know that."

"With what?" said Lady Killigrew, but I never heard the reply, for a servant went by with a clatter of dishes.

"With what?" whispered Belemus. "With frog's kidneys and chicken's eyes and the soft parts of a tortured dog. That's all he has to pay with, for his mother is a witch."

Ink-horn was leaving the hall again, and I realised thankfully that tonight we were to be left undisturbed instead of hurried away to bed.

"Six fits of a quartan ague," my father said sulkily. "Many would have recovered from it. But Walter was of too fine a stock. The fine are taken up to God and the coarse are left here for the Devil's work."

"I think it was more than the ague," said Lady Killigrew. "Like as not he was liver-grown. I lost two of your sisters that way and the second I suffered to be opened. The liver was rust-coloured and swollen, no pretty sight."

My father thrust his platter violently away from him, but did not reply. No one wished to be the object of his attention now. In the uncomfortable silence Lady Killigrew motioned a footman and sent him with a message to the players to strike up another tune.

"You were saying, Captain Elliot?"

"I was saying, your ladyship? Oh, yes, I was saying that there is no ship of war in the Irish Sea, or but rarely, and there are valuable cargoes afloat every day. I wonder Mr Killigrew does not petition for one."

Lady Killigrew adjusted a pin. "It is not in Mr Killigrew's commission to command the Irish Sea, Captain Elliot. He is hard set because of the parsimony of the Privy Council to defend one castle and a strip of coast, and to keep down pirates."

"Such parsimony," said Burley, "I can hardly conceive'll run to the lengths of depriving so important a post of common ordnance."

"Indeed it does, Captain Burley," said my grandmother. "You'd be surprised at the constant efforts Mr Killigrew makes, by letter and by personal appeal, for sufficiency of small armaments of all sorts. He does not get them. Even today, with the Spanish threat in no way abated, we are pared to the bone. Mr Killigrew receives twelve pence a day as captain, which is the same sum as is paid to the master mason at Boscastle Pier. We have our deputy captain—Foster here; a master gunner—Carminow there; two other gunners, and the musters of Budock to call on in need. To supply them we have not above twenty calivers, four barrels of powder, and three culverin mounted.

Mr Killigrew has spent a fortune out of his own pocket, as he has told you."

"Your ladyship has my deepest sympathy," said Captain Elliot. "It is a bitter reflection that those who serve our country most are the most often beggared by it."

"There's some as find their labours not unrewarding," said Captain Burley, swilling back another draught and wiping his mouth on his sleeve. Everything this man said he said with a sneer.

Soon afterwards the chief guests left the room, and servants began to clear away, picking their way among overturned chairs and spilt wine and a half-dozen sleeping sailors. In one corner three men were gambling and seemed likely to come to blows, among them an evil-faced sailor called Aristotle Totle. Candles guttered and dripped on the tables. The beech-wood had burned dead, and grey ash was scattered in the hearth. The musicians had given up the struggle, and Dick Stable, who was the harpist, was feeding scraps to my father's spaniels.

"See," said Belemus, nudging my elbow, "the captains have gone off for their private talks. You were asking me why these men came here. Now if you could listen you would know."

"Well, I cannot, so I never shall."

"Ah, that depends, doesn't it."

"On what?"

We left the great hall and walked slowly along the panelled passage to the south wing. We passed the door of the drawing room chamber where our guests were likely to be. Light came from two cracks in the door. After we were past Belemus said in a low voice: "There you are, witless, you can see in."

"But someone might come."

"If you're interested I'll watch for you."

I hesitated, breathing in sensations of doubt and conspiracy; then I went to the door. The top crack was about a foot below eye level. The wood had shrunk and split, and one could see through. I heard my grandmother's harsh cough.

Captain Burley was talking. ". . . if to that we add five pounds of Levant silk dyed watchet blue, and two cases of figs, that's more'n the value of two paltry barrels of powder."

"I cannot strip my poor defences any barer. If the Spaniards come. . . ."

"Oh, if the Spaniards come, Mr Killigrew. . . ." This was Captain Elliot, whispering, not quite audible. "Ten barrels of powder would not suffice. If they come . . . Armada double the size of the last . . . come with whips specially made for the naked backs of Eng-lishwomen . . . but no attempt in the coming summer."

"What information?"

"Private but authentic, your ladyship. *Dolphin* travels widely . . . Blavet last month, the Groyne in December. . . . You could dispense with your last demi-culverin and suffer no hurt."

One of the dogs, Christian, stirred and growled in his sleep. I could just see my father's head as it rested on his hand, his fair moustache drooping over it. Somewhere behind him there was the clink and bub-ble of wine in a goblet.

"Make us a better proposition. One that we can entertain."

"Well, Lady Killigrew, you know what it would entail as well as I do—"

"Nay," my father cut in, "I do not know that I am in the mood for it tonight. My child lies upstairs, but just gone from us. . . ."

Elliot whispered his sympathy.

"My position," said my father, "is one of vast responsibility with scant, paltry, minimal resources. Every month I embase myself writing to Cecil . . . England's safety, England's very survival may depend on the quality of her few real commanders in the south-west. Grenville agreed with me—God rest his soul. Ralegh agrees and has prom-ised. . . ."

Something passed then that I could not catch, but Captain Burley must have made a remark which was instantly resented. My father broke into one of his sudden angers, which were always nearer the surface than one suspected.

". . . I'm not a lackey to be gibed at! We've served four monarchs in our time at the castle and lost half an inheritance in the process! To be so accused in my own home. . . ."

"Well, your honour, it's commonly so spoken, and that Lady Killi-grew herself was involved and that two of her servants was hanged for it—"

A goblet of wine rolled on the floor. "If that is the sort of calumny to which I am to be subjected—"

"Begging your ladyship's pardon," came William Love's voice. "Rich-ard Burley meant no offence, I'll wager. If so—"

"Let it be discussed as you will. I'll no longer be a party to it."

Conversation passed back and forth, cooling and calming and smoothing over. All the same I should have taken warning. I did not, until a shadow moved across the crack of the door. Then too late I stumbled back as someone opened it for my grandmother, and I stared into her cold grey eyes.

There had been little to see through the crack, but now all the room was there beyond her shoulder: the brace of candlesticks, flames bobbing, the heavy, pale-haired figure of Burley sneering angrily in the leather studded armchair, Love standing behind it; Elliot fingering the gold ring in his ear; my father pouring wine, face flushed, his quilted yellow doublet open and awry.

Yet all the time I was staring into my grandmother's eyes. One of the dogs had come after her, its tail wagging unsteadily. She pushed it away with her foot and without speaking to me swept on.

CHAPTER 2

ELLIOT and Love and Burley and their friends stayed feasting all the following day, but they left at nine in the evening and caught the midnight tide. The day of Walter's funeral they were gone and the waters of the river mouth were so still and glassy that no ships might ever have been there to break the reflections of tree and hill and distant fort. To my surprise, my grandmother never spoke to me about her discovery of me that night.

Spring came, and we children worked reluctantly through the long bright mornings longing for the afternoon hours of freedom and adventure. Usually we stayed within the palisades, but sometimes we ventured abroad in the keeping of a groom called Rose who not seldom risked a thrashing for allowing us to wander farther than we should. We had a tiny boat with a single sail and a pair of oars; in it we sometimes sailed well up the river.

Both river banks, except for enclaves where houses or villages stood, were covered with thick dark woods, cut through here and there with miry tracks. Squirrels, badgers, foxes, and hares abounded, and sometimes underfoot the viper would lift his head. Venturing into this wild country was explicitly forbidden us by Parson Merther, but sometimes we penetrated a few hundred yards. Many strange stories were told of these woods, that they were old, old as the birth of the world, and that they had an influence on all people born or living in them. Strange sects flourished there; witches lived in the far reaches of some of the narrower creeks. These smaller creeks filled up with glimmering oily water at high tide but twice daily sank away to silent yellow mud on which the only sound was the cry and flutter of birds. Many an unsuspecting child, we were told, had strayed up them never to return. Some of the bigger birds were like children, lost children crying, and who was to say they were not?

In the summer we proved the age and magic of the woods by diving and swimming under the water just at the edge of our enclosed land by the entrance to Penryn Creek. There you could see the trees that had grown there before ever the river was. Clusters of tree stumps still existed three fathoms under water, hazel and oak and beech and fir, and at low tide you could see the flag iris and the ferns.

On the promontory of land dividing Penryn Creek from the Fal River proper lived the Trefusis family, of Trefusis, but we seldom visited or spoke. I did not then know any reason why and as a matter of course took my father's part, but the two families had quarrelled over the generations, and it was well known John Trefusis did not at all approve of Killigrew high-handedness. My father used to say that with the mouth of the Fal held between the pincers of Pendennis and St Mawes castles, Trefusis Point felt the nip every time the pincers closed.

Farther up the Fal on the left bank, near the ferry across the river, was Tolverne, in which lived cousins of ours, a branch of the Arundell family. Jonathan, the elder boy, was in his twenties, but Thomas and Elizabeth were of our age. Sir Anthony Arundell of Tolverne, the father, had become an eccentric of late, living a recluse's life, often not rising from his bed until five in the afternoon, sometimes not retiring until daybreak. My father said the woods had got him.

One day in early May we children were invited to spend the day there, so we sailed up the river in the company of Rose and another servant. Tolverne was a much smaller house than ours, but it was convenient of scope and less sprawling and would have been pleasant had it not been so dark and close. In front of the main windows was a shallow lawn, but surrounding that were the trees, crowding close, with a path cut through them to the river. Many of the trees near the house were conifers and even in the winter kept the light away. To me, brought up on the airy promontory of Arwenack, the house was always secretive and strange.

We found there today besides the three young Arundells, Gertrude and Hoblyn Carew, the children of Richard Carew of Antony near Plymouth, Gertrude being in her middle teens and Hoblyn two years younger; and also Sue Farnaby from Treworgan near Truro, a slim girl of about fourteen with a piquant tilted face and black hair; and Jack Arundell of Trerice, who at fifteen had been head of the Arundell Trerices ever since his father died when he was an infant.

Jonathan Arundell of Tolverne, though twenty-five, seemed to find as much pleasure in the afternoon as any of us, especially when it put him in the company of Gertrude Carew. Soon we began a game called Who's from Home?, which ranged over the widest area of the garden and grounds, and to my slight alarm I found myself paired with Sue Farnaby. I had never been alone with a girl of my own age in quite this way before, for the essence of the game was that it should be stealthy and secretive, and that led to whispering close to ears and giggling and an air of conspiracy which put you on a familiar footing right off.

Sue had the advantage of having played this game at Tolverne before, so she knew all the best hiding places and all the paths through the woods. Soon we had lost the others and were on a narrow path by the river from which we could see our own little boat with Rose sitting fishing from it, a row-boat crossing at the ferry, and a hoy of thirty or forty tons struggling down the river against the breeze.

"It's best to sit here for a while," she said. "The others will seek each other by the house. After we have given them time to scatter we can creep back and be first home."

She settled on an outcrop of rock and smoothed the thin scarf tied over her ears. "My father is a farmer and merchant. We do not own Treworgan, we rent it from your father. My mother knew your mother in Devon."

"My mother?" I said, and then realised she meant Mrs Killigrew. "Yes. They grew up near each other."

"That is my step-mother. My own mother is dead."

"Oh, I'm sorry. . . . My mother almost died when I was born; that's why I'm an only child."

"Are you lonely at home?"

She turned and gave me a wide glinting beautiful smile. "No . . . I have so many friends."

The smile made her a new one for life. She shaded her eyes with her hand. "Do you know Sir Anthony Arundell? Isn't that him coming across the ferry?"

There were two men in the boat. "The front one in the crimson cloak? Yes, you cannot mistake his white hair."

Sue Farnaby said: "I have been friendly with Elizabeth Arundell for years. I come here often, and sometimes she comes to us, though our house is humble to hers. Why were you called Maugan? Is it Welsh?"

I laughed. "I don't think so. Not this way of spelling it. There was a St Maugan, wasn't there, who founded a church near Padstow? I have never thought about it. Why were you called Susan?"

"Susanna," she said, "after my grandmother."

I laughed again. There was nothing in the conversation, but at the time it seemed light and witty and suddenly joyous. We chatted on until she got up and gave me a hand. "We should be going: they'll have tired of waiting by now."

Giggling together we began to creep back by another path towards the house. I wished I could wander through these woods all afternoon linked to this slim, pale, black-haired creature who led me on by one hand, while the other gathered her skirts together at the front so that they should not be caught by brambles. When she laughed her teeth gleamed like sudden sunshine; her skin was strangely fine; her eyes had twenty expressions from the darkest gravity to grey-green laughter. For me at that moment she was all mystery and enchantment: she was the first woman.

We found ourselves within sight of the house; and there ahead of us crouching behind a bush was Belemus with little Odelia Killigrew who had drawn him as her partner. I had no wish to speak to them, but Sue Farnaby said we must, so in three minutes we had "captured" them and were concerting together how we might get back to our winning point on the other side of the house without being seen.

Sue said we could go through the house: there was an arched door ahead of us in a stone wall and beyond it steps to another narrower door which was open. We found ourselves in a dark room which had a strange look about it, there being ornaments and small pictures and a smell of burnt herbs. Before we could go on Sir Anthony came in followed by the man who had been with him in the rowing boat.

Sue said: "I beg your pardon, sir; we were playing a game and had lost our way."

Sir Anthony had a flat plump face which my father said had once been handsome. The flesh was no longer healthy; it was as if some subtle corrosion of stress had touched it. He waved a dismissive hand, but the man with him said: "These are your children, sir?"

He was a stout man, his stoutness being in all ways different from Sir Anthony's, as a taut strong rope is different from a frayed slack one.

"No. . . . Friends of my children. This is Susanna Farnaby of Treworgan. This is Maugan and Odelia Killigrew, and Belemus Roscarrock, who also lives at Arwenack."

"Roscarrock," said the man. "That is a famous Catholic name."

"My father is a Catholic," said Belemus.

We were about to move off when Lady Arundell came in. Sir Anthony said: "Oh, Anne, this is Mr Humphry Petersen, I don't think you will have met him before. Though you'll have heard our cousins speak of him."

"You come from Chideock?" Lady Arundell said coldly.

"Not directly, my lady, though I know it. I have been abroad for some months."

"You have news of war, then?"

"Nothing that makes good hearing. The English have suffered a heavy defeat in Brittany."

"Ah?" said Sir Anthony. "I hadn't heard it."

"Well, sir, it's serious enough to prejudice English hopes in France for a long time. We laid seige to Craon—a thousand English, some six hundred Germans and some loyal French troops under the Prince of Dombe and the Prince of Condy. A large force of Spanish and League forces—upward of six thousand strong, sir, under the Duc de Mercoeur —launched a surprise attack and cut us to pieces. We lost two-thirds of our total strength, bearing the brunt of the attack. The loyal French suffered much less but fled and found refuge in neighbouring towns, but we had no place of refuge, sir, and were hardly an army at all by dawn of the next day."

Lady Arundell said: "Susanna, in the orchard under the vine bower you will find my lawn cap. Fetch it for me, will you."

"Of course, ma'am."

"Did I hear say you were a Killigrew, boy?" Mr Petersen said to me as I was going past him.

"Yes, sir."

"The Killigrews of Arwenack, hard by the mouth of the Fal," said Sir Anthony Arundell. "John Killigrew has a numerous brood."

"Yes, I know of him well. He governs Pendennis Castle. And are you the eldest boy?"

"Yes, sir, leastwise. . . ."

"Leastwise?"

"Maugan is a pack-saddle boy," said Sir Anthony, peering at me as if I was not there. "John is his eldest, who's twelve or so; you'll see him in the garden. Thomas is a year younger, and Odelia, here, a year younger still."

Just then Jack Arundell of Trerice and Thomas Arundell came in to see what had become of us, so we went off with them and rejoined the others. We lay for a time in the grass, talking and laughing and planning what we should play next.

Suddenly Odelia dropped a little stone into her lap and said: "What is recusancy? I have not heard of it before."

"Recusancy?" said Thomas. "Who used the word?"

"It was your visitor, Thomas. I did not mean it had been spoken out here. Is it some wrong word?"

"There is nothing wrong with the word," said Jack Arundell of Trerice brusquely. "It is what it stands for that's dislikable. Recusancy is being a Catholic and refusing to change, refusing to come to church, refusing to be a protestant of the English Church."

"Are you a recusancy, Belemus?" Odelia asked.

"Recusant," said Belemus, sucking a piece of grass. "My father is."

"Mean to say he would fight for the Spaniards?" Hoblyn Carew asked.

"Of course," said Belemus. "I'm a Spaniard in disguise. Did you not know?"

Sarcasm was too much for some of the younger ones and they wriggled uncomfortably.

"They say there are spies and traitors everywhere," said Hoblyn. "They say that if the Spaniards landed there would be traitors in every town. And they say another Armada is coming."

You could hear the east wind stirring the top of the trees. Odelia picked up two stones and threw them into the air, trying to pick up the one in her lap before catching the two as they came down.

"And what," she said, "is a pack-saddle boy?"

Two of the older ones laughed, and I thought Sue Farnaby was one of them. Belemus said: "When you are born the midwife puts you on a horse, and if you take a toss you are known as—"

Thomas interrupted: "Being a pack-saddle boy means you are a bastard."

Thomas was the second of the Tolverne children; nine or ten years younger than his brother, but still older and bigger than I. The other two were gentle and rather frail and without guile, but he was a thruster, with tight curled hair, a white bland face like his father's but without the sensitivity, a pampered body.

I said: "You are quite a know-all, aren't you."

"Well, it's the truth. It may taste poor, but then the truth often does. It's a pill that has to be swallowed."

"Other things too may have to be swallowed. Like this mud, for instance."

"It means," he said, "that your mother like as not was a light woman and that, for certain, you have no name. You bear the name of Killigrew for a kindness only. I doubt if you was ever baptised."

He got up as I went for him, but I had the strength of anger. I put him down twice and broke two of his front teeth. Odelia and Elizabeth were screaming, and soon the elders rushed out and there was much to do, with no one taking my side except Sue Farnaby and Jack Arundell of Trerice, and the elders were too angry to listen to either of them.

The party did not last long after that. Making the most of a need to catch the falling tide, we left in a subdued silence. I thought I would never be invited there again and probably would never see Susanna Farnaby again or be permitted to roam through the woods with her, with the sun shining and the trees budding and the river birds crying and a light breeze rustling the grasses. I felt as if I had destroyed some part of my youth.

In spite of the ebbing tide the head breeze was so fresh as we came out into Carrick Road that Rose and the other servant had to lower the sail and take to the oars. I only spoke once and that was to Belemus as we neared our landing jetty.

"I don't understand it. Would you not have fought him if he had said as much to you? Then why did he say it? What had I done to offend him?"

Belemus smiled his cavernous old man's smile. "Witless, don't you know you had spent all the afternoon enamouring with the little girl he most fancies for himself?"

Rose was the bearer of an angry note written by Lady Arundell to my father complaining that I had attacked her son as if I were out of Bedlam and had done his looks permanent harm and perhaps his very health; she trusted I should be suitably dealt with.

I was. My father was out, but my grandmother ordered me to be well thrashed, not by Parson Merther, who had no muscle, but by Carminow the gunner, who knew how to draw blood. And then I was confined to my room for three days on bread and water.

The pain and the hunger were things quite light beside the sense of humiliation. Something budding for the first time in my heart had been burned away. I went over the scenes of the afternoon a hundred times, and all the pleasure of the first hours was poisoned by the disgrace of the last.

On the second day of the confinement came a new and unexpected frustration: we woke that morning, which was a Thursday, to find ten ships of war anchored in the roads.

The fleet was under the personal command of Walter Ralegh, with Sir John Burrough as second-in-command, and was being sent out to attack the Isthmus of Panama and to try to capture the treasure ships of the Plate. That night my father was to banquet Ralegh and Burrough and a picked company of officers and gentlemen. They were sailing on the morrow.

All I could see from my window was the passing to and fro of small boats ferrying people aboard and ashore. I paced up and down most of the time, biting the skin round my fingers, and when Rose brought me bread and water at five I kicked it over and ground the bread into the floorboards. When John and the others came to bed at eight he said the guests were still at table, so I pulled a shirt on and a pair of breeches and went to see.

I stole across to a bedroom which was my uncle Simon Killigrew's when he was home and stared out across the river mouth. It was a moonless night but starlit, and I could see the lights of the vessels and pick out their shapes. I wished I was going with them, to glory or to death. If I had no name I must make one.

I took a devious way towards the great hall, avoiding contact with the servants. I had seen Sir Walter Ralegh twice before and could guess which was Sir John Burrough; but I could not make out the others, though I knew one was a Grenville and another a Crosse and a third called Thynne, all west-country men.

Supper was near its end, and for this meal no servants had dined but only the twenty guests and their hosts. Ralegh seemed to take little part in the conversation, his face sombre and as if his mind were elsewhere. I was surprised that he looked so sour and preoccupied, with this splendid new venture just opening for him. Sir John Burrough looked a kinder, more tolerant man, and I wondered if I could run after him when he left tonight and ask to be taken. I thought of Grenville last year who had fought the whole Spanish fleet for fifteen hours alone, withstanding eight hundred rounds of shot before being overwhelmed. Ralegh was his cousin.

I wondered what it must be like to be the Queen's favourite, perhaps the most powerful man in all England; and now leading a fleet against the enemy. I wished fervently that I might grow up. I felt that all opportunity was passing while I was still too young to play any part.

The following evening when they had all gone I went down into the big parlour to see my father and to receive from him what final admonition he deemed necessary before the incident was closed. To my surprise he seemed now to think lightly of it all.

"The Arundells were always touchy as to their looks—not that they ever had none anyway. But you'll have a grief of a life if you fight everyone who calls you bastard, my boy."

"No, father, it was not so much that; it was what he said—"

"Never forget that there have been others such as yourself who have left their mark. William the Conqueror was one, and people tumble over their own heels to claim him as their ancestor."

I watched my grandmother, who was adding some accounts. It was due to her, though I did not realise it until years later, that there was little risk of my having to seek for my mother among the servants. It was a rule she had enforced with an iron hand even in her husband's time. What her menfolk did outside the house was very much their own affair—but they did not, in peril almost of their lives, embroil themselves with the servants.

"Remember one word," my father said, yawning and stretching his legs across a footstool. "Success. If you are a good success in your life people will forgive you far worse things than a little matter of your mother's wedding. You may do murder, you may betray your country, you may savage women, you may steal from orphans, you may have pillaged and perjured and burned—only let the outcome be success and the world will fawn on you."

"Yes, father."

"But don't consume your substance in your country's service, or you'll be brought near to beggary. To hold office in our age is to hold your purse over a hungry mouth that takes all and gives nothing in return. Even your great-uncles Henry and William who are as close to the Queen as a pair of father confessors—in and out of her bedchamber, running secret errands for her—even your uncles admit themselves to be deeper in debt with each year that passes. At least, one has a knighthood for it, which is more than I, though I *am* head of the family and my father was knighted and his father before him, and they living in less troublous times than this. . . . By rights I should have had it ten years ago."

"Leave the boy be, John," said my grandmother, coughing harshly. "Leave him to learn his own lessons."

My father drank deep from his mug. "We all learn, but some of us leave it a trifle late. If I had the last twenty years over again I should do one thing or the other: till my own soil and never budge from it and become a wealthy vegetable, like the Boscawens over across the river; or live all my life at court and reap the benefits the way Ralegh has done. Half and half gives you the sour edge of both worlds. . . ."

"The best way to teach the boy," said Lady Killigrew, "is not by book or precept but by sending him into the world to taste it for himself. The confines of Arwenack are too restrictive for him."

"I don't see it," said my father.

"Others see it."

My father took out his pocket mirror and began to turn up the ends of his moustache. "Presently. In good time."

"Who is my mother, sir?" I asked.

"You see," said Lady Killigrew.

"Your mother, boy, has gone to make one of the blest above. She did so at your birth. Who she was is neither here nor there. Be content that I am your father."

Lady Killigrew said: "Many a lad has fended for himself before he

was Maugan's age. You have a young, multiplying family of your
own, John. Saplings grow frail if they are overshadowed by taller
trees."

Later that night I heard them talking about Ralegh; Henry Knyvett
said he was overproud and contemptuous, sitting so silent over supper
as if no one here were good enough to mix with him.

"I am not so sure it was that," said my father. "He was angry at
having raised this expedition and commissioned its crews and part
financed it, then to be deprived of the leadership and ordered to
return to court so soon as he saw the expedition properly under way."

"When did he tell you that?" asked Lady Killigrew sharply.

"Just as he was leaving. Frobisher is to follow and take over command in his stead. With Essex in some disgrace Walter is now supreme
with the Queen, and she wants him home. But it is a tightrope he
walks with such a changeable woman."

"I would have his tightrope if it were offered to me," said Henry
Knyvett, picking his teeth.

My grandmother's son by her first marriage was a ramshackle man
of nearly fifty with a long nose and a receding profile. He walked
as if there was water in his joints, and always wore a skull cap at
meals to prevent his hair falling in his food. Things were never easy
between him and Mr Killigrew.

"Oh, you are all for Ralegh," Mr Knyvett said, "but we know he is
the best hated man in London, and I could give more than several
reasons why. He has pulled himself up from nothing by his own shoe-
laces. He is a near-convicted atheist and a blasphemer. Now he
lives richly on wine patents and cloth licences, domineers over the
Queen as Captain of her Guard, and treats ordinary men as if they
were dirt under his feet! D'you suppose he is disappointed to be
deprived of a chance to fight the Spaniards? I do not. He gets all the
Spanish adventures he wants in the Queen's bedchamber."

"Envious tongues will always twist the courses of a man's rise," said
my father. "He has done much for the tinners of this county and none
could be more popular with them. As for him domineering the Queen,
if you'd seen so much of her as I have you'd know better than to
suppose any man is her master. She pulls the strings and others dance.
Believe me."

All June was supreme, with no rain and gentle warm sea breezes.
It was the last fine summer for several years.

Half a mile from our gates, and on the river bank near the town
of Penryn, was the old Collegiate Church of St Thomas of Glasney.

In my great-grandfather's time, when England was Catholic, this had been the centre of church life for all the far west. The establishment had been large and wealthy, with a refectory, a chapter house, dormitories for the canons, a hospital, many outbuildings. Now, except for the church, it was in ruins. Of the college chapel, dedicated to Thomas à Becket, only the tower stood. When you walked through the cloisters you could see how roofs had been robbed of their lead, stones carried away to make farmer's walls, windows broken, coloured glass stolen, doors prised off their hangings. Even many of the big paving stones had gone, and nettles and cow parsley and vipers bugloss grew rankly in their place.

We children did not often go there: it was too near Penryn, and the Killigrews were not popular in Penryn. But on the rising ground above the ruins was a windmill which had been used by the monks for grinding corn. This had been taken over first by one and then another of the millers of Penryn; but it was known to bring bad luck, and the last man to use it had hanged himself from the great beam. Now it had been allowed to fall into ruin like the college buildings, and a witch lived there called Katherine Footmarker. She was a woman who had been driven out of Penryn for having turned a neighbour's pet into a toad; but here in this ruin she had been allowed to live, partly because of men's fear of her, partly because she was known to be able to cure cattle and sheep of the murrain, and the evil she did was suffered for the good.

Although the Arwenack children were terrified of her, we were drawn sometimes towards the mill by the attraction of the forbidden and the dangerous, and twice we had seen her, a woman as tall and thin as my grandmother, walking with long strides through the bracken, once with a jackdaw on her shoulder, once followed by a black dog, which Belemus swore was no dog at all. We would have thrown stones at her if we had dared.

I had in the last year grown fond, perhaps overfond, of Meg Levant, the serving maid. Sometimes around eleven in the morning I would sidle into one of the smaller kitchens where I knew I would find her helping to get our dinner. She would be cleaning the trenchers or scouring the knives—often I would steal a piece or two of marchpane to keep my stomach quiet. She was a jolly girl of seventeen, soft and pretty and auburn-haired, and it was good to be in her company after the solemnities of Parson Merther. In the evenings too in the summer after prayers there was a half-hour before we had to be abed, and I would help her get the candles and the snuffers ready.

One evening I said to her: "Who was my mother, Meg?"

She stared at me as if I had asked her the riddle of the Sphinx. "Your mother, Master Maugan? How should I know?"

"You're older than I am. You've been here for years. Someone must have whispered it to you."

"Why should they?"

"Servants talk. What do the other servants say?"

"Have a care for that candle: you know your grandmother won't abide a crooked one. . . . The servants say you was brought here as a mite a few months old. Your foster-nurse was old Sarah Amble who took the dropsy three years gone. You should've asked her while she was here to answer."

"D'you swear you do not know?"

"If twas my way to swear, I'd swear, but since it isn't I won't. Now, out of my light, boy, or Rosewarne will be after us both."

I barred her passage. "Who would know, Meg?"

She frowned and looked me over. "How you d' grow. You'll be more longer than me afore Christmas. Dare you not ask your father?"

"I asked him but he wouldn't say."

"Maybe tis a secret best kept."

"Not from me. Who else would know?"

"I'll think on it an' tell you."

"Think now."

She tried to push me out of her way. I put my hands under her armpits. She squeaked petulantly. "Don't touch me that way! If someone catches you you'll be for a thrashing."

"It would be worth it."

She looked at me sidelong and picked up a large bracket sconce which held five tall tallow candles for the kitchens. "Saucy. If you're so curious and so brave, why not go and ask Katherine Footmarker."

I let her pass then. "She would know? Really? You truly think so?"

Meg looked back. "If she did not she would know Who to ask."

At the end of the month my father's younger brother Simon and his wife and two children came to spend a long summer holiday with us, as they usually did when there was plague in the capital. Simon was a lively man, hearty and noisy, and when he was on a visit he and my father would spend endless hours dicing together, or when they could persuade Henry Knyvett to join them, Gleek. He and my other uncle, Thomas, were in some way attached to the court. Unlike my father's uncles, William and Sir Henry, they seemed not to have any precise appointments, but they lived well and kept their creditors at arm's length.

Simon brought us news that Ralegh had secretly married one of the Queen's Maids of Honour and in due time had confessed his error to the Queen. A week later he and his bride were in the Tower—in separate cells, Uncle Simon explained with a roar of laughter; quite inconvenient for lovebirds. Simon did not like Sir Walter.

With the arrival of two more children in the house, the pace of our learning slackened and we spent much time on the river and bathing from one of the sandy beaches of the bay. Life was pleasant and easy that warm August and early September. Talk of invasion had abated, and no enemy ship was reported all summer. Sometimes in our wanderings we would come within the sight of the old mill above Penryn, and I thought of what Meg Levant had said. It was a temptation and a challenge.

In mid-September Mrs Simon Killigrew and her two children left for Somerset, but Uncle Simon still stayed on. A few days after his family left he rode out with my father on one of my father's expeditions, and they took Belemus with them. The other children were to spend the afternoon by the swan pool, but I had a slight fever and had been leeched and told to stay in my bed. I knew no one would seek me until supper time.

I left the house by way of the bakery, the walled garden, and the stables, which lay between the main house and the approach. From there I followed the deep rutted track past our own windmill to a part of the palisade where a broken wall gave me a foot up and over.

It was very little more than a mile to the mill over the fields and through the woods. At first I saw no one; but at Three Farthings House Paul Gwyther was ploughing a field and his son Oliver was following behind sowing the seed of winter wheat and rye. Behind Oliver were the two younger boys armed with slings and stones to keep the birds away. Oliver recognised me and waved a hand.

The woods were thick around Glasney. I skirted the edge of them up the hill. The sails of the windmill were broken, but one of the arms rocked gently in the breeze. From behind a tree I stared across the brambles. I picked a blackberry and chewed it, got a seed in my teeth and felt for it with a forefinger. A dog barked once inside the mill.

Silence fell then. In the clearing there were two grey granite millstones the size of dairy cheeses, and propped against them was a broken wheel. Thistles and docks grew among the grass, and with them shoots of barley and oats. A trampled path led to the door of the mill, which leaned on one hinge.

"Who's there?" said a voice. "Come forward if you have business. If not, leave us be."

Just inside the door and well within the sunshine a woman of thirty-

odd, in a faded blue kirtle, was sitting cross-legged on the floor. On a
stool beside her a rabbit sat eating some lettuce leaves, and there
were two or three cats lying in the shafts of the sun.

"Well, boy?"

I tried to speak but some spittle of fright formed on my tongue and
I could only swallow and stare.

"What d'you want?" she said again.

"I'm . . . I came to see Mistress Foot—Footmarker."

"You're as near her as you'll ever be."

I shifted from one foot to the other. A black dog was lying beside
a wicker basket and a jackdaw was perched on a beam.

"What's your name, lad?" I told her. She got slowly to her feet,
brushed the dust off her skirt, picked at a stain on it with her long
forefinger. "I thought I'd seen you before. I thought so. You're from
Arwenack. Of course. You're from Arwenack. I thought so."

It was like being accused of something. "Yes."

"Ah. . . . And what can I do for a Killigrew?"

I watched the rabbit pick up a piece of lettuce and put it in his
mouth. You could hear the crunching and could see his fat little
cheeks swell up and down.

". . . Is he a pet rabbit?"

"Not a pet, lad, because he's free. He comes here when he is so
minded."

I stood half in and half out of the door.

She said: "Does your father know you've come?"

"No, ma'am."

"You mean you've come to see me all on your own? Who suggested
it?"

"I—just thought I'd walk this way."

She blew out a breath and with her foot stirred a big grey cat which
was asleep in the half shade. "Well, it's a surprise to be so visited. It's
very strange. If there was to be any call from a Killigrew I'd have held
a penny it had been your father with his armed band of ruffians to
set the place afire over my head."

"Oh, no, he'd never do that."

"Would he not!" She scratched her bare leg above the knee where
there was a tear in her skirt. "I'm between one and the other here,
lad, as you should know. On the north side is Penryn and on the
south side Arwenack, both wishing me ill, but each waitin' and
watchin' for the other to stir first." She smiled, showing strong white
teeth in her long brown face. "Don't you believe me?"

"I don't know."

"Tell me what you've come for then."

I said: "I want to know who my mother was."

The big black dog suddenly barked again and this disturbed the jackdaw, who fluttered his wings and edged along the beam staring at me with a beady eye.

"Hush, Moses!" the woman said, turning suddenly on the dog, and the dog got to its feet and slunk away into the darkness with its tail curving between its legs. "Noisy animals I can't *abide!*" she said. "Silence is where you learn things, not in noise."

She poured herself some milk and drank it, extended the mug to me. I shook my head.

"How old are you, Maugan Killigrew?"

"Fourteen."

"And base-born? Fourteen. That's 1578, isn't it. Why do you suppose I can answer your question?"

"I thought—you might—find out."

"Ah-hah, and when I find out you'll run back to Arwenack saying Katherine Footmarker is a worser witch than ever you suspected and that she has a black dog that sings lewd hymns and five cats dressed in cassocks and surplices!"

"No, no, I shall not! Really I shall not."

"So you say." She put the mug down and came slowly forward into the light again. "Fifteen seventy-eight is a long time since. John Killigrew has been rovin' over the countryside for long enough. How can you expect anyone to remember—except maybe your mother?— and perhaps even she's forgot."

"She is dead! My father told me."

"Ah . . . well, then. So he remembers. And he won't tell you? Maugan Killigrew, born in 1578. Well, well."

The rabbit has stopped eating and was watching her.

"What'll you give me to find out?"

"I've two shillings here."

"I saw your father ride out this morning," she said, "with his band of servants. What mischief is he up to now?"

"He is not 'up to mischief.' He rides out to hunt and hawk, that's all."

"That's what you believe, eh? Truly? Let me look at you." She put a hand under my chin, but I shrank away. "I believe you're as innocent as you look. . . . Give me a shilling."

I gave her one of the coins.

"This is the half," she said between her teeth as she bit at the silver. "Come again in three or four weeks. Time of the next full moon, maybe."

"But I may not be able to get here again! I thought you would—
I thought you could. . . ."

I looked across the harbour. Two small cogs were luffing out of
Penryn Creek, and another vessel had dropped anchor off Trefusis
Point. She looked like one of the bigger fishing boats from Fowey or
Looe.

The woman said: "If you think I am of the dark then you must
come in the dark."

The rabbit hopped off his stool and moved out of the hut.

"Here, let me look at your hand." Before I could put them behind my back she had caught one and had turned it palm upward.
"How hot you are. A touch of ague, maybe? . . . Well, leastwise
you waste nothing needless on soap and water. Here, spit on them,
boy—not to clean them, but the way the spittle dries tells me as much
as the lines themselves."

I did what she said. She was too close to me with her long black
hair drooping over my hands. She smelt of damp hay.

She said: "You're a Killigrew whether you like it or not. There's
the eagle on you—stamped, see? No escape. You've an interesting
hand, boy. There's blood on it. There's blood on both."

I tried to wriggle my hands free.

"Don't go yet. It's different blood and all. Can you not see it?
Here, here, by the two fingers and thumb of your left hand and a
streak across the palm of the right."

"What does it mean?"

"Ah, that I can't tell you. Time will tell you. You're going to
travel, lad. I see you back and forth to Arwenack all your life—in
it but never of it. There's wars—and women, though only one or
two that mark deep. But always Cornwall and Arwenack, whether
you like it or not, in your vitals. You'll die here, I'm thinkin', here
or hereabouts—but not at Arwenack. You see, that's the last time it
shows; your life line goes on after that."

I took my hands away as soon as she gave a sign of releasing
them. She laughed.

"I think you'll make a comely man, Maugan. The women will like
you. Nor will the men despise you. It takes courage to seek out such
a woman as I'm whispered to be."

I tried surreptitiously to wipe my hands down the back of my
jerkin. "When must I come again?"

"Today the moon is two days after the full. Come in a month or
thereabouts; I may have somethin' for you then, though it's no promise."

"I'll try to get away."

"You'll get away. Most of the things you want to do you'll do. I can see it in your face."

The gate that was the main entrance through the stockade to our land was on high ground which dominated the approaches to the house from the south. During daylight there was one or another man-servant on duty there to see no unwanted person was admitted—beggars, tinkers, pedlars, they all got short shrift; as indeed did other more important personages if my father had reasons for not seeing them. At night the three boar hounds, Charon and Scylla and Charybdis roamed at large.

But today I knew that by now a servant called Penruddock would be at the gate and that he would let me in without telling on me, so I was making straight up the uphill path when I heard a horse whinny. I ducked behind a gorse bush just as my father and Uncle Simon came over the brow of the hill.

With them were eight of our servants and Belemus and Rosewarne our steward. Their horses were sweating, and all looked as if they had ridden hard. But they could not have been hawking for none of the falconers was there, no hooded hawks on wrist, no game tied lifeless over saddles. It was true that four spaniels followed, tongues lolling sideways, but these were my father's favourite dogs that went with him everywhere.

I watched my father's face when he went past. The easy contours had temporarily gone; he looked self-willed and preoccupied. Rosewarne carried a book, and a bag was slung over his saddle.

As I came up to the great gate Penruddock was just shooting the last bolt home. He raised his grey eyebrows. "Was you with your father, Master Maugan?"

When I slid in there was the usual noise and confusion attending my father's return. Dogs barking, servants scurrying, a man to pull off his boots, another to bring a dry linen shirt, and a third to give account of work that had been on hand during the afternoon. But today a new voice could be heard.

It was another cousin and neighbour of ours, Digby Bonython, son of John Bonython of Carclew, a small estate seven miles distant. Digby was on his way home from Exeter. He was a quiet spoken man of twenty-five or six, so it was unusual to hear his voice raised.

"It was Ralegh's ships that made the capture. His second squadron under Borough has taken a Portuguese carrack on its way to San Lucar, and they brought her in to Dartmouth early last week. Nothing is more unbelievable than the scenes since she has been brought in. It was half market and half riot. Pearls, diamonds, vessels of China—"

"How was she taken?"

"Only after a desperate battle. But this carrack! In Dartmouth she towers over the town. Seven decks she has, five times the tonnage of her captor; thirty-two guns, upwards of seven hundred men aboard. They say every trader for miles around has converged on the port. And over a thousand buyers and merchants from London! One has to fight one's way along the streets—and fight is the word. I wished I'd been there two days before. Cecil has been sent down himself, but you could not stop it then—"

"What name did you call her?"

"*Madre de Dios*—and she has all the riches of the Mother of God. Cinnamon, spices, cloth of gold, twisted silks, Turkey carpets, musk and ambergris, jewels of all shape and size. I saw a sailor selling fine porcelain at a shilling a piece—"

"Is it still going on?"

"No, it has stopped or I should not have come away when I did. Ralegh stopped it."

"Ralegh? But he is in the Tower."

"So he was, but when it was found no one could control the men, he was released and sent post to Dartmouth in company with a gaoler called Blount who is to watch over his return. I was there when he came and you would not believe with what pleasure and joy he was greeted. In the end he took control, and from then on, aided by Cecil's men and others, order and discipline was brought."

Henry Knyvett shuffled across and pulled the lattice window to and resumed his seat, brushed some dog hairs off his dusty black coat, crossed his knock-knees. Everyone watched him but no one spoke.

Dorothy Killigrew, my step-mother, who had baby Peter on her knee and was eating her favourite sugar-coated caraway seeds, said in her mild voice: "You will lie with us tonight, Digby?"

"Thank you, no, cousin, I'm bound home and am two days late. I must hurry on if you can favour me and my man with a couple of nags. I would have come post but was short of money. Seven of the Plymouth fishing fleet were just leaving for the Newfoundland banks, and two were putting in here on their way west, so I thought to cheapen my journey and at the same time bring you the latest news."

"You must sup with us, then. It would be a cold ride on an empty belly."

She got up, handing Peter to a nurse, and went out dropping her

kerchief as she left. She was scarcely two months from her eighth
confinement. My grandmother watched her go.

"And you came away from such a feast empty-handed?" said my
father, puckering his brows. The bitter mood in which he had returned from his ride had not lifted; the world was persecuting him.
"Why, in God's name? If there were pickings. . . ."

"Well, not quite empty-handed, cousin, as I'll show you."

Digby fumbled in his pouch and took out a necklace. It was of
pearls, threefold, interspersed with gold buttons, each button being
set with a diamond. My father took it and one of the spaniels, May-
flower, thinking it was something to eat, nosed up; but Mr Killigrew
shoved him impatiently away.

"And what did you pay for that?"

"Ten pounds. It cannot be worth less than a hundred."

There was no sound then except for the spaniels scratching.

Lady Killigrew passed the necklace to her sister, Mistress Wover-
stone. "And what else?"

"All I had money for. No, no more jewels. But I have a parcel
at the door of fine taffetas and some unwrought China silk that will
delight them at home. I wished I'd had a fortune to spend. Much
of it had been already snapped up, but you could still find sailors
who were uncomfortable with their loads and willing to lighten them
at a cheap rate."

So then he was persuaded to have the package brought in and
unrolled on the table, and we gathered round staring and exclaiming.
Presently he gave a small piece of silk to my step-mother; but none
of the family was very gracious, except Dorothy on receiving the
gift. I could see they were all picturing the scene Digby had spoken
of and eating out their hearts because they had heard nothing until
too late, though it had happened less than ninety miles distant.

After supper, Digby went off together with his servant and one of
our men whom my father, pressed by Dorothy, grudgingly lent him
for extra safety, since the way they must travel though short was
hazardous in the bends of the river beyond Penryn. At the gate where
they mounted my father said:

"D'you know if Ralegh is to remain free?"

"He says he is the Queen's captive, and Mr Blount's presence would
seem to confirm it. But I would not put it beyond him to use his
enlargement in such a way that it will continue."

"Neither would I. What has he done? Sometimes it is a touchy
business having a woman on the throne."

"He changed his allegiance from one Elizabeth to another," said

Digby. "That was his crime. And unless we know how inward he was with the first we can't estimate the degree of the offence."

Someone laughed. My grandmother, who had come to the door with us, was staring across the harbour. The wind, which was rising and chill, blew her ochre silk gown about her tall thin figure. She coughed harshly.

"That was the vessel you came in?" She pointed towards Trefusis Point.

"No, that is the other, the *Buckfast*. The captain of the *Totnes* who brought me had a commission in Penryn which he discharged at once and left by the same tide, following the others while the wind was fair. I have my own thoughts about *Buckfast*."

My father laid a hand on the saddle. "Which are, cousin?"

"Which are that some of Ralegh's fleet put in to Plymouth and that they all had had their pickings of *Madre de Dios* while she was at sea. Not all the rich booty was confined to Dartmouth. So my supposition is that the captain of the *Buckfast* most probably has by barter laid hold of some of the spoils for himself, and not wanting to face the hazards of a long voyage to Newfoundland with fragile things in his hold, he chooses to dispose of them where prices are still unaffected by the glut of riches, before he leaves England."

"You think that, do you, Digby?"

"Yes, I think that. Otherwise his delaying here would be unaccountable. . . . Well, I must be off. Goodbye."

Mr Killigrew relaxed his grip. "My loving thoughts to your father and mother."

We waved until the three were out of sight, which was soon, for the night was lowering and the moon not yet up. When I turned, my grandmother's eyes were on the river again. My father followed her gaze.

Parson Merther had come to usher us inside, but the last I saw of Lady Killigrew and my father they had not moved; their two figures were black against the cloudy evening sky. Below them the water was slightly greyer than the land, and a yellow light glimmered on board the *Buckfast* as she swung at anchor near Trefusis Point.

We had eaten salted beef for supper and I was very thirsty and felt a small matter sick. So about midnight I crept out of bed and went down to the kitchens where the pump was. The house should have been in darkness, but a light came from the great hall. The door was ajar, and four figures sat around the empty fireplace: my father, my grandmother, Uncle Simon, and Uncle Henry Knyvett. They were talking in low tones but I caught the word "*Buckfast*."

Then I heard Henry Knyvett say in an irritable and therefore louder voice: "Sometimes, mother, you talk in knots. Untie this one."

Lady Killigrew coughed. "John's middle course would give us the worst of both worlds—"

"But in this case—"

"I know. And I say *you* must do nothing, John. How do you know, when all is said, that there is so much as a roll of calico aboard? It is only Digby Bonython's thought."

My father said: "There are all manner of dangers in such a project. Whereas if I go aboard in the Queen's name none can question my right. The other way—"

"I understand mother now," said Simon. "Be taken sick, brother. Call Merther to your bedside. Then later we can have our way."

The scrape of a chair made me quick to move this time. I slid away in haste and stole back to bed, my thirst unsatisfied.

CHAPTER 3

I SLEPT poorly. A dozen times in the course of the night I slid out of bed—quietly, so as not to disturb John who was a light sleeper— and stood at the long window peering out. Arwenack was such a dispersed house that one part of it could be quite in ignorance of what was going on in another; but I did hear voices now and then, and once something in the back courtyard fell with a clatter.

By leaning out of this window and craning my neck I could just see Trefusis Point and the thin black masts of the *Buckfast* on the moon-silvered water.

As the moon sank behind the rising ground at the back of the house, the colour of the water in the harbour became bluer and colder with the first streaks of dawn, and I fell into a heavy sleep from which I was only wakened by the footboy, Stevens, shaking my shoulder. I must have slept only for two or three hours in all, and I felt heavy and unprepared for another day. In the morning lessons I dropped off over Euclid and received a stinging rap across the shoulders from Ink-horn. Then I had to construe from Horace and stumbled many times and at last dried up.

Parson Merther said: "Out here, boy."

His beatings were so common that a day never passed without one or another bending over his stool, and little eight-year-old Odelia suffered with the rest. It was his custom to give the older boys five or six strokes, but this morning, when he had dealt me four I straightened up and turned.

He paused with his cane half raised, his little sword-point eyes red with the effort. "I did not tell you to rise, boy."

"No, sir, but I think it's enough."

Parson Merther said: "Such brains as you have been given, boy, which are few, you may use on learning more of the Latin tongue, not on instructing me. Bend down, or I will double your punishment."

"I have had my punishment, sir," I said, and moved back towards my seat. Before I could get to it he grasped me by the arm and hit me across the face with his cane. I snatched the cane out of his hand and threw it across the room. He would have struck me again with his fist, but I caught his wrist and turned it away.

"I have had my punishment," I said again, and turned and went back to my seat. This time he did not try to stop me, but walked across to where I had flung his cane, picked it up, and went back to his desk.

"Continue the chapter, John."

In a close-bound community such as ours, news from outside the palisades could come early or late according to the merest chance. Rumour was always rife, but news as such hung on the chance caller or, more often, some messenger we might need to send out who would bring back what he had heard.

Today no one left the estate. Our head falconer, Bewse, had a cut over his eye, but when I asked him how he came by it he grunted and said it was none of my business.

Neither Uncle Simon nor Uncle Henry Knyvett was in to dinner, and Mr Killigrew was still in the mood when all the world, instead of being of no consequence, had become his enemy. In the afternoon it began to rain, and a curtain of wet mist shivered across the bay. The house itself seemed to drowse off to sleep in the clammy damp. When the mist lifted a little before supper I saw that the *Buckfast* was still there, swinging gently at anchor. As I watched, a ship's boat cast off and three or four men in her were rowed ashore at the point.

At supper both Uncle Simon and Mr Knyvett came in. Uncle Simon was walking with a limp, and during supper Henry Knyvett grew very drunk.

As we were going upstairs Belemus said: "And how does the little rebel feel?"

I shrugged. "Well enough."

"Ah, you see how easy it is, once the first step is taken."

"What first step did you take, Belemus?"

"Oh, much the same as yours, Maugan, except that I did not advertise it so publicly."

As I undressed and got into bed I peered out again, but the mist had returned and suffered me not to take a full view of the harbour.

On the following morning before we broke our fast Stevens came in and said: "Master Maugan, your father wants you in his chamber."

Few were summoned to the small room in which Mr Killigrew kept his private papers and to which he often retired, occasionally to work but more often for peace and quiet or to dice against himself when there was no one in the house to play with. Today he was sitting behind his iron-clamped desk, and four spaniels were sprawled like a discarded fur coat at his feet. I stood just inside the door and listened to the scratch of his pen and one of the spaniels sighing.

He was wearing the tarnished buff jerkin and the broad greasy shoulder belt which was his usual work-a-day attire; but his hair was always well washed and combed and his moustache pomaded and unstained.

He finished the letter and put the quill back in the pewter inkstand. "Damned ink," he said, and dusted the paper and leaned back in his worn leather chair to look at me. His eyes were almost empty of expression, as they so often were. He could smile charmingly and his eyes would stay cold; he could shout with anger and his eyes would stay cold; it took something from his good looks.

"You are growing big for your boots, boy."

I stared at the pistolets on the walls.

"Answer me."

"Yes, sir."

"You would do well to remember that but for me you might *have* no boots. On that I'll say no more. . . . But you're yet fourteen, Maugan, and at that age you do as you're told by your elders, whether it's by me or by a little horneywink like Merther. See?"

"Yes, sir."

His eyes strayed to a pack of cards lying on the desk, then reluctantly came back to the matter in hand.

"If you don't know how you must learn how. But you've had beatings enough, so today you'll spend in the kennels chained along with the hounds. They know how to come to heel when you tell 'em. Neither food nor drink till cockshut, unless you fancy their food. When we've supped I'll think whether to keep you there the night. Follow?"

"Yes, sir."

"But use your hands on Merther again and I'll have all the skin off your back. That or you'll be turned out of the house."

He got up and pulled the bell rope by the window. All the spaniels woke and tumbled over each other. "I've a taking for you, Maugan. You're my eldest, so far as I know, and though there's other base ones about, you're the only one aside from my own family that I've cared for. Maybe that's because I cared more for your mother. . . . But don't overtry my patience. A child or a span'l more or less: what's that in a large household?"

I was cold and hungry. The hounds did not seem at all to mind my being among them. It rained until three, but I would not crawl inside the kennels so I got wet. When the rain cleared a thick high fog came down again so that even the chimneys of the house could scarcely be seen.

No one came near me and no one dared speak. On the rising ground behind the cobbled yard four men were sawing and stacking logs for the winter. Each year trees were cut down from the wood just to the west of the castle and the thin weakly growths thinned out. The better pieces were kept long to make planks for repairing the upper rooms of the north wing, for here during the building they had run out of good timber and green wood had been used. Coming across my view from time to time were three girls carrying apples from the orchard to be wiped and stored. Between me and them was a great pool of liquid manure lying where it had drained out of the stables and the cow-houses.

In the late afternoon I heard a quiet hiss and swung on my chain to see Meg Levant who had sidled round the edge of the yard keeping within the shelter of the bakery until she was near. She had a bowl of hot soup. I glanced quickly about, as did she, at the windows of the house and at the four men sawing wood. Then the bowl and the soup changed hands and she squatted down in the shelter of the wall almost invisible against the brown stone, while I gobbled up the soup.

It went down into my vitals like thick warm wine. As soon as I had finished I handed it back and she snatched it and subsided again.

"Someone will remember that in Heaven," I whispered.

"So long as no one d' discover it here on earth."

"Go then before they do."

"I can hardly be seen 'ere. Do you want for aught else?"

"No, I shall live now to torment you again."

"I was afraid so." She took out an apple and began to eat it. "Meg."

"Yes?"

"Jael Job brought me here. When it is dark jog his memory or I may be forgot for the night."

She promised. I was glad of her being somewhere by for a few minutes.

"What should you be doing now, Meg?"

"Peeling rushes for the candle wicks."

"Have a care you're not put in with me for disobedience."

"I shouldn't mind; 'twould be a welcome rest."

The three maids carrying the apples clattered across the yard. When they were gone I said: "What news is there today?"

"News?"

"I've been here since early morning. Is my father in or out?"

"In. They be all in. . . . There was trouble in the river the night afore last."

"What sort of trouble?"

I had to listen to the crunch of her teeth on the apple while she chewed it and swallowed.

"Harold Tregwin come over from Gluvias. You know what a gossip he be. Thursday night off Trefusis Point a fishing hoy was boarded and robbed, and one of the crew falls overboard in the commotion and is drownded. Yester eve his body floats up by St Thomas's Bridge."

I let out a slow breath. "Why should anyone wish to rob a poor fishing hoy?"

"That's what Harold d' say. By his account the captain have put in a complaint to the justices o' the county and asked that the murderers be traced. 'Twas quite a tale he told, but you d' know Harold, how he loved to make a plaguey long history of it. Here, can you catch? I'd best be going."

On the next day, which was Sunday, we all walked as was customary to Budock Church, my father and mother leading the way followed by the other members of the family, then the children, with our servants in a long crocodile behind. Mr Garrock, the vicar, by mischance chose as the text of his sermon St Mark, Chapter 3, Verse 27: "No man can enter into a strong man's house and spoil his goods, except he will first bind the strong man; and then he will spoil his house."

My father slept through most of it, but I knew I dared not because we should be examined on the content of the sermon by Parson Merther that evening and whipped if we could not give a fair outline, and I was in no position to court further trouble.

When the sermon was over my father yawned and said in a loud

voice to Uncle Simon: "Let us not tarry for the prayers," and so el-
bowed his way out.

Perhaps he had not slept so soundly after all, for over dinner he
was downright in his criticism of the state of the clergy. Will Garrock,
he said, was an ignorant unlettered scoundrel better suited to keep a
taproom than a church. Hawken of Philleigh, he knew for a fact,
spent all his days and nights dicing and wenching; it was said that
the parson at St Issey had been burnt in the hand for felony; and
Arscott of Cubert was a drunkard and kept a whore and six bastards.
It was time there was a clean sweep in the church of pluralists,
felons, and ignorant rogues.

I do not know how or in what way it came to be understood in
the house that our part in the affray of Thursday night was not an
innocent one; but it crept up like cold in the bones. Perhaps it is not
possible for five or six men, some of them with wives, to go out after
dark and to come back unquestioned.

On the Tuesday Sir Francis Godolphin called.

Sir Francis, who lived near Helston, was Vice Warden of the
Stannaries and lately Sheriff of Cornwall. His first wife Margaret had
been a Killigrew and my father's aunt. Sir Francis was nearing sixty
at this time, a grey-bearded man, short of stature and quiet of
manner, temperate and sober; he and Ralegh between them, so it
was said, had done much to improve the lot of the tinners in the
county, and through it Sir Francis had become rich.

With him tonight was our neighbour, Mr John Trefusis, a sharp-
voiced man with a skin as brown as snuff. My father was up at the
Castle when they came, so Mrs Killigrew, in a fluster and with
babies and needlework to be rid of, had to greet them in the withdrawing room, and I and young John and Odelia were permitted
to stay on unnoticed. By the time my father came in, close followed
by Lady Killigrew, our guests were supping white Rhenish wine
and eating sweet almond biscuits.

Since Mr Killigrew and Mr Trefusis did not at all esteem each
other there was a stiffness about their greeting which left an awkward
silence when they sat down. To fill it Mrs Killigrew began to ask
about Sir Francis's eldest son who was fighting in Ireland; but the
exchange of polite talk was brief before Sir Francis with less than his
usual smoothness said:

"You will have heard, John, of the boarding and robbery of the
Buckfast last Thursday night?"

"Who has not? They have trumpeted it abroad sufficient for all to
hear."

"And should they not," said Mr Trefusis sharply, "when they are robbed of sixty pounds in gold, and when one of their number is hit on the head and dropped overboard? Should they not complain? You cannot be unmindful of your responsibility."

"I?" My father crossed his legs and squinted down at a stain on his stocking. "I suppose you mean because it happened in my waters? Well, I regret it, but I do not see what I can do beyond taking depositions if they wish to make them."

"They have already made depositions, John," Sir Francis said. "Yesterday, before they left."

"They have? Then they made them improperly. They should have come to me."

"They preferred otherwise."

"One has not always the good fortune to be able to please oneself. In any event I should have thought the captain on very shaky ground for complaint if it's true what is rumoured, that the money was stolen from this Portuguese carrack which has been brought in and which is the Queen's prize."

"According to the captain," said Sir Francis, "they brought goods here which they had purchased in fair trade at the quay at Plymouth. They spent the afternoon and evening of Thursday visiting Mr Trefusis, Mr Thomas Enys, and divers traders of Penryn, to whom they sold most of these goods and received payment in money and in bills. At about four of the clock on Friday morning seven armed men boarded and took possession of *Buckfast*, and in the struggle one of the crew, Ezekiel Penwethers, was struck on the head and fell overboard to his death. The ship was searched from prow to poop and everything of value taken, including of course the gold."

My father had not listened patiently to this. He had closed his eyes and sighed and opened them to look again at the stain. "So I've heard, Francis. So I've been told. For my own part I doubt very much if the captain's story will bear a close quizzing. But if it is true I am sorry he has suffered this misfortune—though not overly surprised. Vagrants and thieves roam the countryside committing all manner of outrages; and they are on the increase. Who is to check them?"

"If the captain's story were true I'm sure you would not be overly surprised," stuttered Mr Trefusis, "since one of the robbers was seen to be wearing Killigrew livery under his cloak!"

Into the stretched silence came a sudden burst of shrill weeping; little Odelia had slipped from her chair, and she rushed to her mother for comfort. By the time Mrs Killigrew had carried her from the room the flush had faded from my father's face.

"The spleenful thoughts of my neighbour never surprise me. But I trust that you, Francis, don't cradle such suspicions?"

"Well, I should be glad to have—"

"A reassurance? Are you saying that I did it? Do you think if I had committed this robbery I should have been such a fool as to take men aboard dressed in my own livery? But in fact on Thursday night last I was ill."

"Ill?"

"A seizure in the stomach. I had to rouse my chaplain, and I think he can reassure you that I was not out of my bed that night."

Mr Trefusis grunted his doubts. "Then if it was not you in person. . . . This has—"

It was a mischance that at that moment Simon Killigrew should enter the room. He looked curiously from one to another of the tautened faces. "Welcome, Uncle. And you too, Trefusis. Is this private business?"

"Oh," said Trefusis, "I did not know you were here! That might well explain it all!"

"Explain what?" asked Simon.

"They're all the same, the Killigrews," said our neighbour. "They all have morals as accommodating as a Greyfriar's sleeve."

"You came to this house uninvited, Trefusis," said my father. "If you don't leave under your own sail you are likely to be helped to go."

"A moment, John," Sir Francis said quietly. "You may put Mr Trefusis out; but these depositions have been taken and will presently find their way to the appropriate quarters. Whether they are true or not, I'm afraid they will have to be sifted. Therefore—"

"Then sift them, Francis! But I thought I had enough jealous ill-wishers in the county without supposing one of my own kinsmen to be among them. What is your interest in this? With all your broad acres and prospering tin-works, what can you covet of mine?"

"I covet nothing of yours, as you should know. This accusation is no doubt false, but it shows the reputation you bear."

"My reputation, by God!—"

"Yes. If you think because I speak you words of warning I am your ill-wisher, then you misread me. But it comes to a pretty pass when mariners shun the river you command and only put in here under extremity of storm and stress, when armed retainers rule the countryside instead of the Queen's law. Things cannot go on like this. I speak as your kinsman and your friend. Good night."

On the Thursday after this Uncle Simon said he must leave on the morrow for Greenwich were the court then was. My father said he had been thinking it over and had decided he would ride with him; then my grandmother decided to go too. This caused harsh words. My father said Lady Killigrew was not strong enough to sit a horse with them for ten days. She answered that if she tired she would hire a coach. My father said that in their present beggared state they could not afford it; best if she waited and took a passage by sea. My grandmother said she was an indifferent sailor and the autumn gales were due; she wanted to go now; she was sick and tired of a country bumpkin's existence; if he wished to go chasing Lady Betty again she would not stand in his way; all she wanted was to see for herself what they were wearing in London and in Westminster; she wanted to meet all her relatives and friends; besides, she had a little money now.

When Friday morning came Lady Killigrew was ready at sun-up with the others, her two bags packed, her little black mare saddled, and no one dared say no.

The house was very different without them. Rosewarne the steward did his best, but he was given such scant authority when the two ruling Killigrews were at home that he did not have the way of it when they were gone. Then my step-mother took to her bed with an attack of jaundice, and just at this time Henry Knyvett chose to pay one of his rare visits to his wife at Rosemerryn, so the ordering of the servants fell upon Bethia Wolverstone, my grandmother's unmarried sister, and upon Mary Killigrew, my father's unmarried sister. But Mistress Wolverstone spent much of her day reading and praying and my aunt Mary lived only for her hawks and her falcons, so discipline relaxed, meals were late, and work went forward at half speed. Even when Mr Knyvett came back there was no improvement for he went into one of his drunken spells.

All this slackness was aided by the great storms which blew up as October came in. There were ever more excuses for not going out, for postponing work in the yards and on the roofs of the barns. It had been a good year for apples, and the cider presses were much in use. Catching Henry Knyvett's complaint, servants were found drunk about the house, and one was thrashed for trying to force a kitchen maid. One day the webster came and bargained for our surplus wool but I do not think my grandmother would have let it go at so low a price.

One evening, having been helping with some hides, I went up to say good night to Mrs Killigrew later than her own children; and she told me to sit and talk with her for a while; then she read me a chapter from the Bible.

There was no malice toward me in her such as I found now in my grandmother; indeed Mrs Killigrew was too gentle and too absent-

thoughted to feel malice for anyone. She spent much time in reading
and meditation. The books beside her bed were Latimer's *Sermons*
and *A Treatise on the Resurrection of the Dead*. Yet she did fine
wrought stitch work, was skilled in gardening and in preserving fruit,
and if one of the servants was ill or hurt she would tend on them herself. I thought my eldest half-brother John would grow up to be like
her.

When she paused to take a sip of water I could hear the rats
scuttering behind the wainscot and the bang of a loose shutter in
the wind. I stared curiously at the wire hoop of a farthingale with a
pair of silk stockings hung over it, at a purple taffeta nightgown behind the door. I thought: what if my mother had been here instead;
would she have been content always to take second place?

Mrs Killigrew said: "Tell me, Maugan, are you happy here?" When
I looked up startled, she added: "Of late you have been in trouble
more often than out of it."

"Perhaps it is a Killigrew shortcoming."

She lifted her head. "You're growing old before your time, Maugan."

"Do you want me to go away?"

"Away?"

"To leave Arwenack."

She smiled. "No. You are good company for my own children. They
would miss you greatly. We all should."

"It's a big family now."

She closed the Bible though she had not finished the chapter. "I too
come of a large family, Maugan, with many sisters. My father ruined
himself in providing dowries for us all, so lack of money is no new
problem to me. There are many greater misfortunes."

I said: "I wish I knew who *my* mother was."

"I wish I could tell you."

"Does Father ever speak of her?"

"No, Maugan, never. Or not to me. Perhaps it is not surprising that
he does not speak of her to me."

There was something on the bed on which Mrs Killigrew had
been working when I came into the room: a piece of fine purple cloth
enriched with gold and silver lace. There was a short length of pleated
silk cord dangling from it over the side of the table.

"Have you often been to London, ma'am?"

"Once only." She put a coriander seed in her mouth and chewed
slowly. "To Whitehall, when your father's uncle, Sir Henry Killigrew,
presented me to the Queen."

"Is my uncle, my great uncle, high in favour still? How comes it that he stays constantly in the Queen's favour when others go so much by ups and downs?"

"I think the Queen has two kinds of servants, those who are her favourites . . . and those whom she trusts. Those whom she trusts are those to whom she gives her most laborious and responsible positions of state; their lives and careers are not so subject to change—if they serve her well. Your great uncle Henry has served her well for thirty-five years, and your great uncle William for scarcely ten less."

The wind leaned and pushed against the house, and the loose shutter slammed in the next room.

"And," she added, "your great uncle Henry married well. His new wife is French and I do not know her; but his first wife's sister is married to Lord Burghley and is the mother of Robert Cecil, whom everybody supposes Lord Burghley is bringing on to succeed him as Chief Secretary. And a second sister, Lady Bacon, is the mother of Anthony and Francis Bacon, both young men of gifts, I'm told."

I got up to go. "I'll tie that shutter. Do you want anything for the night?"

"Your aunt Mary will be in soon, thank you."

I fingered the material on the bed. "What is this, a new canopy for the cradle?"

She seemed to hesitate. "It's a Spanish cloak belonging to your father. I'm repairing it."

"The material is fine. I don't remember him wearing it."

"No. . . ."

I picked up a string of corals that had been dropped by one of the babies and put it on the carved chest beside the bed.

"Good night, madam. I hope you sleep well." I kissed her cheek, which smelt of some herbal tincture.

"Maugan," she said as I got to the door. "Do not mention this cloak. Mr Killigrew would be angry."

CHAPTER 4

THE evening of the full moon was the second Thursday in October, and my father and uncle and grandmother had been gone three weeks. It had been a windy day, but as night fell the wind fell and left only the high white clouds moving across the sky like afterthoughts. By the time ten o'clock had come and the house was asleep, the moon was riding high and the harbour water was greying and whitening with the passage of every cloud.

Almost as soon as I was out of the house Charon found me and growled his suspicion, but he soon stopped to eat the pieces of meat I brought. But away from the house it was not the hounds that had to be feared. I could appease them and shake them off but could never lose the shadow that followed at my feet or dodge the giant imprints of the trees that cut across the drive with silhouette images of witches and skeletons, of blood feasts, of human sacrifices, and of damned souls.

Once over the palisade I ran for some way along the rutted muddy lane, before breaking through a tangle of bramble and bracken to the more open land beyond. From here the river mouth lay like a forked quicksilver tongue thrust into the dark flesh of the land.

Near the mill a stop for breath. There was a light. I went on through the brambles and then more slowly across the open ground. The door could not properly close because of its lost hinge, and the light inside was cut off briefly as a figure moved across it.

The light came from a small open lamp like an early Christian lamp with oil in the shell and a wick burning from the lip. There was a brazier near the centre of the room with a pot simmering on it.

"So you have come, lad."

The lamp though dim spread a more uniform light over the room than the bright sun had done. On a shelf against one wall was a pile of books, and on the millstones behind the brazier were rows of bottles and jars and tins. The roof of the floor above had given way in one place and the wooden steps led to a hole which had been nailed across with old sacks to keep out the draught.

"I came . . . have you. . . ."

She shut the door. "It's a fine full moon but a small matter withdrawn. Sit down. . . . Let's see, what is your name? Maugan?"

I sat on the edge of the stool where the rabbit had been last time. She said: "Are you not afraid of comin' here?"

I nodded.

"Well, courage is no bad thing and deserves a reward. I'll try to help you."

I held out the other shilling but she shook her head. "Wait a little. In time we'll see." She took a spoon and stirred the pot. The glow lit up her long, cautious sun-browned face. I realised it could once have been pretty.

"Do you know, I have lost my rabbit," she said. "He was killed by a stoat."

"Oh . . . I'm sorry."

"Have you ever seen a stoat dance before he kill?"

"No."

"Animal nature is not kind, but kills only for food. Human kind kill for the pleasure or from a strange evil notion called principle. Was your mother's name Maugan?"

I stared at her. "Why?"

"There's an M in this pot. It would not be unnatural that you were given her name."

"Oh. . . ."

She looked up at me. "Have you ever seen a glow-worm in the day time?"

"No."

"One day if you will come again I'll show you what they're like. Like a little beetle. The female have more light than the male. When she be bearin' her eggs, she is lit up by them from within, like little embers from the fire. Do you know you can read by the light of three or four glow-worms?"

"No."

She stared into the pot again. "You must learn of nature, Maugan. It will help you to find content such as no mixing in the company of men can . . . I think you were born by a river, lad."

"*This* river?" I said.

"Bigger than this. Wider and deeper."

"Where?"

"I have not seen all the rivers of England. Bristol, maybe. Plymouth. London. I see love there—and hate—and greed—and disease. But neither poverty nor riches. It's likely your mother was of good stock. You've no call to be ashamed of it, if that were ever in your mind."

I said nothing in reply.

"They were not of a kind, your father and mother. I can see that. But it's not always just money or breed. . . ."

"How—how did she die?"

"Of the plague, I'd lay a guess. There's sickness and death all around. It is a wonder you survive. I see no relatives left. I see only your father—riding with you—up a narrow lane. . . ."

There was a long silence. She seemed to have come to the end.

"Greed, did you say?" I ventured at last.

"Yes, greed. But ask me not what part it played. . . . It could be that your father was greedy, grasping and plucking at the flowers that were not his."

She stood up and folded her hands on her elbows. The light flung her shadow across the room like the shadow of a great cat. "D'you know, lad, what this bowl contains in which I have been reading your past?"

"N-no."

"My food for tomorrow. . . ."

I did not answer.

"Rabbit bones for stew. If you don't believe me, here, take this spoon and taste it."

"No!"

"Afraid it's some ungodly brew? It matters not what you look in if you have the gift of sight. I could have told as much by gazing in a cabbage heart, no more by using the skull of Paracelsus."

She went over to the bottles ranged on the millstones. "D'you know who Paracelsus was, Maugan?"

"No."

"They stuff your head with Greek and Latin and Logic and never tell you how to cure a sore place or heal a cut finger. Here, come here, beside me."

I got up slowly from my chair and while she was not looking I glanced into the bubbling pot. I thought I saw a face in it and moved back.

"Betony," she said. "Saffron for measles, saxifrage for the stone, neat's foot for chilblains, comfrey and liquorice for bronchitis, marjoram and aniseed for megrim . . . they make a pretty list. Few here come to me for ailments of their own; they're too affrighted. They only come—four at a time for protection—when their cattle or sheep be sick. See what courage you have, Maugan, treadin' where fools dare not tread."

"You spoke of hate too," I whispered.

"Love and hate, I spoke of. There is always love and hate between every man and woman. You'll learn that it is so. And when the love is stolen it's the more passionate for that. And when betrayal follows, hate flourishes like tares in a cornfield. In a manner you are fortunate, Maugan Killigrew."

"How?"

"You spring from passion, and so must be more alive than those who come of duty, routine appetites, or the boredom of long livin' together. In the fullness of time it may be you will come to love and hate, just as your father and mother did."

The moon had moved some way across the sky before she would let me go. In the end she took my shilling. She talked much more before I left, and each time I made a move she began some new subject. But she told me no more of my mother.

I came away with a sensation of discomfort and distaste—and with little feeling of relief at an ordeal over. While she had talked to me I had felt both drawn to her and repelled. I felt she had tried to put a spell on me and that she had in some measure succeeded. Soon or late I should go back, drawn by this attraction-repulsion as to the edge of a cliff.

The night had clouded as it grew old and the way home was no more friendly than the way out. I had left a short stout length of rope looped over the palisade and marked it with a broken tree, but as I got near I heard voices, low and gruff, and then the shuffle of feet.

They were coming on the track by which I had come, a group of figures in the uncertain moonlight tramping up the hill. Six men. The first wore a grey hat with upturned brim and had a bandaged hand; another was a negro. They were all ill dressed, two almost in rags. They might have been any band of robbers that roamed the wide commons of England, but they walked too confident, their gait was purposeful.

When they had passed I rose and moved slowly from bush to bush in their wake. They stopped at the closed gate of Arwenack and rattled it and tried to force it open. It was only then in the brilliance of the moon that I recognised the man in the grey hat as Captain Elliot.

They had dropped anchor, they said, in Helford Haven but two hours ago. *Dolphin* only was here. *Neptune* had been sailing with them but they had been separated by storm. *Dolphin* had been badly damaged and was in need of repair and refit. Also Mr Love, the mate, was ill.

"Rouse your father, boy."

"He's from home. Also my grandmother."

"Who's in charge, then? Your mother?"

"My—mother is not well. My uncle, Mr Knyvett—he's here."

"Go summon him then. Can you brave the dogs?"

"Yes. But it is long after midnight. Mr Knyvett will be abed."

"Tell him who's here and that we've urgent business with him. In the end we shall persuade him it has been worth a disturbed night."

So my return was not at all as I had expected. I went over the palisade, pacified Charon, found my way in through the sleeping house, and woke Uncle Knyvett. He was far too heavy in the head and confused to care how I knew of the callers. He grumpily pulled on his night shirt and breeches and over them put his shabby black velvet dressing gown. Then he stumbled in his ramshackle way across

to the other wing, kicked Long Peter and another servant into some
sort of wakefulness, and instructed them to call in the hounds and
open the gate.

As soon as he saw Captain Elliot, Henry Knyvett began to complain, but he was cut short.

"It's no time for the amenities, Mr Knyvett. We've had a pretty
brush off the Carmarthen coast. Then we ran into heavy weather off
the Land's End and near foundered. Captain Burley was beaten back
towards St Ives and may be drowned by now with all that barren
coast on his lee."

They walked away from me then, but I could still hear portions
of their talk.

". . . four barques, there were, on passage from Bristol to
Pembroke. . . . We'd been beating about for some days, but that
morning the wind was coming fair from the south. Burley sighted
them first and gave chase. We was in the wind of them and cut
them off. We summoned them to surrender but the first two gave
fight. . . ."

The sailors had come into the great hall and had dropped their
bags beside the fireplace in which a great log dully smouldered in
a desert of white ash.

". . . I got this in boarding. My master gunner is a leg short, and
two others hurt. . . . Love? Nay, Love came through unscathed but
fell sick after. After being at sea three months we all need a
thorough rummage—and are not unentitled to it, I'd say. . . ."

The man with the gun was the pock-marked sailor who had been
so quarrelsome in February, Aristotle Totle.

". . . then when will he be home? But no doubt you can undertake the necessary measures. . . . Silks and velvets mainly, with a
substantial loadage of wine . . . we could not transfer the cargo in
mid-ocean. . . ."

"Maugan, to bed now."

"Yes, Uncle Knyvett."

"This stuff you have here, this is some of it?"

"A sample. Just a sample. . . ."

I moved towards the door. The negro was feeling the Pavia tapestry that hung to the left of the fire.

". . . There's little to be done tonight, Elliot. Do you wish to lie
here?"

"You must send word to Truro. Also we have need of vegetables,
fruit, fresh water. And an apothecary. Some of my men are sick too.
These things are why I didn't tarry until the morning."

"Maugan. It is time for you to go!"

"Yes, Mr Knyvett."

I went, shutting the door after me, climbing the stairs, suddenly feeling weary and alone.

Dolphin lay in Helford Haven, five miles away. This was a small river running into a sizeable broad estuary with safe land-locked mooring for vessels up to three hundred tons and densely wooded banks. Beside the *Dolphin* was another vessel of about the same size but not so lean a trim. I saw them both on the third day when I slipped away with Belemus and we climbed across the headlands to look for ourselves.

But by then there could have been nothing more peaceful than the sight we saw. It was far more peaceful than Arwenack where more than a dozen seamen sat at table each day and made free with our food and the comforts and cordialities of the house.

Others came to the house too. John Penrose, a cousin of ours from Kethicke, John Michell from Truro, and John Maderne. They came and talked in private, together and separately, they ate and drank and got drunk with the sailors and then left again. On the fourth day William Love arrived, much thinner for his illness, and sat in a chair in the great hall and watched our servant girls with strange and cloudy eyes.

Some of the other sailors were less content to watch, and a few of the servant girls were not backward in secret meetings in the hay lofts. They blossomed in new silks and velvets, and two babies were born the next July. But the visitors roamed further than the unpromised, and thunder more than once grew up around a wife or a sweetheart. A long-haired sailor, Justinian Kilter, was in trouble all the time. Meg Levant had been seen of late with Dick Stable, the tall delicate boy who played the harp, but one day Kilter turned his attentions to her and Stable would not be put aside and he was sent sprawling across the yard and fell and cut his head on a mounting stone. Later that evening I heard a scuffling in the passage and found Meg struggling in Kilter's arms. I took a breath and ran at him full tilt. The charge knocked them off balance, and in the confusion Meg wrenched herself free and bolted into the next room.

"Oh, ask pardon!" I said. "I didn't see you," and was about to go on when Kilter seized my arm.

"Pup," he said, "you collide overeasy for my liking. See this fist?"

"Yes."

"Have a care it don't collide with your nose or it might spoil your chances in a more permanent way than you have just spoilt mine." He laughed. "There's too many meddlesome folk in this house."

But all did not treat it so light nor did many carry their drink as amiably. There was more drink than I had ever seen before, the visitors having brought two casks of wine into the yard where any might sup who chose. The yard smelt like a tap-room, and the house little better.

Annora Job, the seventeen-year-old daughter of Jael and Jane, was pretty and tall with long golden hair and thought much of herself. Jael Job, as senior retainer, on conversational terms with his master and much in his confidence, was a step or two above most of the servants and had not looked with pleasure on any of the young men who had so far come forward, so she was still unpromised. She was not herself above a side glance here and there, but she had none for Aristotle Totle, who on the fifth evening got up late from the supper board, leaving a number of his fellows in a drunken stupor at the wine-spilled table and carefully climbed the stairs to where he knew Annora would be. When she came past he tried first to persuade her and then to take her by force. Her father was the first to reach her, and finding her still shrieking and with her clothes in disarray, he gave Totle a great blow and threw him downstairs.

Totle picked himself up with blood spurting over his face and went roaring up the stairs again, to be met by Jael Job coming down. They locked, and fell together, and burst open the door into the banqueting hall. Neither Mr Knyvett nor Captain Elliot was there, and the others in the room, seamen and servants alike, stood back while the two men reeled across the room, upsetting stools and trestle tables and fire irons and chairs. The negro, tipped off his chair, suddenly leaped cursing at Job from behind, but Carminow, the master gunner, snatched up a candlestick and, spilling lighted candles about the table, hit the negro across the head with it.

In the semi-dark women screamed and men shouted and trampled and swore. Dogs too took sides, snarling and fighting among the scuffing feet. The seamen, outnumbered by two to one, would in the end have been badly used by the Killigrew men whose tempers had smouldered for days; but in time Parson Merther, who had scuttled out at the first blow, brought in Mr Knyvett and Captain Elliot.

Captain Elliot fired his pistol over the heads of the fighting men, and in a while some order was let in; men were picked up, a fire of burning tallow and rushes was stamped out in a corner, new lights were brought and dogs kicked out of doors to cool. The negro came round quickly, but a falconer called Corbett was badly hurt by a blow he had taken late in the fight, and he lay in a stupor for several days and was never quite clear in his head again until he died in '95.

It might have been that such an explosion would have cleared the air, but it did no such thing; the seamen thought themselves set on unjustly, and quietly whetted their long knives and waited. It was clear that Elliot must get them away as quick as possible, so there were long hours of hasty bargaining behind closed doors. It was not until one of the seamen who had been ill quietly died that we woke to realise there were other perils in their visit besides drunkenness and rape.

His body was carried down to our landing stage and taken out to sea by four of his fellows and put overboard. An hour later the last bargains were struck and Elliot and Love left. Elliot carried two heavy bags which clinked. Then the others began to go, bearing their belongings with them. One sailor looked unlikely ever to make the five-mile trek to Helford.

Last to leave were Aristotle Totle and Justinian Kilter. Mr Knyvett had gone in, but Carminow and Rosewarne were there to see them away.

"Well, we'd best be off now," Totle said. "But we'll be back—eh, Tinny?"

"Like as not," said Kilter.

"Like as not in my own barque next time," said Totle. "Or I should be if right was right. We poor Jacks never get our desarts."

"Who knows," said Carminow.

"Aye, just so, who knows. Maybe next time we'll be along of the Spanish, and come blow you out of your little 'ole."

"I'll wait for the day," said Carminow.

Totle showed his broken teeth. "Then we'll *really* get among your women, gales. Eh, Tinny?"

"Already have," said Kilter, shouldering his bundle with a quiet grin.

A gale is an impotent bull, and the two insults, I could see, were all but more than even the quiet tempered Rosewarne could stand.

In silence the two sailors were watched until they had tramped down the leaf-covered path towards the gate. Then Carminow cleared his throat noisily and spat.

"Good rid to they. They only just left in time."

"Maybe they didn't leave in time," said Rosewarne.

CHAPTER 5

FOR several days life went on as usual. Letters arrived from Nonesuch, where the Court had moved, telling of my father's life there but vaguely worded and avoiding mention of a date of return. I heard

Henry Knyvett mutter that if "John's doxy" was amiable we should not see him until his money ran dry.

Then about a week after *Dolphin* sailed Mrs Killigrew's personal maid, a girl called Ida, complained she had a headache and could not sleep. The next day a dairy maid and Dick Stable the harpist were taken with a high fever, and the day after two more went down. Attacks of quartan ague were common enough, and the outbreak might have been a seasonal one, but on the Sunday I heard two of the older women whispering together. One of them, Maud Vance, who was the midwife for the house, told the other that an hour ago she had gone to the room where Ida was ill and found her in a stupor, and had stripped the shift off her and found a rash of purple spots on her belly and legs. It did not take long then for word to spread that the sailors had left their disease behind.

What name it had no one knew, or how to treat it. We put the sick people in one big room and closed the windows and nailed black sail-cloth over the windows so that there was no difference in the room between night and day. We had the walls washed in vinegar, and smouldered herbs in pewter dishes held over the candle flames. My step-mother, though still frail from her last illness and great with child, insisted on directing the care of the sick.

At the end of the first week the dairy maid died, and soon afterwards a saddler. By now there were twelve sick, but so far it was all among the servants. There was great divergence in the degree of the illness. Ida was still out of her senses, but Dick Stable was up again and helping to wait on the others. Some broke out in a rash. Some were troubled with shivering and fever for a day or two and then mended. One man died in wild delirium; two or three lay for days having lost their senses but with eyes wide open as if awake. Maud Vance muttered about "the putrid fever" while Henry Knyvett even mentioned the dreaded word "plague." But Mary Killigrew, my aunt, who was so shaken by the illness about her that she quite forgot her hawks, said it was not either. She had been through the London plague of '63, when twenty thousand had died, and this complaint bore no resemblance; she ought to know. To her it was, she said, more like the spotted death; those noisy drunken pirates; no good ever came of giving evil loose men house room. It would not surprise her at all if this were a judgment.

At the end of October twenty-one people in the household were sick with the disease, including Thomas Rosewarne, our steward, and three had died. Twelve were mending. Then, at last, one of the children took it. It was Paul Knyvett, my cousin, who was near sixteen. Then Maud Vance took it. Then Mrs Killigrew.

Maud Vance had it very bad and lingered for days between life and death; Mrs Killigrew had it just as light, though it pulled her down and caused her to look more frail than ever. Paul Knyvett had fearful pains in the head and could not pass water. His tongue was covered with sores, and on the second of November in great pain he died.

So another long walk, this time in showers of hail, and this time behind a coffin of polished pine made by Timothy Carpenter, the house handyman and furniture maker, who had to use up wood for it he had been saving for new cupboards in the still room. Death I had always conceived of as something which could happen to other people, not to me; but Paul's dying so suddenly, while I still had his metal pencil case, and while we had been carrying on a make-believe feud, came too close home.

In the middle of November, when many were at last recovering and there had been but two new cases in the last six days my step-mother was brought to bed of her ninth child. As Aunt Mary said, it was an inconvenient season. Mr Knyvett, since the death of his son, was never out of a drunken stupor—he wanted to return to Rosemerryn but his wife would not have him for fear of the infection, barring the windows and doors against him; Maud Vance our midwife was still too weak to walk; and with Rosewarne in the same condition, the last discipline had fallen out of the house.

Belemus told me about Mrs Killigrew, whispering it behind his hand when we were supposed to be listening to Elizabeth reciting a passage from Cicero. Mrs Killigrew had been taken with the first pains during the afternoon and Jane Job and Kate Penruddock were with her. "Trembling in their shoes, I'll lay a crown, and not knowing what to do next."

"And would you?" I asked.

"When I grow up I shall be a surgeon. It's a useful trade. And the first belly I shall open will be yours."

"They've families of their own," I said after a minute.

"Who?"

"Mrs Job, Mrs Penruddock."

"Oh, yes, that's true. I've no doubt we shall soon have another little cousin. Ink-horn will come around and tell us in the morning as if he'd done it all himself."

But in the morning Parson Merther had nothing to say. Outside it was blowing a half-gale and the wide river mouth was frothed with white. The house, as usual when the weather turned wild, was full of draughts and creaking windows. As we went along the passage to break our fast we could hear Mrs Killigrew moaning, and Odelia burst into tears and wanted to run in to her.

After lessons and just before dinner I wandered into the kitchen. Instead of preparing dinner they were baking bread, which should have been done early in the morning.

The great bread oven into which the faggots of wood had been put hours ago was just open, and the ashes were being raked over before the loaves were thrust in. I hung about not speaking, not getting in anyone's way. The heat from the oven quickly spread all about the kitchen, and it was a relief when the last batch went in and the door could be shut. Sarah Keast, who was making the bread because Simon Cook was ill, went across and thrust her bare feet into old felt slippers and took a long drink of buttermilk.

"Rose back yet?" she asked of Stevens, who came in carrying a cauldron for the soup.

"Aye. Ten minutes gone. Pendavey won't come."

"Why not?"

"Afraid of the fever, he say."

"What an' him a leech. Shame on 'im. What then?"

"Rose went all around Penryn. Glapthorne he d' ask next. Glapthorne say he've no skill wi' lyings in. He say to send to Truro."

"They'm all scared. That's what's trouble wi' they. Mrs'll have to manage as best she may."

Another woman in the kitchen said: "Reckon she'll be as well wi'out any of 'em. I was twenty hours wi' my third. They leeched me twice, but twas no help. Twas the rowan berries Sam hanged over the bed that give me the strength to bring the child forth."

"But Jane d' say tis all the wrong way round. If the child be the wrong way round there's no 'elp for it. I tell 'ee tis they men coming 'ere, as Mistress Mary d' say. Tis they coming as put the evil eye on we. Four dead already, and gracious knows where it will stop. Two more afore nightfall, like as not!"

"Well, if tis so, I shouldn't wish to be in Jane's shoes. If Mrs and child was to die, God knows what Master would say; fault or no fault, it isn't in him to take it kindly."

"Reckon he should be 'ere to look after his own, stead of whoring after others. Like as not none of this would've happened else."

They stopped and one of them glanced warningly at me. I went out into the larder, which was lined with flour barrels and salting tins and earthenware preserving jars and deep wooden tubs of meal. No one was there so I made my way back by another route into the house. Then I saw Meg, but she was carrying a posset of colewort up for

Mrs Killigrew and would not stop except to shake a scared head at me. Upstairs I heard Mrs Killigrew screaming.

I did not like the sound. Dinner was late and we were nearly forgot. I wandered into my father's private study. Mr Knyvett had used it of late. It smelt cold and stale and it had not been cleaned for days; a dozen glasses were littered about the room, some still stained with the remnants of wine. The rain was beating on the lattice window like a birchen broom.

On the desk was an open book, in which Mr Knyvett had been writing. I did not think he had touched it since the day when Bewse, the head falconer, had come to him with the news that Paul was dead.

I looked at the writing.

21st Oct rec. John Michell sale of 200 yds fine velvet cloth at 18/- per yd. £180. Paid Capt Elliot one fifth = £36. Paid J. Michell one fifth = £36. Divers other payments = £18. Nett £90.

29th Oct rec. T. Roscarrock 80 yds purple silk cloth at £2.10.0 per yd. = £200. Pd J. Roscarrock one fifth = £40. Divers other payments = £12. Aside for Captain Elliot one fifth = £40. Nett £108.

I shut the book. I did not know who else was in and out of this room; in any event few could read; but it seemed a matter best kept private.

On the desk was a smaller book bound in black leather, and I opened it where a straw was stuck in to mark the place. Entries this time in my father's hand.

Paid John Harris, Lamrest, £15. Owe him £235. Owe John Heale £1000, Mr Challenor £250, Hugh Jones £550. Paid Mr Coswarth and his uncle £50. Owe Wm Gilbert of London, haberdasher, £26. Mr Siprian of London, farrier, £100. Paid Mrs Arscott £15. Owe Her Majesty by the report of Mr Reynolds of the exchequer, £1700. Borrowed of Mr Stanes £200, owe him now £1400. Owe Anthony Hony, £150.

There was a long list of smaller entries, some of them household items of expenditure, some debts, some rents received.

I wandered through the dark passage into the hall, where the servants were now laying the cloths for dinner. Parson Merther was passing down it with his thin ferret face a-tremble.

I said: "How is Mrs Killigrew, sir? Is the baby born yet?"

He gave me a distraught glance in which he scarcely seemed to recognise me and said: "*Musculorum convulsio cum sopore.*"

I turned and looked after his hurrying form. For the second time since he had gone I wished Mr Killigrew home.

At dinner that day Rosewarne reappeared. He looked thin and still sweaty as if the ague had not yet left him. Mistress Wolverstone had also come down; I heard Aunt Mary say in an undertone to Miss Wolverstone:

"She will not live long unless something be done. The child's head has descended but these convulsions will kill them both. She is quite out of her mind between the fits, and nothing we can do brings her aidance. I think tis more a spell than a disease. We have rubbed her face with my topaz and given her saxifrage root and motherwort. What John will say when he returns I know not."

"There is a young woman lives near Penryn," said Mistress Wolverstone, pulling up her fur collar against the draught. "Has she been asked?"

"None of them will come. They have no fancy for our household while the fever is among us."

"I am of the opinion Maud should get up, even if it is only to sit in a chair and give her counsel."

"Have you seen Maud? She can as yet no more put foot to floor than fly."

I had to go then to my seat because Parson Merther was about to say grace. But after the meal I pretended not to see his beckoning hand and slid away towards where my aunt and my great-aunt and Mr Knyvett and Rosewarne and Jael Job were standing, talking together. I knew what they were talking about, *whom* they were talking about, and I *had* to hear.

". . . I've heard tell she is very skilful with medicines and herbs, and if it's a spell been put on my sister, then this woman is as like as anyone to know the cure. If she would come."

"Oh, Katherine Footmarker is afeared of nothing."

"Well might she be afeared of nothing," said Rosewarne, "seein' Who she serves. To bring her in the 'ouse would call down worse misfortune than we now suffer."

"There's some as do good as well as harm," Mistress Wolverstone said, folding her gouty hands. "I was once cured of the stone by a girl witch in Suffolk. It was magic the way she did it. Did Rose ask this woman?"

Mr Knyvett took the toothpick from his mouth. "You may be assured if Rose was sent he went no nearer than to throw a stone. Rose would take fright at the first flap of a black cloak."

"'Twould be true of any of we, sir," Rosewarne said doggedly. "There's bad tales of Katherine Footmarker. They say she dance naked in the full moon and if once she touch a youth he be lost for ever."

"I'll go for her," said Jael Job. "If so be as you've the mind to send for her. I'm not afeared. I'll go and ask her if she'll come."

Everyone looked at him. Perhaps it was in their minds that he was ready to go because as yet his wife bore the weight of responsibility for what happened in the upstairs chamber, and he would rid her of it. John Killigrew's return hung over them all.

"I think she should be asked," said Aunt Mary. "It is the least we can do, and what worse can a witch bring than what those men brought? Foulness and liquor, lechery and gluttony, poison and pestilence. A child dies every time they come to this house. Take someone with you, Job, if you want company."

"I think, ma'am, Rose would come if I done the talking. Maybe if I go straight away she can be here and gone again afore nightfall."

Katherine Footmarker came.

I saw her from a window striding up the long approach, a black caul over her hair against the rain. She carried a cloth bag drawn together at the top by a red string. Behind her, at a distance, followed Job and Rose. When she came into the house she must have been watched from all points by eyes as curious and as frightened as mine. All work came to a stop.

What happened I learned later. It seemed that my poor stepmother was still having fits, and the child was as yet unborn. In the fits Mrs Killigrew was becoming violent, and between them she lay like one dead except now and then for a long shuddering sigh. Katherine Footmarker looked over the sick woman thoroughly and in silence. Then she opened her bag and sent Mrs Job for a cauldron of hot water. All this while Mrs Killigrew lay quiet, but at this stage she began to shake with her next convulsion. Footmarker thereupon caused a crystal of salt or nitre or some other unknown element to be inserted in the sick woman's rectum, and at the same time rags were soaked in the water, a strange yellow flower powdered over them, and wrapped around, and the steaming hot bandage put about her head.

Kate Penruddock said that when this was applied a strange draught came into the room and caused all the candle flames to flutter and darken. At the same moment Mrs Killigrew gave a piercing scream and her struggles began to subside. Afterwards there were strong faecal evacuations before the birth pangs began again. For an hour this continued, then Footmarker sent for a needle and with this pierced the jugular vein, drawing off a little poisoned blood. At about four o'clock Mrs Killigrew came to her senses and asked for a drink of wine. This Katherine Footmarker refused her, but instead she mixed her a posset in which were dissolved some fennel and poppy seed and terrible things out of two bottles that Mrs Penruddock could not bring herself to describe. At five o'clock Mrs Killigrew was delivered of a strong male child, perfect in every part.

A little later, just as darkness was falling, the child went into convulsions of its own and died. They said it wore such an expression on its face as if it was a damned soul.

Much against our wishes we had been herded in by Parson Merther to wash ourselves and tidy for supper, so I knew nothing for a time except that Katherine Footmarker had triumphed. I was full of a strange exaltation as if I had been a party to the magic. After all my fears, this proved that the woman I had been to was good and not evil. I had done no wrong by going to her. I was delighted for Mrs Killigrew that she was through her ordeal. Perhaps if Katherine Footmarker had been summoned earlier she might even have been able to save Paul Knyvett's life and those others who had died from the fever.

We trooped into the hall a half hour later than the appointed time of six, knowing the meal would not be ready yet; fifteen or so of the servants were standing about in groups whispering, and Mr Knyvett was already seated at the top table, waving his toothpick and talking to Rosewarne who was standing behind him.

Belemus had slipped away on the walk downstairs and he rejoined us now and moved into place beside me.

"The child's dead," he said.

Then I had a strange and terrible feeling in my vitals as if the fever had struck.

"How? When?"

"Of fits. Of the foulest most fiendish fits ever you saw. They say that as it died its body contorted and changed into the shape of a black dog."

". . . How could that be?"

He looked at me with his craggy face twisted wryly. "I don't know how it could be, cousin. I only know that that is how it is being spoken about the house. It may be—as Rosewarne and others swear—that the Footmarker woman is as she is because she's kissed the naked buttocks of the devil bent over the altar at black mass. Anyway, if she can grow wings and fly, now is the time for her to do it."

"How long is it since she left?"

"She hasn't left. She was leaving when the change took place. She was stopped. They was to have taken her and locked her in one of the dungeons of the castle, but Foster would not have her—said it would ill-wish him in any fight with the Spanish—so she is in the cellar under the Gate Tower. It was the furthest away they could put her overnight for safety."

We all stood. "Oh, Lord Jesus Christ," began Parson Merther, "almighty and most merciful Saviour, we the most sinful, the most errant of Thy creatures, do humbly beseech Thee. . . ."

When all were seated I said: "Why overnight? What will they do with her?"

Belemus shrugged. "That will depend on your father, no doubt. He's not likely to be kindly disposed."

"But when is he back? Perhaps not for—"

"Tomorrow. I thought you knew, witless. John Michell has had word that he lay last night with George Grenville at Penheale and should be home by this time tomorrow."

Supper was customarily noisy, but the hall was quiet that night, more so than at the height of the fever. Miss Mary Killigrew did not appear at all and Mr Knyvett was drunk. Afterwards, while Parson Merther waited impatiently for me to follow the others, I spoke to Mistress Wolverstone.

"What?" she said. "What? Well, your step-mother is asleep now. She breathes peaceably; pray God when she wakes she will be in her right mind and not overlooked. What? Well, I know not what evil came from her, but evil came from somewhere, did it not. She is best shut up, poor creature. All such creatures are best shut up, lest they do more harm than good."

"Come, Maugan," Parson Merther said. "The knowledge of good and evil comes late to some people. You are such a one. With prayer and due humility toward your elders—of which, alas, I see few signs as yet—you may come to a full understanding. You must thank God that you are not alone to judge for yourself."

For an hour I sat with the other children translating Virgil's *Georgics*. When at last I got into bed beside John I lay for a long time with my head propped up so that through the undrawn bed curtains I could see the narrow oblong of the window, greyer than the rest of the room. It was still raining and blowing hard, but from the southwest, so that in this room you could only hear the rumble of the wind in the distance as it leaned on the house over the shoulder of the hill.

Presently John, whom I had thought asleep, said: "Do you think Mama will die?"

"Not now," I said.

"Do you think the witch will be burnt?"

"I don't know."

"I heard Ink-horn say he knows of tests so that you can tell if she has sold herself to the Devil. What sort of tests?"

"If you stick pins in her and she does not bleed," I said; "if you throw her in the river and she floats; if you tie her thumbs and her toes crosswise and she sheds no tears; if you shave her head. . . ."

"But is that not like torture?"

"If she's a witch it will drive out Satan from her and make her confess. . . ."

"And what if she confesses?"

"I suppose they will hang her."

"What do you hope they will do to her?"

"It's for them to decide."

Soon after that we must both have fallen asleep, but I did not sleep long and wakened in utter terror, the way one can from a dream, with the belief that I was in a coffin and the lid was coming down. I sat up in bed and could see no light and breathe no air. The feel of the bed curtains only convinced me it was a shroud. I crawled to the foot of the bed and nearly fell out, then groped towards the window. It was not until I heard the familiar sound of water gurgling off the roof and saw a single light of a fishing boat, that it came to me I was in my own room, looking from my own window and that John still slept undisturbed in the darkness.

It took minutes standing there by the window while the dream fell slowly away like slime dripping off after crawling out of a bog. It took more minutes standing there before I began to pull on my breeches and hose and jerkin and a pair of shoes. . . .

The passage outside was no lighter than the bedroom; from the opposite room came Parson Merther's snores. In the great hall a few gaunt shadows lurked, fathered by a flickering log; dogs stirred and grumbled. I picked up the poker that lay on the andiron in the hearth.

I had to stand on a chair to unfasten the iron bolt, and when the door came open a gust of damp air wafted in from outside. I did not shut the door again but left it swinging, and I could hear the stirring of the rushes on the floor as the wind moved over them.

It was lighter out here, and the warm night cloyed. There was only one light to be seen in the whole house, where Kate Penruddock sat up with Mrs Killigrew.

The door leading to the cellar of the Gate Tower was in the right-hand wall and was not locked. I went down the ten steps and came to the cellar door and knocked. There was at once a stirring inside.

"Who is it?"

". . . Maugan Killigrew."

"Ah, Maugan, I looked for you today when I came. Were you hidin' from me?"

I looked at the door. Last year a man had been put there, a beggar, who was not worth a place in the castle, and the same stout padlock had been used then as now.

"Or did you suggest they should send for me in the first place."

"No!"

"Ah, well, it is good to have a friend. Have you water? I'm thirsty."

I slid the end of the poker through the padlock and began to pull.

I heard her laugh. "It's hard to be an apothecary if you be a woman. And it is hard to do good by savin' one life because then you are rough treated because you did not save two."

The poker slipped and I slipped with it, so that the metal clanged.

"You trying to release me? Well, that's a kindly act, and I exempt you from all the curses I've been mutterin' these past hours. Ignorance is a sorry thing, my dear."

I was sweating so that my hands could hardly grip, as if I was still part of a nightmare. I felt I wasn't doing this just because I wanted to but because she was making me. She had awakened me in my room and brought me here.

Although I was so thin I was always very strong, even in those days, and I could feel the poker beginning to bend. I stopped and then noticed that while the padlock was not giving, the staples let into the wall were. Another heave and the staples gave way and the door swung free.

She came out. Her face was an unnatural white in the darkness.

"You're a true friend, Maugan Killigrew."

"I *had* to come."

"That's how it should be."

I could not tell whether her vivid smile was loving or wolfish.

I said: "You must not go home across the fields. The hounds would be on you."

"I have no fear of dogs."

"They would raise the house. It's safer to go through this gate if we can get it unbarred."

"And then?"

"This leads direct to the jetty. Behind the jetty on the stones you'll find a small boat. You can row round the point and beach it down the river below our land."

"How far is it round the point? I could swim."

I thought of witches who never sank. "Take the boat. There will be a strong outgoing current."

"You'll not come with me to bring the boat back?"

"It will be found in the morning. I have left all the doors open behind me."

"Come here, Maugan. You're not afraid of me?"

I did not answer, but when she moved closer I could not step away. She kissed me on the mouth.

"If that's a witch's kiss, then you're accursed, no doubt. If it is a woman's, then you'll come to no harm because of it. Time will show."

CHAPTER 6

"WELL," said my father, "she was left to go by someone in the house, there's no doubt of that. She could not have forced the lock from the outside and bent a poker in so doing, and then left by sea, bolting the gates after her."

"Anything is possible," said Parson Merther, "if you have Satan on your side."

"Oh, stuff and nonsense, man . . . I do not believe every woman who bows twice to the moon has all the power of evil at her beck. I doubt if this Katherine what's-her-name is likely to know any magic beyond mixing a brew or two."

"Your son died under her hand, sir, and you saw his face."

"Mrs Killigrew thinks she did no ill, but rather good in delivering her when no one else could."

"Mrs Killigrew, sir, if I may make so bold, has so generous and Christian a nature that she seeks only the good in the darkest deed."

"Well, since you mentor us, or should do, in the faith yourself, perhaps you should pick a leaf from her book."

Parson Merther blew his nose and lapsed into offended silence.

Mr Killigrew said: "It has been an ill time for you all while I have been away: Paul dead and Clara and Basset and Wilson too; and now this. But you can't visit all the blame on this woman who came in only yesterday. I'd say, leave her be—but for one thing. I don't relish a traitor in my house. Whether it was right to detain this woman overnight or no, it was done. That being so, the justice of the case was left to me. Follow? Properly to me. Someone who will let a prisoner out can on another day creep down to let the enemy in!"

"Send some men for the woman," said Henry Knyvett. "She cannot have gone far. Bring her in and we can question her."

"I'll think it over," said my father, coddling his moustache. "I've much on my mind today. She'll be at the mill, never fear; women like that don't run far. No, I'll ride over myself tomorrow or the next day and question her there."

"Suppose she will not say?"

"She'll say."

For the next week I lived in an agony of fear lest Mr Killigrew should put his threat into practice; but for a week he did not leave the grounds. He was in one of his feckless, indolent, agreeable moods. Always when he came back after some venery with a woman he would show a more lively affection for his wife and children—though I did not perceive the connection until I was older.

Also, perhaps almost to his own surprise, his other affairs had prospered. Money had come into Arwenack through the visit of Elliot; and while in London he had received some private assurance that there would be a blockage in the inquiries into the boarded fishing vessel.

In spite of his extravagances on Lady Betty he was in funds. Uncle Sir Henry had lent him money, and the son of a wealthy draper called Henry Lok had taken over a substantial number of his bonds. This to Mr Killigrew was almost the same as being given money; the problems of repayment were too far ahead to trouble his mind. He was loud in the praises of both men, and Sir Henry and his lady were to spend Christmas at Arwenack. It was to be a great occasion.

Mrs Killigrew had no setbacks after her ordeal and in two weeks was about again. The fever dragged on until mid-December with one or two new cases and several slow convalescents, but no one else died.

One day at the beginning of December my father rode out with his men, but it was only collecting rents, or so Belemus who rode with him told me. I asked Belemus, trying to be casual, whether they had stopped to collect a rent from Katherine Footmarker; but he only grinned and said no. Then followed a week of good weather when Mr Killigrew was out hawking and hunting every day. He would be away by eight and back at dusk, so the house hardly saw him and the daylight hours were each day a long lull of sunny quietness between the shouts and clatter and bustle of morning and the clamour of late afternoon. I knew at such a time Katherine Footmarker was safe unless she got right in his tracks.

On the fifteenth of December, which was a Friday, he said he was riding on business to Trerice to see Mrs Gertrude Arundell, and said would I ride with him. Though I had several times been to Fowey and once to Penzance by sea, this was the farthest I had been on land. My father had a younger sister called Katherine, who after being a widow for three years had just married Sir Henry Billingsley of Totnes. My father and Katherine quarrelled incessantly; they never wrote unless they were disputing over something, and this visit to Trerice was over property held in coparcenary, as it is called, with Aunt Katherine, in which Mrs Arundell had an interest. That is the way of the Cornish gentry; by threads of property, marriage, and inheritance they are for ever intertwined.

We left with five servants riding with us, crossed near the old mill, which to my relief showed no life, dropped into Penryn, and then skirted the wooded valleys up which the creeks of the river ran. We forded one narrow neck of the river and crossed Carnon Bridge which was the limit to which the Carnon stream was navigable at low water. Farther up you could see the tinners working, and the stream under the bridge was a muddy yellow. My father told me the river was silting up and that there was now no more than four fathoms at low water at Daniel Point. It was on account, he said, of all the trees being cut down and the soil washing away into the valleys.

We passed through Truro and climbed the steep hill at the other side, with the horses falling to a slow walk, bits and stirrups clinking, hooves slipping in the mud; my father said we were first calling at Treworgan, for he had business there.

"Do you mean where the Farnabys live?"

"Yes." He looked across at me suspiciously. "Do you know them?"

"I met their daughter, Susanna Farnaby, at Tolverne in May."

"Ah. I follow." His horse shook its muzzle and snorted; the air from its nostrils rose like steam in the crisp sunshine. "Well, they were there but are there no longer."

"Where have they gone?"

"Gone? How should I know? To live with some sister of hers better circumstanced, I believe. He was a shiftless fellow from whom I could get no rent."

"Do you mean he was—they were turned out?"

"He'd put me off long enough with this or that excuse. A man's a fool who thinks to pay the same rent today as fifteen years back. Prices have flown up everywhere. When you were born you could buy a dozen yards of cloth for £4, now you cannot buy the half of that. Wheat was £1 a quarter, now it's £3. You could get an ox for £5; now it's £12. It is his own fault; he can sell his produce higher. Why, the farmers are the lucky ones! It's sloth has put him out."

We were nearly there before I said: "He was ill, I think. Sue mentioned it when I met her in May."

"Who? Oh, the Farnabys, you're still chewing the cud over them. Yes, he's been ill; everyone's ill sometime. It did not excuse me from my obligations when I had an ulcer on my leg. The world's no place for lent-lilies, boy."

It was a pleasant house with mullioned windows. At the gate, to my surprise, one of our own servants met us, and there were two more at the door. My father dismounted and went in. I stared about, fancying that in spite of what I had heard Sue might come running from one of the outbuildings. I suddenly noticed that there was no front door; then I saw it propped against the wall of the house.

Penruddock was one of those who had ridden with us and I said to him: "What has happened to the front door?"

"Twas took off last week, Master Maugan."

"But why?"

He rubbed his thumb through his beard. "Mr Killigrew ordered it. Mrs Farnaby was not for moving; ye see, she says Mr Farnaby is too ill to be moved. Mr Killigrew had been over once afore but the rent was not paid, so we was ordered to take all the doors off, and Mr Killigrew puts an hour-glass on a pole and says if they're not out by the time the sand is run we're to go in and put 'em out."

There were two white doves cooing in a cote.

"Have our servants been left here since you came last?"

"Aye. The house and furniture has been seized in non-payment and will all be sold. If we'd have left it unguarded news would have got around, and other debtors would've stepped in and claimed a share."

I walked slowly into the house. My father was in what must have been the big parlour. With him was a clerkly man with a book.

"Tis all down, Mr. Killigrew," he was saying, giving a little bow now and then as he spoke. "One Turkey carpet, £3; two window cushions, 10/-; two looking glasses, £1. 3. 4; nine pieces of hangings, which rightly belong in the dining chamber, £3.10.-; twenty-nine pewter dishes, twelve saucers and a candlestick, £2.16. 8. Tis all down in the greatest detail."

My father grunted. "Nevertheless kindly walk with me through the house. I want to have a fair idea of the total value."

"The total value, Mr Killigrew, the total value. . . ." They disappeared through the farther door, the little clerk trotting behind Mr Killigrew like an eager puppy.

I went back into the hall. Behind the door was a cloak and a hat with a feather. Had they not even been allowed time to take their personal things? I thought of slender, pretty Sue as I had seen her last laughing among the trees at Tolverne.

I went upstairs and opened one or two of the doors. In the second room there was a faint perfume: I think it is sandalwood, for to this day if that scent comes to my nostrils I am back in that empty house walking hesitantly into Sue's chamber.

I never for a moment doubted that it was hers. The long narrow bed with the taffeta curtains, the floor covering of a once bright yellow, now much faded and worn. The canvas sheets were still on the bed. On a table beside the window was a sugar box, a cup of mother of pearl, a candle snuffer. By the table was a pair of worn slippers of blue velvet. A looking glass lay face downwards on a chair, as if dropped in haste.

I picked up the slippers and thrust them inside my jerkin and ran out of the house.

We were expected at Trerice, and Jack Arundell came out to meet us, with his mother, younger brother and sisters not far behind. I liked Jack as much as any boy I knew, and little realised what the years would bring. He was staunch, opinionated, frank, and had a great belly-laugh which his new-found deep voice made the more startling. His father had died when he was four and he had been under the wardship of Sir Richard Grenville until Sir Richard was killed.

Trerice was a new house, enlarged and rebuilt by Jack's father, and was handsome and ornately gabled though not so large as ours. Mrs Arundell was good looking and, being a second wife, much younger than her late husband; and I was a little startled to see my father suddenly begin paying court to her. No doubt it was all done expertly and with breeding, but to me, being so young, it seemed maladroit and was greatly embarrassing. He invited them to spend Christmas with us, and Mrs Arundell, blushing, thanked him and said she would try to make the necessary arrangements. "Do not try, Gertrude, just make 'em and come." "Well, John, I have four stepdaughters to consider, two of them yet unmarried, aside from my own family." "Bring them all. We shall be very jolly this Christmas, so the more the merrier."

I slept in the same bed with Jack, in a square dark room black-panelled to the ceiling, and we talked long after the lights were snuffed. Jack said he knew where the Farnabys would be, her sister's husband was called Maris and owned a farm on the high ground behind the river.

Jack had just returned from Exeter College, Oxford, and next year after he had matriculated was to read law at Lincoln's Inn. He told me of his life at Oxford, the sixteen shillings, eight pence a year he paid for his chamber, of dicing at the inns, of long talking late into the night and arguing all the problems of the universe with like minds, of disguising himself in a workman's smock to go and see the plays in St Mary's Church, of the cold after Cornwall and the load of wood he had ordered for when he returned on the eighth of January, of the logic he read, of the laws against beards and long hair, of the lectures on rhetoric and theology.

After a while he fell silent, and then said: "What do you think of the Arundells of Tolverne, Maugan?"

"I have not been since my—the dispute I had with Thomas. Why?"

"I esteem Jonathan myself. But like you I am not very inclinable to Thomas, who is something of a cot-quean and will rule them all before long. Did you know Jonathan is to wed Gertrude Carew next month?"

"No. She's very young."

"It will be a good match. Even his father favours it."

"Why 'even his father'?"

"Because Sir Anthony, I believe, is getting addled in his age and does not know his own mind two days together. Have you any hankering after the old faith, Maugan?"

"The old faith?" I said, astonished. "No. I am a Protestant, as we all are."

"As we all should be. Catholic is another way of spelling Traitor these days. How many of them are in the pay of Spain no one knows. But we Arundells are a mixed bag. Our cousins—"

"Oh, the Arundells of Lanherne, I know."

"My grandfather happily believed otherwise, and we are as staunchly Protestant as the Killigrews. So are the Tolverne Arundells one would say."

"Have you reason to suppose. . . ."

"Do you remember the man we met there? The man called Petersen?"

"Yes. I had forgot you saw him, too."

"Do you think he looked like a priest?"

"No. At least: I never thought of it. What are you suggesting?"

"These priests are still coming in from France, with their intent to overthrow the Queen, or to organise sedition until the Spanish land. What more suitable entry than Tolverne hidden in its quiet creek in the woods?"

"It would be suitable but that the Tolverne Arundells are as loyal as we are!"

"Perhaps I imagine things. Perhaps I am oversensitive about someone who bears the same name as myself. But it—but the change is not so hard as you may imagine. There were some lectures at Oxford . . . a man named Curry . . . it calls many of one's beliefs in question. I can understand a man like Sir Anthony, a thought eccentric at any time, perhaps driving himself so hard that at the last he finds he has worn out his new beliefs and is left only with the old. Like someone with a wooden board trying to rub away a stone. . . ."

A rat squeaked in the wainscot; after a moment it went hobbling away. We became drowsy and warm. I remember thinking before I dropped off of the difference in our positions; I without name or lands or independence, a base son of a great family much in debt; and he already master of this fine house and estate, rich and un-encumbered, sure—so far as one could be sure—of a life of activity and distinction.

Two or three days after we got home I was alone with Mrs Killigrew and said to her:

"Did you say you knew the Farnabys, madam?"

"I knew Mrs Farnaby in Devonshire when she was a girl. Her father was my father's steward."

"Have you heard they are in distress?"

She had not. I told her what I knew and she bent over her lace.

"Your father does not always tell me of the day to day happenings on the estate. . . . I wish I had money to send them, or gifts, but alas. . . ."

I swallowed something and said: "You might perhaps invite the daughter, Susanna Farnaby, to spend Christmas here, ma'am."

She looked so surprised that I went redder than before. "I might, Maugan. Do you want her to come?"

"I don't think she would. I mean I don't think she would come here after the way they were turned out of their farm."

"It was harsh, you think."

"I don't know what they were owing, what had gone before, but. . . ."

"Your father, too, Maugan, is beset with problems of money. There is now a temporary easement, for which God be thanked, but I see no such happy issue as a permanency. So he may seem harsh in his own straitness. I will invite the girl if you like; I can write to her mother. She could come with Gertrude Carew."

"Perhaps Father would not want it, even if they were willing."

"I don't think he is in the mood to cavil at an extra guest or two. Indeed, among so many, he is hardly likely to know she is here."

I caught her gaze. In another I might have thought there was mild irony in it; but it was not in Mrs Killigrew's nature to be disillusioned; religion and meditation were her steady comforters.

"Thank you, ma'am. I don't think she will come."

"We shall see."

One day in that week I was able to slip away on my own and go
to the ruined mill above Penryn. It was empty. Katherine Footmarker
had left and taken all her belongings with her. Only a jackdaw
fluttered in the darkness as I pushed open the door. I called once or
twice, every moment more glad that I should not have to see her
again. The bottles and packets had gone, the wooden mug, the brazier,
the iron pot. Only the burnt circle on the floor and the litter of fallen
ash, a broken stool. . . . I went out again into the open air, dragging
the door to after me.

It was only on the way home that I found my relief vaguely tinged
with disappointment.

The first of our guests to arrive were Sir Henry and Lady Killigrew
on the twentieth, and they brought my grandmother with them. I do
not remember that I had ever seen Sir Henry before. He was, I suppose, about sixty-five or six, but he looked younger, a dapper man,
not tall—few Killigrews are—but he had been handsome before a faded
greyness had stolen over cheek and beard. He had a cold careful
assessing eye like a judge or an attorney, beautiful hands much be-
ringed, was spare of figure, and dressed like a dandy. Lady Killigrew,
his second wife, was half his age, dark eyed, pale skinned and beautiful, but there was something hard about her; she had a strong accent
and lapsed with relief into French when she spoke to her husband or
to my grandmother.

Sir Henry had four daughters by his first wife, all now married,
and all married to knights, and one more daughter by his second. But
this year at last to his great joy the second Lady Killigrew had given
him a son and heir.

He seemed then to me to be immensely old, for in his late teens he
had ridden to London with his father and been introduced into the
court of the late King Henry. He remembered the news coming into
Cornwall of the execution of Catherine Howard and of Henry's re-
marriage to "the discreet widow" as he called Katherine Parr; he had
been twenty-three during the great uprising in Cornwall against the
new Prayer Book led and encouraged by Humphrey, John and
Thomas Arundell—I felt a prick of discomfort at these names. When
he was twenty-six he had been placed by his father in the service of
the Duke of Northumberland and had become Member for Launceston in young King Edward's last parliament. When Edward died he
had on instructions from the Duke ridden to Launceston and there
had Lady Jane Grey proclaimed Queen. After the plan failed and the
Duke was beheaded, my uncle had had to flee the country.

"Walter Ralegh put a barque at my disposal," he said. "Not this

Walter but his father; it was his own barque, he was a merchant, you know, and traded with the French ports. The *Joan* she was called, after his first wife—she had but the evening before put in and was scarce unloaded but Wat knew I had no time to spare. There were men looking for us. Not just the Queen's men but others who owed us personal revenges: if we were caught it was to be a Roman harvest. We put out in the dark before the moon rose; with me was Andrew Tremayne, John Courtenay, Peter Carew; we none of us saw England again until Mary died. . . .

"I was seasick that night," he added, "and all through the days that came. Like Brother Peter, I was never a sailor."

"It does not follow," said Mrs Killigrew. "Sir Walter is often sick, they tell me."

"I doubt if Sir Walter is ever as comfortable at sea as he pretends to be. Oh, he has great gifts, I know, including a gift of the gab, but he's a soldier first and foremost."

"Is he still confined within the Tower?"

"No, he and his Elizabeth were released last week just before we left, but he's still banished from Court, and no easement of that. It will irk him, I know, for he frets to be at the centre of things."

"He should do as Essex does and keep his wife quietly in the country where no one notices her," said my father. "In due time the Queen will forget."

"I think it is a greater offence on Walter's part," said Sir Henry. "Her Majesty, I know, showed a greater choler; she spoke harshly to me of his deceit and ingratitude. I believe she thought a man who stayed unwed until he was forty should stay faithful to her for life. Also I think it is her feeling that my Lord of Essex is a nobleman of the most distinguished blood and as such owes less to her favour. Walter, as a commoner, owes all."

Sir Henry had himself seen service in the field as a young man, and had been with the English army under Poynings which landed at Havre in 1562 to support the Huguenots. He had been wounded in the battle of Rouen and taken prisoner, and he would have been put to death on the orders of the second Duc de Guise but for the intervention of one of the Montmorencys. Twenty-five years later he had been sent under Leicester to the relief of the Netherlands and had witnessed the brilliant, crazy charge at Zutphen which had brought Sir Philip Sidney to his death.

I noticed when he was talking to us he would speak freely of things long past, but if talk moved to the present his face would close up and he would turn the conversation. Only on the evening of the twenty-third, when many of our other guests were due on the morrow, did I hear him talk much of things of the present—and then it was to my father and step-mother when he thought there was no one else within earshot.

They had supped less fully than usual; my father said he had stomach pains, so Sir Henry said he would keep him company at a smaller meal, and they had eaten a shoulder of veal well larded and the loins of a hare dressed with a special black sauce. Afterwards they drank malmsey and ate roasted pears, while my step-mother picked at her favourite sweetmeats.

My father had been telling him that Sir Walter Ralegh had taken a great fancy to Sir Richard Grenville's younger son, John.

Sir Henry said: "No doubt then he'll be sending the boy off on one of those wild-cat adventures to Roanoke or some other point in North America, and staying behind himself, writing exhortations from afar. After all it was Ralegh who should have gone in the *Revenge* in the first place, not Grenville at all."

"You are imputing him with cowardice?"

"Oh, Walter's no coward! I should be a fool to call him anything but violently brave when the occasion prompts. But by chance or design of late the occasion has not prompted."

"And Essex?" said my father, stretching his legs indolently over his favourite footstool. "What of him?"

Sir Henry sipped his wine. "We see Essex's influence as more dangerous than ever Walter's was. And nowadays he has better brains to guide him. . . ."

"There was talk in London that he might be appointed to the Privy Council."

"Oh, I would not be surprised at that any day. Last week at Nonesuch the Queen and he were happy and flirtatious together; then one or other says the wrong thing; a great quarrel arises and Essex stalks off in a passion. When I left the Queen was agitated, touchy, would fly into anger at the least thing. When Essex returns, as maybe he will have done ere now, she will rant and curse at him like a fish-wife, but then will come the reconciliation, and just after the reconcil-iation is the time when she grants him new distinction."

Sir Henry looked across the big room to where his beautiful wife was sitting before the fire plucking at her lute.

"The Queen gave orders that Christmas was to be spent at White-hall: the whole Court has been half packed and in a fret to be gone. Three times they have called the carrier in charge of the wagons to move the royal furniture and wardrobes, and three times she have changed her mind. It will depend on Essex what sort of a Christmas the Court will enjoy!"

"You spoke of the earl having good brains to guide him," Mrs Killigrew said.

"Well, yes, I mean advisers, and the wisest of them are my two nephews, Anthony and Francis. Indeed, if he took more heed of their counsel, I think we should have more to fear."

"We called at Gorhambury on the way down," said Lady Jael Killigrew. "That mother of theirs!"

"There are many whispers about Francis's morals," said Sir Henry, with a wry expression. "But Lady Bacon does not whisper, she roars. We were scarce in the house and the door shut on the servants when she burst out, 'Fornicators, and adulterers and perverts shall bring the wrath of God upon 'em! Francis has no shame! Keeping that bloody Percy as coach companion and bed companion! And those wanton Welsh boys besides. Hell fire will fall upon him, mark my words!'"

"And much more, so very much more," added his wife. She plucked a note from the lute. "All day the old woman talks me a sermon on the corruptions of the court. As if I do not know!"

My father scratched a flea bite on his hand. "You'd have thought the Bacons would have stuck to their own instead of going in with Essex."

"I have lived too long to believe that relationship or loyalty have any weight in the modern world," Sir Henry said. "Brother is against brother, friend against friend. It is little for the son of a slain man to become the ardent supporter of the murderer, for husbands and wives to bear witness that will see the other to the block. There are only two motives which reign undisputed, advancement and survival."

"You're a thought cynical tonight," my father said. "And I've no doubt you're right. . . . The Queen looked well, but she grows no younger. Whatever comes now she is the last of the Tudor line."

There was a short silence.

"And what follows? James of Scotland? Arabella Stewart? Philip of Spain?"

Sir Henry's face took on its closed-up look. "The Queen is only fifty-nine. Who knows what changes a few years may bring?"

"I wish it would bring peace with Spain," my father said. "You'd think that even Philip would see the war's not paying either of us to continue."

"There are always feelers out," said Sir Henry, still cautious. "The peace party in both countries is growing."

"Is it true that another Armada is building?" Dorothy Killigrew asked.

"Our spies say so."

"Even more reason why we should come to a just agreement before it sets sail," said my father. "The last one missed success by a narrower margin than is trumpeted abroad."

A log rolled from the fire, and I moved quickly to push it back, then shrank back into the corner lest I should be noticed and sent away. The new flames cast a flickering light on Lady Jael's white hands.

"It's always a mystery to me," my father was saying, "how the Spanish soldiers have such superiority on land while we hold it at sea. Think you it was all Parma's doing?"

"I am not so sure either will hold good that much longer," said Sir Henry, "since each nation is learning from the other. It is discipline, technique, leadership that tells. Often we've showed ourselves superior in courage but the organising has been inferior. But we've learned and are still learning."

A servant—Rose it was—came in with a pottle of canary sack, which my step-mother preferred to the heavier wine the others were drinking. Sir Henry got up and knocked out his pipe and refilled it. I watched him fascinated; no one in our family yet smoked.

Lady Jael laughed. "What do you do with your life here, Dor'thy? At other times than feasts and festivals. Are you not so—so quiet? So on a desert island?"

"I have my books," said Mrs Killigrew. "And many tasks—pleasant tasks—in this house. There is no town near by, but *this* is a town, this house, the people who live here, within the palisades. It is just the same but in a smaller, more closer way, for everyone is known to us and we are known to everyone."

"Well, I think it would not suit me for a long time, though I grant you it has more of the rest and the beauty than Lothbury, eh? Soon I should sigh for noises and laughter in the streets."

My father grunted. "Ralegh said last time he was here why did we not build a town in the arm of the river? There's ample space for docks and warehousing. I've thought of it myself since. It would give me pleasure if it cut the throat of Penryn."

"On fine Sundays now," said Lady Jael, "it is quite the height of the fashion after service at St Paul's to climb up upon the roof and stroll for the air and the view."

"Men do not build towns," said Sir Henry, "towns grow where there is need for them. If Penryn were not there there might be reason for one to come into being at the mouth of the river. Not otherwise, I should have thought."

"Yet I'm not sure," said my father. "There is a Dartmouth, there is a Plymouth, there is an Exmouth. . . . Why not a Falmouth? It

would be profitable for us as a family, but I fancy it would need a
greater outlay of money than I could ever gather. I will sound William
sometime. He has the Queen's ear."

"You will get no help from William," said Sir Henry with that affectionate asperity with which he spoke of his brother. "William is
knee deep in debt, though prospering withal. The Queen might
lend an ear but she will certainly lend nothing else unless she sees
hope of profit. Her funds at present are stretched to fortify her coasts,
not to build new towns for the Spaniards to sack."

My father drained his cup. "Our best hope is peace. And in the
meantime . . . well, Christmas is upon us! Sing us a song, Jael. It is
the Eve tomorrow."

CHAPTER 7

MANY times since 1592 I have celebrated Christ's birthday—in happiness, in sorrow, and under the stark severity of the narrowest Puritans, but this was the only one of its kind. My father shrugged off such
minor problems as his ever-growing debts: money had come in and
he spent it. Perhaps he remembered the days of his own youth when
life had been easy for the head of the house; perhaps he only remembered his early Christmases with a child's memory and tried to recapture something that had never been.

Lady Killigrew had not been well while she was away, and spent
much of Christmas in her room; this freed my father—and perhaps
all of us—from some restraint.

On Christmas Eve, Mrs Gertrude Arundell and Jack Arundell arrived from Trerice. Then came Digby Bonython and his sister Alice
from Cardew, and a few minutes after them Hugh and Grace Boscawen from Tregothnan. Hugh was two months younger than I, but
Grace was twenty-four and unmarried.

After dinner two of our cousins arrived from Fowey, Tresithney and
Abel Treffry. Tresithney was twenty-one and Abel was fifteen. We
waited then and that was all until dark. At six when we were sitting
down to supper Mr and Mrs Richard Carew came with their daughter Gertrude and her husband to be, young Jonathan Arundell of Tolverne. Sir Anthony and Lady Arundell had not come, nor Thomas, so
it looked as if we were but part forgiven for my attack on him. I did
not mind that because in the party that arrived was Sue Farnaby. . . .

I think, along with the sinking sensation of pleasure at seeing her again, came the realisation that her family really was of inferior status to ours, or they could not have been brought so soon to overlook the deadly act of eviction.

From St Thomas's until Christmas Eve the children and a half-dozen servants had been decorating the great hall and the principal chambers. Holly and ivy had been brought in from the woods near the river and the apple trees stripped of their mistletoe. The window sills were bowered with bay leaves, and rosettes made of dyed rags were strung across the hall. Belemus, given his way for once, painted some of the window panes crimson and ochre and vivid green, so that in the day coloured light fell in, and in the night coloured light shone out. Oranges and lemons were tied together in bunches and some crimson cloth found to hang upon the walls hiding the duller arras.

To make room for our visitors we children were turned out of our bedrooms and slept five in a room on straw at the back of the house. At table we were crowded closer together than ever before, for none of the parties came with less than two servants to company them.

Christmas Eve there was a fine supper, and the Yule log was dragged in and laid across the hearth. It was expected that it would burn for four days. After supper we sang madrigals and carols; then at midnight the Lord of Misrule came in in a gaudy yellow robe followed by twelve attendants in all the colours they could find. Dick Stable, because he was a lively comic lad, and because he had a sense of how far he might go without setting my father on him, had been chosen for the part, and he was crowned by my step-mother amid much cheering and laughter. Henceforward he was to command the merry-making and to keep his throne for twelve days.

On Christmas Day nearly the whole household went across the fields in procession to communicate at Budock, and after a great dinner at which there was pigeon-pie and a boar's head and mince-meat pies and plum-porridge and saddles of mutton, the afternoon was spent in a torpor. In the evening presents were given all round, and we danced until ten o'clock. Apart from little things for my own family, I had only two presents to give, for I had scant money—or for that matter scant opportunity of spending it. But I had had Rose buy me in Truro a pair of stockings of fine wool dyed scarlet, and from one of the sailors I had bought a little cap made of delicate bone lace from Antwerp.

Having bought them I spent an agony of time deciding which to give to Meg and which to Sue. Because the stockings had cost more I esteemed them more, but I was not sure whether Sue would regard stockings as a proper present from me. I could not make her out at all: she looked so shy and pale and hostile.

So I gave the stockings to Meg. I did this before supper when she was trimming the candles, and she took the stockings from me and let them slowly unroll out of her hands.

"For me? . . . Dear life, boy. . . . Where did ee get 'em? Bought 'em? For me? Proper *ladies'* they are. Well, my blessed parliament! Thank you, Master Maugan. I'll never bear to *wear* 'em. But I'll put 'em on. Truly. Not that you can ever *see* 'em." She giggled. "Well maybe once, so long as Dick don't catch us." She took two dancing steps up to me and put her arms, stockings and all, round me and kissed me on the lips. It was the first time she'd kissed me on the lips. There was much more taste and it was more exciting.

Suddenly she drew away. "Do anyone know about this?"

"No."

"Then nary a one tell, will ee, Maugan. Tis better that way, boy."

"I won't tell," I said.

"My dear life, ladies' stockings. You're a real gentleman, Maugan. When you d' grow up there'll be no holding of you. And thank you."

I went away feeling as if I had done something I should not have done. Yet I was not ashamed for it.

I carried the little cap for Sue in my pocket all through supper and through the dance after, but was shy of giving it to her in front of others. Meg's attitude had added to my shyness and reserve. But when the dancing broke up there was a lot of talk and movement and no one attended to what others were doing, so I edged over.

"Sue, I bought you this, I thought it would perhaps pleasure you, it was the only thing I could think of, and. . . ."

She was flushed from dancing, and the many conflicting and coloured lights in the room gave new expression to her face. I remember how white her eyelids were as she took the lace cap and looked down at it.

"It's very . . . kind of you, Maugan. This lace is . . . fine." She turned it over and her fingers suddenly trembled. "But should you not buy me a gown too? A pomander ball, a muff, a mirror? It's the least a Killigrew should give a Farnaby, now that my father is bankrupted and may go to prison."

"It was not my doing."

"Do you know we were given an hour? We were allowed to take nothing but the clothes we were in, and one small valise besides among the three of us. Do you know that your father had raised the rent four-fold since we went there? Do you know that my father wrote six letters asking for time and promising to pay? And it was all just two weeks before Christmas, a time of peace and goodwill toward men—and among neighbours. See all this: all the luxury, the table, the wines, the jewellery; we don't begrudge it to others if we could have had an understanding of our own straits."

She looked up, and her eyes were full of tears.

I said: "Oh, Sue, Sue. I *know*. . . . I know it all, but it was done before I heard. But if I had known I couldn't have stopped it. . . . Why did you come?"

"Because my aunt thought it best. I was one less for her to feed."

The next day, which was St Stephen's Day, most of the men went hawking, and it was good to have them out of the way. The rest of us, after longer prayers than usual—which were to suffice the day—and a quick breakfast of brawn and mustard and malmsey, set about preparing the hall for the mummers' play in the evening.

The nature of the play was such that, although we all knew who was taking part in it, each player should be so disguised that the watchers could not easily name him, and work had been in hand for two weeks making new and remaking old masks. Some looked like unicorns, some like bears; others wore deer's hides and antlers, and a few with no other disguise must black their faces. Dick Stable was to be St George and old Penruddock the Devil.

I do not know if many guessed the identity of the boy who played the young companion to St George. He wore a white skin-tight mask, a black cap, a green jerkin, tight grey breeches with gaiters just above the knee and brilliant scarlet stockings. Meg was not only showing them to me, she was showing them to all the house. I was afraid for her because she risked a beating. I kept looking at her legs as if they were something beautiful but forbidden that I would never see again.

The play would have been a greater success if so much double beer had not been drunk before it. Twice it had to be halted because the stage was giving way from over-many persons on it. When there was a fight to the death between St George and Satan, Satan forgot that he was mumming and encouraged by the shouts of his followers laid St George over on his back with a Cornish wrestler's throw and looked up with a drunken grin of triumph beneath his loosened mask. St George's boy tried to drag him off, and a fight broke out. In a moment eight or ten figures were wrestling and punching; but there were some sober enough to stop them before it became more than a matter for passing laughter among the distinguished audience.

When the dancing came, mummers mingled with audience, and although at the beginning there was a pavane and a coranto, no one was in a mood for courtly airs, and soon the players struck up for a country dance. Lady Jael Killigrew was closely attended by Digby Bonython, and she seemed not at all to mind. She had shocked us by coming down to supper in a gown of tissue of gold lined with velvet, so low cut that her breasts were scarcely covered. Her eyebrows were plucked and her eyelids fresh treated with kohl, and she wore perfumed lavender gloves. My step-mother did not dance as yet after her illness, and my father constantly led out Mrs Gertrude Arundell, Jack of Trerice's mother.

Mr Killigrew was in his liveliest, most arrogant mood, and insisted that everyone should dance a new dance he had brought from Court called a lavolta, whose chief step was a high leap in the air. What with demonstrating and then dancing it, his face became flushed, his thick blond hair fell over his face, sweat glistened round his nostrils and in the cleft of his moustache. It was strange to see him so animated yet with so little animation in his prominent eyes.

Sue Farnaby had avoided me all day. In the play she had been one of the signs of the Zodiac, and she still wore her parchment mask and two wooden fishes on her shoulders. There was a jig, and I went suddenly across and caught her by the hand and we were into the dance before she could stop. For a while she seemed to be making little effort, but after a few minutes she brightened her step. I saw Jonathan Arundell of Tolverne watching us.

"I have been wanting to speak to you all day," I said.

She looked up at me quickly but did not speak.

"After last night," I said, "it was almost more than I could do to ask you for a dance."

She giggled slightly.

"I'm sorry," I said. "It was on account of me that you were asked here and I realise now it was wrong of me to ask. I hope some day—some day to be able to put things right between your family and mine. I can only do my best."

She seemed to be thinking of this as we went round again but when the dance came to an end and we paused breathless before another began and still she did not speak, I said:

"Sue. . . ."

She patted my arm. "Maugan, dear, it was naughty of me to deceive you but I am Gertrude Carew."

I went very red. "All evening I thought. . . . Which is Sue, then?"

"She says I was not to tell anyone."

"Did you change your costume on purpose to deceive folks?"

"Sue wanted it. I don't know why."

Jonathan Arundell had come up. "Gertrude, is that mask not irksome on you now, dear? I shouldn't think jigging in it so comfortable."

She laughed. "Nor is it comfortable to Maugan, Jonathan." She pulled off the mask and showed dishevelled hair and a shiny happy face. "I must withdraw and cool myself."

"Do you know which is Sue Farnaby?" I asked when she had moved away.

"I think she left the room a half hour gone," Jonathan said. "She was the black girl in the turban. I think she went to take the colour off her face."

I walked slowly down the passage leading to the north wing. The wind outside was not strong tonight but every now and then it would raise its voice like a lost dog and howl round the big straggling house. I thought of this building teeming with life and colour and music and little human beings, and all about us were the great empty spaces of sea and river and sky and wood and star. In the grim castle at the end of the promontory two men remained on guard through the night as a precaution against surprise; but in the dark of the night it was impossible for that watch to be sure. The safest protection and the surest watch dog was the wind and the treacherous unquiet sea, for ever ready to pounce on men and drive them on the Manacles or Dodman Point. They said there was the wreck of an Armada ship to be seen on the north coast not far from the Arundell house at Trerice. Wrecks from that Armada still littered the sea coast below Dover, so passengers to and from France did not pass unreminded.

There was a light burning in one of the rooms upstairs, and from it Annora Job came out, her fair hair in long plaits down the front of her bodice. She glanced at me with slant eyes and went on down the passage. As I reached the other end I heard a door close again and saw that someone else, a man, had come out of the same room. It looked like Tresithney Treffry, my cousin from Fowey.

At the end of the passage were two rooms given over to the mummers where we could dress; they were no more than attics under the eaves. One had been set aside for the men and one for the women. The men's room was empty except for piles of clothes; in the women's room was Sue Farnaby. By the light of the single candle she was combing her hair before the square piece of mirror propped against a wooden box. She turned round when she heard me.

She was still wearing the borrowed frock but she had washed the burnt cork off her face and hands.

I said: "I was confused tonight. I thought you were Gertrude and Gertrude you."

"She has just told me. Don't you know I am an inch taller?"

"I thought it was the shoes."

"And she is two inches more round the waist."

"I'm sorry."

"That we differ or that you made the mistake?"

"That I made the mistake."

She put the comb down but did not look at me again. "I think I was wrong to speak to you as I did last night, Maugan."

"Oh, no, it was well deserved. I'm ashamed for my family."

"Gertrude says it was you who got me invited here."

"Well. . . . Yes."

"It was kindly meant."

"I wanted to—see you again. So perhaps it was selfish."

"I don't think that selfish. I've enjoyed it here."

"You can stay another seven or eight days yet."

"I'll have to go when Gertrude goes. I think it will be before January."

"What will you do then?"

"I don't know. Something will come. Do not spoil your Christmas with our worries."

"Won't you come back to the dance?"

"I wanted to take the black off my face. Already it has made this lace dirty."

"You still have a mark on your ear."

"Where?" She turned. "Where? I can't see it."

"No, not there. It's very little."

She picked up the cloth towel. "You take it off for me, will you, Maugan?"

I stood beside her; I was two or three inches the taller and I lifted away a piece of her black hair and rubbed the towel gingerly round the rim of her ear. I rested my hand on her shoulder and it was like touching something magic. I felt sick with pleasure. Her breath was on my cheek. I wanted life and time to stop.

I laughed loudly and stepped away. "There, all's well!" I swallowed and dropped the towel and turned away.

"Thank you, Maugan. Let's go down."

She took my hand and we went slowly along the first passage and turned into the second. Here we surprised Stevens the footboy who was kissing one of Carminow's daughters. They broke off and fled when we came round the corner.

I said: "Not all are dancing."

"It's a merry house. I hope the Carews will stay over into January."

"When is Gertrude marrying Jonathan Arundell?"

"In May. She'll be fifteen then."

"So shall I be. I'm fifteen in February. And you?"

She said: "I was fifteen last month. Soon we shall all be old."

"I can't bear the thought of your being old."

Her hand tightened on mine. "I wish I were a man. I could go out into the world and make my fortune—or at the least try to make it— I could help my father and mother in some bigger way. A woman is such a useless thing!"

"No!"

She said: "I have known for years that nearly all my friends are different circumstanced from me. It was by accident perhaps that I made such friends. My mother knew yours and she knew also the Bonythons and the Arundells. So it happened that I sometimes—often —came to be invited where my father and mother were not, because I was of a suitable age for their children, because my manners were not amiss, because I have been taught well. But all the time there was this difference which now my father's bankruptcy or your father's ruthless ways has pointed. I'm not of their world, Maugan."

"Do you think I am?"

"Well. . . . I don't suppose in your case it will make so much difference. Although your—your mother is unknown your father is the biggest man in all these parts. He'll be able to establish you in some way; or you will be of value to him here. While he lives you cannot want. And if he dies you will remain a Killigrew, with relatives in the highest places in the land. . . ."

As we got to the great hall Belemus came out with a jangle, for he was wearing the cap and bells of a jester.

"Ah-ha!" he said on seeing us. "There's more than one skirmish going on about the house this night. My, your tongue must be black, Maugan."

"What do you mean?"

He peered at Sue and laughed and went bounding along the passage.

I said: "I'm sorry for my cousin. Becoming a jester has shaken his wits."

She stopped and looked up at me with that sober elfin stare. Then she opened the door into the hall. At once all the light and heat and noise rushed out like a furnace flame. They were dancing a round dance, and my father and his guests were in figures of eight at one end of the floor, while the mummers and servants were at the other. Job and Carminow and Foster were gulping beer out of the barrel by the farther door; my mother was talking to Parson Merther who had come to call the younger children to bed; in a corner beyond the fireplace Henry Knyvett and Lady Jael and Digby Bonython were at dice together. One of the candelabra had slipped askew and the candles were smelling rank and dripping grease: it was the game in that

particular figure of eight so to manoeuvre that your partner was hit by
the grease and you were not. Three dogs had slipped in through an
unguarded door and were quarrelling over the bones of the swans
which had been thrown on the floor.

Sue, who had released my hand when Belemus came out, took it
again.

"D'you wish to join in?" I shouted.

"No, let's stay here and watch."

I was happy just then, feeling her fingers in mine. I was content
that she was my friend again and not at all concerned that Belemus's
conclusions were wrong or to think how much happier I might have
been if they had been right.

Mr Killigrew sat up all that night dicing with a succession of his
guests. They one by one took themselves off to bed until at dawn he
was left only with Lady Jael and Digby Bonython. He was in pocket
on the night, and so was happy about it, but as a consequence few
stirred until well into the afternoon of the following day, which was
St John's. At dusk John and Sinobia Enys arrived. He was three
weeks younger than I but she was just twenty-one. They matched
with the Boscawens, except that Sinobia was pretty and feather-
headed while Grace Boscawen was plain and intelligent. In the evening there was another procession, headed by the Lord of Misrule and
tonight he was followed by a hobby horse, who was Rose the groom,
and after him came Maid Marion, our kennel man, Long Peter, the
tallest man in the house, dressed in woman's clothes. It was the night
for practical jokes. Someone sawed the back legs off Penruddock's
stool and melted the ends of two candles on to the stumps, so that
when he sat down, he collapsed backwards into the fireplace. Little
Odelia Killigrew was terrified of spiders, and her brothers John and
Thomas captured three hairy ones out of a loft and released them on
her platter just as she was about to eat. Six of the servants were
served with small beer which turned out to be cow urine.

Nor were the guests exempt. Jack Arundell was given a meat pie
which contained a live mouse. This ran along the table and caused
upset wine cups and shrieks of laughter. Digby Bonython's chair was
smeared with wet paint. Henry Knyvett contrived to set off a fire-
work under the table between Lady Jael and himself, but Lady Jael
was too concerned for the sparks on her skirt to join in the loud laughter.

The next night, which was Holy Innocents' night, we danced "Kiss
in the Ring," "The Spanish Lady," "Lumps of Pudding," and "Up Tails
All." Most of these were kissing dances, and I kissed Sue five times.

But each time she turned her cheek and it was not as exciting as that moment in the dressing room holding her shoulder. Meg Levant with one kiss had spoiled me for cheek kissing for ever.

My father had been shamelessly pursuing Mrs Gertrude Arundell of Trerice all the week, so that the least of us could not miss his intentions; I pitied my step-mother who had little choice but to sit through it all. Jack was boiling, and I could see that he would take his mother away as soon as ever he could. Another affray, subtler and more suspicious, was that between Digby Bonython and Lady Jael, who was far from being so correct as Mrs Arundell. I did not know until near the end of the holiday whether my great uncle Sir Henry was aware of what was going on, but in the middle of the first week in January, Belemus came to me in delight and told of a great quarrel which had taken place that morning.

The Carews and Jonathan Arundell of Tolverne and Sue Farnaby left on the last day of December. The day before they left a dozen of us went over the neck of land dividing the house from the promontory of Pendennis and climbed the hill to the castle. It was a clear bright day with a north-westerly breeze flicking a few white waves beyond the shelter of the bay.

Carminow let us in and we climbed the narrow spiral steps to the topmost turret. In later years I have seen some of the big residential castles of England, and realise that compared with them Pendennis might be more properly called a fort. We admired the guns in the ramparts, walked round the walls, and scanned the wide horizon, chatting and laughing together. Some wanted to see the dungeons under the keep, but Sue said she had no taste for cells and she would like to climb down the rocks to the edge of the water. I said I would go with her.

It was a scramble, but when we got down we were in the sun and quite sheltered from the wind. For a while we sat there watching a barque from Amsterdam furling her sails as she came slowly into the harbour. Neither of us spoke, but as the warmth seeped into us Sue unfastened the tie of her cloak. She knew she was leaving on the morrow.

After a long silence she said: "I have a feeling it will be the last time I ever come here—to Arwenack, I mean. It has been a wonderful week, Maugan, in spite of what went before."

I said: "Write to me, will you, when you've time? I want to hear from you."

She nodded. "But I'm not very smart with a pen."

"I'll come and see you. After all you're only at the head of the river. It will be quite easy to take a boat and go up with the tide."

But I think we both knew it wouldn't be so easy, neither writing nor meeting, and we both knew that, even if we contrived both, it would not be the same as the week just gone. My heart felt like lead. I desperately wanted to say something important to her or to get some declaration from her before it was too late; but my tongue would not frame the sentences. What I felt was not something you could blurt out in a few rough words, but I had not the wit or the experience to frame them in a way that I imagined would be acceptable to her; the alternative was silence.

There is no ache like the ache of youth. I knew Arwenack would never be so empty for me again as it was going to be tomorrow.

She said gaily: "Would you like to be a sailor, Maugan?"

"I think so. I'd like to go west and fight the Spaniards."

"My father says voyages of purchase or reprisal swallow up more sailors than they breed."

"Has your father been to sea?"

"Yes, he went twice with Captain Amidas to the Canaries."

I stared bleakly out at the horizon on which were two vessels hull down. "And did he like it?"

"Not so much that he was not willing to leave it afterwards to others. He says that some come home with wooden legs and some with none, leaving body and all behind, and that those who return learn little but to eat tallow and drink stinking water from the ship's pump."

"Some gain honour and a great name."

She also was staring over the water. I think neither of us was attending seriously to what the other said.

"I *wish* that I were older."

"It will come, Maugan."

"Perhaps not soon enough."

Both the ships on the horizon were now closer in.

"We must go," Sue said. "Dinner will be on the table. The rich man's guests must curtsey and say 'Thank you, God be with you,' and your serving men will be ready with the wines and the meats and we shall all be called to say grace."

She got up to leave but I did not move.

"Maugan." She held out her hand.

I took it and got up; she smiled at me. I bent and kissed her cheek, which she turned to me. I moved my head quickly and kissed her lips. It was a poor kiss, a child's kiss with a man's meaning in it, one stolen rather than given.

She smiled past me. Her lips trembled and she said: "I had wild dreams last night that the Spanish were here. I dreamed of snakes and angels. D'you know what that means?"

"No."

"It's an omen of some sort. Maugan, I'm afraid. Afraid for the future. Will you take this and keep it for remembrance?"

She unclasped a small gilt bracelet from her wrist.

"I'll keep it, Sue. Here, will you take this stone, it's all I have."

"I'll keep it always."

We began to climb slowly back out of that warm corner of the world, up towards the castle.

Young John, my eldest half-brother, who was now thirteen, was climbing down the rocks towards us followed by Thomas and Odelia.

"Did you see that?" he called as he came within hearing. "She's *Frances* of Fowey being chased by a Spanish galley, Carminow says. From Blavet, Carminow says."

We swung round. The second ship had turned away, and without the spy-glass one could not tell her identity.

"Carminow says she's been lurking off here all week; two barques, he says, was chased by her yesterday and were forced to hazard themselves almost on the cliffs to be free."

Thomas and Odelia were chattering beside him, but Sue and I gazed out at the sea with not a word to say.

"Carminow says if she had come another half mile he would have fired on her. I wish she had, don't you? The guns have not been fired since April last when they stayed a suspicious Frenchman. D'you remember, we were reading from the *Georgics* and Ink-horn would not let us go to the window and see!"

"Part of your dream," I said to Sue in an undertone.

"Yes," she said. "Part of my dream."

CHAPTER 8

For me that was the last of Christmas, though I played my part to the fag-end. By the first days of January our party was winnowed away. All the Arundells had gone, and Digby and Alice Bonython—Digby with a flea in his ear, having trespassed, not without a welcome, on Sir Henry Killigrew's preserves.

Perhaps now looking back I am more aware than I was at the time of some feverishness in my father's festive mood. It emerged more than ever as the first days of January came in, for he tried to hold each parting guest a while longer. As Twelfth Night drew near preparations were set afoot for a special evening to bring our Christmas to its close. If the weather favoured there was to be a bonfire out of doors with some fireworks my father had bought in London cheap after one of the Court festivities had been rained off. The Lord of Misrule was to be dethroned, with lots of horse-play, and an effigy of him was to be burned on the bonfire.

But the project seemed ill-wished from the first. It was as if the enclosed, blinkered, private festive days were too near their end and the cold sharp edges of winter and reality were pushing their way into our lives. In the morning three hoys from Devon came into the harbour to join the *Frances* of Fowey, and later two barques, one from Bremen and one from Dieppe, made a cluster in the crook of the bay which demanded my father's urgent attention. He was busy till dinner time. In the afternoon Thomas Rosewarne returned from Truro with news of difficulties over the disposal of Treworgan, the Farnaby house, which someone was now trying to seize by execution of a bailiff's order on a debt owed by my father. In the evening Sir Walter Ralegh arrived.

We were just ready to sit down to supper, the cloths laid, the cold dishes on the table, when Stevens and Penruddock came quickly up to Mr Killigrew, both sweating with the need to tell urgent news. Mr Killigrew had no time to move or issue orders before our visitor came into the room on clanking feet, followed by his personal servant, while two other servants came no farther than the door.

"I disturb you," he said. "Why, Sir Henry, and my lady. Mistress Killigrew, your servant." He lifted his eyes briefly to the decorations. "I had forgot it was still Christmas, Mr Killigrew, pray excuse me."

After the silence all was commotion. However much Sir Walter, drawing off his gloves and warming his hands before the fire, might protest that he wished in no way to disturb us, his presence was like a tiger shark thrust into a pool of minnows. Although he was not above six feet in height, the old illusion was again created that he was taller than anyone else in the room. It was not just his reputation, nor was it his voice which was thin and rather high with west-country overtones. Nor was it any charm of manner, for he smiled seldom and his manners barely hid an impatience to be done with the courtesies of the evening.

It seemed he had been at a Stannary Court at Helston and had been charged by the Privy Council to report on the fortifications of Pendennis on his way home. This he proposed to do in the first light of morning, having lain here, so that he might also visit St Mawes later in the morning and be at Fowey by this hour tomorrow. As my father said after his departure, Sir Walter, in his offices of Lord

Lieutenant of the county, Lord Warden of the Stannaries, and Member of Parliament for St Michael, did nothing but good for the county in his appointments, but his visits to it were always in haste and he always seemed glad to be gone.

My grandmother, on hearing of his arrival, hastened down to be of the party, and no one dared proceed with the jokes that had been planned. Later it was heard that the bonfire and the fireworks had been cancelled because Sir Walter thought they might start a false alarm of a Spanish invasion.

Sir Walter ate sparingly and drank less. He talked much in fluent French to Lady Jael who alone bloomed under his conversation. But in a few minutes my father excused himself to his other guests and he and Ralegh and Sir Henry went off together, followed by my grandmother, who refused to be left out, and Henry Knyvett, spavin-shanked and skull-capped, carrying his wine cup.

For an hour games were played but everything had gone out of the night, and I wandered moodily off. At the withdrawing chamber door I heard voices, and Carminow came out.

"Where's Wilky?" Stephen Wilky was my father's personal servant.

"I don't know, but I think he is in the hall."

"Mr Killigrew has been pulling the bell and no one has answered it. Tell Wilky to bring the map of Europe from Mr Killigrew's private chamber."

I nodded and ran off down the passage, but after a moment's hesitation fetched the map myself.

They were grouped round the long oak table at the end of the room, Ralegh at the head of it. ". . . if you are aware, Sir Henry," he was saying, "whom you are suggesting we make peace with, for in this you cannot negotiate with Spain, but only with the man who speaks for Spain."

"Difficult, I'm aware, but not impossible—"

"I would have thought more and more impossible. Philip is a fanatic on the verge of mania. Look at his ancestry. His parents were first cousins, both grandchildren of Ferdinand and Isabella. He carries in him hereditary taints. His grandmother, Juana the Mad, lived three parts of her life in a melancholy torpor. His father, for all his gross appetites and power of mind and body, became in middle life a prey to moods of religious exaltation and black despair. Philip might make a peace, but it would only be on terms that a fanatic would approve."

"Burghley is not unaware of the hazards," Sir Henry said. "But throughout his life, in spite of all, Philip has striven for peace with England. He cannot be unaware of the great need for a respite in Europe, for time to let religious passions cool—"

Ralegh interrupted impatiently. "Do not forget his own claim to our throne. Plantagenet blood and a direct descent from John of Gaunt, son of Edward III. He was married to Mary Tudor and has already virtually been King of England for a short time. And Mary Stuart by her last will disinherited her son in favour of Philip. He still dreams of inheriting England when Elizabeth dies, or of conquering England before. As he grows older and our Queen still lives his mind will turn more than ever to conquest."

My father saw me. "Oh, you've the map, boy."

"Were all else in favour," Ralegh went on, "this is no moment to make peace. Had our forward policy been favoured after the Armada was beat back, Spain would have been brought to her knees. *We* should have been dictating peace, not feebly negotiating it through secret channels. It is too *late* for peace, Sir Henry. Four years ago Spain was in dire distress, her fleets scattered and destroyed, her coasts open to the massive counterstroke which we could have mounted the next year. But instead we did all by quarter measures, by petty invasions and timid retreats. Now we are no longer in the strong position we were."

My father began to unroll the map along the table; the others held it down with their hands but as yet paid little attention to it; Sir Walter was not now to be stopped.

"The Spanish are a noble and a clever race. If one thing was made plain to them by our defeat of their Armada it was that our ships, our training, our gunnery were better than theirs. Since then they have been building feverishly, and every one of their new ships is built on English lines or putting to use the lessons of their first Armada. In some cases even the designers and builders have been English. Twelve great galleons, called after the apostles, have been built in Biscayan ports, another nine laid down in Portugal. There are at least another twenty nearing completion, with many fly-boats, galleys, and pinnaces to escort them. Look what happened in '91, when Howard and his fleet was nearly caught off the Azores. That was new tactics, not old. And the only one to stand and fight, by the living God, was my friend and dear kinsman, Richard Grenville! It was two of the "apostles" that in the end destroyed him. No . . . the defeat of the Armada did not signal the end of the Spanish navy, gentlemen, it marked its beginning!"

My father made love to his moustache. "All that may be better reason to come to peaceful agreement with Spain rather than a bitter fight to the death."

"And I tell you, they'll not make peace now on any terms acceptable to us. Not under Philip, not under the new leaders of the fleet. If you and the Cecils believe otherwise you are living in a fool's paradise!"

In the hostile pause which followed Lady Killigrew turned her head and saw me. "Go, Maugan, this is no place for you. You intrude."

"If you please, ma'am. . . ."

Ralegh looked across at me. "Who is this boy?"

"My son. My base son, Maugan."

He seemed in an instant to forget me and stared down, frowning at the map.

"Look," he said. "The Spanish now hold Blavet on the Brittany coast. Troops can be massed there and brought over at will, not in helpless barges to be shot at or rammed by the Dutch. We have sent a new army to Brittany this autumn, but in November the Spaniards landed upwards of two thousand fresh troops; they outnumber us three to one. Of course King Henry has promised to join us, but he will not; he is not ready and without him Norris is too weak to hold the field, certainly too weak to attack. . . . Now look up here. Because the Dutch are enfeebled Denmark rules. Foreign ships must strike their topsails to Danish men-of-war as a token of her supremacy. She possesses all the rich Norwegian fisheries and can close the Baltic to us at will. At present there is a minor on the throne. Protectorates are dangerous—as we know too well. We suspect—and I believe—that Denmark has signed a secret treaty with Spain. . . . Then consider the position in Ireland. . . ."

So he went on, dealing in turn with each country as its position and policy affected our struggle with Spain. I noticed that the hands with which he pointed to places on the map were long and slender, the hands of an artist rather than a soldier.

"Henry of France has undertaken to make no separate peace with Spain," my uncle said. "Verbally in a direct promise to me. And by treaty last June. He can gain nothing by breaking it."

"Henry walks on a wire," said Ralegh. "He fights his own Catholic Leaguers everywhere, the Spanish in Brittany or in Flanders, the Savoyards in Provence. In Normandy rival parliaments sit at Caen and Rouen. North of the Loire the Duc de Mercoeur is his bitter enemy. Picardy is for the Catholic League. Burgundy is a stronghold for the Duc de Moyenne. Champagne is governed by young Guise. Even in Navarre and his ancestral lands he is not unchallenged. And he distrusts the English whom he asks for help. You cannot expect any undertaking given in such plight to last beyond its usefulness."

"Damme, even if he's but half a king," Mr Killigrew said, "there's no one left to challenge him. And I believe he'll see his best hope of prevailing is with our help."

Ralegh drew moodily at his pipe. "The Estates meet in the Louvre

this month. The Spanish Ambassador I think will be instructed to
revive the idea of the Duc de Guise as King of France, with the
Infanta as his consort. Such an idea would divide France more than
ever, but with Spanish aid it *could* prevail. . . . Henry has one counter
to that, and one only."

My uncle shrugged but did not speak.

Ralegh said: "Henry could counter it by turning Catholic."

"By God!" said my father; "he wouldn't dare!"

"I had heard the rumour too," Sir Henry said impatiently. "He
might gain much by so doing, but it would be such a vile betrayal of
all that he and his people have been fighting for that I do not believe
he would seriously consider it even if his conscience permitted him to
do so. He would be discredited for ever. A commoner might do it and
live. A king would no longer be considered fit to be a king."

"Well, I do not think Henry is such a zealot that he will not weigh
the issues carefully—nor should I blame him if he did."

"You would not *blame* him?"

"I would not blame him for weighing up the gain and loss. No."

"Even in an issue of religious conscience for which blessed martyrs
have burned at the stake?"

"I think we are apt to forget that all our grandfathers were Catholics.
I do not believe they went to eternal damnation because of it. We all
try to serve the same God."

Ralegh did not seem put out by the shocked and angry glances
round the table. I had heard before that he was capable of saying
dangerous and outrageous things. My father, who admired and envied him, said it amused him to be outspoken. But these remarks
were on the verge of blasphemy and on the verge of treason.

Talk had broken out at the table again, and Sir Walter, still in
spate, was speaking of his wish to send other expeditions to the New
World; but for me, and perhaps for all there, the alchemy had gone
out of his words.

"If you read the Spanish documents of the last forty years you will
find that they have more than once almost reached the hidden empire
of the Incas but been driven back by hostile tribes, by disease, or by
treachery among themselves. There can be no doubt that between
the Amazon and the Orinoco lies the lake of Manoa, a lake conceivably
as large as all Europe, and on the shores of the lake is the city of
Manoa with its gold mines. This *dorado*, as the Spanish call it, is surrounded by mountains and peopled by intelligent and resourceful
natives who, from evil experience, loathe Spain and the white man.
Therein is England's opportunity."

"Guiana now, not Virginia," said Sir Henry.

"Yes. And of equal import for the future. Look on this map again. Which are the three countries of the civilised world with long western seaboards and a seafaring tradition? . . . Spain, France, and England. Of these only Spain has made use of her opportunities; and look at her strength, look at her wealth! In spite of all her setbacks she remains mistress of half Europe. And why? Not because of her own national resources but because of this life-blood of treasure which she draws from across the ocean. Look at the spoils of this single ship *Madre de Dios,* which Cecil and I and your brother William are still computing. Imagine what England could be if she drew such treasure regularly and as her right! All that opportunity we should now lose if we made peace with Spain."

"My uncle Peter was of the same view," muttered my father. "Rest his soul, he was an adventurous rascal, always fighting; and I'd have you know he proposed a voyage to the Grain Coast and the Ivory Coast ten years before Hawkins made it. It was not his fault he didn't go, it was lack of the means to mount an expedition."

"And such work of adventure should offer far more than prizes and spoil," said Ralegh. "The Spanish in their empires seek only gold and diamonds and spoil. It is a short view. I would set colonies of English down to live and breed and make their homes there and to live in amity with the savage and the Indian. That way there are greater riches than gold to be gathered in years to come—prizes, by the living God, that will make not just the adventurers rich but which will make England great, and greater by far than Spain."

Just then my grandmother turned and caught my eye again, and I knew I must go or suffer a beating. I took two backward steps towards the door. And then I found that Ralegh was looking at me. I was suddenly pinned there.

"You go to join your playmates, boy?"

"No, sir," I stammered. "Leastwise not willingly. But I must go to bed."

"Stay if you wish," he said. "We are not talking secrets."

So, very astonished, I stayed.

My grandmother looked at me once more, and I knew that sooner or later she would take it out on me for disobeying her.

But I had to wait until my fifteenth birthday before she paid me back.

CHAPTER 9

ON MY fifteenth birthday my father apprenticed me as a clerk to his
cousin, Mr Chudleigh Michell, of Truro, who was a merchant and
brother of the John Michell who had helped dispose of Captain Elliot's
haul.

"It is time you were striking out for yourself, boy," he said, staring
at himself uneasily in his hand mirror. "It will be of service to you,
this experience; and who knows, you may make a niche for yourself
there; he needs a handy boy to help him."

I left Arwenack the following week. Little Odelia wept bitterly,
and I was sad myself because it seemed the end of my childhood
and the end of a phase of life. Chudleigh Michell was a thin sharp-
nosed man with a pock-marked skin and rheumy eyes. His wife was
deaf, though only twenty-six, and the five children, the eldest barely
seven years old, seemed to take advantage of her handicap by crying
all the while. I had a garret under the eaves, and the house was so
built that the wails of the babies rose up like cries of lost lambs.

More than anything else in this changed life were the different
noises and the different smells. At Arwenack one had grown accustomed to the smell of dogs and damp rushes and new bread and sour
tallow and burning chestnut logs and sea breezes and salt air. In
Truro the river smelt of mud and tar and rope, and the house of
babies and urine, and the warehouse, which was really a part of the
house, of woollen cloths and hides and wine. I heard less of the wind,
and when it blew its voice was muted; and I heard much of running
water, for a leat flowed under the house. The most unpleasing noise
of all was of a founder in the house next door who cast candlesticks
and copper chafing dishes, for after they had been cast he would
turn them until they were smooth and bright, and the shrill scraping
set one's teeth on edge.

I had had the hope that to compensate for the change I might see
something of Sue Farnaby, but my hours, which stretched from seven
in the morning until nine at night with half an hour for dinner, left
neither leisure nor energy to go far afield. Mostly my work was ledger
work and copying in the office and handling the bales of cloth or the
hides in the warehouse below. Chudleigh Michell exported coarse
undyed woollen cloth and hides to Brittany and imported unsweet-

ened wines in return. For a man of thirty-five who had begun from nothing he was doing well.

It was May before I had a day off—except for Sunday when church-going tied me close to St Mary's—and I went at once to find the farm. First directions were quite wrong, for it was not by the river at all but in a fold of the hills behind St Clement's Point. It was a poor place when I got there, muddy with recent rains, the track to it overgrown, the gates in need of repair. The woman who came to the door wiping her floury hands was clean enough and startlingly like Sue.

No, she was not Mrs Farnaby, she was Mrs Maris. No, the Farnabys no longer lived here: Mr Farnaby had died in March, and Mrs Farnaby had gone back to Tiverton to work for a cousin who was a lace-maker. No, Susanna had not gone with her; she had taken service at Tolverne, having been offered a place there as Elizabeth Arundell's personal maid and companion.

I walked back to the town in some discomfort, for the name of Tolverne had come to have sinister meanings for me. It was a bad house, I thought, an unlucky, unhappy house for Sue to be connected with. I remembered too what Belemus had said on the way home after the fight. "Don't you know that you have spent all the afternoon enamouring with the little girl Thomas most fancies for himself?"

I saw nothing of my family and heard only from time to time of their doings; but I learned that my father had succeeded in selling Treworgan in spite of the claims of his creditors. It was the second manor he had had to sell within the year, and Chudleigh Michell was of the opinion that at least two more would have to go. I learned too of the great unpopularity of the Killigrew name. Over and over in the first half year I saw the change in countenance that came over people when I told them. Almost always their first question was, "From Arwenack?" and if I answered yes, it was like confirming some mortal affront.

The town of Truro, though it has grown in my lifetime, was then no more than six streets; but even those I hardly explored, being content to spend my few leisure minutes on the quay, which was built out on the tongue of land splitting the streams Allen and Kenwyn. It was early June before I wandered north of the town where one or two houses and shacks had begun to climb the dusty hill amidst the gorse bushes and the foxgloves and the litter of bluebells.

When I was clear of them I sat on a boulder and looked down on the roofs of the town from which a few lazy whorls of smoke curled upwards like a fire that is almost out. A woman with a dog was picking flowers among the stumps of trees to my right, and beyond her four men were cutting down another scrub oak.

One thing I greatly missed in my new life was the sense of being up with events. Ships were always putting in to the Fal with news which had not yet reached London—we were their first landfall—and the constant coming and going of people great and small with tidings from Court or from the Indies made Arwenack something of an exchange and a clearing house. Here in Truro I was cut off from everything but the gossip of the town.

I got up from the stone as the woman with the dog came towards me. It was Katherine Footmarker.

She had already seen me, so I could not turn away. "Maugan Killigrew! I didn't think to find you here!"

Perhaps it was the sun, but her sallow skin seemed to have flushed. She was wearing a cloak with the hood thrown back, and her hair was half down in a coil that disappeared under the cloak. Stumbling, I explained.

"Well, so we are neighbours then, or more or less. I have a little place near the foot of the hill. Are you walking my way?"

It was hard to think of an excuse, so I turned and went with her. I felt again she had this spell over me, because sight of her had made my heart thump.

"After you played saviour to me I thought the mill might grow perilous with all your father's strubbers roamin' the countryside; so I came to Truro. Things would have gone hard with me here had I not been taken in by a friend, Mistress Larkin, who blows hot and cold in her friendship for me, and this, praise be, was one of the hot times. Alas, it was her last exercise in charity for in April she died, and I live in her property now, a small matter on sufferance—since it is not accorded a good sign that my friend should pass away so sudden— but at least I am not molested or have not been as yet. And there are enough brave folks in the district who will come and buy my simples."

She asked about Arwenack and how Mrs Killigrew was; what my father had said when he came home. She asked why I had been apprenticed to a pinch-purse like Chudleigh Michell who must she thought have been pock-marked from birth as a prophecy of what he was to become. When we got to her house, which was a tiny cob cottage built for support between two trees, she said:

"Will you come in, Maugan?"

"I have to go back. I must be back by five."

"Since we're neighbours and strangers in this town, will you come and see me again some time?"

". . . Mr Michell is strict about his hours."

"I believe that. . . ." She put her basket down. "These will cure warts, and, suitably mixed with other ingredients, will avert chill bladders, strangury, and colic. . . . D'you still think I am a witch, Maugan?"

I did not know where to look.

"My father was an apothecary," she said. "I have cousins who are apothecaries still. But my father taught me more than he ever taught them. There are ways and wisdoms that can only be passed from man to woman and woman to man. He learned me these before he died. It is perhaps a small kind of magic; but I don't think it is witchcraft. I don't feel myself a witch. I fail utterly to fly or to change my shape. I have experimented to try to change Moses, here, into a toad, as I was accused of doing in Penryn, but again I failed. I don't think you will come to harm associatin' with me. I have never wantonly harmed anyone in my life, and I certainly would not harm you. If you are lonely ever or in need of help, will you come?"

"Yes."

"After all," she said, "I am in your debt. Never forget that."

Perhaps I was more lonely than I knew, for I saw her again, once or twice by accident and then once or twice by design. Deep down, I still did not know whose design it was, mine or hers—no more did I yet know whether I had released her at Arwenack of my own choice. But I found my visits a break from the monotony of book-keeping and letter copying. They helped to keep my wits alive.

She lent me books. *The Most Pleasant History of Tom-a-Lincoln. The Red Rose Knight. The Noble Birth and Gallant Achievements of Robin Hood; in Twelve several Stories.* These were books of a kind I had never seen in Arwenack, where all reading under Parson Merther was a drudgery. She lent me *The Delightful History of Reynard the Fox and Reynardine his Son, every Chapter illustrated with a curious Device or Picture representing to the Eye all the material Passages.* And she lent me *The Compleat Book of Knowledge,* compiled by Erra Pater, made English by W. Lilly, a heavy volume full of information on Astronomy, Medicine, Weather, History, and Cooking.

With my twopence a week spending money I bought rushlights and read far into the night.

One day in her cottage I told her that the eldest Michell child had burnt her fingers on the stove and she said: "I'll give you some salve to take back with you. It's a simple diaculum and will take away the hurt. If you soothe the pain out of a wound it is halfway to healing." She went to a shelf. "Perhaps you'd like me to show you how I make it, then you can assure the Michells lest they think the ingredients unholy."

"I have never told them I come here."

"They'll mislike it?"

"I don't know."

But I soon did know.

"Where?" said Mrs Michell, cupping her ear. "Where did it come from? *Who?* Foot-what? Foot*marker?* . . . *That* woman! If she be a woman. No one be safe from she! Put that on my Emily's fingers! Sooner I'd thrust 'em in the fire 'gain! Fire be where *she* did ought to be if Christian men and women knowed their duties! Toss 'n out of window, boy. . . . Nay, nay, come to think on it, fire is best. Wait now while I stir 'n up, get a reg'lar *bluaze*. Now then, toss 'n in."

"There's no *harm* to it," I said. "I saw it mixed. It is all clean herbs, pounded and blent."

"What say? What? Green? Clean? *Clean!* Naught can be clean that *she's* touched! She's supped wi' the Devil, sure 'nough, and them as touches pitch. . . . Throw it on the fire! Maugan, if I tell Mr Michell 'bout this. . . ."

"You burn it if you want to," I said.

"What? What're ye mumbling for? Speak up. Here, if ye're feared to do it I will!"

Mrs Michell picked up a pair of tongs and with them gingerly clasped the pot I had brought. She dropped it and it rolled under a chair, but with a cry of fright and rage she pursued it and caught it up again and at last dropped it into the fire. There it slowly turned black while the pot broke up and then suddenly flared into coloured flame.

"*There!*" she shouted in fear and triumph, waving the tongs in my face, while three of her babies cried piercingly. "There! What did I tell ee! Eh? What d'you say? Mr Michell *shall* 'ear of this!"

Chudleigh Michell said cautiously, picking at a pimple on his cheek: "Not as we've proof positive against she, but tis dangerous work, Maugan, tampering wi' such like. What I say is, them as is not *against* Satan is like to be for 'im. Witchcraft and such like is no call for 'alf measures, and Mrs Michell's rightly afeared for the mites. Five little souls we got in our charge, Maugan, and a sixth conceived lately. It don't do to take chances, and I'll thank you to keep away from such like. I've only had cause to beat you twice, Maugan, for lateness and such like; but this is devil's work, and tis my duty not to spare the rod lest evil have got into 'ee. Take off yer shirt."

"Poor Maugan," Mistress Footmarker said when I told her. "I am for ever causin' you trouble. So we'll not meet again."

"Oh, we'll meet. But I fear for your books. I hide them under the bed, but sometimes he roams about late at night and he may surprise me."

"I care nothing for the books if they please you, but have a care for yourself. He has the cruel face of a weak man."

"I must stay with him two years; then I shall be old enough to seek work in London."

She said thoughtfully: "That may be best. That may well be for the best."

I hesitated and then, because she had been much on my mind, I spoke about Sue. Katherine Footmarker listened attentively while she stirred the fire, which was burning turf and only smouldering on that dank July day. Then I found I had to tell her about my quarrel with Thomas Arundell and my reasons for it.

She laughed harshly. "So that was how you first came to me. But you'll be much occupied, lad, if you try to kill every man who speaks the truth about your birth."

"So my father said."

"Did he. Well, for once he was speakin' wisdom, a rare enough occurrence to take heed of."

"It was not what Thomas said of my birth, but what he said of my mother. . . . Do you know my grandmother?"

"Lady Killigrew? Not but by reports. By reports, well."

"I think it was through her I was sent here. She does not like me."

The woman picked up a piece of the turf with the fire tongs and turned it over. "If there be a witch in Kerrier. . . ."

"You'll not get your fire to draw that way," I said. "Turning turf over only encourages the smoke."

She put the tongs down and straightened her back. "I don't know where the bad comes from in the Killigrews. They have wit and charm, most of 'em, and courage and a forthcomin' manner, and sometimes great good looks. But there's a wild and wasteful streak, like a crack in a good wall—and there's a hint of slipperiness and the weathercock about them too. D'you know what some folk say about the Killigrew coat of arms?"

"No."

"That it's a two-headed eagle so that they can always look which way suits them best. . . ."

All through the wet summer and autumn I visited her when I could. She was the one person I could talk to. The other apprentices of the town had fought shy of me as soon as they knew my name, and one or two attempts at a sort of persecution had not prospered for them, so they had learned to leave me alone. It was a bad year for everyone; the hay was ruined by storms and the harvest late and blackened by rain. Prices mounted, and midsummer wheat was eight shillings a bushel. By the autumn it was unsafe to venture far out of the town because of the bands of desperate men who roamed the moors terrorising travellers and stealing sheep. The constables were afraid to proceed against them for they were so greatly outnumbered.

Confirmation came to the town that Henry IV, of Navarre and now France, had changed his religion and turned Catholic, as they had talked of at Arwenack. It meant, said my father, when at last he came to see me, a new weighing of the struggle in Europe. Henry swore he would be true to his treaties, and the first effects of his apostasy had been to unite his people rather than divide them further; but he was not yet master of Paris; when he felt himself secure who knew which way he would jump?

Mr Killigrew said I was growing into a great beanstalk and I looked too sapless and scrawny; it was high time I came to Arwenack for a week or so; I had another half-sister, Elizabeth, born last week and no fuss at all, not like last year when they called in that woman from the mill.

There was to be nothing special about Christmas this year. My father said it was time some of our guests invited us back. I asked him if he had seen or heard of the Arundells of Tolverne. He said he had seen some of them at Antony, the Carews' place, in May, where he and Mrs Killigrew had gone for the wedding of Jonathan Arundell to Gertrude Carew, but the old man—by which my father meant Sir Anthony—was as queer as a jay-pie. He had refused to leave his home even to be present at the marriage ceremony; it was said that Lady Arundell had difficulty in getting him out of the house at all. "It's the trees," my father said. "They've been there too long, before ever the country was Christian. If I had that house I'd cut 'em all down."

When he left he slipped me two shillings and kissed me on the forehead. We were not a demonstrative family, and I did not remember when last he had done such a thing.

A week or so after his visit I went as far as Powder Street with a message for Mr John Michell and saw a crowd come up the narrow way going towards High Cross. In the middle of it was a stout man shackled and walking between two guards. There were three others with him, the rest were all sightseers following behind or others who pressed in to watch the procession pass.

"Who is it?" I asked of a notary's apprentice.

"Don't really know. They d' say he be a Romanish priest caught red-'anded down to St Ives. He be going to be examined afore the Bishop of Exeter who's up to parsonage house. I 'ear tell he was caught wi' a mass book an' a cross 'pon him. Tha's all I d' know."

The stout man was Humphry Petersen, whom I had seen rowing across the river with Sir Anthony Arundell.

I was to travel home by wagon to Penryn and from there walk. Mr Michell personally saw me aboard with my pack, and said I must be back not later than January 1. As the two-wheeled wagon began to move, he stood with his cap over one ear, picking at a spot on his chin, his narrow eyes following me suspiciously as if he thought I might jump off as soon as we rounded the first corner.

Indeed I got off, but not for three miles more until we had taken the long, slow pull up from St Kea. Then when we stopped to give the five horses a breather I told the wagoner I was going no farther with him.

The track through the woods was miry with all the recent rains; crows and jackdaws were zigzagging over the bare tree-tops; in my path were trees bright with holly berries and young oaks with brown withered leaves and rusty fronds of bracken and here and there Aaron's-beard powdering the branches. There was much rustling and stirring in the undergrowth, but I saw no man all the way to the ferry, and when I got there, glad to break at last from the overhanging wood, I had to knock four times at the cottage door to rouse the ill-favoured ferryman.

There was welcome at Tolverne. Even Thomas's smile, though grudging, parted his lips sufficient to show the stumps of the broken teeth. Sue Farnaby went scarlet and then white. The now Gertrude Arundell had not changed at all with marriage and was the same laughing bouncing girl.

I must of course stay the night. To put me on until supper they brought cold game pie and some powdered beef spread with Dijon mustard, and this was so appetising after the food in Truro that I ate it wolfishly. By the time it was finished, the rest of the family had drifted out of the dining hall—all except Sue Farnaby and young Elizabeth; and Elizabeth, in spite of hints from Sue, stayed on and on chattering.

Sue was not so pretty as I remembered her; she had dressed her hair in some different, new way, and she had gone even thinner. But it didn't matter, that was the strange thing, it didn't matter at all.

Suddenly, forgetting Elizabeth, I said: "Sue, you are happy here?"

"Oh, yes, of course." I knew then that she was not.

"I went to the farm behind Malpas where your aunt lives. She told me you were at Tolverne."

"I came when my father died."

"She told me. That was in May. But I haven't been able to visit you before. I have so little time free that it has not been possible."

Elizabeth had stopped prattling and was listening, looking from one to the other. She said: "Sue is very happy here, except that Thomas is tiresome from time to time. I tell her to take no heed of him."

There was an awkward pause.

"I take no heed," Sue said lightly. "And I have you, my sweet, to guard over me."

"He has been better since I told Jonathan. But Jonathan should put his foot down firm. After all he is—well, he is almost master of Tolverne."

We sat down twelve to supper that night at the main table: there were several relatives I did not remember having met before and as soon forgot. Sir Anthony did not come in until the meal was half finished, and then he appeared at the door in his dressing gown, with a servant at his back carrying a candelabra. I did not think he had changed much in looks, but his presence cast long shadows of silence over the table, which had not been lively by Arwenack standards when he came in.

When the meal broke up, Thomas was with me; I wanted to shake him off and seek out Sue; but he said: "Come in here a minute," and led me into another chamber where there was a spinning wheel and other evidence of women's occupation.

"My dear cousin Jack has sent you?"

"Jack?"

"Jack Arundell of Trerice. I imagine he is employing you to spy on us."

"I don't know what you mean."

He stared at me with his angry little eyes, which gleamed red in the light of the single candle. Slowly his expression calmed. "Oh, no matter then."

"But it does matter. What are you talking of?"

"Nothing. Forget I spoke."

"I can't do that."

He stared out of the window a moment and then flicked the curtains across. "My father, as you will have seen, is becoming of unstable mind."

"Oh, *no*. Eccentric maybe. . . ."

"If he is not incapable of managing his affairs this year he will be so next. It is a rotting of the vital matter which is going on all the time. It is not to be wondered at."

"What makes you say that?"

"We are a doomed family. Some of us at least. It is an evil seed in our inheritance. My grandfather's two eldest brothers, Alexander and Richard, *both* became idiots and incapable of managing their affairs while still in their twenties. That was how my grandfather inherited. My father has been lucky: he is near fifty. So it will go on, I fancy."

"Perhaps you take too gloomy a view."

"Perhaps. But the disease has taken a religious turn in my father as it did in my uncle Thomas who went on a pilgrimage to Rome thirteen years ago and has never returned. That's all. That's why it's more important."

"Your father is deeply troubled over religion; many are, and it doesn't mean they're insane because of it. I think your father is swaying towards the old religion again."

"Swaying! He would have us all swaying on the gibbet in Launceston gaol if he were not restrained. . . . That's why I thought you were a party to Jack of Trerice's scheme to spy on him and have him attainted. You seem a likely type for Jack to employ."

Thomas stood with his hands on his hips ready to fight, fair hair curling about his face. Already he was running to fat, and his chin was so smooth he could hardly have begun to shave. But he was no weakling.

I said: "I cannot for the second time abuse your hospitality."

"What? Oh, I see; that way. You rushed at me unawares that time. Well, why did you come, then? To see Sue?"

"Why do you suppose Jack has any scheme to spy on you?"

Outside an owl was screeching. There was no moon tonight and I knew it would be very black among the trees.

"And if anything happens to my father," he said, "look at Jonathan. Another such. Weakly and insecure; he'll as like as not run on the rocks himself in one way or another. . . . And then there's me. Well, I tell you, I hate this house, for it's dank and lush and ungodly. If it comes to me I shall drop it through my fingers and move away. I'm not like th' others, thank God. I take after my mother who's solid Godolphin stock. If I have my way we'll make an end of the Arundells here!"

"You're not likely to have your way," I said.

"All right, bastard, tell me why."

But this time I would not be provoked. "Your brother is well enough and young. He's just married and will have a family. They'll inherit here, not you."

The boy laughed harshly. "Jonathan. . . . I wonder. . . . That's another unhealthful symptom of our family. My grandfather had three brothers and a sister: none of 'em married. My father has two brothers and a sister: none of 'em married. Well, you can work that out as you fancy. But I can tell you, whatever was wrong with them, it's skipped me!"

As he finished speaking his mother came in, and with her was Gertrude and Sue. Talk was general until just as she was leaving Sue was able to get a word alone with me. She whispered: "Meet me in the herb shed at eleven. Move quiet, for Elizabeth sleeps light."

It was dark but not cold in the herb shed, and aromatic of thyme and rosemary and marjoram. I lost count of time, waiting. There was one faint light I could see through the door and it helped to break the blackness. At last I heard her light footstep. I hissed faintly to show her I was there and she crept over to me. I made room for her beside me on a low bench and for a moment or two she was quite silent. There was a sweet sick delight in the moment for me: all the thrill of meeting shadowed by the realisation that it might be the last meeting for months and that we were, by our lack of age and position and money, as far apart as ever.

Then she made some slight movement, and I realised she was shivering.

"Are you cold?"

She shook her head. I put my arm round her and felt her quivering against me.

She said: "Hold me, Maugan."

I held her and felt an exaltation steal over me. It was like being a father and a lover and a prince all in one. I was strengthened and uplifted by her weakness until I could have sung.

"Sweet," I said. "Sweet Sue. Sweet Sue. Sweet love. Sweet darling. Sue, Sue, Sue." It was a love song to me as beautiful as the Song of Solomon. I kissed her and found she was crying.

"Oh, my love," I said. "Don't cry. Don't cry." I half-knelt beside her, trying to comfort her.

In a few minutes she said: "Sorry. I'm sorry. But it was seeing you again after so long. I was afraid you would g-go and I should have no word with you."

"That wouldn't have happened because I came only to see you."

"You did? But I wondered, I never heard, I did not even know you had been to Aunt Kate's, I thought you'd forgotten me. Why didn't you write, Maugan?"

"Each week I thought I should be able to come, and each week could not. I thought there would be no welcome for me here, and therefore. . . ." I tailed off, too dazed with her to be coherent.

"Why are you so unhappy? There is Elizabeth and Gertrude. . . ."

"Oh, I'm not *unhappy*. I know I'm lucky to be here; but it is the thought that my own home is broken up and will never return, and being away from my own people altogether, nothing of my own. . . . And then it was seeing you. I'm sorry, Maugan. I'll not embarrass you again."

"And Thomas?" I said.

"Well, yes, he can be tiresome. But it's nothing. Elizabeth should not have mentioned it."

"Isn't that really why you are uncomfortable here? . . . Sue, answer me."

"Oh, what does it matter? I have other things. Let's not spoil this moment."

I took her hand and she stood up beside me. Her hand moved up to my shoulder. I drew her to me and kissed her for the first time not like a boy but a man. She kissed me back, leaning against me. At that moment I could have conquered the world. I kissed her tenderly, fiercely, comfortingly, experimentally. It went to my head like a drug.

She began to speak against my shoulder. "He has been three times to my room. Of course I have only allowed him the barest liberties under threat of screaming for help. But it is so degrading, I never know what to say, what to do. . . ."

"Have you told Lady Arundell?"

"No, I dare not. If she knows he is seriously interested in me she'll find some excuse to be rid of me. She has different plans for her favourite son."

"But could you not go elsewhere?"

"My mother says she can earn barely enough to support herself and urges me to stay. The girls are kind; Jonathan is good; it's something I can put up with."

"Does he—what does he say to you?" Already I was beginning one of the familiar self-tortures of love.

"Oh, he speaks kind enough, but his eyes give him away. And what is most degrading, I know that his mother need have no fear: Thomas would never marry a girl without money; he only sees me as someone he would like to take his pleasure of."

"Sue . . . we're both—soon we shall be both sixteen. While I am home I'll talk to my father. I'll tell him I want to go to London, not to be apprenticed but to find work at once that will enable me to live—somehow. Then when I get to London I have relatives at Court. It *must* be possible to find some occupation for you too, so that we can be not too far apart. I'll talk to him. I promise I'll persuade him to let me try!"

I began to kiss her again. I could not believe that this was not a unique thing happening to me, that it could ever have happened before in just this way since the world began. I am not a complete fool; but the sweetness of first love is over-toppling to mind and sense. Whatever it was I had gained, it was priceless, beyond earthly valuation, to be cherished, venerated, tasted and drunk of. Above all, it must not be lost. No exertion, no risk, no enterprise was too great.

I said: "Even at sixteen there is nothing to stop our running away together."

"Except that all the laws of the country are against us. We cannot even be betrothed without the consent of your father and my mother. I think . . . Maugan, I would want to run away with you but I should be afraid."

"Sue, Sue, we must not be defeated."

"Your father will surely help us."

"I think he may help me to go to London. But I think if I mention you he'll be angry and call it a moon-calf passion."

The joy was suddenly gone and reality had its cold finger on us. She said: "Go first to Arwenack, see what you can persuade your father to do for us. If he will help in some way, go to London and I'll wait. I can manage here. If it becomes impossible I will leave and go to my mother. . . . But if your father will not help you, if you think it is a time to be desperate, then we will be."

"You'll run away with me?"

". . . Yes."

Before we separated I had promised her that if I could extract a promise from my father that I need not go back to Chudleigh Michell I would come up the river and tell her; if he would not help, then I would call in on my way back to Truro, since it would be easier to return to Truro and concert our desperate plans from there.

I saw Sir Anthony in the morning. He was still in his dressing gown and smelt slightly of incense, but he seemed very far from the incapable person his son Thomas adjudged him. "Give my obliged duty to your father, boy. I have not seen him for twelve months or more. We are neighbours and relatives but I do not stir from here and he does not call, so we might be hemispheres away."

"Yes, sir."

"At one time there was much traffic between the houses. Your grandfather was my guardian. Did you know that?"

"No, sir."

"My own father died when I was two and a half—much as Jack of Trerice's—leaving me with two brothers younger than myself. I was named ward of John Killigrew. Then my mother re-married almost at once to Dick Trevanion of Caerhays. She continued to live here with her new husband and spawned an eightsome of little Trevanions who've all swum away with the passage of years. All swum away. A grasping lot, the Trevanions, a wild and grasping lot, without reverence for the things that are God's. And the Mohuns, their cousins too."

"Indeed, sir."

"Yes, indeed. My lady would betroth Thomas with one of the Mohuns, but I say no good will come to them in the end. There is but one Church and but one Vicar of Christ. The heresy and blasphemy rampant in England today can never prosper, Maugan. It can never prosper."

I did not speak.

He put his hand on my shoulder. "I pray you will be given grace to see your duty as Christ's will."

"I pray so, sir."

"In this critical time Cornwall, unpopulous and poorly endowed though it is, must play a leading part, for we are thrust out like a lance into the western seas. All that is done here is of greater moment than in any other part of this island. So we must search our souls: you, Maugan, a young boy; I, an ageing man; John Killigrew, your father, who keeps guard over the greatest harbour in the west."

"Yes, sir."

"I think one day soon I will break my habit and call on him. We used to play together as boys. I have sinned greatly in the past, Maugan, but it was from mistaken convictions, never from greed."

Lady Arundell came to the door. "Come, my dear, you will take cold standing there. The servants are waiting for you at the steps, Maugan."

CHAPTER 10

I SAID nothing to Mr Killigrew for the first few days. My grandmother seemed always to be about; and also he was in a temper which boded ill for any requests I had to make. It might not have been the same house from last Christmas. The servants were preparing some mild junketings, but we had no guests, few decorations, no plans for dancing or plays. Meg told me eight servants had been discharged last June and although at first they had hung on, grateful for the charities of the more fortunate ones and feeding when possible from the leavings after each meal, they had gradually drifted away; three to the granite quarries of Penryn, two to service with the Boscawens, one to work at the Godolphin tin mines, two she thought to join the bands who roamed the moors. Everyone, Meg said, was in fear of the least mis-adventure, for it was common knowledge that Lady Killigrew wanted to be rid of more.

I noticed that the armed retainers were no fewer in number.

Belemus Roscarrock was away with his mother, but I saw how my half-brothers and sisters had grown. John, though still the same sober, earnest, un-Killigrew-like lad, had shot up three inches, and Odelia was turning very pretty. She put her soft arms round my neck and smothered my face with kisses. Meg Levant also kissed me, though in private, and I noticed guiltily that my passion for Sue did not prevent me from enjoying it.

I had only ten days all told, and three of them passed in a flash. I gradually realised that if I had any ally in this house at all, anyone with any influence on my father, who might be prepared to listen with sympathy to my troubles and aims, it was my step-mother.

St John's day was clammy and foggy—but not with the harsh damp I was later to know in other parts of England—it blotted out the harbour at dawn, dusk fell an hour early, and a low drear wind sighed over the house. In the afternoon, glad to be near the sea again, I walked along the cliffs to Helford River and back through Rose-merryn, sometimes losing my way but never far off direction because I had known all the land since childhood. If I was to ask Mrs Killigrew's help, I must carefully rehearse what had to be said. I must put my problem to her in the most appealing way, asking her first only for advice. Instinctively I was reaching towards that axiom of human affairs that if you seek out another for advice you often get help as well.

On my way back to our main gate I met Harold Tregwin of Gluvias. Tregwin owned a small boat, but it was too ill-found to venture far to sea, and sometimes he seemed to do as much trade in gossip as in fish.

Today he had a tale that while out trawling last night for mackerel off Shag Rock, which was near St Anthony's Point, he had nearly collided with an unknown vessel close in upon the rocks and under oar. He had exchanged shouts with her and an English voice had answered, but he was certain he had seen men in armour aboard.

I repeated this story to my father when I got in, but he took little notice; he said if he paid attention to every story that reached him of Tunisian pirates and Spanish galleons he would have been at arms every day.

I had hoped to see Mrs Killigrew before supper but she was busy with her second youngest who was ill. In after years I often thought it strange that Peter, who was delicate as a child and constantly demanding of attention, should prove so strong and resilient in later life that he stood the hazards of his manhood and of the torn and combative world in which he grew up better than any of his brothers and sisters. His deceptive stamina, his ability to bend without breaking, to trim his sails and ride out every contrary hurricane, drew something perhaps from a childhood in which he learned early to husband his strength and to give ground like a fencer.

We sat down about thirty-five that night. Because I was no longer a child I did not sit with the others at the side table, but had been given a place at the top table not far from my father.

They began to speak of Ralegh. His first child had just been born, a boy, to be called Walter after him. There were rejoicings and there was to be a great christening at Sherborne. Sir Walter, they said, had not been well, had been taking the waters at Bath. He'd been active throughout the year in Parliament, making speeches, sitting on committees, putting fresh projects before the Privy Council for setting up another colony in Virginia; but he was still not permitted to appear at Court, to see the Queen, or to take up his old position as Captain of the Guard.

There was a story too that Sir John Borough had been active again, landing on the island of Margarita, and that the Spanish governor had been killed in battle—

The boom of the explosion was muffled by the rocks and the situation of the house, but there could be no doubt of its nature. In a minute my father was on his feet shouting orders, and the great hall was in confusion, men rushing off to gain their weapons, women calling to each other, children crying, dogs barking.

For the first time then I missed Belemus as a companion. I knew what he would have done—slipped out quietly on his own to see what was toward, no doubt with me as his companion. I proceeded to do just that, but perhaps because of being on my own I ran into disaster.

After the first haste and confusion things quieted down quickly. Carminow was already at the castle, but Foster was in the hall, and he went off at once with four of the senior retainers bearing calivers and pistols. Since the explosion could mean several things, an attack on the almost unfortified house being as likely as an attack on the fortified castle, my father wisely did not order more of his men out of Arwenack but instead posted watchers in the two towers. The women and children he said should stay in the hall, and those not already there should assemble there, with Jael Job and his four remaining best men in charge. My father then picked out Penruddock and Carpenter and two other servants who normally never bore arms, and furnished them with pikes. A similar number of men he gave to Henry Knyvett, and told the two parties to move off in the direction from which the explosion had come.

This was as far as organisation had gone before I slipped from the hall. I raced up to my bedroom to get a sheath knife and was down again and out well ahead of the search parties.

There was a moon somewhere making opalescence of the fog. The first thing when clear of the house was the smell of gunpowder. As soon as the explosion occurred I had thought of Harold Tregwin's story, but now it occurred to me that it might be that someone had accidentally discharged one of the great culverin in the castle—or still more likely have dropped a spark into a keg of powder.

I ran quickly through the trees and bushes towards the head; the fog seemed more like smoke drifting from a fire, but at the edge of the rocks below the castle it was as if I had come past the smoke-laden area, for the fog blew chill and clean.

I looked up towards the castle. The two lights were what one would expect on any night. The sea was blanketed and impenetrable. This was much where I had come with Sue that day twelve months ago—only we had climbed farther down—

There was another explosion directly under the castle wall where it ran back towards Arwenack. I was too late to see the flash, but as the sky flickered I turned and the noise struck me. Figures moved between me and the darkness where the light had been.

Someone fired a musket, but this quickly died and there was silence. A man began to shout. The sound of oars.

I was still some twenty feet above the water but turned to climb up again because the sound was so close; they must have been coming in right beneath me. I took a sharp step up, and two figures on the rock above converged in the mist. I grabbed at my knife, but a man caught my arm and twisted it round. Something glinted like a shield or a breast-plate, and then my head seemed to split open with a blow that reached down to my chin.

I woke in a ship's hold, sea-sick and with a vile headache. A rope ladder was swinging like a pendulum and bilge water was slapping backwards and forwards with the rolling of the ship.

After a while a man came down and left me a bowl of bread and milk, but I was too sick to eat it, and the rats had it instead. I must eventually have slept, for I woke to find a dark foreign man bending over me and fingering the bump on my head. He nodded at me but said nothing and climbed the rope ladder and disappeared.

I was wondering whether to make the effort to try the ladder myself when the hatchway opened and another man came down. He was big and fair-haired with a lean fox face. He was Captain Richard Burley of *Neptune*, who had feasted at our house in company with Captain Elliot and Mr Love on my fourteenth birthday.

Book Two

CHAPTER 1

IT was the twenty-fifth of February, 1594. The small and shabby cavalcade was dwarfed by the mountains that raised their shattered tips into an ultramarine sky. Leading the party on foot was a tall peasant called Bartolomeo. He took long steady strides, using his crooked stick as if to divine the way. On his almost shaven head he wore a wide brimmed black hat with a broad strap under the chin, and his great black coat was wrapped tight around him against the wind.

I wished I had such a cloak for protection. The wind had blown for four days. Although the snow was ankle deep where we walked and clutched crisply at every step with a fine powdery film misting up to our knees, most of the peaks far above us were bare. They had been blown bare.

There were two carts in our procession, carts drawn by mules whose high wooden collars were painted with flowers, and whose shabby harness, held together with hemp and cord, was decorated with tiny bells and rosettes of vivid coloured wool. But I did not ride in them. The second cart carried produce necessary for our survival from day to day. The first carried Captain Richard Burley and Captain Juan Rodrigo Alazar, a Portuguese gentleman I had met while still at sea.

It was the twenty-fifth of February, and my sixteenth birthday.

We were near Madrid.

I have never been able to remember the details of the time at sea. The ship was not *Neptune* but *Santa Ana,* a Portuguese vessel under the command of Captain Alazar, with Richard Burley acting as navigator. Captain Burley explained to me that *Neptune* had foundered with her prize at the time when Captain Elliot and his crew had reached Arwenack; and, needs must when the Devil drives, Richard

Burley had since found employment where it offered. Beggars, he said, could not be choosers. He was as full of saws as an old wife, but empty of explanation as to why they had chosen to seize me.

All the rest was plain. Spain would pay well for a first-class navigator who knew the rivers and harbours of England: such were not easy to come by. Captain Alazar, a freebooter of some note and anxious to please his Spanish masters, had asked permission of them that he should be allowed to raid Pendennis. Permission was given and three engineers and twelve barrels of gunpowder were supplied to blow it up.

The attempt had failed. From the look of things on the night of my capture I did not think that the attack had been pressed home with any enthusiasm or vigour. Burley said that as well as damaging the fort they had struck across the peninsula and fired Arwenack, but from the way he told it I knew he was lying. The details were not true: this was sop to please his new masters.

I could not see that taking me back with him to rot in some dungeon or die in the galleys would ingratiate him further. I wondered if he had done it out of spite; he never spoke of my father without a gleam of venom in his eye, but he knew I was not a legitimate child and my death was not likely to bring my father in sorrow to his grave.

I had been two and a half weeks in prison in Lisbon but had been given a cell to myself and supplied with passable food and English books. Captain Alazar had visited me but had refused to comment on what my fate was to be. Then one day I was released to join this cavalcade bound for Madrid, and Burley was of the party.

We had been two weeks on the way, twice snowbound in tiny villages, huddling in a single hut and crouching about a smoky brazier for warmth. Last night we had left Talavera, and tomorrow they said we should be in Madrid.

Presently Bartolomeo called a halt, and the half dozen walking peasants and the two tartanas drew in at the side of the truck in the shelter of a great rock where the wind could only stab spitefully in back eddies from the other cliff face. Here we ate a frugal midday meal, though the sun was well on its way down. And here both Burley and Alazar sat beside me eating in silence. When I had finished I took off a shoe to look at the raw blister on my heel.

Alazar said: "In Madrid you will have new boots. Those are of poor leather, they do not wear well."

It was not his practice to say anything to me at all. I said: "Why are you taking me there?"

I certainly expected nothing in return, for I had asked the question before, but this time Alazar shrugged and glanced at Burley and said:

"Because, boy, you happen to be a proof of the success of our raid on Falmouth Haven. You or another would have done. But having got *you*, we now see you as a piece of merchandise to be disposed of in the most favourable market. See?"

"No. I don't see. . . ."

"For you for the galleys I could get a few *reals*, less than a seaman since you are too thin and too young to last. But it has occurred to us that you may have a small value of another sort. It depends. . . ."

"On what?"

"A little on yourself. Being who you are, like. To be of value at all you must help a little. Do you wish to die?"

"No."

Captain Alazar took a long drink of red wine. "Well, to stay alive you must help a little."

"What does that mean?"

He put the goblet down. "Spain and England are at war, yes? As countries, as nations. But every person is not at war with every other person. That is for the person to decide. If you have nothing but enmity in your heart for Spain—and show it—you will rot in a prison quick enough, and I shall wish I had left you to the overseer's lash. But if you will take life as it comes—if you will see Spain and the people in it as just people like yourself, among whom you must live and work, then it will be of more value to me, and you may not go to prison or the galleys at all. But it is for you to decide."

I said nothing for a long time. Bartolomeo was already on his feet again, for there were only a few hours of daylight left.

"Well?" said Burley in an aggressive voice.

I said: "I have no wish to die."

"Good. Good."

"But I don't know what you expect. I don't know what you are suggesting."

Burley's savage face quickly clouded, but Captain Alazar got up and patted me on the shoulder. "We have a proverb: 'If you run too fast you may trip over nothing.' Be content to greet each day with an open mind—judge it as it comes. That way we all make progress."

We reached Madrid late the next day almost as dusk was falling and lodged at a shabby crowded inn in the centre of the city. Five of us, including Bartolomeo, slept in a room under the eaves. Bartolomeo had still to be paid for the hire of his cart, and the next morning there was a violent and ugly argument over payment. Then there was another quarrel with the keeper of the inn. After Bartolomeo and his companions left, still grumbling and unsatisfied, Captain Alazar went out. I kept the attic all day, and Richard Burley was my companion. He seldom spoke but lay all day on one of the pallet beds picking his teeth and taking snuff and dozing. Twice he sent down for food. The first time a black-eyed barefoot girl with silk bows in her hair brought it, but Burley looked at her so lewdly that she put the food down and fled, and the second time it was the innkeeper himself.

I could see very little from the tiny window. A slope of roof hid most of the narrow street and opposite a taller building was just going up so that it cut off any view there might have been over the city. All day, except in the afternoon, there was the clank and hammer of the workmen, and somewhere below the rumble of carts, and the shouts and laughter of people in the inn.

Captain Alazar came back an hour after sundown and the two men went downstairs together. I gathered that he had been trying to gain an audience with somebody and had failed.

He tried the next day and the next, and the third long vigil was lucky, for he came back heartened by his meeting, and the following morning I was taken out into a handsome square near the inn, and cloth was bought to replace my tattered suit. There were churches all round the square, and all the bells were ringing and the open space was thronged with people. Beggars crouched at every corner and water-carriers rang their own bells as counterpoint to the churches. Bargaining and argument went on over the purchase of the cloth, for Captain Alazar had no money to pay for it but only a promise of money for the morrow. As soon as the measurements were taken I was hustled back to the inn; but by evening the suit, of blue worsted yarn with a thick blue duffel for a cloak, was at the inn and I was being fitted.

The next morning was a Saturday, and the tensions between the two men showed that this was a highly important day for them.

We set off at eight, the three of us only, passed through two smaller squares, in both of which the houses were still being built, reached a third which had at its opposite side a building like a Turkish palace. The great doors were guarded by soldiers in armour, and the flanking sides of the square were given over to armouries and stables. Captain Alazar pushed his way through a crowd of sightseers and suppliants and went up to a man dressed in black velvet, who glanced at the parchment we carried and then passed it over to a guard.

Inside the place was gloomy after the brilliant sunshine. Here and there torches burned to give light in the corridors. Passing along I got glimpses through open doors of chapels with candles burning, of soldiers eating, of monks sitting writing at a table; now and then we came out into a courtyard or passed along a gallery which had one arcaded side looking out over a fountain or a garden with statues. The guard led us into an antechamber hung with paintings of battle scenes, and here were a dozen other people already waiting.

We too settled to wait. We waited from a quarter before nine until a quarter after twelve. Nobody else in that time was attended to, only the number in attendance grew. Then a liveried servant came through the farther door and passed through the stirring expectant throng until he reached us. He spoke to Alazar and we followed him.

Beyond was another antechamber in which a man sat writing at a desk. He was tall and middle-aged and his face was square and bony and discreet like a carefully closed fist. Two young pages with long black hair stood at his elbows.

Alazar said in English: "Excellency, this is the boy."

Eyes like olives dipped in water made a very careful scrutiny of all that I was and wore. "He speaks Spanish?"

"No, your Excellency."

"What is your name?" He asked in a harsh, accented English.

"Maugan Killigrew."

"Whence come you?"

"Arwenack House, beside Pendennis Castle, in Cornwall."

"You are the natural son of John Killigrew, governor of the castle?"

"Yes, sir."

"Tell me the names of his other children."

"His—my. . . ." I stared a moment. "The—the eldest is John, who is now fourteen. Then comes Thomas, who is thirteen, then Odelia, who is—who will soon be—twelve. Henry is ten, will be eleven in June. Maria is four, Peter nearly three, Elizabeth is a few months old. . . . That is all."

"What is your mother's Christian name?"

"I do not know, sir. I never knew who she was."

An impatient gesture. "Your—second mother. How do you put it? Step-mother."

"Oh. Dorothy. Her maiden name was Dorothy Monck."

The Spaniard rubbed the sleeve of his crimson velvet jacket. As he got up the pages jumped to draw back his chair. He left the room by a tiny door let into the tapestry. The pages came across to me, and their hands searched impersonally for hidden weapons.

"Who was that?"

"Señor Andres Prada."

"Who is he?"

"Quiet, boy."

Señor Prada came back; I was to go with him. Alazar wanted to accompany us but the Spaniard brushed him contemptuously aside.

We went into a small room with a long window looking across the city towards the snow peaks thirty miles distant. Another man, whom I took to be a junior secretary, sat writing at a desk piled high with papers. When we had stopped moving there was no sound in the room but the scratching of his quill. He was in black; an elderly man with pale red-rimmed eyes, a drawn ascetic face with a heavy under-jaw which a grey beard did not disguise. Altogether he looked less Spanish than any other I had recently seen.

I had expected he might have jumped to his feet but it was Señor Prada who made the obeisance. I think he said: "This is the boy." One grew used to the sound of a sentence.

The elderly man said in a very good English: "You think he is bona fide?"

"Yes, sire."

"Come here, boy."

I took two cautious steps nearer the table.

"Know you who I am?"

"No, sir."

The elderly man put his pen down and rubbed his knuckles together as if he was cold. The papers on his desk were elaborate lists and statistical tables, many of them annotated. "He is certainly English. It is a type I well knew once. . . . Are you a Luterano, boy?"

"Sir?"

"Are you an apostate? . . . What they call a Protestant?"

"Yes, sir."

A glint came into the tired eyes. "If you are to stay here that must be changed. It must be changed, Prada."

"Yes, sire."

"You come from a western county which, alas, I never visited but one which I always held in esteem. You are Celts and have affinities with the Irish. A sturdy, faithful stock among whom fidelity to the religion of Christ dies hard."

"We too—" I began and stopped.

"We too?"

"No, sir," I said, seeing danger in argument.

"Throughout England," he said, "good and saintly people groan under the yoke. It may be that, God guiding and strengthening our hands, they shall need to wait but a short time now."

A brilliant band of sunlight lit up the Hapsburg coat of arms on the carpet by my feet. Was this the man Ralegh had spoken about at Arwenack last Christmas twelve-month, this quiet, clerkly, dedicated, elderly person?

"There is much unrest in England," he went on. "Oh, I know that, boy, everyone is agreed on it. She is shaken by religious feuds to the point that many parts are on the verge of revolt. There is pestilence and other internal troubles, too. It is a judgment. . . ."

"Your Majesty—" Prada began.

The knuckles cracked. "Tell me, boy, where is Drake, now? We have seen nothing of him these later years."

"I think he lives near Plymouth, sir."

"You are right. He superintends its fortifications. He works on schemes for improving its supply of water. He has been out of favour with the Queen. He grows old—as we all grow old. If he came forth he would fare less well."

"Yes, sir." I was startled by his sharpness and his detailed knowledge.

"Yet I have information that he still yearns for adventure. I have information that the Queen is regarding him more kindly again. Knew you that?"

"No, sir."

"Well, let him beware if he comes forth again. He will fare less well. He will find our fleets greatly changed."

"Your Majesty," Prada said, "the two men who brought this boy are in the next chamber and ask some reward for his capture."

The King picked up a sheet of parchment and held it in hands of the same colour. "Is it true, boy, what they say here, that they fired your castle?"

"Yes, sir," I said, after a moment. "Yes, it was the explosions that brought me from the house. Of course I do not know what damage was caused."

"In due course we shall have word on that. Is your castle well prepared to resist invasion?"

"Yes, sir."

"My information is that it is not. My information is that your father neglects his defences, selling the powder and shot where best he can. . . . Prada, can you use this boy?"

"I think, sire, he may be of some value."

The King turned the parchment over and over in his thin fingers. "Give this Portuguese a gold chain of a fair weight and quality. And grant him an annual pension of fifty ducats. . . . The Englishman . . . give him a hundred ducats and some employment with the fleet. He can continue to be useful in other ways."

"Yes, sire."

The King extended his hand, it seemed for me to kiss, and then withdrew it. There were little beads of saliva at the corners of his mouth.

"You will keep this boy in your service, Prada?"

"Yes, sire. So long as we can see use for him."

"Then attend to his soul. At that age a course of instruction may do all that is necessary. . . . But whatever is necessary, let it be done. . . ."

Before we left the room the pen was scratching on the paper again.

I separated from Alazar and Burley in the middle of the following week.

Whatever the value of the reward, they were not unsatisfied with it. Alazar's gold chain was one for which he said he could get two-hundred ducats anywhere. Their interest in me finished from that day. They were to hand me over on the Tuesday to Señor Prada; I had to be there and I had to be alive, that was all. Burley was drunk all Sunday.

On the Monday while Alazar was out Burley brought back a woman and made love to her, with me in the room. It confused and frightened and troubled me as nothing else could have. This grabbing, tittering, grunting struggle between two half-naked human beings almost made me sick. No one could have grown up in Arwenack ignorant of sex, but I had never seen it happen before. That this was all part of the same tender feeling that I had for Sue Farnaby, as it were the other side of a coin, seemed to darken and poison what I had thought of as true and good. The woman was stout and her flesh was white and flabby, her breasts heavy and sagging, her thighs coloured like the underside of dead fish. They made little attempt to hide themselves from me, and at last I turned to stare out of the window trembling and breathless. What made the whole hour worse than insupportable was that while with part of myself I wanted to bludgeon them both to death, obliterate them as one does a disgusting slug turned up under a stone, another part of me was curious and lustful and fascinated.

I realised that day what the Puritans meant when they spoke of lust as an abomination and a secret blasphemy, a lechery put in men's minds by Satan himself.

So on the Tuesday I was glad to be rid of them. Whatever the future, I was glad to see them go.

Señor Andres Prada had a small house at the corner of the great square with all the churches, the Puerta del Sol. I was put in the charge of a young man called Rodez who spoke English and I was given a garret room at the top of the house, but mercifully was

to have it to myself. During the first weeks I used to look out of
the window and think, well, this is one way, there is just room for
me to squeeze through, and so long as I do not land on something
that breaks my fall I should die.

I learned much from Rodez; we talked much, and while he improved his English I began to pick up a smattering of Spanish. Rodez
was a nephew of Prada and was attached to the Court as a page.

Prada was one of the two chief secretaries to the King. It seemed
possible, Rodez said, that in time I too would become a page at the
Court. When I asked him why, he shrugged and said that had been
decided, why should I quarrel? Would I rather have my bones
stretched by the Inquisitor?

Prada spent most of his time at the Palace or escorting the King
on long journeys of religious penance to the royal monastery of St
Lawrence of the Escorial, a giant mausoleum to house his father's
remains which the King had just built on a spur of rock among the
mountains fifty kilometres distant; so Prada maintained but a small
household for himself. Señora Prada was much younger than he, a tall
dark, bold woman with a wanton way of speaking and dressing. Rodez
also had two sisters in the household, Isabella and Mariana, young
women of twenty-odd who aped Señora Prada in their manners.
I had thought of Spanish women as strictly brought up, carefully
chaperoned, discreet, and demure. These were not. Mariana, the
younger, in particular had a wild way of talking and looking and
seemed to care nothing for convention or accepted behaviour. Even
Father Rafael, the priest who lived with us, was unable or unwilling to curb her.

One day he called me into his little room on the second floor,
which was half a study and half a cell, and began to question me as
to my religious beliefs, but his English was too bad for us to make
progress. After two hours, he gave me some books written in English
which he said I must read and study within the week. He did not
seem interested in his task, which was a relief. At table he ate and
drank as heartily as the rest, and his clothes were of the finest.

Not so another priest who came three days later from the Holy
Office. A man with a face like a vulture, his grimed hands folded
behind him, sandals of hide-thong on bare grey feet, and smelling
of decay, all the house—even Mariana—fell silent on his coming and
remained so until he left. He too spoke little English, but I heard
him questioning Rodez about me. His small rodent eyes kept looking
me up and down. When he had gone I asked what he had said.

Rodez smiled quietly. "He says it is a dangerous heresy on our
part to keep company with a Lutheran, even at the King's command.

So I would have you look to your soul's well-being before others do
it for you."

"And if I do not, Rodez?"

"Our friend says you will burn everlastingly in hell."

"Do you believe that?"

"Of course. But what I am more concerned for is that you should
not burn temporarily on earth. Have you ever seen a man at the
stake? It is an interesting sight. I believe there will be an *auto de
fé* some time this spring. If you are still with us I will take you."

Every morning I would be wakened at five by the sound of the
city stirring to life in the great square. Often the first noises would
be the clop-clop of tiny hooves as the first donkeys went past below
driven on by the harsh *"arre"* of the drivers. Sometimes their loads—
brushwood or straw or piled crops—would scrape and whisper against
the sides of the house as they went by. Then the bells of the churches
would begin. There was the church of Buen Suceso on the far corner
between two streets; near it was the Convent of Victory. Opposite
was the church of Our Lady of Solitude and the foundling hospital
of La Inclusa, and, nearest to my bedroom and out of sight from it,
the new church of San Felipe el Real.

The bells would start the tethered goats bleating; carts would begin to rumble in, and soon the whole square would hum with life
and noise, while the first rays of the sun struck fire from the windows opposite.

We rose at six and washed in the icy water from the well; at
seven we ate bread and syrup and drank steaming bowls of coffee,
and so the day began.

For a week Mariana never spoke to me. She was a tall girl with
a lovely skin; overplump from eating too many sweetmeats, but at-
tractively so. The heavy spectacles she put on and off at intervals
were the fashion and did not indicate that she needed them to see—
though for a week she might have been blind where I was concerned.
Then one day I came into the room where we dined and found her
squatting cross-legged on the carpet telling her beads and muttering
her prayers. Many women in Spain sat in this fashion. I was turning
to go out when she said:

"Do not run away, *pincho*."

I was startled at her English; until now I had thought only
Rodez spoke it.

"I am sorry. I thought—"

"That I was saying my prayers?" She tossed the long string of beads back so that they rattled against each other. "So I was. Do you dislike that?"

"No. . . ."

"Spanish girls—we tell them at many times. It is just as we fancy. We tell them for luck when we play at *Ombre*. We finger them for the *ennui*. We tell them even while we make love."

I said: "I did not know you spoke English."

"You think we are barbarians in Madrid? How old are you?"

"Sixteen."

She whistled. "*Dios mio*. And very sick for home, eh? Why have they brought you here?"

"That is what I want to know."

"My uncle will tell you in good time. All things he arranges in good time. No doubt he may find you useful."

"I do not know how I may be useful."

"You can come with me shopping and carry my basket. That is a beginning."

"They will allow that?"

"Assuredly. You'll not run away?"

"No."

When we went out I did indeed carry her basket, but as her negro slave went with us, together with her usual duenna, this seemed an excuse. It was the height of the morning, and along our side of the square were rows of little booths where every trifle and foolish luxury could be bought. Gallants in the richest finery moved among cripples and beggars squatting on the uneven cobbles in poverty and squalor. Beyond was a long wall where painters were exhibiting their pictures. Small shops and coffee houses abounded.

Mariana bought a fan, a blue cravat, a bundle of white candles, two boxes of sweetmeats. As we turned to go home a shabby man of about fifty carrying some rolls of cloth stopped and spoke to her. A sardonic handsome man with grey-brown hair, a big moustache, and a withered hand. Mariana bought a piece of the cloth and moved on.

"My uncle is much in demand with old friends," she said curtly. "They remember their schooldays when they have favours to ask."

"Who was that?"

"An old soldier who escaped three times from the Turks and was three times recaptured. He lives now by writing ballads for blind beggars to sing."

A man went past in a brown cassock carrying on his back a great cross that seemed too heavy for him to bear. There was a mask across his face.

"A penitent," said Mariana impatiently. "His confessor has imposed this on him, and, since he is a person of quality, he does not wish to be recognised. Come, *pincho*, you've seen enough for one morning."

"Why do you call me that?"

"Assuredly it is just a fancy."

"What does it mean?"

"It means a louse."

When we got back to the door of our house I opened it for her to go in. She looked me up and down with her brilliant eyes. It was like standing under a shower of cold spray.

"Do you like the name?"

"No."

"Perhaps one day you will prove it is not true."

"Perhaps."

"Have you ever had an *amencebada?*"

"What is that?"

"What would you guess?"

"Something to eat?"

She laughed. "Let us go in."

That night Señor Andres Prada returned, and the following morning he sent for me. He was sipping chocolate in the study he used above the patio, and wore a gold embroidered morning gown. With him were two other men, one much younger with dark copper hair and the eyes of a zealot, whom I later learned was called Pedro Lopez de Soto; and a stiff-haired, cautious faced, stout man called Estaban de Ibarra.

"This is the boy Killigrew."

Both men spoke halting English. They began to question me.

All the questions related to England and many of them to my father. Some of them seemed designed to trap me, as if they were privately testing the accuracy of what I said against information of their own. They spoke of our neighbours, of Hannibal Vivian: how often did he keep the fort at St Mawes, and when he was away, who took his place? Then they worked up the river to the Trefusises, the Enyses, the Arundells. It was fascinating how much these men knew already, and in what detail. But sometimes their interpretation was quite wrong, and I was careful not to correct them.

After a while they broke off and began to talk among themselves. Although I could not follow all they said, five weeks of careful listening had given me a smattering of Spanish.

I was dismissed and went down into the patio itself, which was tiled in blue and green, with a tiny fountain playing. Vines and other plants climbed up the walls and across the trellis which almost cut out the sky. Rodez was there idly eating a green walnut, and Father Rafael sat in the rocking chair reading his breviary.

I found my hands and knees were trembling.

"Mariana has been telling that you walked out with her yesterday," Rodez said.

"Round the square, yes."

"Mariana has a taking for you. Have a care."

"I don't think so, or she would not call me *el pincho*."

"Why not?"

I was still thinking of the three men upstairs. "Well, it means a louse."

Rodez laughed. "Never believe it. *El piojo* is the louse. This is Mariana's amusement."

"What does *el pincho* mean, then?"

"It means the Handsome One."

"Oh," I said, surprise for a moment gaining over apprehension. "And what is an *amencebada?*"

"Now I know she has the fancy for you! Perhaps I should not say take care, for perhaps it is already too late!"

"Rodez." The voice came from the balcony above, cutting through Rodez's laughter.

"Sir?"

"I want you."

When Rodez had disappeared I stood for a minute or two watching the goldfish moving lazily in the pond beneath the fountain. I heard a page of the breviary turned. Father Rafael, no doubt, was keeping an eye on me as well as on his prayers, but I felt unequal to the task of addressing him.

Señora Prada came into the patio and asked Father Rafael a question. Their Spanish was quick and colloquial, but I gathered that she asked where Andres was, and he told her he was upstairs and the names of his callers. She said, was he going to the Palace tonight and Father Rafael said, yes, there was to be a meeting of the *Junta de Noche*. She said, oh, that was *good*. More passed between them that I could not follow at all; but because I could not I had more time to notice the intimacy of their conversation.

Rodez came down again, and I heard Señor Prada showing his visitors out.

"Who were they?" I said to him. "Who were those men?"

He shrugged. "Two who order this country, my friend. Like my uncle: behind the stage."

"Yes, but what did they want with me?"

"We Spaniards do not fail for lacking the attention to detail. You? You are just one of the details."

"Details of what?"

"Who knows? The information you give us is filed away. If it is ever needed, then it will be used. See?"

"What is the *Junta de Noche?*"

"A committee, an inner council, which works under the King."

"Are they—do *they* belong to it?"

"The young one, Captain de Soto, does not. He is an outsider, but is secretary to the Adelantado. The Adelantado of Castile is the highest military officer of the crown. Does that satisfy you?"

"And the other?"

"Estaban de Ibarra? He, with my uncle, is joint secretary of the Council of War."

I said: "I do not understand. I am a boy of sixteen. In England I could not, would not, be interviewed by—by Sir Robert Cecil, by the Earl of Essex, nor even by his secretary. I am a nobody. What is my value here?"

"Little enough, be assured. But be thankful for your own sake that it is something."

CHAPTER 2

THAT night I dreamt of Sue Farnaby. She kept crying: "Maugan, Maugan!" her voice lost and hoarse. I began to cry out: "Sue, Sue, Sue!" in reply, panting each word in effort and in agony. When I woke some sound was ringing in my ears, and I think I must have been crying the name aloud. I was soaked with sweat and for minutes could not shake free of the dream.

It was dark in the room but a light was flickering from the square, three wavering bars on the ceiling. I got up and went to the lattice. There were no lights in the houses opposite but there was a lantern glimmering on the cobbles below. Yesterday an old horse struggling to drag a load of gravel had died there and the body had been left where it fell. Now two beggars were hacking at the carcass for what they could take away.

Sue's cries were still ringing in my ears. I could not stay in this house any longer letting time and opportunity slip away: there must be some escape.

First, first I must improve my Spanish, at least to the point of understanding and being understood. Second, I must lay hold on some money, for in any country there were people who would give their services or hold their tongues for gold. Third, I must plan a way back.

I had to *begin* to make plans now. Madrid was right in the *centre* of Spain, impossibly situated for a fugitive, but it would be better to die on the way than to stay on here in weak luxury until one's uses were done.

The beggars below snatched up their lantern and their knives and faded into the gabled shadows. Two men were crossing the square; they were monks walking silently, hoods up, arms folded in sleeves; they went into a building beside La Inclusa; the clang of the door echoed across the square.

It was cold, and I went back and sat on the bed, then on impulse pulled on my stockings and went to the door and opened it. The house was built round the patio and some light came in through the passage window as I went down the first flight of stairs.

My only thought tonight was to see how easy or how difficult it might be to leave this house when the time came; one did not know what would be bolted and barred or whether any guard was kept; but when I reached the first floor where the two main bedrooms and the living room were I heard the murmur of voices and saw a light under the door of the Prada bedroom. I had time only to squeeze into the shadow of a heavy Cuban mahogany chest when the door opened and Father Rafael came out. A woman's hand came through the door; he bent and kissed it, then strode away, the only sound being the scuff of his sandal heels and the rustle of a silk robe. Immediately he had disappeared the light under the door went out and I was alone and could almost have been persuaded that this was a part of the earlier dream.

I leaned on the stone balustrade and looked down into the patio. I had found these Spanish people far kinder than I had ever supposed them to be; for all the danger and the unspoken menaces that surrounded me I had not lacked for casual friendship; I had even wondered what Catholicism meant that men should fight it so bitterly. Now in this moment I remembered again the words of the Puritans at home.

I was about to go down the last flight when somebody moved in the patio. It was Sebastiano, the negro who often guarded the door. He had been squatting beside the fountain, and if I had gone down he would have caught me. His keys were rattling as he moved to the great door and presently he opened it and Señor Prada came in followed by his personal servant carrying a lantern. There was a conversation; Prada sounded tired and irritable. To stay on this balcony would be to invite discovery, so I stole back up the stone flight and then up the creaking wooden flight to bed.

Over the next week I worked day long at Spanish. When Rodez tired I went to Mariana.

Mariana had beautiful teeth, and it was not hard to make her laugh. Always she called me *el pincho,* but I never challenged her translation, knowing well enough that if I did she would shrug it off or somehow turn the point against me.

I went again to the Palace; once to help Rodez with moving and arranging some English books. But on the second occasion I was confronted by the terrible priest with the face like a vulture and spent two chilling hours in his company being instructed in the tenets of the faith. I wished fervently that I had the true learning of a Protestant. I lacked the knowledge to confound his specious reasoning, yet instinctively knew it must be evil and corrupt; I had been brought up on the evils of Rome. That night I prayed for guidance and courage. There must come a moment soon when I must refuse to hear any more of his sly and perverted arguments; to listen to them was almost as much of a blasphemy as to heed. Yet to stand up and tell him he was an agent of the Devil needed a cold courage, a desperate faith that was hard to come by.

The third time at the Palace I was called in, again with Rodez, to wait at the table of Captain Lopez de Soto, the copper-haired young fanatic who was secretary to the Adelantado of Castile. De Soto was entertaining some dozen guests in a party recently arrived from Italy. Three were priests and five were Genoese naval officers, members of the entourage of Prince Giovanni Andrea Doria, who had just arrived in Madrid. Talk was sometimes in Spanish, sometimes in Italian, and for the most it was of naval power and the Spanish building programme and the prospects of an early attack on England.

After it, one of the civilians called me to him. "They tell me you are a Killigrew."

A narrow sun-tanned face, a mop of brown hair, the eyes blue, eccentric, slightly squinting; it was a different face from any seen of late.

"Yes, sir."

"And a prisoner, I'm told. Fresh out of England. The trees will be budding there soon."

"You are English!"

"Much better than that, boy. Do they still dance the Hal-an-tow at Helston?"

"You're . . . from Cornwall?"

"Yes. Though it's more than thirteen years since I was there. I think sometimes of the pleached alleys, the primroses, the violets. How is your father?"

"You know him?"

"As a young man. I was born at Tolverne up the river from your place."

I choked with delight and relief at seeing a friendly face. The three months away from home might have been three years. As I grasped his hand I remembered what young Thomas Arundell had said that night at Tolverne. "And Uncle Thomas who went on a pilgrimage to Rome thirteen years ago and never returned."

"This means—much to me. . . ."

"Oh, aye, I well know. I was thirty when I left, not a boy in his teens, and I stayed away from choice not because I had to; but the old place still has its pull. Always, always I've promised myself a sight of it again. But that nasty old woman lives too long."

"I saw your family, sir, just before Christmas. I was coming from Truro and spent the night at Tolverne."

"Ah. . . . My brother's family, you mean. And how fares Sir Anthony? Now that Hell is nearer I suspicion he is making efforts to avoid it."

I told him about his nephew Jonathan's wedding and all the family news. Even though my pleasure drained off a little as I realised this man had cast in his lot with the enemy, just knowing he was a kinsman was an encouragement to hope.

I said: "Do you know what they intend with me here?"

"I? Nay, I've just arrived. But there are many English scattered through Italy and Spain. You may take heart."

"Protestant English?"

He gave me a look. "You must change that. Oh, I know the Killigrews have always been on the side of the reformed church, but I can tell you why: it was for what they got out of it, not from religious fervour. Three quarters of Killigrew land was church land. I do not suppose many of your ancestors would cling to a faith that it was not in their interest to cling to—and I'd advise you to change while this Spanish forbearance lasts."

I said: "What did you mean, sir, by saying that Sir Anthony was nearer Hell?"

"As all heretics are when they grow older and nearer death. But if there is God's justice he'll not escape by amending his ways now."

"I don't understand."

"Ah, boy, you're too young to remember. There was a saintly Jesuit priest called Cuthbert Mayne arrested in Cornwall just before I left. He was hanged, drawn, and quartered at Launceston. My brother was on the jury that tried him. An Arundell, by God! To bring such shame on the name! By Christ, all the saints in Heaven must have turned away their faces!"

I stared across at a picture of the Virgin; she had a strange wide-awake expression like some newly opened flower, and she seemed to be listening.

I said: "Mr Arundell, can you help me?"

"What in?"

"I want no part in—in religion or in war. I only want to go home."

His face hardened. "Then it is time you grew up. No one now, of a surety no one with your name, can draw aside from the greatest issue of the age. Are you for Christ or anti-Christ? Is that not important enough to kill indifference? There's no choice in between, and I cannot help you to one."

I said, curiously: "But sometime don't you hope to come home?"

"I have told you yes, and sometime soon! But not as a suppliant. I have not lived all these years in exile to creep back under the festering cloak of Calvin. In England there are hundreds of thousands who would rise tomorrow if they received the call! One day it will come."

Rodez was waiting for me impatiently by the door.

"Sir," I said, "where are you lodged in Madrid? If I'm permitted may I wait on you sometime?"

"Your friend has my address; I shall be here for some weeks. I have spent much of my exile painting and there is a Greek living in Toledo whom I wish to see."

As I walked away down the long passage with Rodez he said cynically: "A relative?"

". . . Distant. I had never met him before."

"Spain has a good sprinkling of them—English who have clung to the faith. But they are not popular. We are never sure if one or other of them will not turn out to be a spy."

"Who is Captain de Soto?" I asked. "Why does he entertain in this way?"

"I have told you: he is the secretary of Don Martin de Padilla, the Adelantado of Castile."

"And what has the Adelantado to do with naval matters?"

"He is the supreme commander of our fleet. A seasoned veteran, not a weakling like Medina Sidonia who commanded in '88."

"He is assembling another Armada?"

"Ah," said Rodez, "have a care you do not ask too much or we may take *you* for a spy."

That night Señor Prada was called again to the palace and sent word back that he would not be home. Rodez had gone with him; and Señora Prada went off to the theatre with a gallant. Father Rafael retired early to his room, and Isabella, who was in love with a young officer who had been posted to Valladolid, spent the evening in the patio plucking moodily at her guitar.

That left Mariana and me, and of course her duenna sitting cross-legged in a corner. We spent an hour on our language, but Mariana soon grew tired of it for she had less to learn than I and less incentive. Because of our lessons our friendship had ripened. In the course of work she had told me much about Spain and about herself; I had told her of England and Cornwall and of my own life. But with an understandable reticence I had never mentioned Sue Farnaby.

Now she suddenly said: "Have you ever been in love, *pincho?*"

I hesitated. ". . . In a way."

"In what way is that?"

"Well, yes . . . I have been in love."

"With who? Tell me now. A little girl of sixteen? a big girl of twenty? a married woman?"

I said: "Oh . . ." and laughed self-consciously.

"And this girl—you have loved her?"

"I said so."

"But there is different—*si, claro . . . depende. . . .* If you love perhaps like Isabella down below you swoon and sigh, you worship, you adore; very beautiful, but it is in the heart, no more. Or you may love—make love, is that it?—with the body, with the senses—you are in passion. That is fierce, the thing itself. Which was yours?"

"The first."

"Ah . . . so I should have think."

We said no more for a time. Then she said:

"Do you know what an *amencebada* is?"

"You know I do not."

"In Spain, boys when they are twelve or thirteen are given a con-cubine mistress who teaches them about love. That is what such a woman is called."

It was the first warm evening, and the gentle plucking of the guitar was sonorous and sad, punctuating the faint plash of water from the fountain. Mariana stood up and leaned over the balcony. She called something in a harsh voice to her sister and the playing stopped. She turned to me with gleaming eyes.

"*Muy bien.* If you will have the goodness to watch."

Her black hair was parted in the middle, tied at the back with a ribbon and wrapped up in a carnation-coloured taffeta scarf. She unwrapped the scarf. While she was doing it Isabella began to play again, but this time differently, fiercely: a strange music that I had heard before but only in the distance coming from lighted taverns or from a group of gypsies around a fire: a trembling passionate music full of sadness and sliding semi-tones. Mariana stood by the balcony's edge, eyes closed, with a hand clasped to her face as if in torment; and she began to dance.

She had no castanets, no high heels. She danced on a tiny piece of tiled floor, twisting round, holding her hands on high and clicking her fingers. Even in sandals she was able to make a rhythmic rattling with her heels. She shook and swayed as she danced. She writhed like a serpent, weaving her hips as if round an invisible rope. She used her hair like a Gorgon's till it came alive and turned me to stone.

The music stopped and she stopped and hung over the balcony looking down at her sister. You could not see her face for the cloud of hair. And in the corner her duenna sat quietly sewing.

"That is what I show you, Maugan. That is what I mean by love."

"It's a different thing."

"It is the real thing."

"I don't know."

"You should know."

"Yes. . . ."

She took up the scarf in which her hair had been bound and wiped her forehead and face with it. Then she began to wind up her hair in its ribbon.

Isabella began idly to pluck at the strings again. One of the black slaves came along the balcony on some errand but he did not glance at us; servants in Spain are well trained. Mariana gathered up her books, her gold embroidery—on which she seldom worked—and brushed past me. Her sandals slip-slapped away and I heard them going up to the next floor. In a few moments the old woman in the corner also got up and followed quietly after.

I tried to read but could not. Three images were in my mind: Sue; and Captain Burley; and Mariana. Were they all different sides of the same cube? I did not know. To me they were as different as pure air, foul water, and fire. Every time I looked at the book, I saw Mariana. At last I decided to go to bed.

On the next floor I had to pass several doors to reach the wooden stairs to the attic. One door was open and Mariana was sitting in front of a mirror braiding her hair.

I went in. She laughed gently.

I whispered: "Where is . . . ?"

"Tartara? Dismissed, as she should be. I thought you would come."

"I. . . ."

"Wait." Mariana rose and shut the door behind me. Then she stood against it, her hands behind her waist, still quietly, cynically smiling. I went nearer to her. She took a step from the door and put her arms round my neck and kissed me, her breasts against my rough shirt. She was the same height as I was. Her mouth sought out mine.

I ran my hands up and down her back, feeling the warmth and liveness of her through the satin, then slipped them round and grasped her breasts. But while we clung to each other in a voluptuous hunger that drowned my free will, a strange thing happened. I found I wished to escape from what I had seemed most to desire.

I remembered Sue Farnaby; I was *hers* not any other woman's, and I *wanted* no other. And I only wished to go at my own speed in love, not to be dragged along down an ever steeper slope.

I jerked my head up and tried to unloose her arms.

"What is it? There is no one."

"Mariana, it was someone, I'm sure." She had given me the only possible excuse.

"No one will come in here."

"*No.* Mariana. It is not just that. It—it would bring disgrace on you—"

I at last got free of her and went to the door. I did not dare look back, for I knew if I looked at her again I was lost.

"Maugan!" she said.

I went out.

For days after that I was a swimmer in cross currents too strong for me. Much of the time I was glad of what I had done, glad of a fidelity to Sue Farnaby and to an ideal of love more important than a hot groping passion in a shadowy bedroom. But ever and again I would be swept with a feeling of shame, as if by denying Mariana I had denied my new manhood.

I knew too that by turning away from her I had done my hopes of escape a mortal disservice. If any one could have helped me it would have been she if she were my lover; she had just the generous reckless nature not to count the risk to herself.

As the days passed dissatisfaction and self-criticism grew. Could

I have been slightly less fastidious, slightly more calculating, I would have had the best of all worlds.

Thomas Arundell was staying in the square in front of the palace, and I went to see him with Rodez to keep me company. I found him admiring several pictures he had bought, and for a time he seemed reluctant to drag himself away from them.

"So, Maugan. You are going to the *auto de fé* next week?"

"I do not know."

"Yes, he is," said Rodez.

"As a spectacle," said Mr Arundell dryly, "it may be interesting. But in Rome they gave up such displays about a thousand years ago."

"Sir," said Rodez, "this is a solemn act of faith, not a vulgar wild beast show."

Arundell went across to the easel in the corner of the room. "There are blues and greens here which defy analysis, which seem to come of a supernatural commingling of colour. I have seen such colours again and again this week on the canvases of the painter, Dominico Teotocopoli. They are a *revelation*. D'you know anything of painting, young man?"

"No, sir."

"A pity. Some of the Killigrews have a turn for art. And piracy, of course. A strange family. Nearly as strange as the Arundells, and we, God knows, are devious enough. Passionate in all things, even in wrong-headedness. You think my brother is serious in his reconversion?"

"He risks his freedom for it."

"Well . . . well. You seem widely informed in some matters. Do you know my sister Alice?"

"No, sir."

"She lives now, I'm told, in seclusion in Tregony, having like me never wavered in her faith. The family split, young man, she and I true, Anthony and Henry turncoats. I am glad Anthony is trying to save his soul even if so late in the day; not so Henry, I'll warrant, a damned stubborn dyed-in-the-wool heretic if ever I saw one. Alice was my favourite—she's still unmarried I'll wager, like the rest of us. I'd like you to take this letter to her if you return."

"If I—"

Mr Arundell glanced at Rodez. "No, well, it's no more than a rumour but there's a rumour abroad that you may be sent home."

"Sent *home?*"

"Oh, I know nothing of it. There was talk of an exchange of a prisoner or something of the sort. Of course that may well come to nothing. But if it should, then I want you to take this letter, for I have had no word from Alice for five years."

"Gladly." My mind was in some sort of leap-frog.

Mr Arundell went on talking; he was a great talker and I stayed for nearly an hour. For a time I was in a half world of my own, yet ever and again I would make a desperate effort to attend to what he said, lest some further hint might be dropped. For the most part he talked about painting, which seemed to be the subject nearest to his heart. I wondered if he would ever come back to England, as he clearly hoped, and if he came whether it would seem too grey and cold to him after so many years in the southern sun.

I ventured at last to interrupt him again with a question, and he said:

"Come back to your true religion, boy; that's the important thing, and if you're a good Catholic the Spaniards will be far more likely to release you, since they'll be sending home a Christian and not a heretic. Tis only a matter of time, boy, before this secession of the northern countries comes to an end; there is no wisdom or reverence in it; they fight for the Devil. Have you had instruction since you came to Madrid?"

"Someone—I don't know his name—from the Holy Office has seen me several—"

"Oh, they are far from being the best teachers. They're auxiliaries of the King of Spain—saving your presence, Mister Rodez. Get you a good Jesuit, who draws his spiritual message straight from the Vicar of Christ in Rome. You will find such a man infinitely persuasive and infinitely comforting. Ask Señor Prada, he'll know such a one."

"We have a Benedictine in our household," said Rodez sullenly.

Mr Arundell had picked up a small painting. "See this, Maugan Killigrew. Done by the same artist in Toledo. Observe the slender elongated figure of Christ. Do you not get from it an impression of a supernatural being, of an earthly form transcended by the Holy Spirit? It is supreme painting, such as I have never seen before. Some day I will hang it in my *own* house in my *own* country, when religion is preached there once again! May it be soon, for I grow no younger. My father died at twenty-nine, and we come not of a long-lived stock."

On the way home I pestered Rodez to explain what Thomas Arundell meant, but Rodez said he had heard nothing of my going home. Rodez was in a sulky mood for he had not liked Mr Arundell's outspoken words on things Spanish. I asked Rodez about the *auto de fé*, and Rodez said, yes, it was to be in honour of the sixteenth birthday of Prince Philip, the heir to the throne and the King's only surviving son.

As we came to the door of the house the old soldier with the withered hand who had spoken to Mariana was waiting there. Rodez told him brusquely that Señor Prada was not in and would not be in; if he wished to see him he must come again in the morning, and be here early. The old soldier muttered: "It is all very well, but my employment has ended. Hunger drives talents to do things which are not on the map." He slouched away.

I had been only three months in Spain, less than two in Madrid, but by now I was fully understanding the language; it had come suddenly in the last two weeks as a result of all the concentrated effort.

When we got in we found the house in a great commotion. Mariana storming through the kitchen in one of her moods had upset a pan of boiling water and scalded foot and leg. Maids and servants were still running with unguents and smelling salts, and two apothecaries were in attendance.

I did not sleep well that night. With Mariana in pain servants were kept at the stretch, and footsteps sounded on and off until dawn. But what really kept me awake was another dawn—that of hope. Even now one hardly dared to speculate lest it was some trap set to weaken resistance. Supposing I was now confronted by the grey-faced priest: would I be right in dissembling one more time? Whatever happened, he must be avoided now.

During the next days I was not allowed to see Mariana, for she kept her room and apothecaries visited her almost hourly. On the fourth day after her accident, Rodez going in, I followed him and was startled by her pallor and evident pain. No one had told me if the scald was severe or slight, and I had felt that Mariana, being Mariana, would have made a commotion in either case; but I saw that she was feverish and ill. Rodez going to one side of the bed, I approached the other where her duenna sat stitching, but when Mariana saw me she turned on her side and began to talk brightly to Rodez of the week's entertainments that she was missing. When at last there was a pause I said:

"I am sorry you have had such an accident, Mariana."

She said to Rodez: "How is it the little *piojo* is in my room? Did he creep under the door?"

I said: "Last summer I was shown how to make a salve to cure burns. I was shown it by a witch."

Mariana said: "And no doubt cured the Queen of England with it when she burned her fingers on a candle-snuffer."

"No, I have not seen it in use. But she was a wise woman who taught me."

"Well," said Rodez, "it could do little worse than these apothecaries have done."

"I swore never to tell the ingredients. But I do not think you have them all here."

"That is a very good excuse," said Mariana. "You can work magic but not now."

"I could *try*. Is the scald healing?"

"Hah! Healing!" said Rodez.

Mariana said: "Tell the little *piojo* to go away; he makes my head to ache."

"Let me see the scald," I said.

They looked at me as if I had said something indecent.

"See it?" said Mariana. "It is on my *leg*."

Considering what I had seen of her in this candlelit bedroom a few nights ago, I thought her modesty a small matter overdone.

Rodez said: "They poultice and poultice and it grows worse. Maugan has sisters of his own."

"Don't let him touch me," said Mariana. "I could not bear it!"

"If part is on the foot," I said, "suffer me to see the foot."

"A child of your age," she said contemptuously over her shoulder. "What have you had to do with witches?"

"Does flax grow in this country? And bog moss? And indigo? I don't know if I could find the ingredients?"

For the first time they seemed impressed.

"There are a dozen quacks selling their nostrums every morning in the square," said Rodez. "I do not know if they have anything you want or would sell it. See tomorrow. Mariana, do not be a stupid pig; if Maugan knows something you can hardly be worse off to try it."

"Let him mix it first," she said. "Then I will decide for myself. Now go away; his voice makes my head to ache."

It was lucky that I did not see the burn then or I might have been afraid to try. Even so I wonder at the courage. But youth is reckless and confident; something of my faith in Katherine Footmarker gave me faith in myself. The next morning I was out early with Rodez. Often I could not be sure; the names were different and I was no expert at knowing herbs on sight or smell.

We came home with a dozen things: oil from the flax, lime-water, powered bark of the red elm. I diluted and sprinkled and mixed them with a salve which had a white soap from Flanders as its basis. When it was done it was a pungent unassimilated mess very different from what she had given me in a box for the Michell child. But I spread it on moss and that all on a white cloth and carried it upstairs.

She was less vituperative this morning after another feverish night, and allowed me sight of her leg as far as the highest burn which was on her calf. The blisters had long since been pulled off the burns and left festering sores, rank and raw and almost bleeding. They were still discoloured with the dressings of the latest apothecary, and Katherine Footmarker would have said this had first to be cleansed away; but a look at Mariana's bottom lip told me that if once she was put in more pain she would refuse to be touched. So I cut the poultice into two parts and put one on her foot and the other on her leg. She muttered something under her breath, and the tears which came into her eyes she shook away. I waited for an explosion but none came, so was in haste to tie a light bandage around each burn to keep the salve in place.

Later that morning there was an angry commotion in the bedroom when one of the apothecaries came and protested against his not being allowed to see the wound. Supported by the duenna, he warned Mariana and Señora Prada of the dire risks they were running in allowing a heretic—and a child heretic at that—to meddle in such matters. They were imperilling not merely Mariana's life but her soul. It was well known that the Devil used such people as one of his most favourite instruments.

But Mariana, once set on her way, would not be moved. They had had their throw, she said; now, by good Jesu, let another be given the chance.

In the evening she sent word down that I was to prepare another such poultice for the morrow. I heard privately that the morning application had brought some relief.

So for three days it went on. Each day another mixture—never, I thought, quite the same as the last, and each day I put it on a leg and foot that were growing cooler and less inflamed.

So was she. She took now to calling me "Doctor Leech," with that irony of voice which absolved her of any risk of being thought serious. Yet others in the house knew of her improvement, and both Rodez and Isabella used me with greater consideration. Looking back now, I am in wonderment that I was not more surprised. Perhaps I have not ever been as surprised or as grateful for this gift as I should be.

On the day before the *auto de fé* she hobbled downstairs and I told her she had no more need of ointment.

She said: "But the best apothecaries never finish. *Siempre seras bien recibido.*"

Rodez and I went to the *auto de fé* alone. He was by nature late for everything, so when we got to the Plaza Mayor just after dawn two or three thousand people were already there, as well as hundreds crowding the balconies of the four-storey houses. At one side of the square was the King's balcony, and opposite on a raised dais two cages in which about sixteen prisoners were housed. I could see all this plainly, but the floor of the square was cut off from my view by the heads and shoulders of the people in front of me, and the wooden stands which had been built for the occasion were swarming with people who clung to them like flies to a meat bone.

About 7 a.m. the King and Queen and Prince Philip and a number of people of the Court began to take their seats, and towards eight the procession began. Peering through heads I could see perhaps a hundred charcoal men carrying muskets and pikes, and two or three hundred Dominican monks with banners, led by a man on a white horse carrying the standard of the Holy Office, red with a silver sword in a crown of laurel. Then there were halberdiers and grandees and three men bearing a crucifix wrapped in black crepe. The crucifix and the standard were fixed on the altar and prayers began, led by the Grand Inquisitor.

I stood back on my heels and stared at the crowd, listened to the great murmur of voices, the chanting. In the centre were solid ranks of glittering soldiery, the massed squares of monks. This was the generative core of a nation far richer and more populous and more famous in arms than ours. If England were ever conquered scenes such as this would take place every week in London, and there would be no lack of fuel for the fires.

After another parade the Grand Inquisitor began to preach. It had been cold in the square in the early morning, but as the sun rose the heat grew until the air was foetid and stifling. From here it was impossible to hear what was said and the patient crowd began to shuffle and fidget. Some took out rolls of bread and began to eat it with garlic and leeks. Stallholders had set up trestles at the foot of the stands, and they did a good trade selling cups of cordial and bowls of broth. A monk with the strange hood of a Capuchin was collecting *maravedis* and gifts in kind for the poor.

It was past noon before the Grand Inquisitor finished. The King rose to reply. Although the voice was dry and thin there was a quiet passion and fervour in it; several times he roused his listeners to murmurs of approval, and once there was a grumbling roar when he said something of reconversion by fire and the sword. As soon as he had finished, the royal party went inside to eat and to rest. Most of the ordinary spectators squatted where they were, trying to take their sieastas in the hot sunshine. Monks were still chanting and singing, and lesser penitents made endless processions round the square.

As the afternoon wore on the shadows of the houses formed new geometries across the crowded square. About five the royal party reappeared. A procession of monks made a circuit of the amphitheatre bearing statues and effigies of saints and a dozen coffins with flames painted round them. These, Rodez said, held the bones of heretics who had recently died in prison.

Now the prisoners were brought forward one by one and their crimes read out. I could not hear the sentences, but one of the four women prisoners and five of the thirteen men were condemned to death; the others went to the galleys, to imprisonment, or to be scourged. A fight broke out in the crowd near by us: a woman with a man had looked at another man, and knives were out; people surged and pushed; we were trampled and moved five or six yards before the pressure eased.

Mass was celebrated in the growing dark; then people settled to eat again. Litter and dirt were everywhere, and even though the chill was returning it did not take away the smell. Bags of wine were passed round, and I drank deeply. The scene was like the Day of Judgment, the flambeaux smoking, the Inquisitor on his dais. The King had not gone in; it seemed he could wait to dine until the ceremony was over. Already it had lasted more than twelve hours.

I was tired now and ready to go. My legs were tired with standing, and there was nothing but stale warm air to breathe. Rodez muttered something and I said: "What is it?"

"Four of them—and that includes the woman—have said they prefer to die in the Christian faith. That leaves two to face the fire alive. Ah, well, it's not an ordeal I would relish myself, even for a seat in Heaven; and for them, who merely make more certain their descent into Hell. . . ."

The crowd surged forward and we with it as the prisoners were bound to stakes in the middle of the square. Faggots and charcoal were piled around them by black-coated burners and priests of the Holy Office. Heads bobbed in my way; someone was coughing and spitting; two women in front of me were arguing about the price of wool. Columns of charcoal men with lighted torches were in procession to make obeisance to the King.

Now the flag with the white cross was leading them back to the six pyres. One of the prisoners was shouting at the top of his voice; in a quiet that had fallen it was easy to hear the words, but they were in a strange tongue: German or Dutch perhaps. It looked as if a priest were counselling each of the prisoners, advising them; but the shouting man would have none of it.

"He has gone off his head," said Rodez. "I see they are to be merciful to him."

A man was trying to get his little boy of eight through to see more clearly. Most were willing to move aside, but a woman complained angrily that the boy was standing on her dress; a torrent of angry argument broke out; in the arena charcoal men were passing cords round the necks of the four prisoners who had recanted; the one was still shouting, another was reciting the Lord's Prayer in Latin. A long brass trumpet reared its mouth and a shrill blast was blown; it silenced the quarrellers beside me as the charcoal men pulled on the cords and the cursing and praying of the prisoners ended in a strangled coughing. Soon all were dead.

The people sighed; a monk's high voice intoned a prayer.

The trumpet blew again, torches were raised where I could see them clearly, and then were plunged. People pushed me forward against the people in front, straining to see, all wanting to see the two living victims as the flames licked round their feet. It seemed that they were not yet to be deserted by the monks of the Holy Office, who risked burns in order to hear any recantations that might fall from their lips. One of the prisoners was dressed in tattered black slops, and as these caught fire he began to scream in a high-pitched almost whistling voice like a horse I had once heard being clumsily slaughtered. The other made no sound, but as the flames licked up him blisters rose and burst quickly on his skin like bubbles in a boiling pot. Then as they burst, so blood poured from them, and also from his nose.

As life left them, their bodies twisted and crouched against the wire thongs as if they were wrestlers in some game. The four who had been strangled before burning had taken on the same contorted attitude of defiance.

The screams of the last living man came to an end, and then the only thing was the hissing as blood and fat ran down into the flames.

Pressure slowly eased; breath came back; people stretched and yawned; there was room and time to feel one's aching feet; but it was nine or after before the last prayers were said and we were free to go. Noisily, sweatily, untidily, like people coming from a cockpit or a bear-baiting we made our way out. At one of the entrances to the square there was a great crush as more tried to pass through than there was room for; women screamed, blows were struck. Rodez and I were like sticks in a current, one minute idly moving, the next caught tight in a log jam, inching forward a half step at a time. I thought, if anyone should block this crowd at the other end there would be no need of the judgment of the Holy Office for me or for a hundred others.

Suddenly we were through and walking back towards the Puerta de Sol in a laughing, talking, jostling company.

CHAPTER 3

WHEN we got back Andres Prada was at home and with him was the old soldier with the withered hand who had at last insinuated himself into the house. Father Rafael was there also, and the three men were sitting at a table in the largest of the living rooms drinking wine. After the hot day the night had turned sharply cold and a brasero bowl was under the table warming their legs and feet. The soldier had a rough duffel cloak thrown around his shoulders.

"Well," said Señor Prada to us, "so it is over? I confess I find the ceremony tedious these days. How His Majesty—a man suffering from gout and ulcers—can endure the long day I know not."

He was speaking in Spanish as Rodez and I took seats on cushions on the floor and were given wine to drink by one of the servants.

"For *my* part," said the old soldier, who was called Miguel, "I have never seen one through. I witnessed a part of one in Seville when two English soldiers were to perish for their heresy, but to melt a man slowly away like a candle lit at the wrong end has always seemed to me a poor testimony of Christian charity, so I came away before the flames were lit."

"This boy is English," said Prada.

"Ah. . . . Yes, he looks it. Yet twas my colouring when I was young: fair-haired; and he's not unlike I was, thin and lively and strong, with wide-awake eyes not short of a glint of mischief. You remember me as I was then, Andres?"

"It is a long time since."

"And you were ever a dark-skinned boy for contrast. And prone to sickness. The years have advanced you and retarded me. . . . This English boy, now—why do you keep him here?"

"He was brought in by two sea-rovers who kidnapped him as proof of a raid they made on the English coast. But it so happens they have laid hold of the base son of this man who guards a key fortress on the coast of England. . . ."

"Have a care, sir," said Rodez, "he follows Spanish now."

"He's like I was then," mused Miguel, plucking at a hole in his slops, "but scarcely like I am now after a lifetime of soldiery and five years a slave to the Turks. My hand shot through at Lepanto; a prey to feverish agues that rack the bones I have left. Over thirty years of honourable service for my country. It is no employment for such a one to hawk cloth from door to door or to write doggerel for broadsides. That is why I petition you, Andres, and through you His Majesty for some honourable commission—"

"You have had them in the past—"

"Pittances, Andres, pittances of the most degrading kind, ill-paid and often unpaid, as you must know. A Naval Commissary is expected to live off his peculations and I will not do that, Andres. I still believe in the ideals of patriotism and honesty, however much in this age they have become empty words."

The door opened and Señora Prada came in. When she saw the company she seemed likely to turn and go away again at once.

Her husband made a half-irritable gesture. "Oh, my love, I am not sure if you have met Miguel de Cervantes, a playmate of mine in student days. A distinguished soldier who has also turned his hand to plays and poems—"

Miguel rose to his feet and gave her a bow, which she barely acknowledged. "My lady, I knew your husband, as he says, in the days of his youth, and I come to pay a call long overdue—"

"Oh, you have called before," said the lady. "Twas you, was it not, who escaped three times from the Turks and was thrice recaptured; but that is old news: Andres, this is the second time I have come home and Sebastiano is not at the door to hand me down! I think in the morning he should be beaten."

"I'll see to it, my love," said Prada cynically. "No doubt you found the *auto de fé* tiring. There is wine and food laid in the next chamber."

"I am going out again," she said. "I came but to change after the day. Don Diego will be calling for me within the hour."

She left the room, and an awkward silence fell, in which I thought the old man would take his leave. But clearly he was used to being treated as of no account; perhaps his condition had long been too desperate for him to be too tender of his honour. Yet as he sat down again I saw that he had not lost his bearing or his dignity.

"I say to you, Andres, I still believe in the old ideals, rarely though they emerge in the present Palace and Court. From what I have seen of it since I came to Madrid from Andalusia—"

"Oh, it is a superficial blemish that you exaggerate," Prada said impatiently. "The King could scarcely be more holy—"

"Oh, the King, yes indeed, he turns his Court into a monastery. But under the assumed piety of the religious form every sort of immorality and corruption exists. Spanish ladies, once a model for the world, are loose and immodest in their lives. The behaviour even of many of those men who have taken the vows of a priestly life, the behaviour of many such is licentious and evil."

"Señor," said Father Rafael gently, "you speak harsh words which would be dangerous outside this house. Even in it they give offence."

"As for you, Father," said Miguel, "if I speak ill of your cloth I mean no personal slight. But many others say as I do. The treasury is empty, and the riches of the Indies flow into it and then out to enrich the peculators in Spain and the bankers and Jews in other lands. Under the cloak of the church the state decays!"

He reached for the buckskin bag containing the wine, and poured himself some and drank it. Then he wiped his long moustaches with his withered hand.

"And if you were in my position," said de Prada, "you would contrive to change it all?"

"Nay, friend, I have no easy remedy; do not mistake me. But I think no country can prosper while corruption is so widespread, while the worst poverty and the most lavish luxury are separated by a street's width. I think no country can fight a just war while it is being bled white from within; and while it is dominated by 22,000 spies in the habit of the Holy Office! We have many wars on our hands. The Netherlands remains a cockpit. Henry of Navarre has entered Paris by a ruse and our troops forced out. Did you hear he stood upon a balcony of Porte St Denis and saluted them as they marched away, calling, 'Commend me to your master but never come back'? He'll be at war with us ere long, you mark my words. . . . And as for England—every preparation for the Second Armada is hampered by lack of money, lack of supplies. You know that, Andres, without my telling you. . . ."

"I know, Miguel, without your telling me."

Prada's cold voice at last made an impression on the other man's eloquence. "Aye, well, you should be far better informed than any of us. . . . No doubt I talk out of place. Did I not see Lopez de Soto leaving here the other day? If so, you will know all about the naval preparations."

"You did—and I do. Captain de Soto says it is due to the corruption of minor officials such as yourself that the Armada is not more ready to sail."

Miguel de Cervantes's face went a deep colour like the faces of the burning men; an old scar whitened on his cheek. "Of many it is true. I have said so. That way they live. Because I would not

so tarnish my good name I am reduced to beggary and to suppli-
cating help from old friends! As you know I have been in prison,
but never for any act injurious to my honour!"

"Well I will help you if I can," said Prada. "But perhaps I cannot."
He rose. "You must excuse me now."

"When may I see you again?"

"I will let you know. Have you no other friends?"

"None so close to the Court. While men like Lope de Vega strut in
society I am—destitute."

"Tut, tut, we'll meet again, no doubt. But I'm not the King, you
know."

The old soldier was edged towards the door. As I also rose Señor
Prada spoke sharply in English.

"I wish to see you, boy."

"Now, sir?"

"Yes. Wait there. You may go, Rodez."

Father Rafael picked up his rosary and followed Rodez from the
room. I was left to wait alone.

Andres Prada's face was irritable as he sat down again at the table.
He took up a palm leaf and fanned the brasero bowl to make the
charcoal glow. He coughed as the smoke caught his throat.

"What would you say, boy, if I offered you your freedom?"

I stared at him. "I would—would thank you from my heart!"

"There would be conditions."

"What conditions?"

"You would be required to convey a message back to England."

"Gladly—" then I stopped. "Where would I have to take it?"

"That matters?"

"Yes, sir. If. . . ."

He put the palm leaf down. "The message would be to your father."

"To my—"

"Would you carry a message to him?"

"*Willingly.* . . . To my father?"

"Yes. Verbally."

"If—yes, I think so."

"There would be other conditions—concerned with the message."

The charcoal had died again, being nearly burned through, and
the chill of the night seemed to come out of the white plaster
walls.

Señor Prada said dryly: "We thought to convert you to Christ before offering you freedom. The King was unwilling to make any move

to restore you to your family until you had come to see your error. But I prevailed upon him otherwise."

"Thank you, sir."

"I will be plain with you, boy. I did not intervene on your behalf out of love for you. Those freebooters who brought you here hoping for a reward, got it because you were of some small use coming fresh from England, and that part of England, for the information you gave us. But there is this second use to which you may now be put. Have you been well treated here?"

"Yes, sir."

"Fed, clothed, used as a guest?"

"Yes, sir."

"Put in chains, beaten, starved, stretched on the rack?"

"No, sir."

"An attempt has been made to persuade you to reaccept the old religion. That failing, has coercion been used?"

"No, sir."

"Well, remember those things. If God sees fit to favour us in war, and we take England, there will be clemency and justice shown as well as the rigour of holy law. Remember that and tell your father."

"Was that what you wished me to tell him?"

"Not that alone." He paused, biting his finger thoughtfully. "Answer this, boy, I know little of your Calvinist religion. Do you still use the Bible of Christ?"

"Yes. . . . It is in all our churches."

"So that an oath sworn on it would be binding upon you—as we should swear upon holy relics?"

"Yes."

He peered hard at me as if trying to assure himself.

"Tomorrow then we will see if a way can be found."

"What are you asking me to swear, señor?"

"To secrecy in the message you carry."

"To my father?"

"Yes, it must be learned by heart and must go to him only and then not be spoken of again."

Sleep for less than an hour. The pageant of the day, with its ponderous, tedious progression to the blind automatic spectacle of the end, was of the stuff of nightmare. Mingling with all this were sudden wakings full of panic hopes and fears, and long minutes when everything was clear with the feverish clarity of illness.

About eleven that morning Mariana limped down the steps to the patio.

"So, Maugan, I hear you are to leave us?"

"There is no certainty of it yet."

"Perhaps you will be returning to your girl, and you can say to her, 'Oh, those Spanish women, how I despised them!'"

"If I say anything to anyone in England it will be that Spanish women have courage and beauty . . . and one, among them that I knew, more than any of the others."

She looked surprised. "Sweet Jesu, you are becoming a courtier. It must be true that you have two uncles close to the Queen."

All that day I waited, but it was not until six in the evening that the summons came. Rodez arrived to say we were to attend at the Palace at once.

There was no ceremony to being admitted, no waiting, no ante-chambers crowded with favour-seekers. We entered the palace by the side door through which the pages came and went, crossed the width of the building by musty passages most of them below ground, here and there coming out level with little green courtyards.

I was led into a chapel with savage stained glass in its Gothic windows. At the back of the chapel was a writing table, and seated at the table were three men: a priest I had never seen before—he had been chosen because he spoke English; Señor Prada; and Don Juan de Idiaquez, whom I had seen once before and whom I knew to be, after the King, the most important member of the *Junta de Noche*. Rodez withdrew and left me with the three men. The light from one of the windows threw a bloody streak across the table and across the well-kept hands of Idiaquez.

"You will sit here, Maugan Killigrew," said Andres Prada. "Father Vasco will read to you the message you are to learn by heart. When you have learned it he will take your oath, then you will be free to go."

CHAPTER 4

It was July before I saw Cornwall. I travelled back to Lisbon in the company of two couriers and there waited four weeks. A provision ship carrying supplies for the army in Brittany at length gave me passage, but three days out we were struck with a great storm which after a week drove us back, a battered leaking wreck, into

Coruña at the Groyne. More weeks passed in repairs and we did not reach Blavet until early June. Then began the most contrary wait of all, with only two hundred miles of sea between myself and home. Great gales blew across the Bay with rain and biting winds. Enormous waves dashed against the mole and damp powdery balls of spume tottered through the narrow streets. I had been given some money but this ran low, and I worked in a shipyard for three weeks unloading planks.

In the end a man I knew brought me home—in the sort of secrecy in which he always seemed to move and have his life, a secrecy of which his thin whispering nasal voice seemed an essential part. Captain Elliot said:

"I'll run you as far as Helford, put you ashore there; *Dolphin*'s bound for Plymouth but twill be no great way off course. I'm never above doing a favour for an old friend, and your father has long been a well-wisher of mine."

"Taken by Burley, was you," said William Love, laughing heartily. "He's turned his hand to many things, has Richard Burley, but child-snatching is a new one and not, you'd ha' thought, so richly profitable. One day he'll find his neck in a loop o' rope, and then he'll dance to someone else's measure."

"Seen him?" said Captain Elliot. "No, young man, we have not seen Captain Burley since just before that time we visited you. You remember that time when we came on you late and you roused the house, and we stayed with you four or five days."

"Aye," said William Love, "and there was some fever in the house among the servants that more'n one of our hearty lads took. I wished we'd never come."

"But that—"

"What," whispered Captain Elliot, "what was the name of the one that died of it? We buried him off Gyllyngvase. Mark Jarvis, that was it. . . . Nay, I have not seen Captain Burley since we parted off the Land's End the day before we made Helford. And then I had no time to bid him good day for I was afraid any minute to feel the Runnelstones under my keel. His prize foundered, you say? I thought we all should have. How long ago is all that, William?"

"Nigh on two year. September or October '92. The boy's grown since then. He's already taller 'n his father."

"Ye've grown since I saw ye last," said Justinian Kilter, "but I mind you well. You was ever interfering 'twixt me and that girl, what's her name, Meg something. But last time we called you wasn't there to thrust in your oar so I made free with her to my heart's content."

"Dick Stable would see you did not."

"Ah, that's his name, that skim-milk of a man. I never can mind whether he be Dick Harp the stable boy or Dick Stable th' harpist. Poh, he could not protect a lent-lily from a bumble bee. Meg had her fill o' me last time I was there. I should not wonder if I've fathered a brat on her."

"Muscle?" said Aristotle Totle. "Why ye've no muscle yet; you should be ashamed at sixteen; why at your age I could lift two grown men. 'Ere, feel my arms—no, not there, 'ere. There's strenth for ee. I've killed twenty men in my time wi' my bare 'ands. Twenty or twenty-one, I lose the count."

"How is her Ladyship your grandmother?" asked Captain Elliot. "I'll be bound she'll be glad to see you back. You're a lucky young man, Maugan Killigrew, being sent home like this. Many will say, how did he accomplish it? What special service did he render to receive such special favour? Like as not, you'll be asked that, and then what will you say?"

"The truth. That it was because of an exchange."

"Ah, but what exchange? they'll say. Did we release some Spaniard? Did we?"

"I think so."

"I'll hold a penny Richard Burley plays some continuing part in this," said William Love. "He's a deep fish and contrives much to his own profit. We must seek him out."

"No," said Captain Elliot. "Burley now has truck with the Spaniards, and that is treasonable work. Eh, young man? Who sups with the Devil. . . . Let us have no thought for Burley and his evil ways."

We sighted the Manacles about four-thirty on a wet and gusty Sunday afternoon. After the towering Sierras the dark coastline looked low and unimposing, but a lump rose in my throat and for a half hour it would not be swallowed down. Though the sea had little vicious heads on it and the wind was shifting and backing treacherously *Dolphin* reefed her sails and made scarcely any headway towards the shelter of the land.

"We'll slip in as the day wanes," said Captain Elliot. "'Twould not do to rouse an alarm, for there's been much nervousness all summer on account of a Spanish attack."

I could not wait to get off this ship, and there was more than homesickness to it. For one reason or another they were all lying to me. Whatever element of truth escaped them was by accident and not design. They even contradicted each other. Totle boasted of impossible prowess; Kilter spoke so of Meg to goad me; Elliot untruthfully disowned Burley; Love, perhaps most dangerously of all, twisted his own memory.

We dropped anchor after dark in the deeper water above Durgan. Two men rowed me to the bank of the river. It was raining still, a Cornish rain, an English rain, different in feel and taste and smell from what fell in Madrid or Lisbon. I thanked the men and scrambled ashore knee wet, pushing aside the branches of an overhanging tree, scarcely looked back. In moments the sound of their rowlocks and the plash of water was blanketed off by the dripping wood.

I began to run. It is about five miles, through woods, across moorland and along narrow tracks from Durgan to Arwenack. I ran all the way. When within sight of the palisade I lay down under a tree in the long wet grass trying to get back lost breath. The grass smelt sweeter than it had ever smelt before. After seven or eight minutes I went to the gate of the palisade and hammered on it. There was no reply, and I knew that one might knock there all night.

But you don't keep a boy out of his own home however carefully you guard it. I followed the palisade down to the river's edge, then lowered myself carefully into the water and by clinging to the ends of the last poles I swung under the great fence and crawled up the other side on to the grassy sward that led to Arwenack House.

They were astounded to see me, aghast, frightened. To appear after six months dripping water in the hall, dirty and emaciated, out at elbow and knee, with sores round the mouth, swollen feet and blue marks like bruises on my legs, was perhaps sufficient to startle anyone. They had given me up for dead, so some came near to thinking it was a ghost.

It is the only time in my life that I remember my father's eyes lighting up on sight of me—those eyes in which a light so seldom showed. The children were all abed, but the older ones were wakened and came tumbling down clustering round and showering excited questions. In no time I was surrounded by forty odd people, a mixture of family and servants, while dogs licked my feet and leapt up at my face and others barked and quarrelled and urinated among the rushes.

The only absentee was Mrs Killigrew who was in bed with another child born a week ago, named Simon and already christened, for they thought him determined to slip away.

After the first clamour had subsided, the voice of Lady Killigrew could be heard. She had not moved from her chair when I went to kiss her, but now she looked down her long prehensile nose and said, enough of greetings, the boy must be fed and *washed*, he stinks of bilge water and looks as if he's lived on nothing else for a week. She set the servants running and continued to stare at me with her cold blue eyes while others did the questioning.

It was a rich homecoming. I fell on the food when it came and wolfed it, still talking, answering, laughing and half crying, joking, trying to explain.

Not only were they astounded, they were vastly impressed at the story. Even my father was impressed that I had been received at Court. In among all the happy conversation there was a questioning note. And I had to keep a guard on my tongue and on its explanations.

It was midnight before anyone thought of bed and nearer two before I found myself again in that long narrow room I knew so well with its tall window overlooking the river's mouth—and the security of it and the constriction. I was back in my mother's arms, in my mother's womb, held firm where none could attack, protected, supported, confined. Every board, every panel, every stair, every creak of bed and crack of wall and squeak of shutter was familiar and friendly, part of an eternity of childhood which belonged to me for ever.

But happy as I was, there was something to ask my half-brother before his chatter stopped in sleep.

"John, have you seen the Arundells of Tolverne?"

"No, scarce anything. Why?"

"You remember Sue Farnaby? She was staying with them in December when I called there."

"Ah. . . . Is that how the wind blows? Well, she's pretty enough, I grant you, if only she had money. But she has none and you'd do well to think on that. Maybe it's less important for you; but father never fails to impress on me the need to marry an heiress. I believe he can scarcely wait until I am old enough."

"Have you seen anything of her?"

"Of Sue Farnaby? No. . . . Of course, being near fifteen, I *am* now old enough. . . . It's not pleasant to think one has to wed for duty. Grandmother once told me she saw her first husband only twice before they was betrothed, and she then but thirteen. And Uncle Henry to cap it says that's nought, he knows of a boy of six who was carried to the altar and coaxed to say his vows so that after he might go and play. D'you think that's true?"

"Have you seen Jonathan and Gertrude Arundell? Have they issue yet?"

"I've seen no one but Thomas. Thomas came down the river all on his own one day in May. He has grown so *gross*, Maugan. But so strong with it. While he was visiting us the tide fell and his boat was caught in the mud. Sawna and Penruddock went to draw it into the water but the mud was deep and they could not stir it. Down goes Thomas and by himself lifts the boat bodily and thrusts it into the water. I'll vow you could not knock him down and break his teeth now."

"What did he want?"

"It was some business to do with his father who he says is softening in the head. You know Sir Anthony was a ward of Grandfather, and it was some legal business, I believe."

"Then why did Jonathan not come? He is the eldest and next head of the family."

"That I don't know. I don't think Thomas has much respect for his brother."

"I don't think Thomas has much respect for anyone," I said, and after I had spoken wished I had not, for it brought old apprehensions to the surface.

Next morning my father was out early seeing to the shearing of the lambs. Belemus was still away, and I found myself depending on my half-brother for all the news. John said it had been another unnatural summer: the hay had been cut but would not dry, sheep were dying of the murrain, oats and corn were flattened by the rain and wind. This was true throughout the country and there would be great distress. There was also great fear of a Spanish invasion. Uncle Simon and his family were coming next week; there was plague in London though not nearly so bad as last year. Odelia had had a quinsy in May and had been lanced by Glapthorne of Penryn. She had been tedious sick and Mother had saved her by riding into Truro and bringing back some draught. Penn, the falconer, had died in March: he had cut his finger and the poison had run through his body like quicksilver. Stevens was promoted in his place. Oliver Gwyther of Three Farthings House was paying court to Annora Job. Meg Levant was married to Dick Stable these three months. Yes, said John, *Dolphin* had called in in April, but after the trouble last time only Captain Elliot and William Love had come ashore.

So he talked on and on about the everyday things of life at Arwenack just as if I had only been away working in Truro. He talked about life as I had known it for sixteen years, while the familiar sounds and smells and sights seeped in. A girl in the laundry was starching and blueing my grandmother's ruffs; another carried a wooden iron-bound pail full of buttermilk; in the yard Long Peter was tending a sick dog; Parson Merther led the younger children upstairs for an hour's Greek; seagulls wheeled and cried in a sky of washed blue and broken cloud; the wind blew sweet off the sea; I was home and in a few days it was going to be hard to believe that the six foreign months had ever happened except in a vanishing dream.

Yet there was one intimidating task still to be undertaken.

At eleven my father came into the house with Rosewarne and Job and five dogs, and they all went into his study. I hung about outside and after twenty minutes the two servants left.

The last time I had been in this room was nearly two years ago when fever was rife in the house and Paul Knyvett had died and Mr Knyvett had left all the account books open on the table.

Mr Killigrew was sharpening one of his quills; he glanced up briefly and nodded me to a seat. His waist had increased this year and his fine complexion had become higher toned and a trifle blotchy. His thick fair hair was losing its colour and becoming an indeterminate shade of pale straw-brown.

"Well, boy, so you're home again, by the mercy of Christ. Or by the mercy of King Philip. I thought you were dead. We all gave you up for dead. I'm gravelled at this honour done a son of mine."

"It was not exactly honour, father. I spent the first three weeks in a Lisbon jail."

"I call it honour not to be sent to the galleys but to be received at Court and well treated, to be later released and sent home in comfort. The Spanish respect the name of Killigrew more than I thought. D'you know who was released on our side by exchange?"

"No one was, father. That was an excuse to avoid the need to explain."

"To explain what?"

"My coming home."

He laid down his pen. "There is more to this than your coming home?"

"Yes, sir. I was charged with a message."

"To whom? God's face, what sort of a conspiracy is this?"

"A message to you, father."

"What d'you mean, to me? Who could wish to send a message to me?"

"The Spanish Council of War. Andres Prada, Don Juan de Idiaquez, Estaban de Ibarra—and others."

"Well, well, I never thought to hear a cub of mine so pat with Spanish names! You're telling me they released you in order to carry a message to *me*?"

"I was required to learn the message by heart and to repeat it. Then I was required to take an oath on the Bible that I would repeat it to you only and to no other. This I swore."

Mr Killigrew unfastened a button of his jerkin and began to scratch inside; his heavy lids came down once or twice as if the light were too strong for him. All the dogs sighed together.

"And this message? You have written it down?"

"No, sir. It was a condition that it should not be." I moistened my lips. "I am required to—to deliver to my father, John Killigrew Esq. of Arwenack House, Governor of Pendennis Castle, the following message from the *Junta de Noche*, supreme War Council of his Imperial Majesty Philip the Second. Render up to Spain, at a time to be later assigned, the Castle of Pendennis, the river mouth and bay and all defences under your charge. Raise no arms, assemble no musters, give all aid to the landing forces as and when required to do so. For reward, on success of the mission, ten thousand pounds in gold, a knighthood, and a grant of the lands and properties of Godolphin, Erisey and Trelowarren, Enys and Trefusis."

I stopped speaking. Mr Killigrew still had his belt knife in his hand, and his thumb was absently testing the sharpness of it. He got up and walked to the window. His thick figure was silhouetted against the diamond panes, with the rain trickling crossways down them.

"Brother of Christ," he said, "that I should be so insulted!"

I did not speak, but let out a slow breath.

"Sometimes I think I've slipt low in the respect of my friends. I did not know I was esteemed so low by my enemies!" He laughed lightly. "For three and a half centuries the Killigrews have served England and her Kings as soldiers, as diplomats, as poets, as courtiers. We fought for the House of Lancaster and have never wavered for the Tudors—except when Mary took to her papist ways, which served her right, shrew that she was. I and my father and my grandfather have *beggared* ourselves in the service of her sister. And we're for her reformed church, every one of us—not a backslider in five litters. Yet a half-dozen powdered strutting grandees from Castile suppose they can buy me and my fidelity as if I was a strumpet set up for sale to the highest bidder! No wonder they treated you well, boy! Did you *tell* them I was in debt?"

"No, father. They already knew."

"Ah, their system's got its spies. How did you consent to bring this pretty message? Did you think I should be interested!"

"Oh, no! But I wished to come home."

He turned at last from the window. "Well, it was a way of coming. It was a way of coming! A knighthood, indeed! That would not be outside my deserts. . . . They know their geography, too, it seems. . . . Godolphin, Erisey and Trelowarren, Enys and Trefusis. And how much money? Ten thousand pounds? They knew their finances. But they did not know their man. That was their failing, boy, they did not know John Killigrew of Arwenack!"

"No, father."

"Ralegh shall hear of this: we'll laugh over it together. And Cecil.
It will show how high my position and responsibility is rated by
Spain." He hesitated a moment, sat again in his chair, which creaked
a welcome to the familiar weight. "No, well, we'll think of that. . . .
In the meantime breathe no word of this outside."

"I am sworn not to."

"For see, Maugan, I have malicious enemies whose tongues, given
taste of this offer, might wag to bad effect. So have a guard on
yourself." He laughed again, again lightly, but the timbre was metallic.
"It is as well if Godolphin does not hear of it or he might have some
fear for his estates. And Hannibal Vivian. . . ."

I said: "There is one more thing I was charged to do. It was to
give you this."

"What have you there—an amulet?"

"No, it is a ring with a seal on it of the Spanish royal arms. I was
told to give it you and to ask you to return it with your reply. This will
prove that it comes from you."

"So they expect an answer? And who's to carry it?"

"That they would not say. I was afraid for my life they would wish
me to carry it back, in which case I should have been no better off
for the journey. But they did not. They said they would send a
messenger when the time comes."

"When the time comes. . . . From that I'd gather they mean no
attempt on England this year. Or perhaps it is a trap to lure us to
sleep—as in '88 when the news was spread deliberate that they had
given up the attempt, just as they set out."

"It will come," I said. "They are all set on it. It is the one thought
in their minds."

"Ah. As Ralegh said. Unless they can be stopped. The forward
party at Court presses for a preventive raid on the Spanish ports—such
as Drake performed seven years ago. But whether it will come to
fruit I don't know. Cecil plays for time and peace. Essex breathes
fire and would fight the world. Ralegh brings up his new-born son
and plants trees at Sherborne. We shall see."

"Yes, sir."

"A knighthood, indeed," said my father. "Godolphin and Trelowarren, Enys and Trefusis. . . ."

Now that the message was out I felt immensely lighter—and relieved. And the relief, though in part because the message was safely
delivered, had also to do with its reception. I would not have admitted it then in so many words, for to be a traitor is unthinkable.
So one did not think of it. All one thought of was the many men in

financial straits or torn by conflicts of conscience who would not have
flung such an offer contemptuously away. And although Mr Killigrew
never suffered with his conscience, there was no question but that
he was in straits. More servants had gone since Christmas and meals
were the poorer by half.

Of course, having been myself in straits often since, I can see now
that his economies were half hearted and without method. He had
the true attitude of the aristocrat towards money: he was never really
able to learn to see his wants as governed by his means; it was always his means which had to be adapted to his wants. He would
buy an expensive horse or a jewel that took his fancy or dice with
anyone who called. Only the best wines passed his lips. I soon discovered that he was involved in another complicated affair of the
heart with a Mistress Margaret Jolly of Tregarden and spent much
time and money in her pursuit. These were activities he made little
effort to curb. Yet his smaller economies cut into the comfort of the
house, and there is no doubt that he intended them to save more than
they did.

"Yes," said Meg Levant. "We all thought you was dead. Drowned
or killed or put to the galleys, which is death deferred. I cannot
b'lieve tis you safe, unharmed by all they foreigners. Did you get to
know the Spanish girls?"

"Some. They seemed much the same as ourselves."

"Fancy. And how you've growed! And how thin y'are. I mind tis
no time since you was below my shoulder. Now I'm beneath yours."

"There's been times, Meg, when I've wished you were."

"Naughty. But twas always your way to put on some mock."

"It is not all mock. So you're wed to Dick after all, eh?"

"What d'you mean, after all? We were pledged at Christmas and
wed proper in church, St George's Day. There's no after all 'bout
that!"

"Dear Meg, it was but a turn of speech. He is away today?"

"The old wagon broke Saturday, so he's gone Truro with Tom Rose
to buy some new axle pins. He'll be 'ome 'night."

"He's a fine fellow, Dick. I'm sure he'll make you a good spouse."

"Ah, hark at the old man! Give me your blessing, will you, Maugan?
Dear life, I mind you since you toddled and you was always old-
fashioned. This Spanish time has not changed you. But then *all* our
babies be growing up."

Ever since I first knew her Meg would retreat behind a superiority
of age if I took liberties. Yet today there was a shrillness in her
voice as if she meant it—or wanted to mean it—as if she was willing
herself to draw away from me. Now she was married there could

never be the same easy comradeship again. Something in her look today gave the impression that all was not well about the withdrawal, or as if perhaps she was not quite at ease with her new life. Dick was a good fellow, but perhaps the vein of buffoonery in him took the romance out of his love-making. Meg was a romantic girl, living when her endless duties allowed in a world of knight errants and fair maidens imprisoned in castle keeps. If a story-teller came to the house she was always the first to listen.

"All our babies are growing up." I saw this on the next Sunday, a week after my return, when we walked to church. John was already as tall as his father. Thomas, a year younger, was square-shouldered and squat with his father's cleft chin and a rolling bandy walk, a musical boy who played the lute well and sang; Odelia, auburn-haired and frail looking—yet in fact a tom-boy—pretty with dimples and a wide, bewitching smile; Henry, aged eleven, had eyes so thin-set over a hawk nose that he looked sinister and sometimes the oldest of the lot. Then came Maria, just six, bulging with puppy-fat that squeezed up round her eyes and swamped her pudgy nose; nobody could detect the beauty she was going to be. The last to walk in the procession was Peter, not quite four, and he cried because it was so far, but as his mother was not there no one took notice of him until I set him on my shoulders, and then Father glowered. Perhaps he knew that Peter cried often and got his way. Perhaps he foresaw that Peter in some measure would always get his way. The two youngest of all, Elizabeth and Simon, were permitted to stay home.

I wonder now what my father would have thought if he could have seen into the future that Sunday morning as he strode vigorously along followed by his clutch of young eagles. Would he have been surprised and pleased to know that three of his sons would receive the knighthood which he had missed, and whose missing he so much resented? And would he have guessed which? Stiff, sober, formal John for whose betrothal he was already scheming? The morose but artistic Thomas, half-doer and half-dreamer? The acquisitive Henry, old before his time and full of claws? The sinewy Peter, slender and quick and noisy as a weasel. Simon, now attached to life so insecurely but later to be the fighter? William yet unborn?

Perhaps he could more easily have foreseen his own shabby end.

CHAPTER 5

DIRECTLY after church I told my father about the letter I carried for Thomas Arundell's sister and asked permission to deliver it. Mr Killigrew was then much occupied with a Baltic hulk which had just been brought in by a Plymouth fly-boat. The hulk was carrying pitch, tar, wood and cordage; these being contraband of war were subject to seizure, and my father was in haste to go down in case there might be some pickings for us, so he nodded impatiently to my request.

Mrs Killigrew, down for the first time since the birth of her eleventh child, said I might borrow Copley, her favourite pony. I was at the ferry by six, but the ferryman, a black-bearded dwarf with hands like squids, at first refused to get the larger boat out. We wrangled but when I had paid him fourpence he pulled the boat away from the side and I led Copley trembling into the box at the back. Then I had to help row, for the tide was strong.

The sun was sunk into the trees before the thatched roof of Tolverne showed. The last hundred yards of the path was much overgrown with brambles as if it had been scarcely used this summer and Copley was nervous as small animals stirred in the undergrowth and birds twittered in the low branches above his head. Even though there had been no rain today the track was miry, and ferns and weeds were rank with moisture. In the yard of the house the cobbles were slippery with mud, and a great pool submerged the half of it. As I jumped down Jonathan Arundell ran out. When he saw me he stopped and looked nonplussed, but by now I was used to this greeting.

"Maugan! But we thought you were dead! You were taken by pirates or Spaniards!" He peered past me. "This is a happy surprise. Since when are you home?"

"Seven days ago. You see I've not waited long to call."

"No. . . ." He looked past me again as he patted my shoulder. "This is good news. Come in, come in. Did you come by the ferry? You saw no one on the way?"

"Except the ferryman who scowled like a murderer. You were expecting visitors?"

"Yes. My uncle. And Thomas. They should be here before night falls. What brought you safely home?"

I told him as he led the way in. The house was dark and seemed empty but while talking I hoped and prayed Sue would suddenly step from some doorway. He stopped to call a servant, who came with a lighted candle and began to light others. Jonathan looked thin and ill. In the galleried hall the remains of a meal were on the table. The candles stained the greying daylight, and portraits grimaced on the panelled walls.

"Is Sue here?" I said, breaking into his talk because I could wait no longer.

"Sue?" He frowned and rubbed a hand over his forehead.

"Sue Farnaby."

"Oh. . . . No. She left. She left in May. Maugan, there is much to explain, and since you must lie here the night I shall try to explain it. Throw your bag on that chair. Sit down. You've eaten?"

"Not since dinner. But I can take something later. Why did she leave? What is wrong?"

"All is wrong, Maugan. Our lives have been sliding downhill for two years. You remember how Sir Anthony was at Christmas when you were here. Well, it has gone from bad to worse. Thomas swears he is mad but that's not true; my father is torn apart in conscience and belief, and his struggle has become our struggle so that we as a family are torn also, brother against brother, sister against sister-in-law!"

"It is all to do with religion? What had Sue—"

"As a young man my father was as staunch a Protestant as any Killigrew; but as the years have passed the old religion has attacked him like a canker, creeping upon him and upon us." Jonathan twisted his face. "For my part, Maugan, I cannot seem to feel religion that deep—if the truth were told I do not find myself hostile to some of the old forms and beliefs: for me they have a beauty that the new way of worship lacks. . . . But I would not live or die for either. Perhaps it's a weakness of mine. Thomas thinks so. All I'm concerned for is a happy home, especially for Gertrude, my wife, who has the feelings of her father. So. . . ." He shrugged. "So it went on for a time, a smouldering pot sending up the occasional bubble of steam. As Thomas has grown to manhood he has hated all the things my father is now devoting his life to. A sterner Protestant than Thomas never drew breath. . . . Oh, he has some reason on his side: Sir Anthony has become less cautious; people have talked; it's a matter of time before he comes into conflict with the sheriff's officers. . . . Thomas has lived on tenterhooks, says it should not be left to a sick man to lead his family into disgrace. My mother . . . well, you can see how she is torn. Then in January a Godfrey Brett came to stay. He is still here and pretends to be my father's secretary. I trust I can tell you this without fear of its being repeated?"

"Of course."

"He came, and—well, one has to acknowledge that he is a fine man, and little Elizabeth has been much influenced. Her father naturally encourages it. So that is the way of it. Gertrude at loggerheads with my sister. I with my brother. He with my father. Oh, I tell you, it's a picture of a united family that I draw for you, Maugan!"

"And in all this," I said, "why did Sue Farnaby leave?"

"Her aunt at Malpas was ill, and she went to nurse her. But I think she wasn't happy here. Who would be?"

"And she is there now?"

"I don't know. Maugan, things have come to the boil this week. Thomas has become more and more restive and yesterday he made some discoveries which set him blazing. He stormed off to Uncle Francis with the idea of having Sir Anthony put under some restraint. It's an impossible position for us all, Maugan! In a manner I agree that Thomas is acting in the best interests of the family; yet it is not his place to do it! Neither mother nor I will move; but Thomas has no love or respect for anyone—except himself. Sometimes I feel I would rather go to prison with my father than prosper in Thomas's company. . . ."

A servant came in. "There are horses coming, sir."

"It will be them, I imagine. Stay here, Maugan, I'll go and greet my uncle."

I had not seen Sir Francis Godolphin since he came to Arwenack with Mr Trefusis. With him was Thomas, grown almost as tall as I and half as broad again, Thomas of the round soft face and the bland eyes and the hard mouth. They exclaimed at sight of me, and then when the ladies came downstairs there were more cries of surprise and pleasure. At least, give Thomas his due, he put on no pretence of being pleased to see me; I think he had no feelings either way; there was other business on hand.

All the women looked haggard. Gertrude was still not with child: it was going to be perhaps as Thomas had predicted. Elizabeth's eyes were red, and her mother's too. Lady Arundell, although she must have borne the brunt of all this trouble, greeted her brother with composure, indeed rather coolly. It became clear that Sir Francis was here at his young nephew's invitation, not at hers. After their first congratulations to me there was an awkward silence which was broken by an offer of food and wine, which Sir Francis refused until he had seen his brother-in-law.

"Oh, Anthony?" said Lady Arundell, as if her husband had been far from her thoughts, "he is upstairs. He's well, though he was not

quite in the best of spirits when my—my *son* rode for you yesterday.
Yes, he's well enough. You shall see him presently."

"Thomas brings me sombre tales. It is true, is it, that Godfrey
Brett is still here? He must be taken, Anne. It's no longer safe to
house such creatures, as you must know. . . ."

He stopped at the sound of a foot on the stairs. Sir Anthony in a
long blue silk housecoat led the way, and behind him, stepping on
his shadow, was a tall thin man of about forty in the correct black
milan fustian of a secretary. Sir Anthony walked with a stick now
and in some obvious difficulty, but he would accept no help and
greeted his brother-in-law in a composed and controlled way.

"Maugan, too? But I thought you were lost to us. Well, happy
that you're not. Let Thomas take your cloak, Francis; you must be
tired after so long a ride. I trust all's well with you." To a servant:
"Cover the table, Banbury, and bring food and wine, and water for
washing."

We talked a few minutes, and they all found some outlet in questioning me, until two servants returned with a basin and ewer and
towels. Sir Francis washed, and after him Thomas and I, while the
table was set. Presently we sat down to eat, while the others stayed
at the table talking to us. In all this Godfrey Brett sat politely at
Sir Anthony's elbow, not speaking but discreetly present.

It was not until I mentioned that I had met Thomas Arundell in
Madrid and had a message for his sister that Sir Anthony showed
any signs of stress.

"Ah, so Thomas is well. We parted in anger many years ago. Perhaps now we should see things more as one."

"It is on that subject that I come to talk to you, brother," Sir Francis said. "Later when the meal is over we should retire together and
talk it over."

"Talk now if you wish," said Sir Anthony. "I have no secrets from
my family. Maugan Killigrew is the grandson of my guardian. Godfrey Brett is my close confidant."

"Too close," Thomas muttered, but Godfrey Brett though he must
have heard did not even raise his eyes.

"Thomas," said Sir Anthony, "though yet eighteen, thinks to grasp
the reins I hold—though if they were to drop from my hands they
would go to Jonathan. Thomas affects to believe that the stresses I
have been under have affected my judgment. Oh, do not deny it,
boy, I'm not blind yet, nor deaf."

"I don't deny it, Father," said Thomas grimly. "It is why I went
for Uncle Francis."

Sir Francis Godolphin stroked his grey beard. "I think, Anthony, in spite of what you say, that we would do better to talk of this in private."

"It will not be without Brett, that I can tell you."

The servants had gone from the room. Elizabeth was breathing sharply as if she had been running.

"Then so be it," Sir Francis acknowledged patiently. "But since it must be in front of Brett, then I have to tell you that for the sake of your family you must be rid of him."

"You presume to dictate whom I shall employ as my secretary?"

"Oh, come, brother. You know he is more than that."

I saw Sir Anthony's hand begin to tremble on the stick he still held. "What passes between Brett and me is the concern only of ourselves."

"There you err. In these days it cannot be. To rid yourself and your household of his—his tutelage must be the first step."

"A first step to what? To eternal damnation?"

"I'm not expert at theological argument; but I know, as you do, the laws of this land. We know what happened to Tregian when he was found harbouring a papist priest."

"Whom I helped to condemn," said Sir Anthony.

"All the more reason why you should not condemn yourself."

"All the more reason why I should, if that's what you call condemnation."

Sir Francis gave a slight shrug, and glanced round the table. Is this, his glance said, a man incapable of ordering his own affairs?

"Father," Thomas said, "you've no right to imperil the inheritance of your children. We have our own lives to live. Look at the Tregians, the Beckets, the Tremaynes, and all the rest—beggared and imprisoned, their estates seized and their prospects ruined. That's well enough if they're all of one mind. We are not."

"Nor are we all of yours, Thomas!" Elizabeth burst out shrilly.

"Ah, well, you have been influenced, bewitched by all these priests—"

"Silence!" said Lady Arundell, suddenly. "I will not have my children talk in such a way! Francis . . . Thomas has presumed on an overkindly upbringing to disgrace himself by speaking against his father. He exceeded his rights by sending for you. You are welcome, of course, but. . . ."

"I think Thomas has some right on his side," said Sir Francis quietly. "I would disown a son who behaved as he has done, but I pray I should never give him such reason. Is it true, Anthony, that you have been disposing of lands and farms to give the money to the priests that pass this way?"

That word had been spoken again—and this time not by an angry boy.

"The money is my own to do with as I will."

"Some must be held in jointure with my sister. She brought you property worth one thousand pounds a year."

"It has not been touched. My mother, who was Margaret Chamond of Launcells, left each of her children personal property, and it is that which I have sold."

Elizabeth was opposite me. She was not a pretty girl but she had grown quickly to womanhood in the last year. She was wearing a severe frock of brown velvet with a doublet like a man's but with much longer points. It was suddenly as if her bodice was too tight. She put her hand up to her throat, trying to loose the standing collar. She wrenched it open and pulled out the chain about her throat. On its end was a gold crucifix.

She said in a loud broken voice: "Holy Mary, Blessed Virgin, Blessed Mother of Christ, pray for me!" and burst into tears. Then she pushed back her chair and ran from the room.

Both Sir Anthony and Godfrey Brett crossed themselves at her words. You could hear her feet clattering down the stone passage towards the other stairs. A servant came in bringing more claret wine. We all waited in silence until he had gone.

As the door closed Thomas began to speak, but this time it was Sir Francis who waved him impatiently to silence.

"My brother—for so you have been by marriage for twenty-eight years—my brother, your life is your own to do with as you will, and I have long held you in esteem. But there is a point at which it is the duty of every Englishman to take issue with you. It is especially my duty as a Deputy Lieutenant of the county. In harbouring Jesuit priests from Rheims and Douai you are guilty of a treachery against the realm. By receiving them, by sheltering them, by dispensing money to them, you are furthering the interests of Spain and making more possible the conquest of this country—with all that would follow. Whatever you may feel, I must arrest this man and deliver him in custody to the Sheriff."

Sir Anthony made some convulsive movement as if trying to stand up, but all he did was upset a goblet which rolled across the table spilling the dregs of red wine on the cloth.

"So that's it, eh? That's why you come to call attended by no fewer than four personal servants. And do you intend to arrest me also?"

"This man is your secretary, no more, you say so yourself. Culpable fault need not attach to you. You were mistaken in the man, that's all."

"And having discovered my mistake, I am to denounce him? Oh, no, Francis. The spirit of Cuthbert Mayne, the first martyr in this holy war, will see that I don't do that. I will go in chains with Brett, make no mistake. Even to the rack."

"You need denounce no one," said Sir Francis, "only keep silent for the sake of your family."

With unsteady hands Lady Arundell picked up the overturned goblet. She did not look at her husband.

"Sir," said Godfrey Brett, "I have a suggestion to make."

Everyone looked suddenly at him, at his narrow ascetic face, at his deep set unyielding eyes. He too was now fingering a crucifix. "Well?"

"I think you are reckoning without me. That would be a mistake."

"We are reckoning that you will soon have lost your power to harm, to corrupt, to subvert. That is the important thing."

"I have not lost my power to harm this household, though it is the last thing I would wish to do. Others have passed through Tolverne before me. One at least—Humphry Petersen—was caught and put to the question. He gave away no secrets even to the end. It would be unwise to suppose that I would be so brave."

Sir Francis Godolphin pushed aside a candlestick so that he could see the other man more clearly. "Explain yourself."

"I have a mission, Sir Francis. You have a mission. We meet, by misfortune, under the roof of a common friend. That constrains us both. If I am caught here or hereabouts I shall necessarily implicate Tolverne and those in it. Sir Anthony, as you see, will not deny his part, so you cannot help but cause his family's ruin."

"And your suggestion?"

"My suggestion is that I leave tomorrow unimpeded by you. Twenty-four hours afterwards you come to seek me. By then I shall be well away from here; if I am caught there will be no need even to mention the name of Arundell."

The grease had spilled with the movement of the candlestick and was running down the brass base. Sir Francis turned to his brother-in-law.

"You see, Anthony, how your secretary thinks first of his own skin."

"That is untrue," said Godfrey Brett. "We all come prepared for martyrdom, but only as a final resort. It is our duty to do our utmost to avoid it—especially when it would involve others of the true faith. It's a simple bargain I'm offering you."

"Bargain!" shouted Thomas. "D'you think we should—"

"*Silence!*" said Sir Francis. ". . . And how do we know that if you are caught later you will not betray your patron when put to the question?"

"I cannot *promise* you that," said Brett; "for we none of us know our own endurance. But I can promise you that I would rather die. Therefore that way you have much to gain. If I am taken here you are lost already."

"And if you evade us, as you clearly hope to, then another spy remains in England to spread blasphemy and treason and perhaps assassination!"

Brett inclined his head. "It is a risk. You must weigh the advantages of one course against another."

Sir Anthony said gently: "Godfrey, I don't like this talk. I'm not afraid of prison or shackles or disgrace. Our blessed Lord suffered more than we ever shall. It is an honour to follow in His footsteps. Let us be taken together."

Brett patted his hand. It was a gesture very out of place in a secretary. "We have not only ourselves to think of, sir. We have to consider our loved ones, our cause, the greater good. It is only considering the greater good that constrains me to make this bargain with my enemies."

Sir Francis poured himself a half glass of wine. It was a first sign of a lessening tension. "Are you an Oxford man?" he asked.

Brett inclined his head. "Yes, sir."

"You argue like one. And seem to have given my brother a like disease." Sir Francis carefully ignored Thomas and looked over his head at Lady Arundell. "I exceed my duty if I agree to this, Anne, I do indeed. No doubt there are hot-heads here who are for immediate action; but I think this proposition should be considered. It might well be considered until the morning."

CHAPTER 6

I AWOKE thinking at first that I had dreamed the noise, that someone was slamming a door in my face. Then I heard voices, someone screaming for help.

I was afoot at once, struggled into my slops, and had passed through Thomas's room while he was still shaking the sleep out of his eyes.

On the front landing was a light. The wide bannisters of the stairs threw bars on the panelled walls from the single candle burning in the well of the hall. Elizabeth was down there, fully dressed, bending over a crumpled cloak. As I slithered down, bare feet slipping on the polished oak, I saw that beside her was the fallen figure of Sir Anthony.

When she saw me she stopped calling and trying to raise him. "Maugan! He fell! I think he's. . . . Maugan, he fell from half-way up. I—I was behind him but I could not catch him. . . ."

Sir Anthony was still breathing but in the flickering light his face was soap-grey and very old. As I tried to drag him into a better position others of the family came, including servants, and presently he was lifted and carried back to his chamber. There he lay stertorous, a trickle of saliva damping the corner of his mouth, while talk and argument eddied over him.

Elizabeth's story was that she had been awakened by her father who had told her to dress and come downstairs, as he had a message for her to take. It was only when Thomas pointed out that Godfrey Brett was not roused and they went to his chamber and found the bed empty that she burst into tears and told the truth. Sir Anthony had not fallen on the way downstairs: he had fallen backwards as he was going up after seeing Godfrey Brett on his best horse and away.

"So!" shouted Thomas. "The rat's gone! By morning he'll be half across Cornwall! But if he's taken Hilary she's a distinctive mare and maybe we can trace him. Come, Uncle, what did I say? If we leave now we might even catch up with him before he leaves the woods!"

"No," said Sir Francis. "Leave him go."

"But—"

"Leave him go. The bargain that he made still stands. But I did not expect that he would run tonight. I thought his courage would have stuck till morn."

"It was not that way," said Elizabeth, wiping her eyes with the back of her hand. "It was my father who insisted he should go at once. It was against his own wishes that Godfrey Brett left."

I stepped back feeling myself an intruder in this scene. I pictured Godfrey Brett spurring towards Truro, looking for the next family who would hide him. There were others, no doubt, and plenty.

Old Henry, one of the ostlers, was brought in and stared helplessly at the sick man. He fingered the livid bruise at the side of Sir Anthony's neck and said in a whining voice that he would draw off blood to give the Master some easement.

Gertrude Arundell, Jonathan's wife, came to stand beside me as he began. She too had gone thinner this summer; at sixteen she looked mature. Then I saw her glance towards the door and draw in a sharp breath; Godfrey Brett was standing beside Elizabeth.

The only sound for some moments was the drip of blood into the bowl.

Sir Francis straightened up. "Well, sir, did your horse go lame?"

"Yes," said Brett, and came into the room. "Yes, sir, it was lamed by the sound of a fall as I was crossing the yard to the stables. So it never started. I have been waiting in Sir Anthony's study until Miss Elizabeth brought me word. It seems that my old friend is mortal sick."

"I think he has had an apoplexy."

"Then he will need me."

"You come back at your own peril."

"We do all things, sir, at our own peril. It is man's privilege and destiny." He walked to the bed.

By the morning Sir Anthony had come round, but he could not speak and lay listlessly, eyes dulled under the white brows; but now and then a gleam of intelligence showed, like someone coming to a window and peering through the shutter. Lady Arundell and Godfrey Brett never left him.

Toward evening the sick man recovered enough to know what was being said to him and to nod emphatically when Brett asked if he should administer extreme unction. Only Lady Arundell stayed in the room while the anointing was performed; later when others went in it was possible to see a dampness round Sir Anthony's eyelids. Shortly afterwards he relapsed into a state of coma. When you passed the door of his room you could hear the slow heavy snore of a dying man.

He lasted through the night. I half expected Brett to make good his escape this time, now that all that could be done had been done, but he was still there when dawn broke.

It was a warm heavy day. The trees had encroached on the house in the last two years; the gardens were neglected and flies hovered over rotted branches and damp ferns. Foxgloves and nettles and brambles fought for light and sun under the silent trees. When one opened the window there was no fresh air, only a smell of dank vegetation and the buzzing of flies and bees. It had rained again in the night.

About seven the family was called to the bedroom. Sir Anthony's eyes were open and he had stopped snoring. Godfrey Brett stood by the bed holding a crucifix for him to see. Thomas stood by the window, his faint shadow darkening the floor.

After a while the dying man moved his head an inch to take in the people about him. Brett was intoning in Latin. Sir Anthony raised a hand—and made a gesture which might have been the sign of the cross. Outside rooks cawed in the tall cypress trees. The hand came slowly to rest and the mouth slowly opened, the lips parting reluctantly as if stuck with glue; the head rolled.

Thomas uttered a strange noise at the window. I do not know if it was grief, or if it was satisfaction at being one step nearer his inheritance.

To arrest Godfrey Brett at once was now the obvious course, since Sir Anthony would no longer suffer from the disclosure. Thomas was all to see it done. Sir Francis hesitated.

Thomas said they now had nothing to fear from an inquiry; his father had not been in his right mind when employing this man; no one could prove otherwise; no one else was to blame; Brett could hurt no one. Thomas further argued that there was now more danger in letting him go since, if he was later caught, he could accuse not Sir Anthony but Sir Francis Godolphin of abetting his entry into the kingdom. What high officer responsible to the Queen would dare to give such a man his freedom? Or suppose Brett got clear away, how would everyone feel then? Sir Francis rubbed his grey beard.

I do not know if consideration for Brett's decision to stay and be with Sir Anthony to the end had any bearing on Sir Francis's doubt. Largely I think it was still consideration for the house of Tolverne. If an inquiry were ever held the house and its occupants, even if cleared, would remain under a cloud. And Jonathan, now head of it, was not a man to bear up stoutly under disgrace. There was a frailty in him, a lack of conviction, which would stand him in ill stead before a court of inquiry. Then there was Elizabeth, a convinced Catholic now and in a hysterical frame of mind. Even Lady Arundell, with her attachment for her late husband and in early bereavement, might not stand up well.

Because there was no further excuse to stay, I left before a decision was come to. But I learned later that Sir Francis with typical discretion had found a middle way. He kept Brett under house arrest for four days until after the funeral, and in the meantime set afoot discreet inquiries in Truro. Two days after Sir Anthony was borne to his last resting place in Philleigh Church, where he still lies, a Breton vessel, the *Violette*, of forty tons, bound from Truro to Dieppe with a cargo of uncoloured woollen cloth, took in sail at Tolverne Pool just long enough for a row-boat, which had been loitering in her path, to put aboard one tall black-clad Catholic who temporarily was to be allowed to be neither missionary nor martyr. I understand

that Brett took it calmly, as he took most things calmly in his dedicated life. It was no policy of the Counter-Reformation to sacrifice its
sons without good cause.

Mistress Alice Arundell now lived at Tregony, so it was scarcely
out of my way to call first at the farm in the hills behind St Clement's Point. It was raining hard and blowing, on the first of August,
1594. As I rode Copley up the last ridge to the farm, his hooves
were squelching in brown mud. The trees on the other side of the
river near Malpas were hung with a widow's veil of rain. I had passed
field after field in which the corn was beaten flat; sheep huddled
for protection under dripping and waving trees; cattle hung their
heads; here and there men and women worked about the barns, sacks
over shoulders and tied round legs; it rained as if it would never stop.

At the first gate a dog barked savagely and Copley reared, but I
made peace with the mongrel and we plodded together up the
squelching track to the front door of the farm. I knocked and waited.
My heart was thumping. Water dripped off my hat, off the thatch
above the door, off Copley's saddle, off the mongrel's slimy muzzle.

A woman came to the door wiping her floury hands. It was exactly
what she had done last time I had called.

"Mistress Maris? You remember me? I came to see you a year last
May. I have called to see Sue. My name is Maugan Killigrew."

I forgot that the last time I had not told her that. But the name
seemed to convey nothing to her.

"Sue? She's not here. She's in Paul."

"In Paul? Near Penzance?"

"Yes."

Mrs Maris was of a sudden involved in keeping the mongrel out
of the house. It had tried to slip in unobserved but she saw it and
blocked it first with her foot and then with her hand. There was a
struggle, and then she grabbed the animal by the tail and turned it
and thrust it out. It slunk off down the path, and Mrs Maris, breathing hard, straightened up to regard me again. She did not ask me in.

"Why has she gone to Paul?" I asked.

"Why not? That's where she lives now. She's wed. Did you not
know?"

So I saw the inside of the Maris farm after all. She was not unkind
when she saw I was ill and took me in and gave me a cup of buttermilk.

It was a small poor room with a low ceiling heavy beamed so that one could barely stand upright, and on this dark day and with the small windows overgrown it was twilight at noon.

"Aye," she said, "it was last Wednesday. A week since today, so perhaps it's not surprising that everyone does not yet know. The betrothal was very short. She was wed at St Clement, down the valley from here. You take the turning by the old stables that Richard Robartes has just now bought and follow the trees down the hill. Her uncle, my man, stood for her, since her mother has but recently herself wed again and could not travel. I loaned her my own gown that I'd had since better days. The silk was turned yellow a small degree, but it fitted her, and it became her well. Mrs Glubb who's quick with her fingers, made her cap and gloves. It was all done very handsome, as you've a right to suppose."

There were signs of a faded gentility about the room: goblets on an oak dresser, a cupboard cloth of Venice work, brass pans well scoured and polished, two brazil armchairs.

"I saw how it was directly he came to call. And I saw it was a chance for her. She was always a bright child, quick as silver, sharp as a needle, and lively company, and she'll make a good wife. When she came home from Tolverne she was listless and lacking spirit; but when he called all that was changed. I saw how it was going to be, and how fortunate she was."

I sipped the buttermilk but could hardly get my throat to swallow.

"Oh, it is a good match for her. Mind, he's not so young as he was, but there's money and land and connections. He's not one of these shiftless paupers who eke out their living as best they may. And he's a godly man, not a drunkard or a dicer, as many are. As I said to her: you're alone in the world now your mother's wed again, and you've no dowry nor no hope of one. Here's the chance of a fine house—though I've not seen it—and a horse to ride; and he says he keeps five servants—he never came but with one beside him; and a fine old name like Reskymer. Mind, no one ever pressed her. When my man thought she was overlong in answering he said, Does she know what she's about keeping him waiting like this? There's many a maid would leap at the chance. But I said, go to, it is part of a woman's way to hesitate; it does not do to be too eager, lest you be taken for granted ever after. A matter of a few days' patience. And sure enough it was."

A heavy patch of damp on two of the low beams; the room smelt of mildew and rot; afterwards that smell would recall to me the darkness in that room and the dripping rain and the darkness in my soul.

"I believe he's a Reskymer of Merthen, a cousin of the main family, that is. There's always been Reskymers in the church. He says he met Susanna at the Arundells two years back when she was fourteen. He was then a widower by some ten years but he had no thought for Sue, thinking her then a child. Since then he has seen her three times; but the last of these, chancing to call at Tolverne in May, he was much struck by her beauty and called there again last month only to find her gone. So he pursued her here, and so it fell out. If you have a thought to see them they live in the rectory at Paul, near Penzance, which I'm told is a handsome house quite worthy of his position and name."

I could not sit here for ever. If I could get out into the rain again, mount the pony, just the effort and the buffeting of the wind. . . .

"Thank you, ma'am. If you write to Susanna, give her my respectful regard."

Copley welcomed me with a snort and a shake of his bridle. The mongrel dog was sniffing at a piece of bone on the edge of a muddy pool of water. A man was in sight coming over the fields driving a pair of oxen before him. The rain blew in fresh clouds over the dripping trees. Nothing in the landscape had changed. Only I had changed. And I had changed for ever.

Book Three

***

CHAPTER 1

THERE is no proportion in memory. Months of happiness or misery can suffer an ellipsis which no effort may fill; yet moments or single days linger in the mind from a choice that seems not one's own and have an endurance beyond their worth. Selection is as difficult as sequence because one's memory has already acted.

I know there has never in my life been a time of greater misery and resentment. A young man of finer fibre might have permitted himself to feel only sorrow, but I have never been one to take adversity well.

One always feels most for the first illusion lost; but this was more than illusion; it was the linch-pin of my faith in life. Belief in Sue Farnaby and our love for each other had become for me in a few short months the constant around which everything else revolved. That destroyed, there was no centre for any loving kindness to attach to. I was lost, groping in the dark of my own nature, clumsy with pain, and liable to break anything with which I came in contact.

The attitude of many people at Arwenack changed towards me during that year, and this can only have been reflecting the change that was in me. I quarrelled violently with Belemus when he returned, and we fought it out in the wood behind the house. I was uncouth and and unpleasant to my half-brothers and sisters. If my grandmother had been about there is no doubt I should have been sent away again to Truro, but the damp weather did not suit her and she spent most of each day in her chamber coughing.

Yet I fared altogether better with my father. I was inches taller than he now and tireless, filling out a little but still very thin. He set me to work about the house or in the fields or to ride with him on one of his dubious outings, and my new mood only made him smile derisively. He never asked about the change or why all the world had suddenly become my enemy; Dorothy Killigrew of course did, but I returned her evasive answers and presently she gave up.

Perhaps my mood found a responding chord in Mr Killigrew; I know he forbade any inquisition when Belemus and I came to the table with our features puffed and scarred. I have since thought—though I did not perceive it then—that my father was a man who was himself lost and without beliefs in a world that seemed to him full of enemies. He had grown up in an age when lawlessness was near to a patriotic duty, when armed retainers were the accepted instrument of privilege, when one lived by force at home and by bribery at Court. But time had caught him up and passed him by. He was in a bog of his own and my grandfather's devising, and casual efforts to struggle free only sent him the deeper. To thwart his enemies he went to shifts that created more enemies. Godolphin was a greater power in the land, but Godolphin never rode abroad followed by a half score of armed men of his own. Nor did Sir Reginald Mohun nor did a Grenville nor a Basset nor a Boscawen. Their only armed forces were the musters they gathered for the defence of England.

Times were changing. My father's way of life stood out in a dangerous prominence. And he was not prepared to change it. Creditors were pressing, but his need of Mistress Margaret Jolly pressed harder. His debts demanded close personal attention, but it would not always be such good hawking weather. A number of his fields were fallow for lack of farm help, but he saved with having fewer servants to feed and so could spend more on the occasional feast.

I began to know all he did. The expulsion of the Farnabys was not an isolated act. When he rode abroad to collect his rents there was no nonsense tolerated, and I was the witness of three scenes in which tenants were turned out without ceremony and without mercy. Twice I was in brushes with bailiffs who sought to put a distraint on property. I learned to carry pistols and to practise the use of them. Sometimes Belemus came with us and then we would ride together immediately behind my father.

Belemus's father was still in prison and his lands under seizure by the crown, so that he too was a young man without proper restraint. After our fight we became closer friends and took part in ventures of our own.

At the end of that summer Belemus fell in love with a girl called Sibylla who was the daughter of Otho Kendall, a burgher of Penryn. In the town Killigrews were never popular, but Belemus and I took to frequenting Cox's Tavern which was hard by the harbour and next to the Kendall house. This way he could sometimes catch a glimpse of Sibylla as she came and went, and presently he found a wall which he could climb on, from which he could carry on a whispered conversation with her out of her bedroom window.

It was all fraught with a good deal of hazard. The local quarry-workers and townsfolk knew who we were and resented our being there. Otho Kendall was a fiery man, and his father Sebastian Kendall was an old sailor, be-ringed and one-eyed, whose reputation for violence had not lapsed with age.

Sibylla was a slender black-eyed girl, more beautiful perhaps than pretty, and she wore her hair under its cap in long black braids. But there was nothing demure about her eyes when she raised them, and Belemus was afire with passion.

It must have been one afternoon in early September when, sitting in the Tavern, we saw the girl leave her home alone and walk up the hill carrying a basket. She had gone no more than a dozen yards before we followed her. The sun was shining after a morning of heavy rain, the tide was out, and the town drowsed in the warmth as if deserted. But once or twice I thought there were faces quietly withdrawn from windows as we passed.

They were bell ringing in St Gluvias church across the narrow creek: they had been at it all afternoon, practising or just for the sport.

We followed Sibylla until at the first thicket out of the town she stopped to pick the blackberries which glistened still with the drops of rain on them. Belemus gave me a nudge to stay where I was and went over to speak to her.

At eighteen Belemus had grown into a powerful and personable young man. His buff leather jerkin with its brass buttons showed the breadth of his chest. He had grown a short black beard and a tiny wisp of moustache which he kept carefully trimmed and which softened the wide flat angles of his mouth and cheeks. He walked with the swagger of a man who hardly knows his own strength. He gave the girl a great bow, his long hair as he uncovered blowing in the breeze. She turned her head away and continued to pick blackberries. I could not hear what they said for they spoke in low tones, but every now and then she would break into a shrill excited laugh. The church was a few hundred yards away across the muddy creek and up the hill, and the bells clashed and clanged ever more violently as if themselves agitated by some compulsion of excitement.

Belemus was trying to persuade Sibylla to take a walk with him as far as the hill above the town. It seemed an innocent invitation, but she knew that the paths through the hazel and nut trees were narrow and winding and one might easily stray. Others had done it before, and the bold and the brazen walked up there of a summer evening hand in hand. All the same, something in her manner suggested that sooner or later she would yield; it might not be today, but a persistent courtship would have its reward.

The bells at last stopped with a final clang, and in the echoing sunny silence the only sound was the crying of the gulls as they fought and flapped about refuse which had been thrown in the mud for the next tide to carry away. I glanced back and saw two figures coming up the narrow cobbled street. One was limping and had a black patch over his eye.

Belemus scowled at me as I came up. "What's amiss? Leave us be."

"There's others who'll not."

"Who's that, man?"

"Miss Sibylla's father and grandfather will walk with you right away. They're equipped for climbing, for they carry sticks."

The colour fell out of the girl's flushed cheeks. "God save us, go away, Belemus! Hide yourself, you and your friend. Go, go quick, leave me to my berries!" She turned sharply and began to clutch at the fruit; ripe and unripe went into her basket together.

"It would take more than a couple of such to flight me," said Belemus, pulling at his beard. "A damned old miser and a limping one-eyed lobster-catcher. Why—"

"Come, man, you'll only make it worse for the girl. Come away while there's time."

I pulled at him, but by now the two men were near enough to see us. As we moved farther up the hill, putting distance between us and Sibylla, the roar of Otho Kendall came after us.

"Hi! You! Killigrew trash, I'd have a word wi' ye!"

Belemus stopped and fingered the short knife in his belt. "If I were a Killigrew I should feel some choler at that."

I said: "You are included."

We waited until the two old men had come up with the girl. We were then some twenty yards away. The sun, already watery for the morrow, glinted on the three gold rings on old Sebastian Kendall's gouty fingers, on the ear-rings trembling under his grey wig. He had been hard put to it to keep up with his son.

"Killigrew dung!" shouted Otho Kendall, and spat. "Keep off of my dattur!"

"We were not on her, old man," said Belemus.

"Filthy whorers! Keep out of Penryn. Go back to your own midden over th' hill. Come nigh us again and we'll tear yer tripes out."

"Old man," said Belemus, "old man, when I choose to come to your scabby little town, I shall come, and not you nor any of your smutty fellows shall stop me."

At this moment Sibylla unwisely made some movement, and her father swung round and hit her on the side of the head. She collapsed in a sudden wailing heap, bonnet going one way, basket the other.

"Bravo," said Belemus, "strike your women! It's common, I know, among offal such as you!"

Old Sebastian could restrain himself no longer and came up the hill, his great stick swinging and murder in his eye. Otho at once followed. We should have had our skulls laid open before ever we could get near them; so we turned and went up the hill.

And there stopped. The eight bell-ringers had come out of the church, and while we were exchanging insults with the Kendalls had surrounded us. Except for two who carried sticks they were not armed, but four or five were grabbing up stones.

"Hold 'em, boys!" shouted Otho. "We'll give 'em a rare cooting this time!"

A stone struck me on the shoulder. Behind us the two old men would be on us within a count of five. Together we rushed uphill towards the two men who chiefly barred the way home. Another stone struck me on the back of the head, and a great shower sprayed over Belemus. Faced by us both charging them with drawn knives, the two men backed away. One swung at Belemus's shin with a stick as we went past. He stumbled but I grabbed his arm and we were through.

But though we ran we did not outdistance them. It was close on two miles to the palisades, and each time when we thought we were clear they would catch us again with another shower of stones.

When we got to the gate of Arwenack and the shouts and yells of our pursuers had at last died away, I was bruised in a dozen places and bleeding at the back of the neck. As Belemus leaned against the gate gulping for breath he bared his teeth and said:

"They think to drive us away, the rogues."

"And so they have."

"But not for long, dear Maugan, not for long."

"Well," I said, "I do not fancy your love affair will prosper, but let me know what you have in mind."

That night we went back with a half-dozen armed servants. We walked along the little cobbled main street. Cottagers at their doors watched us resentfully and mothers called their children in, but no one blocked the way. We went into Cox's Tavern and stayed drinking for an hour. Then Belemus went out and hammered on the door of the Kendalls' house. The windows were shuttered and no one came. Belemus thought to break down the door but I counselled that this would not endear him to Sibylla however she might be suffering at the hands of her parents. So we came away.

Thus the affair simmered for two or three weeks. Then we began to revisit the tavern, though not without rapiers in our belts. Sometimes Belemus would get a word with the girl, but she was close-guarded. Then came another day when, leaving as darkness fell, we were stoned again.

Belemus said: "These rats need a lesson."

We went back that night and broke open the door of the church. I climbed up in the belfry and cut the four bell ropes so that but one strand of each remained. Some of the ringers would likely fall on their scuts at the next practice.

We splashed lime-wash on the walls, carried out the pews and chairs and dropped them in the mud of the river. We rounded up a flock of sheep, drove them into the church, and shut the door on them. Then we dug a pit outside the door and went home.

A scandal there was but none could bring the fault home to a Killigrew. We continued to go into Penryn twice a week. Sometimes Belemus would get a word with Sibylla but most often not. Then one day he met her by chance on St Thomas's Bridge and it all fell into place. He came home exultant, but at first would not satisfy my curiosity. Two days later he took a private chamber at Cox's Tavern and spent the night there. Then I knew "it" had happened but not how. The next time we went together he showed me the window of the chamber he had hired. It looked directly into Sibylla's window. There was a high wall between the two buildings, but if you were already on a level with it it could be used as a stepping stone between.

So for three weeks he took the room at Cox's Tavern, selling two of his rings to pay for it. His absences did not go unremarked at Arwenack, but he was eighteen and thought able to look out for himself.

Then one day he was not back to help with the reaping, and since it was the first fine day of the week my father was angry. I went up to my chamber about noon and found Belemus lying on the bed.

He said: "Ah, well, Maugan, I had a little trouble," and moved. The bed was soaked with blood.

On his way home he had been set on by two men in the wood above the town. He had a knife wound in his ribs and a purple cut on his head. He did not know either man—had barely seen them—but he had been left, perhaps for dead, and had not come round until the sun was high. Then he had crawled down towards Three Farthings House, and Paul Gwyther had brought him home in his cart.

He was weak from loss of blood and the knife had gone deep, but he had not bled from his mouth, and I thought he was not wounded to death.

There was a rough-and-ready treatment followed at Arwenack for injuries of all sorts, but I thought of what Katherine Footmarker had told me and used first a strong solution of salt and water, at which he complained greatly; then I put on a plaster and hoped for the best.

He said, would I keep it quiet from my father, so I went down to dinner and told a story that Belemus was staying the day with the Arundells; but I did not think the deception would work long, for too many servants were in the secret. Belemus spent the night in my chamber, while I slept on the floor and John squeezed in next door. Belemus had a fever, but all his cursings and ravings were of a quite logical turn, on the theme that Sibylla would be expecting him and he would not be there.

The following day he was hardly able to move, but he crawled down to dinner somehow and told how he had fallen from a horse. It was clear that any prospect of visiting Sibylla was remote for at least a week. I said, well, I would go and tell her.

He said: "Go after dark. And take Long Peter. He is the roughest man I know when it comes to an ambush or a tavern brawl."

"Are you in love with Sibylla, Belemus?"

He stared. "Of *course*. I worship the ground she steps on. She is like Thisbe walking in a woodland glade! . . . She is so beautiful I lose my breath every time I look at her—"

"Yes, yes, I understand. And does she love you?"

"Mother of God, how could you doubt it? D'you think she's a whore? D'you think she would have given herself to me otherwise—"

"And shall you wed her?"

He tried to catch his moustache with his bottom teeth. "I think it is possible, Maugan. I think it is likely. But with my father in prison a deal may depend on my marriage. I'm not as free as you. But I would wish to; I would certainly wish to."

"She will have little money and no position. It is something to think of."

"Oh. . . . That is in the future—we are both young. I love her, and she loves me, that's all there's to it now. If things go wrong betwixt us I shall wed her, you can be assured of that. You were always one to look on the black side."

I patted him gently on his unsore shoulder and said: "It's all very plain now. I will give her your message and your love."

The nights were drawing in, and when supper was over it was dark. I did not ask Long Peter to go with me; I thought he might be in the way.

I walked to Penryn and Cox's Tavern. Only four men were in the taproom, and they were all fishermen of a harmless sort, not toadies or bullies. I drank a pint of small beer. Cox had a heady ale known as "lift leg," but the business tonight demanded clear thinking. After an hour I asked for the chamber which my cousin Belemus had reserved. With some side glances I was shown up into a tiny room, so low beamed that you could not stand upright. The window was already shuttered, and the pot boy who showed me up set down the candle on the chest by the door and quickly left.

I shot the rude bolt on the door, unlatched belt and sword and put in on the pallet, then beside it I set my leather jerkin. The situation was as Belemus had described it: a shuttered window opposite, with a wall between which came no higher than the sill.

Most people were now abed, but there was a chink of light showing through the shutters opposite. Below all was silent and black. I set the candle down so that the light was entirely shaded from the window; then climbed out, stepped on to the wall, and redistributed my weight so that instead of leaning back against the wall of the tavern I was leaning forward against the wall of the Kendall's house; then gently tapped.

The light went out. Now except for the reflected light from the candle in my room it was pitch dark.

The shutters parted. I could see an arm. I put one foot up and swung myself in. In a moment not one arm but two were round me. I put my hands about Sibylla. She was wearing only a night smock. After a little pleasant groping in the dark I found her face and kissed her.

She began to scream; but my fingers on her mouth and her quick mind stopped her.

"Do not be alarmed. I had no time to grow a beard."

"*Maugan!* . . . Tis you! Where is Belemus?"

"Abed with a knife wound in his ribs, got by being set on in the woods. Shall we be heard?"

She drew herself away. "Nay. . . . Nay, not if we whisper. Love-a-duck, you give me a scare! Is he serious sick?"

"Not serious, but he'll be laid away for some days. It was some of your tribe who set on him?"

"How should I know? They d' know naught of this—"

"It cannot be unknown that Belemus still comes to the Tavern, even if Cox keeps his mouth tight over the hiring of the chamber."

"And—and why've you come?"

"To bring word from Belemus. Have you a light? It is pitch in here."

She moved, and a cupboard door opened to show that she had not put out the rushlight but had only hidden it. She looked nice in her thin smock with her long black hair over her shoulders.

"Give me the message." Conscious of my look, she picked up a shawl and wrapped it about her.

"You have the message: that he's wounded and cannot come. He sends his love."

"And also his friend. Did he tell you to climb in here and make yourself free?"

"How else could I give the message?"

"By writing it and throwing it up."

"Can you read?"

She hesitated. "Well, I would ha' guessed what twas! You'd no right to give me such a fright. I'll tell Belemus of ee."

"If you tell him so much he'll think the more. He says you're a passionate girl."

"How dare he speak of it!"

"We are close friends. We share many things."

"Ah, but there's some things you cannot share, and I'm one of 'em, Maugan Killigrew."

"Well, a kiss more or less is no killing matter."

She eyed me up and down, but I think the rushlight was too frail to show up my uncertainty. A draught from the window made the flame lurch, and I pulled the shutter to with my hand.

"Well, saucy," she said. "Grow a beard an' I'll think about it. Why, you're half a boy yet!"

I knew then. "Oh," I said, "that's dangerous talk."

"I don't see."

"It would be easy to prove different. And you could scarcely scream."

She backed away. "If I screamed I'd be for trouble, but not like you. Love-a-duck, they'd truly kill you! Nay, *quiet*: they'll hear you movin'; that board d' creak!"

I had followed her. "I'll confess to you it was no hardship to come."

We talked for some minutes in whispers, I persuading, she refusing, yet each refusal on slightly weaker ground than the last. Presently by little degrees I was able to put my hands on hers and then to kiss her, she still protesting. However, I remained so brushing her face with my lips, and thus got my arms about her. For a first time it all, I think, had a fair appearance of expertness.

"Ah," she whispered, "what a scoundrel y'are. Have you no loyalty to Belemus, eh?" But she did not now move much in my grasp.

We sank back on the bed. It was of stout planking and did not creak. My hands began to caress her through her night smock. "Nay," she whispered, "wait. Untie me this knot."

I did as she said, and she began to kiss me in return. Then I felt her body stiffen in my arms.

"What is it?"

"Listen. . . ."

"Oh, it's the wind—"

"Nay! Listen. . . ."

The shutter of the window was not properly caught. I heard some-one cough.

She got up from the bed and reached for the rushlight. Then we were in the dark.

"It's someone outside," I whispered, "some passing fisherman. It is of no import—"

"Oh, yes it is. I think—at least, I fear. . . . Wait."

She slipped away from beside me, and I heard a board creak as she stepped on it. Then her shadow showed by the slit in the shutter. She was there some time.

Her breathing was very quick when she came back. "There's two of 'em Tis Lawson, the sexton, and my Uncle Reynold! They'll be armed!"

"And what makes you think they're concerned for us?"

"Because I *know* now! Father yesterday dropped hints that I didn't follow!—Maugan, they'll beat me half to death and they'll *kill* you! I know it! I *know* it!"

"Ssh, ssh, quietly does it. Let's think. We're not found yet." But for all my show I was beginning to sweat. I had left my sword in the tavern. In the pockets of my slops there was a folding knife: that was all.

From this window the shaded candle in my own chamber oppo-site was the only light. The shutter swung loose, no doubt telling its tale. Almost directly below, two men were standing. I went back to the bed.

"They'll get tired waiting there until the dawn comes."

"Nay, Maugan, nay." She put her hand on my knee. "They'll wait and wait. And if the light breaks it will go the worse for you. But I been thinking."

"Tell me."

"I been thinking. . . . Outside this door tis but ten steps down and then a front door bolted only at the top; the bottom bolt be broke.

. . . They'll think to surprise you as you come out of the window—if they know you be in—but they'll not think you've the sauce to come out of the door. Tis like to be unguarded."

I hesitated, frustrated, wildly angry, but the anger was a defence against fear. So long as I could be angry I could see myself as a disappointed seducer, still as the hot spark who had begun the evening, not as a boy surrounded by dangerous men and in hazard of his life.

She said: "Shall I open the door and see if the way be clear?"

"No, wait a while."

But after waiting I agreed, seeing no better way. She described the small house, assured me there were no turnings: it was straight down and out.

So she went to the door. I unfolded my knife and followed. One moment there was her soft warmth beside me. The next I was in the passage outside listening in the silence.

Someone was snoring. It was the comforting sound of a house harmless and asleep. But there was another sound, nearer, less harmless, though at first I could not name it. Then I knew it for someone's breathing. And whoever was so breathing was awake. And near me.

Whoever was so breathing must know that I had come out of Sibylla's room and must be waiting for me to make the next move before pouncing.

I did not move but stared in a sickly fashion into the shadows. Some faint reflection of light there was, and I made out what looked to be the head of the stairs. I suddenly went down on hands and knees and crawled towards it.

At once there was a thunderous clatter over my head, as if someone had swung a club and hit only wall; then a figure fell across mine. A groping hand caught my foot and when I kicked free the body twisted itself and fingers tore at my face. I stabbed with the knife. There was a grunt: I kicked clear and half ran, half fell down the stairs.

Grope for the door; there seemed only hinges. The wounded man was crawling down the stairs. I turned into the next room; this was all there was to the house. The shutters were poor here; they fell apart; I jumped into the yard. After the dark of the house the night was clear. On a bin, pulled myself over the wall.

A lane. Away from the town; away too, it must be at first, from Arwenack. Panting like a hound at the end of a chase, I went up the hill, leaping from cobble to cobble and slipping and sliding in the muddy pools.

At the top I stayed long enough to swallow and look back. Three were coming. I ran on then, making for the mill where Katherine Footmarker had lived; but before I got there they had lost me.

CHAPTER 2

Soon after this my father left for London. His affair with Mistress Margaret Jolly had prospered, and, so prospering, had come to die a natural death. His visit to London was to be a routine one to see his friends and to attend at Court. So he said. But in fact everyone knew that he was to meet a Sir George Fermor of Northampton, and that Sir George, an army man, had a daughter called Jane. Jane was fifteen and an heiress. John, my half-brother, was now fifteen.

By the time Mr Killigrew left the scratches on my face were forming scabs, and by the time he returned they had healed. But after all these years there is still a white mark where finger nails went deep.

The man I had wounded was Sibylla's father, Otho. There was much whispered talk about it all, but the justices were not invoked. The Kendalls were not people to go to law, being too cautious to risk a case against one of the great landlords. They would have their own revenge in their own way and in their own time.

We never saw Sibylla again. We heard she was beaten with a wooden rod until she bled, then was packed off to an aunt in St Austell, and very soon we heard she was wed to a cousin there. It was the safest way for them of covering up the scandal.

I took all the blame and notoriety, Belemus none. He was amused, and although he bore Sibylla's loss ill for a few days he soon rewon his spirits. He had not been so deeply involved.

My father said to me: "Well, boy, we all have our rigs and sprees, and I'm the last one to be stopping you in your youthful pastimes; but you could have chosen a better place to play the turkey than Penryn —and among those Kendalls. Awkward rogues, every one of them. Lucky to escape as you did."

I muttered something.

"And watch your step when away from this estate. All Penryn men have long memories. I don't want more trouble just at the present— they have ways of running to Westminster and telling tales behind my back. Were you a party to this prank in the church too?"

"Sheep are always straying where they don't belong, sir."

"Yes, well, you've done enough now. What was the girl like?"

I looked up and saw him watching me with a speculative, envious gaze. I felt myself flushing. "Why . . . like most girls, father."

"God's breath, you've had so many that you lump them all together? You must have been active in Spain!"

"No, I—"

"Well, I see, it's just an evasion. I agree she was a pretty little thing. I saw her—or I think it was she—with the nets when they was being mended after the Easter gales. I thought to myself: there's a catch for some young fisherman; but I never thought to think it would be you! You hadn't thoughts of marriage, I hope?"

"No, father."

"I should think not. You're only half a Killigrew, but a half of one should look for something better than a Sibylla Kendall. Before ever you went away Mrs Killigrew said you had thoughts for the Farnaby girl. Is that true?"

"She's wed now. To a man called Reskymer, who's rector of Paul."

"What, Philip Reskymer? That tall thin man with the sad yellow face? If that's so he's a kidnapper, for he must be fifty if he's a day. She's gone for a safe place no doubt—the Farnaby's were ever a shiftless timid lot and Philip Reskymer has lands and money in a small insignificant way."

"They say he was married before," I said, turning the knife.

"Oh, yes, twice I believe. The flowers sicken quickly when planted in *his* bed."

My father waited until he had seen all the corn, such as it was, stooked and dried and gathered in. The week the threshing began he left, and Thomas Rosewarne rode with him. This left three who might give orders in the house: Lady Killigrew, Henry Knyvett, and Mrs Killigrew. But Lady Killigrew was still confined to her chamber with bronchitis; Henry Knyvett, having come to some temporary remission with his wife, was at Rosemerryn when sober and unsober when at Arwenack; and Mrs Killigrew although not at the moment sick with her usual complaint, was much concerned for her two youngest, who ailed often.

That left me. Mr Killigrew had said nothing but he had implied much by the confidences he had reposed in me over the last two months. After all, Belemus was not of the family, and John, however valuable as a pawn on the marriage board, was still too young for authority. I would soon be seventeen. . . .

I liked threshing, and this year it fitted with my wild restless mood. All the time we were doing it the rain came down. The great barn where we worked was open at one end, but when the gales grew too strong the doors were closed and we threshed in semi-darkness. We used handstaffs of pliable ash about five feet long so that we could

work standing up. Tied to the end of the handstaffs with leather
thongs were the short clubs which struck the corn. We worked,
twenty of us at a time, standing over the corn spread on the floor,
worked to a regular rhythm, a blow, a pause and then a blow. Sometimes we sang songs together. We sang

> Over the mountains
> And over the waves,
> Under the fountains
> And under the graves.

And

> Why does your sword so drip with blood, Edward, Edward?

We laughed and joked and told tales. Dick Stable told the story of
the miser of Market Jew who met the Devil and was granted three
privileges: to sit in his own light, to sit next to the parson, and if he
saw a pig in a gutter he might turn it out and take its place. Dick
was always one for comic stories, but I did not think his new wife
Meg laughed so heartily as the rest.

When enough of the grain had been beaten the straw was raked
away; but the gale outside persisted so high that we could not let
it do the winnowing: if we had opened the doors it would have taken
the roof off. So we made our own draught with goose-wings on long
poles and then gathered up the corn into baskets before carrying it to
store.

I worked for a time beside Meg, and thought she went at the corn
much as I did, as if it served to work off an inner hurt. Out of the
corner of my eyes I watched her movements as she swung her staff:
her slight yet comely figure, the breasts raised under her grogram
shirt each time she lifted her freckled arms; what caught my eye most
was the slimness of her stomach and waist. Now and then her dark
auburn hair would fall over her brow and she would shake it back
impatiently; it was hot working in the closed barn, and there was a
dampness of sweat on her forehead and on her upper lip. The sight
of her was something I could not ignore.

The gales abated as the threshing was completed but it stayed dark
weather with flurries of rain and clouds hanging low on the river.
The autumn killing of cattle began, and the salting of the beef to see
us through the long winter months. We ate our fill at this time for
there would be no more fresh meat until the spring.

Having been helping with the cutting up and salting of a carcass, I
washed my hands and arms at the pump outside and went through
the house to my room. On the stairs I met Katherine Footmarker.

In the half dark I thought she was some illusion of the rain-dripping windows.

"So, Maugan Killigrew! . . . Well, lad, you're back. I'm glad. Truly glad." She spoke as if I were the visitor here.

"Yes. How is it—"

"You've not been to see me since you came safe home."

"It is only three months. What brings you here?"

She laughed gently. "Your step-mother thinks I've a skill or two that's useful."

"Mrs Killigrew invites you?"

"She sent for me first when your sister Odelia had the quinsies, but I would not come on account your father was here. So I sent a syrup which I'm told gave her ease. Then after, I came when Mrs Killigrew had an ailment, and again to see little Peter. It surprises you?"

I did not know what to say.

"Peter's sick again," she said. "He has the autumn fever. But I tell Mrs Killigrew to save her fears for him too. He shivers and quivers in every wind, but he's like to outsee you all."

It was on my tongue to tell her of the salve I had made for Mariana's scald.

"Does my father know you come?"

She shrugged. "There's servants here who rail at me comin', and one or another may drop the word. It's no concern of mine."

"But you would not come when he's here?"

"I don't like your father's ways. I believe the Killigrews have no good destiny here, and he is sealin' it. Each time I come it's like a clenched fist over this house. It slopes, Maugan. The whole house slopes towards the pit!"

She seemed herself a part of what she prophesied, a bird of ill-omen flapping its wings in the dark.

"Take care for yourself," she said. "I told you there was blood on your hands."

I stared down stupidly, thinking for a moment she meant from the carcass of the animal we had just slaughtered.

"There's blood on each hand," she said, "and I'm none too sure Otho Kendall's is marked on either. But it's a warning. Follow not your father, lad. You've better things in you than to become one of his bullies. And as for women, the way for your happiness is not to pull down any maid within reach of your fingers, as your father did and I hear you're doin', but to live for one or two. Each bauble you seize and throw off tarnishes and debases what you can feel for the others. Love is like gold, it should be spent in sum and not frittered away."

That she was talking in such ignorance of the truth set all my anger alight. "I've a life to live, and how I spend it's of concern only to me! I'm part Killigrew and I owe all to my father! If I can give him some service I shall do it. As for women . . . that's my concern too, isn't it?"

She swung her scarlet stringed bag gently back and forth. "Well, I see there's been a change in you, Maugan, and that in less than a year."

"Don't come here again. If you're against my father you're against us all."

"That's not true, boy. I'm not against your father. I'm 'against' no one. I see trouble comin' to this house as rain comes with a cloud. That don't mean I shout welcome to it. I speak warnin'. If you've no time or patience to heed it, more's the pity."

"There'll be less trouble with you out of it."

She put her hand on my arm; I tried to shake it off but it had a firm grip.

"In Truro we were friends. Who's slid poison in your veins?" She peered more closely. "Ah . . . I remember. You were sighin' for that girl. . . . How's she done you ill?"

I shook her hand off at last.

She said: "I've many cures, but not for the one that ails you now. Time only can help. But remember that if one man robs you it don't make all the world a thief. Nor one woman neither."

"Keep your advice."

I saw she was suddenly angry.

"As for me staying away from Arwenack," she said, "I'll see you damned ere I do that! So long as your step-mother calls me, I'll come. I have a finger in this house, lad, and not you nor your father shall root it out. I give you warning of it!"

She brushed past me. I almost laid hands on her but something held me back, some old awe. I watched her till she was out of sight. Then I went on clumsily, noisily, up the stairs.

I began to want Meg Levant. I wanted her not out of love, not at first wholly from desire, but out of seething black-minded misery and frustration. Because of loyalty to Sue I'd rejected Mariana; because the alarm was raised I had been robbed of Sibylla. I had no hard thoughts for Dick Stable; everyone liked him; but I was in the mood to ignore the feelings of others. If he could not keep a pretty girl content for six months of marriage then he should not be surprised if another tried.

With some cunning I changed my attitude to her. I began to use her with a respect which I saw she at once appreciated. I did not hurry; there was time. I contrived to meet her once by the castle steps when she was coming back from an errand there, so we walked home together. I was carrying a copy of *The Noble Birth and Gallant Achievements of Robin Hood*—it was Katherine Footmarker's book which had never been returned—and on the way I suggested we sit on the stile and she could listen to the first of the twelve adventures. She sat very quiet all through the reading. A week later I did the same again; and when this was over suggested she should try to find an errand to come this way each Wednesday to listen to the rest. She looked at me out of her long hazel eyes, but did not say either yes or no.

The next Wednesday she was not there, but I said nothing when we met in the house. I kept to my new civility and left things to simmer. The following Wednesday she was there, and as it was raining we sheltered in the granite look-out which was at the narrowest part of the land. When the third chapter was finished she stretched as if coming out of a dream.

"Laws, tis all very strange. Is it all true, d'ye think—all this trade about Friar Tuck and Maid Marion and the rest? Did they ever live?"

"Surely they lived. Doesn't it speak of King John?"

"I wish I was like Maid Marion," she said, pulling at a thread in her skirt. "I wish I was a man or could dress like a man. . . ."

"You did once."

"*When?*" She looked at me. "Oh . . . that were in a play, in jest. 'Tedn the same 'tall."

"Meg," I said, "what did you do with the stockings?"

"Those? Oh, I still *have* 'em. But I wore them last Christmas and tored a hole in 'em. They're mended, but I couldn't get the right colour o' wool."

"I never gave you a wedding gift. When next I'm in Truro I'll buy you another pair."

For a few long seconds she looked through the rain towards the house. "Can't you get a good view from here! Tis as good or betterer'n from your father's window."

"Would you like that?"

"I might like it but Dick might not."

"Dick would never know. He does not see all you wear."

She giggled slightly. "Aye, that's true."

"Meg, I'll buy you two pair, one red pair, one green—on a condition."

"What?"

"That you let me put 'em on for you."

She went a sudden blushing scarlet. "*Really*, Maugan!" She stood up. "What d'ye think I am—a common quean? *Well* . . . my life . . . tis too insulting of you. I thought you'd mended your ways—"

"So I have."

"So you have *not*—"

"I've mended my ways because I don't joke with you, Meg. It's dead serious."

"Then all the more *shame!*—"

"D'you truly think so? But I've a great taking for you, Meg. I mean it not rudely but as a compliment."

She stared down at me, angry and flushed of face. Then, as usual with Meg, she saw the comic side of it and burst out laughing.

"Well, you're some caution, boy. My blessed angels! Is this how you went on in Spain?"

"No. For I saw no one there I liked so much as you."

"Then you learned it from that rig, Sibylla Kendall."

"No, I did not, I learned it from no one and have never asked it of no one else in my life."

"Oh!" She swung away, her hair shaking loose under its coif. "I'll leave you here wi' your lewd thoughts. I believe twas all a put-on to mock me."

"No mocking. Think it over, Meg."

"That I shall not," she said, and left me.

The next day it came on to blow from the south-west. There were those in the house who said the sea had been calling for three days. It blew a gale out of the south-west, piling the sea up in mountains on the rocks, scattering twigs and branches over our roofs and plucking thatches off the barns. Two fishing boats which should have come back to Penryn never came back, and a barque was blown on the rocks of Pennance Point and was lost with all hands. As soon as the news of this came a party of us went to see if we could help, but although the point was sheltered from the worst of the gale, there was little to be done. The bay was tossing and seething with a tangle of rigging and spars, and all the sea rolled yellow with the cargo of corn. As the tide fell we picked up a dead sailor on the sand, then two lifting and falling in a pool stained red and still encroached on by the sea; then found one so wedged under a rock that no leverage would release him. A dozen spars, an old chest and a few lengths of sailcloth were worth salvaging, but it was uncomfortable work, for the wind was shifting north and the rain fell continuously and ever colder. When we reached home, soaked and tired and ready for a swig of brandy, we heard that another ship, an Irish ketch called *Kinsale*, had run for shelter into the Fal, both her masts spent and her captain lost.

The mate, a man called Garvie, had already come up to Arwenack and was full of his woes and a good deal of usquebaugh. Temporary repairs, he said, would take ten days, and he might have to sell some of the cargo to pay for them. The ketch, he said, was the property of two brothers called Ferguson who lived in Dublin, but until he reached there he must act on his own authority.

When he had gone grumbling off, mopping his flat face with a red kerchief, I said to Belemus: "What did he say she carried?"

"You heard. Unsweetened wine, with some Holland cloth and silks and perfume, from Bordeaux to Dublin. She is sailing under French letters of marque, which I find a little strange. I have a thought she may be doing a little privateering on the side."

"I have a thought we might think so."

Belemus looked at me. "Were you in mind to interfere?"

"Not with the wine."

Belemus always opened his mouth wide to laugh. "I believe the Spaniards changed your soul while you were out there and sent you back with another man's. The Maugan of other years is still languishing in some friar's prison in Madrid."

"He died," I said, but did not specify when.

That evening after supper we took Long Peter and Tom Bewse, the head falconer, and Dick Stable, and set out in the small Killigrew pinnace for Penryn. Even the river had choppy waves on it, but it took us only a few minutes to reach the shelter of Penryn Creek. There we soon picked out the *Kinsale*, a vessel of maybe eighty tons. She was in a sorry state, but so far as could be seen there was no one aboard her as she creaked gently at her ropes. Laughter and loud voices echoed along the quay from Piper's Tavern, and no doubt Cox's round the corner was busy too.

A rat was nosing among the nets at the end of the pier. Lights from the cottages showed pools of water among the great uneven slabs of granite which made up the quay. We shipped our oars and rubbed up against the side of the *Kinsale* as gently as a cat making friends.

Altogether we took out sixteen bolts of Holland cloth, nineteen bales of silk, and twelve boxes of perfume. This was all the cargo we could get at without taking the ship apart. We had not the space or the time to unload the wine, and in any case the bulk was too great to handle unless we stole the ship as well.

So in two hours we rowed slowly and heavily home.

None of our booty, I decided, should go into the house. As it was unloaded from the pinnace the stuff was piled in the grass in front of the tower facing the harbour. There Long Peter and Tom Bewse had mules and horses assembled. The cloths, the silks, the scents were slung over the withers of the animals and by the early hours of the morning a train had left for Truro. Belemus went with it. I stayed behind. I did not know what the outcome would be, and I was curious to discover it.

CHAPTER 3

THREE days later my grandmother sent for me.

I seldom went or was invited into her chamber, which was the finest in the house because she had refused to vacate it in favour of her son when my grandfather died. Each time I went in I was impressed by the richness of the bed hangings, by the arras with the scenes of the Nativity and the Passion wrought upon it, by the Turkey carpet beside the bed. She once told me that these were things she had brought with her marriage portion, but so unblemished were they that I could hardly believe it. What gave credence to such a claim was my grandmother's intense care of anything personal to herself. She used as expendable anything in the house except those things which were actually her own.

When I went in this November day in 1594 I remember being impressed by something else for the first time: the close disagreeable smell of an old woman near to her term, and the noise of her breathing which sang its own tuneless swan song.

But there was no sign of any change in Lady Killigrew's outlook on life. She knew all she wanted and wanted all she knew.

"Maugan, I hear of another robbery in Penryn Creek."

"Yes, ma'am. Two or three nights gone it happened. A ketch had run in for succour."

"Do you know who robbed it?"

"I think it better not to guess, ma'am."

Lady Killigrew coughed. "Silk was stolen, they say, and cloth and perfume. Where is it now?"

"What, ma'am?"

"Do not fence with me, boy. What have you done with the stuff?"

I glanced at the door. "It is all with—it is all in safe hands."

"Where?"

"In Truro with John Michell."

Diamonds winked as she fumbled restlessly with the sheet, for she was never without her rings in bed. "What have you kept here?"

"Nothing, ma'am."

"Nothing! How dare you! Was it good perfume? And silk too? I—"

"Who told you, ma'am?"

"God damn you, boy, think you I have no eyes or ears?" She paused to get her breath. "Who instructed you to convey it to Michell with such speed?"

"No one, ma'am. It was a precaution. What is not in this house can never be connected with this house."

She stared at me with utter contempt. "Think you Arwenack could be searched?"

It came to me then that, just as my father clung to habits and attitudes now going out of date, my grandmother lived even more firmly in a world that was past. Mr Killigrew on his feckless course had intimations enough of danger; from time to time he lifted his head and looked uneasily about. But Lady Killigrew, perhaps because she was of a generation earlier, never questioned the grandeur and safety of her position and name. What she said was of course still true: Arwenack could not be searched. It never had been. But with open defiance of the law the risk would grow. To me the solution was a simple one. Defiance of the law could well continue but it must be more carefully contrived.

I realised she was shouting at me. "You'd neither right nor leave to order this to be done! Who *gave* you leave?"

"The mate of the *Kinsale* has already been here complaining," I said sulkily. "There is commotion in Penryn. Nothing now could be moved. But there is no need: it was all gone before the alarm was raised."

"In future, Maugan, come to me before you take decisions on yourself. My sister and I always have first pick of any cloths or jewellery that come in."

She began to cough again, and this time could not stop. Her long pale face crimsoned with the strain, the old veins bunched at temple and at neck; she sat up and shook convulsively. As the spasm went on she became less the tall lean fierce woman I had known all my life and instead was just an animal fighting for life and breath. Her eyes ran, her bottom lip stuck out quivering, her long broken teeth were parted in a snarl.

I patted her on the back, I brought water for her to sip. It seemed that no human frame, especially an old one, could endure the strain, and I thought she would die.

But at length the spasm began to subside, and finally nothing was left but the old tired wheezing of the lungs. She looked up at me with no more favour in her eye than before the attack began.

She said: "When—I die, boy—when I die, then you shall draw the shroud over me as you will. But so long as I occupy this bed, this room, this house, then direction as to the affairs of the house come from me—they *do not* originate in *your* mind. *Understand?*"

"Yes, ma'am."

She wiped her cheeks with a square of silk. "I shall tell your father and ask him to punish you. . . . But perhaps you do not care. You are young. *Anything* can be borne when you are young; nothing when you are old."

"May I go now, ma'am?"

"*Nothing* when you are old, Maugan. D'you *hear me?*" She was shouting again.

"Yes, I do."

"But you do not understand. You don't listen. Why should you even try? . . . People talk of the consolations of age. . . . They do not *exist.*" Her fingers went slowly along the sheet, creasing it into a ridge, the nails leaving a line on the linen. "They do not exist. It is not just illness, infirmity, loss of husband and old friends, loneliness, the contempt of younger generations—it is *not* just these things." She coughed again but this time checked it. "Age does not only take away the things one prizes, one by one; it takes away the sweet taste of *life itself.* Understand: the sweet taste. When you are young all sensations have savour, all the fruits are for plucking. In age one by one the fruits begin to lose relish. At first that does not matter; there are always new ones to try: but quickly, oh so quickly, the new ones pall and fade and turn pulpy like the others. The flowers *droop* as soon as picked. Are you *listening?*"

"Yes, ma'am."

"You're listening but you're only waiting to go; you think, here is an old woman, in her grey hairs, drooling nonsense that does not concern me. . . . But it *will.* Mark me, if you live long enough it will. Pray each night, boy, to die at forty. It is better to lose the world while it is worth losing. That way your last thoughts can be regret."

"And religion, grandmother? Does that not bring you consolation?"

"Do not be insolent. . . . In a week or so your father will be home. I will tell him of your disobedience." She narrowed her eyes moodily at the candle flame. The heavy gold brocade of the bed curtains was dark with age where they merged into the shadows of the beamed ceiling; they made a canopy over her as if she were riding in a litter or a royal chair. "It will be an important day for the Killigrews when he returns for he will bring back with him the future mistress of Arwenack."

"Oh . . . I didn't know that."

"You don't know everything, young man."

"It is settled, then?"

"It will be settled."

"Jane Fermor. . . . When are they to be married?"

"Not yet, but soon; within the year. It's time, and I want to see the succession."

"I trust she will be pretty." I got up to go.

"Pretty?" She spoke the word with distaste. "There belongs more to marriage than two pair of bare legs. She has been carefully chosen. She will bring money and influence. That is what matters."

"Perhaps, grandmother, John will think otherwise."

"I wonder how she will feel, coming to this house. I remember how I felt as if it were yesterday. I was a widow of twenty-three with a child of four. We had rid all day over rough moors, and darkness was falling. Our escort of six seemed scarcely enough. . . . When we reached this house I thought in the dark that it was in ruin. . . . Your great-grandfather and great-grandmother were at the door to meet us. I recollect how they were dressed. . . . Yes, how they were dressed. He had a curled moustache like your father's but was a bigger man and wore a gold chain to his knees. She had golden-yellow hair and a gown of tawny velvet. After the bleakness of our journey the elegance of their living was a great comfort to behold."

"But the house was in ruin?"

"Ah, no. In the morning I saw it was still building. This room was complete and all this wing; but the north wing was not above shoulder level. And the great hall was not finished for many years, not until your father was thirteen. . . ."

I went to the door. "You have memories to look back on, grandmother. Why should you have wished to cut them short?"

She was a long time answering and she seemed to have forgotten me. But as I took the door latch she said:

"Perhaps that is not so. . . . Perhaps it would be better never to have been *born*. For what has the effort been worth? Memories or no memories, what has it all been worth?" She lifted an unsteady hand. "A few needs met, a few ambitions gratified, a few pains suffered. . . . Food and wine and the coarser appetites. A leap from the womb and a plunge into the grave. . . . Then—well, then it is gone and there is nothing to show, nothing worth showing, nothing to leave, nothing worth leaving, only tho—only the carved stone in the church, a stale Latin tag, bones mouldering, and the end of a life which need never have begun!"

I could hear her begin to talk again after I had closed the door.

We had all waited with a sense of anticipation to see Jane Fermor, this girl who had been chosen by my father for his eldest son—I in particular, for except for an accident of birth the girl would have been chosen for me. Yet when she came I was out hawking and the first intimation was extra horses in the stables and strange servants in the hall.

Supper was almost ready, and Sir George Fermor came down first in company with my father. Sir George was an erect fierce man of around five and forty, with the tight mouth and bowed legs of a captain of horse. He was a man, you would think, who would regard an enemy pikeman, a wild boar, or an unleapable fence with the same haughty and fearless stare. His voice was harsh and made itself heard above everything like a carpenter's saw; his footsteps clanked as if with the echo of spurs.

Behind him in a few minutes, accompanied by Mrs Killigrew, came his fifteen-year-old only child. She wore a gown of silver lace with puff sleeves of white taffeta, and had a carcanet of seed pearls round her hair. Everything she wore was expensive but nothing she wore could disguise her thick figure, her big feet and hands, the solidity of her stride. Nor was she pretty, being very pale with little dabs of red ochre on her cheeks. Her hair was jet black and fell down either side of her face like curtains through which her ears peeped. Her eyes were green, small, but bright and magnetic. Her skin was milky and fine. She spoke little through supper and seemed indifferent to the embarrassed boy, a month younger than herself, who sat at her side. But I saw her eyes move assessingly about the hall, taking in the livery of the servants, the Pavia tapestry, the quality of the plate we used, the sprawling dogs like a breathing undulating rug before the fire.

Lady Killigrew had somehow contrived to control her ailment and was at the table in her best gown. She had uncanny powers of recuperation and a will of the same order. She and Mr Killigrew engaged Sir George Fermor in conversation through supper, but even they were talked down by the rasping voice. When it chose to utter, which was frequent, nothing could live with it. In the main it indulged in self-congratulation, but sometimes it dealt with the sloth and evil nature of servants. Thrashing was the only thing good enough for most of 'em, he said; all his servants were thrashed regular whether they'd offended or not; it kept them up to the mark. While he so spoke he stared meaningly around, leaving no doubt as to his thoughts.

The betrothal was celebrated next morning in the presence of Parson Garrock of St Budock and Parson Merther. The two young people stood in the centre of the hall, with Mr Killigrew on one side of them and Sir George Fermor on the other. Young John was required to speak first, and this he did, faltering over the words:

"I, John Killigrew, do willingly promise to marry thee, Jane Fermor, if God will and I live, whenever our parents think good and meet, till which time I take thee for my only bethrothed wife and thereto plight thee my troth. In the name of the Father, the Son, and the Holy Ghost. So be it."

Having said this he put a gold ring on the girl's right hand. Then it was her turn to speak the oath—which she did in a deep voice— and to give him a ring in return. This done, they kissed and the union was celebrated in rhenish wine. My father was in great spirits, and even Sir George weighed light upon him. Jane, in a tight-laced bodice with a green kirtle and a red petticoat edged with lace, looked as dumpy as before. After the plighting she began to talk with the children, not animated still but sober, almost fierce like her father, and Odelia and Thomas were listening to her open-mouthed. I drew nearer, thinking what if I were being asked to marry this girl, how would I feel? And I suddenly met her gaze.

She said in her deep voice: "Who are you, fellow?"

I stared back at her, and before I could think what to reply, little Odelia said: "This is our brother, Maugan."

"Brother?" She looked me over. "If he be not older than John then I'll eat all the dam' dogs in this hall."

"I am older," I said. "However, your inheritance is safe. My father was not married at the time."

"My father has seven by-blows to my knowledge, but they're not kept in the house, fellow."

"This is a special occasion, girl," I said, "for which they have let me out of the kennels. If treated well I seldom bite."

Her smile showed very white, very even teeth and small hard dimples. "More's the pity. . . . And this? Another of the same?"

Belemus had come up. "No, I am a cousin, cousin—and neither illegitimate nor safe."

We talked for a few minutes, she over-towered by us both but in no way out of countenance. I had never met a girl of fifteen like her; she had a self-possession beyond measure and a determination and vigour in all things.

My father pressed them to stay for the Christmas festivities, but

Sir George could not and Mr Killigrew breathed out his relief in private. The money that had come to us from my raid on the *Kinsale* had helped him to order this week with all the old flamboyance and extragavance, but it could hardly have lasted through the twelve days of Christmas.

On the morning before they left I came on Jane Fermor walking with her maid on the edge of the woods behind the house. I would have avoided her but she beckoned.

"Your name's Maugan, isn't it, fellow?"

"Yes, girl." I suddenly saw that behind her back she held a pipe which she had been smoking.

"Then tell me. I want to know. How many fallow-deer have you on this estate?"

"Two score maybe. And the same of red."

"A poor number. They should be bred up."

"No doubt."

"And shall be. Tell me something more, what are those woods on the hill?"

"Just woods. They lead towards Budock and Constantine."

"Are there any wild boar or wolves?"

"We have few such animals in Cornwall."

"No?" She brought her hand round to the front and glanced up with a smile to see if I had noticed. To be quite certain she put the pipe in her mouth and drew on it. "Nor have we many wild animals in Northampton; but sometimes Sir George my father purchases a boar and sets it free for the sport. We have woods much taller than these. All these trees are so stunted."

It was on my tongue to refer to the height of human beings.

"We have bear-baiting, too," she said. "With bulldogs most times, but the latest craze is greyhounds. It gives the bear more chance. I'm disappointed not to have seen none here. Do you not ever have it?"

"My father is too fond of his dogs."

She wrinkled her nose. "So I should think from the stink of 'em. I'd have half of 'em thrown in the sea."

I did not speak.

"You're a rude sort of fellow, aren't you," she said.

"We know little of your polished manners in Cornwall."

"Have you ever been to London?"

"No."

"It's an education which would profit you. I was there last month. I go regular."

"That must be—profitable."

"Last month I saw a woman scourged naked. Next I'm waiting to see a man."

"I once," I said, "saw the entrails of a dead sheep being fought over by seagulls."

She drew at her pipe and puffed smoke thoughtfully in my face. "Maugan Killigrew. Who was your mother?"

"A woman. Like any other."

"Maybe she too was scourged naked at Bridewell as a whore."

"If you go four miles up the river you will find a boy with no front teeth. He lost them for saying less than that."

"But you can't do it to me?" She laughed and put a hand on my arm. "But perhaps he meant it—while I did not. I was seeking a chink in your armour."

I moved enough to let her hand fall away.

She said: "When a boy is as hostile as you it is natural to probe. A girl is not strong enough to wield a sword, so she must use a pin."

"Oh, you make a great mistake," I said. "I am not hostile."

"But you do not approve of me, eh? Do you smoke?"

"No."

"You should try it sometime. It soothes the *temper*." She patted my arm lightly. "Or perhaps you don't like seeing a woman to smoke? Sir George my father does not, so I must take it out of doors. This is woundwort, of course. Smell it." She wafted the pipe under my nose. "I cannot afford tobacco at three shillings an ounce while my father holds the purse strings."

I muttered something, more embarrassed now by a friendliness that cloyed.

In spite of her crude abrupt way of talking she gave the impression of being greatly concerned what men thought of her; and in spite of her thick figure and big hands and feet she was not without attraction. That surprised me but it was true; and not only for me. I saw Belemus looking at her. John did not seem awakened to those ideas as yet, and he parried all questions about her with an uneasy smile.

The day after they left, I went into my father's study and found him still in good spirits. He rolled up the map he had been looking at and tapped me on the shoulder with it.

"Well, Sir Maugan, our troubles are at an intermission—perhaps altogether over. At least we shall need to look at this no longer." He tossed the map into a corner and made the dogs bark.

"What is that, sir?"

"Tell me, what d'you think of our guests?"

". . . They are rich?"

He laughed. "The wedding's to be here next May, and she brings as her dowry twelve thousand pounds in gold. In *gold*, Maugan! It's a commodity we've seen little of, this decade. I've been tempted to have my ring and snuff box melted down just to see the plain virgin colour of the stuff once more before I die!"

"John will still lack a few months of sixteen then."

"Yes, and she the same. D'you like her, Maugan? D'you think she'll be a worthy mistress of this great house when I am gone?"

In the last months our relationship had been cordial and frank to a degree I had never imagined possible; but this was a delicate matter.

"She—I think she may be inclined. . . ."

"No, talk plain. I give you leave."

"I think she'll be a holy terror."

He grunted, not pleased with my frankness now he had it. "She's raw now. She'll weather. Life'll give her a few hard knocks and the corners'll be less sharp. Mind. . . ." He stopped and smoothed his moustache. "Mind, I think John's scarcely man enough to handle her yet. But boys grow up more slower than girls. It will work out all right. Why, look at yourself."

"Myself?"

"Yes. Twelve months ago you were no more than a child—though often an awkward child, I'll grant. Now—well, now you're a man. *You* could manage her. I believe that."

"I believe I should not want to, father."

"Oh, we'll find you a wife soon, boy. God's lungs, I wish you were legitimate, I'd put you to good use within the year! We've still need of all our assets!"

"Perhaps I can help in other ways."

"Perhaps you can. So you have. But a word of warning to you on this Irish boat: I can afford no scandal."

"I'll have a care."

"I mean it. No more adventures when I am away. I can afford nothing that will damage my credit with the Privy Council. My debts put me on a tight-rope; and until this marriage I must take great care not to fall."

"I'll remember."

He was turning over the papers on his desk. "You know, I'd have liked to link you to Jane Fermor." He smiled sardonically. "I'd have sat back then and watched the storm. John I'm a trifle afraid for. But he'll grow to his tasks!"

When I left the room I was still wondering what map it was he had thrown in the corner.

I remember nothing of Christmas that year except that I bought Meg Stable two pairs of stockings, one green, one red, and that she refused to accept them on my conditions. It was a cold January, with ice on the swan pool and everyone keeping as much as possible indoors. The house became oppressive and stank more than usual of dogs and wood smoke. Each morning the windows were steamed over so that one seemed to live in a world of fog; in the afternoon moisture ran down them and down the walls. Everyone wore two or three coats, but even this could not keep out the cold airs which moved everywhere just out of reach of the fires. It was a time when mischief brewed, when old feuds among servants sparked into life again, when jealousies and lustful fancies had their freest rein.

In February I rode into Truro and went to call on Katherine Footmarker.

It was strange how far behind my stay with Chudleigh Michell had fallen. It was as if some lost forgotten boy had served a year in my place. I found Katherine sitting at the back of her cottage caring for an adder which had been beaten with a stick and left for dead. Her greeting was very cold and unfriendly, as I could but have expected, and it took some time to come to the purpose of my visit.

"That harsh and evil woman," she said. "Why should I help her if I could?"

"She is my grandmother. If she has to die I'd prefer her to do it in some less distressful way."

"See his tongue?" she said. "He does not open his mouth to flick it out, but pushes it through a slit in his lip. Hearin', smell, taste, he does it all with that tongue."

I had taken a seat on a tree stump at a respectful distance. "Are you not afraid of being stung?"

"Bitten? No. Birds, animals, reptiles, they all know their friends. Which is more than humans do. It's more than Maugan Killigrew does."

"I'm often perplexed as to that. I'm often perplexed, for instance, as to my feelings for the woman Katherine Footmarker."

"What *are* your feelin's for her?"

"I am drawn to her and repelled. There's no middle way, no mean of feeling."

"See how he touches ground with his jaw. It's said snakes can't hear, but I suspicion they touch the ground to feel the vibrations travellin' through and over the earth. You could never come on him from behind without him knowin'."

"Nor could one come on you."

"Still a sharp word in your mouth? You're like a young goat trying

his strength for the first time and hitting his head against everythin'.
Do you love your grandmother?"

". . . No."

"Then why ask this?"

"I have a fancy to help her breathe if I can. You're helping a snake."

"Ah," she said. "But I've a fondness for this poor snake who I doubt
did no wrong in all his life. Let me see . . . bronchitis and tissick.
That would not be so easy."

She stretched her long back and went into the cottage. Presently
she came out again carrying two bottles but at first she would not
give them to me.

"This one, a simple remedy of horehound and comfrey, is to be
taken durin' the day. This second at night. But I warn you this second is likely to make her sleepy—and I can promise no cure."

"She can be hardly harmed by it—or be worse and live. What is it?"

"A diacodium. I give them you both on a condition—that she never
knows where you got 'em. It's a fancy I have."

I agreed, but when I offered to pay she laughed harshly. "You and
I have an open exchange, Maugan. First one pays something and
then th' other. The time to strike a balance is not now."

There had been a small frosty sun just after midday, and now on
the way home shafts of it broke through the clouds and fell like
dipped lances over the moors. By the time the woods above Penryn
were reached the day had closed in and the light was moist and
grey. The church bell was tolling; the breeze bore the sound up the
hill; someone was dead.

Just past the ruined monastery buildings I came up with two men
on foot, one helping the other who seemed ill. One was Timothy Carpenter and the other Dick Stable. Dick had a great cut across his
head and was spitting blood. Timothy, though in better shape, limped
at each step.

I put Dick on my horse and walked beside Timothy. They had
been to Penryn on business for my father and had stopped for a drink
at Piper's Tavern. There they had heard that old Sebastian Kendall
was dead. Three or four Penryn quarry men had been in the tavern
and one had shouted it was that virgin-thief Maugan Killigrew who
had really killed the old man.

So the result. When we got in Dick was found only to be bleeding
at the mouth only for lost teeth, but the cut on his head went deep
as a crater, and they had both been hard used. I took the story to
my father and suggested I went with ten men to Penryn that night
to teach them a lesson.

He shook his head.

When I looked put out he shouted: "I've told you before! I do not fall over only for two reasons: the forbearance of the Queen, which Uncle Henry sees to; and a similar forbearance on the part of the Privy Council, Cecil chief among them. But I have had my warnings. They'll not abide mischief. The war's too tense. So Penryn must go unpunished. Let them be."

"Give me leave to do something in private."

"You could not, for nothing ever stays private where the Killigrews are concerned. When this wedding's through things will be different. Once *start* to defeasance your bonds, and your creditors become no longer pressing for payment! It's a sorry paradox. Have patience. May will soon be here."

I took this message back to Belemus, who pulled his little beard. "Well, that's that, I suppose. It all goes much against the grain."

"Imagine Sebastian Kendall being dead. I wonder if it *was* I who killed him."

"Nonsense, he died of a tumour, that happens whether or not. I wonder if they buried him with his gold rings."

"Well, they could hardly get them off short of filing them; his knuckles were too great."

"Filing through gold is a long business," said Belemus, "and disrespectful to the dead. The Kendalls had a great veneration for the old ruffian."

"Which we have not," I said.

"Walk so far as the point with me," Belemus said. "I think we should talk."

CHAPTER 4

By the sea night is seldom so black as inland; it is as if some reflection of the long sunk sun glimmers in the sky. But this night was perversely an exception, and the churchyard of St Gluvias was an unwelcoming place when we reached it. Our horses had been nervous all the way and had had to be urged forward into the dark. I had calculated that a third-quarter moon would rise about three, and that if we arrived at two much of the spade-work would already be done by the time the moon got up. In fact it must have taken us fifteen minutes longer than calculated to cover the short journey, and then, stumbling over headstones and groping among tall grasses, it was another ten before we certainly located the grave.

We worked for a while in silence—although the thud of our digging, the rattle of the stony earth as we shovelled it out seemed to fill the night around. Once or twice Belemus's mattock struck sparks off stones, and to us they looked bright enough to raise an alarm.

There was no house nearer than the parsonage, which was across the other side of the lane, and our most likely discoverer was some tin-streamer returning from Carnon or a rogue marauding for himself and unlikely to make his presence known.

Imperceptibly as we worked the graveyard grew lighter. Delicately by fine balances the weights grew less heavy on our eyes. I found it possible to see Belemus, up to his knees in the hole we had dug, to notice the gnarled elm leaning askew like a tired witch across a view of the town. An owl which had been out all night with shrill melancholy cries was no longer invisible. Then as my spade struck on something which gave off no sound, the clouds broke over the east and a gibbous moon peered across the river.

It could hardly have been better timed, but now we had to go slow, for though I was not squeamish I had no wish to impale old Kendall on the mattock or the spade.

Eventually we cleared enough round the cloth-wrapped figure to try to lever it up, but stones and earth kept showering down, and the corpse was as limp as a dead rabbit. So we had to dig more, and then distastefully brush the clay and earth off the wrappings with our fingers.

I had remembered Sebastian Kendall as a gnarled, powerful-built old man with straggling grey hair. This stinking mummy seemed half the size; the face as the dirt fell away looked withered and grey, the eyes peeped out of slit lids.

"Faugh!" said Belemus. "Have you a knife?"

I fumbled in my belt. The owl fluttered round again, his wings black against the upturned moon.

I passed the knife to Belemus, who was now standing in the grave. He got to work, and the foul stench of decay rose into the night. He at last sawed through the cloth and reached the corpse's arms, which were folded across the chest. We were able to see both hands together, and Belemus lifted one of them. "Look."

Before being buried Sebastian Kendall had been deprived of his fingers and left only with the stumps. It seemed that whatever veneration the Kendalls might have for their grandfather it did not extend so far as we had supposed.

The next morning early my uncle Simon Killigrew arrived, having slept with the Arundells at Trerice. His coming was unexpected and not welcome to my father, who knew that he seldom saw his brother when Simon was in funds, and who, as he said to me, had enough hungry mouths to feed without another and one of extravagant tastes added to his board.

Simon was interesting for the news he brought. Ralegh had at last obtained a patent for further adventure and only last Thursday had left Plymouth in command of five ships, bound no one knew whither. Accompanying him were seven score gentlemen adventurers, among them many from the west country including John Grenville, Sir Richard's younger son, a cousin of Ralegh's called Butshead Gorges, and Ralegh's nephew John Gilbert. There was a rumour they had gone in search of El Dorado.

Sir Francis Drake and Sir John Hawkins were also known to be fitting out an expedition which was to seek plunder in the West Indies.

All this filled me with an intense restlessness. I would have done anything to sail with Drake. The Spanish would be in terror if they knew he was out.

Much was feared at Court, Simon said, of the situation in France. Although Henry of Navarre, now undisputed King, had declared war on Spain as he had undertaken to do, he was not prosecuting the struggle with any vigour. Indeed in the last weeks he had signed local truces with the Spanish, in Brittany, in Normandy and else-where. At any time such truces might culminate in a treaty of peace which would take France out of the war altogether. The Pope, it was said, was only too willing to mediate.

Moreover the Archduke Albert, now the first soldier of Spain, had been sent to take over the government of the Netherlands. And the remaining English troops in Brittany were being withdrawn, leaving the way clear for the Spanish sea-raiders to prowl the narrow seas. All this pointed to increased danger for the exposed counties of the south-west.

Fresh money was being voted, Simon said, for the further fortifica-tion of the Scillies. The fort, half completed on St Mary's, was to be hastened forward and two sconces added. Another four hundred pounds was to be granted out of the customs of Plymouth and Corn-wall to help towards the cost. (My father sneered on hearing this and said, Why was it Godolphin got all the concessions? Whose ear did he have access to that he should always be treated with such priority over the legitimate and more pressing needs of others, such as the Killigrews of Pendennis?)

In the middle of this interchange Parson Merther came in with terrible news of happenings in Penryn. An old man buried yesterday had been dug out of his grave and his fingers cut off for the rings he

wore. What was worse the corpse had been carried out of its grave
and left in a sitting position in one of the front pews of the church
where a woman this morning had found it, almost to the loss of her
reason. This act, said Parson Merther, would of course be a hanging
matter if the culprits were ever found. My father, on being told that
the old man's name was Kendall, raised a fish-like eye in my direction,
but such was the offence that he did not dare ask if I had had any
part in it.

The news Uncle Simon had brought of the withdrawal of the English troops from Brittany was a great blow to the west. That evening
after supper Hannibal Vivian came hastily from over the water, and
we talked long into the night. My father said it would have served
better if Ralegh and Drake and Hawkins were at home at this time
instead of jaunting off in search of the plunder of the Indies. Hannibal
Vivian, a gaunt high-nosed man, had not seen me since my return,
and I was the subject of a cross-fire of questions from him and from
Simon on what I had seen and heard in Spain. It was agreed about
midnight that a joint letter signed by my father and Hannibal Vivian
should be sent to the Privy Council urging that money, new levies,
and better armaments should be allotted for the defence of Falmouth
Haven.

The next day Dick Stable was taken ill of the blow he had received,
which was more grievous than we had supposed. Each time he got up
his senses swam and he shivered and shook and had to lie down. I
tried my hand with him, though where the brain is damaged there is
little that medicaments can do. About this time died the falconer,
Corbett, who had been injured in the head at the time of the fight in
the hall in 1592. It made us all anxious about Dick for fear he might
go the same way.

Lady Killigrew was sleeping better and, imperceptible as the rising
of a tide, vitality began to creep back. She wrote letters again and
talked of visiting her daughter Lady Billingsley in Devon. She
plagued her elder and unmarried daughter Mary with proposals that
they should go to Westminster together. She took a new interest in
terrorising the servants with threats of dismissal.

She continued to pick at me. When the bottle she had been taking
was done I fetched her another and another from Mistress Footmarker,
saying to my grandmother there was a new herbalist in Truro. Mrs
Dorothy Killigrew guessed different; and a conspiracy grew up between her and me that when someone was ill in the house I should
ride and describe the symptoms to Katherine Footmarker and bring

back her salves or balsams or simples. It helped me to understand more about sickness and its cures.

When Uncle Simon left, my father rode with him, taking Stephen Wilky and Thomas Rosewarne. While he was away Belemus and I were up to one wild prank after another. Nothing was too rash for us to attempt, and no questions of morality troubled our sleep. I persuaded myself I was enjoying this new and unfettered life; but instead of allowing experience to happen to me I pursued it with the feverish joyless energy of someone seeing his days foreshortening and anxious to savour them while there is still time. I persuaded myself I had forgotten Sue Farnaby, with as much success as comes to a man who tries to ignore a knife in his guts.

It was the first of May, and the last day of a spell of weather which had brought summer too soon. If you could get out of the south-east wind, in a valley or behind a rock, it was warmer than many a July. In the haven white wavelets danced a coranto all the way from St Anthony Point to Arwenack steps.

In the morning I had been with three men scattering wood ash on the meadows, the wind doing much of the work for us; and then in the middle of the day instead of returning to the house I ate a rabbit pasty and walked out to see how the sheep were faring which had been set to summer early on the moor between Pennance and St Budock. On the way home near Mongleath I heard quarrelling voices and came on Meg Levant, very fiery but very terrified while two beggars menaced her for money she had not got. They were sturdy men and armed with sticks, but I had the advantage of being more ready to fight, so after a short set-to they made off.

"Well," I said, breathless, "so this is how you behave so soon as my back's turned!"

Her hair had come loose, and the wind blew it in tails across her face.

"Oh, Maugan! That grab-thief wi' the beard. . . . I been over to Menehay to get a moonstone they say's good for the dizziness. Old Sarah Pound has loaned it me for a week to try on Dick."

"You have it now?"

"Aye. I was afraid they might steal it, though they'd ha' had to take mortal liberties to find it."

"Show it me."

"Turn your back then."

I looked across at the sea and listened to rustling clothes behind me. "There."

I turned it over, a glistening bauble, worth a rose noble perhaps but unlikely to have curative value. "Why, it's warm!"

". . . Well, I wanted to carry it safe!"

"You're not afraid of my stealing it, then?"

"Nay, I'm not afraid o' that."

We began to walk home. I realised that the event which had just taken place could hardly have occurred more favourable for me. All her romantic instincts would be gratified.

I looked sidelong at her as we walked. Her breasts were high and her stomach slender; her blunt freckled face was distinguished by the fine long eyes. We sat on a bank that looked towards the sea, while the warm wind streamed past us. I wondered if honesty might pay the best result.

"Meg, would you believe something to be true if I told you it was true?"

"Ah . . . that depends."

"Would you believe at least that I'm not joking?"

She frowned and pushed hair away from her eyes. "What is it?"

"I have never made love to a woman."

She stared at me for several seconds. Then she burst out laughing. "Who-ee! What d'ye take me for—one of they lambs up there? Baa-aa!"

"It is true!"

"And Sibylla Kendall? No doubt you played Primero on the bed wi' she!"

"Sibylla was Belemus's girl. The night I was surprised with her, Belemus had been wounded and I'd gone to tell her of it."

Meg continued to laugh, though I could see a flicker of interest somewhere at the back of her eyes. I took calculated offence.

"Very well, then. You can find me of use when set on by thieves but in the next breath you call me a liar, which is cousin to a thief and hardly better. Take your stone and find your own way home!"

I threw the stone in her lap and went off. She called "Maugan!" but I took no notice. However, I strode not so fast as I might have done and could hear her after me. On the right was a thicket of white hawthorn which I knew well, and I plunged into it, made for the glade in the centre of it and flung myself down. She caught me up.

"I'm sorry, Maugan, 'twas not meant as an offence. Truly, I thought you was joking. Truly I thought that. Is it strange that I thought it? You was in Spain a six month, and then everyone believes you was Sibylla's lover, that's believed by all! If you say 'twas not so I believe you, but I always thought it, and so I thought you was joking."

I did not answer.

After a silence she breathed out. "I fancy I ha'n't been here before. Look at all they bluebells! And the May blossom! 'Tis like a wedding."

Within fifty yards the open moorland began again, but here you might have been in a forest. Sheaves of bluebells fisted up among the trees, and the hawthorns were white with blossom which was falling as constant as snow. The wind whistled through the trees like wind in the rigging of ships. Even here in the centre of the glade Meg's hair was blowing over her face; but it was a filtered wind, sifted of its violence, and warm. The sun beat down.

"Maugan, I believe you."

I said: "When I was on my way home with Captain Elliot, Justinian Kilter was aboard. He said he had made free with you on his last visit."

"Who? That fair man that was 'ere afore the fever outbreak? I never *seen* him since! If he was aboard when the *Neptune* last called he never shown his face at Arwenack! What wickedness to say such a thing!"

"He said you have a mole on your left breast."

"Oh, what lewdness! Well, I have not, and you can tell 'im next time you see him!"

"I have to believe you now?"

"Yes!"

"Seeing's believing."

A shower of petals floated down between us. "That's lewd talk from you again, Maugan Killigrew."

"I don't think it so."

"Well, it is so."

"Is love ugly, then?"

"I didn't say twas."

"Then is it lewd?"

She plucked a bluebell and put it against her nose and smelt it. I moved to her and took her hand. She pulled it away, so I took the other which was holding the bluebell. She looked at me, less certain of herself than was usual in Meg.

"Tell me," I said, "what is it like?"

"What's what like?"

"Making love with a woman."

"Maugan, it's not nice to speak of it so, in broad daylight, in the sunshine, in the open air."

"Then it *is* ugly?"

She pulled her hand away again. "Oh, poh, you're joking now. As if you're s' innocent as all that! I'm not th' only girl you've kissed an' fondled."

"I never said so. But love doesn't end there."

"No, it does not."

"Well?"

She put both hands up to push her hair away from her forehead. "Oh, it's nothing special—nothing to get excited about. The best part is the kissing and fondling."

"Not everyone says that."

"There, I tell you, and straightway you contradict!"

I said: "Meg, perhaps it is loving the right person. Like kissing the right person. For instance if I kiss you I take much pleasure of it. But if I kiss, well . . . if I was to kiss Annora Job, who is a pretty girl, just as pretty as you, it would not pleasure me at all. Why not? I don't know. But that's the way it is. Now perhaps that is the way it is with love—"

"Are you telling me I don't love Dick?"

"I'm not saying anything. I don't know. Perhaps *you* don't know. But might it not be part true? That you love him one way and perhaps not another?"

"No, it is not! 'Ow dare ye say such things, Maugan! I only said . . . oh, tis no ue talking! I'll *go*."

As she got up I got up. As she turned to pad away on angry sandalled feet I caught her arm and pulled her round.

"Meg."

"Leave me go!"

I kissed her a few times, not well, for she struggled, but on the eyebrow, on the ear, on the lip. "Now you're no better than they thieves!" she said breathlessly.

"Stay a while," I pleaded. "*Please* stay. No one'll miss us for an hour."

She looked at me, again uncertain, but there was a glint of kindness in her eyes. "If you promise not to be lickerish."

"I promise."

We lay there lazily for ten minutes in the sun. I sucked a piece of grass and looked up at two choughs planing into the wind. The sun was gilding their black wings, transforming them. I wished it would gild ours.

Meg went across and gathered a sheaf of bluebells, then came to sit beside me again.

"A pity you ha'n't your book, Maugan. Then you could read to me again."

"There's nothing so good in books as there is in life."

"Such as love I suppose."

"Such as love, you rightly suppose."

"Which you, never 'aving 'ad it, d' know all about."

"I'll know if you'll teach me."

"Hoh, some teaching you'd need."

"I'd be a quick learner."

"Quick learner! I reckon in no time you'd be trying to give me lessons!"

"Maybe we could both learn."

"Oh, Maugan, change the talk. It's carnality—so to go on all the time."

"I don't think so. I'm asking a favour of you, that's all."

"A favour! My dear life!"

"Well, wouldn't it be?"

She stared at me with compressed lips, breathing deep. But she could not keep up her exasperation and began to laugh. I leaned over and kissed her teeth.

She stopped quick at that. "Maugan, *please,* what're ye trying to do? I'm *married.* Do that mean naught? Have ye no thought for Dick? Have you no—"

"Maybe I shall have thoughts for him—sometime—later. Not now. I'm sorry, but not now. I want you, Meg. I'm asking you. Truly, meekly, as a *great* favour."

She put her fingers on my mouth. "Don't speak so. 'Twouldn't be fair. And"—she glanced round—"you can't mean *here?*"

"Here. Safer than any dark corner of Arwenack. There's no one in a mile, and no one ever comes here for no one knows of it, except Belemus and me, and he's in Fowey visiting the Treffrys. Here in the warm wind where it's light and clean. . . . Prove to me love's not ugly."

She stared at me and for the first time I could see temptation and indecision in her eyes. It almost staggered me, now that she was so near yielding, that I had got so far. I waited, not taking even a deep breath.

The temptation faded. "No, Maugan, what can I be even thinking of? *No!*"

She began to get up and I caught her shoulders and pulled her down. She struggled and then was still. We lay there looking at each other, while the wind thrust through the trees and the May bloom drifted down. I began to smother her face with kisses, and then, with some instinct that at the last she would rebuff me in this open place, half-pulled her, half-caressed her into moving under the branches of an old elm where there was privacy and shade. The young bracken was crushed with our weight. At the last when I knew I had almost won there was a horrible fumbling with clothes which might even then have brought hesitation and self-doubt back. She turned towards me and tried to speak but I said:

"Sweet Meg, now I know Kilter lied. Oh Meg, let me love you. Sweet Meg, don't deny me now."

And she did not. In later years I was to learn that a woman's attitude to love is only an extension of her attitude to life; and Meg was never one in ordinary dealings to measure or grudge a gift.

When my father came home next day he was in a black mood that found fault with everything and everyone. I was at a loss to account for it.

Now he took me really to task for having laid hands on the Irish vessel. It seemed that she belonged to Sir Denison Ferguson, who had been raising Cain to have a commission appointed to investigate the robbery, and it was only by strenuous efforts that he, Mr Killigrew, had blocked the appointment. He had done this by accepting the task of opening up an inquiry himself, jointly with Mr Hannibal Vivian, to discover the culprits. This was going to be a delicate matter and a tedious one, for there were people in Penryn, he had heard, who were prepared to stand up and swear that the raid was the work of his bastard son. They had no proof, of course, but the accusation would look bad. Care must be taken so to arrange the inquiry that the trouble makers should not be called. A report must be in the hands of the Privy Council by July, or they would send Sir Ferdinando Gorges from Plymouth to complete the inquiry. Gorges, being a creature of Essex, must not be allowed to come.

However, the full and real cause of his angry mood emerged later, when he told me that Sir George Fermor had postponed the wedding. Sir George, he said, had come to the conclusion that John and Jane were yet too young for marriage—let them wait another six months. He would reconsider the matter in August when Jane was sixteen.

"There is some deep device behind the postponement that I like not. It was all arranged for next month, and I went up there expressly to discuss the details. This was a thunderstroke."

"D'you think it is the money, sir? It's a vast amount to find, and all in gold."

"I think not. I made the carefullest inquiries before ever proposing the match. He is very wealthy."

"D'you think it may be that he has heard we are in debt?"

"I told him as much—but not of course the extent. No one knows the extent, for my debtors are well scattered and unknown to each other. That is what preserves me at all! . . . Anyway, it will add acutely to our problems through the summer. . . . Perhaps by August the Spaniards will have landed, and then we shall have no debts, nor no life neither!"

Loving a woman is not an act in isolation. No fences of the mind or body screen its effects from everyday life. Meg and I lived in the same house, ate in the same room, could meet by accident three or four times daily. Yet while we were often near each other there was little chance of true conversation and no privacy for anything more. May brought in the rain and no further meetings were possible in the whitethorn glade.

For ten days she kept me in ignorance of her true feelings. With greater experience perhaps I would have known, but I did not then. For ten days she kept out of arm's reach. Then one evening I was sitting reading by the fire in the big drawing-room chamber. My grandmother and Mrs Killigrew were there, the latter working a sampler, Lady Killigrew poring over a letter which had come by the wool stapler that evening. Supper had been done an hour and dusk was falling. Someone came into the room with a branch of candles, and I knew it was Meg. Without looking up I heard her move to put the candles on the side table where they usually stood and then for a few seconds she did not move to go out. I glanced at the mirror on the wall and saw she was looking at me. I turned my head and she quickly lowered hers and went out.

That old room at the end of the north wing where we had dressed up for the junketings of three Christmases ago. In the old days servants had slept there, under the eaves where a man could not stand. But now because we were the fewer to house the room was empty. I wandered up and looked it over. I remembered it vividly with Sue standing in front of the looking glass tucking in a strand of hair. She had just taken the burnt cork off her face and one smear had remained under her ear. I had wiped it away. Now the room was empty except for some old sacks and a sea chest. Green timber had been used up here when the house was built, and the door was warped. The window, having been shut with difficulty in 1590, had never been open since. One of the beams had got beetle. It all smelt of sacking and cobwebs and dust. But it was an empty room.

There was special danger in all this—if my grandmother ever learned of it we should both be turned out of the house without hesitation—and at first Meg would have nothing of the idea. Indeed she was so hostile that if it had not been for that betraying look I would have thought it hopeless to press her. Then suddenly she gave way. Embarrassment, shyness, hostility, desire, they were all there in her eyes as she nodded and said maybe, in the hour after supper, in the long hour of twilight, in the hour of dusk. I was to go first. She would perhaps be able to slip away. But, mind, I wasn't to wait—at least, not long.

I went up. I said I was going out and instead turned up the stairs. The maids were washing dishes, scouring pans; I tried to walk quietly but tension made me clumsy; I seemed to have four feet and hobnailed boots. I reached the room out of breath and lay there on the floor gazing out at a fleece of cloud moving over the grey slit of the sky. I lay there, my heart thumping, my body alive, my mind full of concupiscence. So she came, and instead of young bracken and the wind and the high sun, I laid her on the sacking, and her small body was the warmer and the softer and the more vivid for the contrast with the dust and the dirt.

I do not know even to this day how much I was truly loving Meg and how much the memory of Sue. At least, although there was still much bitterness in my heart towards Sue and in a sense towards all women, none of it escaped upon Meg. Perhaps I too, like Meg, was a romantic and this emotion transmuted what might have been a shabby coupling with a maidservant. Surely inner experience is all. The gold and the dross exist together in the same ground; it depends which you find.

In those days I knew myself to be changed, and wondered that others did not remark it. I looked at all women with new eyes. Confidence and imagination had grown overnight. I was stabilised, more content. I was not happy but so much less unhappy than before that it passed muster. And some of the wildness had gone.

All this time Dick Stable had been making a slow mend, and when one day he asked for his harp we knew him to be truly in recovery.

Then Belemus came home and at once perceived what others had not. "Well, what's to do with you? You look wide-awake. Have you been conquesting over some woman?"

"I don't know what you mean."

"I'd lay a curse you know well. Is it Meg Levant you've spurred? I've thought for some time—"

"You've thought! With what? There's nothing in your head but dried blood and crow droppings. Just because—"

"But soft. He who denies most roundly accuses himself. What if you have been tampering with some wench? Is it a matter for anger between friends? If you will tell me nothing, well and good; I shall know in quick time. You admit you can keep nothing from me. Come, I tell you all my adventures. To share 'em makes 'em live again."

"I'm sorry, Belemus, you're mistaken this time."

He looked at me cynically, pulling at his beard. "I thought you'd changed, I thought you'd left your other soul in Madrid. But now and then it pokes out as if begrudging your better self free play. How does it profit man to take things serious? You were like death after

Sue Farnaby had married elsewhere. I tell you, there is only one philosophy in love: to kiss and fly. Take your pick this morning—and tomorrow start over again. It's the one solution, boy. Love is fun. Don't tie it up in all manner of tedious ribbons labelled faithfulness and truth and honour. You'll weigh it down and sink it. And what's true of love is just as true of life. Spit in its eye before it spits in yours. It's spring for us, witless, and we must make the most of it. It lasts no time. We'll be gouty and palsied soon enough!"

"You're preaching to the converted," I said. "I've no time to waste, no more than you."

CHAPTER 5

THAT day a Spanish shallop appeared in daylight cruising along the shore of Falmouth Bay. She carried lug sails on both masts and in spite of her ungainly build had a turn of speed. From what we could see with the glass her full complement must have been more than forty, perhaps half of them soldiers. She came close in but when our demi-culverin fired twice at about six hundred yards, which was near the limit for accuracy, she turned sharp about and made away. Carminow cursed his own precipitancy then, for if one of the 9-lb. shot had struck her it might have disabled her.

Instead we had to stand and watch the Spaniard chase and over-haul a fishing vessel which had come in-shore unsuspecting. Foster said he thought the smack was from St Keverne. She was boarded and her crew of six taken off. Then the shallop shook out her sails again and moved away with the empty smack in tow.

My father, who had come hastily from the house, said that with the Spaniards so close Sir Francis Godolphin should be warned, so Belemus and I left for Godolphin. It was a twelve-mile ride, and to reach it we passed over high and desolate moorland from which it was possible to see the distant prospect of Mount's Bay glittering like a dish in the slanting sun. Over there, I thought, across the other side, just beyond Penzance, is the church of Paul on the hill, and there lives a girl called Susanna Reskymer.

Godolphin was a mansion built around a square courtyard with gardens surrounding it on three sides. On the fourth side and shadowing it from the late sun was the hill on which some three hundred tin miners were employed and from which the family derived its wealth and stability; and I wished that the Killigrews could have had some similar source so that, irrespective of personal extravagance and royal favour, there would be a steady replenishment of resources to pay off old debts and to guarantee new ones.

Sir Francis greeted us graciously enough and we spent the night there. He had the news, which we had not heard, that the new master of Tolverne, Jonathan Arundell, was sick and was more often confined to his bed than managing his estate. When Belemus was not there Sir Francis said he thought Jonathan was still suffering from the effects of the crisis at the time of his father's death; Jonathan was a sensitive man, and the humiliation and melancholy of that time had bit deep. I thought of Thomas's prophesies, and asked about him.

"Grows fat and ever more vocal. When a younger son is so strident it is good for all that he should leave home early."

"Does he propose to do that, sir?"

"Not as yet. I advise his mother, but she seems set on an early marriage for him to Bridget Mohun. Marriage may tame him."

I got up to go but he said: "Stay a while, Maugan. Talking of taming. . . ."

"Yes, sir?"

"This Belemus is a wild spark, and I hear rumour that you are outvying him."

". . . Sometimes we ride together."

Sir Francis pulled his beard. "Your father lives the life he does perhaps of necessity now. He is in a tide-race and must swim with it. But it is a pity if his sons should become so committed."

"Is not a son committed to sustain his father?"

"Not in activities outside the law."

"The law is hard to come by in these parts, sir. Sometimes one has to assert one's rights."

"It is the distinction between right and wrong that I draw your attention to, Maugan. Have a care for it, for a happy life and the hangman's noose are closer together than some realise." When I did not speak he went on: "But this is a bad time for differences. With the Spanish so close all men of good-will should draw together. If they do not they will be lost."

"You think there will be an invasion this summer?"

"What will stop them? Only perhaps the fear of Drake and Hawkins. The command of the narrow seas is no longer ours. You who have been in Spain must feel the same. Were they not preparing even last year?"

With June there were several false alarms round our coast, and during the month at least four fishing vessels disappeared. Then a great to-do was caused by the return of the crew of the St Keverne smack which had been taken in Falmouth Bay. One man, a gunner, had not been released, but the others were sent back in their own boat. They were examined before Godolphin and Sir Anthony Rowse with other deputy-lieutenants present.

It seemed that the Spaniards had captured them only to press them for news of Drake's fleet, now almost ready to sail from Plymouth. They had told what they could but knew nothing, fortunately, of Drake's objective. (Few did.) So they had been set free again, and themselves brought back valuable information, namely that there were eleven Spanish galleys and twenty ships of war in Blavet alone.

In late June two Lizard fishermen came in with reports that there was sixty sail just off the Manacles. They swore the exact position and approximate number, but whether it was true or not the fleet disappeared into the summer mists.

One night I plucked up the courage to ask my father whether anyone had yet called at Arwenack for his answer to the message I had brought.

He looked at me out of swimmy, prominent eyes and said: "Well, what do you think, boy?"

"I think you'd have told me. But if they bothered to release me with the message they surely must sooner or later send for your reply."

"Well, when they do their messenger will receive an answer as plain as the nose on his face."

"D'you not think, then, that that shows the Spanish mean no invasion this summer?"

"Oh, I'd reason nothing from it. Maybe they thought they'd try you out with this message to see if you'd deign to carry it. Maybe they had no thought except to mock us."

But I knew this had been an offer made in deadly earnest, and I thought from an expression on my father's face, as he bent to pick up a puppy, that he too was not deceived either. Sooner or later someone would come.

Sometimes in the night, especially during those long fair nights of late June, I would lie awake and think of the elderly, scholarly, grey-faced fanatic in the Escorial, with his tiny junta of powerful, clever, dedicated men around him; and I would think of the milling crowds in Madrid, and especially of the crowd gathered for the *auto de fé;* and I would think of the warships lying at anchor in Lisbon waiting for the word to sail.

All through June and early July I was making love to Meg. Meetings were difficult, sometimes hurried, and the more difficult as the nights grew lighter and as Dick recovered his health and spirits. One night, the last of June, we were able to meet out of doors at nearly midnight in the woods behind the house. It was not dark, it was never dark those nights, with a pale blue reflected light over the northern horizon blending into an ultramarine sky in which the stars were never bright. We lay and made love in the long dew-damp grass, and afterwards walked across to the headland looking over towards France. I had never tried to fathom her feelings for Dick, but I knew that, whatever it had been at the beginning, now she was in love with me. We talked little. When we met there was the need for each other which grew no less with indulgence. I do not think we either of us thought much of the future. She was the stableman's wife; that could not be altered. I was in love with her because she was pretty and kind, because she was my first woman, because I needed love, because at that age there is no other way to be. Perhaps she wanted it like this always; but if I wanted it as a permanence it was *time* that I wanted to stand still; a perpetual summer when I was seventeen; when everything is new and crisp and soft and brilliant; when the boy's eye and the poet's eye have the same vision. If time moved on, then that created other vistas. Soon or late, I was prepared to move with it.

On the way home that night, climbing the palisade, she fell and turned her ankle; so I picked her up and carried her the rest of the way.

"How strong y'are, Maugan," she whispered, and I enjoyed my own strength and the feel of her firm thighs, and her warm arms round my neck. We got in somehow limping and conspiratoral and giggling in the dark. When I tiptoed to my room John woke but he did not ask where I'd been; and I lay for a long time beside him in a delicious healthy uplifted lassitude of muscle and mind until as dawn crept in sleep came with it.

In early July my father, burying his differences in the emergency, went over to Godolphin and there conferred with Sir Francis, together with Bernard Grenville, Sir Richard's eldest son, and Jack Arundell of Trerice, Sir Anthony Rowse, Hannibal Vivian, and others. As a result Sir Francis addressed a letter to Lord Essex asking for more men to be sent into the west country. "I still rest of the same mind," he wrote, "that a stronger garrison be needed for all these parts, for the gathering of the Spaniards seems as a cloud that is like to fall shortly in some part of Her Majesty's dominions."

In the middle of the following week, before any reply could be

got, galleys appeared off the north coast of the county, near St Eval.
They came in close on that forbidding coast in the calm clear
weather, making their soundings as they edged nearer the black and
emerald rocks; but they had been seen and watched from early morning, and by the time they were within reach of shore Bernard
Grenville and Jack Arundell had mustered a group of ill-assorted
and ill-armed men to oppose the landing if landing had been in the
Spaniards' minds. So the galleys sheered off.

Thereafter no more alarms. The weather broke and the emergency
passed. Haymaking began, and all set to to get the meadows cut
before the gusty dust-raising wind turned to rain. When the hay had
all been cut and been left to dry and turned with pitchforks from
day to day and then gathered and finally built into ricks, there was
a night of carousing and celebration. Most of the men and boys, including all the Killigrew boys old enough to work, had been out all
day and every day, having had food brought to them to save returning to the house; so now all was noise and laughter, with jokes and
lewd banter and traditional songs. The girls were put into two carts
and dragged by the half-drunken men round and round the yards,
while Dick Stable preceded them on an ass, plucking unsteadily on
his harp and singing:

> With Hal-an-tow! Rumbelow!
> For we are up as soon as any day, O!
> And for to fetch the summer home
> The summer and the May, O!

My father was pleased with the hay, but his oats and wheat were
thin because of the dry weather and because the land had not rested
enough. We needed *rain*, he said, not this damnation wind.

I remember on the twenty-first the weather set fine again because
it was the day I rode into Truro for more medicines for my grandmother. Every time I went to see Mistress Footmarker I stayed an
hour or two learning fresh things about herbs and their mixtures and
administrations; but she never let me see her mix the diacodium.
She was so generous of her secrets that I sought for some other reason
and thought that she found satisfaction in doling out bottle by bottle
the physic which did so much good for the woman she disliked.
That way Lady Killigrew remained beholden to her, even though
she might not know it. That way at any time, perhaps, the remedy
could be withdrawn.

At dawn on the twenty-second three shallops, easily identifiable
as Spanish, were in Falmouth Bay. They never came close enough to

be fired on and after a morning of tension turned away and disappeared towards the south-west. Towards evening, in accordance with
the agreement of two weeks ago, my father sent Belemus to tell
Jack Arundell and me to Sir Francis.

At Godolphin all was quiet. Lady Godolphin was unwell with an
attack of the stone. For that she had been prescribed in London to
take saxifrage root steeped in the blood of a hare, and she esteemed
this as a remedy. My great aunt Margaret had been dead some years
and I did not know Sir Francis's second wife well enough to query
her cure; nor did I know Katherine Footmarker's, though I remembered it had something to do with a prolonged diet of goat's milk.
Sir Francis had as yet received no answer from Essex.

At Godolphin the family supped in one room and the servants
afterwards in another. Sir Francis himself when busy with his papers
ate frugally and alone. My father said he was mean to eat so sparsely
when so rich. That night we had a lonely meal, for Lady Godolphin
was upstairs, his daughter was long since married, while his sons were
all away, one still soldiering in Ireland, one commanding in the
Scillies, a third at Westminster.

Sir Francis said before I returned home tomorrow he would show
me the tin works on Godolphin Hill, and so we went early to bed.
I slept dreamlessly and was wakened by a thunderous knocking
shortly after six. I thought I had overslept and pulled back the bed
curtains as a servant came in.

"Begging your pardon, sir. Sir Francis's compliments and the Spanish have landed!"

"*What?* Is it true? *Where?* How many?"

"'Tis thought about a thousand in the first landings. They come
in by first light and captured the village of Mousehole. Word come
five·minutes gone!"

I turned to claw into my clothes. Every button, every tie took
twice the length of an ordinary day. Mousehole. I had never been
there but I knew it as a fishing village horseshoed around a tiny
harbour. And just above it, on the hill above it, was the twin village
of Paul.

We were not above ten miles distant here. An hour's gallop on a
good horse . . . I bolted downstairs, found Sir Francis fastening his
doublet while a servant buckled on his sword.

"Ah, Maugan, you slept well? You have heard the news? So it
has come at last. I have a commission for you."

"Yes, sir."

"Ride and tell your father what is happening. Tell him to raise the alarm throughout his district and to gather his musters for instant use. Then I shall be obliged to him—"

"Sir," I said, "I ask to be excused from carrying such a message." He looked at me straightly from under his level brows. "Let one of your servants carry it. It will not matter who bears the tidings. I wish to ride in the other direction."

Sir Francis looked down at his sword and lifted the hilt an inch to be sure it was free in its sheath. His face was grey with a tension that he did not allow to show in his words or speech. "That is the way I am riding."

"Yes, sir, so I thought."

"It is more important that the country should be raised than that the invasion should be at once resisted."

"How many soldiers have you at call, sir?"

"Soldiers? None. Nor any relatives of combat age in this house. I shall take eight of my best servants, and I have sent to St Aubyn at Clowance, who is my nearest neighbour; there will be others coming across country as they hear."

"What arms will they have?"

"Arms? Oh, we shall have some shot. And there will be billhooks a-plenty."

"I shall be more useful accompanying you than spreading the alarm. Another sword may not be unwelcome, and if you have pistols I can shoot."

Lady Godolphin came in. "Do not go, Francis, wait until the alarm has been generally raised. What can you do against the best soldiers in Europe?"

"Oppress them by weight of numbers."

"You have no numbers. And what if the invasion spreads along the coast—as the day goes on there may be other landings—it is perhaps planned to take the whole of West Cornwall. Who is to guard this house?"

Sir Francis put his gloved hand on his wife's arm. "I like the choice no more than you, my love. . . . But we are five miles from the nearest coast. And the miners with their pickaxes and shovels would be a stumbling block at the last."

"Oh, Francis, have care for yourself. You are not so young but that you must lead all the charges."

"I am not so old that I can stay behind." He kissed her. "Be rid of your fears by the time I return. I'll bring you a Spanish helmet for a cooking pot. Come, Maugan."

There was Sir Francis and myself and a yeoman farmer called Rame and eight servants. At the hamlet of Relubbas we overtook John St Aubyn who was going at half speed until we caught him up; with him were four servants, and presently we met Thomas Chiverton, who had fled his property at the first alarm but now took courage in our presence. Thereafter we picked up no more reinforcements while we circled Mount's Bay.

It was a splendid morning with a low fur of white fog hiding some of the sea. As we rode the three gentlemen talked in urgent tones. Mr St Aubyn was a rosy-faced, white moustached man of fifty, and he looked anything but a soldier. Sir Francis before setting out had sent off five messengers: one to Sir Anthony Rowse, one to Bernard Grenville, one to my father, one to the Privy Council in Whitehall, and one to Drake and Hawkins in Plymouth asking for immediate action to save the country.

As we skirted Market Jew we found the first people fleeing in terror; women leading small children, old men hobbling, and young men too, just as intent on getting away. Sir Francis spoke sharply to some of these latter, and a few turned about. But most pressed past us without pause. The Spaniards, they said, were pillaging and burning whatever they found and putting women and children to the sword. The dreadful fate of Antwerp—where seven thousand had been slaughtered in a night—was in everyone's mind.

Smoke was rising round the bend of the bay. I jumped off my horse and caught one straggler urgently by the arm. "How are the Spaniards heading? Are they set this way?"

"Aye, master, they'm comin' this way and every way. There's thousands of 'em landing! They come in a dozen great ships! There were no wind at dawn an' they oared in under cover of the fog. They was on us afore we could gather our wits!"

"Are they going inland towards Paul?"

"They'm goin' all ways, master." The man shook himself free.

I caught the others up where they had stopped on the slope into Penzance and were talking to a group of a dozen men headed by a constable called Veysey. Veysey was plainly a level-headed fellow. He said the Spanish had landed several hundred men to begin and had thrown forward a slow moving and slow expanding semi-circle of picked troops, with pikes and guns. Behind them, behind the screen thus formed, came a second force which appeared in truth to be burning and pillaging everything it found. Lacking officers or gentlemen to command, the group of Cornishmen forming round Veysey had accepted him as their leader, and the numbers swelled to about fifty men while information was being exchanged.

Sir Francis wanted to organise a defence about the market place, but a dozen of Veysey's followers shouted their dissent; these were men of Mousehole who knew that all they possessed in the world was being destroyed. They had fled to save their lives but now that they were reinforced they wanted to turn and fight.

Sir Francis by right should have taken command, but I could see that he was swayed by the general mood and by the bold manner of Veysey. For my own ends I edged my horse nearer.

"They're fighting for their homes, sir. If they are left three hours to cool in the market place waiting for an attack they may go too cold to resist at all."

"What do you think, St Aubyn?"

"We might do one as well as the other. I don't see neither is likely to stay an army."

What swayed the choice was the arrival of some thirty more men, a half of this number armed with old guns and eager to come to grips with the enemy. Like new water in a stream blocked with twigs, all suddenly gave way; and we began to move towards Mousehole.

It was an unorderly throng, sixty or seventy afoot, with about a score of horsemen, mostly centred in the middle around Sir Francis, but a few like myself edging forward after Veysey who knew and led the way.

And it was a strange march too, for we traversed the open green which skirted the sea, and the fog, capricious as always, had come down in a sudden cloud on the water so that we could not see fifty yards from shore. As always with fog the world seemed the quieter, and here were no stragglers nor fleeing women. Our march was deadened by the grass; seventy men scuffled across it, twenty horses clumped into the turf; there was only the sound of creaking leather and shaking bits, the occasional clank of a pike or the rattle of a caliver.

When to save time we cut off a corner and tramped across the shingle, the sudden noise of stones, of tramping feet, of slipping and clattering hooves was like an outbreak of giant hailstones. We reached the other side and tramped into silence again.

The carpet of fog lifted its corner off the sea and we could see some of the invading fleet. They were four long black galleys, their masts stark, their oars out like the feelers of sea animals. On the foremast of each vessel a red and yellow flag hung. Small boats were ferrying soldiers ashore.

An acrid smell of burning. We were still two miles from Mousehole; between us and it the fishing hamlet of Newlyn was in flames. The nearest of the boats was putting down its load a quarter of a mile away. As the soldiers jumped out they fell quickly into line, the thin sun glinting on their breast-plates.

Veysey came spurring back to Godolphin. "Sir, our way's barred. If we're to go on at all we'd best take to the 'ills and make a circle."

Sir Francis said: "No. . . . We'll deploy here. We may hold them for a while."

As he spoke there was a puff of smoke in the prow of the leading galley, then the clap of a gun and a ball whistled overhead. We had been seen and saluted.

Just as the press to go forward had been a common choice, so now was the halt. These galleys would carry twenty to thirty cast pieces each, and if they began to fire them on us we should be disposed of very quick. A marching body of men is a fine target for a 5-lb. shot.

This must have occurred to everyone at the same time, for there was now a general move to retreat. The gentlemen did their best to stop this, shouting Godolphin's order. But just at the wrong moment a second ball whistled over, and this was a more cogent argument than any we had. In a body the men gave way.

But as they moved, two of the galleys began to move also, fifteen oars a side propelling the long hulls through the water, more than ever like sea animals after a prey.

And the prey was us. They used their main armament no more. Perhaps with the prospect of a sea battle against Drake and Hawkins within the next few days they felt they could not afford to waste shot, but small-arm fire flew after us and there was always the greater threat in reserve.

Being on horseback, all Godolphin and the other riders could do was keep pace with the retreating men. Just before we turned the corner of the bay I stopped and looked back and could see the Spanish soldiers slowly advancing in two lines about fifty paces apart. Over to the right a glint of armour betrayed where a party on reconnaissance were climbing the hill from which they might discover ambushes and overlook Penzance.

At that moment Constable Veysey was shot from his horse beside me and rolled over in the grass. That finished his followers; they broke and began to run in all directions away from the enemy. Sir Francis swore and drew his sword and sat his rearing horse shouting at them, but apart from his own few all fled.

Veysey was unconscious but not dead, and we could find no wound nor bleeding; we rolled him over and saw the back of his leather jerkin torn in three places by the impact of spent bullets; we got him slung over the saddle and followed in pursuit of the flying men.

By the time we came into the market place the retreating force had melted away. A few stragglers, late arriving for the advance, had assembled in the square, but they were almost all armed only with pikes and pickaxes, and a few carried bows and arrows.

It was now ten o'clock and the hot sun was beating down out of a cloudless sky, though the secretive fog still limited the horizon. There was no time as yet for any but the most neighbouring of lieutenants to bring succour. We could certainly expect nothing from Pendennis, since they would have to hold their musters in readiness for an attack on the harbour.

Sir Francis stared at the clusters of houses, now mainly empty but one or two with women or elderly people peering anxiously from between part-closed shutters.

"Thus are we prepared," he said to St Aubyn bitterly. "Scarcely better so, if at all, than when the first Armada came. If they have the force they can cut off the peninsular and be in command of all Penwith by nightfall."

"There's nothing we can do to stop 'em," said St Aubyn. "Nothing till help comes."

An old woman came out of a house pushing a barrow. On it was loaded her personal possessions: some pewter, a calico quilt, a candlestick, a brass chafing dish. She scarcely looked at us as she pushed her burden steadily out of the town.

One of the Godolphin servants came up. "If ee please, sur, the Spanish be advancin' now. They be at the foot of th'ill, no more'n half a mile away."

"In what numbers?"

"Oh, I should say, three, four 'undred of 'em. They be carrying a banner, and more'n half of 'em's in mail."

Sir Francis looked at Chiverton and at St Aubyn, then sheathed his sword.

"We must abandon the town. See that no one stays, you Parker, and you Crinnis. We'll go by slow stages and keep to the higher ground by Gulval. That way we may have the enemy in sight—"

"Sir," I said, "in that case I ask leave to be excused." When he looked at me in surprise I said: "I have a friend in Paul. I don't know in what peril she stands; I must go and see."

"The way is barred, Maugan. That must be plain to you."

"Not by a circuitous inland route. It must be possible to approach the village from the north or west."

"If the Spaniards take Penwith they will take you, and this time your release may not be so well come by."

"It's a risk I must run."

Sir Francis pulled his horse round. "I don't know what your father will say to me, but I cannot stop you if you wish to go."

"Thank you, sir."

So as the Spanish closed in on Penzance from two sides, Godolphin and his small group retreated reluctantly by another. I left by the fourth, striking due north and then turning west as soon as I was out of sight of the town.

CHAPTER 6

THE larks were singing. High up in the attenuated sky they fluttered, beating out excited messages that paid no heed to me or to my sweating horse. The first time I stopped to give my horse a breather after the long rough climb Penzance was still in sight, and it was possible to see curls of black smoke beginning to rise from some of the outlying cottages. The second time it was all hid by the brow of the hill.

Penwith is a strange secretive land, full of unexpected rocks bearded grey with lichen. I saw only one man in the first hour and he was in rags, crouched on his haunches setting a trap for a hare. I asked my way of him and was told it with an accent which showed his native language was Cornish and that he spoke English only with resentment. I did not tell him that we were being invaded by the Spanish; perhaps it was wrong but I felt that at best he would only dimly comprehend. His way of life was nearer to the hare he was trying to trap.

From this height it was hard to tell one's distances, but as I dropped down into the first wild valley full of nut trees and scrub oak, I dismounted and led my horse, feeling that that way one was less likely to blunder upon the invaders unawares. I had eaten and drunk nothing since yesterday, so stopped at the first stream that we might both drink; but there was no food except for the abounding wild life which there was no means of snaring.

The valley led down to the coast and to a deserted bay. The sea here was emerald and turquoise, the rocks a terra-cotta brown and square-fashioned as if worked by a sculptor. We had come too far west and I led my horse up the hill which would divide this from the next cove. Almost as soon as we reached the top the strong smell of burning wafted through the trees.

I tethered the horse and went on foot. It wasn't far to go. A rutted cart track led through a field in which the scent of the growing barley was overhung by the smell of smoke. Black specks floated in the sunlight, and here and there scraps of burnt paper and rags hung in the trees.

At the other side of the field was a broken iron gate ajar, and beyond a wider track with a cottage on either side of it. Both cottages were burnt out, the cob walls standing but roofs and windows gone. There was no sign of life and now little burning, only a wisp of smoke came from them.

But there was something bigger afire. Passing two chickens picking unconcernedly in the tufted grass, I turned the corner and came at once upon what until recently had been Paul Church. The tower had collapsed, breaking down the chancel wall; windows had fallen in, a black column of smoke and flame still came from the interior.

I made a cautious circuit of the building. No one was about; only the dead in their graves were here for witness.

The pall of smoke obscuring the sun moved away on a chance breeze: a substantial square-built house across from the churchyard was also blazing. I ran over the graves and to a lych-gate, panting, though not from running. A charred door lay across the front steps; the heat from inside made entry impossible; I ran round the back. The kitchens and still room, stone built and cool, had survived the flames. Even the timbers of the roof were only charred. Thrust open the door.

"Sue! . . . Sue! . . ."

The sound echoed in the silence. A smock hung over a chair, and beside it lay a scythe. On the table was a bowl full of cold pottage and a spoon. I tried to push open the next door. It resisted and then broke off its upper hinge and leaned inwards. Beyond was a hall, blocked by a fallen beam. The movement of the door disturbed two or three charred pieces of panelling, and they fell to the floor so that the flames leapt again and an eddy of smoke blew across my face.

"Sue! Sue!"

Somewhere outside a dog was howling.

Back through the kitchen and out into the yard. The stables were empty, the dog was farther on yet. A coppice of trees came near the yard, the two closest had been scorched by the heat. I thrust through the tangle of brambles to another cottage which had not been fired. A cross-bred hound sat on its haunches beside a body which lay sprawled in front of the door.

It was a man, I saw with relief, a labourer. He lay on his back, eyes staring wildly at the sky, a gaping pike-wound in his throat. One hand still grasped a pitchfork.

I patted the hound and tried to comfort him, then returned to the front of the rectory and stared about in the smoke. From here you could see where the Spaniards had dragged things out of the house in their search for valuables. But these piles, like the house, had been fired, and only a wisp of curtain, the handle of a warming pan, the charred pages of a book remained.

The village of Paul was a few smoking cottages, a tavern with ale trickling from an upturned barrel, feathers scattered in the road, a broken stool beside a tin-washing keeve, a dead horse.

The hill down into the village of Mousehole is very steep, and I climbed a hedge to get a view through the smoke and the sea mist.

The harbour was empty except for four fishing boats which swung at anchor on the full tide. All the houses round the harbour had been gutted. Three or four of the houses climbing the hill were still alight. No sign of life. Sword out, I went down the hill.

It looked as if the Spaniards had moved on, directing their main drive along the coast to Penzance. There were no warships within visibility, which now stretched to maybe a mile.

I had reached the first cottages before I saw another dead man in the street, sprawling much as the other had sprawled. Voices.

Between the cottages was a narrow passage choked with charred embers. I slid into it, feeling the heat on my boots, crouched in the buttress of a chimney.

Three Spanish officers.

The sight of these Spaniards walking in full armour down the street of a conquered English town, brought home to me as nothing else had—not the flight of the inhabitants, not the burning villages, not the galleys, not even the two corpses—the reality of this invasion of our land. In the year of the First Armada not one Spaniard had set foot on English soil except as a prisoner or as a shipwrecked mariner begging for succour.

But now it was here. The second Armada had landed its soldiers almost without opposition. There would be bitter fighting no doubt and perhaps another sea battle as fateful as the one off Gravelines. Drake would accept this challenge with all his old fire and brilliance. And, although Ralegh was away, Essex or another would lead an army against this invading force. But from now on the long bitter war would reach a new pitch.

As they reached the harbour wall a strange thing happened. A man in a shabby laced jacket with blue velvet slops and a large black-hilted back sword, came from behind the wall, and I expected them to draw on him. Instead they talked for a moment and then all four turned and walked off together. I saw his face. It was Captain Richard Burley.

I went back up the hill.

At the last cottage a loaf of bread was lying in the road, and I grabbed it and ate half. At the church the fire still burned too fiercely to get inside. I sat on a vault, trying to decide what to do. One could only continue to search.

So I went on for two hours, trying to trace a pattern around the village. The Spanish had not penetrated inland more than a mile beyond Paul. I found four cottages, all clearly deserted in haste but unburned.

By five I had returned to the church. The sensible thing was to abandon the search and rejoin Sir Francis, if I could make a way back through the invading army. The mongrel hound which had continued to howl intermittently beside the dead body of his master suddenly changed his note to an angry bark. I went round to the scorched coppice and through the brambles.

"Down, Snuffler, down," said a man's voice. "Quiet, boy! Oh! Now have a care, boy . . . that's very well. That's very well. Good dog. . . . Let me move him, *that's* very well. . . ."

A man in clerical black was kneeling over the corpse, straightening its twisted limbs. Two other men in rough clothes were near by, pikes in hands. Beside them stood Mrs Susanna Reskymer, looking just as she had always been in my memory, tallish and slight, with grey-green eyes and black hair cut short over the forehead and ears, and the clearest of pale skins made paler now by what she was staring at, and a lip caught between her teeth and a wrinkle of horror twisting her forehead.

I said: "Sue . . ." before I could stop, and at once the two servants lifted their pikes.

The man in black also moved, and then Sue saw me. The pallor at seeing a murdered neighbour was nothing to the pallor that came to her face now.

"Maugan. . . ."

I stumbled out of the bushes. "I came to look. . . . Are you safe? I've been—searching since this morning."

"We hid in the quarry. There's a cave. . . ."

"I found the—the church burning."

"Yes, it's all gone."

"Is that your house, just there?"

"Yes. That's gone too."

"I was afraid. . . ."

"We just got out in time."

The thin man was standing opposite me.

"This is my husband," Sue said. "Mr Reskymer. This is Mr Maugan Killigrew from—from Arwenack."

Someone put out a hand. I had to change hands with my sword.

"This a tragic time for us," he said. "Have you seen aught of the Spaniards?"

"I saw some at noon in Mousehole. Not since."

"You went *down* into Mousehole?"

"Not all the way."

"Were there many dead or wounded?"

"One man was all I saw."

"And this one, alas, our faithful Pieton. We tried to persuade him to leave but he would not. No doubt he died as he would have wished, defending his home."

Philip Reskymer looked all of his fifty years, having lined cheeks and grey hair and the narrow shoulders of a scholar. But his eyes were alert and candid and penetrating. This was the man she had chosen, to whom she had given all that she had promised me, in the terrible intimacy of marriage. This old man was the man who had possessed her. He owned her; she lived with him, slept with him, was breathed upon and kissed and caressed by him. Utterly unchanged to look at, she was fundamentally changed within. She was Mrs Reskymer.

I heard myself explaining how I came to be here, what I had done since morning, why I was seeking them, and, now that I had found them, how I hoped they would let me see them to some safer district.

Philip Reskymer said softly: "It is kind of you, Mr Killigrew, but where does safety lie? We don't know that, but we know where *duty* lies, and mine is here by my ruined church to help any of my parishioners who may need me. As dark falls I fancy they'll come drifting back."

"And your wife?"

"Ah, there is another matter. I'd gladly see her out of this if I knew such a way."

"I don't think any of you safe here," I said. "If the Spanish intend to take Penwith, the only real safety is to make our way east before they seal it off. I was near enough this afternoon to hear three officers talking, and they were debating the holding of Penzance. The neck of Penwith between St Ives and Penzance is not above a few miles. If they can defend that they have a foothold in England from which they'll take some dislodging."

Sue had not spoken since uttering my name.

"You speak Spanish, sir?" Reskymer asked.

"I was their prisoner for six months."

"And were badly treated?"

"Not badly. But I am not a woman."

He winced. "I could wish some solution. What do you suggest?"

"That we all leave as quick as possible. Have you horses?"

"There are two in the cave. But my place is here."

"Will it benefit your flock if you are murdered and your wife raped?"

"I. . . . But if you are a soldier do you desert your regiment to protect your family? No more can I leave."

"Then let your wife leave with these two servants. There's some hours of daylight left. It will give them the chance to make a few miles, and then they can wait for nightfall before trying to slip through the net."

Sue spoke for the first time. "I cannot desert you, Philip." Listening to her say that was like poison.

"Oh, yes, you can, if I can be sure that you'll be safer leaving. But is it so?" Reskymer bent to close the staring eyes of the dead man. The cross-bred hound watched him suspiciously. "Poor John Pieton must be buried. There will be others. Susanna, I'm torn both ways."

One of the servants came forward, and together they carried the dead man into his cottage. Sue got up from her stone and went with the other servant into the back of the cottage. There a woman servant was boiling some stew on a fire. We were all faint from hunger, and in twenty minutes we sat down together round the table and ate the hot stew with bread. From the unburned kitchen of the Reskymers' house had been salvaged an Angelot cheese and a cherry tart; these made the meal.

Philip Reskymer wore a white band round his neck in the manner of the Puritans. His hands were veined and nervous and seemed to have a life of their own, like sensitive antennae. He ate little while he told of their awakening that morning with the Spaniards already rampant in the village at the foot of the hill. Jenkin Kiegwin, he said, who owned much of the property in Mousehole, and whose house was the one substantial one in the town, had been surprised before he could flee and killed at his own front door. His wife and son had fled and were thought to be safe, but the fate of a second son was unknown. Most of the villagers, he thought, had got away in time. I watched Philip Reskymer while he talked, and he seemed to me in no way well-favoured, even for a man of his age. I could not conceit what Sue had seen in him, except as an escape from penury. My flesh crawled at the thought of those veined hands touching her body.

Hate which has come out of love burns the brighter for what it is consuming; I could have killed her and wept over her in the same breath.

One of the servants came back with an old woman who had been hiding all day in the bushes above Mousehole. She could tell us nothing of value, being half-crazy with fear. Reskymer took her into the unburned house and Sue ministered to her.

"I am concerned for old Mrs Lavelis," muttered Reskymer. "Arthur Lavelis is away, and the three servants are new and unreliable. Then there are the Lanyons, but they are better able to fend for themselves. . . ."

"Shall I go to Trewoofe and see?" Sue asked.

"It will not be safe."

"It's not safe to wait here," I said. "I ask you to leave while there is time."

"How can I?" said Reskymer. "Already we've old Aunt Betty Coswarth to care for. There will be others. If the Spanish find us—"

"And Sue?"

His long hands took the bowl of hot milk from his wife and he carried it to the old woman. "I think he's right, Susanna. I cannot expose you to this risk if—"

"I'm already exposed to it. There's no proof that I shall be safer elsewhere."

"There's every reason to suppose it," I said.

Sue stood up with her back to her husband. Her eyes were brimming with tears. "I'm sorry, Maugan, this is my home."

Furious, hurt, miserable, I wanted to turn on my heel and leave the girl to her beloved husband and her invited fate, but I could not make the first move. I just stared back at her, knowing myself lost and defeated.

"Your home is in ashes," I said. "I've seen *men* burnt too. But of course it's as you please." The words scarcely meant anything; I had to say something to release the pressure in my throat.

Just then a young woman with a child appeared and almost fainted with relief when she saw Sue at the door. This woman too was taken into the kitchen and fed. She had been crouching in a disused tunnel for thirteen hours. She had seen two Spanish soldiers about an hour ago on the quay.

Philip Reskymer walked across to the ruins of his church and we tried to get inside, but the heat was still too great and some of the roof timbers had not fallen but were smouldering and liable to collapse. Even the great stone pillars had broken apart.

"This is the first church in England ever to be lit by a Spanish torch," he said. "I fear it will not be the last. Do I understand, Mr Killigrew, that you saw an *auto de fé?*"

"Yes. Human beings burn too."

"Tolerance is a rare commodity."

"We do not burn our captives."

"Not of late. We stretch them on the rack."

"I think," said Sue, "I think I will see if old Mrs Lavelis is safe. It's thirty minutes mounted, and since she's half blind. . . ."

"Then take Tamblyn with you. He has a strong arm and a stout heart."

"If your wife wishes to visit this Mrs Lavelis," I said, "I shall be pleased to go instead of your servant."

"Thank you, Maugan, no," Sue said.

"But why do you not all go?" Philip Reskymer suggested. "If the Spanish come in force, none of us will survive. But if they stray singly then Tamblyn and young Mr Killigrew are as good a protection as you are likely to get. You have a horse, Mr Killigrew?"

"In the next field."

It was half an hour before we left.

We rode three abreast to begin, and then as the track narrowed Tamblyn fell behind. But he was still too close for private conversation between us. The sun had gone down into a blood-red haze which looked like a record of the day and a portent for tomorrow. We came upon a stone-built square house mercifully unburnt, with narrow mullioned windows and an iron-studded front door. We rang for a time and had no response, then knocked, then tried the latch and walked in.

We were in a hall with a handsome hammer-beam roof. It was dark and cluttered with heavy furniture, and I bumped into a table.

"Who's there?" quavered a voice.

"Mrs Lavelis?" called Sue. "Where are you?"

"Who's that? Tell me at once."

"Susanna Reskymer with two friends. We came to see if you lacked anything."

"Company, yes. You'll find tinder on the big table. Light a candle."

Eventually light began to grow, flickering and dying and then creeping up. A plump old lady was sitting on one of a flight of broad stairs, holding a musket across her knees.

"So you are real," she said. "I was beginning to doubt."

At the first scare the servants had fled, leaving the old woman of eighty-four to face the enemy alone. So she had stayed all day, though her sight was bad, sitting on the stairs gun in hand.

We helped her to a comfortable chair, prepared some food for her. In the reaction she was suddenly frail; we could not leave her to-night. But Sue was concerned about her husband. She asked me to go and tell him. I said my first duty was to her; Tamblyn must go.

She did not like this, argued that if I would not go alone she would stay here herself; I said where she was there I would stay.

Sue helped the old lady up the stairs to bed. Mrs Lavelis said the bedroom next to hers was prepared and usable; if Sue would take it she would sleep more soundly; the two men could sleep in the room next the hall. Before we closed the door Mrs Lavelis was breath-ing quietly.

At dusk Sue told Tamblyn to go and explain to Mr Reskymer that she would not be back tonight. Then she told Tamblyn to re-turn here with all speed.

When he had gone she stood with her back to the great front door looking at me with liquid resentful eyes.

I leaned across and lit two more candles. "I am real. Even though at first you may have doubted it."

"Oh—I'm—*glad*, Maugan. I only wished it hadn't happened this way."

"The choice was yours."

She came slowly to the table, on which were still the remains of supper. "Was I to know?"

"You thought I was dead?"

"Yes."

"If you had been my widow your haste would have seemed inde-cent."

She flushed. "It's a long story."

"It will be a long night."

She began to pick up the trencher plates, the spoons.

"Leave that," I said.

She stopped. "What do you want me to say? What is there to say? However long I tried I could never persuade you that what I did seemed at the time to be right."

"Oh, Sue. . . ."

She put her hands to her face. I got up but she said: "No, don't touch me."

"Sue, why did you ever *do* this?"

She went to one of the long narrow windows and peered out at the darkening drive.

"Is it safe to have light? Might it not attract the Spanish?"

"They'll not be concerned with us tonight. Also it will help Tamblyn to find his way back."

"Yes, it will help Tamblyn to find his way back." She suddenly went on in a choked voice: "Why did I marry Philip Reskymer? I'll tell you. Because I'm a weakling and a coward. . . . They told me you were dead. Can you understand? They told me you were dead. I could not even *grieve* openly. You were supposed to be nothing to me. Only Elizabeth Arundell guessed. . . ." She turned. "I couldn't stay on at Tolverne—not an everlasting companion to Elizabeth in a gloom-filled house, for ever and ever. There was just an eternity before me of life without purpose. Philip Reskymer came twice to see Lady Arundell, to whom he's related, and I saw he liked my company, but that was all. When I left I thought I should never see him again. I never wanted to see any of them. I wanted to get right away. . . ."

"But you changed your opinion."

"He found me at my aunt's farm and asked me to marry him. He put it to me in such terms that I couldn't refuse outright. He said he would come back in a week for an answer. It was in those days of waiting that I knew my true weakness."

The tears were brimming on her lashes. "Philip is such a *kind* man: that was my undoing. Above all I needed kindness and some sort of comfort. Can you *understand?* Philip asked me to help him in his work, he asked me to be his companion and helpmeet and friend. That appealed, for I felt if I could have some *object* in life. . . . He told me of his work, and it seemed saintly—there are so few like him."

"Also he was rich."

She stopped and then nodded her head, so that a shower of tears fell. "Yes. That counted. I'll not pretend otherwise. He had a house, servants who would tend on *me*. That may be nothing fresh for you, Maugan, but it has been fresh for me. Ever since I can remember we've been in dire straits. My father was always particular to keep up a standard of manners and behaviour—I was brought up to act like a lady—but at what cost behind the stage! The meals we had with only parsnips and carrots! The endless grubbing in the fields! That had already begun again while living with my aunt. How was I to know that if I refused his offer it might not continue for the rest of my life?"

"Have you never looked at yourself in the glass?"

"Oh, no doubt I should do as well as the rest *if* I had a home and money for a dowry. But who wants a *penniless* girl? Nearly all marriages are a question of money. . . . And don't you see? Philip was not taking your place; he was taking some other place, which perhaps my father had once held—or which perhaps had never been filled before! Do you understand that?"

"Do you love him?"

She made a rapid impatient gesture, and took out a handkerchief to wipe her eyes. "What is love? Two or three diverse things. I don't love him as I—as I. . . . But I love him in the sense that he is worthy of respect, of admiration, of help, of service. Until now I have found satisfaction, a new sort of life, in helping him, in being beside him while he worked."

"Did it never occur to you that I might still be alive?"

"When I first heard, the news was that you were dead. It was not until later that I heard how you had disappeared. By then I couldn't bring myself even to hope. That too is a weakness, I know. I have this fault of seeing things blackly. Often in my life I have hoped and prayed—and the hope has never come."

"Does your husband know about us?"

"No. He thinks I'm just of a melancholic nature—which may be true but not to the extent that he thinks."

"And what are we to do now?"

"What is there to do? I'm married."

"If we told him the truth, would he not understand?"

"Maugan, I could not. I entered into my marriage in good faith—as he did."

"You still love me?"

She passed near a candle and the flame eddied in the air movement her body made. I felt I was like that candle, as much subject to her, as little capable of stability when she was near.

"I must go and see if Mrs Lavelis needs me."

"She's asleep."

"The old are always dozing and waking. Come with me. From her bedroom you can see across the fields. It might be as well to look once more before darkness falls."

CHAPTER 7

TAMBLYN returned about eleven. He said the master was safe—more villagers had drifted back but none had ventured down into Mousehole.

Sue slept in the guest bedroom next to that of Mrs Lavelis. Tamblyn and I took it in turns to keep watch from a little turret room which commanded an excellent view to south and east. Tamblyn took the first watch—from twelve until three, while I slept on one of the beds in the room next to the hall. In spite of everything I went to sleep quickly and being wakened at three was like being dragged out of a pit.

I went up, took the rug still warm from Tamblyn, and wrapped it round. The chair gave a view from both windows. The stars had disappeared, and a Spanish army could creep up on such a night.

I sat there holding Mrs Lavelis's musket and began to think about Sue.

My heart was sick and my mind full of fancies. I sat there for a full hour thinking about her, with sleep pricking at my eyelids and my will not quite in control. It was the deepest part of the night when dying men die and the living have their darkest thoughts.

I suppose it must have been near four when I found myself beginning to wake up. There was no longer any struggle with lids or limbs. Yet though I woke I woke not from my thoughts.

I thought of Sue.

I got up and peered out of the windows. A low wind was sighing in the trees. I went downstairs and opened the door into the room beside the hall. Tamblyn's deep regular breathing greeted me.

I went upstairs again, passed Mrs Lavelis's door and listened. There was no sound. I went on to Sue's door and gently opened it. There was no sound here either, and it was not until I was half-way to the bed that I caught her quiet breathing.

She was sleeping with the bed curtains drawn back and woke the instant I touched her hand.

"*Who is it?*"

"Maugan. I thought to see if you were safe."

"Is there anything wrong? What time is it?"

"Near four. No, all's quiet."

"Then. . . ."

"I came to be with you."

"Maugan, you should not."

"Should I not? Have I not that right?"

"Oh, between ourselves, perhaps; but—"

"It's only between ourselves."

"That can't be, my love."

"You'd call me that and yet deny me?"

"I'm sorry . . . I shouldn't have said it. It's the shock of waking like this. You surprise words out of me."

"Love is the only word I have surprised. . . ."

I sat there for a time beside her without speaking. In the accustomed dark my eyes could see the oval of her face, and the shape of her shoulders. She had reared up from the pillows but now lay back, only her head lifted. I took her hand. It was warm and a little moist. I turned it up and kissed the palm.

The hand contracted, tried to free itself, though not violently.

I said: "To whom did you first swear your love?"

"To you."

"That oath to me was binding, a betrothal. For it I forsook all others."

"I thought you were *dead!* I've told you, Maugan!"

"If a woman marries a man and then, mistakenly thinking him dead, marries a second man, to whom is she rightly married?"

"Oh, yes, I know. But we were not married. It was a—"

"It was a betrothal, wasn't it?"

"Yes. Yes but—"

"A betrothal is as binding as a marriage ceremony. Ask any one."

"Oh, no, it isn't so now in law."

"Can you be more cruel than that?"

She sat up again. "Maugan, what can I *say* to you! When I saw you yesterday I thought my heart would stop. Since then I have tried, tried so hard!"

"You have tried so hard to defeat your true feelings. You say you're weak. I think *I* am weak. You are far too strong. . . ."

We looked at each other and I put my hand up to her neck. I pulled her towards me. She resisted, pushing at my chest, but it was the resistance of one far gone in some illness or trial of strength. It was as if she had burned herself up inwardly during the day and now had no reserves left.

I think if it had not been for my experiences with Meg I should not have gone into Sue's room that night. Yet to say that the knowledge of one woman breeds confidence with the next is to state a truism that puts too base a value on it. I was not going from one light creature to another but from a simple romantic scullery maid with whom I had learned all I knew to the girl who should have been my wife.

The first dawn light picking out the gap in the bed curtains showed up Sue's face pale and drowned against my arm. Her hair lay like seaweed over the pillow.

I said: "But I don't understand. . . ."

Her eyes flickered but she did not open them.

"You have been married—how long?" I said. "If—"

She said rather sulkily: "It is not that sort of a marriage. I tried to explain."

"Then what sort in God's name—"

"Before we married, Philip made it clear he sought nothing of me but companionship. He feels that a relationship of the body between a man of fifty and a girl of seventeen is unnatural and wrong. I believe he loves me—I know he does—in the fullest way; but he's a principled man and has never attempted to amend his views as we have grown closer in friendship. . . . So you have found me as I am."

I drew her closer to me. Her body was slighter than Meg's, less rounded, the bones small but more noticeable. I was enamoured and enraptured with her out of my senses. We lay for a time unspeaking.

At last she said: "It's getting light."

I reached up and pulled the curtains closer.

"Maugan, you must go."

I stopped her mouth in the only way. And in that way our rational minds ceased to work. I knew that first light was the most likely time to be surprised by the Spaniards. I knew that Tamblyn might get up and find me no longer in the turret room and raise the alarm. It was possible that Philip Reskymer might come over at dawn. But my brain was submerged; nothing mattered.

But however narrow the slit in the curtains, daylight crept through and was suddenly in possession of our dark fortress, and the curtains were high walls against the world no longer.

She sat up: "I think I hear something."

"No, it's the wind."

She listened intently. Eventually she gave way to the pull on her arm and lay down. She tried to push her hair back from her brow.

A bird was cheeping under the eaves; it was an alarmed sound as if a cat were stalking him. There was a scraping on the roof above us made by a crow or a chough as he edged along the thatch. Far away a cow was lowing.

I said: "We must make plans."

"How can you make plans to defeat fate?"

"Not defeat it perhaps but circumvent it. Sue, you can't go on living this unnatural life for ever. If we survive this invasion, then some way must be found to free you of an impossible tie. It will poison and distort Reskymer's life as well as yours and mine."

"In whatever we do we must go slow."

"I have a feeling," I said, "that if he loves you as you say he does he'll not be able to keep to his principles much longer. Look at you! Would any man?"

"He doesn't see me like this."

"No, but one day he may. Have you separate rooms?"

"Of course."

"With a connecting door?"

"Maugan don't torture yourself! Accept my assurance that nothing. . . ." She stopped.

"What is it?"

"Listen."

I listened.

Outside a horse neighed, and there was the jingle of harness.

I leapt out of bed and began to claw into my shirt and doublet
and slops and shoes. Half clad I hobbled to the window. It was
broad day. Some men on horses were disappearing round to the front
of the house. I grabbed the musket from where I had propped it and
fumblingly primed it with powder.

"Who is it?" Sue whispered.

"Men. I don't know them. Dress but wait here."

This room led on to a landing looking down into the hall. It was
still gloomy here but light fell in from the open front door. Three
men were already in the hall.

"Halt!" I shouted.

They stayed there motionless, but two men coming in the door
raised guns.

"Hold!" said the man in front. "Who the devil calls? I don't recognise
the voice."

"What are you doing here?"

"Since this is my house I've a better right to ask you that."

I lowered my gun. "Your home?"

"It was when I went away."

Arthur Lavelis had been on his way back from Exeter when the
news reached him of the Spanish landings. He had ridden through the
night, collecting as he went a dozen other riders so that the number
now in the courtyard of Trewoofe was twenty. As they rode rumours
had flown to meet them, that a second Armada twice as great as the
first was on our shores and landing soldiery by the thousand, that all
Penwith had already been burned and put to the sword.

Coming closer he had had official word with Godolphin who last
night had encamped on the hills above Market Jew. Four or five
hundred men, Lavelis said, had by now flocked to Godolphin's standard and numbers were increasing hourly and breeding greater courage. All the same they were an undisciplined company to meet any
concerted attack. Skirting the embers of Penzance, Lavelis had come
home without falling foul of invaders. It remained to be seen, he said,
what sights the day would bring.

By now Sue, utterly calm and possessed, was out on the landing, and Tamblyn rubbing his eyes had come into the hall. Old Mrs Lavelis was sleeping peacefully so she was not disturbed.

We breakfasted at once. Lavelis said if he ever found his three servants again he would hang them. A blustering moustached bachelor of forty with a roving eye that lighted with appreciation on Sue, he held a council of war over his cold mutton and galantine sauce. With him was a regular soldier called Captain Poor who had ridden from Liskeard overnight. Poor said Drake and Hawkins had been on the point of leaving for their expedition to the West Indies, with seasoned troops standing by to go aboard at the last minute. These troops under Sir Thomas Baskerville, Colonel General of Drake's soldiers, would probably now be thrown into Cornwall to meet the attack while Drake and Hawkins sailed to take the Spaniards at sea. Until the full weight of the invasion was known no one could do more.

Poor said that as soon as he had broken his fast he would ride back to try to rejoin Godolphin. That way he would be performing a valuable reconnaisance and at the same time reinforcing the main army of resistance. He suggested that the force at present at Trewoofe should split, ten remaining to guard the house and the women, but the younger and the more active to go with him.

I knew then I must part from Sue. I had no claim to a special concern for her; her husband was near, and if I made an excuse I should look a coward.

Before we left I tried to get private word with her, but she was much with Mrs Lavelis and avoided conversation with me. I think she was still unawake from the heady drugs of the night and trying to find some balance within herself. That also was true of me: I wanted talk with her, yet if I had got it it would have seemed superfluous. What had happened had happened and nothing would ever be the same again; but nothing was solved by it, rather greater problems made. One's mind needed time to absorb them.

Just as we were leaving I went to her in front of the old lady and said: "I must go, Sue. If this is over soon, I shall be back. In any case if I am alive I'll come back. Remember that this time."

She looked sidelong at me. "I'll remember."

We rode away, Lavelis with us. The weather had changed, and it was a grey lowering day with a stiff south-easterly wind blowing off the sea. Landing from small boats would be less easy than yesterday.

We came round a sharp shoulder of rock, and the whole of the Mount's Bay was visible. The town of Penzance was in ruins; you could see the roofless walls, but there was no sign of life about it, either English or foreign. The top of the great rock of St Michael's

Mount was shrouded in misty rain; in front of it, in the green plain of Marazion, was a large body of men perhaps five hundred strong, scattered irregularly in groups with here and there a tent and a wagon. Close in to the Mount rode four Spanish galleys. The rest of the sea to the low horizon was empty.

Captain Poor said: "It's hard to tell if the battle is over or not yet joined. At least let us go down and bury either them or ourselves."

But I had seen too much of Spanish discipline to suppose that a landed army would be in the casual array of the groups on Marazion Green. This was Godolphin's mixed assembly.

We found Sir Francis in better spirits. The forces of the Spanish had been exaggerated, and at worst this was not yet a large-scale invasion. Indeed, although other vessels had been reported off the coast, it was from these four galleys only that the landings had been made. Yesterday the Spanish troops had burned Penzance and then had attended a mass celebrated by three priests on the hill above the town. As darkness was falling, and perhaps fearing a counter-attack during the night, the bulk of the force had retired to the safety of their galleys, and there they still were. No one knew if garrisons had been left ashore, but Godolphin would not spare any part of his force to discover this. He saw it as the best strategy to keep his men together to watch the galleys and if need be to follow them and try to prevent any repetition of yesterday.

One or two seamen in our army were watching the weather with experienced eyes. The galleys were mobile so far as oaring took them, but this dead on-shore wind would make it difficult for them to get clear away. If it strengthened they would be pinned within the bay, and if any English force appeared to windward of them they would be trapped. But of course no one knew what superior Spanish forces hovered below the horizon: if Drake suddenly appeared and engaged the galleys he might himself be trapped in turn.

Meantime to wait. We camped on the grass, making the best of the thin driving rain and the lack of food and shelter. Twenty women who had come in were sent to scour the countryside for bread and bare necessities. In the evening some sheep and chickens were slaughtered and roasted over spits, and enough ale was found to keep the damp at bay.

About seven with the fine rain still falling and the wind coming firmly out of the south-east, the leading galley was seen to move. Its oars lapped the water and it turned its snout towards the shore west of us where the inlet of Penzance lay. At once the near-finished meal was abandoned, men cried to each other, horses were saddled, calivers and muskets and pikes were shouldered, swords buckled.

The galley slid through the water followed by its three lesser creatures, and the motley band of men kept company with them along the shore.

Short of the Penzance inlet the first galley turned in-shore. The pinnaces were lowered. At that moment Captain Poor on one flank and Sir Francis Godolphin on the other gave the order to open fire. There was an intermittent rattle of guns, and some of the men on the first ship retreated from the rail to less exposed positions. The galley replied with small-arms' fire. We could see a consultation going on on the poop. If the galleys employed their cast pieces they could of course clear the shore while the first wave of troops were landed. It all depended whether they considered they could spare the powder and shot.

In the meantime a half-dozen men ashore who were armed with the modern muskets continued to fire, and another half dozen with long bows climbed down on a projecting point which brought them slightly nearer the ships and strove to outdo the musketeers.

While this issue was in the balance I noticed an old man and an old woman a hundred yards farther along the beach. He was digging in the sand for bait and she was shovelling seaweed into a basket. I do not know if they were unaware of the imminent conflict or if they were deaf to the sound of gunfire but it seemed they were indifferent to both. They reminded me of the man of whom I had asked the way yesterday. The struggle to exist had reduced them so low that they cared nothing for larger and more general dangers. They had no enemy greater than hunger, no fear beyond an empty belly.

The wind was strengthening and wavelets were breaking all along the shore. Then a man in the crowded bows of the first ship crumpled and fell among his fellows. It was one of the bowmen who had made his mark. Within five minutes of the soldier's fall the galleys began to move away out of range.

A straggling cheer broke out and ran along the groups of defenders.

"They'd best go if they be going," said the man next to me. "'Tis blowin' up dirty."

But once out of range the four ships anchored again in line astern. They were not giving up.

We posted sentries along the beaches, and the main body retired to the grassy slopes behind. Dark fell and two bonfires were set up on the beaches, to give light and comfort. I dozed off for a time, leaning back against a dank and mossy boulder. I dreamed about Sue, nothing else, not Spaniards, nor war, nor burning churches, just Sue. The strength of my desire for her kept waking me and I would start up and shake myself, trying to throw off the fancies. I do not know what alchemy gets to work in a man that one woman's face and lips and hands and body alone will satisfy him and no other.

In the middle of the night I went along to the tent where Sir Francis Godolphin sat writing a despatch. After two nights without sleep he was looking his sixty-odd years. I offered to write the despatch for him, and this he agreed to and leaned back in a chair speaking the rest to me. It was a straightforward account of his actions and of the movements of the enemy, destined for the Privy Council at Westminster. Added was a calm appraisal of the future. I realised as I wrote why the Privy Council set more store by the counsel of Sir Francis Godolphin than that of Mr John Killigrew.

We had finished and he had sealed the report when there were shouts in the distance and one of his servants came running across the grass with news that it was reinforcements from Plymouth at last.

Into the tent came a tall vigorous young man called Sir Nicholas Clifford. He brought with him, he said, two hundred troopers under the command of two experienced captains, and reassurances from Drake that a portion of his fleet would be off the Lizard by dawn. It remained only to concert action here to meet any emergency which the day would bring.

Captain Poor was wakened, and the two new captains came into the tent for a counsel of war. Because I had been in the tent when they arrived they did not question my presence.

Nicholas Clifford's plan was different from Francis Godolphin's: it was a strategy stemming from strength instead of weakness. If the force of the enemy was no more than four galleys, they should be encouraged to land, not prevented. Although they had got fresh water on Wednesday, they had had none since and might now be in need of more. The whole camp should be moved in the night.

By three we were in transit. By five we were in our new positions. About thirty men armed with pikes and bows guarded the beaches on which the Spanish had tried to land yesterday, the remaining seven hundred of us, including the mounted troopers who had arrived over-night, were out of sight in the valleys of Gulval and Ludgvan. If the enemy landed they could land almost unimpeded. If they ventured into the green country behind the beaches they would be attacked from all sides.

Clifford reckoned that Drake's fleet would be in Mount's Bay by noon or soon after. Seven hours to go.

From a vantage point in the hills we watched the four black smears offshore grow into the warships we now knew so well. Clifford had brought a strong glass and through it he studied the movements on board. The sky was lightening with more than the dawn. It was to be a better day.

For a time there was no movement apparent, then the longest galley shook out a sail or two as if trying them against the wind. They were quickly furled. Except by oar, the four warships were incapable of moving out of Mount's Bay, and unless the slaves were flogged until they died, they would not make open water at all.

No fires were lighted in our camps, but we saw the men left on the beaches gathering round their fires, and though the morning was not cold we munched bread and cheese and shivered in the wind.

About eight, three small companies which had been sent out to test conditions to the west of us reported that no Spanish remained at Penzance or Mousehole and that the inhabitants were drifting back. Because they had fled at the first alarm casualties had been few.

By now the day was bright and I watched the sky suspiciously. In this sea-surrounded peninsula changes of weather can be rapid. The wind which had blown from the south-east for twenty-six hours was still strong but was becoming hesitant, lifting and falling in gusts. Broken blue sky let through a fitful sun. The horizon, which had been misty from one cause or another ever since the invasion began, was showing as a hard rim. Complete surprise was now impossible, but if the wind would only hold, the Spaniards were still caught.

At nine Clifford and Lavelis and four others of whom I was one rode down the valley to within half a mile of the beach. Where we stopped it was sheltered and while Clifford used his glass we felt no wind at all. He transferred his attention from the galleys to the horizon, but I could tell from his manner that he had seen no other ships. Just then I felt a breath of wind on the back of my neck.

The others must have noticed it a few minutes later for they all looked up and then Clifford spurred his horse away from the shelter of the trees. The south-east wind had quite dropped and a breeze was springing up from the north-west.

We galloped cursing to the sea, Clifford nearly bringing his horse down in his annoyance. By the time we reached the sand three of the galleys were already unfurling their sails. The fourth, the leader, put out its oars and began to nose in towards the land.

"By God!" muttered Lavelis, "don't tell me our luck is yet in!"

The warship came within musket shot. Men were in her bows and one or two of our defenders took aim at them but Clifford sharply held up his hand.

"Do not for pity's sake discourage them."

The galley swung round and shook out her sails. As she did so about a dozen men dived off her bows and began to swim for the shore. Clifford still refused the order to fire, and by the time the first man stumbled shouting upon dry land, the galley was moving out to sea in the freshening breeze. The voices that called to us were English and besought us not to fire. The Spanish captain, one Amerola, had chosen to jettison some of his captives, seamen and others taken on his cruise and judged of no further value.

Their joy on being released was the only reward we had. By eleven all four Spanish ships were hull down on the horizon. It was not until an hour later that the first sail of Drake's fleet showed.

CHAPTER 8

FROM then on the weather set in foul. Through devious sources we heard of the further adventures of the raiding galleys. In mid-channel they came on a fleet of seventy unescorted ketches, hoys, and cargo vessels freighting towards Plymouth, and ran amok, scattering the little ships all ways. But one galley which caught five found that even ketches have teeth when cornered and a bitter fight ensued. Three of the ketches were sunk but the galley was so mauled that as the weather grew steadily worse she was glad to call off the fight and limp away into the mist of the next squall. As night fell her condition grew worse and by morning she was sinking. Captain Amerola took off her crew and only three warships returned to Blavet.

The shock of the landings was great throughout the country. My father received weekly letters from the Privy Council directing his energies to the training and better equipping of his musters. Drake and Hawkins had word from the Queen that their new adventure must wait until the risk of invasion was past.

My father and Hannibal Vivian jointly replied to the Privy Council that whatever they might do with their musters, such force as they constituted would be little use without powder and shot, and Hannibal Vivian went to the length of demanding a new culverin, four demi-culverin, and three sakers. He did not get them, but in early August a supply of new muskets arrived together with some powder and ball, and these were sparingly shared out. Then there was a great parade held in one of the fields above Arwenack at which some two hundred fifty men, the levies of five parishes, appeared. A motley band, a quarter of them unarmed, the rest no better than those who had met the Spaniards at Penzance. My father was in a fine temper.

He had words with Hannibal Vivian, and then blew off like a powder magazine at a group of four Penryn burghers who came to complain that his musters were stripping their parish of any defense at all.

That evening Meg said to me: "I've scarce seen you since you come home, Maugan. Does the war fret you s'much?"

"Enough."

"There would—I think there'd be a chance tomorrow. Dick'll be gone till midnight. If you've the mind. . . ."

"It's not possible tomorrow, Meg. I must be beside my father all day."

She looked at me searchingly. "You're not tired of me? Tell me if it be so."

"No. No, of course not. Perhaps Saturday. Is Saturday a chance?"

"I believe Dick'll be around, but I'll see."

In the end I avoided her until one howling stormy night a week later when, with the thatch nearly lifting over our heads and the tiny window rattling in its socket, I took her in the old upstairs room where we most often met.

When it was over she said: "I asked if you was tired of me. Maybe I should've asked if you hated me."

"Hated you? Dear Meg, how could I ever hate you?"

"Well, what else d'you mean by this sort of love? Tisn't love with tenderness. Tis love with anger in your heart." She began to weep.

I hugged her to me, trying not to weep myself, for all the pleasure I had had with her had turned to ashes because between one meeting and another I had known the girl I loved. I had tried to hide the change in my feelings for Meg by forcing them to a greater intensity, and the outcome had only been to show her the more clearly that my pleasure in her was gone.

We sat there long, dangerously long, while with all the desperate hypocrisy of someone who is trying to avoid hurting a person they care for, I comforted and cozened her and talked her into half-believing that nothing had changed. Perhaps it would have been kinder over all to have told the truth, to have made a clean break; instead I exerted all the wiles of a professional seducer to save her pride and her love. In the end I all but persuaded myself into believing it.

But the following day I took horse and rode back to Paul.

"You shouldn't have come, Maugan. How did you know where to find me?"

"You couldn't live in the shell of your own house: my next call was Trewoofe. Where is your husband now?"

"In the village. Most of the villagers have nowhere to live, though some are finding shelter at the Kiegwin's, whose house was not burned. Jenkin Kiegwin, as you know, was killed but his wife and two sons are safe. The rest of the villagers are in tents or in cottages farther afield."

"And Arthur Lavelis?"

"He is from home most days helping to dispense relief."

"But you can stay and talk?"

"For a few minutes."

"Why are you so defensive?"

"Only because I'm afraid."

"Of me?"

She touched my hand. "Of what you're going to ask."

We took a few steps down the grass lawn. At the end was a yew hedge which would hide us from the windows of the house. Before we reached it, she stopped.

"Maugan, what *are* you going to ask?"

"For you."

Her eyes in the bright windy sunlight were a cat's green. "You know that can't be."

"Even after what happened two weeks ago?"

"That was—oh, it was something neither of us could fight against! It took hold before we were aware. But now we are aware."

"I'm only aware that I love you more and more."

"But I can't betray the vows I made."

"You already have."

"I have said—that was something out of control—in the deepest part of the night." When I made to speak she hastened on: "Well, what are you suggesting?"

"We could go away together. You were willing to agree to that two years ago."

"But then I was unmarried. We can't marry now. We could live together but you would lose whatever hope you have of preferment at home or at Court."

"I can make my own way. Others have. I am a bastard; my children would be no less."

"And I, Maugan? I have made vows to be the wife of Philip Reskymer."

I pulled her round the corner of the yew hedge but she would not come into my arms. There was a surprising strength in her taut frame.

"Wait, Maugan," she said. "Wait. Wait."

"For what?"

"For time to help us."

"Do you mean wait for your husband to die?"

She winced. "No . . . or yes . . . I don't know. All I know is that at this time I can't let him down."

"As you did me."

"I thought you were dead! He is not! He is working eighteen hours in the day trying to aid the people here. He is working all day, and the work on top of the shock of the raid has made him ill. Not serious ill, but sick and in need of help himself."

I let go of her hand and sat slowly on the stone parapet. "Sue, I can't exist without you. If I'm not sick of body I'm sick of soul. Every night I lie awake thinking of you. Before I met you this time I was living a life which passed for contentment—it was no more but it passed. Now all that's gone."

We stayed thus for a time and were so still that a blackbird hopped along the stone path watching us with a boot-button eye. Then Sue moved and he fluttered away with a chatter of alarm.

"I don't know what to answer, Maugan. Not yet. Not yet. In a year or two—"

"What difference will that make?"

"He'll not need me so much. And you will surely have some profession. . . ."

I put my arms round her. "Did our one night mean so little to you? . . ."

"But this is the only way. The only way now! Don't you see!"

I began to kiss her. At first she seemed to be going under, her hands against me to be weakening their pressure, but of a sudden she thrust me away.

"No, Maugan! Not *now!*"

I said: "If you'll not leave him, then let us at least be lovers. I can ride over. It'll not be easy but it can be done. You say he's often away. . . ."

She groped her way back to the wall and again sat down, taking breaths. "And if I have a child?"

"Then it will be time for you to leave him, for everyone to know of our love. . . . Don't shake your head, Sue. Please don't. Please."

"But I must!"

"Why? Why? Why?"

She did not answer. Every now and then there was a spatter of rain in the wind.

I said: "All this we've been talking of—it's unreal. *This* is the wrong

time, *that* is the right time. . . . If we love each other and you don't
love him—all else is wasted words. . . . Look at me, Sue. Tell me if
it isn't true."

But she would not look at me. I knelt beside her, stroked her hand.
The lace of her sleeve fell over both our hands and covered them.

I said: "*Do* you love him?"

"*No!* I have said so!"

"Yet you will stay with him?"

"For the *time*. Go away, Maugan, for a few months, a year. Forget
me for a year. Think about making your fortune, making a place in
the world. Remember now, I'm quite safe—much safer than I was at
Tolverne."

"How do I know that? If he loves you he won't be able to keep
aloof from you for ever. If you consider it your duty to stay with him
now you may then consider it your duty to submit!"

"He will never press me."

"He isn't pressing you to stay now. You consider you must!"

"Darling, darling, there is so much difference." She put up a hand
to my face, but now a raw anger was bleeding inside me.

"In this house—now there is this emergency—do you have a separate
bedroom from him?"

She hesitated. "Not a—separate bedroom. A separate bed. He sleeps
each night—"

"So each night he sees you undress, sees you unbind your hair,
sees you half-naked—how long can that go on?"

"Maugan!" She stood up. "It isn't so! You're tormenting yourself
without cause. While our own house is rebuilding, it is like this, but
only until then. We preserve a decency—there is nothing of what you
think."

"Whatever you say I don't believe a man and a woman may share
a room for weeks without intimacy growing— It's a matter of *time*,
Sue! It's just the other way from what you say. Time is not on our
side, it's against us! It's on *his!* Come away today, I beseech you.
Let us go as we are. It's of no importance where, so that we're together. Once you said you would. You promised that before ever
you met him. Mine is the prior claim."

She got up and put her fingers to my lips. I struck them away, almost insane with distress. She went very pale.

"Maugan, please don't let us part like this."

"We must part like this or not part at all!"

She shook her head with sudden tightened decision. "I will *not*
come with you. Not now. I think my reasons are the right ones. God

forgive me for making you unhappy. Come back in six months or a year."

"I think," I said, "it would be better not to come back at all."

The weather was wild and wet all through August. According to my uncles, Cecil's spies all reported that no big Armada was assembling to attack England that year, so the Queen reluctantly re-granted permission for Drake and Hawkins to sail. But such permission was only given on the undertaking that they were back by next May.

Thus freed, they now found themselves land bound by rough seas and contrary winds, but at last on the nineteenth of August a brief lull enabled them to get away.

All Plymouth turned out, we were told, to see the great men off, church bells ringing, bands playing, flags fluttering in the breeze. We waited for a glimpse of them at Falmouth but they kept well clear. Harold Tregwin swore he had caught sight of their sails glinting in the sun set when he was casting out his lines off St Anthony Point.

That day my father came in from a brush with the law, two bailiffs having attempted to serve processes upon him while he was in Truro, and he having laid about him with his whip and only just regained his horse in time. One bailiff was thought to be hurt.

I said: "You should not go out without someone of your family who can issue orders and more easily take the blame. This news will travel far."

"I can't skulk behind my palisade all day long. If they come near me again they'll suffer worse."

He turned to kick one of the dogs, which was snoring.

"I have heard further from Sir George Fermor this week, and he has seen fit to postpone his daughter's marriage to John for a further six months. If as I suspect he means the time to run from the end of the first postponement, it will mean no wedding until May of next year!"

"I wish I could help."

"Short of selling the stones of the house and the timber of the jetties there's no way. I have some manors left, including Rosemerryn where my step-brother drinks his guts rotten, but each manor is pledged to the hilt. If I sold them I should do no more than discharge the debt on them and have the price of a few packs of cloth over. I hope Fermor will burn in hell for this!"

"Can you find no other match for John? There must be other rich men."

"Few who would give that sort of dowry. And we might get land or property which all takes time to raise money on. Gold in hand,

I'm altogether stronger placed. Not that I should throw it to my creditors like meat to hungry wolves, the way my father did with your
step-mother's dote. In three years he had cleared all his debts, £10,000
of them, and we'd nothing left except ample credit! I have no such
intent. This money shall be meted out, a bite here, a morsel there.
Let my creditors once see the colour of gold and they'll rest content with small commons. But I have to have some soon or we shall
all perish!"

"What of Thomas? He's now fifteen."

"I saw your uncles about it when I stayed with them in May. But
there's little prospect for a younger son. What has he to offer but a
famous name? It may well be different in a few years when, through
our connections at Court, he may have prospects of his own. But
you can't marry off a boy of that age with any profit unless he's the
eldest and will come into the estate."

"Still less," I said, "if he's a bastard with no prospects at all."

Mr Killigrew went to the old square looking glass and began tenderly to trim his moustache with a pair of needlework scissors. "Yes,
well, that's true, you're small value to me socially, but you stay at my
side. That's use of another sort."

"I would gladly try to make my own way in the world."

"You didn't enjoy your time with Chudleigh Michell. What other
employment is there?"

"Can I be found something with one of my uncles in Westminster
or London? You have given me your name. That should be of value:
I can work, I'm not without aptitude."

My father put down the scissors and dabbed some pomade on his
moustache. "There's something to be said for your idea, especially at
this time. I did my best to clear up the fuss about the Irish ship but
no one's satisfied and they're still threatening me with Ferdinando
Gorges. If he comes it would be of benefit if you were far away.
These Penryn prattlers can do much less harm if the object of their
prattle is not to be found."

"I'd like to go soon, sir."

He turned. "Why, what's pricking you? Have you been up to some
new prank?"

"No, sir, I assure you."

"God help you if you have, for I'll stand for no more."

I spent the afternoon duck shooting with Belemus beyond the swan
pool, and after we came home I lingered in one of the barns helping to bale the wool ready for the webster, and so hoping to avoid
Meg. I was the last to go in, and suddenly Dick Stable was in the
doorway waiting for me. I greeted him casually but he did not answer,

then abruptly he began to talk to me in such a stumbling voice that only a sentence here and there was audible.

Someone had dropped a word or else he had grown suspicious himself; this was the outcome; half-minatory, half-supplicant; Dick had scarcely ever quarrelled with anyone in his life, and he was vastly aware of the difference in our station. The break of laughter never absent from his voice when he spoke was still there, but it was the laughter of a child which is hurt; sometimes near tears and sometimes near rage. His voice and manner deferred while his words accused.

I was oppressed suddenly with a bitter rage in which the hopeless futility and wrongness of everything in the world choked me. I got up from among the bales, and Dick moved suddenly as if he thought he was to be hit.

"What old wife," I said, "has been pouring her evil thoughts in your ear? I thought you'd recovered from your cracked head."

He laughed nervously. "Nay, the story's abroad for all to hear as will. Maybe as always it carries last to 'im as it most consarns. If ye—"

I put my hand on his shoulder and spun him round. Again he half lifted his hands in defence. "Listen, dolt. You were sick, out of your senses for weeks, months. Meg was half crazed herself with worry. We thought you'd maybe sit whittling sticks on your stool for ten or fifteen years. Who was to know? We tried everything. I went to the Footmarker witch in Truro; Meg went to old Sarah Pound at Menehay and borrowed her moonstone; it was under your pallet for a week; are those the acts of a wife and friend behaving lewdly together while your mind is closed?"

"Aye, but—"

"Hear me out. I have seen much of Meg: I admit it. So I did before ever you married her. We used to kiss and be a thought familiar before I was fifteen. But that's different from what you are now vilely thinking. You don't realise what a splendid wife you have in Meg. You do *not*. I'm telling you. She was that worried for you, that rejoiced when you began to recover. While you were sick I saw much of her, I agree; we spent much time together as I have said, contriving how you might be aided back to health. Sometimes she would be deeply worried and in need of comfort. If I essayed to comfort her you need not entertain lewd thoughts on that account."

"I'm told you was seen creeping up to one of they attic rooms—"

"Listen again! I do not *creep* anywhere. If I go I go openly. Show me the man or woman who told you that!"

"Nay, I wouldn't listen t'every tale. But twas common thought—"

"All right, it was common thought. And common thought has erred. D'you understand me?"

He blinked and then stared into my eyes. "Aye, I understand, Master Maugan. I've no wish to offend ye. If so be I've mistook it all then I ask pardon. But Meg 'erself, Meg 'erself do appear different, changed. I think maybe she be no longer a-love with me."

Hating the world, I put my arm round his shoulders. "Listen once again, Dick, and this time most careful. I've known Meg longer even than you, and I tell you she cares for you deeply. But she is a romantic girl, none more so, and love to her is something serious and romantical, not to be laughed at or jested over. Beware of your laughter. Suppress it. Take her serious, be moved by love, be moved by her. She's a comely girl, Dick, young and full of spirit. I have not stolen her from you, but another may if you don't take care. Woo her. It's not so tedious a thing to do. Nor is it so hard. Don't imagine you are foolish to gentle and flatter her; think of the prize. Her love. Her surrender."

He nodded his head, taking in perhaps one word in three but taking, I prayed to God, the general meaning. We walked together, lover and cuckold, towards the house like old friends.

That night two ships anchored in Falmouth Haven. We knew they were English by their build and signs. My father said it was likely to be a part of the Drake and Hawkins fleet: they had no doubt suffered from the general adverse winds and been scattered, so were returning for shelter and rest. We watched them carefully through the night lest this should be a trick and they were roving Spaniards in disguise. Presently there came up one of those rare jewelled dawns which made the blue light on the river seem like some new and magic sky, and we were able to study in more detail the high poop of the larger vessel.

When a little pinnace brought its master ashore we found it was Ralegh back from his trip to El Dorado.

CHAPTER 9

HE was as thin as a board, his handsome velvet suit hanging on him, his skin burned Indian brown by tropical suns. But he was well and abounding with vigour. So were his crews, such as were left; they brought no sickness, only tales of wondrous things.

Many had died, most in combat, including John Grenville, the great Sir Richard's second son, Captain Calfield, the senior naval officer, and Captain Thynne, commander of another barque. It was thought that about eighty were left of the seven-score gentlemen volunteers, and crews over all had been reduced by a third. It was not possible to be certain, for this arrival in Falmouth constituted only half the force.

But their worst losses were six weeks behind them, they had had fair winds home and now were happy to be back. Sir Walter's first act on reaching Arwenack was to write to his wife and send it post telling her of his safety. He wanted to rest here with his crews for two days to recover, then he would ride overland to Sherborne and let the captains bring the barques to Portsmouth.

My father made him and his gentlemen welcome. As many of the crews as could lie under his roof were also welcome—the rest must stay aboard or be put up at the only other house near by, the Gwythers at Three Farthings House, at the mouth of Penryn Creek. (One never asked favours of Penryn town.)

My father was all agog for news of prizes they had taken—he clearly had thoughts of another *Madre de Dios* capture and himself being the first to benefit—but on this Ralegh was disappointing. They had taken no prizes, no prizes which would rank as such; they had gained no great naval victory; they had—on the way home—raided and destroyed three Spanish settlements—it was here that nearly all the casualties had come on them. But all this paled before the significance of their attempt—and near success—in finding El Dorado.

On the first night after supper in the big withdrawing chamber a select company listened in silence while he spoke about it. With him was a spectacled young man with close-cropped hair called Laurence Keymis in whom Sir Walter greatly confided, John Gilbert, Ralegh's nephew, and Ralegh's cousin, Butshead Gorges.

Having left England in February they had reached Trinidad in six weeks and in attacking Port of Spain had captured Don Antonio de Berrio, the governor of the island. Him they had treated like an honoured guest and from him they had received more news of Dorado, or the city of Manoa, which lay some four or five hundred miles up the river Orinoco. Leaving Berrio a captive on board and a garrison to guard his four ships, Ralegh had embarked with a hundred volunteers in five small boats, had crossed a sea as wide as the Straits of Dover with a great tempest blowing, and had attempted to find a way among the maze of great rushing rivers and small treacherous streams which made up the hundred square miles of the Orinoco Delta.

Making friends wherever they could of the Indians, who found this marvellous after the cruelty of the Spanish, they had worked their

way up stream. Often lost, sometimes stranded for hours and de-
spairing of refloating their boats, short of food and water, unable to
land at night because of the dense thickets and forced to sleep in the
boats in heavy dews with no shelter, rowing for days against violent
currents, menaced by serpents and crocodiles, by whom one of the
crew was eaten, they had reached the Caroni, a major tributary of the
Orinoco. There they had seen a wonder land of green grass, abounding
waterfalls, rich plains, vivid birds and fine fruits, and had met Indians
who promised gold and silver in the city of Manoa only another hundred miles up stream.

But by now the rains had begun, the great rivers were swollen. All
efforts to row against the current had failed even with eight oars
aside. Lashed with storms of rain ten times a day, in rags, already
adventuring for a month, and three hundred miles from the safety of
their ships, the men had begun once more to lose heart, and this time
Ralegh had yielded to them. At the village of Morequito he had made
a friend of the chief, Topiawari, who had told him that if he could
return next year with a larger force the Indians would join him in
driving out the Spaniards and would acknowledge Queen Ezrabeta as
their rightful ruler. Above the tributary river called Cumaca, hearing
of a gold mine in the interior, Ralegh had sent Laurence Keymis to
discover it, and although Keymis had not seen the mine, he had come
back with samples of its ore.

So, through storm and flood, landing on islands, seeking and finding
new friends among the local tribes, resting a day here and there to dry
off and get news of the Spaniards, who were in strength not far away,
they neared the mouth of the river again. There, in their tiny boats,
they were caught like twigs in a flood and swept the last one hundred
miles to the sea in a single day. In another violent storm they had
sailed the thirty miles back to regain their ships at Trinidad, carrying
with them treasures and souvenirs of all sorts, gifts from the Indians,
idols in gold, jacynths, loadstones, necklaces.

And so home.

If they had sailed direct they would have come short only of a few
men. But Sir Walter had obligations to those who had helped him
finance this expedition, the Cecils and the Howards and others, and
the venture had brought no big prize. Hence the costly raids on Cumana, Santa Martha, and Rio de la Hacha. From the way Sir Walter
looked when my father questioned him about them it seemed likely
that there was little profit to show for them after all of it. And John
Grenville lost; that troubled Sir Walter most of all.

Ralegh's plans now? To obtain an audience of the Queen and to gain
her support for the fitting out of a far larger expedition next spring.

Everything was in its favour, Sir Walter said. Here was the prime opportunity for setting the English flag in the most desirable part of South America, for counter-balancing Spain's power by settling Englishmen abroad in a country where they were bound to prosper. But, he said, he was already himself beggared with the financing of this one trip. He could not set up a second and larger expedition.

It must be an enterprise of state.

"One day I believe Guiana will become an English nation," he said, "equal to Virginia in beauty and in value. And it could be to England what Peru has been to Spain."

While he was here my father prevailed on Ralegh to try to stop the further inquisition which was being pressed in the matter of the robbery on the Irish ship. I do not know what was said between them but the next time Sir Walter saw me he looked at me with a new interest and a new frown.

All through the second day the interchange of news went on, for Sir Walter was as ignorant of events in England as we had been of his adventures. He questioned my father closely on the strength of the fleet with which Drake and Hawkins had sailed.

"*Garland* and *Foresight?* They served me well in '93 off the Azores. None better. *Defiance, Bonaventure, Hope?* They're good. And *Adventurer?* She's new, likely. That is all except for light craft?" He shook his head. "Its a handy force and with such leaders may achieve anything. But I have fears. Conditions have changed in the last six years while Francis has been kept on a leading chain. The Spanish have learned by their mistakes, and no objective comes easy now, as it would have done after the sea battle of '88. Their ships are better found and better led. Their towns in the West Indies are protected by massive forts—as we found to our great cost at Cumana. What is worse, they know of Drake's coming and are prepared. His old genius may lead him to some splendid victory; but I shall not rest easy on his behalf."

The two barques were to sail on the morning tide and at the same time Sir Walter was leaving overland. On his way he had the sad task of calling at Stowe and telling Lady Mary Grenville that her young son had fallen in battle.

After supper on the evening before he left he was walking with Laurence Keymis on the green sward that led down to the main jetty of Arwenack. It was a fine still evening, and the smoke from their pipes wavered little as it went upward. A dozen seagulls were stalking cautiously across the stonework beyond the lawn trying to reach some scraps of food but constantly put off by the pacing men who, as soon as they were nearly far enough away, turned and came back. Behind this scene was the wide mouth of the river which tonight was the colour of old silk, with the two barques riding silent at anchor on it, and the squat fort and gentle creek of St Mawes beyond.

I was desperate and there was no other time. I went up to the two men and said:

"Sir, may I speak with you?"

Sir Walter stopped in mid-sentence, plainly displeased. "That you are now doing."

"Sir, I am venturing to ask that, if you go to Guiana again next year, I may come with you."

"In what capacity?"

"Any that is available."

"Are you a sailor?"

"Only of small boats. But I could quickly learn."

"Why are you unsatisfied with your home?"

"It is not just that, sir. I'm seventeen and a base son. It's time I tried to make my own way."

"And you think to make your fortune with me?"

"I would hope to be of use, sir; that's the main thing."

"Can you shoot?"

"Yes, sir."

"Read and write?"

"Yes, sir."

"Cook and mend and wash your own clothes?"

"All of these a little."

"Have you ever been under fire?"

"No, sir. Except once only in the recent Spanish landing, and that was little."

"By the time I was your age I had already seen bitter fighting at Jarnac and at Moncontour."

"Had you, bi God," said Keymis. "I had not realised you was so young at that time, Walter."

"I wish I was so young again and purged of the accretions of the world. . . . Why d'you suppose, Killigrew, that I am in need of fellows such as you?"

"I do not suppose it, sir, but I hope it."

"Which with most of us is the same thing. Listen. There's two kinds of men who hunger for adventure overseas. One goes for what he can get, what he can steal, what he can destroy. Are you such a one?"

"I do not think so."

"Even though there's a suspicion you put unwanted fingers into the hold of this Irish boat and pulled out the best of the cargo? What's the truth of that?"

"I think it has all been greatly exaggerated, sir."

Sir Walter put the end of his long pipe in his mouth and drew on it. "You have the Killigrew tongue, I see. The other type of adventurer is he who goes as friend and settler to make a home and marry and raise a family and till the soil and draw richness not by rapine and the sword but from the fruits of the land he farms. Are you such a one?"

"I think so. I hope so."

"The second time you have used the word hope, which is one I distrust, for it lacks a sense of individual purpose. If I go out next year I shall choose two hundred volunteers as I did in Virginia and apportion a piece of land—perhaps five hundred acres—to each. For that it will be necessary for each to share towards the cost of the voyage. Have you money for that?"

I looked out across the bay. "No, sir."

"Not even from the proceeds of your robbery?"

"I do not admit to robbery, sir, and I have no money from that or any other source." I knew now he was jibing at me.

"Ah, well, then your chances of becoming a settler are small. As to being a sailor, I need trained men."

The gulls were taking advantage of our stillness.

Keymis said: "The boy can write. Maybe we could make some use of him as a clerk."

"He does not look the clerkly type. More the pirate I would say. All Killigrews are pirates or poets at heart, and this generation has run to the former. I'll think of your request, boy. Next year when I am recruiting men remind me of it."

"Thank you, sir." I turned away, repelled by his sour and arrogant tone. There was little hope of anything now. Next year when Sir Walter was recruiting men he would be at Chatham or at Portsmouth.

I stood out after they had gone in, long after the light left and the glinting silks of the river estuaries had faded and become threadbare. I felt lost and alone, without future and without hope. Two days ago I had had another quarrel with Meg in which she had accused me of caring nothing for her any more. I had told her of my talk with Dick and used this as an excuse; but whereas a few months ago such a revelation of Dick's suspicions would have horrified her, now she was willing to take the risk almost casually, almost coldly.

Whatever I did I could not get Sue out of my mind and so was no company for anyone. Perhaps Belemus guessed something of this, for yesterday he had drawn my attention to a book of poems Ralegh had brought and pointed out a verse which ran:

To love and to be wise,
To rage with good advice;
Now thus, now then, so goes the game,
Uncertain is the dice.
There is no man, I say, that can
Both love and to be wise.

But wisdom was not what I sought, only release from the pain. . . .

I wandered into the house. As darkness did not come until well on in the evening only a solitary candle was lighted in the great hall. Distantly one could hear laughter and talk in the kitchens. There was a light under the withdrawing chamber door and another under that of Mr Killigrew's private study, but I sat on the stool by the great empty fireplace of the hall feeding a half dozen mixed dogs which had followed me in.

Presently the door of my father's study opened and Sir Walter and Laurence Keymis came out, talking together. They did not see me as they passed but went upstairs to bed. Keymis carried a candle, Ralegh, a book and a pen and a horn of ink.

I went into the kitchens. Most of the servants would normally have been abed, but instead a round dozen of them were laughing and joking and drinking ale with an equal number of Ralegh's sailors. A brief silence fell when I came in, so I walked on not wishing to dampen their fun. In the closet off the hall Kate Penruddock was dusting the shelves with wormwood. Here spare bedding was kept, and when it was taken out for Ralegh and his officers it had been found to be infested with fleas. Not, as Kate said, that anyone minded a few, but it would ill-flatter the house if great men were unduly bitten during their stay.

I found myself back in the hall and suddenly confronted with Thomas Rosewarne.

"Ah, I was looking for you, Mr Maugan. Your father wants you in his chamber."

I went along and tapped at the door, speculating whether some minor misdeed had come home to roost. There seemed none. Since parting from Sue I had not even had the incentive to break out.

My father said: "I have news for you, boy. Ralegh wishes you to ride with him tomorrow. He has offered you a post as a secretary in his household."

Book Four

CHAPTER 1

LIFE sometimes is like the phases of the moon: one dwells in deep shadow without expectation of change, rootless and motiveless; then in the term of a day the shadow has gone and one is startled and quickened by the unsheltered rays of a new sun.

The environment into which Walter Ralegh took me, besides offering me a partial escape from the cold and barren futility of my passion for Sue, was as foreign to life at Arwenack as the de Prada house in Madrid. At Arwenack there was a constant coming and going of important folk, and a thin layer of culture was laid over the bare exigencies of life like a linen cloth on a dining board. But it went no deeper and it had little or no substance. At Sherborne the demands of material forces were no less present and no less urgent, but here culture existed as a separate and independent unit, and intellect for the first time came into its own. Doors of the mind were opened looking upon new and exciting country as vivid and as unexplored as anything in Guiana or the colony of Virginia.

Here were books treating of every subject from astrology to campaigns of war, from botany to Greek history, from chemistry and experiments in alchemy to poetry and philosophical speculation.

Nor were they ranged along the walls of a single room; they proliferated about the house, left open on tables and settles, dropped where they had been temporarily abandoned and where they would be most convenient picked up. Globes and maps abounded and musical instruments and paintings and busts, and old parchments and vivid tapestries, and boxes and tables made of strange spice-smelling wood.

The Raleghs' house was just new built, and they had barely moved in. Unlike the low design of Arwenack, this stretched out tall into the

sky, supported by slender turrets at the four corners. No floor was of
great expanse, but their being five gave much more space over all than
at first seemed.

The kitchens were in the basement. Above them a splendid blue
dining chamber looked through tall stone-mullioned windows across
the formal walled gardens to the stables. Two of the turrets were
incorporated in this room like ears, the others being utilised for the
staircases. Here also was a narrow but handsome hall and two smaller
rooms.

On the next floor was the green withdrawing chamber with the
Ralegh coat of arms—the shield with the five lozenges—on the ceiling
and over the wide fireplace. Behind was Ralegh's study and a ladies'
withdrawing room with closet and close stool. Above this again was
the Raleghs' bedroom, but here the turrets were separate rooms, and
behind on this floor were two guest chambers, one now given over to
little Wat and his nurse. On the fourth floor were the principal guest
chambers, while above that was a warren in which slept and lived the
indoor servants.

The accommodation was none too ample, for there were always
extra people staying in the house, not relatives like Arwenack or
casual callers, but men visiting and staying with Sir Walter to discuss
some project, mathematical, theological, parliamentary, or colonial.
They would sit long into the night, their talk ranging far beyond the
confines of the subject they had come to discuss. Perhaps a dozen
such men visited regularly and these I came to know well; a few would
stay for weeks at a time, a part of the household and of its intellectual
life. Such intimates were George Chapman, a poet; Thomas Hariot, an
astronomer; Matthew Royden, a free-thinker; the Earl of Northumberland, an alchemist; Dr Dee, the Queen's astrologer; and of course
Laurence Keymis, who was an Oxford fellow and a mathematician and
was closest to Ralegh of all these men.

Lady Ralegh was a tall fair-haired, blue-eyed woman of about 30,
with a slender neck and a subtle smile. Although many more beautiful
women came to the house I never saw Sir Walter look at any one of
them with that interest which betrays a straying fancy. Lady Ralegh
was the ideal hostess for him, taking all incursions upon her hospitality
with determined calm. Sometimes she would sit through a stormy
intellectual argument, her head slightly lowered, taking no part yet by
her presence keeping the argument from becoming an outright quarrel; sometimes she would rise and go to her household duties or to
care for baby Wat, and the talk would be less sparkling for her
absence.

Yet she never contributed to it, and indeed I believe the talk most times went too deep for her. Sir Walter also most times went too deep for her. She could not follow the great imaginative flights of his mind. Her subtlety was comparative shallow but her judgment was more sure, and watching her, one could see the way her wits detected the working difficulties of what he proposed. When she did criticise a plan or a notion of his, he paid her too little regard.

They both doted on their son who was now near two years of age and a vigorous happy boy. Indeed their life, one would have thought, was idyllic. Their love for each other was manifest. Their magnificent four hundred and fifty acre estate set with fine trees and full of wild life was large enough to occupy any country man's love of land. Ralegh bred horses and sometimes reared them, his falcons were the best in Dorset, he planted trees and shrubs and supervised with all his rare energy the cultivation and the improvement of his land. And he kept a new kind of open court to which came not the aristocracy and the powdered gallants of Westminster but the cream of England's art and thought.

An idyll, but there was a worm in the bud. Sir Walter was still excluded from the Queen, his office of Captain of her Guard was in abeyance; he had no power in the land. And Sir Walter, I soon saw, joined with his splendid intellect and towering imagination a festering ambition to be back in the Queen's favour.

Adding new poison to the first months of my stay with him was the reception given to his adventures in Guiana. The Queen was not impressed and still would not see him. Cecil was cold and unwelcoming, asking what profit Sir Walter had to show for the money invested. Howard, as became a sailor, was more downright about it, saying Ralegh was a fool to have pursued legendary gold mines when there was gold on the high seas already mined and waiting to be seized by a bold man.

But worse was to come. A rumour spread—no one knew whence it came but Keymis was of the opinion that it had originated with the Bacons—that Sir Walter, a man of action in his youth but a courtier tied to the Queen for far too long, had thought better of personally undertaking such an expedition with all its hardships and hazards and at the last had not accompanied it at all but had spent the summer with his relatives the Killigrews in Cornwall and had rejoined the ships at Falmouth when they returned.

I remember the evening when Sir Walter came back from Westminister and first told this story to his wife and Carew Ralegh and Laurence Keymis and Arthur Throgmorton, Lady Ralegh's brother. Sir Walter was a man of considerable temper; but under strain he went white, his skin more sallow, that was all. However neither Keymis nor Throgmorton—a great supporter of his brother-in-law—were so concerned with restraint. Their anger overflowed like lava from the lip of a volcano. Carew Ralegh, Sir Walter's elder brother, was quieter in his manner and more sophisticated.

"It is at best a foolish story," he said, "for it can so easy be denied. Slander is most dangerous when it's hard disproved. We have a hundred men who can swear where Walter spent his summer."

"My hundred men are in Portsmouth and Weymouth and dissipated over the west country. Where this calumny will do harm is at Westminster and Greenwich. Those of influence in those places who can answer for me are relatives and friends whose word may be suspect."

"I'm surprised that Robert Cecil does not speak for you," Lady Ralegh said. "I wrote him so soon as I heard you was home. And none could be closer to the Queen."

"Oh, Cecil," said Arthur Throgmorton, contemptuously, "you rest too much on his goodwill. His only concern is for himself, and his friends can go hang."

"You're wrong, Arthur," Ralegh said sharply. "Robert Cecil is our friend and always will be. But his position is delicate, with the Queen still favouring Essex. In any event he could only recommend my case to Her Majesty, he can *prove* nothing of my whereabouts since he only has my word for 'em."

"And your word is not enough!" said Keymis explosively. "That's what I find hard to stomach. They even choose to cast doubts upon the whole voyage by saying we picked up Topiawari's son on the Barbary coast. One is truly staggered to observe the lengths malice will go to!"

"You have kept notes and diaries, Walter," Lady Ralegh said. "Why do you not send them to the Queen or to Cecil asking that they be examined and pronounced on? It's impossible to fabricate such pages, thumbed and stained with the marks of travel."

Ralegh tapped out his unlit pipe. "By the living God, Bess, I think it is an idea! But I would improve on it: the story would be better writ up and published, not as diaries but as a sober account of all we saw and did. If they pretend to believe I could conjure out of my imagination all the wonders of that voyage, then they'll defeat their own object by making fools of themselves!"

"Even then it will not succeed unless it reaches the Queen," murmured his brother. "There will be jealous hands ever ready to snatch it away."

"She cannot fail to read it!" Sir Walter said, getting up sharply and moving about the tall green candle-lit room on his long legs. Again his height seemed greater than it was, and the flames scrawled calculating shadows over his face. "The problem is not how to get it to her but how *quickly* it may be got to her. If I'm to prepare for a full expedition next spring, things must be set in train before the turn of the year."

"I'll help you, Walter," said Keymis. "There must be a good map drawn and all scientific data. Is John Shelbury free?"

"No, he's in Islington on business for me and will not be back for two weeks. If—"

"Can this boy write?"

Sir Walter looked coldly at me. "That's what he was brought for."

"And is it readable what he writes?"

"You've read it in letters already without hardship."

"Try me," I said.

"That we will." Sir Walter in his pacing passed by his wife and laid a loving hand on her shoulder. "And tonight."

"Tonight?" said Lady Ralegh. "But no! You've rid all day. Supper is waiting."

"I'll sup lightly with a glass of canary in my chamber. So'll Laurence. So'll this lad. There's no time to waste."

I did not normally sleep in the house, but in the small Norman castle on the other side of the stream where Walter Ralegh had first lived when the estate was granted him four years ago and where he now housed the outdoor servants and any servants visitors might bring. But for the several weeks during which the account of the voyage was being written I slept on a couch in an ante-room off Sir Walter's study, and I saw that couch too seldom.

At ordinary times Sir Walter retired to sleep at midnight and rose at 5 a.m., from then on driving through the day with immense and consuming energy. But this was not an ordinary time, and while he was writing the account of his experiences in Guiana his endurance was limitless and he expected ours to match. I recollect chiefly hours with aching limbs and pricking eyes, sitting copying or making notes or sharpening his pen or standing at his elbow for new instructions.

Although it was all done in a fever of inspiration most pages were written twice and many more often. I remember one lovely day in late October we had worked from six until twelve, and then broke for dinner and a rest. There were a few personal belongings I had left in the castle, so I hurried over in the hot afternoon to fetch them.

The narrow valley between the two houses was threaded by a trout stream, and at the higher end amid a copse of trees Sir Walter had had the stream dammed and a pool created where the Ralegh family and their guests—and sometimes the servants at stated

hours—swam in the summer. At the lower end the stream was spanned
by an old stone bridge which also carried the London road on the
other side of the wall bordering the estate. Here was a big raised stone
seat sheltered by an ancient durmast oak, where Ralegh sometimes sat,
and he was already there this afternoon and beckoned me. I saw that
he had an inkhorn and some sheets of paper with him.

"It's a good point of vantage, this," he said when I climbed up.
"Here I can watch the stream and the bubbles of the trout. Or I
can see the keep and think of England's past, or turn to view my
house which I trust will play a part in England's future. As for the
present," he looked over the wall, "it passes by from time to time on
horseback or in coach and four, and if I mind to I can greet it as it
goes! That's all helpful to thought and meditation."

"You have written some more, sir?" I asked, looking at the pages he
held.

"I have redone a page or two. The break of dinner gives one a new
sight."

"The break of dinner always sends my father to sleep."

"That's a hazard of nature that comes on in later life. . . . Not,
I imagine, that your father is so much older than I. Here, see what
you make of this."

I squatted on the wall and read the page he handed me. It was a
description of a day when they had almost reached the limits of their
endurance.

When we reached the tops of the first hills of the plains adjoining
the river we beheld that wonderful breach of waters which ran down
Caroni: and might from that mountain see the river, how it ran in
three parts about twenty miles off, and there appeared some ten or
twelve waterfalls in sight, every one as high over the other as a church
tower, which fell with such fury that the rebound of water made it
seem as if it had been all covered over with a great shower of rain:
and in some places we took it at the first for a smoke that had arisen
over some great town. For my own part I was well persuaded from
thence to have returned, being a very ill footman, but the rest were
all so desirous to go near the strange thunder of water, that they drew
me on by little and little until we came into the next valley where we
might discern the same. I never saw a more beautiful country nor
more lively prospects, hills so raised here and there over the valleys,
the river winding into divers branches, the plains adjoining without
bush or stubble, all fair green grass, the ground of hard sand easy to
march on either for horse or foot, the deer crossing every path, the
birds towards the evening singing on every tree with a thousand
several tunes; cranes and herons of white, crimson and carnation

perching on the river's side, the air fresh with a gentle easterly wind, and every stone that we stopped to take up promising by its complexion either silver or gold.

For a moment the sonorous prose carried me with the scene he described.

"Copy that, will you."

"Yes, sir."

He must have caught some hesitation for he said sharply: "You have some suggestion?"

"Oh, no, sir. . . . Except perhaps . . . if I may venture it, wasn't the last line as you wrote it before superior to this one."

"What? Read it to me."

"Before, sir, you ended: 'and every stone that we stepped on girt with grasses and strange flowers.' Is that not more in keeping with the whole than: 'and every stone that we stopped to take up promising by its complexion either silver or gold'?"

"You have not lived as long as I."

"No, sir. Shall I write this now?"

"In a moment. Sit where you are."

I sat and waited.

"It's possible, Killigrew, that the interests of style would best be served by the gentle cadences of the first ending. But you must educate yourself to discover that other aims must sometimes be served. This is not merely a journal recording the quest for empire. It is a broadsheet of persuasion, and so one weighs in the balance the virtues of rare flowers against promise of profit, the values of a ringing sentence against the musical clinking sound of coin, and in such case the former gives way." He took the sheet from me and read it through again. "No, I think there is little wrong with the new ending. It has style of another sort. It lifts the end instead of letting it fall. I don't fault it on any count."

"Very good, sir."

"One thing that's not very good, Killigrew, is your obstinacy in not conceding a point when it is won. It's a grave mistake in a secretary."

"Yes, sir."

"Even if you maintain your own opinion against the opinion of your betters, maintain it so in secrecy, not by an expression on your face like a flag nailed to the mast as the ship sinks."

"I'm sorry, sir."

"Did your father find you a handful?"

"I don't think so."

"He told me he did. And now and then even here I have noticed

that the rebel stirs. We have no ships to board here, boy. Have
you found yourself a wench?"

"No, sir."

"Did you have one in Cornwall?"

I hesitated, and wondered if he had been told something. "I had
one but I lost her, sir."

"By death?"

"By marriage to another man."

Sir Walter turned to gaze over the wall into the road, but it was
only a wagon passing drawn by two oxen, with an old man drooping between wisps of white hair leaning forward in his seat, whip
held cross-wise like a bow.

"It is never too young to be a rebel, but it is bad to feel too much
about women too soon. At seventeen they should be a pleasant jest
or a means of advancement."

"As you said, sir, I am not educated."

He glanced at me, his eyes assessing. "Your acceptance of that
fact, boy, would carry a greater conviction if you admitted it with
a show of humility. The way you speak suggests that you think your
ignorance is a better condition than my wisdom."

I did not know what to say so said nothing.

"Not that I have paused always," he said, "to give myself the best
advice. Or I should not be here, reduced to pen and paper to explain
myself at tedious length when a single audience would do."

I picked up the sheet he had dropped.

"This journal, Maugan, is in effect a letter to the Queen, who still
holds me in disfavour for my marriage. She was my great love and
remains so—on a queenly level. Knowing her with some closeness
through the years I have come not only to an esteem of her brilliant qualities but to an understanding of her susceptibilities. And
I have met few women with a greater susceptibility to the colour
of gold. Now get off with those sheets and make a good copy. I have
no liking for arrogant secretaries."

When the manuscript was finished he took it to London to find a
printer, who must, he said, set it out before the New Year. He was
much up and down to Durham House in those months with Keymis
and Carew Ralegh; but I was usually left behind. Only once did I
go with him and stayed three days. I saw then what state he still
kept in London.

On the second day I had time off and went with an apprentice
staying in the house to a performance at the Blackfriar's Theatre.
There I saw a Greek play performed in English. It was called

Oedipus and was about a young man who had incestuous relations with his mother and murdered his father, not knowing until too late who they were. This made a profound impression on me. Partly perhaps it was because it was the first play I had ever seen, but mainly the subject of the play bit deep into my mind. It was as if the story laid bare knowledge I had never reached to before but which I had always had.

All that winter Elizabeth Ralegh stayed at Sherborne with her son, so I attended on her often. Sir Walter was a deeply complex character, difficult, volatile, unpredictable, of sudden tremendous energies and equal depressions; his wife had a resolved calmness which cushioned these explosive forces. It was only when he was away that one discovered how much the effort cost her; she would herself be irritable and exhausted and at a low ebb—though she never ceased to count the days till his return.

Before I left Cornwall Mrs Killigrew had been much concerned for my spiritual safety at being put in Ralegh's charge. Sir Walter, she said, had more than once come near to being brought to trial for atheism; not long ago a commission had sat to determine what evidence there was to proceed; it was acknowledged that he had been a close and loving friend of that noted rake and blasphemer, Kit Marlowe, and there were rumours of much evil in his home; that a friend of his had been seen to tear out leaves of the Bible to dry tobacco on, that God was as often cursed as praised in his presence. I wondered if Mrs Killigrew would still think my soul in peril if she had seen me walking with Lady Ralegh on the green terrace below the house of a winter's afternoon, or playing ball with Wat in one of the pleached alleys, or trying to help Lady Ralegh with her spelling when she wrote an important letter, or fishing for trout with Hardwicke, a cousin of theirs, or listening to George Chapman putting forward his profound Christian convictions at the supper table.

What did obtain in this house, as distinct from any other I ever knew, was that *no* dogma was accepted without a fair examination of its merits. Royden, the free-thinker, or Hariot, the mathematician, were as free to express their views and just as subject to examination and criticism on them. No opinions was sacrosanct.

After Sir Walter in importance in the house and greater in intellectual stature was this Thomas Hariot. Of Lancashire blood but Oxford birth, he had first been Sir Walter's mathematical tutor, though himself by eight years the younger; then later he had been steward for the new Sherborne estate. Now, though no longer living permanently in the house, he was still Ralegh's personal accountant and adviser. Few knew the limits of his genius. The scandalous Marlowe had once asserted that "Moses was but a juggler and Hariot can do more than he," and there were others who thought him little less capable.

It was round him, I thought, rather than round Sir Walter that it seemed likely that accusations of blasphemy might centre, for in talk one night I heard him cast away the whole of the Old Testament and throw grave doubts on the divine inspiration of the New. Nor, he said, did he believe in the story of the creation of the world nor in any of the miracles. Natural laws, he said, could not be disrupted by spiritual forces—nor, if there *was* a God, would it be in the divine interest so to disrupt them.

Recently he had accepted the patronage of the Earl of Northumberland, and now divided his time between Sherborne and Isleworth where he was building himself a telescope on the principles laid down by Roger Bacon three hundred years ago. When it was finished he hoped this telescope would magnify the sun and the moon and the stars by fifty times. He was an enthusiastic believer in the atheistic theory that the earth revolved round the sun, and he often strove— vainly I am glad to say—to convince Sir Walter of this.

According to Keymis who was himself a mathematician, Hariot was turning topsy-turvy the whole science of algebra. Keymis tried to explain to me something of his new methods. Equations had long existed but for the most part were cumbersome and unusable; Hariot, again by some magic which I could not follow, brought all the symbols over to one side and equated them to zero. While I could not see quite how it was done I could just perceive the gateway that this opened and the vast empires of unexplored thought which lay beyond.

Hariot, though so brilliant, suffered from ill-health and lassitude. Keymis said he was a fool not to publish more of his speculations and conclusions—otherwise lesser men or later men would seize upon his ideas and take the credit—but Hariot would not bestir himself. Ideas were of the brain and needed only intellectual energy— of which he had a plenitude. Promulgating those ideas in written form needed application at the desk and physical effort.

No less than Hariot, Sir Walter too was prone to ill-health and lassitude. Running along with his great energy, his intense application to whatever he had in view, his enthusiasm for the new idea or the splendid conception, was a narrow streak of hypochondria. He would of a sudden and without good reason become utterly depressed about his prospects of success and about his health. Once in a month or so he would be taken with pains in his abdomen or with serious digestive disorder or with gout in his back which would prostrate him and, when it was gone, leave him in complete melancholia for a day or so. Not even his wife or son could shift him out of it before it was due time. He would never be seen by an apothecary but would dose himself with infusions of bark or herbs brought back from his travels.

Even when in good health he was fond of experimenting on himself with dosages and brews; sometimes out of scientific interest, sometimes I believe out of a morbid curiosity in his own body's strength and weakness. All around him who were unable to refuse were dosed from time to time, I among them; and I believe it was his sudden discovery that I knew something of the uses of herbs that weakened the barrier which my youth and his great position put between us.

The samples of strange medicines and infusions he had brought back from the Indies filled half a room, and where Katherine Footmarker would have been satisfied to make from them a salve to cure a burn, he would delight in heating the ingredients in a crucible to see if they would explode. Many times he burst tubes and bottles and the mixtures ran to waste on the floor. Sometimes he would laugh like a mischievous boy at the result.

It was strange to see him so, because most times the shadows sat upon his face as if they marked it for their own.

After he came back from Cornwall he was much busied writing a forceful report of the deficiencies of the defences of the west country. He also wrote constantly on war matters to the Privy Council, bombarding them with ideas and suggestions and warnings. His policy was always that offence was the best defence, and he argued that if an attack on England were to be warded off, a resumption of active war was the best way to avert it. He even offered to send a pinnace at his own expense to discover so far as it could the present state of Spanish preparations. For the most part it seemed that the Privy Council paid no heed to his advice.

I remember one night at the turn of the year he was absent unexpectedly and Lady Ralegh was worried for him. He returned in early morning, and told that all yesterday he and the Lord Lieutenant of Dorset with a group of servants had been hunting a Jesuit priest. In the night they had caught him and now he was where he could do no more harm.

One knew and averted one's thoughts from the later processes of the law; but Sir Walter was restless all day and the following night was absent again. When he returned it seemed that he had obtained permission to see the priest in his cell and so, having spent one night hunting him, he now had spent all the next arguing with him on religion—and listening too.

I heard him say to Keymis: "Such men have to be *stepped* on, *stamped* out—they would betray England, assassinate the Queen—but I found his beliefs vastly interesting. This is the other end of the scale from the Brownists whom I spoke for in Parliament recently. . . . Whence *comes* the certitude, the morbid *infallibility* of such men, each convinced of a passionate dogma that allows no compromise, each believing in the same God but ready to perpetrate all injury upon the other for a set of interpretations! It confounds me. I believe intolerance to be one of the cardinal sins!"

Hariot was at the table but he did not speak then, a quiet plump man with a bland pasty face and eyes screwed up as if unaccustomed to the light; but that night a great debate developed, first at the supper table and then later in the green drawing chamber.

It began on the nature of the soul and ranged over all the quarters of the mind, passing this way and that with the quickness of a ball between tennis players. Ralegh asserted that there were three divisions of the soul, which consisted of the animal, the reasonable, and the spiritual. The souls of beasts rose only to reason and consciousness through the perception of what was before their eyes; man achieved a closer kinship with God by perceiving, though dimly, the reality beyond the material world. Christ, he said, was of the same substance as God, as far spiritualised beyond man as man was beyond the animals. Through Christ only could man begin to apprehend the wisdom and the purpose of God, for God by His nature was pure and eternal and therefore never to be wholly discovered.

"How do we know what we may or may not discover, Walter?" Hariot said suddenly in his soft cushiony voice. "Where are the limits of human reason set except by the human himself? Except by his sense of unworthiness, except by prohibition of the church or state, except by his own *lack* of reason. We are yet at the birth of knowledge. If there is a God, then, as sceptics, we are all agreed that He is Transcendent, above the universe, beyond human experience. But He may well not be beyond knowledge."

"I don't deny the value of what knowledge we may get Tom," said Sir Walter. "But I don't fret myself at its limitations. I don't believe we can ever measure the infinite, plumb the bottomless, adapt our conception of the nature of time to the beginning or end of the universe. We are joined to the earth, compounded of the earth, and we live on it. The heavens are high and far off. Eternal grace can only come by revelation."

"But how do you define eternal grace, Walter?" asked the Earl of Northumberland, a thin, younger man with sharp brown eyes like a thrush. "I'm with Tom on this, though we seldom see eye to eye on philosophical matters. Where does human aspiration end and divine grace begin? If by observing Tycho's great star we may foretell the second coming of Christ, are we not reaching to a knowledge beyond the normal limits of our powers? If by studying the aqueous sign of Pisces we may calculate and predict the excessive rain which has fallen on this land in the last three years, are these not—"

"Yes," said Sir Walter, "we're reaching to a knowledge beyond the normal limits of our powers, and often failing, as we shall always fail. There has been no second coming of Christ—yet. When He comes I do not think we shall have to study the heavens to be forewarned. God is above nature. We may accept His existence or deny it, but we shall not get nearer Him by an excessive marshalling of fact or an excessive exercise of reason."

Thomas Hariot filled his pipe. "We are all groping, friends; Henry here most of all. To him the horoscope and the telescope are equal servants of philosophy and as worthy of trust. It's a common view. Even Johann Kepler appears to hold it, alas for him. I do not hold it. Until a firmer line is taken we shall make no sure progress. Once the division has been made I believe there is no limit to what we may know and what we may do. The capacity of men to reason differs as much as their sensibility to material things. But because knowledge may be stored, each pioneer may leave his discoveries behind him like a ladder leading to the next loft, waiting for another to climb. In the world of science there should be no need of prediction—which is a form of guesswork—only of speculation which can be susceptible of proof. That is true science, and it is the true destiny of man."

"I think," said Sir Walter, "there cannot be a true destiny of man which rests on intellectual pride."

"Ah, but it is not *personal* pride. As men we are insignificant, temporary—we carry, a few of us only, the bricks of knowledge one or two rungs higher. If there is pride, then it is pride of species, that in this great universe where God seems increasingly remote we ask nothing of ourselves but to be worthy of our reason and worthy of our place. Mortality, that is certain; immortality, that is the gift of God."

Towards the end of the year Lord Northumberland married Lady Perrot, the widow of Sir Thomas Perrot. Lady Perrot had in her maidenhood been Lady Dorothy Devereux and was the sister of the Earl of Essex. As soon as they were married Northumberland brought her to the house and reconciled her with Sir Walter.

Fifteen years ago, I was told, before either of them was married, Sir Walter had had a quarrel with Sir Thomas Perrot which had

resulted in a duel and in their both spending six weeks in the Fleet
as a punishment. But the swordplay had not let the bad blood, and
there had never been any reconciliation. When Lady Dorothy married
Sir Thomas she had done so without the permission of the Queen, so
had been banished from Court. She had taken up her husband's
attitude towards Ralegh; so a year or so later when she had come
secretly into the Queen's presence at Lady Warwick's hoping for forgiveness, Ralegh had drawn Her Majesty's attention to her and she
had again been summarily banished. This had led to the first great
quarrel between Sir Walter and Lord Essex, when Essex had
violently denounced Ralegh to the Queen while Ralegh was within
earshot.

Sir Walter, though quick to take offence and quicker to give it,
was never one to remember a grievance beyond the next sunset;
and the new Countess of Northumberland seemed ready enough to be
his friend. However, what Henry Percy was really angling for was
bigger fish. He wanted a reconciliation between Ralegh and his new
brother-in-law. Changing in all speed, as the rest of this strange circle seemed able to do, from philosophy and necromancy to hard
politics, he argued that there was now nothing but old memories
dividing the two great men. Essex, I heard—or rather overheard—
him say, had suffered several recent defeats at the hands of Robert
Cecil; his standing with the Queen was not so secure as it had
been a year ago; and above all he was for a forward policy against
Spain—as Ralegh was. Cecil wanted negotiation and peace. On his
own Cecil was stronger than either of them. United they could outweigh him. Also Sir Walter wanted more than anything a return of
the Queen's favour. If his forthcoming book should fail to gain it
Essex's friendship might turn the scale.

"The only obstacle," said Northumberland, fingering the goblet he
held, "is in the essential similarity between you and Robert—little
as you may think so, Walter. Y'are both proud, both quick of temper,
impatient of others less able than yourselves. You've both got the
energies of three men. And you're both warm-hearted under your
arrogance. Once come together and you may likely become the closest
of friends."

Sir Walter said: "Well, for my part I wish him no ill. He's a man
who has matured and sobered greatly since the days of our quarrels.
I would happily talk with him at some friend's house. But I find
it hard to suggest such a meeting since I stand to gain so much more
than he."

"Let's not be too sure of that," said Northumberland. "At any event
I think this is the time to make the approach. And I can do it direct,

without the knowledge of Anthony Bacon or any of his cronies. He's
a truly generous man, Wat; but he is surrounded by mean advisers."
"I could wish for nothing better," said Lady Ralegh, looking at her
husband. "Lord Essex was my friend before we married, and he
stood by me in trouble when some others did not. But there is one
thing I do not like, which is that this reconciliation would seem to
be aimed at Robert Cecil, who is also our friend. I would not wish him
to feel we were changing sides against him. There is a matter of loyalty
to be considered."
"Oh, loyalty from Cecil!" said Carew Ralegh.
Sir Walter was at his walking again. "I don't think it need be
aimed to anyone, Bess. Anyway, Henry's is a pretty notion and we
must not reject it. As for his wife, having realised my great error in
so short a time, I cannot believe that any brother of hers could but
be worthy of the highest esteem. I'll meet him wherever or whenever
you say."
"As soon as it can be done," said Lady Northumberland. To Lady
Ralegh she said: "We have come a long way. Let us go on in friendship. I think my brother will want it too."

They met for a parley in London, though I do not know where,
just at the turn of the year. Sir Walter's book on Guiana had been
delayed at the printers but a proof copy of it was put in Essex's hands
and he declared himself greatly impressed. The meeting went well,
for Sir Walter came home to Sherborne alive with enthusiasm for the
future. He was certain now that friendship with Essex would not
shake his accord with Cecil. Why, he asked, should they not all three
be on good terms? They had nothing to lose except enmity and out-
worn divisions. At that I heard Carew Ralegh mutter: "Get Essex
and Cecil to lie in the same bed? Get a peacock to lie with a snake."
Essex, said Ralegh, had told him he had some great project on
hand for the coming summer—together with Howard, the Lord
Admiral, which gave some clue as to its nature—but he was not permitted to divulge more. Ralegh, if not too deeply engaged in Guiana,
might be invited to play some major role. This was the greatest of
temptations, for it appeared to be putting into effect the very urgings
that Sir Walter had been sending in to the Privy Council all winter.
And glory close at hand always weighed heavier with the Queen
than glory at a remove of four thousand miles. In the meantime Sir
Walter had invited Essex to visit him at Sherborne; by then the book
would be out and its effects known. All the same he flung himself
with his usual feverish impatience into immediate preparations for a
new visit to Guiana. Even if only on a reduced scale, smaller much

than last summer, it must be undertaken to fulfil his promise to the natives and keep their interest in England alive.

From my knowledge of what went on it will have been guessed that I was treated all through the winter more like a member of the family than a servant, far more like a cousin than a secretary. I shared their board and was as often as not at their private talk. This was done so naturally, almost, one thought, in absence of mind, that I was quite won over.

Sir Walter was a man with high standards for his helpers and a biting tongue when they fell short, and it took time to get to know him. But he had disarming qualities which would take the sting out of his arrogance. For a man capable, as I saw sometimes, of dubious stratagems of business and the most tortuous approaches to statecraft, he yet had a profound candour among his friends, and a frankness and a capacity for trust that I have not seen bettered.

I looked at no girl while at Sherborne, though one or two looked at me, but I made a friend of Victor Hardwicke, a kinsman of Lady Ralegh who acted as an assistant steward on the estate. When Sir Walter was away we would borrow two of his nags and go riding together; he was twenty-four and a great change from the raffish Belemus, being a serious young man with an infection of the lungs, who coughed much and played the lute and wrote poetry and was in love with a married woman at Cerne Abbas, the young wife of the hosier who sold Sir Walter his gloves and his jerkins.

He told me that Sir Walter, in spite of his great incoming from the wine and broadcloth business, was in debt from his expeditions to Guiana to the amount of thirty thousand pounds. He had lost also forty thousand pounds on his adventures in trying to found the colony in Virginia, and this had never been properly recouped.

"The taking of the *Madre de Dios* two years ago should have enriched him permanently but he gave all his profit to the Queen— eighty thousand pounds or more—to buy his liberty. So he is in straits."

"Like others," I said, thinking of my father.

"Yes, but while out of favour he has little opportunity to recover his losses. That's why he must go with Essex. It's his great chance. Unless the Queen relents, Guiana must wait."

At least, I thought, my father has a marriageable son. . . .

Nothing all this while of Drake and Hawkins. Then in the new year came word that they had taken Havana. This set aside all Sir Walter's fears for them. The genius of the old sea-dogs had triumphed over the new organisation of Spain, for Havana was the key to the West Indies.

It was in this mood that he first went down the steps of Sherborne to welcome the Earl of Essex from his carriage. I watched them from a window.

My master always loved to dress magnificently, was fond of diamonds and big pearls and grey silks, and this was an occasion when every magnificence was justified. As they walked up the steps together there was little to choose between them for brilliance and for dignity. They were both big men but Essex, fourteen years the younger, topped his host by perhaps two inches; brown-bearded in a fuller fashion but with a clean-shaven front chin, dark-haired, big-boned, slim-waisted, vital. One saw the magnetism even at a distance.

I saw little else at that meeting, for they dined six only together: the Raleghs, with Carew, Essex, and the Northumberlands. At ten the coach drove away. In spite of all protestations to the contrary, a meeting such as this between the two greatest contenders for the Queen's favour was fraught with significance for all who ruled England and therefore the more secret the better. I wondered if Sir Robert Cecil would hear of it. Some said that a pin dropped in the royal bedchamber at Greenwich would always be heard in Theobalds.

For the next days Sir Walter was thoughtful and moody—not depressed nor yet exalted, as if the meeting had gone but moderate well. In fact, though I did not know it then, he was wrestling with his great decision. Essex had offered him a command in the venture which he and Lord Admiral Howard were planning.

The only comment Sir Walter made in my hearing was: "I wish such power as they are being granted had been put in Francis Drake's hands. If he has captured Havana with his meagre force, with what Essex is mounting he could have won the war."

That month was published by Robert Robinson a book entitled *The Discovery of the Large, Rich and Beautiful Empire of Guiana, with a relation of the Great and Golden City of Manoa (which the Spaniards call El Dorado). Performed in the year 1595 by Sir Walter Ralegh, Knight, Captain of Her Majesty's Guard, Lord Warden of the Stannaries and Her Highness's Lieutenant General of the County of Cornwall.*

Its reception could hardly have been more gratifying. Four printings were sold in as many weeks. The Germans, the Dutch, the French, the Italians wished to bring out editions. Many in England spoke of it. Cecil, to whom the book was dedicated, politely praised it. But Sir Walter found no happiness or satisfaction in this at all. He lived each day on tenterhooks, for the one person who counted gave no sign. She might not yet have read it. For all he knew it might have been deliberately kept from her. He waited on Cecil to enlist his help;

Cecil was polite but cold; his father was unwell; he could not leave
Burghley House except on the business of his office. Essex—yes, said
Sir Walter, even Essex was more generous than Cecil. Warmly and
impulsively he commended it to the Privy Council and promised to see
that the Queen received her copy. Still no response.

There was also some laughter, and in time this seeped through to
Sherborne. The Bacons led the scornful whispering. Men without
heads? Amazons who consorted with men for only one month of the
year and if they conceived male children returned them to their
fathers, though females were brought up to be as warlike as themselves? This was Sir Walter at his usual game. He would sell his soul,
perhaps already had sold his soul, to gain advancement. A pretty piece
of fiction, this relation of supposed travels in a remote country.

One evening at supper Thomas Hariot said to him: "I wish you had
let me see the manuscript in some early form, Walter. It's ill to me
that these statements should have been allowed to pass into the
printed book, that you, the apostle of scepticism, should seem to ask
your countrymen to believe such wonders."

"My countrymen, Tom, are as obtuse as you. Read the book again.
I am saying these are the *stories* I have heard from the Indians.
Whether they are true is another matter; but often such legends have
a solid substance of fact behind them. Further visits will provide opportunity to prove or disprove them."

"Then I think it would have been a strategy to have made this
crystal clear. . . . But these oysters growing on trees. You saw them?"

"If Laurence were here he would confirm it. Ask him when he returns."

Laurence Keymis had been away three weeks in Portsmouth. Sir
Walter had been able to fit out one good and seaworthy vessel; Keymis
at least was to go. If Sir Walter went with him then he turned his
back on the great Essex and Howard enterprise. Now was the last
moment of choice.

"For my part," said Lady Ralegh the evening Keymis returned, "I
as little welcome one adventure as th' other. Each is fraught with
separation and loneliness for me. Each is fraught with danger and
hardship for you. Here we're happy. Let younger men bear the edge
of these enterprises."

"Oh, younger men," said Sir Walter, restlessly. "Yes, that's true. Yet,
by the living God, at forty-four a man still has something to give. And,
maybe, less to lose—though I doubt that. Each year I find I've more to
part from. You weave your silken ties, Bess."

"I wish they were stronger." Her discerning eyes followed him as he
got up and stood scowling into the fire.

"Well, the choice tonight is not neither but either. And, Laurence, the choice is made. You must go alone."

Keymis's spectacles flashed in the fire light. "So be it."

"If my expedition with Essex is a success, I shall stand a chance of sending a fine fleet to Guiana next year. You must go as my envoy, Laurence. Tell them I shall be with them soon!"

CHAPTER 2

A DAY after Sir Walter's decision he said brusquely to me: "Well, Killigrew, you see how the wind blows for me. For you there are three choices. One, you go home, two, you stay here, three, you go with Keymis. Tell me within the week which it is to be."

"If I stay with you, sir," I said, "what of this seafaring adventure? Is there a place for me on that?"

He smiled thinly. "It's early days to promise but I should have thought it likely. If the worst befell I could take you as a personal attendant."

"I should be happy to be that."

"There may be bitter fighting. I can't tell you more."

"That I'll be glad to see."

He inclined his head. "Yes, well, then, is that your choice? You'd be advised to sleep on it."

"No, sir, that's my choice."

It must have been some time that week that a first letter came from Belemus.

Dear Witless (it ran),

All goes badly here as usual. In a world of constant rain and wind we keep warm and fed and allow our vassals to venture out into the half light and the mud of winter, but I wonder often how long the roof will be above our heads.

Your father departed at the break of the year for Westminster, but I learn at his first arrival in London he was pounced upon by some of his creditors and thrown into the Fleet. He was there two weeks, but from his last letter it seems that a friendly hand at Court has got him released and if nothing more has befallen he is now on his way home. Your grandmother, dear Lady K., has taken on a new chapter of life and directly she heard of your father's plight left for London with her personal maid in tow. She looked frail enough to sink in the first gale, but I seriously believe it would take a tidal wave. Anyway they are likely to have passed each other en route or collided ere this.

John's marriage with little chimney-smoking Jane comes no nearer, and, ever as a mirage, retreats as we advance towards it. Your Meg bites excessively at everyone, including poor Dick. I believe that in everyone she sharpens her teeth on she sees the image of you.

Another old friend of yours, Captain Elliot, put in to the Haven last month and came ashore. For a pirate he is well informed, bringing us news that King Philip is ill with gout and ulcers and a double tertian fever. I hope the news is in no way exaggerated. His usual mate Love was with him and I learned from him the way they have been making money of late: they have been buying guns and powder in Hampshire stolen by the profiteers who are arming and supplying our ships; then they have taken them to Spain and sold them to the Spanish at a fine profit. So if another Armada sails it is like to be partly provisioned with English cannon and shot. Neat, is it not?

Your father was no sooner out of the house than who should pop up but your witch friend from Truro trailing prophecies and little spiders wherever she strode. She appears to have put a spell on Mrs Killigrew who sweats more night fevers over her two youngest than over all earlier hatchings. Though I wish no hurt to Footmarker I like not so much this affection that has grown between her and Mrs Killigrew, for it smacks of the evil eye. Footmarker sees a doom on the house, and your step-mother, poor wight, cosseted by debts as high as her pink ears, is hardly to be blamed if she believes there's a truth to it. It is not a healthy friendship. . . .

On the last day of January Laurence Keymis sailed. The night before he left for Portsmouth there was a party at Sherborne, but Sir Walter was in no mood for it and went early to bed. He commanded me to bring him up some books, and as I was collecting them Laurence Keymis came to me and gave me a note that I was to deliver with the books. The note was open and was a short poem of farewell.

"Put it on the top book, Killigrew. He'll see it there."

"Yes, Mr Keymis."

The other took off his spectacles and polished them. When he did this he always frowned as if angry, but tonight I could see he was full of emotion, and his eyes had tears in them.

"I hope you realise," he said suddenly, "your privilege in serving such a man."

I muttered something and he put on his spectacles, looping them energetically round his ears.

"Such men as he are born once in a century. The w-warriors who are thinkers. The scholars with the courage to fight. In times of peace they rot, presumed upon by lesser men who fear their brilliance and their superiority. They are banished into obscurity by their fellows or their monarchs, pursued by envy and spite or ignored and derided. Only in need and in time of great peril do other men turn to them. L-look at your master! A man chock full of faults—I who know him so well would not deny one of them—but also a man so full of talents and inspiration that he is like one with a quiverful of arrows, each sharp and true. A born leader, the greatest living strategist, a poet, a philosopher, an essayist, an orator, a skilled musician, a s-soldier, an explorer, a founder of new Englands overseas. The crowds hate him, the leaders of the country ignore him, the Queen banishes him. But we who know him—we who know him, Killigrew, live to serve him!"

I thought as I climbed the spiral staircase that Laurence Keymis would never have spoken to me so freely if he had not been full of wine.

After Keymis had left Sir Walter remained in very low spirits. He felt, he said, that he had turned away from his true mission in search of a more immediate prize and a less enduring glory. Then, as often, he fell sick. He was certain he had a stone in the kidney, and sent for works on anatomy and surgery to see how it might be removed. Bess Ralegh waited on him personally, and on the fifth day he was suddenly well again and writing a long urgent personal message to Essex on the recruitment of sailors for the fleet.

This done he turned to another interest. While ill he had had two young dogs for company in his room and he had been observing their behaviour.

"Animals," he desired me to write down, "of a certainty can communicate one with another and have reasoning powers of a lower but similar order to man. Their senses, however, are more highly refined. Therefore I cannot see that my perception or any man's perception is better than theirs. In so far as perceiving *is* a matter of sense—and what else can it be—then I can advance no reason why my apprehension of reality is preferable to theirs. If our perceptions differ, *they* may be in truth and *I* in error just as well as I in truth and they err. If I must be believed before them, then my perception must be *proven* truer than theirs. Without proof none should be asked to believe it. Even if by demonstration it seem to be true, then will it be a question whether it be indeed as it *seems* to be. To allege as a certain proof what of its nature must be uncertain is absurd!"

That night none of his favourite companions was in the house and he had only Lady Ralegh and me and Victor Hardwicke on whom to sharpen this argument. He paced up and down in his black satin suit, discoursing at us and expecting us to challenge his reasoning while we sat for the most part helplessly by.

It must have been about the fifth or sixth of February, and a gale was howling outside. A log fire burned in the hearth and half up the chimney. The two dogs, the object of his argument, lay well fed and dog-sleeping before the fire, their ears twitching once and again as their master passed, but giving no other sign of superior perception. The firelight flickered on Lady Ralegh's composed face, on her dark velvet robe with its tufted sleeves and long hanging cuffs, and the close gown of white satin under it, on the chains of pearls at neck and waist.

I wondered if this gale would be blowing round the Cornish coast and whether my father was safe home after his experience. His creditors were becoming more desperate. So therefore would he. I wondered what it was like in Paul and where the Reverend and Mrs Reskymer were sleeping. Perhaps it would be cold and the Reverend Reskymer would say "Come into my bed—this way we shall keep each other warm." And Sue would slip out shivering in the dark, her hair like seaweed, her face like a water lily drifting in the dark, her night shift a reflection of the moon. So she would lie beside him, soft and slim and straight and he would put out his hand and stroke her thighs. . . .

"Well, Maugan," said Sir Walter, stopping in front of me. "What have you to say to that?"

"Sir," I said, "I believe my apprehension of reality to be preferable to any, for I have not heard a word of what you've said."

Lady Ralegh drew in a sharp breath at this insolence, which was greater than at first appeared, but Sir Walter after looking surprised suddenly laughed. He seldom laughed.

"You assert that my philosophical speculations have no validity outside the brain that breeds them? A stinging rebuke! Well, it's true that intellectual speculation may run ahead of reason. But the reason of man in itself ends and dissolves like a river running into a sea. What do you advocate—an end of curiosity? You at your age? Between birth and death, Maugan, there's little time. What there is is not entirely wasted if it strikes a balance between questioning and faith."

That week he rode again to London and supped in the company of Lord Admiral Howard, Lord Thomas Howard, the Earl of Essex, Sir Francis Vere, Sir Conyers Clifford, and our cousin Sir George Carew. It must have been a strange meal, for I knew that Sir Walter was on bitter terms with Lord Thomas Howard and he seldom saw eye to eye with Sir Francis Vere. However, he came back a Rear Admiral for the purposes of the expedition. The Queen still would not see him, but her consent to this appointment showed that his disgrace was less deep than it had been.

In the succeeding weeks the whole house was caught up in feverish preparations. Sir Walter was more often in London than at Sherborne, but without warning he would suddenly arrive, mud-spattered, out of temper and on edge, sometimes alone, sometimes accompanied, but always turning the house upside down.

With his second-in-command, a grizzled sailor of forty called Robert Crosse, who was Francis Drake's favourite captain, Sir Walter had been given the responsibility of enlisting or otherwise obtaining crews for such of the ships as were to commission in the Thames. Most of these ships were transports and victuallers; they were scattered from Gravesend to Greenwich, and some were in poor shape and needed serious repair.

In March Cecil received secret confirmation of Drake's capture of Havana, and he withdrew his opposition to the expedition, though he warned the Privy Council that a serious obstacle was appearing from another quarter. King Henry of France was bankrupt and weary of war. In order to keep him in the field at all he needed support. He needed, he said, an English army.

What was worse, he knew it existed. Massing some ten thousand strong under its finest commander, it was preparing to embark in English warships on one of the biggest enterprises ever to leave England—not, however, to succour the French but to aid some secret adventure farther afield, perhaps to defend Ireland or to attack Blavet. This was not good enough. Though Henry distrusted English intentions to the extent that he would not grant them the port of Calais, which he held with a strong garrison, he wanted their troops inland at this crucial time. Meantime he edged nearer and nearer to that ominous peace treaty with Spain. The only way of preventing such a treaty might be to accede to his demands.

Sir Walter was in a fever lest the whole expedition should now come to nothing. The sixteenth of March was a Saturday and the day, I learned, when Sir Robert Cecil was drafting the Generals' commissions which would give them authority to take this formidable fleet away from English shores. The Queen, said Sir Walter at dinner, though the most gifted and the most brilliant woman he had ever met, was much given to indecision. Now of all times she might be excused for hesitation in the signing. On her choice might hang the future of the world.

When home he would usually find respite from his activity in London by other activities of body or mind, all undertaken with the zest of youth; but now he drooped. One of his sick spells loomed. It rained all Sunday morning, and after divine service he retired to his study and sent word that he would take a light dinner in his room. Arthur Throgmorton and Carew Ralegh played at backgammon all afternoon, a game that was never now brought out in Sir Walter's presence. Once he had played it largely but since his friend Christopher Marlowe had been killed in a duel originating at the board he would not have the draughtsmen near him.

The rest of us spent time in the stables admiring a white gelding Sir Walter had bought and a sorrel mare which had foaled last week. Little Wat, having received no encouragement from his father, toddled with us. Lady Ralegh stayed indoors and helped Mrs Hull, her sempstress, line a stomacher with grey cony's skin.

Ralegh's depression bred restlessness in me, and I had a return of the acute malaise of last August. I felt that wherever I went I was an animal in a cage—and the cage was my love and desire for Sue Reskymer. Somewhere in the world there *must* be escape for me. Before supper I went for a walk with Victor Hardwicke but strode along so violently that he ran out of breath and had to call a halt.

"One would think the devil was after you, friend. Remember my age and infirmity!"

I stared at him moodily. "If you cannot walk a mile across a park you're not in good state for a campaign at sea, Victor."

"Oh, pooh to that." He coughed. "Who ever had to walk a mile on a battleship? That is the beauty of the form; superior to soldiering; one is *conveyed* into the fight. Much to be preferred."

"There may be soldiering in this too. De Vere's men are not coming with us for the pleasures of a sea voyage."

"Well, then, they can fight on land. . . . I'm to keep a diary of the trip. Tell me I shall need breath to write! That's what Cousin Bess would argue!"

"Who? Lady Ralegh? She doesn't want you to go?"

"No, she's superstitious. She's a mixture, is Bess. To her Sir Walter can do no wrong; but all the same she considers him unlucky. She says on each voyage he loses some splendid youth. John Grenville last time. Who this? She doesn't want it to be me."

"I wouldn't call you a splendid youth," I said.

"Agreed! The dangers which threaten don't threaten me. Tell her so." He linked his arm in mine. "Let us walk back at a more endurable pace."

That evening we supped frugally. Sir Walter came down but his presence cast a blight on the table. At the end of the meal he said, well, tomorrow, unless he heard to the contrary, he would return to the Thames-side to continue his recruitment. It was, he said despondently, a task like gathering sand in the fingers; no man had stomach for the job; as fast as crews were brought together they slipped through his grasp and ran away.

He was about to go upstairs to his study when Bell, one of the servants, brought in a dripping rider with a message from Essex. It contained only four words. "Her Majesty has signed."

In the melancholic mood that still hung over me—like some miasma I had caught from my master—I watched and listened to the rejoicing and the toasts that followed without ever becoming a part of them. Much wine was drunk and everyone was joyful. Victor Hardwicke brought out his lute and they sang songs. The victory might already have been won. In fact this was only the preliminary victory—over a monarch's indecision. Whatever the project, I had already seen enough of the Spanish to know that the expedition was not likely to bring an easy or a cheap victory. Sir Walter himself must have known that, for he it was who was constantly warning his countrymen against underestimating the strength and courage and determination of the enemy. Yet tonight he was transformed and as happy at the news, it seemed, as any heedless boy.

All thought of retiring to his study was gone, and instead maps were brought and he watched smiling while the others pored over the charts and speculated as to the destination of the fleet. Their first objective, he said, would be to cover Drake's and Hawkins's triumphant return. Afterwards they would sail on to seek glory of their own.

"It's clear, Cousin," Victor Hardwicke said, "that you know exactly where we are bound and will not tell."

"I am Rear Admiral only of the White. Lord Admiral Howard will command the first squadron, the Earl of Essex the second, the Lord Thomas Howard the third. It will be for them in conference to decide the movements of the fleet and what the crews and officers shall be informed of and when."

"What is your flagship to be?" Arthur Throgmorton asked.

"*Warspite*. Our newest."

"And *Ark Royal?*"

"The Lord Admiral's."

Voices crossed and recrossed. Victor picked up his lute again and smiled at me. His angled, hollow-cheeked face was haloed by the candles. He began to pluck gently at the strings.

If love were mine, who pray would seek for valor?
For love is warm, and courage listeth cold.
If love were mine—

"Victor," said Sir Walter. "D'you know the song 'Weep not, my wanton' which was all the rage last summer? Here, let me have your lute. It goes so. . . ."

He took the instrument and began to play with nearly as accomplished a touch as the young man. Carew Ralegh, the cool and cynical, of all people, took up the refrain and sang in a fine clear voice, and soon the rest of us were joining in. I saw Lady Ralegh, her small determined head a little on one side, her lips moving but no sound coming from them as she watched her husband, her brother, her brother-in-law, her cousin, all men close to her. Then her eyes lifted towards the door. Sir Walter stopped in mid chord.

Bell stood there with another messenger, he even wetter and more mud be-spattered than the first.

I think it was in all minds that perhaps between church and dinner the Queen had veered away from her early resolution and had sent to countermand the first order. Sir Walter tore open the second message which was much longer. One could see as he read it that it was unwelcome news, but he said nothing as he read.

"What is it, Walter?" Carew Ralegh asked. "More from Essex?"

"No. . . . No, it is from John . . . Sir John Gilbert, my step-brother. He writes from Plymouth. A picket boat, he says, has just come in bringing news of Drake and Hawkins. The–" he stopped and cleared his throat. "The report of their having captured Havana is false. In all their enterprises they were heavily defeated. And Drake is dead."

CHAPTER 3

IN April the remnants of Drake's fleet began to arrive in Falmouth. In this disastrous expedition the great Hawkins had died too, and the remaining officers and men, of whom only four hundred were left, were in much sickness and want. (My father said bitterly that the failures always put straight into his haven—like the survivors of Sir Humphrey Gilbert's last voyage in '83; if a success the captains sailed straight for Plymouth or Dartmouth, and those towns got the spoils.)

In April too occurred another event of great consequence. The Spanish in Picardy abruptly changed their front of attack and with a brilliant and unexpected thrust invested Calais and then took it, massacring the entire garrison. By these thunderbolts the face of the war was changed. More than had ever been admitted had been expected of Drake's being at sea again; now he was gone and there was a

Spanish port at our throat. It was the one thing the Armada of '88 had lacked.

Twice in the month I rode with Ralegh to London. By exertion and exhortation the naval expedition was kept in being, though none knew if it would ever leave our shores. In early May, I sailed with Captain Crosse in *Swiftsure* to join the fleet assembling at Plymouth. Sir Walter was to follow with the main body almost at once. At Plymouth the bay was alive with warships. Lord Admiral Howard had arrived with *Ark Royal* and *Lion* and six other great ships the day before us. His kinsman, Lord Thomas Howard, was expected later in the week aboard *Mere Honour* and with a squadron in his wake; the Earl of Essex in *Due Repulse* had been the first to arrive and kept princely state aboard her. He was also, it was said, feeding the whole fleet out of his own pocket in order to save the sea stores.

Hardly had we arrived than a message came overland from Ralegh to Captain Crosse that he could not hope to be at Plymouth with the rearguard for two weeks yet. Half the victuallers were still unready, and stores could not be brought to the dockside and loaded in time. He would, he promised, sail from Gravesend on the sixteenth with every ship in his charge, if he had to hang the captains and sail with farmer's boys.

"The Generals will not like it," said Crosse. "There are murmurings against him already that he does not make sufficient haste. When they stop quarrelling among themselves they see Sir Walter in the background, not yet arrived, the great eccentric, and they use him as a convenient peg for their grievances."

In the same bag came a letter from my father which had reached Sherborne after I left.

Son Maugan,

This is to advertise you that your grandmother is likely to be gone from us ere this reaches you. She journeyed to London early in the year and was seized with heart cramps on making her return to us last month. The condition has continued and worsened since: I do not think she can survive another seizure. She has been a noble woman and will take her place with the blest above.

I trust you are finding profit in your employ. It is a fine opportunity for any young man; especially for one such as you.

We have lost eight lambs of the murrain and I fancy there is an evil eye upon the house. Trudy, my bay mare, is ill of the botts. We have sown the castle fields with oats this year. Pray God they do well, for we are sore put.

Your affectionate

Father.

I had received a small monthly wage at Sherborne. It would pay for a horse. I asked Captain Crosse and he said: "I have nothing for you here. If you are back by the eighteenth you should be in safe time."

When I reached Arwenack it was the afternoon of the tenth and sunny and warm; after being away for a few months the beauty of the land and bay caught at my breath. The chestnut trees in the drive were almost out and lifting their candles towards a blue sky innocent and remote. A yellow-sailed hoy was luffing out into the bay; sea-gulls were crying their lonely lament; the sea was a glistening mirror which the distance breathed on and made hazy.

The first person I saw was my grandmother sitting out on a chair on the front lawn.

My father said:
"She's better, yes, she's better, though for how long. . . . I truly believe her ailment was brought on not by shortness of breath but by shortage of money. For her return home from London she wished to hire a coach, but your Uncle Henry being in Holland and William refusing, she was constrained to attempt the hire herself, whereupon her great debts—and mine too—all but prevented her. For a man and five horses she was asked six shillings a day—so prices go ever up— and she engaged one Foster to have them for a quarter of a year— your grandmother was never one to pare her cheeses—but it was all but lost because Foster demanded a surety for their return and there was much to-do—your grandmother weeping tears of rage, she says— before Mr Atkinson stood surety for her. By then anger had so taken hold of her that the first of many seizures came on before she reached Basingstoke."

My father hunched his shoulders as if cold. The year had not dealt favourably with him. In a face grown fleshier his eyes looked smaller, little prominent blue stones with pink under-rims. The life had gone out of his fine hair; it might have been gathered from some threshing floor.

"Have you news of the Fermors, Father?"

"Ah, yes, I'm advanced in that direction. When I was set free of prison I went to see Sir George and had it out with him very straight. Either a date was appointed, I said, or he must look elsewhere for a sire for his grandchildren. So he has stated October next. The eighth will be the day, God helping. Hearing this, and determined that there should be no other delay, I stayed on at Easton Neston until the marriage contract was drawn up and signed."

. . . And Lady Killigrew said: "They can have taught you no manners at Sherborne, or you would have come straight to me on arrival, knowing how mortal sick I've been. Is there opportunity for advancement there? Whom do you meet? Is Lady Ralegh following this new fashion in French hoods? . . . Your step-mother, you will observe, is *enceinte* again. You would have thought we had enough brats to feed. You must look to no further help from this house, boy; I never thought we would have come to these straits. A Wolverstone in penury! Times have changed for the worse when a man may not make use of his authority to some purpose. . . . The Queen has lived too long: government has become oppressive and parsimonious—though God knows who will come after her—not, I pray, that pole-shanked drivelling Stuart: if so I shall be glad to die before her."

. . . "So you're home for a visit, Master Maugan," Meg said. "I thought you'd runned away for good. Do not be scared o'me; I've never asked nothin' but what I thought was freely given. Indeed, twas th'other way round most of the time—as I trust you've not forgot. Have you found some nice wench at your new home who'll just be at your beck and call when youd' want her and no other time?"

. . . "Sometimes I wish I could go in the church," young John Killigrew said as he unloosed his shoes in the bedroom that night. "Have you ever thought of it, Maugan? No, well, it might not suit *you*, but I should not dislike it. I have small interest in my father's life here—it is not a godly life nor one I'd willingly copy. I believe I should be happier if you were my full brother and could inherit in my place. . . ."

. . . And Belemus said: "*Dolphin* was here last week, with your old friends aboard. But they were all but caught. It was a great to-do."

"Caught?"

"By Jonas in *Crane*. Elliot had barely time to slip his anchor and take the tide up river."

Crane was a crompster, a type of vessel fairly new to the navy, a ship of some one hundred eighty tons: three masted and low built, with speed and an armament of two 18-pounders and fourteen smaller cannon, so that she could catch and kill all but the biggest. She was the terror of the Elliots and the Burleys of the coast.

"The difficulty," said Belemus, "was that the man aloft aboard *Crane* reported a suspicious vessel slipping away in the dusk. Captain Jonas, of course, has received many favours in this house; but this was altogether a trifle—well, blatant. Other people would know of a ship sheltering in Mylor Pool. Your father could do nothing personal so I was sent aboard *Crane*. After some delicate negotiation one hundred pounds changed hands—God knows how your father found it—and

Crane went off to investigate a report that there was a pirate ship in the Helford River."

I whistled.

Belemus went on: "By the way, d'you still hanker after little Mistress Reskymer, for I hear her spouse is sick. . . ."

. . . All yesterday I had been resisting a desire to go to Paul. I knew it must end in frustration, yet, now the excuse existed, I had to go. When I got to the church Philip Reskymer was from home and only Sue was there with a black-browed hairy man who topped her by a foot. She changed colour at sight of me.

"Do you not know each other? This is Maugan Killigrew, Mr Arundell, Mr John Killigrew's son from Arwenack. Mr Henry Arundell of Truthall, Maugan."

"Formerly of Tolverne, sir?"

"Formerly of Tolverne." Mr Arundell let breath escape from between thick lips indecently red by contrast with his black beard. "I know of you, boy. I'm told you saw my brother in Spain."

We walked slowly round among the hammering masons as I gave an account of the meeting. So I knew them all now, Sir Anthony, dying for a lost faith with his white wispy hair haloing a fading brain; Thomas Arundell, narrow-faced, blue-eyed, faintly squinting, an artist and a passionate exile; Alice, to whom I had delivered his letter, thin and eroded and grown to a carved chair in which she overlooked her green lawns: now Henry, fat as a king, bearded like a footpad. I knew now of whom he reminded me: his nephew Thomas waiting to inherit from his ailing brother Jonathan in the tree-smothered house by the river.

Yet under or over these thoughts, distinct as a thread of crimson in a dull fabric, was awareness of Susanna Reskymer, of what she wore, of how she moved and breathed and spoke.

Mr Henry Arundell was a close friend of the Reskymers and had come on a similar mission to my own, to which Sue replied: "Oh, he is not well, but I don't think his disease would be dangerous if I could persuade him to a greater ease and an increased rest. Today he is in St Ives on matters to do with this rebuilding. He would suffer no one to do it for him. I expect him home any moment. You'll sup with us, Maugan?"

"Thank you."

To my relief Mr Arundell would not wait; blowing breath and importance, he said he had business with the St Aubyns and must go; Philip and Susanna must visit him at an early date and spend the night. Mr Arundell rubbed his black beard and looked Sue over. Philip must appreciate his luck and take advantage of being alive. . . .

When he had gone off with his two servants riding behind him a silence fell between us. I could hardly believe my good fortune at having her alone, yet I did not know what to do with it. Eleven months ago I had slept with her. We had parted in anger and not written since. That parting was a barrier I could not climb.

We walked back to the church, which was being slowly raised again.

"Where do you live now?"

"In the cottage which John Pieton rented—he who was killed. It's convenient to be near the building. . . . You have been with Ralegh, Maugan?"

"Still am. I came back for a week only because my grandmother was sick. Then I heard Mr Reskymer also was ill. . . ."

"He is more ill than he'll acknowledge, but to his friends I keep up the pretence as he wishes. It's a bloodlessness which troubles him. But he has a rare inner strength, Maugan, arising from his faith, and I believe it will carry him a good way yet."

Two men, broad shouldered, with the thick haunches of the Cornish, were lifting a huge stone into position at the foot of a pillar. We stopped to watch them. So far our words had been as formal as if Henry Arundell were still here.

"And you?" she said.

I spoke constrainedly of my life at Sherborne. "I go now with Ralegh on a naval commission which leaves this month."

"I had heard rumors. Where are you bound?"

"That we don't know. It's a small armada with soldiers aboard."

She was silent for some time. "How much are you committed to it, Maugan?"

"Committed? Oh, completely. Besides, I want to go."

She knitted her brows. We walked slowly round towards the ruins of the vicarage. "I don't like it, Maugan. There is bound to be danger. Think of Drake and Hawkins and so many others. It's not just danger from combat, though that may be great; there is danger from fever and other disease."

"Where there is danger there is usually hope of profit."

She looked up, eyes green behind their lashes in the falling sun. "There could be profit nearer home. I was glad you came today. I wondered if you had met Henry Arundell before. You see. . . ."

"The connection? No, I don't."

". . . I wonder if Philip could help. It might well be arranged."

They had not yet begun to rebuild the Reskymers' house, but the kitchens were being used, and horses were standing in the stables. A servant ran out to ask Sue about supper, and she answered composedly, mistress of the house and the situation. Her circumstances were changing her, giving her greater poise and assurance.

She said: "Henry Arundell's steward died last month. He is looking for a new one and seeking someone well learned who can take over much of the management of his estate. He says it is difficult to find the right man. I know you are very young for such a position, but it might be possible that he would take you."

I suppose I should have been happy that she was concerned for my safety but with the perverseness of the rejected lover I thought the proposition smacked of condescension. "This is not a time when I could apply to him."

"It would be the only time, while he needs one. Philip was at Cambridge with him and with his persuasion the position might be got. It would be a big move for you, with a prospect of advancement."

"An *advancement* from being at Ralegh's side?"

"From what you tell me it's only as a writer that you're employed. Henry Arundell is a bachelor and getting up in years. He's looking for someone young and energetic and reliable. One way or another, you could make your fortune there."

"You're still anxious I should make my forture?"

"You know the reasons."

"Tell me them."

"Perhaps you think I've forfeited the right to be interested in your life, to wish to advance it."

". . . Never that. But I think the advancement must be along my own route."

She bent to rub some grass off her shoe. "Henry Arundell also has close connections with the Howards. They are relatives, of course, and of great influence in and around the court—different from Ralegh, who many think will never return to influence and power."

I did not speak and we moved on through the coppice to the cottage.

She said: "As it happens my father was at one time in the employ of a Howard—at least, it was the same family though a Devonshire branch. This was before he was married. He often used to talk about it—to say what a powerful family they were and what connections they had."

All the brambles had been neatly cleared.

She said: "I have a strange feeling about this naval voyage, Maugan, a premonition. I wish you would not go, but stay here, in your own country."

"And near you," I said harshly.

The wind blew a flicker of hair over her eyes as she straightened up. She blinked and seemed to shiver as she turned away.

"My marriage cannot go on for ever, Maugan, that's now clear."

I stood beside her, already part wishing I had never come.

"Sue, when your marriage ends, then you must think it all over again. Until it does you laid down for yourself prohibitions that I asked you to break and you would not."

"Yes, but it need not prevent our being within distance. . . . Truthall is not so far from here—"

"It is too near—yet. Besides I cannot and wouldn't leave Ralegh for any Arundell or any Howard. I don't always admire him, but being in his company is living in another air. I can make it no plainer than that. . . ."

"Oh, you have made it very plain!"

"Yes, but don't mistake me. You are the wife of Philip Reskymer. If at any time you become the widow of Philip Reskymer, then that's a new situation." I touched her shoulder. "Until then I go my own way, and immediately my own way leads me on this voyage."

"Which I say you should not take!"

"Which I shall take. I may come out of it with some prize."

"Maugan, you could find a greater prize here."

"There's only one greater and that's out of my reach. When it's not, give me first news."

"You're dead to all—all reason."

"Reason was never a complete answer, Sue. It never can be, between us."

I did not stay to sup after all. When it came to the point I could not bear to see Philip Reskymer again. To wish a man dead, to rejoice in his ill health, is a damned thing. I rode home in the dark. Always, I thought, it was a mistake to come this way.

CHAPTER 4

SIR WALTER reached Plymouth aboard his flagship with the supply ships straggling out behind him at nine o'clock on the morning of Friday the twenty-first. I transferred at once to *Warspite* where I shared a tiny cabin with Victor Hardwicke, but I saw little of Sir Walter during the next ten days, he being more often on some other ship than on his own. A great quarrel broke out at dinner aboard *Due Repulse* the first night Sir Walter dined there, it being concerned with some question of precedence between himself and Sir Francis Vere, leader of the land forces. Victor said he thought Sir Walter, bent on unity and agreement among the commanders, had been prepared to smooth the thing over; but his brother-in-law took up the quarrel and if Essex had not intervened there would have been a duel. As it was Arthur Throgmorton, though a Lieutenant-Colonel in Gerard's, was dismissed the army and put under guard. It was not a pretty omen for the success of the expedition.

Even less so was the fact that the Lord Admiral and Lord Essex were almost at each other's throat. Only my master's new harmony with Essex was unimpaired.

Every day the army drilled on the Hoe, forming squares, advancing in line, wheeling in strict formation, while the gentry sat their horses discussing strategy or partook of dummy charges across the green. Two deserters were hanged by Essex's command as a warning to the others.

At length orders were issued that all land companies should embark on the ships, this on the thirty-first, and the embarkation was complete by midnight. I have seldom seen a finer body of men: veterans nearly all, well clothed and well armed, over six thousand strong, though short in cavalry: the army had perhaps two hundred horses and the gentry a like number.

In the night three-quarters of the great fleet warped out of Catwater into the Sound. At four o'clock in the morning of the Tuesday a gun fired from *Ark Royal* intimated that the fleet was ready to leave. At six Sir Walter was rowed back from a last conference saying that on Essex's generous intervention Arthur Throgmorton had been released and allowed to rejoin his company.

It was a fine sunny morning with a fresh breeze from the northwest, not warm but invigorating. We had finished prayers and breakfast when Lord Admiral Howard flying his crimson flag set sail, followed by his squadron; the Earl of Essex, fluttering the biggest flag of all, orange tawny on a white ground, was next to go. The Hoe and all the land round was bordered black with tiny people waving and watching. Next came the Dutch fleet and then Lord Thomas Howard flying blue. It was after midday before we ourselves were under way, bringing up the rear.

Out of the harbour the wind had much freshened and the sea ahead was dotted as far as the eye could see with lurching and tossing ships. This was to be an exercise in manoeuvre before the fleet sailed in earnest. We warped and tacked all day between Rame Head and Fowey, for the most part in confusion but as the day wore on falling into a greater order.

Sir Walter went quickly to his cabin and was not seen again—they had joked at Sherborne that he was a poor sailor—but I had no better fortune and vomited from four in the afternoon until nightfall. Hardwicke, the delicate, stood the pitching and tossing without discomfort and laughed at my antics.

We passed the night uncomfortably off Blackbeetle Point near the entrance to Fowey Haven and all the following morning plied up and down in pursuance of orders from the Lord Admiral; then, the wind backing about four in the afternoon, the whole fleet put back into Plymouth Sound and anchored in line all the way across to Cawsand. At eight a counsel was called aboard *Ark Royal*, and Sir Walter, his hair and beard looking blacker against his sallow face, commanded me to go with him.

It was a full Council of War, and for the most part I stood on deck with midshipmen, secretaries, and others in attendance on the great men. But towards the end I was sent for and carried up papers Sir Walter had brought setting forth his views on fire-power in relation to shore batteries, a subject on which as usual he had controversial views.

In the great cabin were yellow lanterns hanging and gently swaying; lattice windows still light with the evening light; ten principal captains and five admirals; gold braid on blue velvet, silver braid on scarlet; jewelled sword belts with wrought leather. Wine cups stood on a baize-covered round table like sentinels about the littered charts; a few men were smoking and the smoke rose to mix with the hazy breath and argument and wine fumes and the smoke of the lanterns.

Essex was speaking, his face flushed, as if argument had ruffled him. "Let us remember, my lords, that this is a sacred cause, undertaken not primarily in search of gain but to preserve our country and our religion. To remind all of that purpose, services shall be performed thrice daily, in the morning, in the evening, at the cleaning of the glass. . . ."

Presently Sir Walter spoke. I do not remember a word he said, only the tone of his voice. It was a tone I had heard him use only once or twice before. It deferred too obviously; it was full of flattery and ingratiation. For one who knew him well it was plainly insincere and used only with a purpose. In the seat of honour beside Essex sat the old Lord Admiral, white-bearded, hawk-nosed, a jewelled skull cap over his scant hair. On the other side of Essex was Lord Thomas Howard, the third in command. A man in his thirties with a sailor's face, weather-beaten but arrogant and lean, he watched Sir Walter carefully while he spoke. These were the first two Howards

I had ever seen and after what Sue had said I stared at them with a new interest. As if some communication passed between us he lifted his head and his eyes looked me over assessingly; then he turned away and took snuff. A moment later and I was out in the summer evening again breathing a fresher air.

The following morning, which was the third of June, the fleet set sail in earnest, Lord Admiral Howard leading off his squadron at ten, and ourselves weighing anchor shortly before four in the afternoon. The north-west wind had by now returned and it blew intermittently throughout the next days.

On the Friday Sir Walter called me up to his cabin. His desk was littered with books pulled from their shelves, and he was considering the optimum length-to-weight ratio of the galleon. From the behaviour of *Warspite* in the short time he had been sailing in her he had come to the strong conclusion that she was too short for her width, being in length only two and a half times her beam, which in Sir Walter's opinion was a backward step in design; and that she was much over gunned for a vessel of 648 tons: thirty-six guns, twenty of them heavy culverins, being likely to overcharge the ship's sides in any grown sea. On these matters he wrote and talked for upwards of two hours; then, looking as exhausted as I felt, he dropped his pen and rang the bell for a cup of the cordial he had brought with him for sea-sickness; I took a cup as well, though I should have had more confidence if Katherine Footmarker had mixed it.

He was in a natural and approachable mood, and I asked him whither we were bound.

He said: "Our captains, except those at the council, still sail under sealed orders. If any are separated they make for Cape St Vincent."

"Which is not Ireland or Blavet."

"Which is not Ireland or Blavet."

"I have heard it said, sir, that the Spanish fleet is concentrated in two ports: El Ferrol and Cadiz."

The ship lurched over a wave and slithered down the hind side. "You are not ill-informed."

"I was in the Groyne for a week, but never as far south as Cadiz."

"I forget your Spanish adventures. But it does not entitle you to information not yet divulged to others."

"No, sir. I can only guess."

"And keep your guesses under lock and key. . . . By the living God, I feel ill! It would be a humiliation to be laid aside at a time like this."

"There must be many others the same."

"No doubt most of the three hundred green-headed youths in their feathers and gold lace will be wishing themselves ashore again. But it is different for them. The leaders should be above physical frailty. . . ." He took a sip of his cordial, and the whole cabin leaned and creaked as he did so. "Ships stink so foul of bilge water and foetid air, it does not give one a chance. Also there's the heat and stink of the cook room directly under us. In merchant ships they sometimes build the galley in the forecastle. . . . No doubt this does not worry my Lord Admiral, since he is a sailor born."

"Lord Thomas Howard," I said, "is a sailor too?"

"Oh, a fair one. Though no fighter. He commanded at the Azores when my cousin, Richard Grenville, fought the Spanish fleet alone. Howard commanded his squadron away and left Grenville to his fate. His action has been defended because he was outnumbered. I have openly said what I thought of his behaviour and there was to have been a duel fought between us, but it was stopped by the Queen."

The wind was freshening and they were taking in the mizzen which was almost above us, Sir Walter's cabin being four flights up in the poop.

"I should be happier in a world quite bereft of Howards," he said broodingly. "Oil and water . . . we do not mix. But Lord Thomas is far less repugnant than his uncle, Lord Henry Howard. If ever you meet him I commend him to your study."

"At Wednesday's council meeting, sir, I thought none spoke with sincerity or candour."

Perhaps fortunately he did not take the remark as directed at himself.

"Much between the Earl of Essex and the Lord Admiral is jealousy and the question of precedence. . . . But on that I should not cast stones. When I arrived in Plymouth Francis Vere was claiming a position beyond his due, and we had hard words before it was settled."

The ship lurched and the cabin seemed to turn in a semi-circle.

"I know what you are thinking, young Killigrew: that if leaders may endeavour to be above sea-sickness, they should much more be above petty deceptions and small jealousies, over which they have some control. Well, I can tell you they are not. Greatness is a condition of brain and marrow: it is in no way connected with virtue, which is of the soul. Indeed, looking into my own heart, which is in essence the only one I shall ever know, it seems to me that the very faculties which make for excellence of talent and wit make also for a deficiency of patience and humility and generosity towards one's rivals and fellow men. In command I *want* command, not to dog at the heels of some strutting popinjay raised to his position by accident of birth. If there is equal talent in an equal position I do not acknowledge it, save grudgingly—as in the case of Vere—and he no less of me. Never equate the great with the good, young Killigrew, or you will suffer deeper disillusions than you are suffering now."

"I confess I've an anxious thought for the success of an expedition in which all the leaders are at dagger's point."

"*All* leaders are always at dagger's point where there is more than one leader. This is the flaw of so many enterprises. But take heart: some succeed in spite of it. This may; we are a formidable force. Eighteen of the Queen's galleons, twelve great ships from the City of London, eighteen Hollanders, many transports and victuallers capable of fighting on their own behalf. We may meet the Spanish fleet at sea; if not we shall sweep wide with our prinnaces and fast craft to pick up all small vessels as we go, so that none may turn and fly ahead with news of our coming. This is what I have been waiting for for five years, to avenge my cousin Grenville and the men who died with him!"

I saw much of Sir Walter during the next few days. Confined as he was to his own warship, his restless energies had no suitable outlet. Once his sickness had lessened he was ever about, inspecting the guns, talking with the gunners, plotting our course with Captain Oakes. *Warspite* was a fine new ship, but as Sir Walter said, already stinking of the foul water which slapped about in her bilges. I would not have liked to be a common sailor, for it was not possible to walk upright between decks, the clearance being not above five feet, and the men slept side by side on the decks with only some fourteen inches of space to lie in. There was little light or air below because, except in the calmest seas, the gun ports had to be kept closed and there was small hope of healthful rest or cleanliness.

So as to be less conspicuous to the casual sail, our fleet spread wide in extended order during the day and drew together at nightfall with the sound of trumpets blown and cheerful shouts from one vessel to another.

The Sunday was wild, and *Warspite* plunged and groaned like a coach in a muddy lane. Victor fell and sprained his arm. Monday and Tuesday were fair and calm, but this was followed by a gale coming up from the north-west, with rain, on the Wednesday afternoon. Great combers built up under the declining sun and moved after us, overtaking us so that we lurched to the top of them scattering spray and spume over the poop windows, poised high regarding a tossing grey-faced, white-lipped world, and then yawed drunkenly into the valley behind. It looked more awful even than it felt, for while we were riding the crests other vessels around us disappeared into pits from which it seemed they would never climb or swung at such strange angles to the hurrying seas that they seemed about to turn over and sink.

Days passed without sight of land or foreign sail. On Friday, the sea having fallen and the day being fair, Lord Admiral Howard summoned another council aboard his flagship, and presently Sir Walter embarked on a naval barge, this time taking Victor Hardwicke with him. I was left behind to think of Sue and to dream of battle and spoils. When the council was over, which was not until three in the afternoon, Victor took an early opportunity to whisper one word in my ear. It was "Cadiz."

The next day three Flemish boats, two from Amsterdam and one from Middleburgh, were chased and after a fight taken. The captured masters were brought aboard *Warspite*. Though Sir Christopher Blount, who had been concerned in their capture, tried to have them taken aboard *Lioness,* he was brusquely over-ruled by Sir Walter. Three days out of Cadiz, with a cargo of salt and wines, the master of the Middleburgh boat, entertained in Ralegh's cabin with greater courtesy than Sir Walter had just extended to his soldier colleague, was forthcoming enough. Cadiz harbour, he said, was full of shipping, there being twenty powerful galleys of the Andalusian squadron, four of the great Apostle galleons of the Guard, two older Portuguese galleons, and three of the new treasure frigates which were recently back from their defeat of Drake at Porto Bello. In addition there were about forty vessels of a treasure fleet loading cargoes for New Spain. No rumour had yet reached Spain of an English force approaching: it was widely thought that with the death of Drake and the fall of Calais all our energies would be turned towards defence.

News of such import was at once sent to the other admirals, while the three fly-boats were searched and some of their cargo seized. That evening the sun was bloody as it set almost behind us.

We were now beating down the Spanish coast, and the following day about six in the morning we sighted the Burlings, which are islands off Vigo—the first land we had seen since the Cornish coast.

One night my master had Sir John Wingfield, a tall, sombre soldier, and the Earl of Sussex to dine, and after they had gone he stood for a while beside me on the deck staring across at their receding barge.

"The days draw in as we go south," he said. "I fancy if there is one disadvantage to the lower latitudes, it is this. D'you feel homesick for England yet, Killigrew?"

"I have felt so often sea-sick that there's been hardly room for the other."

"Yet you must recall those English June nights when the sun seems barely to set at all; it stays in a blue cloud under the horizon reflecting light until it is time to rise again. There's a harshness about tropical skies that I find less alluring. Perhaps all Englishmen, wherever they may settle, have an enduring picture in their hearts of soft summer cloud and blossom-scented wind and the night skies of midsummer."

"I wonder how Mr Keymis fares in Guiana."

"I wish we knew. Now *there* is a rich and lovely country where I would gladly see Englishmen settle. . . . Yet perhaps he is the happiest man who moves no distance from his birthplace—or only travels often enough to return and appreciate it the more."

We climbed up to his cabin. He seemed to want me to go in, so I did so, and he poured two cups of canary. The sea was slight tonight and the creak and dip of the ship, now one was used to it, was not displeasing. Out of the stern windows you could count the lights on the waters; the stars above were like reflections of them.

"Medina Sidonia is Captain-General of Andalusia," Ralegh said, "and so responsible for the defence of Cadiz. I wonder if he will show a greater capacity for command than he did of the Armada of '88. Though sometimes I fancy he has been fairly judged. . . . Well, we shall soon know. . . ."

"When is the attack planned?"

"If this weather holds we should double Cape St Vincent tomorrow and be off Cadiz by Thursday. I hope the attack will begin on Friday morning, though with caution so much prevailing one can never be certain."

"Is Lord Essex cautious?"

"Oh, by no means: he is more forward than I. But while we are at sea Lord Admiral Howard's word is the final one; and I know it is the Queen's express wish that Lord Essex should not put himself into danger. So the Lord Admiral has a dual and difficult responsibility, to bring off a victory without losing his ships and at the same time to see that his second-in-command and near equal runs no personal risk."

One of the lanterns had blown out and another had smoked its glass, so the room was now in semi-shadow. On the table with my cup was Sir Walter's pipe and a small Guiana idol made of copper and gold which he usually carried in his pocket and which he had been showing to Wingfield. He seldom missed an opportunity of advancing his ideas of empire.

He said abruptly: "Time was, and not so long since, when the Queen was concerned for *my* safety, when I was called back to Court each time I adventured away. There were times when I was beside her in all things and this headstrong stripling kept at a distance or disregarded. I confess they are times I look back on with pleasure and regret. They were times . . . of comradeship with Her Majesty—and inwardness with her such as few men have ever known. She is one of the greatest women who have ever lived—and at the same time one of the most exacting."

I said nothing.

"This talk, this scandal, this poison breath that goes about telling of inwardness of person between a woman of sixty-two and a boy of twenty-nine; these late nights together: they are nothing. I know the Queen. I know her well. . . . Of course she permits liberties; I know that—even intimacies—but never the final intimacy, nor never would. She is the bride of England. . . ."

He walked to one of the lattice windows. His back was bent to look out. The green and gold satin of the cloak drooped like a flag.

"The Court is a cesspool of intrigue and vice. Brother is against brother, friend will cut down friend. But she rides above it in a delicate equipoise. To the outsider it may seem insecure; yet she is firmly held and preserved there by the admiration and trust of five million people. Nor will she ever be dethroned—except by. . . ." He paused.

"Except by?"

"Except by Him who can never be denied. She will be sixty-three this September. Her father died at fifty-seven, her grandfather was fifty-three. May the Living God preserve her for many years yet."

"Amen."

"D'you know," he turned from the window, "the intrigue rages about her and grows with each year. Since I came upon this voyage I have been approached by two . . . gentlemen—I'll not otherwise name them —to discover my opinions and whom I will support if the Queen should die. I said thank God Her Majesty still lives, and while she has breath in her body I am no other's servant. She lives, I said, and enjoys health and still dazzles the day so brightly that all rivals look sick beside her! And so they do. . . . James of Scotland, Arabella Stuart, Lord Beauchamp, even the Infanta is suggested, even Henry of Navarre! Faugh, I'd as soon see England a commonwealth without a king as have any of them!"

His shadow flickered across the table as he moved to his bookshelves and began venomously thrusting back the books. After a while I thought he had forgotten me so I quietly put down my cup and went to the door.

He said sharply, without turning: "The Court is rotten, Maugan, but I would return to it for all its rottenness. Someday you shall go with me."

"Thank you, sir."

"Though you've great-uncles there securer placed than I ever was . . . I wonder they never take you. It will be my first care to place young Wat at Court when he is of age and if I live to see that day."

"Even despite the rottenness."

"Even despite that. For once tasted there is no other flavour. I serve the Queen, if she will have me. But over and above that, even though it may be evil, there is at Court the flavour of power, the smell of government; once having been at the centre of the wheel, life on any outer part is empty and void. If this venture goes well I shall resume my old place and perhaps move into a better. God grant us a good fight! . . ."

On the Tuesday morning we rounded Cape St Vincent, standing close into the land to make the most of the light easterly airs which were stirring there. In Lagos Bay the wind quite dropped and we were hard put to it to make any way at all. Much of the afternoon Sir Walter spent with his glass scanning the distant shore for sign of life, for ours was the squadron closest in; but he detected none.

Unknown to us, however, we had at last been seen. At some moment late that forenoon, two families living in caves in the cliff had sent their men into Albufeira with news. From that village officials came to the cliff edge and counted eighty sail moving slowly south towards Faro. Then, on donkeys and mules, over the rough tracks, they sent messengers east, north, and west: to Faro and Cadiz, to Lagos and Portimão, to the Duke of Medina Sidonia at Castilnova, to Seville and Xeres and all the towns of Andalusia.

In the meantime we made scarcely measurable progress, creeping towards Cape Santa Maria, the last landward point before the bay of Cadiz. The weather had set in too fair.

On Wednesday the sea was glassy; tiny white clouds gathered about the sun and were sucked up in the heat. *Warspite*'s water was rancid by now, the beer salt and foul smelling, much of the butter had putrefied and three hundredweight of cheese had to be thrown overboard. More than thirty men were already down with febrile and stomach ailments. In the morning and evening a mist haze gathered and was thick in patches, so that sometimes another ship would appear near us, its hull invisible and its great spread of dead sail like a mirage floating on still air. Sounds carried far and echoed and were distorted. A gentleman soldier playing a lute on a transport two furlongs away might have been beside us. After dark, for safety's sake, an instruction against music and singing was issued, and even shouting was discouraged except for the issue of orders.

This edict bore fruit just after dawn on Friday when, the mist clearing suddenly, a strange ship was discovered among us, between *Swiftsure* and *Alcedo*. She was as unaware of us as we had been of her, and instantly tried to acquit herself out of it. However, two shots caused her to change her mind, and her captain was taken aboard *Swiftsure* and later *Ark Royal*. This was an Irish ship from Waterford, but one day out of Cadiz, and they were able to assure us that the fleet in the harbour was still as the Flemings had described it.

But the Waterford captain had one other item of news—that a rich argosy of ten ships had left Cadiz at the same time as himself, bound for Lisbon. Ralegh came back from the next council in a doubtful temper, having been commanded to take *Warspite* with *Mary Rose, Quittance, Lioness, Truelove*, and twelve smaller ships towards the coast in the hope of cutting off this argosy. It was not hard to see how his feelings turned. Here was a chance of early and rich plunder which might be as good as anything to be found later; but, with the wind now picking up again, we had just come round Cape Santa Maria and should be off Cadiz by nightfall. The attack might even be al dawn tomorrow, and in that event we should miss it.

However, nothing offered but to obey. All that day, in fitful easterly breezes catching the great sails and then letting them hang again, we tacked and luffed towards the coast, towards Huelva and the long sandy stretches of the Playa de Castilla. With the wind thus fitful, visibility not above a mile and all crews on the alert for instant action, the dominant sound through the rest of that day and the following night was the creak of timber, the living movements of seasoned oak under varying stress, the plash of water rippling and lapping at the bows, the flap of a sail as it partly filled, the thin whisper of the wind in the shrouds.

Saturday dawn broke much as Friday had darkened, though the wind was a trifle more steady. Then at nine, when we must have been almost at the mouth of the Guadalquivir, *Lioness* signalled she had sighted fourteen sail on her larboard bow, and all canvas was bent to give chase.

We knew we were close in-shore but the coast was not visible. About midday we saw a handsome ship some two miles ahead of us—a carrack of five decks and a sitting target for a powerful vessel like *Warspite* if ever we got within range. But this was almost the last break in an overcast sky and a choppy sea, and only *Lioness*, fitfully seen ahead of us, reported she was keeping the quarry in view.

About three Sir George Carew came aboard from *Mary Rose*, with Captain Gyfford of *Quittance*, and Gyfford said he felt it his duty to report, from his knowledge of this coast, that we were hazarding our ships by sailing so close in-shore. Sir Walter replied that where the Portuguese led we could follow, but it was clear that Gyfford's words weighed with him. As commander of this squadron he would be held responsible for any loss or damage. Capturing a convoy of rich prizes in normal weather was one thing; risking shipwreck in a fog to catch them was another. After some little while longer he called off the chase.

The two officers were leaving in Sir Walter's hoy when the curtain of cloud and mist briefly lifted and five foreign vessels were to be seen barely a league away. One was the carrack, the others were all sizeable vessels. We stared at the ships: they were clearly outlined; but before Ralegh could issue an order the cloud came down and blotted them out. We stood and peered and Sir Walter twisted his glass and muttered, but there was no second view. The fog grew thicker every minute. Sir George Carew made a move to leave *Warspite*, but Sir Walter stayed them hoping for a clearance.

None came. Carew said: "If I do not leave now I shall be here until dawn, Walter. *Mary Rose* is lost to sight, and I shall only regain her by good fortune."

"Stay willingly," Ralegh said. "I'd not have you go. This may lift around sunset. What d'you think, Gyfford?"

"I doubt we shall see more today, sir. These fogs come up and cling around the foot of Spain: I believe it is something to do with the Straits and the nearness of Africa. If it thicken more no one will dare move so we shall be no worse off when dawn comes."

"I'm not so sure. Fear is a great spur. They've seen us as surely as we've seen them."

Our nearest neighbour was Gyfford's *Quittance*, a sister ship of *Crane* which Belemus had visited in Falmouth Haven; she was scarcely more than a cable's length astern but by now she could only be seen fitfully as the fog swirled round.

"I'm not for giving up," Sir Walter said sharply. "Go back to your ships—if you can still find them. We'll ride it out here until dark. If there's no improvement by then I have a mind to go and seek out this carrack. She if any will be loth to hazard herself upon the rocks."

"How seek her out without greater risk at night?" Gyfford asked.

"I'll take a few men and look for her in my hoy. Daylight fog defeats us all. In the night lights show."

Sir George glanced at his kinsman. "I don't at all like that. It is no advantage to preserve the ships and hazard the Admiral. Besides if you found her, what could you do?"

"Your hoy won't carry much upwards of a dozen men. You'd be slaughtered, sir," said Gyfford.

"That I'd try to avert. You, Captain Gyfford, must keep in sight of *Warspite* till dark. We'll signal you when we start and we'll show a double lantern on the hoy. You shall follow. *Quittance* has a shallow draught and is unlikely to run on the rocks if she keeps close to our light. *Lioness* shall follow *Quittance* in a like manner, and *Truelove* can come after. *Warspite* will remain here with *Mary Rose* and the rest of the fleet."

"Ah, now—"

"No, George, we risk no galleons. Three lighter vessels can accomplish all we need."

My friendship with Victor Hardwicke had become a singularly affectionate one, but we came near to blows over this adventure. In the end Ralegh, staring coldly at us both and telling us this was no childish game, said we might both go with him.

It was a small party. Ourselves, a ship's bosun called Warnett, Gunner Johns, and four of a crew. Captain Oakes did his best to prevent the expedition, but Sir Walter would have no truck with objections.

When we left the breeze had steadied from the south-east. We had to rely on it for direction and hope it did not change, for otherwise we should fall far off course.

We went slow for fear of losing our followers. We could not see *Quittance*, only her light winking like a widow's lantern behind a curtain. Ahead all was dark.

And it stayed dark. Our course we reckoned was almost due north, following the line of the land. Sir Walter sat in the bows of the tiny boat, his cloak wrapped round him; he spoke little and we followed his example, only staring. The sea was slight but occasionally choppy as if disturbed by shallows. Behind us, we knew, *Quittance* and the others were taking soundings. Once or twice sea birds fluttered across our path.

It grew cold. The sea mist cloyed and clung. We began to lose touch with the light behind and took another reef in our sail. About four Victor opened a bag he had brought and passed round food and ale. Then we saw a light ahead. Food and drink were forgotten.

Gunner Johns made the agreed signal to the ship behind, but in the thick conditions it seemed unlikely they had seen it. The light ahead blinked and wavered and became two. Warnett put the helm over. We were closing rapidly, but then it seemed the look-out on the other ships must have seen us, for we heard distant cries and both lights went out.

"Keep her steady as she goes."

Victor fidgeted with the hilt of his sword.

"We're a sitting target with this light."

Now for some minutes there was no more talk. For all we knew we were passing between the vessels we had sighted. Or we might be leading *Quittance* and the others into a trap.

Sir Walter signalled Warnett to have the sail lowered. We coasted gently along and lost way and began to wallow in the lightly lapping waves. Behind us *Quittance*'s misty light flickered and disappeared.

The fog thinned, and with eyes long accustomed to the dark we saw a vessel on our lee. She was high pooped and foreign, a darker shape in a grey wilderness of water.

Almost at once a shot was fired at us. It was from a light gun, and the splash of the ball was not above twenty yards short. At the same time the vessel turned away and began to disappear into the mist.

Warnett put over his helm to follow, and there was a scramble to raise the sail. Victor waved into the darkness behind him, but there was nothing there.

"We've lost touch with *Quittance*."

"Hark!" said Ralegh.

We listened in silence.

"I can hear the breaking of waves," he said.

"Aye, that's true," said a sailor. "Over there."

We listened again. There was silence for a minute or two and then out of the drab waste ahead came a strange sound like a tree crashing to the ground, like a load of slate being tipped.

Warnett said: "She's struck, sir." Without being instructed he told the sailors to lower sail.

Victor said again: "We've lost touch with *Quittance*."

Out of the darkness ahead we now heard clearly the breaking waves. And then the cries and shouts of men. They sounded like sea birds circling a cliff face.

"Go about," said Sir Walter, "or we shall be ashore ourselves."

Till dawn we stayed in the vicinity, cold and blind. Then as day came we made out through the lifting mists a dark, tall coast and a ship fast upon the rocks near the mouth of an inlet. As the sun broke through the fog we descried *Quittance* standing far out. Captain Gyfford told us he had followed until the lead showed three fathoms under his keel. *Lioness* and *Truelove* had lost contact and were nowhere to be seen. There were three dark blurs to our north, but they were others of the Portuguese fleet. By the time we had been picked up they were out of sight.

On the deck of *Quittance* there was a hurried council of war. If we followed we might catch them, but a single crompster had hardly the mettle to take on three or more armed merchantmen; and a chase extending over a whole day would keep the rest of the squadron immobilised and out of the main attack. Sir Walter decided we should seek out *Warspite* and the rest.

We gained contact about nine, and the whole squadron turned south. That day we made slow progress and through the night. At six the following morning we sighted Cadiz floating like a white ghost city in a pool of blue mist. As we drew nearer the white domes and turrets solidified, the high Moorish walls rooted themselves in shelving rock and sea. And we saw that the attack on the great port had just begun.

CHAPTER 5

THE city of Cadiz is situated on a long thin strip of land like a tongue in the mouth of a dog. It lolls a little out of the mouth as if panting in the sun.

Before this tongue our fleet was assembled, a hundred odd ships from galleons down to caravels, a sight not to be forgotten, tall ship behind tall ship; a first line of them, interspersed with the transports, from which soldiers in full armour were being loaded into boats to make a landing on the beach at the tip of the tongue, opposite a heavily guarded fort, San Sebastian. Drawn up in the shallow water beneath the fort were six Spanish galleys waiting to dispute the landing.

As the sun climbed the wind was freshening from the south-west, and I think Ralegh could not quite believe his eyes at what he saw.

"This—this is madness!" he shouted vehemently to Carew, who had rejoined him from *Mary Rose*. "If it had been begun at four, before dawn broke, it might have had a prospect of success. But this is not a surprise attack! They have been warned, they're ready! A frontal assault in this sea. . . . Do they relish sending troops to certain death?"

Carew seemed surprised at the outburst, and frowned shorewards. "It will be a hard fight, but no doubt we shall prevail."

"I had heard nothing of this! We were going in by sea! It cannot be sense to make a frontal attack with troops on a well-defended shore. . . . By the living God, I'll wager they have fallen out between themselves, Essex and the Howards, and some question of prestige is involved!"

"It would not be surprising," Carew muttered.

"No, it would not be surprising. But if we can intervene we may yet stop this bloody sacrifice—"

"Intervene? Nonsense! It's too late. No one will listen. Essex is the best of them, and he's stubborn as a mule—"

"Well, the mule must be moved. I'll go at once, and you shall come with me. . . . Look! Look there! What did I tell you!"

One of the boats leaving the protection of *Due Repulse* and crowded with men had been hit by the rising swell and had capsized. Many of the men in it, weighted down as they were with armour, sank like stones. Others clung desperately to the upturned keel or floundered for a moment or two before disappearing for ever. A dozen or more swam to the next boat and clambered aboard it. That, pulled violently down and swung off its course by the swimmers, turned broadside on to the waves and likewise capsized.

But Ralegh was already gone. I was after him to the side, but Victor and Sir George were before me and the boat was pushed off before I could argue. So I did not see what followed and only heard it from Victor after.

"He went aboard *Due Repulse* and bearded Essex in front of all his officers. Walter can truly look like the Devil when he chooses. He demanded to know what change of plan this was which had come of a sudden while he was away and how it could be justified since its nature jeopardised the success of the expedition. Essex replied angrily that it was all the fault of the Lord Admiral who insisted that the town must be taken before he risked his ships in the narrow waters of the harbour. Walter said Drake had disproved such timidity. Essex said, ah, yes, but Drake was dead and none like him commanded here. Thereupon they continued arguing but in a gradually more friendly frame, and while they argued Essex sent word that the landings might be stayed.

"Then Walter stormed out and went to see the Lord Admiral. I was not with him there but remained in the boat. In forty minutes he was out and we were rowing back to *Due Repulse*. Somehow—I know not how—by violence of manner, by force of character, by cogency of argument, he had got his way. We are going in by sea, as first arranged."

"But we have not yet gone in."

"No; we've missed the tide, and the next will see us in only an hour before nightfall. Walter himself advised against a night attack."

"So we force the harbour tomorrow at dawn?"

"At dawn."

"In what order?"

"I have forgotten. All I know is that we lead."

I slept fitfully. During the night there was cannon fire from time to time between the Spanish galleons in the mouth of the harbour and the leading English ships, notably *Mary Rose* which under Carew's urging had edged nearest to them and to the shore batteries. All night there was a subtle movement and manoeuvering of the English ships, like men jostling at the start of a race, each captain trying to gain the best position for the assault on the morrow.

I woke a dozen times staring at the stars and waiting for them to wane. At last a faint blueing of the sky was enough and I was up and had buckled on my breast-plate before Victor woke. We only just reached the deck as *Warspite* weighed anchor. It was done slyly, in silence, without fanfare or command; we slipped away as if to some lover's tryst. But the silent ships around us had been silently watching; they were not to be left that way and we were by only some three minutes the first to slip off. The sails of Carew's *Mary Rose* came rattling down, and as he moved close after us he was followed by Robert Southwell in *Lion*, he by Clifford in *Dreadnought*, then Crosse in *Swiftsure* and Lord Thomas Howard in *Nonpareil*.

During the night the Spanish fleet, which first had been drawn up opposite Fort St Philip—which fort formed the north-easterly bastion of the town of Cadiz—had withdrawn a mile or more and were still withdrawing. Soon they would reach the narrow mouth of the inner harbour. Behind them the rich treasure fleet was retiring towards the Port Royal pool, beyond which there was no further retreat.

To reach the Spanish galleons therefore the English ships had first to run the gauntlet of shore fire from Fort St Philip and Cadiz. As the sun came up the wind almost dropped, so that even with all sail set we only drifted gently forward with the tide.

The first ship to draw a concentrated fire upon herself was not ours but a smaller one, *Rainbow*, under Sir Francis Vere, who, aware no doubt of his shallower draught, was making along in the shoal waters nearer the shore in an attempt to be first in action. At this Sir Walter bit at his gloves in anger and curtly demanded of Captain Oakes if he had no studding sails he could set, else we should be leading the attack from behind.

It was clear now that the Spanish were going to stand and fight at the narrowest point of the harbour entrance, between Puntal and Matagorda. Here the water was in apparent width perhaps six or seven cable lengths, but the fair channel was very narrow and almost spanned by the length of four ships. Here the four great galleons, *San Andrea*, *San Felipe*, *San Thomas*, and *San Mateo*, were coming head to stern athwart our passage. Behind were the two big Portuguese galleons and the three powerful Italian armed merchantmen; and in their rear a cluster of smaller ships. Three frigates were taking up their station to our left, while a cluster of galleys lurking under the shelter of Fort St Philip were also retreating, firing at *Rainbow* and keeping pace with her.

Sir Walter need not have gnawed his glove. *Rainbow* had her sails shot to ribbons, and as soon as the majestic *Warspite* came within likely range the galleys and the shore batteries concentrated on us instead. This pleased Ralegh greatly. He stood on the high poop in his purple cloak, staring across at the shore and presently called the buglers to him. The shore fire was just falling short of us, the shot sending up spouts of water twenty to thirty yards away.

"We must not waste our powder, so let us use breath instead. Blow us a fanfare each time they fire."

So the four buglers stood on the poop in line beside him, and each time the shore batteries fired they blew a blast. The sailors and gunners, who had not liked our refusal to answer back, were heartened by this and their cheers followed the bugle notes. Even so, they still winced and ducked when the shore cannon fired, for any moment we might drift within range.

Meantime three galleys, more mobile with their shallow draughts and spidery oars, had crept out of the shelter of the shore and trained their sakers on us. At the first blast a shot tore the rigging above our heads; a dozen thumped into the iron-hard oak of the ship's sides; one landed between two of our largest cannon, missing their crews and skidding the eighteen paces into the sea at the other side.

"We must look to these wasps," Sir Walter said. "Give them a benediction, Mr Johns."

At once the gunners were busy, loading their cannon, priming them, waiting the order to fire. It came, and the ship shuddered and veered; the rattling explosions hurt one's ears.

The shots straddled one of the galleys. Their return fire was less accurate, though splinters flew from the fore yard. We fired again, and one of the heavy 32-lb. balls from a demi-cannon hit the central galley amidships. A half-dozen oars speared upwards like splinters. The galleys turned away.

Amid the cheers and shouts from our men I heard Captain Oakes shout: "In five minutes we'll be in range of the *San Felipe*, sir. We draw more water than she does. I'm not sure of the shoal here."

"Hold on your course. It was she who first boarded the *Revenge*."

"Have we leave to board *her*?"

"No, by God, no, that irks me. Explicit command not to hazard a Queen's ship. Boarding's for the fly-boats. But we have shot."

Over to our right Essex's ship, *Due Repulse*, having gone to the succour of *Rainbow*, had now over-run her and was in furious conflict with the shore batteries. The ships behind us were no longer in line but had spread out so that at the moment of conflict *Warspite* was like the point of a spear, *Nonpareil* and *Lion* on our starboard quarter and *Mary Rose* and *Dreadnought* on our left.

San Felipe fired. Flames and smoke belched from her decks as twenty guns exploded in succession across the narrowing strip of water. A half dozen of the culverin shot hit us above the water line, the bigger shot fell short. We were now about five hundred yards away.

"We're in danger of taking the ground, sir!" shouted Oakes. "Best anchor and wait for the flood."

"If we run aground the flood will float us. We must use our major armament."

A half-dozen balls aimed high and at random flew over our heads. Some desultory fire was also coming from the frigates, and *Mary Rose* engaged them.

"If we take the ground, sir, we'll lose our place and fall out of the fight!"

"By the living God, we *must* make another cable's length! They're higher built than we are—why should we draw more water?"

Our bow chasers went into action. Another discharge from *San Felipe:* this time more than half the shots struck us.

"Very good," said Ralegh. "Anchor now if you must."

Captain Oakes at once bellowed orders, the men on the yards began hauling up the sails, chains rattled. The other great ships were not slow to follow our example; they seemed in no way more anxious than ourselves to risk a murderous small-arms fire without the ultimate sanction of a boarding to follow.

An artist in imagination and perception of danger, Ralegh could yet steel his nerves to accept and even welcome peril: the drama of the battle seemed to appeal to him. While men fired guns and worked furiously loading and fusing them and while sailors ran ducking for cover about the decks, he stood on the high poop with Captain Oakes— who would gladly have moved, I could see—watching the course of the fight. Sometimes he would turn away from the belching guns of *San Felipe* and scan the sea and landscape to make sure that no other English ship should steal a march on him by slipping along in the shoal water nearer shore.

Warspite was suffering. Her main yard had been splintered and two of her guns were out of action. There had also been heavy damage to the captain's cabin and the poop windows. We could not see what we had done in return, for the whole of the superstructure of the *San Felipe* was fringed with drifting white smoke from the cannon fire. Amidships our guns had scored many hits and some of their main armament had stopped firing.

The channel was here so narrow that *Warspite* remained the spearhead of the attack on the big galleons while our four-ship escort clustered closely on our larboard and starboard quarters, exchanging fire with the other galleons and themselves being raked by the lighter fire of the enemy frigates and eight galleys. All the English ships suffered in some degree by being almost bows on to the enemy and not able to deploy all their heavy guns as the Spaniards were doing.

No English fly-boats laden with soldiers were yet to be seen; but a new situation was developing away to our right. The remaining galleys under Fort Puntal had stood and fought *Rainbow* and *Due Repulse* for best part of an hour; but the arrival of *Vanguard* with a half-dozen ships of London had overborne them and the last of the galleys broke and fled for the protection of the Apostle galleons. Now *Rainbow* and *Due Repulse*, with some eddying shore current of air to help, were following them and coming into the area of the main battle. *Rainbow*, still well in-shore, was clearly intent on outflanking the Apostles and thus taking over the leadership of the attack: *Due Repulse* was heading straight for us.

"So!" said Ralegh. "This is not to be borne! We'll see what Essex has to say!"

He spoke to me, and I went with him gladly. Movement now helped to keep thought in check, to relieve tightened muscles, sweat on hands, the griping of fear.

Sir Walter went quickly down the rope ladder to his hoy, his cloak billowing like an opening flower. Four men sat waiting to row. As I joined him a heavy ball struck the sea and drenched us with water.

Due Repulse looked enormous as we neared her. Fortunately the wind had left her sails and she was only drifting forward under her own momentum; Sir Walter clutched a dangling ladder as we went past and climbed rapidly up it. I was too late for the ladder but caught a rope which bruised me against the side of the ship.

When I got on deck hot words had already been exchanged: Essex had taken my master to task for anchoring at a distance from the enemy; Ralegh was saying in a biting voice: "I am a soldier, my lord, and like not these long bowls any better than you; but since I'm debarred from boarding I'd more consideration for my men than to subject them to an endless small-arms fire at close quarters while we wait for the fly-boats. Where *are* the fly-boats? My Lord Admiral was lavish with his promises!"

The Earl of Essex was in white satin under his armour. "The boarding parties were promised when the main guns were silenced. As yet they're not silenced."

"They will be; but not before *Warspite* is holed and sunk, as things go now. I ask Your Lordship's leave to board if the fly-boats are not here within twenty minutes. Better to lose a Queen's ship that way than the other."

Essex stared through the forest of rigging towards the combat he was approaching. "I cannot give you leave, Sir Walter, but I'll not stop you. Indeed, I'm tempted to join you when the time comes."

Ralegh laughed. There was no mirth in it but a sudden release of tension. "In that I'd be greatly honoured. Give me leave to return to the fight."

"We shall be there as soon as you."

We clambered down the ladder again, while the guns of the *Due Repulse* opened fire at one of the frigates. In our tiny hoy we danced away from the side of the battleship and four strong oars took us ahead of her and back to *Warspite*. In the interval of our being away a cannon ball had struck the high poop where we had been standing and had taken the leg off the sailor who had been there to relay the captain's orders to the helmsman. Also Lord Thomas Howard, seeing Sir Walter absent, had ordered *Nonpareil* to weigh anchor and had edged ahead of *Warspite* into the position of honour.

Before Sir Walter, feverish with anger at this, could rail at Oakes for his negligence, *Due Repulse* came sliding into the line, swinging her stern with the tide. She narrowly missed *Mary Rose*, who was in combat with *San Andrea*, but could not right herself in time and crashed into the larboard quarter of *Dreadnought*. This broke the line and for ten minutes neither of the great ships concerned was able to concentrate its fire on the enemy.

Rainbow, with Sir Francis Vere, was now coming swiftly up from the right. Sir Walter ordered Oakes to weigh anchor and at all costs to get ahead of *Nonpareil*. We began to drift nearer the enemy. As we did so a heavy cannon ball split our foremast just above the main yard, and the shrouds fell over the forward chasers putting them out of action.

Drifting with the tide, we came up with *Nonpareil;* then, to the wolfish satisfaction of my master, dropped anchor only by the bows so that we swung broadside on to the Spanish, facing them at close quarters and almost blocking the rest of our fleet from direct contact with the enemy. *Rainbow* had now come up alongside *Nonpareil* and thrown a rope aboard her to warp herself into position for the fight. A hail of shot swept across the deck of *Warspite*, killing men and disabling guns.

Sir Walter was looking back. Some small vessels, a part of the Dutch squadron were advancing, but not the fly-boats. Then Victor drew his cousin's attention to the fact that *Rainbow* had thrown out

another hawser, this time to *Warspite* and by means of it was stealth-
ily hauling herself into the leading position.

Sir Walter shouted in his high angry voice: "Cut that line!" And it
was cut, so that *Rainbow* fell away and drifted off.

It was we three who bore the brunt: *Warspite, Nonpareil* and
Rainbow; all the others behind. The Queen's flag was in ribbons;
men lay about our decks groaning; half our guns were disabled, others
fired through the fallen shrouds. Acrid smoke clouded out the sun.

San Felipe had suffered worse than we. Only two demi-cannon
still fired; there were great holes in her sides and her upper decks
had been swept clear of men.

"Loose that anchor!" Ralegh shouted. "Get a warp aboard her!"

He climbed on the rail and waved his sword as a signal to Essex
and Vere. A thin cheer sounded above the noise of the guns. Both
the other vessels answered his signal and began to drift forward with
Warspite to collide with the enemy.

A great rushing and thunder-clap of noise; Ralegh was no longer
standing but was lying with his purple cloak spread-eagled like a
broken flower; Victor was down too but was crawling to his knees.

I went to Sir Walter. He was conscious but there was blood welling
down one leg.

"Lie still!" I shouted.

"Out of my way!" He tried to get to his feet.

"Let me see!"

"It will wait. Prepare to board!"

"You must stop the blood—"

"Damn you!" He was on his feet again. "Out of my way! Prepare to
board!"

The Spaniards, seeing our advance and having suffered much, were
giving up the fight. *San Felipe* was the first to slip her cable, the others
followed. Some sort of sail was let go on such masts as remained and
the four great galleons began to drift into the port, while the Portuguese and the Levanters retreated behind them.

Then it was seen that Oakes's concern for *Warspite* was not mistaken, for within two minutes *San Felipe* and *San Mateo* had both
grounded. Then *San Andrea* in a desperate effort to avoid a similar
fate, collided with *San Tomaso,* and they both took the ground.
Firing at the guns ceased and the sailors abandoned their posts;
dead and wounded men were left lying on the decks; *San Felipe* had
taken on a dangerous list toward us so that all that happened could
be seen. Pieces of ordnance slid across the decks, and some out of
their ports into the water; men fell with them and others jumped.

Ralegh was holding his leg trying to staunch the blood and at the same time shouting: "Boarding parties away! Boarding parties away!"

I snatched at the shirt of the dead sailor beside me and ripped it up; I went to Sir Walter and bound his leg above the knee where the wound was; he could barely suffer to be held; *Nonpareil* behind us was putting out small boats, some laden with soldiers, some to pick up the struggling men in the water.

A flicker of flames showed amidships of *San Felipe*, either a chance spark or the Spanish Admiral had resolved his ship should not be taken. By the time I tied the knot with a stick to wind it tighter, one deck was blazing.

Now all were abandoning her for fear of an explosion; men leaped into the water in scores, some wounded, some already alight; a few tried to get down by rope ladder; dozens jumped into the water and broke their legs or arms on the scarcely hidden mud-bank; they fell from all quarters.

San Tomaso was also alight and the horror repeated; the other two galleons still kept up some resistance but half their crews were in flight. Many boats the English had put out to capture the galleons were given over to succour.

Sailors from *Rainbow* and from our ship were swarming up *San Andrea* to try to capture her unburned, but so far none had been able to board *San Felipe*. Just then a pinnace from *Nonpareil* shot through a gap in the struggling swarming sea and threw a line aboard. Men swarmed up, intent to put out the fire; but the feared explosion took place on the main gun deck of the flagship, and one of the masts blazing like a fire-brand fell and hit the pinnace square amidships, killing five and burning others. In seconds the pinnace herself was aflame and sinking; men plunged in the water and swam beside their Spanish enemies towards the nearest boat.

Now a group of Dutch fly-boats came on the scene, darting into the swarming channel, and with pistols, hatchets, and knives began to slaughter the Spanish soldiers and sailors as they swam and struggled in the water. Too many years of cruelty in the Lowlands, too many memories of suffering and massacre, too many relatives helplessly murdered in Antwerp and elsewhere, were bearing their grim fruit. Nor did the Dutch take kindly to opposition from their allies, and ugly scenes grew in the melee.

It looked as if *San Andrea* and *San Tomaso* would be ours unburned; boarding parties were already on the enemy decks. Essex, standing plain on the top deck of *Due Repulse* had been joined by Sir Francis Vere; they were turning their thoughts to an assault on the town. Soldiers were being mustered in fly-boats and transports. The admiral and the general went down to join them and themselves embarked on Essex's barge. No signal came to *Warspite* to assist or to participate, but Ralegh ordered the two regiments aboard *Warspite* to join the landing fleet, and then collapsed in the chair Bell had brought up for him.

"The treasure ships. . . . Force our way through now and take them. Nothing to stop us—a few frigates—all in disorder. We should strike now."

"Well, they cannot get away, sir," Captain Oakes said, "except through this narrow channel which we command."

"These canals beyond Carraca? They are deep enough?"

"Oh, by no means. No ship of any draught could attempt it."

"They're moving off!" said Victor, pointing to the transports. "Hark at them."

The landing flotilla was leaving the ships and rowing towards the beach. In the van was Essex's barge with his banner flying, and a dozen gentlemen in armour escorting him. Sir Francis Vere as head of the land forces stood at his side. Behind came a group of boats in three lines abreast in the most orderly manner. All was silence, no cheering, no trumpets, no firing, nothing but the regular roll and beat of drums. Oars kept pace with the beat, and at minute intervals the drums stopped and the oars stopped; with a preliminary roll they would begin again. There must have been two thousand men in the boats.

This was a discipline quite different from the individual bravery of the naval commanders; this strange ominous advance was the stranger in contrast with the wild indiscriminate sea battle.

Ralegh said suddenly: "Victor, go at once and see my Lord of Essex. Ask him to grant me permission to send forces to capture the treasure *flota* while the army mounts its attack on Cadiz. . . . Take Maugan with you."

"What of yourself?" I said. "This wound. . . ."

"It's nothing mortal. The surgeon will see to it. Go. I want the answer."

The water we were rowed through was littered with burning fragments; rags and spars and corpses drifted past. A hand clasped a wooden staff but the owner of the hand was gone. A hat with its soaked feather trailing; bloodstained sail-cloth; bubbles of vomit.

The army had a start of us; they were making for a sandy bay just below Fort Puntal, but no fire was coming from the fort. As we caught up the last line of transports Essex had already jumped ashore and his standard bearer was beside him; regiments began to disembark and quickly assembled in rigid lines on the sand. We had to swing wide to avoid the transports, and by the time we were ashore most of the troops had landed.

We ran towards Essex, who was surrounded by a group of officers, and it was several minutes before we could gain his attention.

Victor saluted. "Your Lordship, Sir Walter Ralegh presents his respectful compliments and asks permission to dispatch a force to capture the treasure *flota* while it is still undefended."

Essex was flushed, his eyes a-glitter with success. "We do not yet know what numbers shall be needed to capture the city. That must be our first thought."

"My lord," said a captain, "I submit that a force be detached nevertheless. Seizure of the city may take days."

"It may or it may not, Monson. Splitting our power now may just mean a failure on both fronts."

"Let Ralegh take it on, sir. The and Crosso and two other ships could overcome the resistance and put skeleton crews aboard."

Essex glanced along the lines of soldiers, standing in their breastplates and helmets and waiting for the next order. "Where is the Lord Admiral? He should be here soon with the rest of the troops. I cannot grant anyone permission to over-ride our original instructions."

Sir Francis Vere said: "He came up in his pinnace just before I left. I think he'll be with Lord Thomas Howard."

"Very well. You go, Monson—and you, Ashley. Convey the Rear Admiral's request—and mine also—that a sufficient force be dispatched to deal with the *flota*. Tell the Lord Admiral also that we wait his reinforcements minute by minute."

"Have we your permission to stay with you, my lord?" Victor asked.

"What? Yes, yes. Monson, send a man to *Warspite* with this message. But remember, I give no sanction to Ralegh. Let it come from the Lord Admiral or not at all!"

Orders rapped out along the lines and the soldiers began to advance towards the city of Cadiz, led by the Earl of Essex with his gaunt tireless stride. It was grim going. The sun was still high and the day at its hottest; the sand dunes that confronted us gave back one step for every two we climbed; our armour became insufferable, our muscles leaden, sweat soaked us and soaked us again, men stumbled and all but fell from the heat.

But we got to the top of the last ridge unchallenged. Before us to our right some half mile away were the walls of Cadiz. A regiment of the enemy was assembled outside the walls, flags waving, horsemen on their flanks and infantry posted ahead to delay our advance.

I could see Vere urging some plan on Essex. What little I had seen of this dark-faced, sardonic man gave me already to understand why he had been a force in the Netherlands.

We began to advance, first over the soft fiery sand, then athwart the shore road to the city. A battalion of two hundred men under Sir John Wingfield was thrown out ahead of us while the rest paused and waited. It seemed that Wingfield's task was to drive in the advance infantry so that a full scale battle could develop; but he far exceeded his orders and burst right through to the main body of the enemy. Then, realising his mistake, and finding himself in danger of being surrounded, he ordered a hasty and undisciplined retreat.

The Spanish, encouraged beyond themselves by their success, counter-attacked with vigor, driving Wingfield's men in a rabble before them. But after a while at a bugle note Wingfield's forlorn two hundred suddenly rallied again, falling into line with a discipline strange in routed men, and another battalion under Sir Matthew Morgan violently attacked the enemy flanks, now themselves exposed. Then Vere sounded the advance for the rest of his army.

It was one of the oldest stratagems in the world of war, but once again it succeeded. The Spanish line broke and fled, horse and foot together, towards the city gates. Here true panic took hold, for the wave of men first to reach the gates crowded in, and then, seeing us so close on the heels of this cavalry, ordered the gates shut, so that some four or five hundred of their own men were left outside. These, abandoning their equipment and their horses, began to swarm up ropes lowered for them. However, the gates were again opened to admit the flood and slammed shut just before the first English reached them.

Panting, swooning from the heat and the fatigue of battle, the group of leading officers paused within musket shot of the gates.

"All but successful, Vere!" Essex shouted. "In another minute we'd have had 'em! By God, I had no thought to attempt the city yet. . . ."

"It's too strong to attempt here," Sir Francis said. But I'll wager it's not so well guarded all the way; I suggest we take a battalion each, you to the right, my lord, I to the left. These fortifications are part new and part old. They'll have their weak points."

"It would be splendid to capture the place before Howard comes," Essex muttered.

"Have a care for yourself, my lord. The Queen will not be pleased with us if we return without you."

So they parted. We attached ourselves to the battalion led by Essex. Some twenty gaily armoured gentlemen surrounded him, but he topped them all, impulsive, ardent, arrogant.

The fortifications of Cadiz consisted of a deep ditch with a high wall behind punctuated by defence towers. As we made our progress round, the defendants were firing at us.

After five minutes Essex stopped. Part of the city wall was ruinous here, and the earth thrown up from the ditch made a mountable slope to reach the top of the wall. But knowing the weakness the Spaniards were guarding it with a line of musketeers, and one of the defence towers overlooked it.

Essex said: "I think we shall find nothing more enticing than this, gentlemen. When I give the word, follow me."

"No, sir!" said Captain Savage. "With respect it is not a place for your Lordship to lead. As your Captain-Lieutenant I claim that privilege."

Essex hesitated, while the officers and gentlemen crowded round him, claiming his attention. "So be it, then. Savage—and you, Evans— and you, Bagnal—take five men each. But we'll follow on your heels. Wait. Musketeers! prepare to fire!"

Shots from the tower were already peppering round us. Eighteen soldiers gathered in three groups. Then the musketeers discharged three volleys at the defenders. Savage shouted and the men rushed forward, first down into the ditch, then clambering wildly up the broken earth towards the city wall. Two men fell but the others gained the wall. Savage at the parapet killed a man and stood with sword raised defying the fire of the city.

Essex and twenty more followed, and we were in that number; behind came a platoon of pikemen, and then the musketeers. It was a hard and anxious scramble: had I been alone I should have been much more afraid.

I gained the city wall ahead of Victor and just behind Essex himself: in the street below us a man driving a water cart stared up open-mouthed: a line of washing hung from the balcony opposite; on a farther roof-top two children played beside a wooden cradle; a mangy dog was eating some refuse in the alley below.

We were in no good place here: the Spaniards had been driven from this part of the wall, but our position was still dominated by the tower to our right; also there was another tower, invisible from below, set back but within musket range. There was no way down to the street except by jumping, and that little short of twenty feet.

Two more of our men had been wounded. Captain Bagnal, one of Vere's veterans, now assembled the musketeers into two lines, one firing through the other, and ordered them to concentrate on the tower. This they did with such accuracy that the tower ceased to fire.

"I do not like this drop," Essex said. "Carrying this armour, one is certain to break a leg."

"I'll try," I said, and began to unbuckle my breast-plate, but Lieutenant Evans sat on the edge of the wall, threw down his sword, and slithered and fell into the street. For a moment after the clatter of his armour he lay still, but before two Spaniards could seize him he got to his knees and reached for his sword. Another English officer with a whoop followed, and then three more. I went over the edge, breastplate and all, and the ground hit me a great blow.

Two dozen were down now and the street was clear of the enemy. There was still some desultory fire from the other tower; Essex remained hesitating on the wall, though only one of those who had jumped was rolling over in pain. Victor landed almost in my arms and collapsed in a heap.

Then I heard cheering farther along, unmistakably English in character. Essex raised his head and thereafter made no attempt to jump. Vere and his veterans had forced the gate.

CHAPTER 6

THE streets were narrow as slits, and the Spanish were fighting for each house. In some cases the women had carried boulders up on to the flat roofs and toppled these down as we advanced. It was murderous work, sometimes by musket but more often hand to hand.

There were about sixty of us to begin, led by Essex, but in no time the narrow streets split us up, like water trickling through a honeycomb; we were all making towards the centre of the city but in different channels and at different speeds.

Victor and I found ourselves with Captain Samuel Bagnal and a Captain Carey and six others. In the street to our left Sir John Wingfield had appeared with a dozen men. To our right was Evans. In our second street three Spanish pikemen had overturned a vegetable cart; behind them were eight civilians armed with staves and axes. We only had one musketeer in our band, and as he raised his gun it was knocked from his hand by a great earthenware pot dropped from a window.

Bagnal bent down and picked up one of the big oranges lying in the gutter. He bit into it, spat out the peel, and took a mouthful of juice and sweet pulp. Then he leaped at the barrier, pulling at the cart's end to swing it round. A pikeman lunged and wounded Bagnal in the shoulder; Bagnal stabbed the man through the throat and sat astride the upturned cart. Three other soldiers joined him and I followed. The civilians did not run but charged us as we climbed; a soldier had his helmet and head cleft open. I thrust at a civilian with my sword; it went in and my wrist jarred as the steel struck some bone. The man's eyes went white and he collapsed, pulling me with him. In a welter of arms and legs I dragged my sword out; we were over the barrier. Carey was driving two men back and the rest fled.

Bagnal smeared the blood down his doublet sleeve and sword in hand stalked to the end of the alley. Three men attacked him. He was stabbed again in the side, but Carey was up with him and Victor and others, and the three men were killed. One of our men was shot through the head from a window.

Another street like the last, except for some acacia trees at the end. Spanish soldiers at windows had it under a cross fire. Bagnal ducked into a doorway, smashed the lattice with his elbow to get a view, and then fired his pistol at one of the windows while two of his own men crept up in the shadow of the opposite wall. They broke in the doors with their pikes and disappeared inside.

There was much firing down a cross alley where Wingfield was engaging a group of Spaniards. A donkey came trotting riderless along this alley, its little knock-kneed legs rubbing against each other; as it turned the corner it spilled its burden of dried palmetto leaves and stopped to sniff at something in the gutter.

Bagnal beckoned to me and we moved on down the street followed by three of the others. At the trees the street split left and right. Since Wingfield was in a pitched battle to our left we turned right and came into a tiny patio with awnings still out, a well in the middle with pink geraniums, two mules tethered, and a dog barking. The heat everywhere was overpowering, and even shade brought no relief.

This patio was empty and we could only hear the fighting like clamour from another world. Victor caught us up, and with him were two musketeers who had got detached from their fellows.

"We'll be short o' powder soon, sir," said one of them to Bagnal.

"Then use your butts," he answered, and walked into the patio towards the door at the other side.

At once he was fired on and wounded again in the shoulder. Doors opened and a dozen Spaniards fell on us with rare ferocity; the musketeers could only fire their guns once and then it was dagger work.

I killed a second man. My side was hurting and I felt sick and Katherine Footmarker was telling me there was blood on my hands.

Bagnal was down and both musketeers; and then Captain Carey appeared with two extra men and fought his way in among the retreating Spaniards, slashing like a madman.

Two of our first group were dead and all the rest wounded except Victor. Why there was blood round my waist I did not know, for I did not remember being stabbed.

Bagnal was up again, though now five times wounded and dripping with blood. He and Carey and a pikeman broke down the door and this led us into another alley. There was a church here, squat-towered, built on to the houses of the street. The pikeman, thoughts on plunder, raised his pike to smash down the church door, but Carey knocked up the pike and we went on.

We had climbed and were near the main square of the city. I felt better now, inspirited by the tattered man leading us. Some women were hurling tiles at us from a roof-top. A tiny Jew, black-robed and white-slippered, stood in a doorway hands clasped, having come out to put up his shutters, caught now between two fires; it was a Spanish ball that killed him; his skull cap rolled at my feet.

We rushed the defenders here, Bagnal as usual in the lead; soon too close for guns, it was bloody knives again. Essex and a gang of ten more gentlemen appeared to our left and the defenders fled leaving bodies all about, Bagnal in pursuit.

Suddenly we came out upon the Plaza, a square with churches and public buildings, shaded by planes and palm trees, some deserted stalls down the centre. Here for lack of opposition there was a pause. It looked as if the main city was almost won, though the Citadel and the Fort would no doubt hold out for some time.

Bagnal's face was a mask of blood, but he seemed in no way weakened. Essex, seeing him so, took out his sword.

"One knee, Captain."

The tall soldier looked surprised.

"You shall be the first knight created on this triumphant day on Spanish soil. Few have deserved better of our nation. Sir John Wingfield is dead, with many others, but it is a great victory."

Victor put his arm round me. "Hold up, boy, is your hurt serious?"

"I think not."

"I trust not, for it would spoil my day if you were to fall out now."

"I'll do my best not. I want plunder, Victor."

The square was filling with English. Among them were a group about the body of Wingfield, who had fallen at the edge of the Plaza. Then I saw that Captain Ashley and Captain Monson were back, talking to Essex, and I struggled up from the stone wall. Too late to hear the message, I plucked Monson's arm; he looked scowling at me and then remembered.

He said shortly: "The Lord Admiral considers the capture of the *flota* must be delayed until tomorrow and orders all forces to concentrate on the taking of Cadiz."

"You delivered that message to the Rear Admiral?"

"Yes, and it was ill received. For once I agree with your master, and that must indeed be a rarity."

"Where is the Lord Admiral, sir?"

"Landing with the second division. I have no doubt Sir Walter will be ashore too before the night is out!"

Firing was beginning again in the square. Some of the buildings around the Plaza were well armed and intended to contest our presence.

At the end of the Plaza beside a church was the town hall. A group of soldiers moved to attack this, and among them were Bagnal and Carey. I saw them meet with resistance at the door and then force it and go in. Victor said:

"Let me see this wound."

"No, I'll do." Remembering my last meeting with Sue, "I want *plunder*, Victor."

When we got to the town hall the ground floor had already been cleared. Pictures and furniture lay wrecked everywhere, books and parchments scattered, one or two wounded lying about. But when we came to the broad central stairs we saw that the whole of the first flight was littered with dead men, and most of them were English. Blood made the steps slippery, broken bannisters stood out like raw stumps; at the top an enormous Franciscan friar lay clutching a pike that protruded from his stomach; like the rest he was dead. The only live one was an English soldier tying up a deep gash on his leg.

"'E stood athwart the stairs," he said, thumbing towards the friar. "Wi' a great axe in 'is 'ands. Nine of us 'e killed afore we cotched 'im. Nine good men gone for one shaven monk. Two o' my friends, Devil take 'im. Reckon 'e 'ad the strength of the Devil too!"

We climbed across the piled bodies. On this floor you could hear the fighting still in progress. I stayed Victor, who was for pushing forward.

"We'll find nothing here that's not broken up or already bespoke. There's a church next door."

"Essex ordered no desecration."

"What he does not see he'll not complain of. Look out of this window. It's no sort of drop compared to the city wall, and I'd guess that door leads into the church."

Victor still hesitated, so I said: "Let me go ahead and I'll tell you what I find."

"No . . . if you go, I'll come."

The church was as dark as the churches I remembered in Madrid. The sun was setting, and only a few coloured shafts came from it high up in the nave; if it had not been for the candles at the high altar and before the Virgin in the side chapel we should have been unable to see our way.

The place was empty, heavy only with the smell of incense and flowers. I knew the orders: no desecration of churches, no women to be molested, discipline even to be preserved in the sacking of the town. The penalty for a breach, at least for the common soldier, was death. But death from either side had in a few short hours become a commonplace.

I went up to the high altar and seized the cross. The whole was too heavy to carry away and was gilt on some common metal, but there were jewels in it, and having lifted it to the floor I began to prize these out with the point of my dagger. Victor after some more hesitation disappeared into the darkness behind the altar, and I heard him hacking at something, but his heart was not in it.

I got eight jewels; five were big stones of a semi-precious nature but the other three were rubies. There were four silver candlesticks beside the altar, and behind these two angels holding jewelled wreaths. These I also stripped, but after lifting the candlesticks down I left them on the altar steps, knowing them too heavy to carry.

Because of having snuffed four of the candles, the church was even darker. Shots and commotion echoed outside. We were as if in a dark pool while the strife of the world eddied to the brim.

I went over to the Lady chapel because sometimes these are as richly ornamented as the main altars. Here about twenty candles burned, some tall like a young man's life, others old and guttering. A few simple posies lay at the Virgin's feet and a ring had been hung on an outstretched finger. She looked out, glazed and dumb, at the corners of her waxen lips a fixed half-smile of compassion but no understanding.

At that moment I thought my loss of blood had overcome me and I was losing my senses, for I seemed to see suddenly not one Virgin but upwards of a dozen, all peering out of the darkness behind her, all with fixed stares and not a half-smile among them. But whereas the first Virgin gazed across the church in contemplation of the polished marble pillars of the Lady chapel, all the other stares were fixed on me.

Then I saw what it was. They had come here for sanctuary, hoping they might be overlooked. They were mainly high-born, richly dressed in fine cloaks and lace mantillas, some wearing jewels; but a few were working women in drab black who had fled here to join their sisters. At any other time such women would not have stood together in a group, huddled close as if for protection; now the prospect of violation and murder over-rode the long distinctions of birth.

I took the ring off the Virgin's finger but could not bring myself to touch the jewel on the Child. There were two small crosses finely wrought in gold, and I pocketed these. No one had moved or spoken.

In halting Spanish I said: "Ladies, we come as conquerors but we shall do you no ill. The Earl of Essex has commanded this, and he will be obeyed. There are always dangers when a city is taken, so you do well to stay here. But, unlike your own menfolk, we do not make war on women and children."

I turned away and went back to the main altar. Still no one had stirred, but walking across the empty nave I had an unpleasant sensation that I might be shot in the back.

At the side of the altar behind the row of saints was a fine, painted screen with some jewels glistening in it, and I went up to see if they were real. They were only painted glass. Then I heard a cry for help from the darkness behind the altar. "Maugan!"

I ran, stumbling over some chairs, groped along the back of the altar. "Where are you!"

No answer but the sound of a struggle. As I got farther in there was a glimmer of light from a half-open door; inside was a round library, candle-lit, two monks struggling with Victor. As I ran forward one of them stabbed him deep in the shoulder where his armour ended.

I sliced at the man's neck, his head wobbled like a stone plinth dislodged; he was dead before he fell. Victor was falling too. The other monk stabbed him as he sank, then raised his dagger to take my sword sweep. Blood spurted from his hand. He brought forward his other hand and with a second knife stabbed me under the arm. I swung again and he was down.

Room was unsteady. The candles flickered as if in a draught, but the draught was in my head. Must not fall now. Must not faint. Second monk was dying; only his hand opened and shut. Victor lying on floor groaning. Get him out of here, back to ship. Beautiful books, illuminated manuscripts: that's what he'd been after; the monks had surprised him. Any more of them? If another came he could finish us off at leisure.

With the deliberation of a drunken man I looked round. Only one

other door and that shut. No one else in the room. I sank to my knees.
"Victor. . . ."

His eyes were glazing. "Go on, Maugan. Take your. . . . I'm very
. . . comfortable here."

"No; let me see."

I tried to get his breast-plate off, fingers fumbling; he was breathing
hard; I prayed the dagger had not gone into his lungs. Off it came, pull
at the cloth of his shirt, soaked first in sweat; blood welling under. I
tore his sleeve up. Knife had gone in through the shoulder-blade downwards. Might be mortal. No blood on his lips. Roll the sleeve into a
pad, press it hard on the wound, bind it with a piece of the other
sleeve. "Kathy," he kept saying. "Kathy." Then once he looked at me
and said: "Go to war in a ship. No marching," and smiled. His head
fell forward.

More blood inside the breast-plate; I tore open the front of his shirt.
The second monk's dagger had glanced off the armour but had
entered over the hip bone.

On the only table not overturned was some wine on a silver tray,
and a chalice. I crawled to it, gulped some down, brought it to
Victor, but he could not swallow; another red stain on his shirt.

I did not like to take off my own breast-plate while there was a
possibility of further fighting. So now the supreme effort. The wine
was warming, brought life and a little stamina; gulped more of it
down. Now. . . . But it was as much as I could do to stand upright.
Never get Victor on my shoulder. I began to drag him towards the
door.

The great stone-dark church: cold after the vestry and silent. Sun
had set and twilight was over. Only the candles in the Lady chapel
and the few left on the high altar. Round the dark corridor behind the
altar, into the nave. Rest there. He was still breathing but very faintly.
Leave him to die, I thought; save yourself.

I dragged him down the great nave. If the women saw us they
made no move to help or hinder. There was still shooting outside but
it had moved away. "Animal nature is not kind," said Katherine
Footmarker, "but it d' kill only for food. Human kind kill for pleasure
or from an evil motive called principle." "I can't bear the thought of
being old," said Sue. "Soon we shall all be old."

The great door at last; I propped Victor against it and groped for
the small door which must somewhere be let in to the larger. "You
are Celts, are you not," said King Philip, "and have affinities with the
Irish. A sturdy stock among whom fidelity to the religion of Christ
dies hard."

Bolts. I shot them back; pulled at the door. Dark outside but light from glaring torches. Wide steps down to the square. A house at the end in flames. A mass of soldiery of all sorts. At the foot of the steps two platoons of English troops were encamped. Other troops rounding up mules and carrying kegs from a captured house.

I clutched Victor and pulled him out on the steps. His face was ashen in the flickering torch light. In one corner of the square were some two dozen wounded; a surgeon and his man looking to their hurts. I staggered down the steps and went towards them, but soldiers carrying a battering ram for a door swept me away, and I ended up sitting on a stone well-edge. People were milling everywhere. The officers were doing their utmost to maintain order, but here and there pillaging was breaking out, and I heard a soldier shout that the Dutch troops were running amok.

Men were drinking from a wine barrel that a sailor was holding for them. I plucked a man's sleeve and asked him where Essex was and he thumbed his hand up the hill towards the citadel. I began to move in that direction and then gave up, realising that, once out of this crowded square, one would be in the narrow alleys where the crush and the fighting and the confusion would be far worse. Better get back to Victor.

I staggered along, pushed this way and that by the press of people; then I saw a man on a horse attended by two servants. He had just come down one of the alleys and was urging his horse through the square.

"Sir Walter!"

Bell heard me and drew his master's attention. Ralegh's face was white with pain.

"Killigrew, you still live? Where is Victor?"

"On the steps of that church, serious wounded."

"We'll go that way. You're hurt yourself?"

"Nothing bad. But Victor is. . . . If we could make some sort of litter and get him back to the ship."

"You'd not get a litter down these damned alleys if the town were empty. Tonight you could easier fly."

With the help of Bell and Myers we came to the church steps. Victor's dark shape showed unstirring. They carried him down.

"He breathes, sir," Myers said. "But he d' look near his end."

"Put him astride this nag. We'll walk him down—"

"Your own leg. . . ."

"Is stiffening on me like a crutch. Perhaps use will free it."

We began a laborious way out of the city. I was in a dream state, half bordering on sleep-walking; Sir Walter was in great pain and had to pause at every sixth or seventh step; Victor lay across the saddle like a sack. Men rushed up and down the alleys, pushed and jostled us, some with booty already, struggling to carry down bolts of velvet and satin to the ships, others fought and argued among themselves in the shops and houses; wounded lay in our path.

Sir Walter said: "I came ashore to urge once more on the Lord Admiral that the *flota*—be taken at once. He is unheeding. . . . It is there to be had at will, he says. They'll have to—treat with him in the morning. . . ."

Great efforts were being made by the English officers to get their men under control, and for the most part the soldiers, although already at the wine, were good tempered and amenable.

"I came too to see the city. So have come all the captains—all except Crosse who stays on *Swiftsure*. Vere has sent part of his army to the bridge of Suazo to guard against a surprise counter-attack. It is as well—some of us preserve a sense of discipline."

Fighting broke out on a wrought iron balcony above our heads. Two Spaniards had retreated on to it and were beseeching their attackers for mercy. They did not get it, but had their throats cut and in a few moments the blood was dripping off the balcony's edge as if from the scarlet geraniums growing there.

"Dutch . . . I don't like their ferocity, but how can you blame them? You stumble, Maugan."

We got down into a lower square. Two English soldiers were disputing over a Spanish woman, one tugging at each arm, but an officer came rapidly towards them with drawn sword, and resentfully they freed her and she fled back into the house behind. There was fighting on a roof, and a body fell with a great thud upon the cobbles; our horse shied away and nearly trod on me; Bell tugged at the bridle and we went on.

At the city gates a new company of English soldiers was marching in. They walked in good order, taking no heed of the fire that raged in a house built beside the gate or of sporadic shooting that was still going on from a nearby tower. Beside the gate was a heap of some twenty dead, limbs sprawling grotesquely; they seemed to have no kinship with us. In the flickering torchlight a few faces peered upwards, mummers' masks without blood or hope; they might have been Spanish or our own comrades'; death had robbed them not merely of nationality but of humanity too.

It was a brilliant night, and lights winked here and there on the surrounding hills. We stopped and lifted Victor down; I moistened his lips and bathed his face. Bell and Myers broke and tied some wood and made a rough litter and put Victor on it. Ralegh could just mount the horse. We ploughed across the soft yielding sand.

We rounded the wall that had hidden us from the harbour. The two great galleons were still aglow but the fire was now within them; ribs showed; they were like brasero bowls burning in the mud. The half-dozen smaller ships which had been afire had sunk and the flames put out. Beyond, our own ships showed like a line of forts built too close together, their clustered masts fenced the sky-line.

Ralegh said: "I'm told that Admiral Portocarrero commanded the galley squadron. I would like to feel they too were accounted for. They are a—spiteful breed of ship and—could do some harm to us if prepared to risk loss."

We reached the water. A few row-boats and barges were fringing the muddy edge. Guards had been posted. Victor was lifted into a boat and Sir Walter helped from his horse. I struggled in the mud, put one foot to the gunnel; Bell took my arm. Pain was throbbing now. It had always been there but as a secondary sensation while other ur gencies dominated.

As we pushed off an old woman came along the edge angrily screaming at us. We steered among the dead, some floating, some stuck in the mud. Burning smoke drifted about; broken spars, charred sailcloth, casks of wine, kegs of biscuit lay under festoons of rigging like netted fish; here and there a voice still shouted and groaned. The water was black and bitty as if itself charred by the fire.

There were lights on *Warspite;* someone was playing a lute and a few unsteady voices were singing, but the men at the ladder sprang to attention when they saw who was back. Somehow we got Victor into the long cabin abaft the mainmast. Dr Wood was sent for. Bell at last unbuckled my breast-plate and it came away with a clack of half-dried blood. He slit the shirt up and the tired blood began welling up again.

Ralegh came in, his face dark. "Well?"

"He's far gone," said Wood, looking up from Victor. "I can do little."

"And this lad?"

Wood came over and began to thumb my wounds. Then he looked at my arm which had a knife thrust through the muscle. "This is nothing. But the other wound's deep. There may be laceration of the abdominal wall. Bind him tight to keep the lips of the wound closed, Bell. If he lives till morning he may well mend."

"What of Victor?" I said, struggling to sit up.

"Lie quiet, sur, I beg," said Bell who was trying to draw a rough cotton bandage round my waist.

"Katherine Footmarker would sometimes mix a cordial—"

"I have my own cordial," said Sir Walter, "but we shall not get it down him, I think. . . ."

An officer who had lost a leg was groaning in his corner.

"Over this way, sur," said Bell; and I turned on my side. The servant had a rough but handy way with him that showed I was not the first he had dealt with.

Lying on my shoulder away from the room, I could look out of the port-hole across the harbour, not towards the town but towards the dark hills. Just out of the corner of my view was a flickering glow, and I edged an inch or two further up the board to see what it was. Bell's remonstrance was cut short.

"Sir," I said to Ralegh. "There's a new fire."

He came at once and peered through the open port-hole. Flames were flickering up in the distance.

"By the living God," he said, "the Spaniards have fired their own *flota*. We are too late now."

CHAPTER 7

CADIZ was occupied, and the Fort and Citadel capitulated. No woman was molested, no church burned. The richest and noblest of the captors were held for ransom, the rest allowed to go.

But the *flota* was lost. With suicidal pride the Spaniards had set fire to every ship stuck in the mud of the inner harbour, and the whole of the great treasure fleet was sacrificed. I lay and watched it burning. It burned for three days. The flames seemed at times to get into my head. The Generals held constant conferences in the city, argument was rife as to whether the port should be held in permanent occupation or evacuated, whether we should instead seize Cape St Vincent and then blockade the Spanish coast, as Drake had once done. But only Ralegh, I think, from the start perceived that we had missed the greatest prize. Essex and the Howards were conscious of the great feat of arms we had performed in thus capturing the first port in Spain, a richer port than London, of the glory and the honour of it. Sir Walter, perhaps because he had once been a poor man, or perhaps because his nature was most similar to the Queen's, thought more of all the wealth of the Indies lost in the flames and perceived what her feelings would be.

One afternoon, returning briefly to the ship for some documents, he came to sit beside me and to peer at Victor, who still lived and was conscious from time to time.

"There's much to be seized in the city—much already has been:

at least the half of it as private spoils. But it will bring no fortune
to England such as was contained in those forty fine ships. They say
the value was twelve million ducats. Spain has deprived us of the
fruits of victory and almost bankrupted herself. Most of the merchants
will never recover—"

"It was not they who fired it?"

"Oh dear, no. They would have treated with us, as Howard
expected. It was the royal officers, to whom any sort of composition
is a disgrace. If we had moved earlier. . . ."

"You did your best."

"Best is not enough if it fails. . . . Now Essex and the Howards
hold princely court in the city. Tomorrow there's to be a state dinner
to celebrate the victory. . . ."

"Have you news of the galleys, sir?"

"Portocarrero retired his squadron into the narrow neck by the
Suazo Bridge and by some mechanical means dragged them through
the shallows and the mud. When the water deepened they were re-
floated and so made their way back to the sea at San Petri. They
are thought to have gone north towards Faro."

Sir Walter fanned himself. The heat in this harbour in the middle
of the day was stifling and the stench from the dead bodies rotting
in the mud made it impossible to keep the windows open. Victor
groaned and tried to turn over.

"Anthony Ashley is to be sent back to England with despatches
for the Queen," Sir Walter said, "requesting her permission for a permanent occupation of the city. Crosse will carry him in *Swiftsure*,
a dozen other vessels will go taking some of the treasure and most
of the sick and wounded. I shall send you both home on that convoy."

"Oh, no! . . . Victor, perhaps, for he's sorely ill; but another week
and I shall be on my feet again."

"Dr Wood thinks otherwise. This fever which has persisted leaves
you in no state for campaigning."

"What of your own wound, sir?"

"I suspect my leg will always be in need of a little aid. Too much
of the muscle was shot away. But I cannot go yet. Tell me, young Killigrew. . . ." He paused.

"Yes?"

"Did you gain any booty that first night?"

I looked at his face, which had narrowed. "Some few pieces of
jewellery. If it is still in my pockets."

"It will be there: only Bell has attended on you. And Victor?"

"I think not. He was looking for some books when two priests
attacked him."

"That's like him. Well, take care of your gleanings. Everyone else is, so far as they can hide them. It's not a savoury spectacle."

"If I go home," I said, "it will be to look after Victor. Having survived all the worst of the fighting unscratched, he came to his wounds through following me in search of plunder."

"Ah," he sighed and got up. "Don't let it trouble your conscience. If I thought of all those who for one reason or another I had led to their death I should not sleep of nights."

Swiftsure left three days later. With her went fourteen other vessels, carrying horses, booty, and wounded men. Victor and I were to have travelled on *Swiftsure,* but at the last Sir Gelly Meyricke with special private despatches from the Earl of Essex to the Queen, and the Earl of Sussex, who was sick with measles, took our places and we were moved to a fly-boat, the *Peter of Anchusen.* So are fates decided.

We left a city still held in complete subjection by the English but a council of the Lords General in no way more decided what to do with it. Ralegh came to see us off. He was on the edge of melancholia: the excitement of battle which had transformed him had long since been lost in the drearier battles of the council chamber.

"For my part," he said, "I believe we waste time here. Our crews sicken in the heat, our victuals rot, our army wastes its strength on futile skirmishes. To retain the city would put a breaking burden on armament and supply. We have done what we came for. Staying will only fritter away the victory."

He was smoking his pipe, more perhaps to keep away the flies than for pleasure. Victor was propped up on his pillows, able now to eat light foods. As soon as he had known what was planned he had protested vigorously; in the end he had accepted his fate but was still displeased by it.

"I believe, Cousin Walter, you're waiting to see us sail so that you can be assured we're safely gone. If I'd a thought more use in my legs I'd dive overboard and swim in again as soon as your back was turned. . . . Even now you cannot be sure of Maugan!"

Ralegh looked at me sourly. "We are all under discipline, and he received his orders. Which are to see you home. He'll do so."

"I'll do so," I said.

Cadiz looked unreal in the hot shimmering light as we put out on the ebb tide. Mottled cloud clustered in a sky the colour of a latten plate. Wisps of smoke still rose from the burned fleet in Port Royal road. Our own ships clustered in the main harbour, pennants lifting in the hot breeze. The Queen's standard fluttered from the citadel, Essex's from Fort San Felipe. Outside the harbour a half dozen frigates cruised as a guard against surprise.

"Well," I said to Victor, "we have not conquered the world, but we live to try again, and as I saw you a week ago I would not have thought that likely."

"Blood-letting did no one any harm. I haven't coughed since we left England. It's all part of the cure."

"Look," I said. "You got no spoils from your efforts. I have a little hoard which will do for two. When we get to England we'll sell the jewels and split the proceeds."

"Split nothing. You got them; I didn't; that's all. But I would have liked those books."

"But for me you'd never have gone into that accursed church, and so no doubt you'd have got your plunder somewhere else and unscathed. Deny that."

"You got me in without compulsion. You brought me out on your back. Deny that."

We wrangled amiably until it was time to sleep through the hottest hours of the day. By the time we woke the city was a dark blur on the distant coastline. *Peter of Anchusen* was a large fly-boat, smarter and faster than most of her kind. She carried a crew of forty, with a black-bearded Captain Smith in command, and there were above sixty wounded and sick aboard, not to mention divers others returning in charge of plunder and horses, so that the whole complement was around one hundred and twenty, about a third Flemish. Besides ourselves there were only eight wounded officers, and we shared a cabin with a Lieutenant Fraser who had lost a leg and a Sergeant Major George who had been blinded in one eye and much disfigured by a flaming spar.

As well as the powerful but cumbersome *Swiftsure* we had two frigates for protection, and every transport was armed, so there was little risk of our being challenged on the way home.

The wind that had got us out of harbour and safely away from the coast hesitated with the setting sun, and the lateen sails of a half-dozen Portuguese feluccas standing well away from the land as they fled south were suddenly flushed with the afterglow so that they looked like flamingoes rising off the surface of the sea. I left Victor and sat for an hour or two on deck in the cooler air of evening talking to Sergeant Major George, who was a veteran of the Dutch wars and in no way cast down by his injuries. While the stars grew ever brighter till they lamp-lit the sky, George told me of bloody encounters at Zutphen and Gertruydenberg. Below I could hear Victor playing, almost for the first time since his wounding.

Weep not, my wanton, smile upon my knee;
When thou art old there's grief enough for thee.

Around us were the lights of the other ships, closest—so close that we could see aboard—being *Maybird*, a very small man-o'-war belonging to Sir Ferdinando Gorges of Plymouth; and behind her, like a sheep-dog central to her flock, the high decks of *Swiftsure*, commanded by Captain Robert Crosse, now Sir Robert, knighted by Essex after the celebrations last Sunday. (The one thing in all this, said Sir Walter, that would have pleased Drake.)

A swell got up later in the night but no wind with it, and by morning our fleet was somewhat scattered. During the following day we crawled slowly west-north-west, wallowing more than we advanced, the land still visible as we made across the gulf. The second night was hazy but the light airs were just enough to keep way on; the third day brought a return of dead calm.

It was a breathless dawn, the sea like pale stretched silk, its limits hardly separate from the sky. The sun came up like a red button which, being constantly polished, at last glittered so brightly one could no longer look. In the night the land had receded. The sails of every ship hung like damp washing.

Although we had drawn together yesterday the scattering this night had been more complete, and the only vessel within hail was *Maybird. Swiftsure* was a mile or more away on our larboard beam, with two transports near by, the frigates and the rest of the fleet being strung out behind. I did not always wake so early, but without helm way the ship had swung so that the rising sun came full on my face, and I got up at once and put a cloak over my bandages and went out on deck to get some cool air while it lasted.

There was a great peace such as sometimes comes at dawn, and the few sailors on deck did not disturb it. I stood there feeling completely at rest. My soul was calmed by the silence and the space, it yearned for the unreachable but without ambition or regret, in part disembodied yet seeming to find a new joy in the senses. I had been in battle and wounded, my wounds were mending, I was young and I was going home.

The chief officer, a man called Lumsden, was on watch with a Flemish seaman at the helm. I went over to them. Three seagulls stood on our main yard but even they gave no cry.

I said to Lumsden: "Do you think we shall double Cape St Vincent today?"

He yawned. "Not a chance while this weather lasts, sur. I doubt if we've made ten miles in the dark hours."

The man aloft in the cross-trees shouted something: it was a long sing-song call in Flemish.

"What did he say?" Lumsden asked the helmsman.

"He says three ships to landward. He think they be Spanish."

"Well, a lot of harm they'll do us or we them while this calm lasts," Lumsden said. "You couldn't sail a skiff."

I peered towards the land but could see nothing. The silk stretched taut and unbroken. One of the seagulls dropped off the yard and planed in delicate semi-circles towards some refuse floating near, but without alighting saw that it was nothing edible and rose again with a lazy motion to resume his position on the ship.

"Was you on this trek to Suazo Bridge?" Lumsden asked me.

"No."

"Oh. . . . Reckoned perhaps that was where you was wounded. They say we lost nigh on two hundred men on the homeward way, most of 'em drunk and fallen on so soon as they was separate from the rest. A nasty piece of—"

The black-bearded Captain Smith was suddenly beside us. "What sort of Spanish ships?" he demanded of the helmsman. "Ask him that, and whither away."

The sailor called a guttural question up to the sailor at the fighting top. There was a pause then, for the man on look-out seemed uncertain. Then he shouted.

"Five or six of them," said the helmsman. "East by nor'-east; four miles or a thought more. In line astern."

Smith shaded his eyes into the rising sun. "I fancy there's something to be seen. . . . Here, Gruyt, tell your man we want the *type* of ship as soon as ever—Nay, I'll go up myself."

He jumped quickly on to the bulwark and swung himself into the shrouds. But before he could go far the look-out shouted again. It was one word and we all understood it well.

"Galleys. . . ."

They came up rapidly. First they were like part of the land, then like islands, then in no time their insect shapes were clear. I wondered how many English prisoners sweated at the glinting oars.

All the English ships had seen them now. *Swiftsure* fired her bow chasers; whether to try to ward off the enemy or as a signal to her flock to group around her we never knew. In any event we were helpless to group at all. Like trees planted on the blue silk we had no power either to challenge or to flee.

Smith sent a half dozen of his crew leaping with orders to rouse the rest of the ship. Major George came up, the unbandaged side of his face bristling with the night's beard.

"So Portocarrero escaped to some purpose. Where's he making for, d'you think?"

"Us," said Captain Smith.

It looked as if he was right. We and *Maybird* were far ahead of the rest and were the obvious prey. *Swiftsure* continued to fire intermittently, being the only ship in the convoy with guns of sufficient range to make it worth a try, but the galleys held on. Soon the first of them was within two miles of us.

Peter of Anchusen had for armament two 5-lb. sakers with a range of fifteen hundred paces, and three small breech-load "man killers" of very short range. *Maybird*, though so much smaller, carried about the same. Both ships were now in great commotion, sailors and such of the wounded as could defend themselves milling about, priming muskets, handing out cutlasses. As soon as I was sure the leading galley was heading straight for us I went below. Lieutenant Fraser, still in much pain from his leg, was lying flat on his bunk and taking little heed of the alarm; Victor was sitting in a chair loading an old pistol someone had given him.

"Well, so it's an ill wind that blows from no direction, Maugan. Move me closer to the port-hole, will you."

I pushed his chair forward. "Victor, I suggest you confine yourself to this place until we have beaten them off. I shall be just above you and no one will come down."

"You were ever one for a bold front, dear Maugan. Confess we have as much chance as a duck among foxes. Then pray for wind."

"I will."

I finished struggling painfully into my breast-plate and patted his shoulder. "Good luck and shoot straight."

I climbed up the companion ladder to the capstan deck. Of a sudden I felt terribly tired of fighting and killing, and fearful of injury and death. Weakness creeps on us unawares. It had come now out of the happiness and content of half an hour ago. I prayed for some miracle to intervene: this sudden unfair attack when we were home bound, and an attack on wounded men, had come at the wrong moment for courage and endurance.

The leading galley was now no more than a mile off. I turned and saw that *Maybird's* captain in a forlorn effort to escape had put down his two ship's boats and they were manned with sailors breaking their backs to tow the little warship towards the safety of *Swiftsure's* guns.

Lumsden came past me carrying a keg of powder, and following

him was Major George. George's cask was broken and spilling powder.
I caught his arm.

"Take care!"

The side of his mouth clear of bandages creased in an angry grin.
"A little surprise for 'em, lad. We want to welcome 'em aboard,
lad—"

"But the wounded—below decks."

"Would you have 'em captives of Spain?"

Both our sakers spoke, and then two from *Maybird*. The shot fell
short. The leading galley had slowed to allow two of her sisters
to catch up; then together in line they came forward again, not
firing, but not presenting any good target with their sweeping oars
and narrow bows. *Swiftsure* fired again, but was far out of range.
Slowly *Maybird* began to draw away from us, as the ship's boats got
her under way. As they neared us the two outside galleys turned in
a slow arc to come on us from either side. This gave our armament
plenty to do. In the distance I noticed one of the English frigates had
adopted *Maybird*'s tactics and was trying to row towards us. I looked
at the sun. It was beating down out of a sky leaden and silent with
heat. Wind. Where is the wind? Wind only will save us. God send us
wind.

As they came up the bow chasers of the galleys opened fire and
two or three balls came aboard doing light damage. On our ship
I suppose there were now seventy men waiting, crouching behind the
bulwarks, lying prone on the quarter deck, up in the fighting tops,
waiting.

At almost point-blank range our sakers began to score; one ball
ploughed through a group of Spaniards; then the first galley swung
against us, drawing in her oars and jarring along our side. Grappling
irons were thrown and at once hacked away, thrown again; the second
galley shivered against our helm; the whole ship reeled and soon the
enemy were swarming over the side.

Thereafter followed a bloody fight such as outweighed the capture
of Cadiz. There was room for no manoeuvre, scarcely could we move
back and forth a yard. On the quarter deck above the main cabins
there was besides myself, Captain Smith, Major George, Lumsden,
and twelve others. On to this deck leaped upwards of a score of
Spaniards in armour attacking with a fury that seemed to stem from
the defeat at Cadiz. Above our heads men fired and were fired on
and then were attacked in hand-to-hand combat by climbing Spaniards.

I stood almost touching shoulders with Major George and we beat
off the first wave of men. All the time as he thrust and killed he was

grinning like a wolf. Lumsden was the first to go, stabbed through the throat; the sailor beside me was then killed by a musket ball; but I wounded the man who had killed Lumsden. Four others died and the deck was slippery. Two Spaniards attacked Captain Smith and his black beard ran red before he disappeared among the trampling feet. Major George seeing the end near snatched up the harquebus he had laid beside the mast, and by firing the wheel-lock close against a pyramid of powder he set off an explosion which scorched the bandages on his face. Bangs like fire-crackers followed as the powder blew along the line of the fuse. A dozen English sailors leapt into the sea, but no others could move before a giant explosion blew all the middle of the ship away. A fountain of bodies and spars and burning sails spewed over the sky. . . .

I was lying beside the dead Captain Smith. Blood was still trickling gently from under his black beard. A weight was across my legs. Men were shouting, crying, cursing in three languages. Major George miraculously still stood upright; his right arm hung useless; his left he held up in a token of surrender. Three Spanish officers climbing over the side were in time to accept it and prevent him from being cut down. I lifted my head: the quarter deck was a shambles, a score dead and half as many grievously wounded; but it was not aslant; the great explosion while blowing the heart out of *Peter of Anchusen* had not yet begun to sink her.

A Spanish sailor bent over me with his cutlass; it dripped spots of blood on my cheek before an officer called him away. I dragged myself from under a fallen body, putting my hand on Captain Jones's shoulder to lever a sitting position; then I scrambled up and stood beside George.

The whole centre of the ship was a mass of twisted wreckage and mangled corpses, more than half of them Spanish where they had been caught swarming into the hatches. All three galleys were around us and further fight was hopeless. The other three galleys were pursuing the little *Maybird*, but I saw her sails flapping, and then looking beyond you could just see movement from the rest of our fleet. But for us the wind had come too late.

We were taken below; Victor and Lieutenant Fraser were unhurt. Twenty English were packed into the one cabin, some of them seriously wounded, and the door slammed. We crowded to the two portholes watching for sign of smoke or flame, wondering if we were to be burned alive in the ship. Presently we felt her begin to move, but it was not the movement of a vessel under sail. A slight pulse to the motion told us that one of the galleys had taken us in tow.

As *Peter of Anchusen* swung round our view swung too and we could see *Maybird,* her sails billowing fitfully, still moving away; as far as could be seen only one galley was now pursuing her, and all the English fleet was converging from the other quarter.

Running feet overhead and Spanish voices shouting; an older man by the door was dying; we dragged him towards the window to get more air. Major George's right hand had lost two fingers and was badly lacerated; I tried to bandage it.

So in the stifling heat of the small cabin we spent the rest of the morning. Although now under sail as well, we were still being towed for extra speed. It meant the English were in pursuit. *Maybird,* Victor reported from the other port-hole, had evaded her pursuers at the last, but he could no longer see any other vessel except one galley keeping us silent company a cable's length away. By the position of the sun we were steering west nor'-west. I glanced out at this consort of ours and watched the regular unrelenting sweep of the oars. The future as I could see it now held no hope. The hideous improbable mischance by which we had been captured when sailing home after a famous victory and escorted by powerful warships was too much to bear.

In the afternoon the wind freshened, and the galleys proceeded under sail only. Towards evening we altered course to north, and soon the land closed in.

Another man died, and the two corpses were laid against the bulkhead. No one had brought us water yet, and the wounded were pressed for lack of it.

When it was dark we could see the lights of a village quite close; we had entered a river or creek. We began to move more slowly and then came to a stop, with the rattle of our anchor chain and shouts from shore.

At last the door was flung open. We blinked in the torch light as we were led out for examination.

I went into the room with Major George. Three officers sat at a table. The centre one, who was smooth-skinned and dark as a Moor, I later knew to be Admiral Don Juan Portocarrero himself. He looked an angry and a worried man.

"Please to tell your name, your office, your nationality," said the man on his left in an English spoken with so guttural an accent that unless one attended carefully the words were lost.

"George. Sergeant Major of Vere's Own. English."

With a fan Portocarrero was stirring the air before his face. Insects droned endlessly round the flickering candles. There was a smell of cooking; we had had nothing to eat since yesterday.

"You have a wife?"

"Yes."

"And after that?"

"Two sons."

"You have rich relations? Friends?"

"No."

The questioning went on for perhaps another three minutes, then the English-speaking one translated what he had learned. The three officers conferred together in undertones.

Portocarrero said something in Spanish which I understood. "For exchange."

As he was led away George glanced back at me out of his one bloodshot eye. "So long, lad. If you're in England before me, take a swill of good beer and swallow it for me."

I wondered what had happened to Victor.

"Please to tell your name, your office, your nationality."

"Killigrew, secretary, English."

"You are married?"

"No."

"Who is your father?"

"John Killigrew."

"Where do you come from?"

"Cornwall."

"You have rich relatives?"

"No."

There were horses moving in the stables under this room. The man on Portocarrero's right had a scar from lip to eye which gave him a perpetual stare. Portocarrero, who had not taken his gaze from me since I gave my name, began to question me through the other officer.

"What is your first name?"

"Maugan."

"Have you been in Spain before?"

I hesitated briefly. "Yes."

"For what purpose?"

"I was brought here by force."

"When was this?"

"Two and a half years ago."

"Were you exchanged or did you escape?"

"I was . . . exchanged in the summer of '94."

They discussed me in undertones.

"If you are a scrivener for Sir Walter Ralegh, why are you sent back to England now?"

"I was wounded."

"But not seriously. You are the least wounded of them all."

"I was to escort back Mr Hardwicke, who is a cousin of Sir Walter Ralegh's."

"And where are the messages you carry?"

"I have none."

"Come, you must bear some report."

"No. Sir Anthony Ashley has the official report on *Swiftsure*."

"And you have an unofficial one."

"No, sir. None."

They talked again, then Portocarrero motioned to the guards. "Aside for further consideration."

CHAPTER 8

THE cell was twenty-four feet long by half as broad with two high barred windows through which a man could only see by standing on another's shoulders. The floor was of beaten earth, the walls of a sort of moor-stone which was as hard as granite.

Ten of us shared it. Besides myself there was Sergeant Major George—reunited with me in spite of his farewells—Victor, Lieutenant Fraser, a Lieutenant Harris, and five others. We were not ill-used, indeed often received small concessions from our gaolers; nor at first was food lacking: dried codfish, maize bread, meal, and rice. All that was amiss was that we were all in greater or lesser degree in need of medical care, and living in mephitic conditions and great heat. And we were the gentlemen; I never knew how many of the crew or the wounded soldiers survived.

Sometimes it occurred to me to wonder if all this had come on me, this capture and all the suffering that followed, as a judgment for the desecration I had wrought to the altar in Cadiz. In spite of the influences under which I have lived my life I have never quite been able to escape from a sense that in the end divine justice is meted out in this world. The sensation comes and goes with circumstance and event, but the old feeling, like a childhood scar, remains.

The first man in our cell died after two weeks. He had been wounded a second time by the explosion and his wound turned gangrenous. The stench in the cell in that hot weather made life for the rest of us unbearable. Victor's recovery was checked but he kept cheerful and, thanks to his lute which he was permitted to retain,

we passed many an insupportable hour. My old wound remained open
and festering and I had a return of the fever at nights. Sergeant
Major George, like the iron man he was, tidied up the ends of his
two lost fingers and the stumps healed. Then he began at night to
work on one of the bars of the window. It was exhausting work holding him up, but there was something in the spirit of the man that
compelled the rest to help him.

To my surprise I had been able to cheat the searchers of the jewels
I carried by passing them to Victor and then recovering them back
again before they turned to him. Both the Portuguese soldiers were
suffering from the prevalent fever and had little interest in us.

News from the outer world scarcely reached us, until I became
friendly with one of the guards, a cheerful soul called Cabeças, and
when he found I spoke halting Spanish he talked freely.

He was a Portuguese, and we were in fact in southern Portugal,
a country which had lost its independence to Spain a decade ago.
Though in name an ally and a part of the Spanish Empire, the
country still had about it an air of occupation: the military governor
and his officers were Spanish, the soldiers Portuguese.

Cabeças told me that soon after our capture an attempt had been
made by the Spanish to exchange us for prisoners taken at Cadiz;
but Lord Admiral Howard did not trust Portocarrero and rejected
the overture. Cadiz had at last been evacuated and instead, a force
landed south of Faro to attack that city. The Spaniards concentrated
their main defence at Lagos, forty miles to the west, where we lan-
guished in prison. Our forces had marched overland and captured and
burned Faro almost without resistance; had they then come on those
last few miles we should have been set free by our comrades; but
they did not follow up their success and re-embarked and sailed
away. No one had seen them since but it was thought they were
returning to England.

One day I asked permission to write a letter home suggesting that
a ransom be paid to set me free; and I was given paper and pen and
ink. I had no hopes of any sum whatever being forthcoming, but if
the letter reached its destination it would at least tell them I was
alive, then Sue might hear and would know I could yet return.

While the opportunity existed I also wrote to Mariana de Prada,
telling her I was again a prisoner. With Victor so frail any device was
worth trying.

So for a time life went on. Nine men, living in a small cell at the
height of a Spanish summer. Few complained. Individual suffering
had to be borne in silence for the common good. All things must come

to an end in time. We were hoping for ransom or exchange. At the
worst, the weather would soon cool. Victor tried to teach the lute to
a young man called Crocker, and often one heard the tune

> Weep not, my wanton, smile upon my knee;
> When thou art old there's grief enough for thee.

I instructed a Lieutenant Mabe in the rudiments of Latin. One
man reknitted his jersey with two old sticks of wood. Major George
worked on his window.

In the middle of August the food grew suddenly almost uneatable:
the fish was rancid, the bread full of weevil, the water foul. Three
men fell ill with dysentery. I complained to Cabeças; he shrugged
and said he could do nothing about it. I asked him for an interview
with Don Juan Portocarrero; he shrugged again and said Portocarrero
had left Lagos and we were now in the charge of Manuel Buarcos,
military governor of the town, who it seemed was the scarred man at
our first interview. I asked to see him. Cabeças blew through his
teeth and said better not, he was a hard one, better leave him alone
or worse might befall.

Two days later Lieutenant Fraser died. Since he lost his leg I think
he had little taste for life, and it is hard to blame him. Sergeant
Major George and I now wrote a formal letter asking for an interview with Buarcos. It was refused. Lieutenant Harris, who had
been sick with a scorbutic condition, became worse, his swollen gums
having so grown about his teeth that he could chew nothing. We
pestered Cabeças again, but he said it was as much as his life was
worth to pass our message through. When we asked if Portocarrero
was returning he said the admiral was now with many others ar-
raigned before a court martial for the loss of Cadiz.

At the end of August, Victor caught the dysentery and began to
lose ground. By giving a small ruby to Cabeças I was able to have
some food smuggled in. My own wound had become an open place
that wept pus and lacked the most elementary cloths. Lieutenant
Harris died. Sergeant Major George, working away at his prison bar,
said grimly that this gave more room and a better chance for the
others; but there were only three of us now strong enough to support
him at the window, and soon he turned to being the support himself and leaving us to pick and scratch at the mortar around the
bar. Some progress had been made, and each morning before dawn
the broken stone was filled in with dampened bread; but the bar
went farther down into the wall than expected, and now we had
come up against a piece of stone which would not yield. We could

not be noisy, for the cell windows looked out on an alley much fre-
quented by the guards when off duty.

Victor now gave up playing his lute. He was often racked with
colic, and afterwards seemed too weak to care. Sometimes I would
see him lying with his hands clasped over his abdomen and his head
rolling slowly from side to side. I did what I could for him, bathing
his face with water, though we did not have enough of it and it
rapidly grew warm and foul from use. I gave Cabeças another ruby
to buy some extract of poppy seed and some starch, and this when it
came helped Victor. The pain was eased and the fever lighter. Cabaças
was sympathetic and brought an amulet stone from his mother which
was good for all distemper of the bowel. He bound us to secrecy in
all this: it would go hard for him if anything were known.

So September came in with blazing skies and unrelenting heat. I
wrote again to Manuel Buarcos, asking for the favour of an interview
After a week's wait he granted it.

We were taken across, Major George and I, the following evening
to the officers' quarters at the other side of the square. It was the
same room upstairs where we had been first interviewed; but this
time except for our escort Buarcos saw us alone.

As the only one with Spanish I had to be spokesman. George spoke
a halting word or two, but by now I was fluent.

This was the moment when I needed all my fluency. Buarcos
sprawled behind the table sweating and picking his nose. Tonight the
scar looked like a shoe-lace drawn taut across the wet brown surface
of his skin.

I told him the conditions under which we were living, and said
that if nothing were done to ease them the rest of us would soon die.
We had all, I said, been put aside for ransom; even the poorest had
been adjudged of some value. But one of the first to die now would
be Victor Hardwicke who was a close kinsman of the great Sir Walter
Ralegh. His would be a big ransom and it would all be lost. The
Government and the Court would not look approvingly on his treatment of us if by it they became the losers.

Buarcos waited until I had finished. Then absent-mindedly, one eye
staring more than the other, he said that in his view war was not
waged thus. In his view war was a matter of blood, not of gold.
If he had had his way when we first came here he would have
impaled us all together on one long pike and left us for the crows
to pick. Portocarrero and his like were weaklings and were now paying the penalty. Had he made his feelings clear?

Perhaps then I should have gone, but I was fighting for Victor's
life as well as my own. So I swallowed and began again. I said it was

accepted and praised in Spain—even we in prison had heard the praise—how the English at Cadiz had been considerate to the sick and the wounded. If war were a matter of blood it could yet be conducted with dignity. Could we not as prisoners ask for fair treatment? If a doctor were unavailable, could I not be given permission to beg herbs in the town? And perhaps one or two of our most seriously sick might be granted some milk and eggs, which might just make the difference between life and death to them.

Buarcos yawned. "Killigrew, you affect my appetite. Do you know that in the fight to capture your miserable ship over forty of my countrymen died? Near on thirty of those were killed by an explosion set off treacherously at the moment of surrender. Another twenty are maimed or grievously injured. Why should I care what happens to you? I am in the confident hope that very soon Madrid will forget. Then such of you as are left can be put to death for sport. It is a dull place, Lagos, and there is too little sport."

Horses stirred in the stables underneath. Tonight the table was set for supper; silver on good white linen; one brown manicured hand toyed with the salt-cellar.

I said: "There speaks a Spanish gentleman. After this a return to the cell will be sweet."

I turned to go, but Captain Buarcos shouted a word to the guards and they seized me. They thrust me round to face him, and he stared at me while thoughtfully picking his nose.

"Killigrew, Madrid knows there are captives here, but one more or less will not concern them. It is St Matthew's day next week and we will have you out of your cell then and will grill you over a slow fire. It will give you something to think of until then besides the tribulations of a poor diet. Remember, in eight days you will be free! You may rely on that—on the word of a Spanish gentleman!"

Now I was thrust out, along with George, but as we left Buarcos bawled after us: "And until then you will all be on a half supply of food and water. You've been living too well in captivity!"

On the way back we tramped in silence. George said at last: "I think we should kill that man."

"I cannot keep my tongue quiet! God, I should not imagine he could deprive us of such water as we've had! It's little enough for bare existence in this weather! . . . So we are back where we were—but worse off!" I was so angry I could scarcely swallow. There was no room yet to consider his threat against me. The anger drummed in my ears like lust.

Sergeant Major George said again: "I think we should kill that man."

It was a hot night, as hot as any I remember, and the smell in the cell was sickening. The narrow windows should have allowed in some air, but the air was too still to circulate. All that entered were the mosquitoes which swarmed everywhere. We had no light, so I could not see Victor's face while I told him. Perhaps he had expected nothing, for he took the disappointment very calmly. All he said was: "I wish Crocker would learn to play in tune."

Crocker was trying to play:

If love were mine, who pray would seek for valor?
For love is warm, and courage listeth cold . . .

In a corner Mabe, my pupil, was near his end. Unlike Victor, he did not bear his pains quietly. I sat up all that night with Victor, wafting a cloth before his face to give him the air he so much needed and trying to keep away the mosquitoes which were constantly settling on his face. My own fever had returned, and I shivered and fretted in company with him. In the morning he looked very grey and drawn, much as he had on the first day after his wounds at Cadiz.

"Maugan, if you see Sherborne again, go, please, to the house of Mistress Katherine Churcher, and tell her that in my last hours I thought only of her. Will you do that?"

"Now, now, I don't like this way of talking. May I ask you, if you reach England first—"

"No, Maugan, let us be practical. For eight weeks I've walked on a thread, and the thread is wearing thin. If the worst befalls I ask you to go to Mistress Katherine Churcher of Cerne Abbas, some ten miles south of the castle. You'll find her married to a man for whom she has neither love nor respect—take her aside and in private tell her that I have always loved her, and, if at death there be any flame in me that does not puff out, that I shall do so for all eternity. . . ."

"Quiet, now, drink this. It will ease the pain. . . ."

On the Sunday Mabe died. That left six of us. On the same night Sergeant Major George dislodged the stone which had been holding up his efforts to move the bar. Now he could make progress again. But I was too sick and sad to aid him. I sat with Victor all day, he now being barely conscious. His face was changing under the strain; the daylight seemed to make his lank fair hair grey and he might have been sixty. Once I got blood on my hand, and it was in just the place Katherine Footmarker had traced it with a long finger that day in the clearing by the mill above Penryn. I thought, if it had not been for me none of this need have happened: Victor would not have gone into the church and we should not have been wounded;

so we should not have been sent home thus and captured. Already, I had killed a half score men in my life, but it was not the blood of my enemies Katherine Footmarker had seen, it was the blood of my friends. . . .

On the Monday and Tuesday, with that tenacity which marked his seemingly frail constitution, Victor rallied and was able to take a little of the precious milk I had bought with another jewel from Cabeças. The coming Friday was St Matthew's day, but so far I had not believed in it: anger and remorse were so great that it cut my mind away from the future. I tended Victor constantly, and visions of the *auto de fé* seen in Madrid only crept in each day with the brazen light of dawn.

On the Wednesday there was a big change in Victor. He seemed no longer to be in pain, and only his breathing was difficult, as if there were phlegm at the back of his throat. His face lost its tensions and the aged look disappeared as if a sponge more cooling than mine had wiped it away. Even his hair and month-old beard became smooth and silky instead of bedraggled and unkempt.

So about two in the afternoon he died.

They took his body away that evening, and left the door of the cell open for a few minutes to create a draught of air through.

There were only five of us now: Crocker, George, Stevens, Fletcher, and myself. I had stared for the last time at features clear cut and thin but already beginning to lose their familiar outlines in the great heat and with the first touch of corruption. George was working away at his window; Crocker was supporting him; Fletcher and Stevens were too ill to help; I sat and fingered the lute.

This was the only symbol of him left, and its strings were silent. It was like the corroding body which had just been carried out, an empty thing without the animating spirit to give it sentience and purpose.

And where was that animating spirit? Not here. Not ever again here.

I seemed to hear Victor's voice in my ear, echoing from three months back: "She's superstitious. She considers him unlucky. She says on each voyage he loses some splendid youth. John Grenville last time. Who this?"

Somewhere a lamb was bleating and it set a mule off whinnying and snorting. Today had been the day of the market in the square, and some peasants were still clearing up. You could hear the sound of earthenware pots knocking together, and sometimes the rattle of a cart. Presently there was another sound much nearer at hand, metal falling, but I gave it no attention until Major George spoke.

"Killigrew! We're through! Killigrew! By the bowels of Christ, we're through!"

"I would not want it to be me," Victor had said. "I would not call you a splendid youth," I said. "Agreed!" he said. "The dangers which threaten don't threaten me. Tell her so."

"Killigrew," said George. "Do you hear me? We're through!"

I got up. "I hear you."

Did a young woman in Cerne Abbas turn and twist that night beside her sleeping husband? "Kathy! Kathy!" That was what he had muttered when I had dragged him half conscious out of the Cadiz church. So life and love are lost, and the lute is silent. . . .

"Killigrew!"

"It's too *late*."

George slipped off Crocker's shoulders and came up. One side of his face was like a riven tree, the eye puckered and sightless.

"It's never too late to get out of here, boy. Remember what you're threatened with on Friday."

"It's too late!" I shouted angrily. "Victor is gone. . . . And these. . . ." I gestured at Fletcher and Stevens. "They can scarcely stand."

Crocker came over to us. "Well? Are we making a dash tonight? Are you with us, Killigrew? Say yes or no. The moon'll be gone in an hour. I say, go now. Who knows what may happen tomorrow?"

"Yes," said George, "there's nothing to delay for." He patted my arm. "Come, Killigrew, you can help your friend no more. He would not want to hinder you."

Tears blinded my eyes. "D'you remember, George," I said, "what you said on your way back from our talk with Buarcos?"

"Yes . . . I said I thought we must kill that man."

"I'll come with you," I said.

We left about eleven. George, as the originator of the escape went first, then I, then Crocker, who was the fittest of the three. We could do nothing for Fletcher and Stevens; to have taken them would have been to set the attempt at nothing from the start. They wished us God speed and a safe journey through a hostile and barren land. Fletcher was able to stand only long enough to support Crocker on his shoulders; then we were gone.

The guard house was beside the gaol, separated by a dusty quadrangle perhaps designed for drilling and the exercise of prisoners. Beyond the guard house at the corner of the square stood the house where we had had our interviews.

All the stalls had been moved and the last of the peasants were gone. A wind was blowing through the town, a dry off-land wind full of dust and heat. It was gusty; whirlwinds rose like ghosts conjured from the arid earth, dipping and swirling in baleful rhythms, then collapsing among the shadows or exploding into the upper air as the wind tired of them.

He dined at ten in the upstairs room—this much I knew because last week his servant had been waiting with the tray to go up as we came out. It was now eleven by the town clock. He should be down to the dregs of his wine.

In a town in an occupied but quiescent country far from any real enemy or risk of surprise, it was unlikely that a guard would be posted at his door; but one could not take the risk. A window into a passage; we climbed in and came to a wide hall. It was empty and in darkness, but there was a candle burning on the stairs, and light came from the kitchens and the ante-room where we had once waited. Major George grabbed up a pike leaning beside the door.

I peered through the hinge slit into the kitchens. A pot was bubbling on the fire, unwashed pans lay on the table, and mosquitoes and flies swarmed round them. The place was empty. I heard voices outside and saw through the farther door three men, the cook and two servants, squatting in the yard playing dice where they had gone for coolness.

On the table, still greasy with the young lamb it had carved, was a long serving knife which through the years had been honed down for sharpness until it was like a stiletto. George was in the doorway, but I motioned him back as I picked up the knife. Captain Buarcos's room was not over the kitchens but over the stables and separated from the kitchen by the width of the hall. We could not tackle three servants in an open yard.

Over the door were two bells. The knife cut the cords working these. I latched the door behind me.

We went up the stairs. A light shone out from his ill-fitting door. In that moment before action I remember the smell of bay leaves, of vinegar and of quinces, the creak of George's military boot on the stairs, the heavy, hesitant breathing of Crocker. A great death's head moth was beating against one of the slits of the door. We let him in.

Perhaps when the body is sick it narrows the mind's preparedness for surprise; one pursues an object with only one's own choices in view. Since we made this plan an hour ago we had concluded without reason that Buarcos always dined alone. Tonight sitting with him was a thin small featured young officer we had sometimes seen about, a young man who wore his hair long and walked with an affected step.

We brought in a draught, and the candles dipped and guttered; shadows curtsied on the yellow plaster walls. Surprise should have been on one side only, instead it was on two; but we recovered first. Buarcos's goblet was overturned as he moved to get up—his sword belt was on a chair four paces away.

"Stay!" said George, lowering his pike. "One word—"

Fine muscatel dripped on the floor. The young officer could reach his sword: he did so as George charged him. At the same moment Buarcos kicked over the table and leaped for the bell-pull. I went after him. He pulled the bell and shouted and got to his sword, but before he could draw it I was on him. It would have been good to talk but there was no time to talk. We rolled over, clawing. His nails reached my eyes as my knife went deep into his belly. Then I ripped him up. Blood spurted two feet; he got to his knees and his entrails were pushing through his tunic as he fell.

I got up trembling. George had killed the young man by running him through with the pike. It was all over in two minutes. I stood there trembling. One of the overturned candles had set fire to the table cloth; it flickered and sizzled as Crocker beat it out. A decent darkness fell on the scene; one candle only burned on the mantel-shelf. Crocker was at the door listening. I trembled like a man in a late stage of St Vitus's dance.

George put his hand on my shoulder. "Well, lad, you opened him like a ripe musk melon. There's nothing more to do here."

It was as if I could not move my feet, as if they adhered to the floor.

I still held the knife; I dropped it.

"We'd best go," said Crocker. "There's no alarm."

George was on his knees groping for the skin of wine. Being of narrow neck it had not all spilled. He slopped some in one of the cups and gave it to me to drink.

"We'd best go," said Crocker. "I shouldn't fancy if they found us now."

I tried desperately to recover myself. It was not at all horror at killing Buarcos: it was the release of a great anger which now, acting on weak nerves and a sick body, left me as if I had myself been stabbed.

"There's horses below," said George. "Think you we could get 'em?"

"No," I said. "They're too precious—too precious not to be locked in."

George took a swig of wine himself, passed it to Crocker. Crocker took it as if it was red-hot, drained the rest in a gulp.

"Let's go," he said.

We heard a frightened neighing.

The blood from the two men must by now be dripping through the boards. George took off Buarcos's sword and buckled it round him.

"Far better," I said. "Mules. We may be able–at the edge of the town—we might get them."

"Come, lad," said George. "I'll help you down the stairs."

We turned to go. When we entered, not three hundred seconds since, two men had been finishing a good dinner, replete, healthy, well wined, at ease. When we left, not three hundred seconds later, they were dead, blood dripping faster than the wine, processes stayed for ever; two corpses spilled among the remnants of the meal. I was sorry I had not had time to talk to Buarcos. I wondered if he had realised it was for Victor.

We got to the top step, my feet halting, George with his arm round me; Crocker was already at the foot of the stairs: I limped down. The kitchen door was still shut. The horses now were neighing and stamping their feet. It was they who would raise the alarm.

The window was still open. It seemed darker outside now. Somehow I got over the sill. Some people were walking across the square: a whole family out late: the father in his black hat, cloak billowing in the wind, the mother in her shawl, five children fan-tailed behind. They took no notice of us.

We left the town.

CHAPTER 9

It was Sergeant Major George's plan to strike south. He thought the Spanish would expect us to go north and so would pursue us that way. South lay the narrow Gibraltar Straits and the Sultanate of Morocco; Ahmed the Golden was on friendly terms with England. It was a long way; but little compared to any trek north.

We found no mules to steal in Lagos; but five miles south on the road to Faro, from an old house which had a half dozen in the stables, we were able to take three without challenge. I do not know quite how we managed to walk that first five miles, since we were all exhausted by privation before ever we began; but fear of what is following and the lure of freedom ahead are the greatest spurs even to sickly men.

Although I was sickliest of the three—in part because my mind was ailing with grief and anger—on that first march I kept up with them unaided. On the mules we made a few more miles before dawn and hid in a coppice of gorse and scrub that reminded me of Cornwall. We lay there all through that hot morning, and it was not until the first hour of the siesta that we moved again—into a village called Lagoa.

There by good fortune we were able to raid a barn and steal leeks and lentils and a few grapes. A mongrel dog woke the village round us and we had to flee into the hills and look down at the peasants milling about as in a disturbed ant-hill.

It was poor food for men long deprived, and during the afternoon while we lay in the shade of a scrub oak I began to be tormented by visions of the food we had left untasted on Buarcos's table. We had been too precipitate: five minutes more would have enabled us to fling the stuff into a bag and carry it away; it would have lasted us two days. The thought was a pain in the stomach, genuinely felt.

As soon as the sun set we were off again, but cut inland away from the coastal track. One could toss a coin as to whether it was the best choice and only hope we did not get hopelessly lost. This was rough barren country, with little cover but little sign of human life.

Towards dawn we descended a long hillside to a giant river bed, dry and strewn with boulders and the trunks of rotted trees. Halfway across we found a tiny rivulet of water slipping downhill and gratefully watered the mules and refilled our own skins. We were able to get up into the bushes at the other side before day broke.

There we lay and discussed for a time the question as to whether, if we moved far enough away to escape capture, we might yet remain in Portugal, slip down to the coast in a week or two and persuade some fisherman, on the promise of a reward, to carry us back to England. As George pointed out, there was some advantage in staying in a country compulsorily annexed by Spain. Many Portuguese to-day were the orphans of those massacred fifteen or so years ago, when it was said so many corpses were thrown in the sea that the fishermen would not go out again until the archbishop had come in solemn procession to purify the waters. For my part I had no preference as to what we did and little expectation as to the outcome, for it was while we were so talking that I knew the pain I had was not hunger after all.

I said nothing then, but about midday had to cry off the search for food and let the others go on alone. They were lucky and came back with a tiny hen. This, cooked and eaten with the fingers, was the first fresh meat we had tasted since capture, but I could not savor it. They looked at me sympathetically and I tried to make light of the trouble. We started off again at dusk, and I travelled until the first streaks of dawn were in the sky. Then I had to give up and lie writhing in the dust.

That I should be attacked at this stage with the dysentery we alone had avoided seemed the harshest turn of fate. It made nonsense of any hope of escape. I knew from watching others that this was only the beginning of an attack. It would get worse until I was prostrate and perhaps unconscious. In five or six days I would die or get better. But five or six days was too long to survive under present conditions.

We moved on again for two hours before the heat was great and then took refuge in a coppice on the north side of a ridge. We had found no water yesterday and the mules badly needed it. The problem of water in this barren land was that such springs as might exist were likely to be the sites of hamlets or villages. We would not probably find another river bed.

I tried to persuade George and Crocker to leave me and go on. This was the clear and logical thing to do. They would not, as I think I should not have. It is when human beings are above human logic that they perhaps show their affinity with God.

They made me a rough shelter from the fierce rays of the sun, put the last of their water beside me, and then split, Crocker to go towards the sea and Major George inland. Whether they found food or not they were to meet here again at dusk.

Sometimes an illness can just consciously be kept at bay while there are others about and while there are decisions to be taken. When the others are gone and the decisions made there is no barrier left. So within an hour I was in a high fever, my belly dissolved into pain and blood.

I thought I was back at Arwenack in the great hall, but it was no pleasant home-coming. A huge log fire was blazing and one could not get away from the heat. All about the room were Dominican monks in the long black robes of the Inquisition. They were staring at the fire and at the pile of logs waiting to be burned in the hearth. Suddenly the one next to me threw back the hood and cloak showing the white woollen garment underneath. It was Katherine Footmarker. She smiled at me, and her teeth had been filed down to points; her eyes held little blazing fires of their own.

"Well, Maugan," she said, "so you are back. Now that this is a Catholic country you must conform or die." "The Spanish have conquered?" I asked. "Oh, yes. They are dragging the women through the streets by the hair." "But where is my family? Where are the

Killigrews?" "They would not conform, Maugan, so they are in there, in there, in there, where all heretics go. . . ."

I looked across at the fire and saw that at the back of it was a heap of skulls and that the logs in the hearth were in fact a pile of dismembered human limbs. I struggled to get towards them in the hope that I might yet save one of them but was held back by the monks, who came to cluster around me, chattering in Spanish and other alien tongues. I shouted and screamed and swore but nothing availed. Then one of the monks came across with a piece of the fire and thrust it into my belly.

The old woman who found me fetched her friends but would not let them cut my throat; instead she had me carried to her hut and laid on her own straw pallet. She disregarded warnings that I had the plague and washed me and dressed the festering sore in my side. Then she squatted down to wait for me either to recover or to die.

It was perhaps forty-eight hours before I began to disentangle her round cautious enquiring face from the faces of fever and delusion. By then she was feeding me on lentil soup which she put into my mouth with a thick wooden ladle. Slowly the phantoms returned less often and I knew where I was and that the disease was on the wane.

The hut we were in was on a hill slope a little removed from the hamlet below. It appeared to be partly built into the rock of the hill, for the roof was of natural stone. On it for a long time I watched a spider in a strange semi-warfare with a colony of ants. And I watched the flies—scavengers rubbing their legs and heads, buzzing around the other insects, privileged by the dimension of flight. Sometimes a lazy bee would bump against the wall, lost and clumsy.

For a long time I lay in this way, gaining slowly in strength but thinking very little, content in utter weakness to let the time drift by, watching day come to the window of the hut, blaze and fade and grow dark again. The woman, whose name was Carla, would come and go during the day, working in the old olive grove beside the hut which provided her with subsistence. Once a day, it seemed, she went down to the hamlet for water; sometimes in the evening curious neighbours would come to peer and question but she drove them away.

She had grey hair tied tight back under a black cloth scarf, and cheeks like an onion, the skin high-coloured and loose; black eyes deep-set and changeless. At first we could understand nothing of each other—her country Portuguese was too much for me, but after a time we began to understand words and simple phrases.

One day I was able to sit up, the next to move to the door of the hut and stare out. I could only speculate on what might have happened to George and Crocker. Thoughts of my own predicament came nearer, to disturb and frighten. Although there might be little direct communication between these peasants and the Spanish, some rumour would be likely to reach them sooner or later. It was not as if we had merely escaped. The sooner I was on my way the better. But where would that way be? The mules had disappeared. The few precious stones I had left had also gone; I only hoped Carla had them. The best one could look for now was some quiet hamlet such as this where one could gradually pick up strength and the protective clothes and manners of the countryside. But much, much farther from Lagos.

While I was so ill I had slept on Carla's pallet and she on the floor. I wanted to change this round but she would have none of it. With an ancient smile she indicated that I was her guest and so must have the place of honour.

She had never asked me who I was, how I had come to be alone and sick under a canopy of thin sacking in a cleft on a bare hillside. I had nothing about me to help her guess my nationality or business, but she seemed incurious. I was somebody who had come into her life and she had cared for me as she would have a sick animal.

I told her that I must be off soon; I could not trespass on her any longer; but she shook her head emphatically; I was not yet well enough, another week perhaps, there was no hurry. I questioned her about the countryside around. We were, she said, about two days by mule from Faro. She had never been that far, but she had heard it had recently been burned by the English and life was not resumed there yet. Much farther east, perhaps three more days, was a big river which divided Portugal from Spain. Between was country such as this, she thought; her nephew had once told her so.

About this time the weather at last broke; a dawn brought ink-blue skies and then thunder. Rain fell all day, drumming like a military attack on roof and trees and cracked earth. The hillside changed into rivulets of yellow mud; dust dry walls within the hut began to sweat, the olive trees bent under the weight. Then the storm cleared away and the following day was blue and sparkling. For the first time I felt a return of full vigour, and was ready to be off.

I asked Carla if she could find me any sort of peasant's cloak and rough breeches, and she said she would try. A skin of water, a belt with some food, a pair of shoes, a stout stick and a knife; it was as much as one could expect, and more. I tried to thank her for what she had done, but she only grinned politely and shrugged it off. I said I wanted to leave on the following day, but she said there were signs

against it. The new moon would be a better time, and that would
be in two days.

The day before I was due to leave I spent out of doors, chopping
and sawing wood for her and stacking it for the winter. From this hut
you could see the hamlet just below and then across the shallow
valley to the hillside beyond. As I recovered I had fallen into the
habit of standing each night at the door of the hut to watch the
sun set. Then as all the hills and valleys flushed with light shadows
would begin to creep along the fissures and up the clefts in the
rock. The light would become more vivid as it was sucked up into
the sky, the land more purple and then grey. There would be a
moment or two of final splendour before the shadows rushed in like
a sea and it was dark.

Tonight I was at the door when I saw five men on horseback
coming down the pewter coloured track on the opposite hill. I at
once called Carla, who came and peered, but then said there was
no cause for alarm; sometimes men went through this way on journeys west; they seldom visited the hamlet and never her hut. My
supper was ready, it would go cold.

So after watching them out of sight round a corner of the hill I
squatted beside her and took the soup cup in my hands and sipped
it. Twice more I went to the door; the first time they were farther
down the valley, the second time they had disappeared.

That day she had brought me an old cloak from the village and
had turned out a grey shirt, worn but serviceable. With these I would
have to do; I was grateful to her and told her so; she grinned and
shrugged and sipped. Night fell and she stirred the wood fire to new
cheerfulness.

I said when I left on the morrow, could she spare some bread to
take with me, a few olives, water, and perhaps a skin of wine? She
said she had it all ready.

At the end of supper she muttered her evening prayers. As she
was finishing a horse neighed.

I reached for my knife, slid away from the fire and crept on hands
and knees to the door. Stars and a still night, two lights winking
in the hamlet, a night bird crying. She was beside me, clutching my
sleeve. I drew away and out of the hut. Nothing. Then the clink of
a hoof.

Men loomed up. The old woman was in my way. As I raised the
knife it was knocked out of my hand. I was dragged into the hut.

An officer, two soldiers, and a peasant. As they tied me up the
old woman began to talk in a whining tone. Perhaps it would have
been better if I had not understood her, for she was arguing with

them, saying she had sent her nephew all the way to the Spanish frontier to fetch them, she was an old widow woman with no money and scarcely food for her belly. Surely she was entitled to a fair reward?

CHAPTER 10

THE dungeon at Seville was much different from the one at Lagos. It was solitary and underground and dark. There were three adjoining cells at the end of a long low tunnel, and the grill in mine looked out upon another passage running cross-wise at a higher level. The other two cells were unoccupied.

It was very silent. Almost the only sounds were occasional footfalls ringing on the hard stone of the upper passage and the prison bell audible in the high distance.

For a while being alone did not matter. I had plenty to think about, most of it unpleasant, but food enough of a sort for an unquiet mind. The guards would tell me nothing. It is difficult when young to wait patiently for one's end, but as time went by the mere loneliness became a danger of another sort and almost as much to be dreaded.

I marked off the days with a wooden spoon that was daily brought and daily taken away. I scratched the wall over my bunk. There was no means of knowing the date when this imprisonment began but it seemed important that time in general should be kept track of.

I asked for pen and paper but this was refused. I asked for books or something to make or do. Nothing came. The guards said the commandant of the prison had no instructions. This struck a familiar note. I wondered what fiesta I was being saved for. Yet it seemed certain that there must be some form of trial first. The Spanish strongly believe in the processes of law—even the Inquisition does —and in this case the law was on their side.

To provide some occupation I began to work on a bar of the grill window looking out on the upper passage. I had two rusty nails out of the bunk, which made little impression. But one went on in deference to the spirit of Sergeant Major George.

Ten scratches became twenty. I tried hard to keep the guards in conversation when they brought food, but nothing would induce them to stay. It seemed likely that they were acting under orders. Stolidly they brought in the dishes of unsavoury mash, stolidly they took them away. The silence of the prison was oppressive. I would have welcomed the shouts of other prisoners. Sometimes I made a noise to reassure myself that I could still hear.

There was a difference between the boots of the guards and the sandal slap of priests. If I ran to the back of the cell it was possible to see the feet passing. Sometimes there would be other footsteps accompanied by the rattle of chains.

Twenty scratches became thirty. Time hung like its own chain about my neck. I recited the "Colloquies" of Erasmus and such Ovid and Juvenal as I could recollect. I sang and tried to compose new ditties or a poem. But it was hard to remember the lines next day. I tried to recall Victor's songs.

> My love in her attire doth show her wit,
> It doth so well become her.

and

> Weep not, my wanton, smile upon my knee:
> When thou art old there's grief enough for thee.

Sometimes I banged at the door demanding to be let out. I wrote letters to people in my head and kept a diary of the capture of Cadiz. The cell, at first stuffy, became cold. The wall on which the days were marked grew damp and water ran down it; I worried that it might wash the scratches away and re-indented them every meal time.

Thirty scratches became forty, and I reckoned it must be December. I kept free from dysentery but my wound would not heal. Victor's are healed, I thought; death is the perfect cure; maybe he's the lucky one.

Little progress with the cell window. Perhaps one had not the dedicated perseverance of George; or it was the knowledge that if one ever got out of the grill it only led to another part of the prison.

One day when the older of the two jailers came to take away the midday meal he dropped a letter on the bunk as he retreated. I snatched it up and stared at it, for it was addressed to me in my father's writing.

I stared at it for some moments, hands trembling. This could only be some ruse. But how could it profit them? I fingered the letter and turned it round and weighed it in the hand.

"Mast^r. Maugan Kyllygrewe, Espana. For delivery." That was all. I turned it again and the seal fell off.

23rd November, 1596.

Son Maugan,

Your letter came one week ago this a.m. It is hard news for us that you are a prisoner again. We had already had this word by note from Westminster in August month. The Spanish asked ransom money for the release of all prisoners of birth, and you were named as so captured; so since then we have known you alive.

There is nothing I can do to bring you to a releasement; that is hard but as God's my judge I could as easy raise the dead as £100 in gold at this moment.

Ruin in its harshest form stares me in the face. By the time you receive this I am more likely than not to be in Exeter or the Fleet and my ancestor's home ransacked by savage creditors. This is the reward that comes to me from twenty-odd years attendance at Court and in the service of the lady our Queen. For the defence of England I have spent money from my own depleted purse receiving as thanks only calumny and neglect. I have travelled far and laboured much in my country's interests, but now even my relatives in the Queen's very bedchamber ignore my pleas for help.

You may by now have expected that an easement of our plight would come by the marriage of young John to Jane Fermor. Well, by evil contrivance it has not. Oh, they were wed as designed on October 8. Sir George came down with a fine band of friends, fifteen in all, a gay, hard-visaged crew all with voices like preachers in a noisy square. They feasted and drank my last £100, by Christ, they did. Little Jane came with two personal attendants who were to stay here and have stayed—not maids as you'd suppose but menservants, army veterans, daggers in belts and the rest—as nasty a pair as woman ever dropped. They bore between them a heavy box—the dowry—they could scarcely carry it, it seemed.

Well, the ceremony was done, a part by Merther, a part by Garrock, a part by some lackey cleric they brought themselves: it was all too long drawn for me: I say stand in the church door and dispatch the business quick. Well, it was done and the gay crew deep gone in my drink and the young couple bedded with all manner of lewd jokes, and the night wore on, many now seeing no more than the table legs where they sprawled on the floor. But Sir George, he drinks with the best and takes no heed of it. And I, being mindful of my purpose, take care to take care. So around three of the clock I suggest to him we go to my chamber where the dowry can be counted and checked.

You can have a notion of all I felt, Maugan, that day: the junketing and the shouting and the lewdness and the ran-tan; while all the time my mind was on things particular to my finances. Here at last was the happy outcome. Well, we went off to my chamber, I and Rosewarne and Sir George and that bent-legged attorney of his who had drawn up the settlement; and after a little preamble in came the two soldier-servants carrying the box. And the box was opened, and inside was a small bag of gold, no more large than the bag Belemus carried aboard the *Crane*.

So I looked into the box, and merciful Christ, it was empty of all else, so I said, What was the meaning of this? So Sir Goerge said, It is my daughter's yearly allowance as agreed in the terms of the marriage settlement. Two hundred pounds a year I pay her so that she is no burden in your house. So I said, but as to the dowry, where is that? And he said, oh, but that is not due yet under the terms of the settlement. So I said, Not due? But it was agreed to be paid on marriage. All such dowries are. So he said, Not this one. It is payable when your son comes of age.

God's virtue, can you guess the scene, Maugan? Can you imagine how it happened? Of course I grew angry and hard words were exchanged. But then Sir George said to this attorney: Produce the settlement for Mr Killigrew to see. And we pored over the parchment, Rosewarne and I, and we saw what in my misfortune I missed at Easton Neston when the contract was drawn. Since Rosewarne was not with me, he being always at my elbow in legal matters, I had permitted all unknowing this evil trickery, this matter of seven words, to be slipped in. On her husband's attaining his twenty-first year.

I have not the time to write all that flew between us, between Sir George and me. I fancy he had not been dealt with so blunt since his school days. But it availed nothing. He told me he had never had the intention of allowing his daughter's dowry to be utilised for my debts, that he knew I should dominate over my own son to this end, and that she'd come to no harm for four years on the allowance of two hundred pounds a year which he would send her.

Well, so as you see, any ransom I might have hoped to pay for your enlargement is in the clouds. I trust you'll have the good fortune to be exchanged some time. There were many more Spanish taken than English so you may yet hope.

For myself there is little hope indeed. I do not think I can prevail upon Jane to ask her father for substantial aid—for that is what he has done his evil utmost to avoid—and she is a hard little thing with a mind and a will like granite. Since her father left she has exerted her temper on several occasions, and, since I feel the only deliverance can come through her good will, she has been given way to. Her two creatures follow her everywhere—more bodyguards than servants. I only pray and believe that Sir George will be unwilling to allow the home of which his daughter will one day be the mistress to be broken up or sold for lack of a few thousand pounds. But that does not protect *me*. He will see me in prison without a qualm and as good as told me so. That I am his daughter's father-in-law and a man of ancient lineage and great personal distinction moves him not at all.

Mrs Killigrew is in foal again, and is much distressed by the danger in which I now stand. Your grandmother, being frailer, more so; her night phlegms grow worse. Young Thomas fell out of a tree last month and broke his leg: we sent for Glapthorne. I hope he has put it to a good setting, for a young man with a limp is much hindered making his way in the world. We have lost more sheep with rot, and are likely to have less ground eared next spring than ever before. God help us.

I send this letter by Captain Elliot, who says he'll deliver it. I have my doubts of its reaching you, though I know he is as much in and out of Spanish ports as English. I pray that Almighty Christ will sustain you in your captivity and lead you to a happy outcome.

> Your affect. father,
> J. Killigrew.

During the next week I read that letter ten times daily. In the end I came to know it by heart, and even after all these years can repeat it word for word. It was a shaft from home, a life line to which I clung in this utter isolation. There might be no comfort in it but it was the connection that counted, a tangible recognition that I was still alive and in touch with the outside world. I felt I had almost spoken to my father—every phrase seemed to come from him, was like a breath of home. I saw it all and knew it all existed and was continuing to exist, and the knowledge steadied and kept me sane.

All the same in January I gave up work on the cell grating. The stone was too hard to make any progress: I was defeated.

For some time now I had regularly talked to myself; it seemed to provide a form of company and a means of ridding oneself of certain insupportable thoughts and fears. But now I began to grow short of breath in the night. Sometimes in spite of the cold I would wake in a sweat, not from fever but from a mind-induced panic. The walls seemed to be closing in so that the cell became a box no bigger than a stone coffin. I would leap up and shout myself hoarse and then beat on the door until my hands were bruised and sore. Then I would collapse on the bed seeking for breath.

One night I could not stop and tore the straw out of the bunk and ripped into pieces the rough flannel covering. I screamed like an animal and knew I was going mad. I wept into bleeding hands and presently fainted or fell asleep asprawl with face pressed against the stone floor.

This happened for six or seven nights. It went dark at this time about six o'clock in the evening and I knew I had at least twelve hours of blinding silent darkness before the next faintest glimmer of light. For half an hour then I would pray aloud: for strength, for patience, for deliverance; for Sue and my father and Mrs Killigrew and the Raleghs; and in so doing a sense of repose would come and some

faint breath of hope. The war might soon be over; I was yet alive;
I would sleep and tomorrow would be another day. But this feeling
would not endure beyond the middle of the night when, with perhaps
six hours' sleep behind me, I would wake in a dreadful panic. I was
blind and deaf and suffocating in a world of unutterable horror. The
thick clay was in my mouth and choking me. I had been overlooked;
the commandant had received no instructions; presently he too would
lose interest and the gaolers would no longer come down the narrow
passage to the three cells and the door would never be opened again.
I was alone and alone and alone for ever.

Each day I pestered the guards; I demanded an interview with
the governor; I must know what was intended. Even death on a grid-
iron seemed less horrible than death from living burial.

One day I found myself sitting on the floor after the midday meal
and realised I had not been marking the passage of days. I had no
memory as to how many had gone since last the wall was scratched,
two or ten or twenty. It no longer mattered. Nothing any longer
mattered. I had just the initiative to eat what was put before me. My
guards perhaps were relieved when they were no longer pestered. I
no longer talked to myself except sometimes in a muttered undertone. I no longer had any thoughts.

Then I did the one thing which I had not thought of to secure a
temporary release. I fell ill. A doctor was brought. He bled me and
administered a clyster. Three days later I was moved to a cell with
three other men and stayed there a week.

A young man's body will put up a fight even when he is himself
past fighting. In a few days I could walk. On the Sunday, which
could be distinguished because of the church bells, two guards came
and led me along a narrow stone passage and into a room decorated
with tapestries and tables and chairs. Two men were talking. One of
them I had seen before, though I was too tired to put a name to the
face: a young man with coppery red hair and fierce, intent eyes. The
other was a stranger. The guards left.

"Sit down, Killigrew," said the younger man in halting English.
"But you speak Spanish now, is it?"

I sat down and stared at him.

"You *are* Maugan Killigrew whom I met in Madrid? But yes, of
course. You have changed. You are much older."

I was much older. The other man was wearing a suit of black velvet
gone slightly green with the years. The sun was shining in the courtyard outside.

"You wrote to Señorita Prada. She told her uncle and the message was passed on. This preserved you when you were recaptured in Portugal. But for that you would have been executed at once."

De Soto, that was the name.

"My time has been occupied, otherwise I should have seen you before. Well, speak up! Have you lost your tongue?"

I swallowed and looked at him. I ran my fingers through my beard and blinked again, feeling the light too strong.

The other man said: "His confinement has been close, captain. After what happened at Lagos I had no choice." He spoke with the guttural accent of a southern Spaniard.

De Soto said: "You seem to have stolen his wits. Well, Killigrew, I have little to say to you at this stage. Many decisions as to policy await His Majesty; others await lesser men. Until these are taken you will be preserved. I can offer you two choices—a return to the cell where you have spent the winter, or a less rigorous life of house confinement only. The last I can give you only on your oath not to escape. If you wish you may have twenty-four hours to decide."

Pedro Lopez de Soto, that was it, secretary to the highest admiral in Spain.

I found myself being led out. I tried to struggle. "No!"

"No what?" asked De Soto.

"I do not need the time. I will take the oath."

"Very well, you will be put in the house of Captain Caldes here as a garden servant—for the time. I can promise nothing more."

I moistened my lips.

"You appreciate, Killigrew, that your escape from Lagos has still to come for reckoning. But the wicked murderers of Captain Buarcos and Lieutenant Claudio have been brought to justice and no more need be made of that."

"Brought to. . . . But I—it was—"

"Say nothing at this stage which will make your case worse. The corpses of the two English soldiers who committed the murder have been found on the Sierra Pelada, north of Huelva. Captain Buarcos's sword was about the skeleton of one of them. Their guilt is established. There for the moment it should rest."

I stared at him. Three years later I was to come across Sergeant Major George in London. He and Crocker had changed clothes with two peasants whom they had fought and killed for their mules, and, altering course, they had eventually made the Biscay coast and a fishing vessel home. But now I felt as if I had lost my two last friends.

"There is one word of advice I would give you at this stage, young man—that is, if you wish to take the best advantage of your time. Are you listening?"

"Yes. . . ."

"Amend your religion," said Captain de Soto. "Embrace the old religion of Christ. Without that no one may save you."

The trees were coming out. The long winter was over and with the suddenness of a woman throwing off a cloak blossom burst in the garden. The cold winds lingered, and there was still snow on the low hills behind the town, but the sun seeped into my bones and warmed them and gave them new life. The dark purple sore in my side began to look less angry and the last stiffness went. I was nineteen years old.

I lived the life of a servant, but this was comfortable and mind-restoring after the solitary imprisonment of the winter. I wrote to my father again, and to Mariana to thank her—and finally a long letter to Sue.

There were five servants in the house of Captain Caldes, two of them negroes, but they showed no hostility and very little curiosity. Perhaps they had learned better; but for me they were human company, and that was what was needed most. The only member of the household to show resentment and suspicion was Father Lorenzo, who was a Dominican, and he had in some way to be won over. I did not at first seriously think of taking De Soto's advice, but it was good whatever the motive behind it. If Father Lorenzo were to complain to the Inquisition, no protection from Madrid, however derived, was likely to save me.

Time passed and his hostility did not change. I thought it all over with care. The heroics of openly defying a Roman Catholic monk no longer entered my head; the practical terrors of the dungeons of Seville had cured all that. So one day I decided to play for time.

He was grudging and did not relax his suspicion, but after some sharp questioning and after hearing there had been some preliminary instruction in Madrid, he agreed to lend me books and to supervise my reading.

This was far from uninteresting, indeed it was a stimulus for an atrophied brain; but I soon saw I walked upon a narrow edge, for the monk was not a man of intellect and he assumed all questions to be heretical unless they could be put down to ignorance. It would have been a much more stimulating discussion with Godfrey Brett.

March and April came, with still no explanation of this treatment. De Soto had seemed to wish to clear me of the killing of Buarcos; this new detention on a favoured basis was nearer in manner to the time in Madrid. They seemed all to be waiting for instructions.

Easter passed with the streets thronged and the bells pealing. The

King, they said, had been ill but was recovered; in Spain all things waited on him. For a governor of a prison, Captain Caldes was a humane man, and mostly his visitors and friends were of a like mind. They all went in fear of the church. The activities of the Holy Office were like the visitation of the plague, something not to be spoken of above a whisper and then only to a trusted friend.

I saw nothing of Seville outside the walls of the house, for the house adjoined the prison and was a part of it. Sometimes I would wake in the night with the stifling fear that I was back in that solitary cell. Then the breathing of the negro on the next pallet would be a salvation and a balm.

In late April Father Lorenzo began to grow impatient. I had read the books and had run out of questions—or questions that could be safely asked. There seemed no way of delaying. One day he asked me when I was prepared to embrace the true church instituted by Christ.

I promised to give him an answer the following week. This had become a cleft stick and one partly of my own making. As a heretic Englishman just released from prison and waiting decisions from Madrid I might just have been tolerated in the household by being unobtrusive and easily overlooked. Now however, having received instruction from a priest, I could not be overlooked by him. Either I became a Roman Catholic or I rejected his teaching. In the latter case he would inevitably report to the Inquisition.

Well, was I prepared to die for my faith, as I had been in Madrid two years ago? Much had changed since then. I had heard the emancipating arguments at Sherborne.

But what of those men who had spoken so brilliantly over the dinner table at Sherborne: Hariot, Northumberland, and the rest; when it came to an absolute decision such as this, how would they choose? How would Ralegh himself choose, a man who for all his openness of mind was a convinced Protestant? Would he be willing to trim his sails and compromise when his soul was concerned? It did not seem likely. But what was the alternative for me?

One morning I was planting out some clove-gillyflowers when Captain Caldes came into the garden with a younger cousin of his, Enrico Caldes. They did not see me. Enrico Caldes, a handsome, open-featured man in his late twenties, was protesting vehemently against the Holy Office.

"Let them lay a finger on you, John, let them but lay a finger on you, and all is lost. No one dare ask what has become of you, or write to you, or ask mercy on your behalf. To call and intercede would be to sign one's own death order. As to the poor wretch—"

"I know. I know it all—"

"Yes, but you do not know that Felipe has been freed—"

"Freed! Well, he is a lucky man!"

"Listen. He was arrested as you know in the dark of the night. He tells me there was no accusation. Someone laid false information about him, he will never know who. So he lies in a loathsome dungeon for six weeks—*six* weeks—protesting his innocence, demanding to know what is his crime, asking for a fair and open hearing of his case—while outside all his property is seized and his family pauperised. Then at last when he has asked for the tenth time to be told the cause of his arrest he is taken out of his cell and brought before his judges. . . .

"Three of them sit there. When he comes in they say nothing. They wait for him to speak, then when he does speak they ask him who he is—as if they don't know his name, as if he is intruding on *them*. What is his business with them, they say. When he asks what offence he has committed to be so used, they tell him first to confess the faults he is aware of. When he says he knows no faults, they order him back to his cell. Knowing what that means—at best another six weeks in a dungeon—he stays there and offers to confess his sins. So in silence they sit and listen while he stumbles over a few irregularities which he has contrived to please them: he has lit candles on a Friday evening, he has changed his linen on the Sabbath—that sort of thing. It does not please them. Now for six hours he is examined before them, promised—mark you—promised pardon if he confesses. So he has confessed to his judges, knowing there is no other way, he has repented and recanted of crimes he has never committed!"

"Well, it is the only way—you know that. Once you are accused. . . . I imagine his penalties will not be light—"

"Light! . . . On three Sunday festivals he is to be stripped and scourged from the city gate to San Clemente. He is to abjure the eating of flesh meat, eggs, cheese, and wine for ever. He must take a vow of chastity, though only thirty-three. He must hear Mass every day of his life. And on one day in every month for a year he must walk barefoot in penance from his house to his parish priest in San Clemente. This is what we have come to—"

"Hush, man, keep your voice down. Lorenzo is out, but one does not know who—"

"Ah, who may be his creature! Who may not? A child is encouraged to betray its father, a wife her husband; no one is safe. . . ."

"Well, that's the way of it. I am no more happy about it than you."

"There is a new torture now, practised in Toledo. Have you heard, it is called *Tormento di Toca*. A thin cloth is thrown over the victim's mouth and nostrils so that he is scarcely able to breathe, and then. . . ."

That night I lay awake for a long time. Did not Henry of Navarre turn Catholic to preserve and consolidate his kingdom; was I more at fault to try to preserve my life? What was my great grandfather but a Catholic? Was he condemned to everlasting torment for that, when the new religion did not exist? So Ralegh had argued once at Arwenack.

That week I said I was ready, and went with Father Lorenzo to the church of San Pedro and met two other priests who questioned me for four hours.

First I had to say in Latin Our Father and the Creed and the *Salve Regina*. Then I was examined closely on matters of the new religion. What were my parents and how had I been brought up? How had I been told to regard the Roman Catholic faith? What had I first been taught of the Mass and what did I now believe? What of sacramental confession? What concerning the orders of friars and nuns such as I saw about me in Spain? What of the intercession of saints? What of Purgatory? What of the eating of meat on prohibited days? What of fasts and disciplines? What of the salvation of the soul? So it went on all through a shining spring morning. At noon a glass of water was brought and then all began again.

At the last I was asked to take a solemn oath, and here almost threw off the whole thing. Yet at the end I dared not.

I, Maugan Killigrew, on the 29th April in the Year of our Lord 1597, being in sound mind and body and under no duress, do solemnly declare that the Church of England is not a church but rather the synagogue of the Devil, and that neither in her, her creed, or matters pertaining to her, can one be saved; and that I, Maugan Killigrew, as a person now received in the Catholic truth of the Roman Church, confess that the said new religion of my country is bad, and in her and all her opinions and ceremonies lies the soul's perdition; and I detest and abominate them and sever myself from them and from the said religion and recognise that the true faith and the Catholic religion is that of the Roman Church in which I have now been instructed, and in which I promise to live and die, never severing myself from her. And I ask with great humility, submission, and obedience and fear of God, to be received by this my conversion into the holy Catholic Church. In the name of the Father. . . ."

On the morning following, in company with the other servants, I took the sacrament in the old faith.

May came and with it the first heat. We watered the garden each
morning but the searing sun sucked up the moisture within the hour.
Plants wilted, eddies of dust moved with the least breeze. We rose at
four instead of five but took three hours siesta in the afternoon heat.
With my acceptance of the old faith came some enlargement, and I
was allowed to wander about the house. From the upper windows
one could see over the town, and in those first hot days the domes
and Moorish towers and arches became part of a mirage shimmering
and unreal, some imagined city on a river's edge existing only in the
spray of a waterfall's rainbow.

Nothing more was seen of De Soto, and I scarcely ever saw Captain Caldes; but one evening Enrico Caldes came into the garden
with another naval captain. As I left the garden the newcomer said
he was just back from Brest, so when it grew dark I made an excuse
of needing easement and stole out again.

They were still talking, and about England. A spy had just come
to Brest from the Court with the latest news. Ralegh was back in
favour at last; it was thought he would soon be allowed to resume
his old position as Captain of the Guard. He and Essex and Cecil
were now working together in great amnity. This meant, they agreed,
that Cecil's peace party had been overborne and that for the time
he had thrown in his lot with the advocates of an intensified war.
Another raid on Spain was therefore likely. Much more now depended on the Armada at present being prepared at Ferrol. It was
essential that England should be conquered this year.

The naval captain was convinced that both countries were nearing exhaustion in this long, drawn out war, and that the one which
struck hardest this year was likely to win. Conditions were far more
favourable now than in '88 for an Armada; it remained only to prepare it and send it at the right time. He was himself returning to
Brest next week with big reinforcements.

He had served under the Adelantado at Lepanto and had a great
admiration for him; a cautious but determined veteran, he said. It
would be a very different story from last time.

Just then the bell in the prison clanged, and I shrank into the shadows and picked a stealthy way back to the house.

On the twentieth of May some decision was at last come to regarding my future.

Captain Caldes said: "You are still on oath not to escape, Killigrew. You have sworn that you will keep this city as a prison and
not leave it either on foot or otherwise in any manner whatsoever.
That is understood?"

"That is understood."

"Then within those limits you may go where you wish. I have arranged for you to have a room of your own in this house until you move to Cadiz."

I stared at him, wondering if peace had come.

"You will be given money, sufficient to live and to buy yourself new clothes. My cousin will see to your needs. Please tell him what you want."

I think I must have looked as stupid as when first brought before this man. "Thank you. . . . I should like a barber. . . . And some soap."

Enrico Caldes got up with a friendly smile. "Come, Killigrew, I'll show you the city."

He showed me the city.

We went to a bull-fight: a wild and noisy pageant in which the leading aristocrats of the city took part, played out under a blazing sky the colour of unpolished steel; we saw the great cathedral of Santa Maria de la Sede and watched the solemn dance of the choir boys performed with castanets before the high altar; we were shown over the Jesuit college; we attended the Eucharist together at San Pedro; we walked the city walls; we sat at night gatherings where guitarists sang and danced the sad, trembling songs of Spain.

From being a captive one had become a guest. With all the grace and courtesy which came natural to him Enrico Caldes was making me welcome. I was quite baffled, and though I tried to get him to talk, on that subject he would not.

On the second of June Enrico said: "Can you be ready to leave for Cadiz tomorrow?"

"Does this mean I'm to be sent back to England!"

"I know no more than you, my friend. Let us go together and see."

We left at six in the morning and reached Cadiz the following night. Even by the quickly fading light one could see that much of the town was in ruins. Enrico said that although it had apparently been the intention of the English to spare the churches, when they left they had fired the houses and most of the churches had gone up in the blaze.

The harbour had more quickly recovered, and all signs of the struggle for the Puntal narrows had disappeared. Some blackened hulks remained in the mud below Port Royal where the treasure fleet had burned.

We stayed at an inn on the edge of the town, and at seven breakfasted off fresh flounders and spiced mutton and small beer. At eight we went on foot to Fort St Philip and there were led to a room overlooking the bay. In the room were three men. One was Andres Prada, Mariana's uncle, another was Don Juan de Idiaquez, that high dignitary of the *Junta de Noche* who had been present when I was charged with the message at the Palace in Madrid. The third was Captain Elliot.

I knew then almost instantly whose decision it had been which had so drastically altered the attitude of the Spaniards towards me. And what that decision was.

I hardly needed to see the ring Captain Elliot was wearing and to recognise it as the one with the Spanish royal arms upon it which had been sent to my father to be given in due course to the bearer of his reply.

CHAPTER 11

WITHIN a week I sailed for El Ferrol.

Expediency I have heard described as a consideration of what is politic as a rule of action as distinct from what is just and right. It is a word with which the idealist has small patience. My idealism tarnished young.

Or perhaps it was all involved in some complex manner with the two-headed eagle of the Killigrews, which could look both ways.

In any event I found that the acceptance of Catholicism could not be made as an empty gesture and left there. I had been too deeply probed by the priests in the church of San Pedro. And this went with me into the confessional. It was impossible to confer with these solemn patient understanding priests and speak of petty sins tongue in cheek; it was impossible not to feel that in withholding from them the fundamental lie one was in a sense giving God the lie too.

The deception was no more palatable on the material plane; for it seemed to stem from the spiritual. The welcome the men gave me in the fort of St Philip was far more open because of this change of religion: it marched with Mr Killigrew's change of allegiance and made my concurrence in it so much more plausible.

Here I had had three courses open. One, to have rejected my father and all that his betrayal stood for. Two, to have accepted it but with amazement and lack of understanding and unspoken hostility. Three, to have welcomed it as if already half expected and to have offered to further his and their plans in any way possible. The first course would have rendered the change of religion pointless and would at best have seen a return to the dungeon. The second was a compromise which might have saved my life but done no other good. The third was a hypocrisy no greater than the greatest already undertaken, and it meant a likely freedom within Spain and perhaps some future chance of escape.

. . . When I did go to sleep I would often wake sweating—sometimes for myself and sometimes for what my father, to save himself from a debtors' prison, was prepared to do.

One could see the scene so well: Mr Killigrew in his study in despair after bringing himself to do what he would so seldom do, add up the extent of his debts. Always before there had been another manor to sell or mortgage, or some rich person he could turn to for a helping hand. Always there had been tomorrow to look forward to; there would be a windfall from Elliot or Burley or some old bond would be extended at the last moment: it always had happened before, and meantime it was a pity to miss such good hawking weather. . . . But not today. There was no way left to turn. A debtors' prison is not a pretty place; my father had already sampled it.

But Captain Elliot was there. "Ten thousand pounds, Mr Killigrew. Not more than your deserts, Mr Killigrew, but where will you get them else? Not from the Privy Council. Not from the Queen. From her you have not even received the knighthood which all the eldest sons of your house have been given as they reached suitable age. Every man's hand is against you, Mr Killigrew: Godolphin, Trefusis, Trelawny, Vivian, they will be the first to trample you down. But there is a way, quite handy to your hand, by which you may triumph over them, and thereby come by your knighthood, together with the ownership of Godolphin, Trelowarren, Erisey, Enys and Trefusis. It is not as if you had to organize an army, lead a revolt, go out in *war*. No, no. You need do nothing—except perhaps rid yourself of one or two of your followers who might be difficult in a crisis. Then wait—that is all—just wait until these ships appear off your coast. All this is a trifle better than a debtors' prison, which is all you will get otherwise. And what does the war really mean to you? Don't tell me you have very strong feelings on religion. And Philip has already once been virtually King of England. There will be a little trouble, of course, some adjustments. But they will come *in any case* when Elizabeth dies, and she is old and not likely to last over-much longer. This is your great chance of fame and fortune. It is really only what Stanley and others did when Elizabeth's grandfather landed. . . . Think it over, Mr Killigrew. But don't think it over too long. I leave on tomorrow's tide. . . ."

It was a strange meeting, that one in the gun room of the castle of St Philip. With my father's answer in their hand they were sounding out Mr Killigrew's base son. He already showed signs of being of the same mind as his father. He had been in Spain before, he spoke the language, he had borne the original message, he had recently become a Catholic: it all pointed one way, and Mr Killigrew's base son had the quickness of wit—or the baseness—to see how their thoughts were leading them and to follow.

It was a strange meeting in other ways because although by the end of it I had been examined thoroughly and much implied, the speakers had been both secretive and vague. I could see that Enrico Caldes had no clear idea as to the object of the meeting; he knew far more than I about a gathering fleet, but he knew nothing of the offer to my father.

Enrico Caldes sailed to Ferrol with me. Captain Elliot had already left for Cartagena, and Don Juan de Idiaquez was returning to Madrid. Prada still had business to conclude in Cadiz; but before I left he sent for me.

"Señor," I said, "I have to thank you—and Mariana—for consideration last autumn when I was retaken after escaping."

He smiled his tight, walnut-brown smile. "Your escape is a matter we have forgotten, for reasons of state. . . . I have a final word or two I wish to say to you, Killigrew, now that we are alone. It is in fact a warning."

I waited.

"When we invade England we are assured of the support of many people in all walks of life. But your father's help, as you'll need no telling, will be of great value to our cause. He was worth buying. However, I like to believe his adherence to us is not solely a matter of gold. Nor, I trust, is yours solely a matter of preserving your life."

"No, it is not."

"So when the time comes you too will help. You speak our language. You will be a sign of our own goodwill towards those of your kinsfolk who do not oppose us. In all this, when all this is finished, you will not be the loser."

I moistened my lips.

He said: "But there is one great danger. The essence of naval or military success is surprise. As our Armada grows here, its presence cannot be concealed from English spies. What *can* be concealed is its objective."

"Yes, I understand."

"So far in all Spain, only five people, including the King, know of the destination of this fleet. None of our senior admirals yet know it.

You will readily see that if this secret were to be allowed to leak out, preparations to meet it in England would at once be made."

"Yes."

"When your father replied favourably to our invitation, it was first intended to keep you in prison. However, you can be useful, and you cannot fail to see that if this information which you possess leaks away to England before we are ready it will sign your father's death warrant. That must be clear to you."

"It is."

"You are fond of your father?"

"Yes."

"I thought so. Then we will leave it at that. Remember, a single unguarded word may ensure his death."

"I understand."

"Goodbye, and may we some day meet again."

I had spent a week at Coruña when stormbound two years ago, but had never crossed to El Ferrol, which is twelve miles away by sea and perhaps forty by road. Now we sailed in through a long and well guarded and narrow channel, and saw the town and dockyard sheltering behind the shoulder of rock which made the harbour in such a way that they were not to be seen from the sea. It was a perfect natural harbour better protected than Cadiz, and one could well understand the reluctance of English admirals to attack it.

Eighty-four sail were there when we arrived, about a quarter of them galleons but clearly not yet in a state of preparedness to sail. *San Pedro, San Pablo,* and *San Juan* were three more of the "Apostles" of which we had destroyed four at Cadiz. *San Pablo* was the largest galleon of them all, being of twelve hundred tons burden.

I was housed with Enrico Caldes, and shared a room with him and two other men in a hostelry in the middle of the town where officers of the fleet had taken rooms. I was allowed to wander about the little town at will, though there was nothing to it except what had grown from the demands of the dockyard. A big fleet had in fact set sail for England last autumn but had been driven back with much damage by foul weather.

One night Captain Lopez de Soto arrived aboard the *Espiritu Santo,* a smaller galleon which he was to command in the Armada, and the next morning I was summoned to see him.

He was sitting in his cabin in a loose shirt under a green silk morning gown, the remnants of his breakfast on the table, a servant combing his coppery hair. He dismissed the servant.

"So, Killigrew, you are well housed? Caldes is looking after you?"

He did not wait for an answer. "His Excellency Don Martin de Padilla is in Madrid, so I am dealing with all the administration while he is away."

"Yes, sir."

"Caldes is to be specially responsible for you, but both of you will come under my supervision. I understand you are to sail with us when the time comes."

"Yes, sir."

"No doubt on duties which will later be assigned to you? . . ."

He waited. There was a faint questioning note in his voice which I did not respond to.

"All orders come in their proper time," he went on. "We shall not, of course, sail yet. There is much still to do here, as you can see. It will be August, I think, before we leave."

"Sir," I said, "I am a good penman and speak both languages. Whatever—duties—may be assigned to me later, can I not be given something in the meantime? Could I not be of assistance to you or to some other officer?"

"That might be. I will give it some thought."

As I got to the door he said: "Killigrew."

"Yes."

"You sailed from England on a great project with a great fleet, bent on the destruction of Cadiz."

"Yes."

"It will be a strange turn of fate to return to England with another fleet but larger, bent on another project but larger."

I said: "May it have the same success."

I do not think it was a wise remark for I noticed a glint in his eyes; I had seen the double edge only as I spoke. But that is the risk of hypocrisy; one must watch one's tongue at every word.

For a month I worked as an under secretary in the Naval Commissariat adjoining the dockyard. The hours were seven to twelve and three to eight; yet sometimes all I did if better organised could have been concentrated into two hours a day. There were twenty clerks and a like number of secretaries and a dozen senior officials dealing with the commissioning of the fleet, but delay and duplication and lack of system set much of their effort at nought. Underneath the high efficiency and devotion to duty of men like De Soto there was laxness and confusion. Every directive had had for so long to be referred to the top—almost always to Madrid—that underlings had become incapable of decision.

And El Ferrol, though supremely secure against outside attack, lacked much for the preparation of a great Armada. It was too far from the centres of Spanish power. The road from Madrid was mountainous and, one gathered, in places scarcely existent; the sea communications were long; the chief centres of population were far away. Small attempt had been made to equip the little town for so great an undertaking. The army lived in tents on the bare hillside, too many of the navy lived aboard ship too soon, consuming naval supplies and falling sick of disease while still in harbour. Streets were unpaved so that no vehicle could move without sending up clouds of dust, and many of the lanes were impassable because of the deep ruts. Ditches were clogged with refuse and alive with flies. At almost every corner cookshops had been set up with great kettles on trivets to supply the needs of the shipworkers and the sailors and the clerks. Often at midday I would have a leek broth at one of them and listen to the chatter of the men standing around. There were Portuguese, Italians, French, and Germans among them, for many of the ships were foreign.

After midday some of the narrow shady streets would be impassable for sleeping men, and other diced in groups or gambled cross-legged over greasy cards. At nights there were noisy scenes and much crime and vice. Militia patrolled the main streets at certain hours, but their times were known and they were easily avoided. Priests were everywhere and kept the churches open for constant Masses.

Over all and above everything was the white dust. It covered the world with a fine film; one's hands were coarse with it, one's teeth gritted, one's hair was powdered. It lay on food and wine and book and seat and bed.

During the month I came to know by sight many of the Spanish admirals and captains who were to command the fleet. Don Diego Brochero, who was to be Vice-Admiral of the expedition, was a fiery and vivid man; Bertendona, who had borne the brunt of the great fight with *Revenge* when Sir Richard Grenville died; Oliste, Urquiola, and Villaviciosa were all men of great sea-going experience, none of them amateurs elevated to command because of their birth. The Spanish, as Ralegh often pointed out, did not make the same mistake twice.

The Adelantado himself was a tall and austere man of fifty or so with a concern for detail, and one could imagine him having little patience with inefficiency; but it was Brochero who had the passion and the fire. Whenever he came through the Commissariat it was as if a vitalising wind had blown through. He it was who was in charge of discipline, and every day a new body would dangle from the gallows on the quay. A soldier had deserted, a sailor had been guilty of indiscipline, a dockyard worker had been caught stealing. Yet no punishment seemed to stop the abuses.

I thought often of writing to my father, but could not find the words. I could not beg him to change his mind without betraying my own. I could not write that I had thrown in my lot with Spain and was glad he had done the same. I could not write without mentioning these terrible decisions, for such a letter would have been without meaning and content. Nor could I bring myself to write to Sue: the main issue was impossible to speak of, yet too great to ignore.

Gradually in settling down one came to appreciate currents of opinion which made themselves felt in the town. The foreign captains were in no hurry to sail. Memories still existed of the battles in the Channel nine years ago; and there were fresher memories of the storm which had defeated them last autumn; they had not so much to gain from a Spanish victory; their own countries lived in uneasy alliance with, or subjugation to, Spain. They would gladly see the Catholic faith triumphant but would have preferred others to play the leading role.

Then there were the fanatics like Captain de Soto who lived only for the day, who smarted everlastingly under the defeat of '88 and the sacking of Cadiz last year, and knew that their destiny and their only fulfilment was to launch another Armada at England's throat. Such men predominated in the leadership. But His Excellency Don Martin de Padilla, Conte de Gadea, supreme Adelantado of Castille, steered a middle course. A sober general with the weight of the whole campaign on his shoulders, he was not to be hurried. Not for him the obloquy which was heaped on the name of Medina Sidonia. He did not underestimate England or the hazards ahead. So every preparation must be made down to the last detail. Then and only then, when the time came, whether it be August or even September, he would issue the orders and the great Armada would sail.

In that first month it built gradually. Three more of the Apostle galleons arrived: *San Bartolomeo,* and the smaller *San Marcos* and *San Lucar; Almirante* from Ivella, the biggest of all; *Misericordia,* the flagship of Portugal; ten German and Flemish urcas, and a dozen other galleons of various sizes. By now the fleet was more powerful than the English one which had taken Cadiz; and in the next week another three thousand infantry arrived, with some five hundred cavalry and field artillery, and mules and oxen and a great quantity of ammunition and stores. Here I perceived the Adelantado to be in a dilemma. Such great forces as he now possessed were self-consuming. If he waited for even greater forces, what he had would likely eat itself away.

That week—it was the last in July and the summer at its greatest heat—several important councils were held and there was dissension at them. De Soto came away from the last of them in a towering rage. That day an English fleet was sighted off Coruña.

If any testimony had been needed to the impression made by last year's capture of Cadiz, it was manifested now in the consternation which ruled in El Ferrol. Orders and counter-orders flew about, ships were manned, batteries mounted, regiments assembled. A screen of fly-boats was thrown out to report on the imminence of attack. On the second morning from a high rock above the biscuit factory I could count a dozen sail. I stood in the hot morning sun talking quietly to Enrico Caldes and silently praying to my Protestant God.

He did not hear. The fly-boats reported twenty ships: five royal galleons, including *Due Repulse* and *Hope*, thirteen other big vessels and two fly-boats. *Due Repulse* had been Essex's flagship at Cadiz but the Spanish said she was not flying his pennant. The fleet was sailing provocatively backward and forward between El Ferrol and the Sisargas Islands, west of Coruña, as if challenging the Spanish to come out. Already half a dozen small vessels had been captured as they came unsuspectingly round Cape San Adrian.

The Adelantado had recived orders from the King that week to prepare his Armada for immediate sailing; to this he had replied that his fleet was as yet far from complete—stores, further military reinforcements, more ships, had all been promised; in particular the thirty-two ships of the Seville squadron under Admiral Don Marcos de Arumburu, another veteran of the battle with Grenville, with the divisions of the Andalusian guard aboard; and Prince Andrea Doria was making his way round from Italy with a fleet of galleys and a strong force of seasoned Italian soldiery; it would be madness to move without all these.

So the Adelantado had argued. Now with the appearance of an English fleet at his very door he might change his mind. Would he be right to do so? Brochero urged an immediate attack, as did most of the captains. But Bertendona was against it, and so in the end was Don Martin. His view was that the English fleet was not big enough. To sail out of harbour at this stage, losing perhaps ten ships in destroying or disabling twenty, giving a fair picture of one's strength and wasting valuable stores and ammunition, would be playing the English game. . . .

So for nearly a week we waited in great tension. Once or twice in every day the look-outs reported the English fleet in sight of Betanzos Bay. Then the alarm would abate as they bore away again. On the sixth day they did not appear. They had left us in peace. El Ferrol began to return to its normal routine of unorganised preparation.

In the first week of August Captain de Soto left for Madrid. On the same date I was transferred to the galleon *San Bartolomeo*, which I was rowed out to daily. There fifty Irish were working on alterations and repairs. None of them spoke Spanish; they had come over in a shallop from Cork as volunteers for Spain, and I was used as a go-between translating the over-seer's orders. In the same week Captain Pedro de Zubiaur, perhaps the greatest living expert on galley warfare, was dispatched for Blavet with seven galleys, two supply ships, and two thousand infantry, where they could wait for the coming of the Armada. It helped in a small way to ease the supply problems of El Ferrol. Soon after this a Spanish spy, an Englishman called Pennell, arived in Coruña aboard a Danish ship and came to report to the Naval Council in El Ferrol. He spoke little Spanish, and I was told to be present to interpret. There were four other men at this interview: Don Martin himself, Father Sicilia his confessor, Admiral Brochero, and General de Guavara.

Pennell had been in Plymouth a week ago, and knew all that had been happening there. The English fleet which had cruised off Betanzos Bay for five days had been commanded by Lord Thomas Howard, and had been part of a much larger expedition—as great as the one of last year—which had been scattered by a terrible storm off Ushant. Sir Walter Ralegh had turned back to Plymouth with his squadron badly damaged. The Earl of Essex, with his flagship *Mere Honour* almost sinking under him, had put in to Falmouth with some thirty or forty other of his fleet in like trouble. (Merciful God, that gave me a twinge!) The Dutch admiral had also given up. Only Howard's squadron, missing the greatest intensity of the storm, had ridden it out and made for the arranged rendezvous. There he had stayed, as we had seen, sailing up and down waiting for the others and daring the Spanish fleet to emerge. Now he was back in Plymouth again, refitting with the rest.

Did they intend another expedition this year? Assuredly, Pennell replied, if the Queen continued her permission. Their intention when they came? It was to attack El Ferrol, possibly with fire ships, and then go on to the Azores to await and capture the Treasure Fleet. One result of the Spanish non-emergence to fight, Pennell said, had been to give the impression that they were still far from ready to sail and indeed would not come out this summer.

Pennell was a well-spoken man who had been a seaman all his life and at some time must have commanded a craft. But his hands trembled now, and one could watch how only the drink steadied him. The questions came near home and I dreaded to hear the name Killigrew mentioned. Once or twice I was tempted to give some wrong emphasis to a reply, for Pennell's information had a ring of truth about it, but I decided it was not a justifiable risk. This was as well, for the next time I saw Father Sicilia he was talking a passable English to the Irish priest who had come over with the volunteers. . . .

De Soto came back from Madrid well pleased with his visit. It became known soon after his return that the Armada would not sail for at least two weeks more. It was puzzling that this delay should satisfy him.

Pennell was lodged in the house where I slept, which was distasteful to me, for the presence of a genuine traitor made me more ashamed of my own position. He would have made a friend of me, but I could not stand the sight of his thin pitted face, the bloodshot blue eyes, the unsteady hands. I knew that the Spaniards, for all they had to make use of such creatures, despised them. Had he been placed here to spy upon me?

The weather had been less settled for some time, and now it set in blustery and wet. Ships putting in from Biscay reported storm conditions and unseasonable cold for early August.

One day when being rowed out to *San Bartolomeo* we passed a pinnace which was being re-painted. Some alterations were taking place aboard and her name *Cabagua* painted out. As we repassed on the way home the name *Mark of Gloucester* was being painted in. I asked one of the Spanish sailors, who shrugged and said: "She was a prize, captured in the spring. She is English built, señor."

"But why is she being given her English name again?"

"The ways of man are inscrutable, señor."

"That is an English style of rigging she is being fitted with, surely."

"Yes, surely, señor."

The harbour and docks of El Ferrol had now become a sea of masts. There were one hundred and fifty large ships besides the many small ones. The bad weather brought in coasters and fishing vessels for shelter, and there were collisions and damage in the roads. A powder vessel sank at her moorings and a Portuguese galleon went ashore on the shoals above the town. Fever had broken out both in the ships and ashore. I avoided it, but Enrico Caldes was gravely ill, and some hundred men died before the middle of August. Many men still continued to desert, and the severest measures Admiral Brochero could apply did not prevent them. I thought of Ralegh's trouble pressing crews in the Thames. Many of the conferences to which the foreign captains were invited—which were not conferences dealing with grand strategy but with ordinary details of supply—broke up in disagreement and frustration.

The Spanish had one advantage over the English: a supreme commander who had absolute authority; but from what I saw of events it became clear that Brochero, always pressing his forward policy, was at loggerheads with His Excellency Don Martin and in this he was abetted by De Soto, Antonio de Urquiola, and several of the other influential captains.

A few days after first seeing the *Mark of Gloucester* I saw Pennell aboard her, and that night, swallowing my dislike, I sat down with him over a mug of burnt wine and encouraged him to talk.

"What?" he said. "*Mark of Gloucester?* Yes, well, I have been useful to them, my friend. You understand? I have brought them the latest news, so in reward they're giving me back a little ship of my own. Of course it's a small and ill-found craft compared to what I commanded in my prime, but I shall be able to eke out a living carrying between one port and another."

"They will release you?" I said.

"Release me? I was never in captivity, my friend. They are *giving* me this ship for myself in payment of services rendered."

"With what crew?"

"Crew? Oh, that offers no problem, my friend. I need ten, that's all. I have already an Irish master's mate, two Flemish seamen, a Dane, and a Frenchman."

"And the Spanish are willing that these men should go?"

"Why not? A dozen more or less, what is that?"

While he drank I watched him. He was a drunkard, but drunkards like madmen are astute enough outside the area of their particular weakness. What if I said to him "Take me"? Would he betray me to the Spanish?

The following day I was called off *San Bartolomeo* to help again in the Commissariat and Captain de Soto was there.

"So Killigrew, you have escaped the fever. Look at this establishment: decimated! I want you to copy out this order for requisitions —three times. They must be ready within the hour. When they are done come aboard *San Pablo,* I have work for you there."

That night I supped with junior officers aboard the galleon and listened to their lively talk. They were a handsome, friendly group. For them the present delay was outrageous. They wanted only to sail and challenge the enemy in his home waters. To them, proud and brave as they were, it was humiliating and frustrating to wait, as one put it, until the English were "knocking on their front gate."

"It is not quite that," said an older lieutenant. "Wars are not won by gestures, they are won by preparation, by strategy, and only at the last by fighting."

"Oh, hark at Rodrigo!" another said. "This is not to be a joust such as you went on nine years ago! We no longer have wax in our ears. We'll fight the English fleets and defeat them before ever we get sight of their coasts. It's said they will sail this week."

"Even so I doubt we shall meet them."

They pressed him then, but he glanced in my direction, so I got up.

"You can speak more freely if I leave?"

"No, no. You are with us, I know that. I can only say that I have heard that efforts are to be made to lure the English fleet away from our shores so that we may sail to England without battle first. If it can be done I'll tell you it will be worth doing. We should not defeat them in straight battle without grievous loss on both sides, and if it can be avoided I have no fancy to continue into northern waters with our sails in ribbons and our bows holed at the water line. However great the victory might be, the weather could be the final victor. It was last time."

There was silence then. My mind flew over the information and found it instantly true: it explained De Soto's willingness to wait.

Next day I again worked on board *San Pablo* to which De Soto had temporarily transferred. At length I could be in ignorance no longer.

"Sir, I see efforts are being made to decoy the English fleet when it enters these waters. Can I not help in some manner? I know my countrymen and their ways."

De Soto finished reading the letter his scrivener had written and took up the wax to seal it.

"Who told you anything of this? Captain Pennell in his cups?"

"No. But *Mark of Gloucester* is not being renamed for nothing."

De Soto pressed the wax down with the naval seal. "So you think I should explain it to you?"

"I hoped I could help."

"You cannot help. There will no doubt be other duties for you; who knows? I cannot tell you, for I am not told."

The scrivener returned then but went out again almost at once.

"But since you have observed this piece of strategy, no greater harm will come of your knowing the rest. As the weather moderates we shall throw out a screen of small vessels to await the arrival of the English. They will be foreign vessels, manned by English, Irish, Flemish, and in due course some of them will be captured. They will all report that the Adelantado has sailed with his fleet to the Azores to

protect the new treasure *flota* coming from the Indies. It is hoped
and believed that your admirals will 'follow' him."

Again we were interrupted, but it was impossible to keep what he
had said out of my mind.

"But, captain, if you succeed in this—this plan, who is to say the
English will not take the opportunity of attacking Cadiz or Lisbon
instead?"

"Two things, Killigrew. One, naval success and greed of gain have
always been uppermost in the minds of your English admirals. Two,
their evacuation of Cadiz after they had captured it last year proves
that the *conquest* of Spain territorially is quite beyond their resources
—or their desires. . . . So we believe they will sail for the Azores and
leave England open for our invasion."

CHAPTER 12

LOOKING back on that momentous time with the aftersight of the years
it is sometimes hard to untangle the sensations and apprehensions of
each day from the knowledge that came later.

I did not at first think there was any likelihood of the Spanish manoeuvre being successful; Ralegh or Essex would sail into the very
jaws of El Ferrol harbour to establish the whereabouts of the Spanish
fleet for themselves. It was not until the ruse had already succeeded
that I began to believe it.

One day I met Richard Burley in the street. It was an unpleasant
shock, for though he greeted me in a friendly way and without apparent surprise, the presence of this man always seemed an ill omen
in my life. He told me he had slipped away from Cawsand near
Plymouth on August 18 and at that time the English fleet was ready
to sail and waiting for the first break in the weather.

Soon after this, *Mark of Gloucester* left commanded by Captain
Pennell of Bristol and manned by a mixed crew. She carried a cargo
of wine and salt from Oporto and Coruña for Weymouth. Other small
vessels left at the same time.

That week I was given a broadsheet written in English to read,
and was asked to go carefully over it for printing mistakes. The
pamphlet was addressed to the English people offering mercy and
advancement to all who turned Catholic, but threatening the sword
to all Protestants. That week also I entered a room at the Commis-

sariat and found it piled with English flags . . . they were to be distributed throughout the fleet.

News came that the King was gravely ill. Temporarily this disrupted everything, for though he was old he held all decisions in his own hands. It was as if a sudden palsy had struck the town. What if he died? Would his son, who must now be about nineteen, in any way alter the urgent command to sail and conquer England? Prince Philip was spoken of everywhere and openly as a weakling and dissolute.

Unknown to me at this time, the English fleet under the supreme command of Essex, was not a hundred miles off the Spanish coast. So far they had progressed well but now they were struck by another of the great storms of that vindictive summer. The two Spanish galleons captured at Cadiz and adapted to English designs were totally disabled and forced to make for Biscayan ports. Sir Walter's *Warspite* was part dismasted and Lord Essex's *Due Repulse* sprang a dangerous leak. The rest of the fleet was scattered, and Ralegh, missing the other ships at the agreed meeting point, and unable in his damaged state to do more than run before the wind, made off south for the second rendezvous above Lisbon. Near Finisterre a frigate of his squadron captured one of the small vessels sent out from Ferrol with the false news.

In El Ferrol, De Soto more and more dropped his guard in my presence. I was competent, discreet, and always willing. So I learned of many decisions almost as soon as they were come to.

Once or twice more he tried to sound me as to my exact purpose with the invading fleet, as if he sensed a plan he was not entirely aware of, but, mindful of Andres Prada's warning, I would not be drawn.

News arrived that once more the King was recovering, and all began to move again. But there had been a full week's delay, and the grinding machinery of preparation took time to gather pace.

The painful decision was reached that bare supplies on all vessels should be cut from ten weeks to five. For a voyage of conquest this seemed ample—but everyone knew the hazards of that reasoning.

Daily fly-boats which patrolled the seas from Cape Finisterre to Cape Ortegal came in to report on what they had seen, and presently we heard that a large English fleet had been sighted off Finisterre. (This was the main English fleet under Essex gathering after the storm.)

For a time we did not know what success if any the decoy ships with their false tales had had. Then the news broke in a flood among the senior officers: three different fly-boats reported that Essex and the rest of the fleet had been sighted off Muros heading south.

They were gone and the way was open. It was the ninth of September.

At once embarkation began. Final stores were brought aboard, messages to the King sent, troops and equipment and ammunition ferried to the transports and the galleons, mules and horses and cattle shipped. To my disappointment I was put aboard *San Bartolomeo* with Enrico Caldes. The fifty Irish were to travel in her as combatants and I was needed as interpreter. Another company of one hundred Irish soldiers under their own captain travelled in the urca *San Juan Bautista*.

Capitan de Mar of *San Bartolomeo* was Ferdinando Quesada, a thin ascetic man, wealthy in his own right, who kept two pages by him to play music in the evenings. The *Capitan de Guerra*, or general commanding the soldiers aboard, was Diego Bonifaz, his rank being equal to that of Quesada; and he had absolute control of his own forces as if army and navy were travelling together only by accident.

Richard Burley sailed aboard *San Mateo*, a galleon just delivered from the new shipyards of Renteria to replace the one of the same name destroyed at Cadiz. Captain Elliot joined the fleet with *Dolphin*, his own crew and his own arms, as an independent privateer.

Embarkation took two days, it was the morning of the twelfth before the first galleon shook down her sails and began to make a way out of the narrow entrance of the harbour.

Orders were to assemble in Betanzos Bay to await a favourable wind. The great fleet took thirty hours to assemble in the bay fifteen miles from Ferrol on the western side of the rocky cape. The weather was still rough and the wind gusty and treacherous when I went up on deck on the morning of the first inspection. The ships were anchored in six lines, each line consisting of ten galleons and fourteen other ships from Easterlings to transports. This made one hundred and forty-four major ships of war. There were another sixty caravels, fly-boats, supply boats, and frigates. In all these vessels, as I well knew from going over the details, there were five thousand sailors, masses of field artillery, mules, horses, oxen, siege trains and over ten thousand trained soldiers.

The Adelantado conducted his inspection from a decorated barge rowed by twenty-four picked oarsmen. From the maintop of *San Pablo*, the galleon next to ours, the Adelantado's own pendant fluttered: a broad swallow-tailed flag in green, so long that when the gusty wind faltered the ends of the standard dipped in the water. The whole fleet was dressed with flags and standards. Men stood in lines and cheered, guns were fired, the galleons dipped and nodded in the swell, the wind clutched viciously at mast and rigging, and the Adelantado's barge lurched and rolled with flecks of salt water glinting off the oars and fine mists of spray lifting and breaking across the bows.

I slept that night in my usual sickly unease of a first night at sea. The Spanish galleon is a much more comfortable vessel than the English fighting ship, there being more accommodation for the men and greater spaces between decks. Of course *San Bartolomeo* was half as big again as *Warspite*. No one in our galleon yet knew our destination in England. I heard the officers speculating at supper and Falmouth was never mentioned. Some thought the Isle of Wight, some Scotland, some Milford Haven; others thought we should sail right up the Thames and capture London.

The next morning it was known that we should wait a few more days for Admiral de Arumburu and the Seville squadron.

We waited until the eighteenth. Instead of the great Sevillian fleet, attended by Prince Andrea Doria's galleys, came a single frigate. It reported that only ten days ago an English fleet under Sir Walter Ralegh had appeared off the Tagus and appeared likely to attempt to capture Lisbon. In the circumstances Admiral de Arumburu had been commanded to remain patrolling the river below Lisbon in case of such a raid. Doria's galleys also, which had in face of severe weather made their way round from Genoa, had been instructed to await the English attack. There was also some danger from the Turks, with whom it was rumoured Elizabeth was negotiating an alliance.

I could picture De Soto's fury. The splendid situation of an England stripped of her fleet and open to the most powerful attack the most powerful nation in the world could muster was slipping away from lack of courage and lack of a single directive mind. It could not be Philip II who had faltered; but because of his recent grave illness his authority had been usurped, and weakness and indecision had crept in.

There were many conferences aboard *San Pablo*. To the last of these Captain Quesada was summoned, and when he returned, he announced that the fleet was to sail without its Sevillian reinforcements. It would weigh anchor at dawn on the twentieth, being still equal in force to the Armada of '88, and still a fleet bigger than any other in the world. No more time must be wasted—except one day in which to take on fresh water and supplies and to deposit the sick ashore.

The nineteenth was a fine day. It seemed that the westerly winds had blown themselves out and we should have a period of quiet autumnal weather exactly suited to the expedition. That evening Cap-

tain Quesada invited two Italian captains and a Portuguese and a
Biscayan to sup with him and Captain Bonifaz. The Frenchman and
one of the Italians spoke no Spanish but could understand English,
so I was commanded to be present.

All day I had been restless, full of a sensation of impotence and
defeat. Though I knew all it was necessary to know of the Spanish
plans I had been completely unable to do anything to thwart them.
One pictured this fleet reaching England and, remembering the destruction wrought by only 4 galleys two summers ago, multiplied
that by 200 to bring this invasion into comparison. In '95 the Cornish
had been in panic, a few good men like Godolphin standing firm and
some hundreds of reinforcements arriving from Plymouth to support
the local musters at a time when the Spanish had already re-
embarked. What of the result now—a great invasion force permitted
to land at Falmouth without opposition? Half Cornwall would be
theirs in a night. Plymouth, unguarded now by Drake and Hawkins,
would fall within two or three days. With the English fleet far away
the command of the Channel would be in Spanish hands without a
fight. Troops could be ferried across from Brittany at will. When Essex and Ralegh and their fleet returned they would be faced with a
strongly entrenched invasion force operating from occupied ports in
England and more able than the returning English fleet to revictual
and call in fresh ammunition.

For a time at supper they talked of music: one of the Italians
played the viol and the cornet, and he and Quesada carried the conversation. But presently the other Italian motioned to me that he
wished to ask Quesada a question. Did the Spanish naval command
know that French Protestant forces had invaded Catalonia? If so, in
what way would it affect their own plans?

Quesada, recalled from pleasanter fancies, frowned and said, yes,
the French Protestants had made some advances in the eastern Pyre-
nees but they would be quickly repelled; it would have no effect on
Spanish plans. The Italian, Captain Conti, then said it was rumoured
that Prince Andrea Doria and his galleys would be ordered back to
Barcelona instead of following the Armada to England.

The Biscayan captain then asked me to say that he had also heard
that Henry of France, so long defensive and static in his policy, had
laid violent siege to Amiens and had just recovered it. If this were
true, if the Cardinal Archduke had surrendered this key city, it would
be a bitter blow to Spain.

Quesada said he had heard nothing of this: rumours were always
rampant, they meant little. Whatever was happening in France it
could not affect the major strategy of the war. Once England had

collapsed, the main centre of Calvinistic and godless resistance would be gone and all other resistance would collapse too.

"Yes," said the Portuguese, spreading his hands. "*Once* England has collapsed. But how long will she resist and with what bloodshed will our victory be bought? Her raid upon Spain last year was not the act of a weak and divided country."

"She is not weak," interrupted Bonifaz, "but she is divided. All our spies say so. This is our great chance while she is without her fleet. We sail tomorrow."

A silence fell. They were all in their different ways considering what lay ahead. Then Conti looked at me and said:

"You are English. You must know your country well. How do you see the prospects of this great expedition?"

I stared back at him, hypnotised by the opportunities his question offered. These responsible captains would pay no heed to what I had to say in reply. And yet. . . .

"I hope, sir, that we shall triumph on this expedition. But there is one matter which concerns me."

I paused and said no more, groping for the right words, praying for cunning and judgment and subtlety.

"And that is?"

"As you know, sir, I was a junior secretary under Sir Walter Ralegh in the Cadiz expedition of last year. . . ."

"No, I did not know."

This conversation was still in English, and Quesada and three of the others listened uncomprehending.

"Well, there was a thing much spoken of at the time of Cadiz, and that was that our fleet must be back in England before the equinox. At that time every year great gales and seas lash our coasts. It is the expected thing. It was the argument much used against our remaining in occupation of Cadiz. There was bound to be a month when no supplies could get through."

"The equinox?" said Conti. "That is—"

"It begins on the twenty-second or twenty-third of this month, sir. In two days' time. That is why I do not believe the English fleet has gone on to the Azores. It is too late in the year. I believe they have turned away from this coast and returned home. I think they are safe in port again; though no doubt they will come out when we reach the English coast—if the weather permits."

Conti turned to the Biscayan captain.

The Frenchman shrugged. "I am used to stormy seas: they come at any time. Equinox, yes more—and stronger tides. But seas are always treacherous, even your Mediterranean, *capitaine*."

Conti said to me: "Have you told Captain Quesada what you have just said?"

"He has never asked."

"Then kindly tell him."

I told him.

Quesada said: "Tell Captain Conti that we are not children to be afraid of every shadow."

Conti said: "Tell Captain Quesada that it was not a shadow which struck us last year and wrecked seven galleons and cost the lives of two thousand men."

Quesada said: "Tell Captain Conti that was November: we sailed unsound and unready at the command of a King who does not understand these things. This is September: we are well prepared and this boy is no judge of what we may expect. I have sailed off Ushant in September seas as calm as a lake."

"Well prepared!" said Conti. "I have complained to the Adelantado that my provisions are faulty and inadequate and my crew brought up to strength with raw youths. He pays no heed. We sail tomorrow —it may be to victory but it may be to destruction!"

The Frenchman leaned across the table. "Do you not know, boy, that a fly-boat reported this English fleet six days ago already approaching the Azores?"

"Then I am wrong."

"Then what makes you say it?"

"Only Sir Walter Ralegh's words last year when conferring with my Lord of Essex."

"Which were?"

"The plan was talked of then, before the Cadiz expedition was mounted—that a fleet should sail from England late in the year and then turn away for the Azores in order to lure an Armada to attack England while she was seemingly undefended. Then the English were to return in secret to England and wait for the weather to disable or damage your ships before they attacked. . . ."

I concluded lamely: "Of course, it may not be so now. It may be true that England is undefended and that we can take her easily. But it makes me uneasy, that this should all be falling out according to a plan the English were discussing last year."

The morning of the twentieth was brilliant and clear, but before midday a strong north-west wind sprang up. It blew straight in to Betanzos Bay. I thought, another day gone. For much that I had said about the weather though exaggerated was true: there was at best a month's sailing weather ahead. No English captain kept his fleet at

sea beyond the end of October. That evening there was another conference aboard *San Pablo* to which all senior captains were summoned. On the following morning the wind had somewhat abated but
we did not sail.

I had an unwelcome visitor. Across a choppy wind-flecked cable's
length of sea six dark-haired Spanish sailors rowed Captain Richard
Burley from *San Mateo* to *San Bartolomeo*. He had a meeting with
Captain Quesada and then I was sent for.

Burley's narrow savage face moved in a sneer of welcome. "Well,
fellow countryman, I rowed across for a word with you. We've been
having a little trouble this last day or so, as you may guess."

"Trouble?"

"Yes, with our foreign captains. Else we'd have sailed."

I looked through the lantern-shaped window. "We were well advised not. The wind has sprung up again."

"Once we was out we could have stood clear of the land and made
some small headway. Leastwise, we should have begun."

"Why did we not, then?"

His blue suit was as shabby as ever; there was a split in his sleeve
and the cuffs were frayed; he always looked a pirate. "Well might you
ask, fellow countryman, since it seems you have been doing your best
to prevent it by spreading lies and rumour."

"I don't understand."

"Not f'rinstance giving it as your considered opinion that instead
of us cheating the English, the English are cheating us?"

"I did not say that, Captain Burley. But it was Ralegh's plan last
year and I thought there was a risk."

Burley spat on the floor of the cabin and then, seeing Quesada's
fastidious frown, rubbed it in with his foot. "You on our side, Killigrew? Or are you trying to make delay worse'n worse until it is too
late?"

"I wish no delay. I only want to get home."

"That's what you say. And there's those at the top as believe you.
Me for my part, now, I'd string you up and have done. Better to be
sure now than sorry later, I'd say. What do you think?"

"I think you're wrong."

"Ah. . . . Ah well, maybe. They've plans at top that I know nothing of. Where we're bound for f'rinstance. But if so be as it was your
idea to put doubts in men's heads, maybe now you think you've succeeded. But I'd not like you to be carried away at the success. The
doubts was there before ever you spoke. What you said was a straw
on a hay-load."

I glanced at Captain Quesada, who I saw was catching a word here and there.

"What is wrong?" I asked. "These foreign captains. . . ."

"They're cautious, see? Jumping at their own shadows, like. Yesterday morning early, two Portuguese fishing smacks came in reporting Ralegh was still cruising off Lisbon with hundred fifty sail. Stuff and nonsense. Lying nonsense. There's not hundred fifty sail in the whole English fleet, nor a hundred. We know that. And three quarters of it is in the Azores, if not all. If Ralegh's not followed the rest, he's disobeyed orders and commands not twenty sail anyhow."

"Why did we not leave, then?"

"They want to be sure. And you and your sort don't help. There's rumour flying through the fleet quicker than fever. Back and forth it go and multiplying all the while. So the Adelantado, to calm them, agrees to wait his next despatch from the Azores, due tomorrow. Meantime he's sent word to the King and waits that also."

"So when do we sail now?"

"Tomorrow or the next day. We can't afford to wait longer. De Soto and Brochero are fuming. Twas De Soto sent me here to see you today; he's too busy himself. He said I was to see you and tell him what I think. What am I to take back, eh? Are you just craven or a turncoat?"

"I spoke out of turn. But I only answered the questions put to me."

Captain Burley rubbed his boot, which he had crossed on his knee. Hair fell over his forehead. "Well, if you'll take the advice of a fellow countryman, answer no more. Else you'll be on that yard-arm. Understand? I'll string you up meself."

He got awkwardly to his feet. He was a big man and seemed to occupy the room. "Right. I'll be going. See you in England—if you're still alive by then. Adios, captain."

We saw him over the side. The sun was sinking into a smear of white cloud. The heat had gone from the day. Captain Quesada grimaced at me.

"Ill-mannered and a knave. What was his business?"

I gave him an altered account, aware that I should have been the knave in Quesada's eyes and not Burley. But sometimes I suspected that with a Spaniard such as this captain even treachery could be borne before ill-manners.

The next two days were fine and warm; there was a strong breeze from the east but that would not have prevented our sailing. On the second day the expected despatch came from the Azores. Ralegh had rejoined the rest of the fleet, which had reached Flores and was making in full strength towards Fayal. There could be no doubt about this; the commander of the fly-boat was a Spanish officer of the greatest reliability: he had seen the squadron himself. Fayal was 1300 miles from Spain. At Admiral Brochero's suggestion all the captains in the fleet were assembled on *San Pablo* and heard the despatch read by the officer himself. While they were assembled there a communication came to the Adelantado from the King, now fully recovered.

This also Don Martin read out to the assembled company. It promised that Admiral Don Marcos de Arumburu would leave Lisbon at once and sail with his Andalusian squadron for England. The Adelantado, though commanding the entire fleet, was not to wait for Arumburu but was to sail without any further delay. The King added that any captain who created difficulties in the way of sailing at once, whether of supply, navigation, or command, was to be summarily hanged from his own yard-arm.

Nothing could be said, no more objections could be raised now, but on *San Bartolomeo* I knew that the delays had consumed a substantial part of the supplies, some of the rest—as always—had gone rotten, and we had no more than three weeks' food and water to begin this voyage.

That night when at last we got to bed I lay awake thinking of home and listening to the wind. Enrico Caldes was asleep in the next *hamaca;* beyond him two young officers and then the Irish priest, Father Donald. The creak and groan of the timbers, the whisper of the water, the whine of the wind, these had all once again become part of every moment and as such were accepted and almost unheard. But there was still the thud of feet overhead as some of the sailors worked on. It would soon be dawn, for we had not retired until four.

Last evening at dusk every member of the ship's complement had assembled on deck and we had celebrated a solemn mass. Afterwards the company of 376 sang a plain chant together. The blessing of Almighty God was humbly asked for the success of this great mission, and my lips had moved with the rest in saying "Amen." Months now in the company of these men had given me a respect for them. Their friendship and generosity towards me was at odds with their behaviour in battle, the fury and cruelty of their reputation. Storm and shipwreck were the only hope now. The only hope, said the creak and groan of the ship's timbers, the only hope. Delay, delay, autumn was coming. Equinox and the high tides and gales. And perhaps in another week or so the English fleet would turn for home. Delay, delay. . . .

The gun woke us at dawn. The first squadron, I thought, under Don Martin de Padilla was already moving off. Still half asleep, I

dragged on my clothes and went on deck. The sky was grey and the
sea heaving; clouds scurried before a howling westerly wind. It was
true that two of the smaller galleons had beaten their way out of the
bay, but their frantic pitching and lurching, the small area of sail they
could safely carry, was proof enough that, whatever King Philip said,
we could not sail today.

It was a week before the gale abated. Twice in that time attempts
were made to leave, but on the fourth day the wind veered north-
west and that, blowing directly into the mouth of the bay, made exit
impossible. Every attempt was made to keep the fleet at readiness to
leave at an hour's notice. Efforts were even bent towards improving
our depleted supplies. Transports which had stood by in readiness
with the rest were sent back into Coruña and Ferrol to pick up more
biscuits from the ovens of Neda and supplies requisitioned from Santiago, Lugo, and the surrounding countryside. Soldiers and sailors, who
were still going down in numbers with sickness and fever, were taken
ashore and six new companies embarked. The strictest discipline was
maintained aboard, not an easy task amid great numbers of idle men;
no day passed without a hanging, and floggings were the commonplace. Perhaps the large number of priests helped to maintain order.
I had by chance been present at the Council aboard *Ark Royal* when
Essex had laid down orders for prayers on the Cadiz expedition and
emphasised that ours was in essence a religious undertaking; but that
was a light dedication compared to the holy crusade on which this
Armada was bent. This was truly a following of the fiery cross, as
fervent as those to recapture Jerusalem from the infidel.

Seven days to the day the wind dropped. It dropped in mid morning, and within the hour *San Pablo*, dressed over all and with its
swallow-tailed green pendant fluttering, weighed anchor and left the
bay, one ship after another of its squadron following in line. By dusk
we were all away.

CHAPTER 13

So began my journey home.

As we came out of the bay and took a nor'-easterly course the
whole great Armada spread out around us. Don Martin led the first
squadron flying his green pennant. Close behind him on his larboard
quarter—always closer than need be, as if pressing him on—was Don

Diego Brochero—flying a yellow flag. Admiral Bertendona with a red pennant commanded the third.

At sunset all the ships of the fleet were ordered to pass before the admiral's galleon. As they did so the crew of each ship shouted three times and sounded their trumpets. Then the master asked the watchword for the night and the course he must steer. This done each vessel fell behind the flagship into its appointed line, and was informed it must not pass ahead of *San Pablo* again until morning.

It was a wild sunset, and the sea was still rough with the remnants of the storm. I remember looking out and seeing all the galleons about us plunging and tossing to the swell of the sea: their high coloured hulls and ornamental bows lit and flushed by the sunset, while each wave as it lifted them showed their streaming sides and white underbellies. As the light faded an iron cresset with a flaming combustible inside was lit on the high poop of *San Pablo* so that all might know the admiral's ship and follow. Then on each ship the crews assembled and sang a hymn to the Virgin before a painted image of her amidships.

All lights were put out except in the cabins of the officers and gentlemen who were allowed small lamps—trimmed with water covered with oil to combat the lurching of the ship; but no candles were permitted for fear of fire.

So I slept wondering if the morrow would bring a return of storm. It did not, and the dawn was kindly and clear. Sunrise brought a fanfare of trumpets, and the whole Armada again came up to salute the Adelantado, *San Pablo* keeping under easy sail until this was done. Then on every vessel was said a *Missa sicca* or dry Mass, with no consecration. The day passed easily and without incident. But the sealed orders had at last been opened and their message communicated to the rest of the fleet. Destination was Falmouth. If bad weather or battle should separate them each vessel was to rendezvous in Falmouth Bay. Strict instructions were issued to the soldiers that when they landed all people in Falmouth Haven must be used well, in all other places the inhabitants would be put to the sword. Caldes told me *San Bartolomeo* alone carried one hundred thousand ducats in treasure, much of it for use in England for bribery and reward.

A second night at sea, and we had made great progress. All day yesterday we had sighted no vessel. I knew this weather from boyhood; often after the storms of September, October would bring in two or three weeks of golden autumn, light westerly breezes, quiet seas, drifting golden leaves, cows lowing, and the smell of wood smoke. From a Spanish point of view all the delays had been worth while.

And my father in his castle must be daily expecting this fleet. Dunned by creditors, cheated by his daughter-in-law, surrounded by a young and numerous family, a renegade and a traitor . . . what would others in the house do? What would Foster think as deputy keeper of the fort when this fleet began to anchor in the bay? What would Carminow the gunner do when commanded not to fire? On how many people would my father be able to rely to obey his orders? Henry Knyvett of course. And my grandmother, if still alive, would be in this. If the fleet arrived flying English flags and my father pretended to know all about them, his commands to welcome the landing parties would be obeyed out of habit until too late. No one really would have the initiative and the courage to defy him. Hannibal Vivian in the other castle might open fire, but he too might be deceived by some false message from Pendennis, and in any event the St Mawes fort could not alone dispute a landing.

I could speculate as to what might happen in a few days from now off the Cornish coast. I could not know and did not know what was happening at that time outside the narrow circle of the invading fleet. I did not know that failure all the way had attended the English adventure to the Azores, so that Essex, disappointed and disheartened, had turned his fleet homewards on the same day as the Adelantado set sail for England and that the two fleets were now on converging courses, though by the nature of the distances involved the English fleet was a week behind. Nor, perhaps, if I had known all this, would I have realised the difference in the condition of the two fleets: the Spanish for all its many shortcomings fresh in manpower and seaworthiness, eager and alert and ready to fight; the English disappointed and losing discipline, full of sickness after two months at sea, unprepared for battle and only anxious to get home.

I remember my great uncle Henry saying that on one occasion a journey from Dover to Dieppe had taken him eight days.

By the morning of the third day the whole Armada undamaged and unscattered was off Blavet in Brittany, which meant that in that time we had sailed a full three hundred miles. And the weather continued fine and favourable. It had been hoped that Arumburu might have arrived ahead of us, but there was no sign of him.

But conscious that all other things were favourable and that time must be seized, the Adelantado would allow no close communication with the shore. Five pinnaces were sent off, one to summon Admiral Zubiaur with his eight galleys and his two thousand infantry, the others to bring fresh water and such extra stores as had been gathered against our arrival.

That evening the sun set into a puckered brown scar of cloud. The wind was freshening off-shore and the sun was swollen to near double its size. An easterly sky. More often than not it signified continuing fine weather. After prayers Captain Quesada sent for me. With him was Captain Diego Bonifaz, and it was he who addressed me. Now at last the cat was out of the bag.

"All orders are issued, Killigrew. *San Bartolomeo* supported by *San Marcos* and twelve lesser ships, will make the initial landing. This should occur on the morning of Thursday next at dawn, if the winds still favour us. Captain Elliot will go ahead of us and should drop anchor off your house in the night of Wednesday after the moon has set. Thus the castle will know when to expect us. Details of the landings will be governed by the state of the wind; but if it continue fair both galleons will anchor in the bay under the castle and I shall land with six hundred harquebusiers and musketeers on the sand beach there. To begin, only fly-boats will enter the harbour because I gather there is another castle which may resist. That is correct?"

Captain Bonifaz was a tight-lipped soldier whose manner was formal and his discipline harsh. I felt some other military man would better have been chosen to lead the invasion if diplomacy must come before conquest.

"St Mawes fort could hardly do more than throw an occasional shot at a landing inside the river mouth, but it could make entry up the river difficult. What action will you take against it?"

"A second force guided by your Captain Burley will land on the sand beach to the east of the river mouth and cross the isthmus to silence this other castle. If it is done by surprise it will soon be over."

"And my part?"

"Your part will be to go in the first landing boat launched from this ship. With you will go a sergeant and twenty soldiers. Your business will be to establish contact with your father and to arrange that he should formally surrender the castle to me."

"And then?"

Captain Bonifaz looked me over contemplatively. "Then when the first operation is complete your part and the part of your father will be over. But I understand you will both be employed in pacifying the country after its conquest."

"What is your plan for the conquest?"

"It is not *my* plan, Killigrew: I accept and obey orders, and I would advise you to do the same. That is what you are here for. That is what I presume you have been preserved and cherished for."

Bonifaz got up and went to the looking glass to put on his muffler; for him the interview was ended. But Captain Quesada said: "As soon as all military and equipment are landed and the landing consolidated, a screen of fly-boats will be thrown out to give warning in case the English fleet should return. It is an axiom of conquest by sea, which Don Martin well grasps, that an enemy fleet must not be left undestroyed. As soon therefore as we have news, our fleet under Admiral Brochero will sail from Falmouth to intercept and defeat it. In the meantime the Adelantado will advance on Plymouth overland."

When I got back to the cabin Enrico Caldes was strumming on his lute, and for the first time for weeks my mind went back to Victor Hardwicke, his body long since rotten in its prison grave.

As soon as Enrico saw me he clearly wanted to talk. "What do you feel, Maugan, to be so near your home again?"

"I persuade myself against it, but some inner knowledge tells me the air smells different."

"I find it hard to understand what you feel, looking forward to being home but yet coming in company with a conqueror."

I bent to untie my shoes; the Irish priest, Father Donald, was listening but I was glad he could not understand.

"I think I know you moderate well by now," Enrico said, "and I would have said you are not of the stuff of which traitors are made."

I kicked off a shoe. "It depends how you define a traitor."

"Oh, yes, that's true. I ask your pardon if I have offended by using that name. I mean that it is hard to envisage myself as leading in an English force against Spain. I have hard things to say of my own country—you have heard me say them; against the obstinacy of the King, against the corruption of the army and navy commissioners, against the tyranny of the Holy Office—all complaints it is not safe to air as I air them. But when it comes to the point I would sooner die than fight against my own country. And, knowing you, I should have thought you were much the same."

I put my shoes in a corner. The ship was lurching more tonight.

"A hundred years ago," I said, "that or a little more, a king of England had usurped the throne in place of his own nephews, and later he murdered them. His rule when established was an enlightened one, but men's hearts were against him. They could not forget. So another man with a much poorer claim, our present Queen's grandfather, landed at Milford Haven to dethrone the other. Men flocked to his standard and the King was killed in battle and Henry was crowned in his place. I feel maybe no better and no worse than those who landed with Henry. They did not look on it as treason for they believed their cause just."

"Ah yes," said Enrico. "No doubt in Spain's history there would be something the same, but I am no historian and judge only by the day before yesterday." He sighed and stretched. "Now we are *all* taking part in history—does that weigh heavy with you? On the success of this Armada will depend the future of generations."

Father Donald crossed himself and began to intone a prayer in Latin for the preservation and success of the soldiers of Christ. He was a hairy man, hair sprouting from his nostrils and ears and sitting like a black halo around his tonsure. He hated the English passionately and utterly, and only spoke to me when forced by occasion. Yet I had seen him joking with his own men and kind and fatherly to the sick. There was something in his attitude towards England that I had only seen in a Dutchman towards Spain.

Enrico's talk of treason had disturbed me, for though I had long since fought all this out, now it was in the open and there was no going back. But I still had no plan to meet the situation. Co-operation such as I had accepted so far was like boarding a coach that did not stop when one wanted to get out. There was nothing to do until we landed, and by then I was stamped for ever before my own people as a traitor—along with my father. To throw away my life in a gesture would benefit no one. Yet to die usefully would need enterprise and resource.

Dawn, and we broke our fast with a mug of wine, some crumbling biscuit and salt fish. The fanfare of trumpets was late today. No parade of ships but a grim preparation for the last lap. Stumble on deck shivering and feeling sick. Dry Mass.

"Laudamus te, benedicimus te, adoramus te, glorificamus te."

"Sanctus, Sanctus, Sanctus, Dominus Deus Sabaoth, Pleni sunt caeli et terra gloria tua."

Wind had shifted a point since yesterday; from a guess it was now north by east. By noon tomorrow we should be off the Scillies, but it would make beating up the Channel more difficult.

We were kneeling on the quarter deck, just abaft the main-mast, below us in the galleon's waist were the soldiers in tight ranks, behind them the sailors and the gunners, then back of all the fifty Irish volunteers under a corporal and a master-at-arms. Two frigates close by were waving their masts out of unison.

"Quoniam tu solus sanctus, tu solus Dominus, tu solus Altissimus— Jesu Christe. . . ."

Men's voices chanting across the ring of ships; they rose above the wind; twenty thousand at prayer.

We rose, still sleepy, stiff with the night, cold and damp with sea wind. The last conference aboard *San Pablo;* I was to go, and when I climbed up the side of the flagship Captain Elliot and Captain Burley were already there. With them were a dozen other Englishmen; some red-eyed, shifty and shabby, sweepings of the sea come to help the Spanish and reconquer England for gain; others plainly gentlemen exiled for their faith and hoping to return to a Catholic England; I looked for Thomas Arundell but he was not there.

We did not go below but were addressed by Richard Burley who seemed for all his uncouthness most inward of us all with the Spaniards. After it was over we stood about eyeing each other, one or two speaking but for the main part distrustful, more suspicious of each other than if we had been of different race.

While we were waiting the sky clouded over, and by the time the conference in the Adelantado's cabin had broken up it was blowing hard. With the peculiarly unstable nature of an easterly wind, it had whipped up the sea into small white-flecked waves which broke as they moved among the ships and cast a drifting spray before them. *San Pablo* catching the wind as she lay was not so much wallowing as leaning over.

We were rowed back to *San Bartolomeo* and clambered wetly aboard, but I could see that other captains going to galleons in more exposed positions were having hard work to make headway. At once sails were let go, and we dipped towards the open sea. Our two galleons led the way, followed by the galleass *Santiago,* four of De Zubiaur's galleys, two urcas, *Aguila* and *Grifo,* six large fly-boats, and seven supply ships. We were the advance guard of Diego Brochero's squadron but had instructions to consider ourselves self-contained and to wait for no one.

As we made away from the lee of the land our ship heeled over, tucking her high bows into the water and throwing out great fans of spray. We were now passing the last ships of the Armada, near the island of Groix, and some of them were already fighting their way into the teeth of the wind to avoid being driven ashore.

We were carrying too much sail, and from the quarter-deck Enrico and I watched the sailors swarming up through the ratlines to the main top-sail yard to take in the sail and then to unclamp the yard itself and lower it to the deck. Others were trimming the foresail, so that presently the galleon settled more confortably on a north-westerly course running across the wind. *San Marcos* was behind us, but *Santiago* and the two urcas were well up.

Towards noon a cold rain fell. Later the clouds broke and although the wind persisted strong and cold, it was not gusty and we were making rapid progress. As the horizon cleared we saw the rest of our squadron on the skyline with Admiral Brochero's yellow flag streaming like a snake.

There was much sickness between decks: the soldiers lay about vomiting, and the swabbers soon gave up their task. By now the whole ship was damp; sea had leaked in through the scuppers and the ports, and the lower gun-decks were running with water that had come down the hatchways. It had been the same on the way out in *Warspite*, but then the weather had been consistently warm; now the damp struck a heavy chill. As soon as we left the shelter of the coast the galley fires had been doused, so there was no warm food or drink.

About four I went below: there was nothing to do on deck, but the tiny cabin was already almost dark, and Father Donald was lying in his *hamaca* telling his beads and being sick. Enrico came in to say that evening hymns would be in half an hour but I made an excuse of feeling unwell and remained below. There I prayed to my own God to increase the wind and destroy this fleet—and if necessary me with it. Twenty-four hours more would be too late. By then the conquest would have begun and at least a part of the invading force landed. Also the act of treason would have been committed. From there on there was no retreat.

An uneasy night. Of the five of us in the tiny cabin three were sick and it was not possible because of the sea to have the port hole open, so the air grew ever more stuffy and foetid. The big ship lurched and plunged, its timbers groaning, ropes and blocks creaking and straining, water slopping in the bilges, and above all the high scream of the wind. I dreamed I was in Captain Buarcos's chamber and that he was alive and sitting across the table from me and I had to kill him over again.

Morning broke in low cloud. The wind had eased but there was a short-pitched smoking sea and *San Bartolomeo* could make nothing of it. She lurched and ducked and trembled like a wild horse tied three ways by ropes. I made a bruised and unsteady way up to the main gun-deck and looked out on a grey waste, with no land in sight anywhere. Three of our ships only had kept with us, the galleass *Santiago*, one of the urcas, *Grifo*, and a fly-boat. We were under storm canvas, a reefed foresail and clewed mainsail only.

I climbed up the four ladders to the poop and found Captain Quesada there while a sailor studied the skyline with a glass. Another sailor moved to cut me off, but Quesada motioned him to allow me through.

I bade him good morning. "We have been scattered, sir."

"It is not to be wondered at. We shall reassemble in due time." For all his calm words he did not look as if he had slept; he was wearing a skull cap instead of his usual high black hat; his beard was grey from the salt in it.

"Has the wind changed?"

"Yes, it is south by east and therefore more to our advantage."

"Where are we, sir?"

"Our calculations put us at ten or fifteen leagues south of the Scilly Islands. If we need the shelter of the Islands we shall wait there until the others come up."

"When did we lose touch with *San Marcos?*"

"Early in the night. Captain Chagres was falling behind at dusk: his ship was never fleet."

"So we should perhaps reach Falmouth tonight?"

"Not tonight, Killigrew. Have patience. At dawn tomorrow."

We made the Scillies at noon, but as by then the weather had moderated Captain Quesada decided his ships did not need the shelter of the roads. One would not hazard one's ship among the many small rocky islets if the need for shelter were not pressing. By four the whole of our advance squadron had caught us up with the exception of one transport. Before this we had been passed by *Dolphin* who stayed to exchange a shouted word and then moved on to carry secret news of our coming.

At five we supped, on oatmeal, salt beef, biscuits, and a can of sack. As the light was fading Admiral Brochero with the rest of his ships came up through the evening clouds, and the squadron spent half an hour in chanting and in prayer. In the afterlight, when ship and sail and spar and gun took on a brief flush of colour, the fifty ships in that tossing sea were like some new vision of creation, seed cast by a hand upon the waters to be swept along by the wind to carry a new life to an alien shore.

We sailed at seven, Brochero allowing a lapse of two hours to the advance squadron before he followed.

As I lay in the pitching cabin one more night—the last night—I thought that by now surely some news of the invasion would have reached England. We had likely been seen from the Scillies: they could send a fast pinnace to rouse the country. Even if no one knew where the Armada would strike they must by now know it was coming.

I thought—and hoped—quite wrongly. No one throughout the length of England had yet any idea at all.

. . . The land slept in complete security. It was accepted everywhere that a part of the Adelantado's fleet was in the Azores and the rest skulked in El Ferrol unable to make any move before the spring. All information from Essex downwards confirmed this. The last despatch from him had told that he was still seeking the Spanish ships and the treasure fleet. By now some great and glorious victory was likely to have been won and only waited the telling. Indeed, orders were then on the way to Essex not to hurry home if advantage could be gained by staying.

The day that Admiral Don Diego Brochero with his fleet joined his advance squadron in the Scillies, the old Lord Admiral Howard at the age of sixty-one, having crowned an illustrious career with the capture of Cadiz, was receiving his patent as Earl of Nottingham; and our Queen had just summoned Parliament to discuss what measures might be taken to meet the threat of next spring. The battleships not in the Azores were out of commission at Chatham, Sir Henry Palmer commanding the Channel squadron was ill, Sir Ferdinando Gorges ruled at Plymouth with a small garrison of trained soldiers; the other western ports were undefended.

In the Atlantic in stormy weather a disorganised English fleet, leaking, full of sickness and preoccupied with its own failure, was steadily gaining on the Spanish. Most of the battleships had stowed away their big guns in the hold to ease their strained timbers after all the storms.

And at Falmouth John Killigrew added up his debts.

Towards midnight the plunging and yawing of the galleon grew worse, yet there was no increase in wind. In after years I have sailed these waters again, and I know how, off the Land's End, seas can build up. Conflicting tides and currents meet here and lurch together as if compelled by submarine upheavals. In the cabin we could feel the galleon climbing up and up as if on a mountain side, and then, as the rudder came out of the water, the whole ship twisted and strained and she lurched down into the trough in a panic slide that seemed to have no end.

I endured it until three and then crawled out past the crowded huddled figures of sleeping men. The decks were surprising dry: the waves were not breaking and they were too big to be split by the ship in her course. A broken ragged sky showed a few stars and the sickly light of an obscured half moon. Behind us our escort of twenty ships was in close attendance, where they could be seen among the lunatic waves. The wind was half abeam and the waves going at

twice our speed, so that we were constantly being overtaken by them
and sailing like a helpless cork along their ridges before falling into
the following trough. It was this which was straining the ship's timbers
past endurance; three men hung on to the helm struggling to keep
her on course; Captain Quesada was beside them.

I did not go up to join them but went for'ard, slipping and sliding
along her low waist, past a group of exhausted sailors hauling on
a rope, climbed over the wooden bulkhead and mounted to the high
square forecastle, slithered past the foremast as we yawed down into
the next chasm, and fetched up against the rail beside the bowsprit.

From here the scene was a terrifying one, and I stayed fascinated
until dawn, shivering and misted with spray, watching each climb
and plunge.

As the sky reluctantly lightened I saw land six or seven miles off
on our larboard bow. It was England, the long dark line of the Lizard
Peninsula, and already we were beginning to gain protection from
it. There would be no easy sailing at any time in this sea, but once
we had rounded the Manacles the cape would shelter us from the
worst and we should be perhaps two more hours from the complete
protection of Falmouth Haven. I looked back and counted fifteen of
our twenty ships in sight. They could all land before dark: veteran
soldiers, supplies, cannon, horses. Brochero too would have arrived by
then and his troops, sure of their landing, could be brought ashore
and fully deployed during the night. By the time the Adelantado
arrived tomorrow the first stage would be complete.

I looked up at the sky. It was a wild and ghostly dawn. Ink black
clouds mounted one on another. The moon had set, but there was a
metallic slash of light where the sun would rise and some stars winking in a patch of clear sky. The Spanish must have read the signs
more accurately than I did for I saw a group of sailors swarming up
the shrouds to shorten sail. They had hardly done so before the wind
struck us like the blow of a fist.

I have heard it claimed by Puritan preachers that the winds which
scattered the Armada of 1588 were the work of Divine Providence
moving to the aid of a godly and righteous cause; if that were so
they did not come to sweep the Armada away until it had been
damaged and disabled in battle. Fewer have claimed the great gale
of October 1597. A menace seen and an ensuing battle make so much
more impress on the mind and the memory than a greater menace
that is struck down just as the battle is about to begin.

San Bartolomeo had stripped her yards just in time. One of the
clouds coming up out of the north-west burst over us, streaming hail

before it in a stinging horizontal cloud, leaping and rattling where it struck, cutting out view of sea and sky so that the ship heeled over as if under the impact of a load of fine shingle flung in a gale. When we came through it the only sail we had carried was in cracking ribbons, one of the yards had snapped, men clung to rail and bulwark and stay, while a livid sun just risen cast a sinister light of brilliance and shadow among the mountains of the sea.

Thereafter in the space of an hour we were struck by three such storms. By then our mainmast was aslant and we were leaking for'ard. Through glimpses of torn cloud we could see twelve of our escort in like straits. *Santiago*, which had stayed close with us all through, being not so high charged as ourselves, had not suffered so severely, but both urcas were in trouble and one of the supply ships was low in the water and green seas were breaking over her.

We were now perhaps three miles only off the Manacles, but wo had no hope of doubling the cape. If the wind held in the present quarter we should miss shipwreck by a mile or so and then be driven deeper into the Channel.

Many of the soldiers had tried to struggle on deck for fear of drowning; bugles were blowing between decks; Captain Bonifaz and three other officers were on the poop with Captain Quesada; groups of men clustered in the lee of bulkheads, now knee-deep in water, now drenched with angry spray. Once or twice men lost hold and slithered across the decks to fetch up against some other obstacle and cling for life. We had lost a half-dozen men overboard.

We were blown past the Manacles, which stretched towards us like a finger reaching out to touch. Our mainmast had torn away part of the shrouds and the main yard pointed half to the sky. Quesada ordered some sailors to cut all away that they could, and men with axes in a lull in the wind slithered for'ard and began to climb. It was a wickedly gusty gale, and as they climbed they were sometimes unable to stir, pinned like flies against the ropes, then a step at a time they'd go.

Once the sun shone brightly on them through a rent in the storm wrack, and their wet clothes glistened against the abysmal darkness of the clouds.

They cut through a mass of rigging, and the main yard swung wide, knocking one of the sailors with it. He writhed on deck before the tangled rigging netted him, then all were caught by a wave and crashed overboard; other figures leaped forward in a smother of sea and hacked at the ropes to free them and let them go.

I was stiff with cold, fingers freezing, stomach contracting. About twelve sailors were huddled on the forecastle near by. Father Donald and another priest had made their way to the poop and were trying to get the men to pray with them.

The supply ship was going. She was filling by the head, and the rolling combing seas toppled over her, burying her ever deeper. Once too often the water held her down; poop high in the air she plunged, masts and rigging lying sideways on the water for a few seconds; then she was gone, men swimming, scattered debris bobbing with them. The fly-boats did their best, but were themselves concerned with survival. I saw a few men swarming up ropes but the rest were left. One rope had five men on it when it was overtaken by the sea; after the wave had passed the rope was clean.

In another hour there were only four of our squadron in sight. The wind had backed more westerly so that between squalls the land was still in sight. I thought, there's Arwenack, somewhere on that low dark land, perhaps I shall never see it now, and I ought to thank God if I drowned. (But what if the Adelantado and his main fleet escaped the worst of the storm and still arrived?)

"Holy Mary, Mother of God," said a voice beside me. It was a big Irishman, his teeth chattering with fright. "Holy Mary, we're sinking. In the name of the Father and of the Son. . . ." His words were whipped away by the gale.

A mountain range of sea came out of a cloud which was already lying on the water. It foamed and bubbled and lifted us, but partly broke aboard; there was a rending sound and I thought we had gone the way of the supply ship. Between the forecastle and the poop there was no deck, only a few spars and struggling screaming men. The galleon heeled and dipped as if her back were broken, then heavily shook the water off her so that the main deck reappeared like a rock in a waterfall.

But mortal damage was done: the weight of sea had broached the hatchways and the galleon was half full of water which was draining slowly from gun ports and scuppers.

As soon as she began to lift, men who had been kept below decks fought their way out through the hatchways, many of them making for the forecastle to lash themselves to the foremast or any other part of the ship which might survive. From the noise and the behaviour of the galleon it was clear that some of the guns had broken loose between decks. The Irishman beside me who had been so terrified left his place of vantage and struggled to drag three of his injured friends to the rail beside me. I helped him tie them to the yard which had been taken down and lashed to the rail when the storm began.

The coast was out of sight except for a glimpse now and then of the Lizard far astern. *Santiago* still kept us company, but having suffered in the same sea as had mortally injured us she was looking to herself and gradually being blown ahead. One fly-boat appeared and disappeared like a piece of flotsam a mile or so on our starboard bow.

The wind was still backing. A tiny rag of sail on the foremast was holding our head up and giving the four helmsmen a chance of control. But we could see the squalls coming up one after another, and each one left us in poorer case to meet the next. Men still worked in relays of ten at each of the pumps, but every wave that came aboard undid the little they could do.

As the day progressed we lost both our last escorts, *Santiago* drew ahead, and the fly-boat sank, disabled by one crested wave and swamped by the next.

It was not long before we followed. By now the galleon was so low in the water that her waist was never clear of it. we existed as two separate ships, the forecastle and the poop, both crowded with men. I was isolated from all the men I knew: Quesada, Bonifaz, Enrico Caldes; by coming to the forecastle I was with sailors and some Irish and half a hundred soldiers.

About noon the sun leered out at us from behind a ragged mass of clouds that darkened half the sky; then the light was gone and the last storm broke.

It fell on us. Wind tore at everything: the last sail went; the foremast collapsed, a double-lashed anchor broke loose. As the sea came aboard it was as if the forecastle were an island about to be submerged in a smother of white foam. The Irishman and his mates beside me were clinging to the yard and were slowly tipped into the sea; I clutched my broken spar, determined not to go, and saw the poop raised high, water and men pouring off it as *San Bartolomeo* plunged. Hatches and wooden blocks and chains slithered past and then the water swirled round and I held tight to the spar as ship and men went down.

The water was no colder than the air had been; perhaps that saved me, for I could hold breath that a sharp chill would have taken. I went deep and only came to the surface after long seconds, among wreckage and cries and the grey wind-angered sea. I saw two sailors trying to hold up Quesada who had been struck by something as the ship sank. The Irishman and his friends clung to their yard near by. Twenty men struggled to get on a hatch that would support five. Two others tried to grasp my spar but I kicked them away. On the crest of a new wave I saw Enrico Caldes swimming away from a mat of twisted rigging. I shouted and tried to make towards him, but the waves hid him and when next I rose to the top of one of them he was nowhere to be seen.

The sea was black with bobbing heads; fully half the complement had survived the plunge, but some were injured, some could not swim, some were already half drowned. It began to rain, a heavy continuous downpour so that cloud and sea became one. Small waves splashed in my mouth, but the rain had the effect of slowly flattening the sea, and in time when it eased the violence of the gale had eased too.

When the rain cleared many of the survivors had sunk. Near by were still the four Irishmen and about eight Spaniards clinging precariously to a raft. Within sight were another forty of fifty, but well scattered.

Nothing else was to be seen but the heaving sea.

Late in the afternoon I was picked up—together with two of the Irishmen and one Spaniard—by a fishing boat, the *Angel* of Fowey, and landed that same evening. Sixteen men were saved out of the 356 aboard *San Bartolomeo*.

Book Five

CHAPTER 1

A MAN at the centre of great events can often at the time see only the small ones which surround him and oppress him with their personal demands. Even an awareness that events have moved past him and left him behind—perhaps to his danger or detriment—can become sunk in a cushion of fatigue which prevents urgency and anxiety from coming to the front of the mind.

Looking back I cannot believe that the whole week I spent with my cousins the Treffrys at Fowey was passed in a state of mental abeyance. There must have been times when I made some effort to learn from them what was happening, and even to get up and go. But all memory is of a sense of being home again after sixteen months away, of dry blankets after the exposure and the sea, of gulping hot drink to combat the cold, of fresh food and good food, of sudden overwhelming collapse after months of tension and alarm. I was alive. I existed. I ate and drank and slept and breathed deep.

So it was days before I knew what had happened in England, and some of it I learned only weeks later—of the panic in Westminster when the news was brought by an exhausted messenger from Plymouth that the whole Spanish Armada was off the Lizard, of the immediate proroguing of Parliament, of the hasty appointment of a new commander for the Channel squadron, of the orders which flew for the commissioning of the remaining ships at Chatham, of orders recalling all English troops abroad, of the mustering of all land forces for the defence of the exposed counties.

In the midst of this emergency rumours of a sea battle off Rame Head vied with others of a Spanish landing on the north Devon coast. Fishermen from the Scillies came in with a report of another fleet assembled there and about to strike. No one had any word of the

English fleet from the Azores. No one knew if it had even started for home.

Then within a few days of the first alarm four galleons appeared off Plymouth. Soldiers rushed to the fortifications, guns were run out, the people prepared to barricade their houses and fight as the Spanish had done at Cadiz; and not even the English flags at the mastheads could reassure them until the ships were recognised by name. They were the first four of the Azores fleet under Lord Mountjoy, who had commanded the land forces of the fleet. He reported a great storm which had damaged and dispersed the English fleet, but thought that the rest of the ships if they had survived should not be far away. By some chance in the wild waters of the Channel he had seen nothing of the Spanish; but he immediately assumed command of the port and ordered his four ships to prepare for battle.

Soon after this Sir Walter Ralegh with remnants of his own squadron was blown into St Ives, and, hearing the alarm, landed and travelled overland to command the defences of Cornwall. Another English ship or two drifted in at the south coast ports of Devon; then Lord Thomas Howard at Plymouth, and finally Essex himself with the rest of the fleet.

None had seen the whole Armada, but some at the height of the gale had seen groups of enemy ships near the Scillies and off the Lizard.

All the English were exhausted with the storm, and Essex and his squadron sailed straight up the Catwater where they were pinned down by the wind and unable to go out again, even had they been in a fit condition to do so.

In the meantime feverish preparations went on while the country waited. The Queen wrote a letter to Lord Essex which years later I was privileged to see. It ended:

Seeing already by your late leaving the coast upon an uncertain probability that no army would come forth from Ferrol until March, you have given the enemy leisure and courage to attempt us. Now take heed according to your duty and allegiance that you do not in any case upon any probability or light advertisements again adventure to leave our own coast whereby our own kingdom may lie open to serious dangers; but that you proceed in this great affair according to the rules of advised deliberation as well as affection of zeal and diligence. For treasure, for victual, and what may be fit for us to send, you shall find that you serve a prince neither void of care nor judgment what to do that is fit in cases of this consequence.

Now reports began to come in of wrecks on the north Devon coast, and three Spanish urcas in great distress put into the Bristol ports for shelter and their crews were imprisoned. A large Spanish fly-boat, leaking and part dismasted by the storm, appeared off Dodman Point with a crew of eighty, of which half were veteran troops. Here it was attacked and captured by a Plymouth vessel and brought back in triumph.

On the last day of October I borrowed a horse and servant and rode to Arwenack. By starting early I arrived before dark. I did not know what to expect; I had no idea. Presumably the Spanish had not yet landed; but Mr William Treffry and his family had no detailed news, and I could not press for it except in the vaguest terms. Until I saw my father under arrest and led out, I must affect to know nothing of treason or betrayal.

There were a few soldiers about in Truro, but as I rode through Penryn it seemed as if nothing here had changed. No sense of emergency seemed to exist. The place looked exactly the same as when Belemus had been courting Sybilla Kendall and we had been pursued out of the town.

It was a sunny day, but bright only with that autumnal brightness which seems to have no warmth or happiness in it. After the storm the month was going out peaceably, like some old man who has wrought havoc in his manhood and now in age assumes an amiability quite out of character. Only the oaks retained their leaves, the rest of the trees had been stripped by the wild and vicious winds.

As we neared the palisades I felt it was not so long after all since I had been home; the flying visit before the Cadiz expedition, the visit to Sue; those for the moment seemed to have all the objective reality I could apprehend; the fierce and bloody sixteen months in between existed only in my mind as a barely accepted dream staining the memory with the colours of nightmare. I was not aware this time of any overwhelming emotional sensation such as I had felt when stumbling over the wet grass and through the bracken towards home in 1594. I was younger then. Or perhaps it was that circumstances made it no longer possible to see home as something unequivocal, clear-cut, safe, a symbol of what was to be desired. My bedroom with its narrow walls and long bright window would no longer offer me protection from the dangers and complexities of the world. Wherever I went now, until the day I died, I carried those dangers and complexities everywhere.

Simon Cook was on the gate. His presence was a reassurance that neither of the worst eventualities could yet have happened. He was astonished, delighted, wished to come with me to the house, but I said no, we'd go on alone.

It was not until we were almost at the house that I saw the tents.

They were spread all around the foot of the hill leading to the castle.
It was a light in one of them in the growing dusk that first caught
the eye. Figures moved about them. They were soldiers.

I came to the house as supper was about to begin.

My father was there, my step-mother, many half-brothers and -sis-
ters, Belemus, Henry Knyvett, Mistress Wolverstone, Aunt Mary
Killigrew, Rosewarne, two officers I did not know. The children
greeted me wildly, with great affection and relief. They were full of the
danger they were in but excited by it rather than frightened; they
clamoured to know how I had come home. My father got up smiling
and knuckling his moustache and saying, By God, I had changed, I
looked twenty-seven if a day, what I must have been through, and now
by God's Providence restored to the family, this was a night to celebrate. By what chance of war and shipwreck. . . . Captain Alexander
and Lieutenant Guildford, this was his eldest son—base son but greatly
esteemed by all—home from Spain, shipwrecked, did you say, Maugan?—aboard the Spanish fleet off our coasts. Come, we must all be
happy tonight, eh, Dorothy? Eh, Henry? Wilky, fetch a bottle of the
best canary; we must break it now.

Never had he been so pleased to see me; I should have been
warmed and heartened. But if I had changed, he had changed more.
He must have been the heavier by fifteen lbs. and this had spread
him without adding solidity or strength. His skin was blotched and
flabby; there were sacks under his eyes, and the lack of feeling in
them had spread to the whole of his face. He had always drunk much
but seldom before had stumbled over his words.

The two officers were studiously correct but little more. They had
arrived only two days ago in charge of five hundred levies thrown
into Pendennis by Ralegh. The men were soldiers disembarked from
the English fleet, musters from the inland towns, some regular levies,
and a few sailors to make the number.

It seemed that my arrival was an embarrassment to my father, so
his welcome was the warmer to deceive others. It was an embarrassment to have anybody arrive from Spain, even an escaped prisoner.

The two officers did not personally question me through the meal
but they attended carefully to what was said. So for my part I weighed
each word before it was uttered, and found this not so difficult as
once would have been the case. The habit of deceit grows.

The great hall had grown shabbier in sixteen months. Two window
panes were broken and were boarded, waiting proper repair. The
rushes on the floor could hardly have been changed in two weeks.
The fire had been badly built and was smoking; a thin fog of grey

smoke hung around the beams. The candles guttered and stank; the
rabbit pie was half cold and the beef tough and oversalt. Servants
looked slovenly and dispirited.

At last I was able to divert attention by saying: "And . . . grandmother?"

"Oh, she's with us still," said Mr Killigrew. "Tenacious as ever;
though much of the time gasping like a landed fish. She keeps her
room these days."

"And John? With his new wife?"

"They're on a visit to her father. They've been gone a month, so
I'm hoping to have word of them before long."

Captain Alexander and Lieutenant Guildford correctly and formally
excused themselves from a game of dice and went off to the castle.
I thought my father would want to speak to me alone but he tramped
off to his private chamber and was not seen again. Mrs Killigrew now
had another daughter, christened Dorothy after herself. A baker's
dozen of children had only cost her her figure and her teeth; but
in the last twelve months something had taken a new toll.

After supper Belemus made a gesture to me and I was able to
detach myself from the children and join him on the ragged lawn
before the house.

"So . . . the bad penny. And never more welcome than now. I had
thought you were done for. But what a change—hollow cheeks, burning eyes: did they put you to the torture?"

"No. . . . But a Spanish prison is no place for lent-lilies."

He looked at me keenly. "There is much that has been going on
here that I don't follow, and your coming seems a part of it. I know
you too well, Maugan. All you say smacks of evasion. What have you
been up to?"

"Nothing that I was not compelled to."

"Ah. That tells a lot. And—"

"And what has been going on here that you can't follow?"

He bent and eased the buckle of his shoe. "Ah, there again, evasion.
You see the house, poverty-stricken, you see your father, bloated
and hag-ridden; there has fallen on us all a conspiracy of whispers.
Things are decided without reason and acted on without notice. This
crisis, for instance. Ever since the beginning of September your
father has been like a fox when the hounds are out. I do not know
if he had some presentiment of it, but one might well think so. As
you know he could always pour the wine down his throat; but this
month he had not been sober. . . . In September he was at great
pains to send John and Jane off to Northampton, though they had no
seeming wish to go. One would have thought, I say, of some presenti-

ment; but if so he has made no attempt to prepare against attack. Carminow had not enough powder to ward away one determined assault. At the worst moment Foster was sent off to Launceston Castle to negotiate the purchase of a demi-cannon; as if we had the money to buy it. I think he will be in trouble for it."

"What trouble?"

"Ralegh was here—a brief tempest and then gone again—but these men, these soldiers have all but taken control of the castle and the fortifications. Decisions are made without consultation of Mr Killigrew; placement of the troops, plans for defence, victualling, arming, powder; we might be in occupied territory. Your father has accepted all this it seems without protest. Unlike him. A few years ago he'd have fought a pitched battle sooner than be turned out of his proper office."

We walked to the edge of the lawn which was ankle deep in wet and tufted grass, and peered across at the black bulk of the castle.

"His debts are no easier?"

"Ha! Look around you."

"And Jane?"

"Jane, dear Maugan, is the wonder of the age."

"How so?"

"If your father had combed the highways of England he could not have found a more unsuitable mate for sober John. A she-wolf! She might be Lady Killigrew's daughter by Captain Elliot!"

"Where is her dowry? My father wrote me something."

"I doubt if we'll ever see it here. But she seems to have some source of funds beyond this mere two hundred pounds a year. She is having a boat built in Penryn—Penryn of all places—and plans to go into business, as she calls it, as a trader around the coast: this at eighteen!"

"Maybe she'll have a family soon and that will tone her down."

"There's no issue yet, and they've been married a year. For her part it cannot be for want of trying."

"What d'you mean?"

"She had not been in the house three months before she invited me to a couplement with her. It's a small matter hard on a man, and no augury for the future."

I hesitated but had to have it out. "You refused?"

"Against the grain. She's no Hebe, but would I fancy be entertaining. However, I have my reservations, as I told her, and one is against coupling with my cousin's bride before even the shine is off the wedding ring."

We paced along in silence. I said: "Susan Reskymer?"

"I heard her husband was sick."

"He was sick before I left."

"Some old men hang on ignobly."

Stars were winking in a cloudless night sky. They were a purer light than the yellow stars winking on the shoulder of the castle hill.

He said: "I leave here next month."

"Oh? Why? What are you doing?"

He shrugged. "For two years now I have worked on the farm here and acted as esquire to your father. Now through my uncle—the one who is not in prison—I have a commission under Norris. I think maybe I was cut out to be a soldier of fortune."

"You spoke of Elliot," I said.

"Oh, *Dolphin*'s been in and out, the last time eight or nine days ago. They had been ill-used by the storm. There were the usual secret conferences and mutterings behind closed doors. As soon as news came that the Spaniards might be landing he left. Not that I blame him. It would not be a happy position to be caught between two fires."

I could not get over a sense of unreality that my home and everything around it should have changed so little. During those desperate sixteen months, while I had seen and done and suffered so much, life had gone on here almost unaltered. Always downhill, yet day by day the same routine. Cows had been milked, sheep sheared, fields tilled, apples pressed, in the unchanging pattern of existence. I and my family had lived in different worlds. It seemed almost as if for them time had not passed. All my nerves had been strung up to a tautness which now would not relax. Egoism in me demanded some greater change in them.

While I was away Meg Stable had had a baby boy, and this or some change had softened her towards me; she seemed no longer to bear resentment for our affair. This was the happiest circumstance of my homecoming; it rejoiced me to able to talk to her again.

Mr Killigrew did not appear the following day and let it be known that he was unwell. In the afternoon he sent for me to his bed chamber. I found him up, sitting before a hissing log fire in a bed-gown which had once been emerald green but was now so faded that it looked as if it had been dipped in sea water. He had a bad cold in the head. All the servants were coughing with an autumn chill that had gone around.

"You haven't yet been to see your grandmother, Maugan. She has complained of it to me."

"I'm sorry. I was busy this morning and expected to see her at dinner."

He was in one of his persecution moods, when he was friendless and alone, and even inanimate things combined to do him ill. The wood on the fire, by being green, would not burn to warm him. His favourite slippers had split only yesterday.

The jug at his elbow contained, he said, an old remedy, fever-few boiled with wine, but I thought the wine predominated. The room was close and horrid.

"Well, boy, it's good to have you back; but you had my letter, so you know all that has gone amiss with us here since you left. A deeper abyss than ever, the Fermors playing their dastardly trick over the dowry, now even my office usurped by these military. It's no pretty picture to come home to!"

"Did Sir Walter order these men to take command of the castle?"

"No one commands the castle except myself; but they control the forces to defend it! There's the rub. For years I have petitioned for money and men; they have not come. Now in an emergency men are *flung* in, powder and shot lavishly provided, but control of the levies passes to an army commander. It's grossly unfair."

"You will, of course, complain to the Privy Council."

He coughed and snuffled and wiped his moustache on a baby's sock. "So I will, so I certainly will. But I'm not a fit man. The anxiety, the tension of this time; you have no idea what I have been through— for a week or more before these soldiers came, *struggling* to gather the musters together, preparing to defend the castle with my own few servants and two trained gunners, constantly back and forth between castle and house, writing despatches, expecting my wife and children any day to be dragged out and raped and *murdered*. It has been a period of great strain, and no thanks for any of it, no thanks; no one cares what I have been through. I'm not at all well; I have been on and off the night-nobby constantly since yesterday. It's very lowering."

"I saw Captain Elliot," I said.

My father glanced at me for only the second time since I came into the room.

"When he delivered my letter to you?"

"Since then."

"Ah, I shall have less to do with him in the future. He's very much of a turncoat, and as such must be kept at a distance."

"He seemed to me something of a go-between," I said.

Silence fell in the room.

Mr Killigrew picked at the frayed sleeve of his bed-gown.

I said: "I saw Elliot at Cadiz and at El Ferrol. Then later still I saw him off the Scillies—little more than two weeks ago."

"When you were with the Spanish fleet?"

"When I was with the Spanish fleet."

"You must tell me all about that sometime. . . . You were ill-treated?"

"No. Had favours. They expected me to be of use to them when they reached England."

"Ah. . . . They did, eh? Never got over the idea that they might be able to buy us. These Spaniards don't understand the Killigrews."

"I could not appear unwilling to help—or I should not have survived. It was a matter of life and death."

"Ah, a matter of life and death. People outside do not realise the stresses—they have no idea. It is necessary to—to trim one's sails to the storm. I quite agree, son, with what you did. Now, praise Christ, you are restored to us and no one the worse for your little deception."

"I trust no one will be the worse at all—for any deception."

My father stared with despondent bloodshot eyes out of the window.

I said: "It was thought—in some parts of the Spanish fleet it was thought that when they landed this castle might be favourably disposed towards them. What they thought, or think, is not important if, as seems possible now, they do not attempt to land at all. . . . But it would be a serious matter if the rumour spread further and was believed in any English quarters."

"Why should it be? Why should it be? No one would dare—"

"I was only thinking, father," I interrupted—something I would not have dared to do a year ago—"that I trust there has been no loose talk in this house, no action which could be falsely construed, no letters written or received, which could give any substance to such a rumour. . . ."

I stopped and waited. I think at last my father understood what I was trying to do—to help if it became necessary without demanding dangerous confidences in return.

"For instance," I said, "I hope there's no one here—Carminow or Foster, for example—who could testify in any way if called on to do so that—"

"There is nothing to testify."

"Nor letters received which have not been burned."

"Nor no letters have been received." He sneezed. "I caught this cold, I believe, through washing my legs and feet last Friday. It is a bad thing to do in the winter, but it was the first time since August, and the weather was unusual mild. . . . Look, Maugan. . . ."

"Yes?"

"You are more inward in this matter than anyone else. You were a party to it to begin and, it seems, have been so to the end. Well, if this is the end then let it be so and no more said. No more will be said by me, I assure you. We've all to gain and nothing to lose by silence. Sometimes there's a virtue in it, as you'll appreciate when you grow older."

"I appreciate it now, father. I was concerned only to know whether silence could be preserved."

I got up to go, but he waved me back to my seat. "Now that we have agreed, there's no haste to be gone, is there? Bring the table over, and we can dice for a while."

I stayed close by the house all that week and the next. If the Spanish still came I wanted to be here. With such forces camped about the castle they would surely be thrown back, and in any event there was no risk of my father attempting to fulfil his promises; but I felt he might yet come to some sort of quarrel with the military over his rights, and I wanted to be on hand to restrain him. Accepting their authority when they arrived was one of the few sensible things he had done.

But as November advanced all England began to breathe again. Mobilisation at Chatham was stopped, the recall of overseas troops suspended, Essex and Ralegh and Howard were summoned to Court to give an account of their mistakes, Parliament met again, the emergency was seen to be over. Two hundred of the musters at Pendennis were allowed to go home, but the trained soldiers stayed and Captain Alexander showed no signs of relinquishing his authority.

I did not know then or for some years after any true or certain facts from the Spanish side. But seven years later, in 1604, peace having been signed and Killigrew fortunes being still at a low ebb, arrangements were made that my half-brother Peter—ever the favoured one— should complete his education in Spain under the care of the Earl of Bristol, and I was sent to escort him and so saw some whom I knew, and heard what had happened to the rest of the fleet in that October storm.

The advance force had suffered the most, and of the twenty ships that sailed under Captain Quesada only nine returned to Spain. The second part of this squadron under Admiral Brochero had been struck scarcely less severely, and the galleon *San Pedro* with Don Diego Brochero himself on board had been dismasted and blown back into a Biscayan port where it needed five weeks' repair to render it seaworthy again. Admiral Brochero had at once transferred to a fly-boat and put to sea again, but at the vital moment the most aggressive spirit in the fleet was absent and his exclusively Spanish squadron scattered far and wide. In the meantime the Adelantado, a half-day behind with the bulk of the fleet, had been met by the storm a little east of the Scillies. There he had fought it out for three days while first one and then another of his great ships was broken and had to run before the storm. When at length it abated his fleet as such no longer existed. He had beside him four other ships only, two of them damaged and his own leaking. He put back to Spain.

In the meantime the remnants of Brochero's squadron, a dozen assorted vessels, had rendezvoused off Falmouth, but being without further orders and themselves exhausted by the storm, they waited only twelve hours and then put back to Brittany. Except for individual vessels which turned up here and there and gave fight or caused alarm over the next several weeks, that was the end. By the middle of November all the Armada which survived was back in El Ferrol.

I was through Penzance by one o'clock and took the coast track, skirting the edge of the cliff through the hamlet of Newlyn and so reached Mousehole. Much was already rebuilding. Up the hill to the church. Copley was tired and I got off and led him, almost pulled him.

The church was still far from complete but the house had been rebuilt. Two horses were standing in the garden in charge of a liveried groom.

The servant who came to the door knew me. As I was shown in I heard a self-important male voice issuing from the principal chamber, and I knew it at once for that of Mr Henry Arundell of Truthall. By chance we had coincided again. I could tell from the way of speaking that his words were addressed to Sue. Then I heard her exclaim at the news the servant brought. I was not shown in: Sue came out.

She was in widow's weeds.

CHAPTER 2

SHE came two steps, held out her hands, ran and then stopped, moved up to me more slowly.

"Maugan! Oh, this is a *blessed* day! Thank God! I hardly dared to hope that for a second time. . . ."

"I should come back? There have been doubts from time to time. This meeting. . . ."

She kissed me, but withdrew slightly because of a footstep in the room behind.

"Oh, *Maugan,* your letter reached me . . . I have *prayed.* . . . You are changed, older—you've been through so much?"

"It's already a dream. This is the reality. . . . Tell me, I didn't know—your husband?"

"In September." She took a deep breath. "Died as he lived, nobly. . . ." She turned. "You remember Mr Henry Arundell? I think once before. . . ."

The stout man had come out of the room and nodded to me. "Of course. This is a pleasant chance. We had almost given you up, Killigrew."

They led me into the room they had come from and plied me with questions. Black suited Sue, as in truth almost everything did. She looked well, a little less thin and pale, warm towards me but constrained in Arundell's presence. I thought he, though superficially affable, welcomed me less than he seemed. I was myself distrait, stunned by the news that Sue was a widow; I had thought it a matter of years. I asked about him, and was told. Afterwards I remembered nothing of it; it was perhaps something in my mind trying to fence off and separate pleasure at Sue's freedom from pleasure at a man's death.

I itched for Henry Arundell to go but he was in no hurry. It seemed that when a new incumbent to this living was appointed Sue would move out to a small house in Helston which had been the property of her husband. She would then, said Mr Arundell complacently, be much nearer Truthall, and he looked forward to the day when they would become neighbours. Anything he could do for the relict lady of his late beloved friend he would do with the utmost pleasure and satisfaction. Puffing through his red lips, he looked at Sue with a benevolence I at once suspected.

She turned to me, hair and eyelashes glinting in the lattice light. "Maugan, my dear, after you called last time I took the liberty of speaking to Mr Arundell about you. As you know, he was seeking a steward of personality and education who could take over the day to day care of his estate. I told him about you, how gifted you were, your experience already gained as a secretary."

I stared at her. One low cut slipper of black satin was tapping gently on the green oblong of carpet.

"Unhappily, because you were so long a captive Mr Arundell has been compelled to find someone else, so alas the opportunity is gone."

Henry Arundell grunted. "Good man I've got. Of course he's married with a considerable family—much older than you, Killigrew. Difficult to know if you would have been able to command the authority."

I moistened my lips, and looked again at Sue, who was smoothing one of the ribbons of her girdle.

"But also," Sue went on, "at the same time when we were talking over this I did ask Mr Arundell if, supposing he felt you were too young for the stewardship, he would intervene on your behalf with his cousins in London. His cousins the Howards. And he promised he would do this. Can I still rely on you for this kindness, Henry?"

There was a long silence in the room.

"That I'll do—for you, Susanna. I have little or no influence with Lord Thomas the sailor. But Lord Henry I know well, and a letter of commendation from me would do much. He has many interests: in art, in letters, in learning, in public charities." Mr Arundell blew through his lips. "He is often on the look out for likely young men. I have no doubt he would find you some employment, Killigrew."

As I opened my mouth to speak Sue interrupted me with her thanks. Every word she said seemed to please Arundell the more. It occurred to me that I had seen Ralegh himself politic and hypocritical on more than one occasion. If I rejected this out of hand and to his face I might mortally offend Sue, who was acting with what she conceived to be my interests at heart. I could afford to be politic. Now that she was a widow my life would begin for the first time.

"Thank you, sir," I said. "I'm greatly obliged."

Mr. Arundell then made a move to go, but Sue persuaded him to stay on a while and before he left she not only had the letter to Lord Henry Howard written for me to present but the promise that a further letter should leave Truthall tomorrow to be sent direct to his Lordship commending his attention to Mr Maugan Killigrew when Mr Maugan Killigrew called. I listened to it all with impatience.

Mr Arundell invited me to spend the night with him. On my declining he was careful to ascertain that I should spend it at Godolphin. I felt that his care for the proprieties was greater than need be.

When we had seen him off and the outer door was shut but two of the servants were present she said to me formally: "You will sup here, Maugan?"

"Gladly, thank you."

She linked her arm in mine and led me into the drawing room. The companion seemed about to follow but Sue said smiling: "I'll ring for you, Florence."

Back against the door as the door closed, my lips against her neck.

Black taffeta rustled; the slight figure seemed to melt even though stiffened by the whale-bone bodice, scent of sandalwood; her fingers smoothing my hair. My lips moved to hers. In two years I had thought I had become cynical, hardened, Not so. I drowned in her, had no conscious life outside this. I muttered wild endearments, unremembered as soon as spoken, trying to give words to wordless passion.

At length she moved to be free, lowering her head, shaking one hand as if it hurt. I looked after her as she walked to the window. She was trying hard to be composed.

"Sue . . . it seems a century. . . ."

"Is nearly. So much has happened. When you came in today I could hardly believe. . . . I've so often prayed."

"Perhaps that saved me. Thinking of you often saved my reason. In prison I used to make up conversations, go over old ones, picture the way you looked. . . ."

"When I heard you were captured again, I thought, *this* was what I was afraid of. I felt it that time you *came;* you remember I didn't *want* you to go! Then your letter. Nothing since your letter. . . . Oh, Maugan."

I followed her, put my arm about her. We stayed like that for a long time. From this window you could see a mason working on the church tower, now nearly raised again.

"Tell me what happened. Tell me everything."

"No, later. When will that woman come in?"

"Wait a little, Maugan. I'm a widow only by seven weeks."

"Is he—buried here?"

"No, at the family church near Reskymer."

"Tell me about that."

She told me. I heard, but again remember nothing. I think she said he had died suddenly. All I know was that I could feel her breathing, watch movements of her hands and lips and eyelids.

We sat down to supper. The woman Florence was there. I used the time to tell Sue of what happened in Spain, again omitting the murder of Buarcos, the pact with Prada, my conversion to the Catholic faith. It seemed to run well enough without these things.

There were differences in Sue, noticed in embryo on an earlier visit. The enchanting person I remembered, without losing any of her enchantment, had come by a quiet maturity and a quiet authority. Servants were at her beck and call, she gave orders smilingly but without hesitation or shyness. Three years of modest affluence. Three years of change. Other people, though living more quietly than I, had lived too.

After supper the woman Florence stayed on, but at length Sue dismissed her. It was now seven, and if I was to reach Godolphin before they were all abed I must leave soon.

I said: "Sue, when can we marry?"

"Maugan, not *yet*. . . . Sometime next year, I don't know when."

"Next *year*. Early next year."

"Yes. But there has to be a little time."

"And until then?"

"Now it's so near, my dear, let's not snatch at it. Secret, stolen meetings, would spoil what we feel for each other."

"Sue, you still feel the same?"

"Can you doubt it?"

"I need you so much that I'm afraid. You seem to look on the prospect of delay with a greater composure than I can."

"Perhaps it's my nature to. The way I have lived has made me so. But what we have waited four years for will not sour with waiting four months. In the first place it will be more seemly. In the second I must settle up Philip's affairs. In the third you'll have the opportunity to see Lord Henry Howard and know if he can propose anything."

"Ah, that I couldn't understand. Last time we met we went into that, and I said I was promised to Ralegh and wished to remain so."

"But that was when you were about to sail. That was a loyalty I could understand. But now you're back, after all this time, you're bound to no one. You've gained nothing from the voyage except much suffering. It's the usual experience for those who follow Ralegh."

"Yet I feel about him as I ever did. If he wants me, I'm his man."

She made a little gesture of distaste. "What has he ever offered you, Maugan? A post as a junior secretary. An opportunity to die in battle or rot in a Spanish prison."

"What will Henry Howard offer me?"

"I don't know. But at least you might go and see."

My last question was a mistake because her answer put me in a position where I must seem unreasonable.

She went on: "When we marry we must have *some* position. How else can we live? If you wanted to remain unmarried then you could stay on as Ralegh's under secretary or sail to Guiana or do whatever he asked you to do. But we may have a family. There has to be a home."

I got up and stared across at the books of devotion on the desk; I felt I was still on enemy territory.

She said: "When I married Philip I did not look for money, except the security from want that he offered. But he was a man of some property. In case you wonder—"

"I won't touch his money—"

"In case you wonder, most of his property was entailed by his father, and as he died without issue it now passes to his younger brother. I shall have some money, enough to live on quietly, but no estate."

"That's not important—"

"Oh, it is, for I would have liked—"

"Sue, I don't know what to say to make you see how I feel. I may have said it last time; I don't know. I have spent nine months or more in Ralegh's service, and it leaves a mark. . . . Over and above that there is a question of loyalty. Sir Walter and the Howards, although they tolerate each other, are fundamentally opposed. If I now took service with one of the Howards I should feel I was—was moving into an enemy camp."

She was hearing but not accepting. "But you want to marry me?"

". . . It's the one thing above all other."

"Then don't you feel any loyalty to me?"

"Loyalty! You have all my—"

"Yes, then. Well, if we marry next April, perhaps, I have a small competence. It will be helpful. But as a scrivener to Ralegh—"

"He may offer me something more."

"He may. But he's not rich. And what will happen to him when the Queen dies? He owes everything to her. The Howards are perhaps the most powerful family in the country, and with both Protestants and Catholics in their numbers they can hardly fail to prosper, whoever succeeds."

I was watching her. "This is a very—practical point of view."

"I am practical. I've had to be."

"Yes, but I think you've been a pupil of others."

"I have talked of it with Henry Arundell. He's very wise on worldly matters, and I seek help where it is most freely offered."

I sat down again near her. "Sue, take care for him, won't you. I think he always envied Philip Reskymer his wife."

She thoughtfully moved the ornate wedding ring round on her finger. "Yes, I think so."

"Then you should see less of him."

Her eyes were black fringed against the delicate skin of cheek and temple. "Ever since my father died, I've had to take care for myself. Accepting the company of someone who wants me honourably is not the worst risk I've run."

"The risk is that he may think you'll take him seriously."

"He's a wise and willing friend. I have few enough."

Jealousy began to claw at me. "Perhaps if I hadn't returned he would have had more to hope for."

She shook her head. "If you hadn't returned—I don't know what then."

"Oh, Sue," I said, "forgive me. Whenever I see you I'm torn all ways. The only happiness will be in possessing you."

She smiled slightly. "Are you sure? Perhaps possession is never what we expect it to be."

"My dear, you've lived too long in the company of old men. . . . When can I see you again?"

"When you please. So long as it's not unreasonably often until the new year. Come on Monday, can you?"

"Gladly. . . . Sue, I still can't get over it. No one can rejoice that such a good man as Philip Reskymer has died, but the outcome is there and I'm still hardly able to sit here and talk with you soberly of it. That you are free again—this for me is like coming into sudden sunshine after so many dark years!"

She put her hand on mine. "And I can rejoice with you—with a whole heart. Now we can start—together—for the first time."

One day I walked up with Belemus to the castle but a sentry would not allow us in. The soldiers had dug trenches and thrown up rough parapets all round the hillside on which the castle stood.

Captain Alexander, while paying lip service to the Governor of the castle, continued to take much on himself. The soldiers cut down twelve fine elms; on complaint it was claimed that they obstructed the view landward; in effect they needed wood for their fires and this was the easy way. Except for occasional visits to the house for official reasons, the officers now quartered themselves entirely at the castle.

On the Saturday we younger ones had a party of farewell for Belemus who was to leave on the following day. There were twelve of us at it, and in the absence of John, Thomas was the eldest true Killigrew present. At seventeen he was a highly accomplished player on the lute, his touch not so golden as Victor Hardwicke's but his range wider. His greatest pleasure was to wander off from the house with his lute and pick up songs and casual dances from the villages round; sometimes he was away for three days. He claimed he knew sixty different tunes in his head. He had grown little and was only an inch or so over five feet, yet good looking in a square-set way. Affected in his manner, quick tempered but generous, he had no interest in girls and had reacted violently to my father's attempts to pair him off in the county. He was in no way interested in this house or the estate or its prosperity or continuance. He was awaiting a summons from his uncle William to go up to the Court, and lived only for that day.

Odelia at sixteen was already quite a beauty, slender and tall, with clear blue eyes like a mermaid's, sloping shoulders, and vigorous slightly ungraceful movements. Somewhere in her growing up she had lost the warm impulsive ways of childhood and not found anything as good in its place. She no longer confided.

Henry already looked the miser he was going to become. His thin face was like a bird's that watched the earth and the sky for food or bright things. He had a sharp tongue and could lash some of the younger children into screaming frenzies of rage. Yet he adored animals and was never without some wounded mongrel at his heels.

Below him the gap. Maria was nine, her fat face reddening with an early adolescence, her fat strong legs bruising together when she ran, her voice never silent, crowing and caressing or raised in high-pitched angry protest. Peter was six but a fair match for Maria in everything except brute strength; and in adroitness and quickness of mind he outdid them all. Elizabeth was five and Simon three, and only Dorothy grizzling in her cradle was absent from the party. The others here today were Oliver Gwyther, who was now betrothed to Annora Job, and two of the younger Knyvetts from Rosemerryn.

After it was over I said to Belemus:

"This is a bad parting—the break up of an old association; I don't like it."

"No more a break up than your flying off to be Ralegh's scrivener. It's just the boot on the other foot, that's all."

"Is it because of Jane you're going?"

"No woman ever made me run away nor ever will. But I confess I would have been happier these twelve months with her out of the house. It goes against the grain to refuse invitations of that nature, and following the refusal an air blows around one as if one had left the window open on a winter's night. . . . No, witless, I've been here too long and go to make my fortune—or to wield a blow or two in in search of it. I hope you don't liken me to the rat deserting the sinking ship."

"Rather to the brave man diving off in order to lighten the boat."

He patted me on the shoulder. "Well said. Watch for me coming aboard again laden with plunder from the wars!"

On the Tuesday I went to see my father and told him I wished to be married.

"What? This is quick since you came home. Who is it? Someone in the house?"

"Philip Reskymer died in September. I want to marry his widow, who was Susanna Farnaby."

He had been startled out of his dejection and you could see him thinking if there would be any advantage in this for him. "Philip Reskymer's widow? Hm . . . well, you would do much worse for yourself. She'll be a woman of some property. Now if—"

"Most of it was entailed."

"Hm. But she'll be no pauper. Well, boy, there's no harm in being wed. It's a proper state for man. You can live here and pay some small sum. There's room in plenty now, and she'd be company for my daughter-in-law. That way you can be a greater help and support."

"Father, I'm sorry; but I want to make my own way. It's not unnatural."

"Have you suggested she should live here?"

"I know she would not be willing."

"She'll have some property. Look after that. Why go into the hurly-burly of up-country life?"

"We both want to."

He sat in offended silence for a while. It was in keeping with his mood that even his base son whom he had befriended so often and so freely should now turn against him. I could see him thinking it: *this* is gratitude.

"I'm sorry, father."

"Well . . . *I* can help you not at all. When do you intend to go?"

"Oh, it's not decided. We cannot marry until next year. I must see the Raleghs and tell them how their cousin died."

"Ah, well, he's the man to be in with. He has the ear of the Queen now, just like in the old days. And even friendly with Essex! God knows, that's not likely to last!"

"I hope it will. Sir Walter and Lord Essex have a generosity under their seeming arrogance that could very well keep them friends."

"In my view, boy, nothing will keep them friends, for they are on two different ends of a see-saw. One or other must be up or down."

"And Cecil?"

"Ah. . . . He is at the centre and so moves little. The Killigrews are hitched to him, and should continue to prosper. It's only I, isolated down here, *neglected* in times of security, *blamed* in times of peril, it's only I who suffer. Never was greater injustice done to a man than by these upstart military—strutting like cockerels over my land, acting out sham heroics in *my* castle, now that the danger is over—when I have borne the brunt of the true peril for so many years alone—quite alone!"

"Father," I said, "I'm glad the Armada failed."

He sniffed and eased himself in his chair to let a notch out of his sword belt. "Well, of course, who is not? For I should have been in the forefront of the battle and one of the first to fall. With the fleet away and her coasts unguarded, England would have been over-run. That great storm was a signal mercy."

"It is better in every way that the Armada failed, father. It truly is, for it saved a—a final decision that I should not have liked you to make."

For a while he did not speak, breathing heavily with relief that his stomach now had more liberty. "Whatever decision was made was made long before, Maugan. But's all dead and forgotten now. Whatever might have been is dead and forgotten."

The following day my father received a letter from the Privy Council. It summoned him to Westminster to appear before them on the twenty-seventh of November to account for his stewardship of Pendennis Castle.

CHAPTER 3

THOSE who were less inward than I to the events of that time must have wondered at Mr Killigrew's attitude before he left for Westminster. He made a new will. He wrote at once to his uncles Henry and William, telling them that he had been summoned to Court and that, since his affairs were in great disorder and his family in distress, he proposed to bring up with him his two sons Thomas and Henry to place in their keeping forthwith. He wrote to John telling him to return to Arwenack in all haste and to take charge of the house and estate. He told me to prepare to go with him so that I could accompany him to the Council meeting and be on hand if needed. He wrote to Ralegh asking him what grievous and unwitting wrong he had committed in his eyes that Ralegh's report should have been so unfavourable. He wrote to Cecil giving an account of his exertions over the last two years in the cause of military defence. He fondled his younger children in a way that frightened them and delivered homilies to Mrs Killigrew that frightened her. He summoned the ramshackle Henry Knyvett from Rosemerryn and for long periods was closeted with him in Lady Killigrew's chamber.

There were some days before we need leave, so I saw Sue again. I told her as much as possible but could say nothing on the larger issues. She said this was the ideal time to present Mr Arundell's letter to Lord Henry Howard. I said my first duty was with Mr Killigrew, but if we stayed long enough I would call. She said: "You *must*, Maugan. It's only fair to us both. Please."

While there I met the Reverend John Tremearne, who was to take over the living of Paul next week. He was a black-coated, serious man, though not of the class of Reskymer. When we were alone he asked me with interest about the Inquisition and Spain's own attitude towards it. It seemed an opportunity to air a matter that had been concerning me.

"While in Ferrol, Mr Tremearne, I met two Englishmen who had accepted the Catholic faith in order to save their lives. How would you regard such people?"

He stared at me angrily, as if surprised at the question. "As traitors to Christ, Mr Killigrew. Men who have sold their immortal souls for a brief lengthening of mortal existence. How else could they accept the teachings and doctrines of the—the latrine called Rome?"

"Yes. . . . Yes, I see. One of these men was much troubled, but the other took it lightly. He was of the opinion that oaths and dedications made under duress were of no importance."

"Denials of God *must* be important, Mr Killigrew—or words and deeds have no meaning left at all. Do you not suppose that almost all the glorious martyrs of old were not so tempted and did not so resist? Latimer and Ridley among them. They rejected these evil excremental fumes from the bog of Roman Catholic Europe. What shall it profit a man if he gaineth the whole world and loses his soul?"

"The other man," I said, "the one who was troubled, reasoned that God, who understood all things, would forgive all things—and resolved when he returned to England to return to the new faith. Do you suppose he could do that?"

"He should go to his bishop and ask advice of him. Legally, of course, there would be no problem. If he attends the services of our reformed church and communicates, that is all required of him by the Crown. Spiritually, he must surely spend hours on his knees every day asking the forgiveness of Christ for his betrayal. Peter was forgiven. Possibly he would be—if he applied himself to his prayers—perseveringly and in all humility."

I could hear Sue's footsteps. My mind turned back gratefully—and perhaps not altogether irreligiously—to her. In three months we should be married. Not any of the subtle problems of conscience, not the decay and deterioration at Arwenack, could touch that exalting thought.

We left on Thursday morning the seventeenth, a party of six, there being Mr Killigrew and Thomas and Henry and myself, and Thomas Rosewarne and Stephen Wilky.

Our parting was not attended by any ceremonial goodbyes. Four of the children and a handful of servants saw us off on a blustering day that lifted tail-coats and clutched at hats and made hairy spray of the horses' tails. We supped the second night at Penheale, but very late and none too welcome, for the last time he had been that way Mr Killigrew had borrowed money from his host. So into Devon and Dorset. Monday night at a posting inn at Yeovil, and on Tuesday morning we clattered up the long stony drive into the estate at Sherborne. My father had hopes of this meeting, that in some way Sir Walter would be able to give him some indication of what awaited him at Westminster; but here he was disappointed—and I too. Sir Walter had been unwell since he came home and imagined he was threatened with a stone, so he had been given leave from his defence duties and he and Lady Ralegh were in Bath taking the waters. Only George Chapman was there and Matthew Royden and little Wat and his nurse and the servants. It felt like coming home. I asked George Chapman if Sir Walter had any new Guiana plans. Chapman said that since the two voyages of '96, the first under Keymis, the second under Captain Berry at the end of the year, Sir Walter had mounted nothing more; but the purpose was there, it only waited a favourable moment.

While my father and the others were dining I borrowed a fresh horse and galloped to Cerne Abbas. It was a miserable task but had to be performed. Kate Churcher was a tall slender young woman, not pretty but distinguished, with long hands and a soft Dorset voice. On a pretext of buying a pair of gloves I was able to speak to her, and fortunately her husband was called out of the shop for a few minutes. When she heard my mission she burst into tears which were the more agonised for being half suppressed. I muttered a little of how Victor had died and gave her his message. While I spoke she looked as if I were cutting her heart out. Talking to her brought up all my own deep feeling for Victor. The meeting was even worse than I had feared, and I galloped back to Sherborne with a swollen throat.

We spent the night at Shaftesbury and another at Andover and Thursday night at Hartley. Late Friday we arrived in London and put up at The French Lily in Mark Lane, where four of us slept in a bed of swans' down eight feet wide.

In the morning we breakfasted off fresh salmon caught last evening in the river and served in small pewter bowls. Thomas and Henry had not been to London before, and after breakfast we went out for a half hour until Mr Killigrew, who said he had slept ill, was down.

We walked down the narrow overhanging street to the river. At the bottom the whole congestion of the city opened out. A dozen boat-men bobbed at the steps asking our custom; upholstered wherries, some open, some covered in, with velvet and satin cushions waited for hire. The river was full of shipping. To our left was the squat shape of the Tower, black against the smoky sky, sombre with the history of imprisoned princes. Cranes stood on the wharves around it, and behind were the towers of churches. Down river was the bridge with its houses hiding the roadway. Just then the tide was flowing and the water mounted against the arches as if it would push them down. All about the boats and in the free spaces, like tufts of snow thrown down by a painter, were the swans.

We were due at Lothbury to dine with Sir Henry and Lady Killi-grew at eleven, so we made our way back and found Mr Killigrew struggling to squeeze his swollen belly into last year's russet satin doublet while Wilky knelt to fit the kid-skin shoes.

It was not far to the Killigrew house but the way was uneven and the cobbles stiff with dried mud. The house was a tall narrow im-posing structure built of brick and wood in a block with three others. The William Killigrews lived farther down the same street but they were away. Sir Henry said he would take charge of Thomas as well as Henry until they returned.

So dinner. With it a careful steering away from personal relation-ships. (Debts do not matter, they are tiresome but bearable; even rogues can be borne if blood relationship demands it; but what rumour has spread that this is something more?) The near success of the Armada was scarcely mentioned. Ralegh, said Sir Henry, was once more always at the Queen's side, tall, magnificent, all the more im-pressive for his limp. Essex, much out of favour anyhow for having taken his fleet to the Azores and left England exposed to invasion, had himself now taken great offence that the Lord Admiral Howard's earldom had placed him in precedence over all other earls, and had retired sulking to Wanstead. Sir Robert Cecil was shortly to leave England on a visit to Henry IV of France, to try to persuade him not to sign a separate peace with Spain.

Irish affairs were giving their usual trouble. It was difficult to know whom to send to deal with this insoluble problem. And conditions in England itself were moving from bad to worse: wild and wet summers, long and dark winters, harvests had failed, prices rose, want and distress stalked the countryside. The Queen, thank God, remained in good health. There were many rumours in Court that she had secretly named her successor.

So dinner. When it was over the two young men, Thomas and
Henry, were shown the room they would occupy, and we took leave
of them. Only then, when Mr Killigrew under some latent fatherly
impulse had gone upstairs with them and Lady Jael was engaged
with the servants, Sir Henry said to me in a rapid undertone:

"Maugan, your father is to appear before the Privy Council, I hear.
How much is there in these unsavoury rumours that are spread
about?"

"What rumours are those, sir?"

He peered at me keenly. "I think you must be more in his confidence than that or you would not have accompanied him. Shall you
return to Cornwall if your father does not?"

That had an ominous ring about it. "Temporarily. . . . But
if there is the opportunity I shall try to find some permanent position
in London or Westminster. John should be back at Arwenack by now,
and if anything should happen to my father he will be the new
master. Besides, I want to marry and am looking for some recommendation for preferment in or near London."

His cautious legalistic mind seemed to take each word separately
and examine it on its merits.

"As to preferment, as you see, Maugan, I have my hands full with
two young men in my charge. And on tomorrow's council may depend
by how much I am able to help them. It's an unpropitious time. Have
you letters?"

"One, that I don't wish to use."

"Why? May I enquire who. . . ."

"It's to Lord Henry Howard."

"A coming man despite his age. You should present it."

"Yet you look distasteful."

"Well . . . privately I consider him ambiguous. More so than the
other Howards, with whom, on occasion, I have been able to work
in amity."

"In what way ambiguous?"

"He has great talent and a real feel for literature and the arts. It
is rather in the private springs of his nature that one suspects some
duality—of religion and of the life of the senses."

My father came downstairs and we talked no more, but as we
left Sir Henry said to me: "We have a chamber here. That at least
I can offer when you need it."

"Thank you, sir."

The next morning, which was Sunday, was gusty with an occasional
flurry of rain. We had to attend at Whitehall at nine. For this Mr

Killigrew hired a wherry from the steps at the foot of Mark Lane and we were oared up river on a nearly full tide, passing under the great bridge, beneath the second of its twenty arches, where the water was now calm, as through a tunnel. At one end of the bridge were some knobs on spikes which were the heads of executed traitors. I trusted my father had not noticed them and was relieved when one of the rowers, anxious to earn something extra, began to point the other landmarks, the tall chapel of St Thomas on the bridge and St Mary Overy's tower on the other bank; then the tower of St Paul's on our right and all the serried buildings of the great city crowding down to the river. The rower said the wonderful spire of the cathedral, five hundred feet in height, had never been rebuilt since the lightning destroyed it. Then we saw the Bishop of Ely's palace with its hall and chapel and gardens.

My father had been silent ever since we got in the wherry. The dejection and the resentment with which he had set out from Arwenack had stayed with him scarcely broken for eleven days. Only twice had it lifted temporarily: once when he had found someone to play Gleek with him at the inn at Shaftesbury, and once when a chambermaid with a large ripe bust and a low-cut frock had leaned over him at Hartley.

Now he cleared his throat and said: "I don't know what's afoot this morning, Maugan. I don't know what I shall be accused of, what praise or blame will be meted out. All I've wind of from the tone of the summons is that my enemies have gathered to do me what hurt they can."

"I trust it will be small."

He grunted and coughed and spat over the side. "God's life, rumour is a dangerous thing; it can magnify and distort the most innocent action. That's what we have to beware of, boy."

"We? You think I'll be permitted entry?"

"As a witness, yes. A material witness. For if some talk of my having truck with Spain should come up, you can testify on my behalf."

Now we were passing between green banks on either hand, but whereas that on our left was dotted with grazing sheep, to our right the grass appeared to be a part of the gardens of the great houses looking on the river from a distance.

"Indeed, I think, Maugan, if it comes to this worst danger of my being so accused, you could very greatly help me."

"How?"

He shifted and glanced around to observe Thomas Rosewarne and Stephen Wilky following in our wake. "I have done much for you, boy, you know that. But for me you would not have lived at all.

Instead you have been treated as my own son, with all the privileges and honour. Through me everything has come to you, learning, the life of a gentleman, service with Ralegh. But for me—"

"Yes. I understand all that and am grateful."

"Well I have been thinking—in the night I was thinking it over. If this charge—this worst charge against me—should by mischance happen to be made, it could well be argued—or *you* could argue—that you alone, in error, were responsible for it. That being captured and in Spain you were forced in order to survive to treat with them, and this you did in my name and without my knowledge. Elliot and Burley, you could say, were your friends, and they so advised you. You might even say that some large sum of money was offered you to land with the Spanish advance forces, and that you accepted it—"

"In short that I alone played traitor?"

"There is no need to use that word in the case of a boy such as yourself. No need at all. You were misguided, frightened, and carried away. That's all. We're of the same name, Killigrew, and so it was thought I might be involved. You, being so young, have little to fear. . . ."

"Except hanging may be."

"Oh, no, no, no. I would not permit it. They would treat a boy very lightly. The error in you would be so much less than if they thought it mine. . . ."

By now we must have passed Durham House where I had stayed with Sir Walter, for we were turning in towards Whitehall Stairs.

I said slowly: "Father, I admit my debt to you. Indeed I acknowledge it gladly. But there are some sacrifices, some payments, which outweigh the debt. You're asking me too much. Besides, the target is out of range: I could not convince them even if I would."

"If you said—"

"But I would not try. Be content that I'll try all else. You know I will support you in any other way you want."

We came into the steps and willing hands caught the wherry, offered help in alighting, brushed off imaginary spray from our cloaks, all hoping for the tossed coin. Mr Killigrew paid the boatman and slowly we began to mount the broad flight of steps. The second wherry was grounding behind us.

"Take heart," I said, "I don't see how the Privy Council may know anything of this matter."

"The Privy Council has many ears and eyes, spies abroad in all countries. You never know what they may know or what they may invent if they are determined on a man's ruin."

We reached the top of the stairs and waited for Rosewarne and

Wilky. It was blowing and my father drew his cloak around him. The brassy daylight showed up the coarseness of his skin, where a once high clear complexion had become pitted and rusty. His eyelids dipped a little at each side like tiny pouting lips. He had wool in one ear against the cold. He looked an old man.

CHAPTER 4

WE waited in a large room adjoining the Queen's presence chamber. It was an ornate room, with a gallery at one end and crystal candelabra like inverted pyramids hanging from the ceiling. Pages and men in varied livery came through from time to time, but no others waited. We had not been searched, though our swords were left at the door. Wilky and Rosewarne had remained outside. At the entrance door to the presence chamber were four enormous men in red, with roses embroidered in gold on back and breast. The floor of this impressive ante-room was strewn with some sort of sweet herb that emitted a pungent smell.

I was vividly reminded of waiting with Burley and Alazar in the palace in Madrid. Only here were no crowds; those who crossed the room did so with a leisurely thoughtful air. It would all have been reassuring if we had been in the mood to feel reassured.

When men left the presence chamber they did so backwards, bowing low. I did not know if Her Majesty attended all or many of her council meetings, but it seemed she was here today.

Nine became ten and ten, eleven. Ever and again a strange and unnerving sound could be heard from the garden outside like a devil in shrill torment. Peacocks screeching on the lawns.

There was a bustle and two men exited, bowing. Following them came a chamberlain, who beckoned to my father. I rose to accompany him, and after a brief hesitation the chamberlain let me pass.

The room we came into was smaller than the ante-room. Light fell from three tall windows upon a narrow table down the centre of the room. A big fireplace with a fire glowing; tapestries depicting battle scenes on the wall; six of the red-clad guard; at the table were about a dozen men in robes of office; at the head a woman.

Near the foot of the table was a bench, with a lower padded bench before it. On this we knelt. While we took up our positions there was complete silence at the table. So we knelt there watched by the twelve greatest men in the land. But not by the greatest woman. She was examining the diamond bracelet on her wrist.

Beside her, on her left, was a small man in black with a humped back: I took him to be Sir Robert Cecil. In the shadows behind his chair were four clerks at a desk writing. It was impossible to know all the other men, but the Archbishop of Canterbury was on the Queen's right, and I recognised the Earl of Nottingham, who had been Lord Admiral Howard. Among the others were the Lord Chamberlain, the Lord Keeper of the Great Seal, the Earl Marshal, the Lord Treasurer, the Lord Chief Justice, and the Controller of the Queen's Household.

So we remained while Her Majesty attended to her bracelet. Silence was not broken until she looked up and nodded.

The Lord Archbishop said: "Mr Killigrew, we have many times in the past had bad reports of you. It would seem that the position of honour entrusted to you by Her Gracious Majesty has not unseldom been used for your private profit. Not two years ago a Commission was appointed to inquire into these abuses. Their report was far from favourable, but Her Majesty saw fit to overlook these lapses, preferring to believe your constant assurances that in all matters touching the safety of the Realm you had no other thought but to serve her. . . ."

At first sight the Queen looked like a young woman; one felt some miracle of preservation had kept her as a maid of thirty. But when she turned her head towards the window one could see the lines under the talcum and the borax. She was wearing a dark auburn wig, and her gown of white silk embroidered with great pearls was cut low showing as much white bosom as Lady Jael ever did. Two pearls in the ears, a necklace which glinted fire at every move, a small becoming crown.

"Nevertheless, in the month now past, when the Realm was in perhaps the greatest peril of all the perils of Her Majesty's reign, your service to her was wanting. Captain Alexander has reported on arriving at Pendennis on the thirty-first of October that there was not half a barrel of powder in the castle, that all fortifications were neglected, the guns in poor condition, the musters unsummoned. Further that your deputy captain was away and such servants as you spared for the defence of the fort were in liquor. What say you to all this?"

My father began a long and rambling defence, which was part justification, part denial. He referred to the many letters he had sent to the Privy Council asking for more arms. He spoke of the difficulties and jealousies he had had to contend with nearer home, when others in their reports and in their positions were judged to be before him. He would have gone on much longer but suddenly stopped. A white gloved hand at the top of the table had been raised.

"What is this young man doing here, Mr Killigrew?"

"He is my eldest son, Your Majesty. A base son but one I esteem. I ventured to ask him here so that in some part his words might be accepted as bearing out my own. If it so—"

"Go on, my Lord Archbishop."

The archbishop turned over a parchment. For a few moments I had met the eyes of the Queen.

"A second charge. Two weeks ago today at Dartmouth, in the examination of one Nicholas Franklin before George Carey of Cockington and Thomas Holland, mayor of Dartmouth, Franklin being aboard the *Bear of Amsterdam* one of the Spanish navy forced in by stress of weather and interned . . . Franklin, a mariner, testified to hearing one Captain Elliot talking with officers, Captain Elliot being a known traitor and long a partner with the Spaniards. Witness says Captain Elliot said in June of last year, he being with his ship in Falmouth Haven and much in the company and confidence of one John Killigrew, captain of the castle, was there surprised by one of the Queen's ships *Crane* and escaped up river. Whereon Mr Killigrew suborned Captain Jonas, commander of *Crane*, with the gift of one hundred pounds to sail out of the haven and so give Elliot time to escape. This money Captain Elliot repaid to Mr Killigrew, and this Mr Killigrew accepted, knowing it to be gold from Spain. . . ."

The peacocks were screaming. The new Earl of Nottingham brushed the end of his pen lightly over his beard.

"Your Majesty," Mr Killigrew said, "my lords, this is an outrage! This is infamy! You, madam, who have honoured me with your confidence for so long, can you accept such a calumny? I, who have laboured all these years. . . ."

"Mr Killigrew," said the Queen gently. "Do not protest. Say if you did or if you did not."

"I did not! On my immortal soul and on my hopes of its redemption through the love of Christ, I swear I did not!"

The Lord Treasurer said: "I think you have admitted on some former occasion to an acquaintance with this man."

"Indeed, yes. My river is an open haven. It is not discriminate in whom it gives protection to. But I was no more inward with Captain Elliot than with a hundred other mariners who from time to time have come to the harbour and dropped anchor there."

Lord Bathurst said: "Could we not have Captain Jonas called?"

Sir Robert Cecil said: "Captain Jonas has already been examined. . . . Not unnaturally he denies all knowledge of this. There is some corroborative testimony from a Coxswain Lloyd who was aboard *Crane* at the time mentioned. But Lloyd, it must be said in fairness, is not an entirely trustworthy witness." Cecil had a delicate voice, careful and low, but every word could be heard.

There was a pause. The Queen glanced at the clock and then turned again to the Archbishop.

"There is a third charge," said the Archbishop. "This is contained in an examination of one William Love, of Weymouth, lately hanged for piracy. Love's statement asserts 'that in the Armada lately sent against us, Captain Elliot, Captain Burley, Captain Lambert, were pilots royal of Spain, all with instructions to land and deal with John Killigrew of Pendennis and Arwenack, with whom they are close acquainted. And in this as in all other respects Killigrew without doubt was faulty and in the payment of Spain.'"

I stared down along the surface of the table—at the hands and the pens and the paper and the wax.

The Queen said: "It seems, my lords, that in this some excess of zeal has robbed us of a valuable witness." You could see the ironical lift of an eyebrow.

Mr Killigrew said: "Your Majesty, my lords, this too is calumny without truth! If this is how I am regarded, then I regret that some few of the enemy did not land so that I could give the lie—and my blood— to this base slander. Your Majesty, this my son was aboard one of the Spanish ships, having been taken prisoner after Cadiz. He spoke with Elliot and others and can bear witness that my name was never spoken by them except as an enemy of Spain to be overcome on landing—never as a traitor, never as a traitor!"

They were waiting for me. This might be the crux of it all. I moistened lips suddenly very dry.

"Your Majesty, because I speak Spanish I was used on this voyage to interpret between the Spanish and some Irish volunteers. I was aboard the *San Bartolomeo* galleon and was one of the few survivors when she foundered in the storm. I saw Captain Elliot three times. He knew me for a Killigrew—and used me the worse for it. He did not regard my father as a friend of Spaniards but as their first enemy to be overcome on landing. Before the Armada sailed I was kept in prison for many months in conditions in which many of my companions died. Later I was in solitary confinement and for a time lost my reason. This would not be the treatment given to the son of someone they counted as their friend."

A gleam of sunlight filtered through the windows and fell on a dark auburn wig.

One man said: "Of what value is a son's testimony on behalf of his father? I would have lied to save my father's head."

"Some sons," said the Queen, "would lie to see their fathers lopped. It does not follow, my Lord North."

The Archbishop folded his hands on the parchment. "This is not the court of the Star Chamber, Mr Killigrew, and we permit ourselves only to deal in summary justice. How we have before us three charges, the first proven, the latter two disputable; but all taken together there is a heavy inference of treason. We have heard your defence, your denials, but—"

A page came quietly across and whispered in the Queen's ear. She looked up, her narrow lips pursed. "Yes, he may come in."

We all waited. She made no attempt to explain to her council who asked permission to enter. There was a heavy clanking step that I recognised before I saw the man bending over the Queen's hand.

"Sir Walter," she said. "We gave you leave to take the waters."

"Your precious Majesty." His eyes traveled over her face. "I had urgent business in London so returned briefly."

"You are recovered?"

"More in two minutes for the refreshment of this reception than for all the time in Bath."

She smiled. Some youthfulness clung to her manner under his admiring gaze. For a few moments they continued to talk together as if no one else were in the room. So far Sir Walter had not even bothered to greet the most powerful council in the land—of which he was not even a member. One could understand how he made himself disliked. It was the Queen who, becoming aware of her dignity, said:

"And this visit to our audience chamber? What is your business, Walter?"

Ralegh looked down the table. "My lords. Chancing to hear that matters appertaining to my lieutenancy of Cornwall were toward, I ventured to request an audience. Your Majesty, if by so greatly presuming I have in any small part given you to think I have exceeded my position or duty, I beg you to say so and I will at once leave."

"No, no. Pray go on."

"You will remember that in the great storm that scattered the Spanish fleet, a part of my squadron, including *Warspite*, was blown into St Ives for shelter. There, hearing of the emergency for the first time, I took horse and galloped overland to Falmouth Haven, reaching there on the twenty-ninth of October in the afternoon. There, finding forces totally inadequate to meet this great threat, I caused five hundred men, some from my ships, some gathered in haste on the way, to be thrown into the defence of the castle and haven. And left them there. Captain Alexander was appointed to take charge of them. So—being in those parts two days before any other officers I am in a position to tell you what I found better than he. I found the defences lax, ill manned, undergunned, with scarcely powder to keep a single company of Spanish at bay."

"This confirms what Captain Alexander reports," the Archbishop said dryly.

"Agreed, my lord. What he did not say, because he did not know, was that your lordships have persistently denied Mr Killigrew money and supplies, though by constant letter and by attendance at Court he has besought you for them. Her gracious Majesty by making me Lord Lieutenant of Cornwall has appointed me to take charge of the defences of that county. With respect I refer you to my letters of August, September, and November 1595, January and February 1596, March, April, and May of this year, all assessing the problem of defence and all arguing that greater forces should be available to the isolated castles of St Mary's, St Michael's, Pendennis, St Mawes, and others, to repel surprise attack. We are a small country, my lords, and face great enemies. Our resources are often stretched to the limits of endurance. But when our scant forces are shown up as such, it is not meet that a solitary commander on the spot should be accused of treason because of it."

The Queen had not liked this. "You appoint yourself defendant of Mr Killigrew? You applaud what he has done?"

"By no means, Your Majesty. I think he has been lax and deserves censure. But—"

"Laxness alone in some circumstances can be treason, Sir Walter. Give us leave to decide that."

"None can decide better, madam. If I—"

"But then there are other charges, of which you may not have heard. Tell Sir Walter the other charges."

Grudgingly the Archbishop told him. My father and I were again required to answer in defence. While I was speaking Sir Walter looked at me but gave no sign of recognition.

"Your Majesty, such charges as these grow for the asking wherever suspicion rests. A man has only to be known to be down for the jackals of rumour to set to work. The tattle of sea-ports makes free of many great names. A noose round the neck is a great spur to reminiscence and invention. John Killigrew has served his country long. Is it likely that he would sell it now?"

"John Killigrew is grievously in debt," said Lord North. "We all know that. A lack of money has corrupted many men."

"It is true also, is it not," said the Earl of Nottingham, speaking for the first time, "that the prisoner and Sir Walter are related and have long been close friends?"

"The relationship is of the most distant, my lord; and I have counted John Killigrew as one link among many in the defence of these islands. In my official journeys through Cornwall—most of them taken at the behest of this council—I have spent a night at his home from time to time. But the implication is scurrilous . . . I would not speak for my own brother if I thought him guilty of treason!"

The Queen nodded. Perhaps she did not approve of the contemptuous way the Captain of her Guard addressed the most illustrious nobles in the land, but the sentiment was good.

"Time passes, my lords. We have other business today, and dinner must be taken soon. A decision must be come to on this man's future. . . . Sir Walter, we thank you for your valued assistance. You have our permission to withdraw."

"Having feasted my eyes this morning, Your Majesty, I do so with a new heart."

He kissed her wrist, and contrived it where the short glove ended. Some of the council noticed this and were displeased, but the Queen was not.

After he had gone a silence fell. Sir Robert Cecil broke it. "My lords, what is your conclusion as to the behaviour of John Killigrew? Might I request a vote. First: that it is treasonable."

Five hands were raised. The Archbishop, the Earl of Nottingham, Lord North, and two others.

"That it has been negligent but not to the degree of treason."

Five hands were raised.

"That he is guiltless of the charges brought."

No hands were raised. Sir Robert Cecil and one other had not voted.

Sir Robert said: "Would Your Majesty graciously favour us with an opinion?"

"That I would, little man, for we are all hungry. Mr Killigrew, you have been accused of negligence in your duties towards me and towards the safety of this realm. We do not consider you have proved yourself innocent. You have been accused of treasonable correspondence with Spain and some willingness to treat with them. You have not shown yourself to be innocent of those charges either."

My father bowed his head, and his straw-grey hair fell over his eyes.

"Nevertheless on these latter accusations the testimony against you is inconclusive and fragmentary. So we are disposed to overlook this most gravest charge. My lords, we would think justice would best be served here by acting on a proven negligence. Would any wish to dispute that?"

No one spoke.

"Mr Secretary, it would seem necessary to deprive Mr Killigrew of of his governorship of Pendennis Castle. Let us have in the next weeks some suitable names from which we may choose a successor."

"Your Majesty," said my father, "I wish to thank you for this clemency. So long as I—"

"Do not mistake this clemency, Mr Killigrew, as any sign of approval. A bad servant is often times worse than no servant at all. Your negligence could have betrayed England. Mr Secretary, I understand that Mr Killigrew is in debt to the Crown."

"Yes, Your Majesty. For two thousand pounds."

"See that it is collected."

"Your Majesty—" my father began in unwise protest, but he was waved into silence. The Queen had risen from her brocaded chair. Gathering around her a mantle of black silk shot with silver threads, she turned and walked briskly from the room. Two pages just had time to dart forward to gather her train.

As soon as she was gone the members of the Privy Council sat down again, talking among themselves; but two of the yeomen tapped our shoulders and we were led out through the ante-room into the palace yard.

There Rosewarne and Wilky were patiently waiting. They started forward on seeing us, clearly relieved.

My father said: "Let us go back at once. There are certain dispositions I wish to make and that cannot be done too soon."

He was arrested at nine o'clock next morning on the suit of Mr Reynolds of the Queen's Exchequer. He was taken to the Gatehouse Prison at Westminster, a gloomy building leading into New Palace Yard. It served the purpose of both a prison and a guard house for all who would approach Westminster Hall.

He had given me what money he had, and his watch and the diamond buckles off his shoes, and his two rings and a gold chain.

"Sell all for what you can get. There is a man called Fulbright in Old Jewry who's as honest as such knaves go. Save only the gold ring, which was my father's before me. Pawn that, for who knows, we may

redeem it some day. Though, God's life, I've little personal hope.
I'm finished, done for, shall be left here to rot. This is what all my
service—"

"You've been arrested before."

"On private suit, yes. But this is different. There can be no intervention, even if any were willing to attempt it. I am at the Queen's
mercy."

"Which may be forthcoming. I don't think she is a vindictive
woman."

"Pray God. I've known her nourish grudges before now. As to finding two thousand pounds. . . . Nor will it only be that. *Watch* the
jackals pounce. . . ."

Anslowe, the gaoler, was a stout dog-faced man with stiff red-grey
hair and a stench about him. He demanded at once three pounds as
garnish money, and said twenty shillings a week would ensure my
father a bed and a ground floor chamber which he would share with
three others. If less, his new prisoner went into the Common Ward. On
the way in we had passed the gratings through which came cries for
bread and meat, and some thin talons stretching through the bars. All
the inside of the gaol, which was small, was dark and stinking, and the
only hope of survival seemed to be to live where some air would
penetrate and one could see out at the carriages and people passing
through the Gatehouse. My father grabbed money from me and
gave it to Anslowe, and he was then taken into a dark foul room
in which already were three men squatting in rags by the single long
window waiting to shout their appeals to any passer-by. They glowered at the newcomer, and Anslowe jerked with his thumb at some
boards and a sheet—"There's yer bed"—then waited for me to go. This
I did with a heavy heart, leaving Mr Killigrew standing like a stout,
sick bird in a circle of vultures.

Ralegh said: "So, Maugan, when we had thought you gone. . . .
The news only reached me in your father's letter. What an adventure you have had!"

It was a splendid welcome, full of good-will and esteem; yet I
fancied I had chosen the wrong time, for Bell was with him, and a
new secretary, and he was preparing to return to Bath. And as always,
when he was with others, even servants, he was less personally
approachable. There were so many Walter Raleghs: the vigorous
enthusiast, the thinker, the subtle politician, the unpretentious friend,
the ambitious statesman, the poet, the strategist, the man of affairs.
Today he was nearest this last.

"Poor Victor. . . . It was a bad day when I sent you both home.

When I sought to preserve his life I lost it. By the living God, how we exist by chance!"

His complexion was sallow and his face lined; the stick was beside his desk though he did not use it to move about the room.

"I came to bring my thanks, Sir Walter—and my father's. Without your help he might have fared much worse."

"Ah, the Privy Council. I should be on it, but Her Majesty knows if I were I should be ruling all the rest. Was there ever such nonsense as suspecting John Killigrew of treating with the enemy!"

I could not speak then.

He said: "Oh, I know he has been no angel. I do not applaud what he does, and some new blood to captain the castle will be a good thing: its condition when I reached it last was lamentable. But to confuse that with treason is to misuse the meaning of words."

His secretary was requesting his attention to some document just signed. While he attended to it I went to the window. A passenger vessel with seven sails was sweeping down river at a fine pace.

The secretary went out, and only Bell remained. The moment was still not a favourable one, but I must have some answer before he left for Bath.

"Sir, my duty takes me back to Arwenack, to see what can be done to help the family. But my half-brother John will soon be home and he must take over this duty. As soon as he does, I—"

"Ah, your father has a young brood, but one or two are old enough to be of value at this time. I would young Wat were of an age." Sir Walter picked up a book and slipped the end of a pen in it to keep the place. "Pack this, Bell, I have other things for tonight. . . . Perhaps in due course you'll be in a position to return into my service, boy—"

"That's what I wished to ask you about—"

The door had opened behind me. "Sir, Lord Cobham has called."

"Ask him into the gallery. I'll be there as soon as he."

The secretary withdrew. I said: "May I take it that you can still offer me a post, sir?"

"Of course. Lady Ralegh was much taken with you. At Sherborne there is much to see to, and there is more than a likelihood that Irish affairs will occupy me for some time. I believe a revolt is brewing, and command of our forces must be given to a soldier of experience and resource. . . . I wonder what Cobham wants now."

"Sir, I have to thank you again for your intervention for my father. It could well have saved his head."

"It was the least I could do when appealed to. Now make yourself at home in the quarters below. I have business on hand."

"Can you spare me one minute more?"

At the door he stopped, his eyes distant and preoccupied. "Two if you have need of them. But Lord Cobham is below."

"Sir, I wish to marry."

"Do you need my sanction? If so you have it."

"If I am married I need a position, Sir Walter. While personally I should be happy and honoured to act as a scrivener or in any other capacity you desired, the need to maintain a wife and later a family—"

"There's room enough at Sherborne. Bring your wife. You can make her happy there."

My tongue stuck to the roof of my mouth, for I agreed with him. "Gladly. Thank you. Thank you. . . . But perhaps I might ask you for the favour of some preferment—or some recommendation. When— when one marries one becomes . . . ambitious."

He twirled his stick impatiently. "Oh . . . ambitious. Ambition is the loadstone that leads us all. Bring your wife to Sherborne, Maugan, if you wish to. Preferment will come later. I am not one to forget my friends."

CHAPTER 5

I sold my horse, keeping Mr Killigrew's, and sold or pawned the jewellery and other trinkets he had given me. Most of this money I gave to Thomas Rosewarne, who was determined to stay in Westminster and take work as a clerk in order to be on hand. He thought that some legal aid might yet be brought to contrive my father out of jail; but personally I wondered whether even a full discharge of his debts to the Queen would see him free again. There was even the risk that new evidence would yet come to light and he would be removed from the Gatehouse to the Tower. How far would the Spanish keep their plans secret now they had gone awry? What if Captain Elliot or Richard Burley were caught?

I saw Mr Killigrew again the following morning. He had spent a restless night and had been badly bitten by bugs. He was very cold, so I left him two extra coats. The covering for his board was rotten, he said, and there was nothing but filthy straw for a pillow. The food he had paid to have cooked in the jail kitchen had come in blackened to cinders. Anslowe had denied him even the liberty of the prison, saying it was against the orders he had been given.

"Go tell Mrs Killigrew how I am situated. Do not spare the descrip-

tion, for there is still some money coming into the house from time
to time and the first claim on it must now be mine. If I cannot
obtain releasement— Leave me alone, man! I have nothing for you!"
This to one of the ragged skeletons who had been importuning him as
he spoke to me through the bars. I threw the wretch a penny. "And
curb your generosity, Maugan! When you are rich you may use your
money as you please. Not now!"

"Sleep in these extra coats, father. Otherwise you'll get them stolen
in the night. D'you want for books or a chess-board?"

"I've pen and paper, that's more important. Already I've written to
Cecil. Tomorrow it will be the Queen. And I have my dice. . . . But
none of these vile creatures are fit to *play* with!"

"I trust soon you may be moved."

"When you see John and Jane make out a strong case to them.
She *has* the money or could get it. And if John can see his father so
languish he has a heart of flint. Get them *both* to understand my
plight. It's a matter of urgency, for with my cough I may not see the
winter through!"

"I'll do everything I can. But take heart, for the case could have
been a worse one."

He blinked at me with bloodshot eyes. "Those old men. Many of
them had grievances against me—*old* grievances. But Cecil! I would
not have thought it of him to sit by like a little frog hearing everything and saying nothing. And the Queen! She's getting old, Maugan, that's what's wrong. She forgets her old friends and makes up
with new ones. It's a common complaint of age. Alas, alas. . . . You
leave for home tomorrow? Hasten, for the sooner I am out of this
the better."

The fish market outside was full of bustle and shouting; beyond,
near the clutter of shacks around St Margaret's church, two women
were fighting in the centre of a jeering crowd. With a sense of
depression and with a sensation of guilt that in some way I should
have been able to help my father more, I turned into one of the many
ale houses and drank a tankard of beer.

Perhaps the sensation of guilt arose from the feeling of pure contentment which ran willy-nilly all the time at the back of my thoughts.
The anxiety of those dark days, the fear of worse to come, was all
the time illumined for me by the thought of Sue. If in two or three
months I married her the world could be what colour it chose, my
own life would be pitched to a new happiness. Whoever was bankrupt,
I would be rich. Almost every morning when I woke this thought
of her was a shock, a stimulus, a vivid flood of excitement breaking

into sleep, as if someone entered a dark room and flung back the curtains.

So now if I was to play fair with her the last move had to be made.

It was a narrow house, not far from Durham House. A supercilious boy with long fair hair took my letter and left me waiting at the door. I waited while my feet grew cold, then he took me in.

"Lord Henry will see you when he is free."

I stood on a handsome marble floor in a high narrow entrance hall. In the distance someone was playing the lute. It was a tune I did not know.

The impudent boy came through the hall again and stared at me. I stared him down.

"Lord Henry will see you."

We went upstairs and into a big room lined with books. A fire burned in an open hearth, and near it, squatting on a rug, another handsome boy was fingering the lute.

In an armchair with a book open on his knee was an elderly man in a fur-trimmed jacket. Although his face was much lined, his hair was black and drawn across the crown to hide his baldness. He had a long nose and sensuous lips. My letter was open on the table. A heavy scent of violets hung in the room.

We waited until the next verse was over.

> Beauty sat bathing by a spring
> Where fairest shades did hide her;
> The wind blew calm, the birds did sing,
> The cool streams ran beside her.

With two fingers the elderly man suppressed a yawn. "Poke the fire, Claude, it waxes cold."

The young lutist dug at the fire with an iron rod. "We have a visitor, my lord."

"That I know. Master Maugan Killigrew." Lord Henry picked up the letter, glanced through it and for the first time glanced at me. "Master Maugan Killigrew, come here."

I came and stood beside the table.

"I have had word about you from my friend Henry Arundell."

"Yes, my lord."

"He tells me you are a young man of parts. One of the Killigrews who proliferate about the Court. Do you know Court life?"

"No, my lord. My experience, such as it is, has been in Cornwall and in Spain."

"Ah, in Spain. Just so. I believe Mr Arundell mentions that. You were a captive but escaped. How did you find the Spanish?"

"Fierce in battle, my lord. Fanatical in religion. Charming in personal contact."

He looked me over. "Ah. A talent for summary, I see. Hasn't he a talent for summary, Claude?"

The boy shrugged and began to pluck at his lute.

> *My wanton thoughts enticed mine eye*
> *To see what was forbidden;*
> *But better memory said, fiel*
> *So vain desire was chidden.*

"A foolish conclusion to a pretty song," said Lord Henry. "Do you play, Killigrew?"

"Indifferently, my lord."

"All young men should learn with their alphabet. My tutor would not permit me, he being a Puritan. Until the regime changed and he was dismissed. I always say I learned under Mary."

"Learned under Mary," said Claude, "suffered under Elizabeth, was pensioned, dead, and buried. The third day—"

"Claude," said Lord Henry, "take your blasphemies off and give Herbert and Arthur the benefit of them."

The boy pushed out his lower lip but did not move.

Lord Henry took up another letter and read it carefully through. "This is the one from Mr Arundell. I learn from it that you have seen service with Sir Walter Ralegh."

"Yes, my lord. I worked as a secretary in his household for six months."

"Why have you left?"

"As you say, I was a prisoner in Spain."

"And now you are no longer welcome?"

"Oh, yes. But it is in the same position. I seek something better."

"Ah, something better. I doubt if I can offer you anything better. I am quite without influence, unwelcome at Court, living in this small style. . . . Claude, I told you, you may go."

The boy sulkily left the room.

"A disobedient youth but engaging. He trades on good nature. . . . I see Mr Arundell says he is hoping to marry."

"Oh? . . ."

"A strange ambition in a man nearing fifty. And one whose tastes have always rather been. . . ." Lord Henry's eyes trembled with malice. "However . . . that should not detain us."

I swallowed and stared at a sacred painting hung between the bookshelves.

"You write and speak Spanish, Killigrew?"

"Yes, my lord."

"That is not a common attribute. It could earn you some interesting post."

"Less of an attribute seeing we are at war with Spain, my lord."

"Commerce and art do not stop at the dictation of princes. Have you any other qualifications?"

"I know something of war."

"I think that will be a diminishing asset, for we are all weary of it. Do you understand—diplomacy?"

He said it in such a way that much more than a single word was conveyed.

"I have had some experience."

"No doubt it runs in the family. Your relatives are supporters of Cecil, are they not?"

"I think, my lord, they prefer to see themselves as servants of the Queen."

"But who does not? Who does not? Our noble Elizabeth—whom God preserve—we all worship and serve. But under her great men sometimes differ as to how she may best be served. I . . . now I am an adherent of Essex."

"Indeed."

"My friends, Francis and Anthony Bacon, and I, we support his lordship when and how we may. Yet am I on happy terms with Sir Robert Cecil and his father, too."

Until now I had not consciously brought to mind Ralegh's conversation in the cabin of *Warspite* that June night on our way to Cadiz. "Oil and water," he had said. "But Thomas Howard is far less repugnant than his uncle, Lord Henry. If you ever meet him I commend him to your study."

Suddenly in the middle of a series of questions Lord Henry said something to me I could hardly credit. I stared at him stupidly, certain I must have misheard.

He repeated: "I gather you are a Catholic, Killigrew."

"No, sir, I cannot imagine where you have—how that misunderstanding can have arisen!"

He unfastened two buttons of his jacket, dusted a little snuff off the fur. His vigorous malicious face was flushed with the heat. "In a country such as ours, my dear Killigrew, misunderstandings are always arising. Consider how they have affected my family. My father, the Earl of Surrey—he came to have a misunderstanding in the matter of religion and the regency in the time of the last Henry, so he lost his head. I was eighteen at the time. A little younger than you."

"If you—"

"And then there was my brother, the Duke of Norfolk. There was misunderstanding about him too, some rumour that he might marry Mary Queen of Scots. He lost his head. I was thirty-three at the time."

I did not interrupt again. Lord Henry settled his slippered feet on the footstool. "Then there was my nephew, the Earl of Arundel, who misunderstood our Queen so grievously as to become a Catholic and not to hide his views. He died in prison two years ago. All these mistakes could perhaps have been avoided by wiser men such as we."

He dusted his jacket again.

I said: "Henry Arundell can know nothing of my religion. All that—"

"Oh, he doesn't. He does not mention it."

"Then in what way—"

"I have heard that you were converted while in Spain."

I still struggled to understand this thing. "What one does in an enemy country is done under duress. There can be no—"

"Under duress?" He raised his eyebrows ironically. "But of course. All decisions are made under duress. That is an axiom of life. In the winter weather I suffer from an affection of the kidneys. Warmth and a dry air prevent it, so I wrap myself about and keep a fire which I see you find too great. I act under duress. In Rome and Florence, which I visited some twelve years ago, the day's warmth was such that one needed no other heat at all. . . . So with religion, my dear Killigrew. In England I am a confirmed Protestant. So I trust are you. Only a fool shivers when the cold draughts blow."

I did not like this man but I could not but be aware of the subtlety of the intelligence probing mine. He appeared quite open, indeed to be forthcoming in the history of his family, but by nuances, delicately calculated pauses, sardonic expressions, he was all the time challenging my responses.

"I wonder, my lord, how you came to have such information about me."

"Does it matter?"

"It well could."

"I am a peaceful man, Killigrew, and pursue peaceful ends. Leave it at that. The value of the incident lies not in itself but in the light it sheds on character. One is given to suppose that you are a politic person."

"My lord, I seek preferment."

"Ah. You flatter me with that original confidence. . . . I have no preferment for you—as such. But there could be employment."

"Tell me of it, my lord."

"Hold hard. Let nothing be done in haste. All young men are the same."

A log fell and blazed. The light in the room by now was fading, and the fire sent dim and secret colours leaping over books and tables and chairs: purple, ochre, and green. Like the conversation the firelight obscured as much as it revealed.

"Sit down, Killigrew. You have certain ductile qualities which I believe could be useful to me. But I sense inflexibilities too, which would have to be plumbed before we proceeded far. A limb will move, but only according to its joints. Mental anatomy needs just as careful study."

I pulled forward a chair of black carved oak. The wood seat had been worked to represent the naked Greek figure of Mercury.

"You go too deep, my lord."

"Oh, no, I assure you, there is no depth in what I say, only a little caution. Tell me, do you admire your uncle?"

"My uncle?"

"Sir Henry Killigrew."

"Why, yes. . . ."

"Do you have his qualities?"

"What do you consider them?"

"An ability above all for secret negotiation, for loyalty to his master."

Lord Henry was watching me with half-closed lids. It was impossible to tell how much he was in earnest.

"Sir Henry is older than I am, my lord. No doubt those qualities grow."

"Not unless they are firmly there at the start. When do you leave for Cornwall?"

"Tomorrow morning."

"Ah. . . . All this is premature. Again haste when haste is unprofitable. I take it you have no further connections with Ralegh?"

I did not know what to answer. "We are going straight home, my lord. My father is in prison for bankruptcy, and my step-mother may need me to help. Once that is done—then it is done. Two weeks, three weeks perhaps."

Lord Henry still had the book open on his knee. "Do you know that old Latin precept: 'There is a time for saying nothing and a time for saying something, but there is no time in which all things should be said.'"

"No, my lord."

"Perhaps this is a time for saying something, but a little only. As

I have told you, the most I can offer could be called maybe a gainful employment. As a secretary, you understand. A secretary and if necessary a messenger. Consider it while you are riding home. Now you may go."

CHAPTER 6

We rode back to Cornwall, Wilky and I, in a succession of days of blinding rain. The farther west we went the more sodden the sky and the more waterlogged the tracks. Rain seemed to become so complete a part of nature that to end a day not soaked to the skin would have been unfamiliar and remarkable. And each day the wind grew stronger as if determined to hold us back.

We got as far as Launceston and then Stephen Wilky, who had taken a chill early, gave up and said he could travel no farther. We were again spending the night at Penheale. The Grenvilles suggested I might well stay a day or two more until the weather improved, but I said no, I would go on. So I left Wilky in their charge to follow at will and went on across the wild moors alone.

Such was the gale here that I could not make fair progress and so slept at Bodmin in a tiny tavern, while the storm howled round the shoulder of the hill and every thatch seemed about to lift off the roof. Next morning even Trudy was loth to start, but we were away soon after daybreak. My mind was pricked on by its own uncomfortable spurs.

Over the Goss Moors, at last into the shelter of the Ladock Valley, a bite to eat in Truro; the short day would soon be drawing in; but one was too near home now to halt at the Bonythons. Set in a cleft of the green hills, Penryn came quicker than expected. Sensing the end of it all, Trudy had quickened her step. Past the old mill and the sun was flaring over the hill.

The gate was open. That was the first thing wrong. Never in my lifetime open and unguarded.

The long chestnut avenue to the house was rutted deep with mud and water, as if more wagons or coaches than usual had been over it. The tents were still on the hill-side. The wind was breaking at last into lost eddies and vicious squalls that grew less frequent with every hour.

At the back entrance by the kitchens were three carts. Two of them were piled with furniture and cloths. I had no need to tether the mare, she was already walking towards the stables as I ran into the house. The first person was Meg.

"Maugan!" she said, forgetting herself. "Dear life, I'm that glad to see you!" And put her arms round my neck.

I kissed her on the mouth, sweet memories in spite of all. "Dear Meg. Is all well?"

"Well? All's ill. Dear life, tis a nightmare. Two days gone a sheriff's officer come and served an order—distraint or some such for a Mr Cosworth. There was none here to stay 'im, so in 'e come. Tis rumoured Mr Killigrew's in a debtors' prison and all London pressing for payment—is it true, Maugan? So afore cocklight yesterday a half-dozen bailiffs was here waving papers in their 'ands—bonds or some such and asking for payment."

"Oh, Meg. . . ."

"And none here to deny 'em. So in they come and begin seizing on this, that, and th' other as part of their debt. All yesterday and today they been carting things away. It's been like a war—men shouting and fighting. They even tore the curtains, pulling betwixt them!"

I went through the kitchens, past a couple of servants, into the great hall. Gone was the Pavia tapestry, the plush chairs on which Mr Killigrew and the special guests sat, the stools, the curtains, the fire-irons. Ash was scattered well away from the fire as if it had been blown about by the gale.

"Young Mr John Killigrew?"

"No sight of 'im."

"Where is Mrs Killigrew?"

"In her chamber, sick."

At the foot of the stairs, two men were carrying down a chest. One was a tall shabby man in black, the other a fox-faced fellow with a big wart on the side of his nose.

They headed towards me and could get no farther; the tall man grunted at me to move. I did not.

"By what right, gentlemen, d'you shift my father's furniture?"

They lowered the chest. "By what right? This no longer belongs to you nor to none of yours. Out of the way!"

"What's your name, man?"

"Who are you?"

"Maugan Killigrew. A son of John Killigrew."

The tall man wiped his forehead on his sleeve. "Oh, I've heard tell of you. Well, there's naught for you to do here. The law of England's took over, and that's ten years later 'n it should have. Your father's a bankrupt and that's all there's to it."

"What's your name?"

"Ratcliffe. He's Challenor. Money's been owing—"

"Where's your proof?"

Ratcliffe stared at me. "We shown it when we was admitted."

"I'll see it again."

"Here." Challenor came round the end of the chest and thrust a piece of paper at me. "See this. Here be your father's bond. Three hundred pounds. Due August '95! Not defeasanced! Not renewed! Nor no interest, neither! Two year it been owing since due and not a penny paid!"

"In time," I said, "you'll be paid in full. But not when you come like vultures—like carrion. What d'you hope to make out of it? A few score—"

"We'll make what we can, by God!" shouted Challenor.

"Get out," I said.

"By God, those days are over, young man, and don't you forget it! I mind the time when your rascally father—and his father!—would ride abroad—"

"Get out," I said.

"Oh, no you don't. We've the law on our side—"

I took out my short dagger and pointed it at Challenor's throat. He bumped back against the chest, slid round it.

"Here, none of that! If you—"

"Two minutes to be out of this house—both of you. If you're not, law or no law I'll let some of the wind out of you."

"You can't do this, Killigrew!" Ratcliffe said. "There's sheriff's officers and bailiffs, aye and justices too, will stay your nonsense—"

"Out of this house and out of these grounds before dark. That gives you ten minutes."

Ratcliffe opened his mouth to protest again, but I went at him with the dagger. He drew sharply back, the two men bumping together, then they turned and went out, leaving the chest at the foot of the stairs. I followed them. Meg was in the hall.

"Bring lights!" This bawled angrily at a couple of shadowy servants lurking in a doorway. Then to Meg: "Where's Job? And Bewse? And Dick?"

"Maugan, you can't rightly blame them. They're not schooled or—"

"Who talks of blame? Where *are* they?"

"In the stables."

I went out, across, kicked open a door. Dick was wiping Trudy, a half-dozen others stood round in dejection, shoulders hunched, dirty and unkempt. With various expressions they said my name. I cut them short.

"Listen. You'd stand by while these jackals rob us? Where's your pride—"

"Tis the law," said Jael Job. "We don't like to go 'gainst that. If a man be broken for debt—"

"But if I say different, you'd follow me, law or not?"

"Well, maybe. There's many a time we've set the rules aside—"

"Let's have these men out, then."

I turned and waited for them to follow me. Challenor and Ratcliffe were standing arguing by one of the carts.

"Unload that stuff."

In five minutes the furnishings were inside the house again.

"Bewse, and you Dick, see these men off our land. And shut the gate behind them."

The rest of us tramped through to the bottom of the stairs and then up. At the top a man was struggling with some bedding and a roll of sailcloth. Long Peter, encouraged now and ready for anything, snatched the cloth away from him and thrust him down the stairs so that he fell half the length. There were two more men at the end of the passage, just coming out of one of the bedrooms.

"Get them out!"

But these, instead of being debtors personally trying to collect their dues, were sheriff's officers and not to be intimidated. There was a short fight in the half dark, a bunch of candles wobbling and dripping from a sconce, grey half-illumined dusk falling through a casement, the rest shadow. In a while we had them pinioned, bruises and a little blood from knuckle and tooth.

"Get them out!"

"Stay. Is that you, Maugan? Yes, it is, I'd a feelin' you were home! But, lad, that's not sense, what you're doin' now."

The voice, the tall lean figure, the long black hair. . . . I was a child again knocking at an old mill door. Spittles of spite came into my mouth: some gland of fear had released them.

"I might have known you'd be here, Mistress Footmarker."

"Yes, well, I'm glad to see you, there's need of a man. This house is in dire distress. I told you years ago it would happen. There's evil like a cloud—"

"If there's evil you bring it nearer. Job, take those two men—"

"No, lad." She came along the passage and I noticed the servants break away as she passed. "You can't fight the law. Your father tried; look where it's landed him. This is not a—"

"You and your damned meddling! Who brought you here!"

Her narrow face was a mask between the long tresses, eyes darker than blue with a kindling anger; often now we seemed to act so on each other; there was no mean, either we were in sympathy or, as now, sparked like flint on tinder.

"As much right as you, lad! Your step-mother, Mrs Killigrew—"

"Oh, she's so dominated by you that. . . . Look, woman—"

"Listen." She put a hand on my arm and I shook it off. "*Listen!* What's wrong with you! Have ears to reason! Leave these men be, else you'll end in jail. Your grandmother wished to resist, to keep these men outside the palisades, but it can't be. I told her so, and Mrs Killigrew the same—"

"By God!" I said. "Now I see it. Not only do you predict the ruin of this house; you see to it personal! . . . Peter, take this woman. If she has a nag put her on it and see her off our land!"

Job and another man began to hustle the two bailiffs along the passage to the stairs. Long Peter was so tall he could not stand upright in this part of the house; he was a man almost without fear, but he hesitated about touching the woman. He licked his lips and glanced at Dick Stable and Penruddock, the others remaining.

Footmarker said: "Touch me and you'll grow worms in your bowels a yard long. Your eyes'll rot out and your tongue'll swell till it bursts your mouth."

Peter blinked and spat on the palms of his hands and made no other move.

She turned to me: "Maugan, you're blind with anger now and full of some spleen. All right, let us not have further words until this mood has passed. There's much to be done. Your grandmother—"

Perhaps in my own feelings was a microcosm of all that men feel when they burn witches: anger trying to hide fear. It was as if I had a sort of love for her turned inside out so that one yearned to destroy it. One yearned to tear out one's own beginnings as a frail human being. I grasped her by the shoulder. She shook me off; that old strange scent of hay; I grabbed her arm and turned it behind her; she clawed with her other hand at my face; scratches and blood beginning to drip; I twisted her arm and grasped the other.

As I pushed her struggling down the passage Mrs Killigrew came out.

"Maugan!" I rushed past her. "Maugan, leave her be, she's here because we *need* her!"

Down the stairs; she tried to kick but her feet were in soft shoes that did not hurt; I felt sick and cold, anger like disease, a dysentery of the mind.

"Damn you, Maugan! If you put me out this'll be the last of me; I'll—never come back again; never again; you'll regret this—it'll be on your soul all the rest of your life!"

We were down without falling. Meg at the bottom, shrinking against the wall. There was nothing *special* in this struggling woman different from any other; panting breath and heaving lungs and reluctant halting feet; she was still talking but the sentences were muttered and broken; I tried not to hear, still fearful of a curse.

In the hall and through it to the kitchens; out into the cobbled yard at the back; a lantern burned at the stable door; I released her with a final push; she nearly fell but caught the door.

"Get your horse or mule if you have one. If you're on foot take a pony. That'll be payment for what you may have done. Take it and go."

She leaned on the door looking at me. "I never thought to see this day. That's one thing I never did think to see."

Now that I was free of her I wanted to shiver.

"Take a pony," I said, "and go."

It was like assuming command of a part conquered fortress. The enemy had been driven out; now to re-organise the forces within.

Most of the curtains had gone, all the best furniture, even some of the beds. The house was like a cold echoing barn. Mrs Killigrew had been in bed with a return of the jaundice and had hardly realised the extent of the loss; she had in any case lacked the courage for open defiance. But she was angry with me for driving out Katherine Footmarker. This I had expected; the woman had grown to have an ascendancy over Dorothy Killigrew which amounted almost to a possession, and it was this more than anything else which I had felt to be dangerous in her continuing here. But what did startle me was to find that Footmarker had been openly treating my grandmother too.

So bad was Lady Killigrew's breathing now that only immobility enabled her to live at all. To move from one side of the bed to the other was sufficient to cause her to gasp and clutch at the air with her mouth. It was a terrible thing to watch, and almost more terrible was to see, trapped inescapably in this useless body, the same penetrating, acidulous mind I had known all my life. It had in no way been affected by illness or disease. It watched resentfully the people who moved round her bed ministering to her wants. Kate Penruddock, Parson Merther, Ida and Sarah Keast, none of them escaped.

When I went in she set on me with a torrent of invective. What business had I to command this house, a nameless bastard brought up here out of mistaken kindness? God, to what depths had the Killigrews and the Wolverstones come? When I said I was only too willing to give up any ordering of this house to John as soon as he arrived back, she said he could not come too soon for her. In the meantime how did I propose to keep her alive, now that I had driven out the one woman who could help?

The servants, of whom there were only fourteen left, rallied round me well and soon the place was cleared up, such furniture as was left made the best of, the gate at the palisade guarded. There was one other risk that had to be considered, for we could not fight an army.

The next morning I went up to the castle and asked to see Captain Alexander. He saw me in the gun room overlooking the harbour. Much had been changed since I was last here, it was like a general's tent in time of battle, with maps and charts on the walls.

"Captain Alexander, you may have heard that my father has stayed behind in London, having been arrested on a suit for debt. I have no doubt that his release will be arranged before long, but for the time being he cannot be here to help you in his position as governor of the castle. I thought I should tell you this."

"I obey orders here, Mr Killigrew. My orders have been to bring this castle to a state of preparedness. So the governorship has not concerned me greatly, my instructions having come from a higher authority. I don't think your father's private misfortunes are likely to concern us here."

"Debtors have attempted to ransack Arwenack. I have driven them out."

"That must be your own affair, Mr Killigrew."

"I am glad you see it in that light."

"Certainly. Unless I receive orders to the contrary."

Having got what I came for, there seemed no virtue in prolonging the interview. He was clearly waiting for me to go.

"Do you intend to spend the winter here, Captain Alexander? You and all the men?"

He shrugged. "That will be decided at a meeting next week."

"Held here?"

"Held here. Sir Nicholas Parker, Sir Ferdinando Gorges, and Paul Ivey, the fortifications expert, will confer here and decisions will then be made. It could perhaps be a convenience if you could accommodate them in your house. As you will appreciate, our quarters here are very full."

"I'll make arrangements."

As I walked back to the house I wondered if enough beds were left and whether we could find food. But the effort was worth making. Alexander was slightly more gracious when I left. His goodwill could be of value.

When she left her last words had not been curses. She had shouted after me as I went back into the house: "Shame on yourself! Shame on you, Maugan, for turning away your only friend! All your life you'll regret this day!"

When I got in I had been violently sick, as if vomiting up buried urges.

My only friend? That evening when the early dark had been upon the house for nearly two hours I sat and discussed the future with another friend who had already forgiven me for my high-handedness of yesterday.

Dorothy Killigrew said: "I am happy for you, Maugan. When she was here for that Christmas I thought her a sweet girl. Pretty and elegant and of a sunny temperament. How lucky for you it has turned out so. I do pray you will be happy."

"Thank you."

"You know I have come to love you as one of my own children, and I shall hope you write to me from time to time. This is a house to leave. I tremble to think what will become of us."

"I don't think father will stay in prison long. He has so many friends."

"Friends who have been alienated, Maugan. If the Queen has gone against him then there is little hope of an early release."

"John will soon be home."

Little Dorothy was grizzling, so her mother turned her over in her cradle.

"I pray we could all take more easily to Jane. She is very—very female, yet strangely unfeminine—without the graces. And hostile to her new relatives. Perhaps time will change her."

"She needs an heir."

Mrs Killigrew sighed. "I am with child again, Maugan. Your father, even in despair, has not abated his demands. With nine children living and four dead, this has at last become a burden on me. Perhaps in wealth and comfort it would not seem so great. But as we are now set, scarcely knowing how to feed ourselves, I am a prey to despondency. Even the consolation of my faith wears thin. . . ."

I patted her hand. "My dear, take heart. Perhaps this is the darkest hour." I could not explain to her by how much it might have been darker. . . . "All the same, I shall be uneasy at leaving you here."

"You must seek your own fortune. This is John's house now—he must redeem it as best he can."

I awoke in the dark of the night thinking that Katherine Foot-marker was in the room. Then that it was Sue. In some inexplicable and frightening way I could not for a time disentangle the two. They were one woman springing from one well of love and hate. It seemed to me that it was Sue I had thrust down the stairs and flung out of the house and that it was she who had said: "All your life you'll regret this day."

Then in asking her forgiveness I was mouthing again the terrible oaths of Seville. "I do solemnly declare that the Church of England is not a church but rather the synagogue of the Devil . . . and in her and all her opinions and ceremonies lies the soul's perdition; and I detest and abominate them. . . ."

I sat up in bed in that long narrow room, brushing my face to clear away the cobwebs of nightmare. Streaks of dawn were in the sky like a woman's grey hair. I got up and dressed and was downstairs by the time Dick Stable, yawning vastly, was raking over the ashes of the fire in the great hall. Dogs fawned about me as I ate breakfast. Soon after sunrise I was on my way to Helston.

I found her house after two inquiries; at the door a stupid servant met me. No, Mistress Reskymer was from home. Two days gone she had left in some haste, taking Florence and Jones with her. She had received a letter and had departed for Tolverne, the Arundells' home.

It was beginning to rain. Sometimes the weather by its persistence wears away courage and resolution. The nearest house was Truthall. I did not fancy dining with Henry Arundell. Sooner than ride home hungry and wet, it seemed good sense to go a little out of the way to be warm and fed.

At Godolphin, Lady Godolphin said Sir Francis was expected back within the hour. Had I come to see him on business, or was it the tragedy at Tolverne which had brought me?

"Oh, but I see you don't know. It has been a great sorrow to us. Jonathan died last week."

CHAPTER 7

HE had been taken with a sudden heart seizure. He was thirty-one. Over dinner we talked of how the tragedy would affect poor Gertrude, a widow at twenty, and Lady Arundell, bereft of her elder son, and Elizabeth, the Catholic, and Thomas, now heir to it all.

I did not speak of Sue, thinking they did not know her, and it was by chance that Lady Godolphin mentioned Mark Reskymer, the head of the family, whose seat was a few miles south of Truthall.

She said: "Oh, I'm *pleased* for you, Maugan. She is a pretty girl, and still so young. You are lucky to get her too, for she'll be a prosperous widow."

"Far from prosperous," I said. "Nearly all Mr Reskymer's estate was entailed."

Lady Godolphin said: "I think you are more fortunate than that, Maugan. It happens that Mark Reskymer mentioned to us that little was entailed. It meant, he said, that because of Philip Reskymer's late third marriage much of the property would go out of the family."

Sir Francis said: "I don't know how Gertrude will be left. The Tolverne Arundells are not a wealthy family, and Thomas must maintain the house."

I said: "It wasn't what I heard—about the Reskymers, I mean. Perhaps I have later news. Or perhaps you have."

"Yes. Yes of course. The proving of a will is always complicated. No doubt the lawyers will have their own say."

I could tell from the tone of Lady Godolphin's voice that she thought she had the right of it. The unease at the back of my mind was always finding some new food. I borrowed a fresh horse and left for Tolverne.

It was seven before we were safely over the ferry, and the night was then so dark that I led my horse up the steep overgrown slope to the house. I thought of Jonathan dancing with Gertrude at our Christmas festivities that happy year. I thought of Gertrude, flushed and happy, pretending to be Sue when I mistook her. I thought of Sue.

There were lights in the hall, none elsewhere. Their supper was late; I was in time for it; Lady Arundell and Elizabeth and Thomas and Gertrude and Sue and five other relatives whom I do not remember and never knew.

Human nature is such that it can stand but so much grief, and I imagine that the depths of unhappiness and sorrow had been plumbed by them all. For more than a week there had been no end to grieving. A new arrival broke the chrysalis of sorrow. Minds turned with relief to look outwards for a time. We talked of war and Mr Killigrew, and the Queen, and the distress in the country and of Jack Arundell of Trerice's betrothal to Mary Carey of Clovelly.

It was clear that Sue had told no one here of our engagement to marry. This was not perhaps surprising: coming to a bereaved household one does not immediately advertise one's own happiness. Her black slightly damp looking hair hung over the narrow lovely bones of temple and upper cheek, the eyes with their green-grey liquid bril-

liance moved reflectively from face to face as others spoke; she sat
a little in shadow, sad and rather vulnerable because of the sadness
about her, yet in perfect repose. When her eyes met mine, which was
seldom, they warmed and searched at the same time.

Through the talk Thomas ate apples, biting with strong white teeth
which lacked two middle ones, munching slowly; his face was broad
and flabby, yet within it like a hammer under a cloak was brute determination, power and stamina, things his elder brother had so sadly
lacked. Through the talk Gertrude, the young widow, watched and
listened, sometimes speaking a word or two, and then falling to stare
so fixedly at the candles that yellow flames burned in her eyes.

No one asked why I had come. At last I was able to speak with
Sue.

"Can we get away somewhere?"

"I'll go out in a moment."

We met in the sewing room. I kissed her face, the grey silk of her
dress, the lace at her throat.

One candle only in this room: it was behind the spinning wheel,
and the spokes of the wheel made bars of shadow on the ceiling. Our
own shadows were one, as soon we should be. We were a strange
amorphous shape on the wall.

She broke from me breathlessly. "Someone may come."

"Does it matter?"

"A week ago Jonathan was lying dead in the room above us."

I took a deep breath. "So be it . . . I'm as grieved as you. But
life in me—in us—is strong . . . to express it is no disrespect. Jonathan
would not begrudge us what he has lost, nor Gertrude if she knew."

"She will know, Maugan, I promise. But just a little time. . . ."
She fingered her black fringe away. "Tell me about London."

I spoke of the meeting with Sir Henry Killigrew and his view that,
though he wished me well, he could not at present offer me anything. I spoke of meeting Ralegh and his suggestion that I could go
back to Sherborne and take my bride with me.

"He suggests nothing more at the moment, but I'm entirely sure
that within twelve months he'll find a means to advance me. Let
everything be said against Sir Walter, Sue, and not his greatest op-
ponent could ever say he was unmindful of his friends."

"And Lord Henry Howard?"

"Oh, impossible. I could not work for such a man." I told her of the
interview. "In effect he offered less than Sir Walter. Not a secretary-
ship but some sort of an irregular employment for unknown purposes.
To write letters in Spanish. To convey other letters—though not, I
think, to Spain; to . . . I think he said to Scotland. It was all so veiled,

so indirect. I only know that I was asked to be a party to some conniving, though he wouldn't say in what direction that conniving was pointed."

"He was suggesting something dishonest?"

"I don't think so. It was hard to say. Clearly he was testing me, trying out the way I responded. . . . But even if his offer were better, I could not take it."

"Why?"

"He is Ralegh's bitterest enemy."

"Ralegh has many enemies. They are not all bad men because of it."

"Also he has some sort of contact with Spain that I dislike and distrust. He had heard of something—events—which had happened to me in Spain that no one, I thought, in England could know. It may not be a treasonable connection but it must be illicit."

"The Earl of Essex has his own informants all over Europe. It could well be so with Lord Henry and his cousins."

I got up, restlessly. "You should see him. He's surrounded by long-haired boys. I grant he has taste and learning, but they are so smeared over with a kind of personal corrosive that they seem to impair what they touch. . . ."

"What was the outcome of it all? Did you refuse what he offered?"

"It was easier just to come away. I'll just not write to him."

"He asked you to write?"

"If I was interested I was to write in January. There was no hurry, he said. I thought in the meantime he might try to find out more about me."

She was folding and refolding a pleat in her dress. After a time I said: "Don't you see how impossible it would have been, Sue? To have accepted any *position* under this man. Yet there was no position at all, only a promise of intermittent employment. What is more, there would not even be accommodation in his house. We should have to live in lodgings or a house of our own. What he would pay me would be useless, to maintain us in such a way."

"In that perhaps I could have helped."

"Do you mean you've inherited more than you thought?"

"What I have, little as it is, would maintain us a year. To be at the centre, at the heart of things, as you would be there, that would be the great advantage."

"This man is repulsive to me, Sue."

She got up. "Darling Maugan, are you sure that part of the dislike is not prejudice because you so admire Ralegh? Even before you met Lord Henry, were you not taking the other side?"

"It is not only that. Believe me."

"Then we are back at nothing, where we began?"

"Not at nothing, if we love each other."

She sighed.

"What is it?" I asked.

"You know I love you, Maugan. . . ."

"I—believe that you do."

"But life has made me practical. Love flourishes where man and wife flourish. If I say more of this now you'll think me mean and calculating—"

"No!"

"Which in a sense will be true. So let us leave it for the time. . . . You can stay a day or two?"

"Until John returns I'm needed at Arwenack. But I can come back. Sue, why is it not possible to take Sir Walter's offer? There's nothing equivocal about that—"

"And live with the servants?"

That stopped me. I looked at her. "I'm not *treated* as a menial. I eat with them. At nights I sit with them except when there is some exceptional guest. Lady Ralegh is a remarkable person; I know she would take to you. There's nothing truly menial about the position. . . . But even if there were. . . . Sir Walter stands at the Queen's right hand. A word from him can find me much greater preferment than I can ever get from the half-Catholic Howards—"

"And how long will he be at the Queen's right hand, Maugan? And how long will the Queen live, Maugan? Everything that he has and is comes from her. . . . In any case, as I have said before, Sir Walter and his friends live a strange life. There is no settled way for his followers, no stability; they for ever adventure in strange lands, or soldier in Ireland, or fight battles at sea. Look at those who have already died."

"There's no sureness in this world. All I want is to serve a man, someone not side-sexed, someone—"

She put her fingers on my lips and I stopped to kiss them. "Maugan we shall never see this the same. But it's stupid to quarrel. We must find a way. Let's sleep on it tonight."

"Sue, there was one other thing. Lord Henry had Henry Arundell's letter before him. From it, or in some way, he had gathered that Mr Arundell had hopes of marriage. I hope it was not marriage to you."

She smiled slightly. "Yes."

"He asked you to marry him? What did you say?"

"What could I say? No, of course."

"Oh, God, I am so deeply in love with you that the smallest danger looms like a cliff. . . . Did you tell him about me?"

"No. It was unnecessary. At present he entertains feelings of friendship for you. Let that go on as long as it can."

I kissed her again. "Little schemer."

She stared at me soberly.

"Yes, Maugan. Yes."

I stayed all the next day just to be in her company.

In the afternoon I had word alone with Thomas who had been out hawking with a half-dozen servants and came out from the stables breathing steam into the still December air.

"You know, do you, that I am thinking of betrothing Bridget Mohun of Hall?"

"I'd heard something of it."

"They're a good family, the Mohuns, no hysteria about them, well set with property, and Protestant of temperament. Bridget's a fine handsome girl. Good firm breasts and round thighs; I like plenty. Though God knows once on a time I'd have thrown it all away for that strip Suzanna Reskymer. Bridget's got the figure and the money too. Her father came in for much of the property forfeited by these recusants."

"I'm happy for you."

He stared at me. "I doubt if you'd ever be happy for me in any *good* fortune. . . . However we won't press that. I used to think you had eyes for Suzanna yourself in the old days. D'you still fancy her?"

"She's almost too recently a widow for the thought to have arisen."

"Well, you'd be lucky if you got her now. I must say I've given her one or two backward glances myself. She's not as well found as Bridget but she's pretty warm with all these holdings in west Cornwall and on the Devon border."

"Most of the property is entailed."

"Who told you that?"

"She did."

"Ah, well, that's a little female delicacy; take it with a pinch of salt. I think from the sound of it you've lost her, Maugan. If you want her, I hope you have."

One of the grooms came to take the hooded hawk from his wrist.

"I own all this now," Thomas said. "I told you I should; Jonathan never had the makings of an old man. I told you there was a curse on us. But by God it's missed me, and I'm going to step away from under it so soon as ever I can. Within five years the Arundells'll be out of Tolverne even if I have to burn it down!"

"And your family?"

"Gertrude will marry again, no doubt of it; Jonathan has not squeezed all the juice out of her, and her father has money and connections. Elizabeth. . . . I would not be astonished if she went to France or Italy and entered a convent. As for my mother—she can go back and live at Godolphin. Or no doubt if she chooses we can find room for her when I found my own line. . . . But not these other old wrecks who drift in and out of the house, hangers-on: aunts and cousins and bastards and the like."

I was no longer simple enough to take up this insult.

We went in. "What's it *like* at Arwenack these days?" he asked, peering at me with his broad white grin. "Not quite the usual robber's lair? Your father has had his wings clipped at last. Are you another doomed house?"

I took my lead from Sue that day and talked of other things. She talked of the rebuilding of Paul Church, of Philip's sister, Amelia, who had invited her to stay with her in Pancras near London, of her mother who was not happy in her second marriage.

I was to leave the following morning at ten. We broke our fast while light was still pushing through the thick spears of the cypress trees. The day was fine with a wintry sunlight, and after I had been to see that my horse was ready I walked back to the house and met Sue coming out to look for me. We walked down to the river.

Thus in silence until we came out on the small stone quay where I and the Killigrew children had tied up that day nearly six years ago when this had all begun. I brushed soil off the stone bench and we sat on it looking out over the river. She was wearing a violet coloured cloak with the hood thrown back.

She said: "Maugan. . . ."

"Yes?"

"You truly believe that I love you?"

"It's a never ceasing joy to realise it."

"Then that gives me a right—a different right from anyone else—to ask favours of you?"

"Yes."

"I have thought so much of what you told me of London. If we are to be married in February, then somehow our lives—at least to begin—must be based on one of those interviews."

"There might be other ways."

"Not well. You could stay at Arwenack, but that is hardly feasible if we married. Henry Arundell might find some employment for you, but the stewardship is gone, and knowing how he feels about me I can hardly ask him more favours for you."

"No, I grant that. Then—"

"If we go to London without any prospect or recommendation I think we should quickly fail. So that leaves Sir Walter's offer and Lord Henry's."

"If you put it that way."

"How else can I put it? And here is the problem. You want to accept Sir Walter's offer—which I see as menial and unworthy of your gifts. I want you to accept Lord Henry's, which you greatly despise."

I stared at her. "You really wish me to work for such a man?"

"I want you to accept his offer. He must have taken a very great liking to you or he would not have made it. I've heard he is a shrewd judge of character. There are not lacking likely young men anxious to be taken up by the most powerful family in England. Must one's *personal* feeling come into this? Must you necessarily admire whom you serve?"

"Not admire. But surely respect, else one loses one's *self* respect. Henry Howard is a dangerous man. No good could come of being at his beck and call."

"Try it and see. Such a steadfast person as you is hardly likely to be contaminated in a matter of months. You would come to know many men—other opportunities would arise."

I looked out over the river, which was a deep oily green. The mass of trees on both banks grew so low that at high tide many of the branches dipped in the water. The undergrowth was dense and few men penetrated it.

"I could not, Sue. You ask me not to go back to Ralegh. Well, I can agree to that if you're set against it. I can agree not to follow Ralegh. But I cannot go from him to one of his bitterest enemies. That would be—a betrayal."

She got up. "Have we not really got to the truth of it now, Maugan? Isn't that really why you will not work for Henry Howard? Ralegh has you under a spell and you cannot or will not break away."

I wondered at the tone of her voice; there was such feeling in it.

"For you I'll break away from Ralegh; I've said so; but I will not be an instrument for attacking him."

"Who says he'll be attacked? And if attacked, who says the Howards will do it? What of Essex? What of Cecil? What of a hundred others? Don't you know how he's thought of in London and at Court? He's the best hated man in England."

"Yet among his own people he excites hero worship."

"Which is what has happened to you!"

"Oh, no. I don't see him as a hero. . . . He has many faults—but also a greatness. I would not follow him blindly. But for me he stands —above other men."

The sun was obscured by a cloud shaped like a dog. The water darkened and a breeze moved over it, ruffling the surface.

"Do you mean you will serve no other but him?"

"Of *course* not. It is only Henry Howard I'll not serve."

"Not even for me?"

"I don't believe you will ask me."

"I have asked you."

"Then I must say no."

CHAPTER 8

ALL the way home I puzzled over Sue's hostility towards Ralegh. It exceeded logic, and in her was therefore to be wondered at. All the rest was reasonable enough, no doubt, if looked on from her point of view. She saw the Howards as the vastly influential family that they were, Sir Walter as an upstart who sooner or later might come to no good. But I could not understand the tone of her voice. *That* was not logic.

There had been no reconciliation between us before I left, nor any promise of a further meeting. There must be some compromise which could be reached, but just at present we were both too heated to give way.

The gate was well guarded today. Long Peter gave me the news that John and his bride were home.

I had it out with them in the big withdrawing chamber that night.

The room was without carpet; the good chairs had gone and been replaced by stools from the kitchens. The table remained because it was so heavy. Candles burned in cheap sticks, a fire flickered with green logs.

Young Jane Killigrew occupied the one good chair and warmed her hands at the fire. She wore a carnation coloured dress of figured velvet, with over it a cloak of fine watered chamlet. It had cost a deal of money. Her jet-black hair hung like curtains beside a stage, and the stage was a milk-white face coloured with two dabs of red ochre, small fierce eyes, a precise well-shaped mouth, all attention as I talked.

"Let's not waste time in recrimination. I was back in time to save something, but the house is as you see it. In another day they'd have been in Mrs Killigrew's and Lady Killigrew's bedrooms. These and four others—which Meg Stable had the forethought to lock—were the only rooms untouched. Even the old aunts have lost some things. They snatched a bracelet from Miss Wolverstone's wrist and took Aunt Mary's clock and outdoor shoes."

"A bag of mine is gone," said Jane. "It contained a penknife, a bodkin, and my seal. The servants must be whipped for ever permitting it."

"The servants have more respect for the law than we have. They couldn't interfere. What right had I to? Only the right of a sword."

"And a temper," said Jane. "One of these days it will lead you into trouble, brother-in-law."

"There'll be trouble now unless we move to prevent it."

"How?" said John.

"Why should we move to prevent your trouble, brother-in-law?"

"Because it is yours too, sister-in-law. Don't think I'm bearing the burden of this house further than I need. It's John's—and yours. So long as my father is in prison John is master of this house, and the privilege bears the responsibilities along with it. John—"

"Yes, Maugan, I know," he said irritably. "But there's little I can do beyond what you have done—"

"There's something your wife can do."

"Ah," said Jane. "I thought brother-in-law might soon come to that."

"It can't be avoided. Examine the situation for yourself."

John got up and sat on the edge of the table. Even so short a time of marriage had greatly matured him, but it had not given him resilience. "What do you want us to do?"

"Well, if we do nothing the creditors will come back. I shall be in the greatest trouble for putting them out the first time; but don't consider that. Consider only that what is left in the house will be taken, our fields and barns stripped. Expect no quarter from any of them for your father gave none when he had the whip hand. All will go, sister-in-law. You may be able to defend your own gowns and jewels, but I wouldn't rely on it. We are fortunate to have been given this breathing space of a few days."

"Well," said Jane. "What do you want me to do?"

"It may not be too late to buy them off."

"I doubt it."

"Most creditors will withhold from snatching goods worth a tenth of their debt if they are offered cash of a value of a fifth with some promise of later payment."

"And what do you suppose this will cost?"

"Perhaps a thousand pounds."

Jane watched me with narrowed, concentrated eyes. Then she laughed once, harshly, and got up to kick at a log. "You must be a fool, brother-in-law."

"Well, that's as you think. You might stave off the most importunate with eight hundred."

"I haven't eight hundred shillings."

"Your father has. It's yours in a year or two."

"Damn the logs: why don't they split 'em! We always have 'em split: it gives a face for the fire to eat at. . . . My father will not waste my dowry on salvaging the debts of old men who should have known better."

"I would not offer comment on that. Except to say, he must have had some notion of John Killigrew's debts when he contracted the marriage. After all, he traded—did he not—an ancient name for a newer name with gold to it."

"That is insolence, brother-in-law. Offensive insolence."

"Well, express it how you will, that's what it adds up to. However, the money we are considering now is not to salvage your father-in-law from prison. It is to keep your own home with some sticks of furniture in it and food and wine in the kitchen. If you begrudge that then you must let the creditors rampage and learn to live in the loft over the barn."

"Your voice spills as much contempt as fermenting beer in a cask." She picked up her pipe from the table beside the fireplace and began to fill it from a linen bag. "I don't know. I will have to consider the matter. After all. . . ."

"After all what?" said John.

"These debtors have no rights over our personal property, yours and mine. And since the only property I have here is personal I should lose nothing. Bucklan and Skinner would stand guard and he would be a bold man who passed them."

"My mother is likely to be stripped of everything."

"And she is pregnant again," I said.

A twitch of distaste went over Jane's face; almost the first true emotion I had seen there this evening. She stared down at the pipe, her big fingers turning it round and round.

"And you expect my father to protect ten Killigrews for the sake of cushioning me? It's a notion he is not likely to be delighted with."

"It's a notion I think you should put to him."

She glanced at John. "And you, husband?"

He shrugged. "You know that I would like it."

I said: "To send a message to your father and back will take the better part of two weeks. We're unlikely to be undisturbed that long. Is there any money you have which would keep these men at bay until then?"

"D'you think I have a gold mine in my pocket? Or what do you think?"

"That a boat is being built for you in Penryn. That you may have resources we know nothing of."

It was a remark made at random, without any preknowledge, so I was surprised to see her look at me with a darting suspicion. "I've some small money of my own, fellow. Not enough to satisfy you or these creditors. . . . Very well, I will write to my father."

She turned the bole of the pipe over towards a candle flame and drew at the stem; she moved back as the pipe caught, inhaled, and let a column of smoke escape from pursed lips. "If I renew some of these miserable bills it will be on condition that I have more to say in the ordering of this house."

John said in a controlled voice: "This is not a market where bargains are struck. There have been too many such already."

"Well, this is another, whether or no. First of all, I want a half of these mongrel curs destroyed. They breed and interbreed and stink out the house. . . . Then I want a different system of feeding in the hall, so that we no longer have the servants slopping porridge into their own mouths while pretending to wait on us. . . . And I want your grandmother out of her bedroom, which is the only one with space to live and windows looking two ways. . . . And I want the children to dine at another hour so that one's ears are not assaulted with the whine of babies and the chatter of others who should long ago have been taught silence. . . . And I want Parson Merther's endless prayers cut by the half. . . . And I want. . . ." She paused and looked at the bole of her pipe to see that it was glowing. "But you see . . . they are but modest demands."

I waited for John to speak. He had slid off the corner of the table and was picking at some grease which had fallen from a candle. "I cannot turn my grandmother out of her room."

"Give her ours. That will be a sensible exchange."

"She—she is near death. If we waited, it's unlikely that we should have long to wait."

"I understand she had been near death for five years. Surely her breathing will develop a worse turn if the debt collectors burst in and carry away her handsome rugs." Jane smiled at me. "This is real tobacco, not woundwort. Now that I am out of Papa's hands I have money enough at least for that."

"They were talking in London," I said, "of a man who smoked so much that after his death he was opened, and his lungs and veins were covered with soot like a chimney."

John was walking up and down. "Jane, please consider; it would be the mortal insult you would offer to an old lady. She didn't even give up that room to my mother. She must have used it for fifty years."

"Well, have it as you please. I will not help without some satisfaction from the help. Really, John, you cannot expect me to."

I said: "She who pays the piper calls the tune."

"Yes, brother-in-law. I'm happy you agree."

"I did not say I agreed. I'm only thankful that there are some among us who do not have to dance."

Often it was hard to tell whether little Jane Killigrew was smiling or whether she was baring her teeth.

On Friday the three distinguished visitors arrived with an escort of servants: Sir Nicholas Parker, a handsome man in his forties; Sir Ferdinando Gorges, just turned thirty, tall and full-coloured with a west-country voice reminiscent of Ralegh's; Paul Ivey, spectacled, narrow shouldered. The first two men were distinguished soldiers, Sir Nicholas having been master of ordnance for the forces in France, Sir Ferdinando captain and keeper of the castle and fort at Plymouth.

While we were supping I saw Jane eyeing Sir Nicholas Parker appreciatively. More than once when he spoke her metallic little laugh rang out, and before the end of the meal his deference to her was marked with a cynical regard. Henry Knyvett had come over from Rosemerryn, but he had already drunk much when he arrived; his long, loose-jointed, knock-kneed figure, the skull cap over the long grey hair, the increasing deafness, were no help to any party, and the task of entertaining the three guests fell on John and on me.

It was Gorges's ship *Maybird* which had narrowly escaped capture when *Peter of Anchusen* was lost, and he took a great interest in my stay in Spanish prisons, for at the age of twenty-one he had himself been captured by one of the ships of the First Armada and had spent a year in captivity before being ransomed. A relative of Ralegh's and as passionately interested in the idea of founding settlements overseas, he differed as to method—being an advocate of a feudal type of rule in a colony, as against Ralegh's belief in the equality of all men. Early on he had parted company from Sir Walter and chosen to follow Essex.

Before we left the table Sir Nicholas Parker fumbled in his cloak, which he had worn all through supper because of the draughts, and took out a sheet of parchment.

"This is something to your interest. It's an order from the Privy Council which I'm commanded to deliver you." He passed it to me.

The order appointed Sir Nicholas Parker governor and captain of Pendennis Castle in succession to J. Killigrew. Further, all J. Killigrew's personal possessions and habiliment, if any, were to be removed from the castle and taken into his house of Arwenack, and thenceforward neither he nor his representatives were to have access to the castle or its defences.

When I had read it I passed it to John, who by right should have had it first. He read it slowly, with Jane frowning over his shoulder and trying to spell out the words. When he had done he got up and handed the parchment back across the table.

"You come on no friendly mission, Sir Nicholas."

"I come as a servant of the Crown. I obey orders, Mr Killigrew."

"Then we must do the same." He bowed but continued to stand. The other men one by one had to stand also, Sir Nicholas Parker the last, and the supper broke up icily.

The next morning John and I and Carminow and Foster went up to the castle to receive from the officer such possessions as Mr Killigrew had left and we could lay claim to. Paul Ivey was already at work, spectacled and earnest, taking measurements and levels. Soon teams of horses and gangs of men would be at work tearing up the rocks and the trees and putting into effect his designs for reconstruction. We walked back in silence, each one of us perhaps reflecting on the end of an era—nearly sixty years of Killigrew governance. *Sic transit*. . . .

I went in to Truro to collect a debt that my father had told me was owing from Chudleigh Michell's brother. On the way, out of curiosity, I passed Katherine Footmarker's cottage and was startled to see it no longer there, instead a black patch on the grass, the two trees burned half way up their gnarled trunks. John Michell said:

"She was drove out in September. Folk thought she had an evil eye. She went west, towards Penryn. Then two weeks since she come back. . . . When twas spread about, this news, there was nasty feeling in the town. A score of men and women went for her wi' sticks and stones. She was just away in time, black dog an' all. She must have been hit but she outdistanced 'em. They set fire to the house, thinking twas the safest way of securing themselves against ill."

I licked my lips. "Which way did she go this time?"

"She was seen in St Erme, heading east. I reckon she've left for

good, and that's as it should be. I haven't the strong feelings Chudleigh
has for such as she, but there's much palsy and scrofula about, and
who knows where it d' come from."

Before I left Truro I called on another old woman whom Footmarker
had named as a friend. The woman could tell me little, except that
Footmarker had often spoken of a niece in Bristol. No doubt she
was now making for Bristol. But it was a bad time of year.

The river at Truro is so forked that except by a great detour there
is no way to Tolverne but by crossing the ferry. . . .

Sue was with Lady Arundell when I arrived. It took me half an
hour to get her alone. Then wisely I did not try to take her in my
arms but sat talking quietly, telling her of what had passed since we
last met.

I could feel her restraint going. In another ten minutes we were
just as close as we had ever been. I told her about Katherine Footmarker; for there was a sense of guilt and disarray in my emotions
now. What seemed a justifiable act in expelling her from the house
had become magnified and out of shape.

Presently a long silence fell. It would have been restful for me if
I had not felt something still tense in her manner.

"Maugan, I have some news for you."

"Tell me."

"You know I have been invited to go and stay with Philip's sister
near London. I've decided to accept."

"You mentioned it. It will be a good experience. But will you be
away long?"

"It rather depends on you."

"Then let it be as short as possible."

"But I thought you might come to London in January too. . . . We
could—if we wanted—be married there."

"Oh, my dear, *gladly!* If that's your news. . . . We seem to have
been separated for a lifetime—"

"No, that's not my news. But perhaps I need not ever tell it you.
Maugan, what I plan is that I shall stay with Amelia Reskymer. I
could have the banns called in that parish. If you—if you felt you
could take the position Henry Howard offers you I could advance
you sufficient money to set up in some small house, and we could
be married in middle February. It might be necessary later in the
year to return here to settle up Philip's estate, but we could look
on London as our permanent home."

It was queer that one came to her full of determination to sweep away all petty divisions. But the nature of our love seemed to emphasise it, as the sun will a chasm.

"Darling Sue, I know how you feel. But let me put another suggestion. Have you enough money to maintain us for six months?"

"Without your earning? Perhaps."

"Lady Godolphin told me that Philip had left you very substantial property."

She fingered back her black fringe. "I've told you. Almost all was entailed."

"Lady Godolphin said Mr Mark Reskymer was complaining that it was not."

"Mark would always complain, even if one cottage went out of the family. But do you prefer to believe Lady Godolphin's word to mine?"

I met a gaze suddenly glinting. "Of course not. In any case whatever you have is yours to do with as you will. My suggestion is that if you could support us for six months without consuming all the money you have, it would give me an opportunity to look about before committing myself."

She smiled. "You would have committed yourself in February by marrying me."

"I commit myself only to marrying the woman I love. Not to serving a man I despise."

"Would not one compensate you for the other?"

"To marry you I'd scavenge in the waste-bins of Bedlam. And be happy to do it. I only ask that our first months of marriage should not be—be tainted by a feeling that I have had to—to compromise, to counterfeit. . . . It's a feeling of buying what is most precious with what is debased."

I got up, angry again, part with her, part with myself. In the middle of speaking I had been seized with the realisation of all the submissions I had made in Spain merely to stay alive. Now I was straining at this less important one. Fundamentally, what had I got against Lord Henry Howard? What was the objection except sheer obstinacy? He was intelligent, able, subtle, artistic. Was it my repugnance which was really counterfeit?

Yet the earlier compromises I had made in Spain, instead of making this more easy, got in the way of it, hurting and tormenting and pushing me towards a defensive anger. And *was* this one less important? Before I had been prepared to bargain with the enemy. It was much harder to bargain with the girl I loved.

She had stood up too.

I said: "What was this news you had for me?"

"You'll not like it, Maugan. Thomas has asked me to marry him."

This window looked over the back of the house, and in the yard outside a servant was splitting logs with a beetle and a wedge. It was a monotonous but irregular sound and hollow, like a spade on a coffin.

"And you said?"

"I said I would give him my answer in January."

"You said—you told him nothing about us?"

"Not yet."

"Why not?"

"It seemed better. There was no hurry."

"Better? Better for whom? . . . Sue, this confounds me. I—I. . . ."

"I'm sorry."

The room had become short of air. "Thomas . . . the man you have always—avoided, disliked. This doesn't make sense. He's almost committed to Bridget Mohun."

"He'll betroth her next month if I refuse him."

"*If* you refuse him? God in Heaven! Sue, look at me: what are you saying? What are you doing to me?"

But she kept her head averted. "I thought first I should not tell you. But then. . . ."

"Sue, do you love me?"

"You know I do."

"But this—you must mean something *else* by love than I do. . . . Do you mean you haven't yet decided anything? That all this talk of. . . ."

"No, I mean it all, but I'll not go into marriage with you, Maugan, unless you can offer me some security, some hope of advancement. I've told you often before that my life at home has left me with some moral scar. The penury, the anxiety, the drudgery, the hand-to-mouth living, the illnesses. . . . All these have made me resolve. . . . My life with Philip, instead of making me bolder, has made me more afraid. Sometimes I think I'm not the right wife for you. You need someone with greater strength of purpose, who'll not shrink from hardship or—"

"I need you. No one else."

"You need me because you love me. It does not follow that my temperament is right for yours. Or my character—"

"Sue, I can't understand this. I'm sorry. I thought you hated Thomas!"

"I never *hated* him. He has become a more mature person of late. I don't love him—"

"But you'd marry him?"

"How many marriages are based on love? Do they all fail? I am under some pressure. . . ."

"*Pressure!* What in God's name do you mean by that?"

"Perhaps it's the wrong word. Mark Reskymer has tried to persuade me to it—because the Reskymers and the Arundells have been linked once before, and the property would stay within the family. And of course, though I don't love Thomas, I'm bound by ties of affection to Elizabeth and Gertrude, and also to Lady Arundell. This for long has been my second home. I know it and love it."

"And you would trade that for a marriage with someone. . . ." I shook my head to try to clear it. "Does Lady Arundell know of this?"

"Not yet."

"You said years ago that she'd never allow Thomas to marry you because you were penniless. I suppose that no longer follows."

"Of course I'd be a less good match for him than Bridget Mohun. But we're both older now. She could not stop Thomas if he wanted to marry me. I don't think she would wish to."

"So what is your price? What are your terms?"

I stared at her with a sheer hostility that it was impossible to hide. For the first time she flushed.

"Well," she said, "now you see me as I am. Last time you were here you called me a schemer and I did not deny it. I scheme for everything—for my comfort, my happiness—and yours."

"Mine!"

"Yes, for it's better to break with me now than to leave this discovery until too late. I'm not a monster as you clearly think; but I am— logical . . . and determined. In all things I weigh one thing against another and then decide. Even in marriage. Even in love. If that revolts you—as it clearly does—then it is better to leave me and go."

My fist kept clenching and unclenching until it hurt.

"What is your—price?"

"Do you mean on what conditions will I agree to marry you? But do you still want me to?" Tears were glinting in her eyes.

"At least permit me to know the terms."

"You make it sound at its worst. . . . I'll marry you, Maugan, if you undertake to accept employment with Lord Henry Howard for at least one year and at the end of that time allow me to decide if it shall be for a second."

"Anything else?"

"Nothing else."

"Are you not better advised to play safe with an Arundell?"

"Yes. But I'll take that chance."

"The eldest son of the house now. He's not rich, I know, but his father was knighted. He may well be. And you have a better home than I could ever provide."

"Who knows what you can yet provide?"

"Some day possibly you'll be Lady Arundell. Better than a marriage to a base son of the Killigrews, who as a family are in any event bankrupt and destitute. You must be logical enough to realise you'd be ill-advised even to consider me."

She blinked away the tears on her lashes. "But there *is* logic in considering you, Maugan. First, I *want* to marry *you*, not Thomas. There is logic in considering one's own wishes. . . . Second, I believe that if you have the opportunity you will travel farther than he will."

In the silence I licked my lips. "Oh, Sue, I came to this meeting in such joy and hope. Now there's a taste to it all that makes me want to retch."

She turned away. "If that's how you feel, I can say nothing more."

"What more *can* you say?"

"Perhaps I can say, don't decide now. Especially if it's—against me. Think it over. Go away, spend Christmas at Arwenack, come and tell me before I leave for London. It will not be until after Twelfth Night."

The man outside had loaded a wheelbarrrow with the split wood and was wheeling it towards the shed. A sleek grey boarhound came to lick at his heels and he impatiently kicked it away; but in so doing he upset his barrow so that half the wood rolled on the cobbles. Was there some wry metaphor in this for me?

Sue had picked up an old doll with a grey dusty face and was turning it over, smoothing out the crumpled musty skirt. I stared at her unbelieving. I felt like one of the men I had stabbed at Cadiz— surprised, incredulous. Was this *his* warm blood?

Whatever I did or said now, my relationship with Sue would never be the same again.

She looked up through her lashes. "You have no further use for me?"

"No. Not that."

"Will you think it over, Maugan? Think if it is so *much* that I ask."

"Not that." What we had disputed over seemed small and unimportant now. What she threatened, the fact that she was *prepared* to threaten, cast an immense shadow over all else.

"You will think it over?"

"I'll think it over," I said.

Before I left next morning I had agreed to her terms. But I had made one condition of my own. If I agreed, we were to be married by early February, no later.

I no longer trusted her to keep the bargain.

CHAPTER 9

I TOLD Dorothy Killigrew about Katherine Footmarker, and she shed a tear at the thought of not ever seeing her again. She had never looked on Footmarker as a witch but only as a friend gifted in healing. She had never feared her as stronger characters had feared her. She felt for her only the attraction I felt, untainted by the superstitious dread that in my case went with it.

In this new century of which I have now seen too much, with its rabid laws against witchcraft since the Stuarts came, and thousands— at the very least a thousand persons every year—burned, drowned or hanged on the flimsiest of suspicions, Dorothy Killigrew's tolerance towards Katherine Footmarker stands out like a harbour light in a storm.

While I had been away the transfer of authority over the castle had been completed and the three men had moved from the house. Captain Alexander remained the serving officer under Sir Nicholas Parker, but a hundred more of the troops were sent back to Plymouth. Ratcliffe and Challenor had returned together with two sheriff's officers, determined to force an entry; but Jane had seen them and had paid them something to arrange for a forbearance of the bills. Where she had found the money no one knew—least of all her husband—but it had saved the day. Her threat of rearranging the household still hung over us.

Christmas Day passed misty and damp. Most of each day and night, under the ordinary businesses of living and sleeping, I thought of Sue. Sometimes I persuaded myself that her threat had been an idle one, that she had used it out of a mistaken determination to help me, yet with no intention of ever carrying it through. At others, I weighed the alternatives as she might weigh them and saw that if it were not that she preferred me—if it could be put no higher than that—Thomas Arundell was likely to be an easy winner. Then, suddenly coming out in a sweat, I would want to ride to Tolverne right away to be sure she would still have me.

I pondered much on her character, which had opened new petals—

or was it thorns?—to me since our last meeting. One thing was quite
clear however much she might deny it: Philip Reskymer had left her
a wealthy woman. Though Thomas might prefer to marry Susanna
Reskymer, he would never have considered throwing away an
alliance with the powerful Mohuns for a penniless widow. Sue had
been confident too that Lady Arundell would raise no great objection.

Why then had she repeatedly lied to me? Because she wanted
still to have the excuses of poverty for marrying Thomas? Because she
could not allow me to feel independent of money lest I put up an even
greater resistance to accepting the offer of Lord Henry Howard?

What was behind her insistence on my taking this employment?
A chance connection with the family endorsed by childhood memories? The singleness of mind of a person far distant from London
and knowing only one important name, having only one recommendation? An obsession with security, a determination to build from a
known foundation?

Perhaps I was reading too much calculation into what she thought
and did. Perhaps instinct and feminine illogicality warred with her
cool objective brain so that, seeking her reasons from the outside, one
over simplified them, seeing them as single lines where they should
be as complex as a Hariot equation.

Yet, whatever motives were sought or excuses found, she emerged
as a formidable character, intent with the sweet reasonableness of an
unyielding determination on moulding her own life as she chose and—
if I consented—moulding mine with it. She loved me—after some
fashion—she had confidence in my abilities, she believed in me, and
was willing to link her life with mine at a price. She was willing to
trade her body, which I had possessed once and therefore could desire
the more, for my compliance in occupation and direction. Sometimes
I wondered if the fierce little animal my step-brother had married
was in fact less formidable for being so much more obvious.

On St Stephen's Day Sir Ferdinando Gorges came down and over
supper began to talk about Ralegh and the one brilliant action of the
otherwise futile Azores voyage. Landing at Fayal with two hundred
and fifty men under a murderous fire from twice that number of
Spaniards, he had led an attack personally through the surf and
captured the beach, then when his men held back from attempting
the heavily defended fortress town, he had led the way staff in hand
and wearing no armour but his gorget. Accompanied by one officer
and followed by only ten men, he had limped without haste a mile
up the rocky slope, while bullets tore his clothing, the other officer
was wounded, and two men lost their heads. When he reached the

fort the rest of his troops seeing him still alive took heart and followed, and in an hour the town was taken.

I had been quite unable to understand Sue's animosity towards Sir Walter; but in the light of her ultimatum certain suspicions began to take root while Gorges talked. Sir Walter was the only person who competed with her in my deepest admiration—and in influence. It did not matter that the competition should be of a different kind. She wanted a clear field.

The next morning I received a letter from her brought down the river by a fisherman. It said:

My love,

You have promised to marry me, on my terms, but I know think harshly of me for it.

I have never claimed to be a good person or an admirable one, and if you have thought me so it has grown out of the goodness of your own thoughts. So I will still release you if you wish.

But remember this, Maugan: I want only your welfare; I love only you, and if we marry I will be faithful to you and a true wife until death us do part.

Susanna.

That day, in a revulsion of feeling, I wrote to Lord Henry Howard telling him I would be happy to accept the employment he had so graciously offered, and I would be in London by mid-January, when I hoped I might have the honour of waiting upon him.

I remained his humble and obedient servant, Maugan Killigrew.

Thanks to Gorges I was able to send the letter in the military bag. I also wrote to Sue telling her what I had done.

Dorothy Killigrew, given the information that I would be leaving in early January to marry Sue in London, said would I escort my sister Odelia as far as Totnes when I left?

"She is the last of the older children, Maugan, and it is hardly right that she should be left here at this time; the rest are all so young that they will grow up together and not notice the change. At Totnes your father's sister, Lady Billingsley, has offered to take her. It will be good for her to get away."

At nights I woke and thought of Sue in the same house as Thomas. Not that she was in any physical danger from him—I realised now how capable she was of caring for herself—but the material temptation was there. How long would she allow her head to be swayed by her heart?

. . . Yet at a price she was still faithful to me. All through she had been, after her own fashion. If I took her down off the pedestal on which my idealism had placed her, and saw her as a human being, fallible and errant, could I not learn to be grateful for this fidelity? By how much did I deserve more?

On Innocents' Day two more debtors arrived and were again bought off by Jane Killigrew. Afterwards she said to me: "You will be seeing your father at Westminster?"

"I think so."

"Then let me warn you, brother-in-law. I am paying some money here to buy my own and John's convenience. Let it not be supposed by you or your father or any of your ilk that I'm proposing to meet the generality of his debts. I am giving it out to his creditors here that he has been seized by his London creditors and will never return to these parts to the end of his days. So far it had served. But if your father lets it be known there is money to be had down here, I swear to you he will kill the goose that lays even this small egg for him."

"I'll not tell him."

"In the meantime my man Bucklan has been going through the details of John's estate here—"

"Of Mr Killigrew's estate, you mean."

"Yes, well, but prisons are not long-lived places . . . there is, it seems, in spite of your father's extravagances about one thousand pounds a year left to this estate. It will be necessary for him to give John a warrant of attorney, which he should have done before he went to London. Will you see to that."

"I'll see that it is put to him."

"Be sure he looks at it in the proper light. He can never be clear of debt, but many of his debts will die with him. If his children are not to starve in the gutter the little money coming in to him must be conserved in some way and not altogether thrown after the rest."

"I'll not quarrel with that. But would you do me a favour, Jane?"

She raised pencilled eyebrows. "What could you want from me?"

"I learn that your demand for Lady Killigrew's bedroom is to be delayed a week or two. May I ask that your—reduction in the number of our dogs be also left until after I'm gone?"

"You have a weak stomach? I should never have guessed it."

"Oh, I agree that the house is over-run. But most of the dogs I know by name and I'd prefer not to see old friends slaughtered."

"Not slaughtered; I think to put them in the harbour and see if they can swim to St Mawes."

She had turned the curtains of her hair to me, so that now I could see little of her face.

"Perhaps you would like to do that with the children also."

She laughed gently. "What a monster you think me, brother-in-law. . . ."

"In jest of course."

She nodded. "Naturally. In jest. But it would be pleasant to live with a man who has no illusions—even in jest."

I said: "There's always someone for whom we are blind."

That night Lady Killigrew struggled miraculously down to supper. The occasion was the visit of Hannibal Vivian from St Mawes Castle. He still remained in control there and had come over uneasily to consult with Sir Nicholas Parker on the new arming of Pendennis. Night fell before he could leave, so he supped and would sleep with us. Hannibal Vivian had long been a friend of Lady Killigrew and was always very gallant towards her.

She had been so long dying that there seemed something uncanny in her appearance tonight, as if a ghost supped with us. Yet, emaciated and haggard as she was, and huddled in a great white cloak, she could temporarily breathe—and a very mordant breath it was.

We ate a Banbury cheese towards the end of supper; it was one that Vivian himself had brought; and he said he had carried a similar one up to the castle, where it had been well received.

"So it would be," said Lady Killigrew. "They lack up there all the refinements of life and ride roughshod over our rights and privileges."

Parson Merther said: "I don't know if it has been noticed but the rough soldiers passing our gate tower this forenoon flung mud all across our coat of arms. It stuck and dried but has not fallen off. I would have gone out to report them but knew my mission useless."

"I'll go up in the morning," said John. "It's intolerable that we should be so insulted!"

Lady Killigrew said: "It may be that the soldiers were saluting the disgrace that has come on our house. We should not quarrel with them for expressing what we all know!"

"Oh, come, my lady," said Mr Vivian. "It is not so bad as that. We all suffer misfortune from time to time. In the end the strong and steadfast will prevail."

Lady Killigrew took a trembling gulp of canary. "Strong and steadfast, Mr Vivian? These are commodities which do not exist in the Killigrew family. Or have not among the men in the fifty years I have

THE GROVE OF EAGLES

known them. Strong it may be in seeking their own pleasure, steadfast perhaps in ignoring all else. Well . . . this is where it has led us!"

"Your son has been unfortunate, madam. . . ." Mr Vivian began to
mutter polite excuses, but his voice was swept away in the flood of
the old woman's bitterness.

"All is lost now—yet it has not been lost by too strict adherence to
a set of principles. Oh, no. Oh, dear no. Some great families have
risen and fallen for a *cause*. The only cause we have held to has
been self interest and we have fallen just the same, but the more
ignobly because of it. I tell you there has never been a Killigrew who
has not been willing to trim his sails to the latest breeze, to turn his
coat if another were more in favour. . . . But for all, it has done us
no good. No good at all. There is a weak, self-indulgent streak in us,
my friend, and not my blood, nor little Dorothy's, nor that termagant
who has just left the room, can stiffen it to fight or die for any principles at all—not religion, not family, not Queen, not country!"

An embarrassed silence fell. She hunched her cloak against the cold
airs and looked like an old white cormorant waiting for the fish to
rise.

"Mary, I think you will upset yourself," said old Mistress Wolverstone. "You should retire to bed."

"Retire? I will retire to my grave soon enough to rest beside my
husband, who was perhaps the best of a poor litter. Not that his
brothers haven't done better than he did. They have stuck close to
the Queen and forever said: 'Yes, Your Majesty.' 'No, Your Majesty,'
and run at her beck and call. So they have big houses in London
and are excused their debts."

"Ah, perhaps soon she will forbear towards your son, ma'am. No
doubt she has been ill-advised—"

"Killigrew," said my grandmother broodingly. "Know you what the
name means, Mr Vivian? The Grove of Eagles. A two-headed eagle
is our crest. Where are the eagles, I ask you! My son has bred as
fertile as a parson, but I see no eagles among his brood. This bastard
of his has more spread of wing than any of the true ones."

It might have been appropriate to thank her for this compliment
had she not been looking at me with such obvious dislike.

I said: "I think you expect too much too soon, grandmother. Because I am not true born I have had more liberty. Give them time."

"Time is a commodity in which I am getting low. Deeds are of
today. Promises are as fickle as next year's harvest." She crooked a
finger like a talon at the parson down the table. "Merther, I will go
up now. Give me your hand. . . ."

When she had gone and the others had risen I walked out on my own for a breath of air before bed.

An unfair estimate, that of an old and sick woman whose temperament for years had leaned towards the melancholic. Killigrews had fought for the Lancastrian cause; they had had difficult times under Mary and one at least had lived in exile during her reign. Yet there was a ring of truth about a part of her accusation. Most of them lived on the surface of life, like fish snapping at passing flies. And when they got hooked they were deeply injured men, harshly done to by the world.

Illegitimacy had not saved me from this prevailing flaw.

On the steps below the gate tower leading to our quay a man was fishing. It was Dick Stable. I sat with him for a while. It was a chill night but my cloak was proof against the light easterly wind. Dick had caught five mackerel and an eel. He told me he and Meg were thinking of looking for something in Penryn. There was a vacancy in the granite quarries, and she might work on a farm near by.

"Quarry work is heavy work, Dick. Go slow on your decisions. Why must you leave here?"

"We may well get turned off, Master Maugan. We b'lieve the new Mrs Killigrew have no taking for the old servants; she d' want new ones like the two she brought, see."

"It's not nice to feel you might go. Enough of my old friends have already left."

"Well, you be leavin' yourself, Master Maugan. There'll be few enough to care whether we stay or go."

I had no answer for that, so we sat a while in silence.

"You be leavin' to marry, I'm told?"

There had always been a slight constraint between us, ever since he had challenged me about Meg, and although they seemed happy enough now I fancied there were little glances of anxiety from Dick whenever he saw me talking to his wife.

"Yes. . . . Next month. Then for a while at least we shall live in London. It is Mistress Susanna Reskymer—Farnaby that was. She came here once. I don't suppose you will remember her."

"Oh, yes, but I rightly do! Twas the Christmas of all the festivities, when I was Lord of Misrule." He sighed. "Dear life, that seem a long time past! How many year? Yes, I remember Mistress Farnaby —slim she is, wi' black hair and bright eyes. I trust, sur, you'll be very 'appy."

"Thank you, Dick, I pray so."

He put his line down and gathered the mackerel together. They glinted in the faint starlight like serpentine rock.

"Yes, I remember, twas the July twelve month following that I seen Mistress Farnaby in Truro. Twas the day after you come back from Spain when we'd all give ee up for dead. She were that glad to know different; that's the last time I seen her. What year'd that be? 'Twould be '94. Dear life, tis nigh on four years I been married to Meg."

The boat which had brought Hannibal Vivian across was bobbing gently at the jetty below us. The water made little sibilant sounds like fish whispering.

I said: "You have your dates wrong there. It was July '94 when I came back."

"Yes, sur, that's what I said."

"Then it could not have been July 1594 when you saw Mistress Farnaby."

"Yes. Yes, twas. See. You come back on a Sunday eve. I mind it well. I been sharpening the scythes for the hay-making on the morrow. Then I went bed and twas Meg woke me to tell me you was in the 'all safe and sound. Then the next day twas wet again—you mind what a summer that was—so Thomas Rosewarne he says, go you into Truro along wi' Rose and get the axle pins for the old cart that broke down Saturday. So we went for the axle pins and in the end for a pile of other things the ladies wished for. When we come Truro the rain were lifting off a bit and I seen Mistress Farnaby stepping out o' that little mercer's there used to be alongside of the church. She were by herself, so, presumin' as you might say, I takes off me cap and tells her you come home safe and well the night afore!"

The last light went out in the fort across the river mouth. All the coastline opposite was black. A cloud had moved up and only a faintest glimmer showed on the water.

"What did she say?"

"Oh, she were fair pleased. Quite overcome at first. I mind well, she was that startled, like. Then she were fair joyful to 'ear you was back."

"Why didn't you tell me you'd met her?"

"Why, sur, I never thought. We was telling everyone!"

"Yes. I suppose you were." I got up. There were lights in the house behind me, but I did not count them. "I think you must have made a mistake, Dick."

"Please?"

"A mistake in identity. . . ." I licked my lips. "Or someone has made a mistake. Let us not talk about it any more."

CHAPTER 10

I WENT by river to Tolverne but she had just left for London. I did not see Thomas, who was out hunting.

Gertrude said: "She'll be sorry to have missed you, Maugan, but you did not say you were coming, did you? I thought the understanding was that you were to meet in London."

"Yes. Yes it was."

"Is something wrong? Can I help in any way?"

"No. . . . No, nothing's wrong, Gertrude, thank you. I just—came to see her."

"Maugan, dear, I'm very happy for you both. She told me in confidence before she left."

"Oh, she told you."

"Yes. Should she not have?"

"No. . . . But I thought she might not have."

"You know—did you know?—that Thomas also asked her to marry him."

"Yes."

"I'm glad she chose as she did. But I don't think there was any doubt, was there."

"Who can say? Thomas has property and an assured position."

"Oh, I think he'll do big things; but he has not made an ideal brother-in-law and I would not wish to be his wife."

"What shall you do now, Gertrude?"

"Stay here with Lady Arundell and Elizabeth until the spring. Then I shall go home for the summer. After that. . . ." She shrugged.

"You'll marry again, no doubt."

"Oh . . . perhaps, some day. Marriage is such a lottery, Maugan."

"Yes," I said.

At Arwenack preparations now to leave quickly while there was still no room for second thoughts. To leave before the clash occurred between Jane and Lady Killigrew, before more creditors came with more legal sanctions, before the dogs were drowned. I was ready by the tenth but Odelia delayed and it was the thirteenth before we left.

I was glad of the preoccupation of having Odelia to look after. In leaving home she seemed as cool as the easterly wind that blew, but later in the day I saw tears on her cheeks. So at Totnes I spent an extra day with the Billingsleys in order that she should not feel too strange with them.

Thence to Sherborne no company but my own, no thoughts but my own. Grey thoughts they were, with a thread of scarlet.

I had come to see Sir Walter, but he was in London on some committee in Parliament. I supped and slept there, uncomfortable in answering Elizabeth Ralegh's questions. George Chapman was there and Carew Ralegh and Lawrence Keymis. Keymis told me that although his voyage to Guiana in '96 had not yielded what he had hoped, he now had better information as to the whereabouts of the great city of Manoa and Lake Parima with its extensive gold mines. Unfortunately, now that Sir Walter had been reappointed to his old position as Captain of the Queen's Guard, it seemed unlikely at present that he would be able to get away. It was even possible that Sir Walter might be appointed Lord Deputy of Ireland in succession to Lord Borough.

This is the man, I thought, Sue will not let me follow because he is a waning star. (Or one of such magnitude that hers is outshone?)

I stayed with my uncle Sir Henry, and the first morning went to see my father. He was still in the same cell though his companions had changed; he was thinner and his clothes were torn and infested with vermin; his hair and moustache had not been cut; he stank foully. He complained bitterly of his treatment and the closeness of his confinement. The cold and cough he had brought with him from Cornwall was still troubling him and he was convinced he was developing his mother's asthma. He had written to the Queen and six times to Cecil but so far without response.

The faithful Rosewarne came each day bringing a few pence and perhaps an item or two of food; but Mr Killigrew was bitter that his two sons Thomas and Henry had only been to see him twice since November.

He eagerly read the letter that I brought from his wife and expressed a sudden desire to see her again. Could it not be arranged that Mrs Killigrew should come to London?

Before I left I saw Thomas Rosewarne and tried to understand and help unravel the tangled skein of my father's financial affairs. Rosewarne had drawn up an account of his present position, but all was now so involved with cross claims and petitions that I could see no way out of it all. His largest creditor after the Queen was Henry Lok the mercer who had advanced Mr Killigrew several thousand pounds on the flimsiest security. Now Henry Lok had himself been attached by other creditors for having underwritten bonds issued by Mr Killigrew. Lok, for his part, was petitioning for some land in Devonshire belonging to my father which the Queen had now seized, and a Nicholas Athol was cross-petitioning and applying for a lease. Other land and property was the subject of suits in the Court of Wards. In all it seemed likely that my father's true indebtedness would be upwards of twenty thousand pounds.

Years after—so many that it is hard to think of them all—I came across some old papers of that time; among them letters of my father to Sir Robert Cecil complaining grievously of his treatment; and one from my step-mother to Mr Killigrew written in April of that year. Since then through many vicissitudes I have kept this letter by me, wrinkled and yellow with age and stained and almost falling apart.

Dear Husband,
  I received your letters by Thomas Rosewarne, wherein you spoke of your want of money. Sorry indeed I am, but help you more I cannot. I have sent to your tenants according to your directions, but none will come near me, neither do I know by what means to get you any money. For I have passed all that I ever had or can make shift for. Good Mr Killigrew, know how poor you left me.
  But nevertheless I have taken order by this bearer that you shall receive ten pounds. My extremities are many, but I will use the best means I may and send you what I can glean. I have written to you of all your business, and now, as for my coming, I am not able because of my greatness with child; therefore I must content myself with my misfortunes. I pray for your early release.
  From Arwenack, 18th April, 1598.
                                        Dorothy Kylygreue.

Old letters always have a pathos; seeing these after so many years brings back that time with poignancy. Perhaps not so much for my father whose fate was not exceeded by his deserts, but for poor Dorothy Killigrew and for all that time of youth and striving and the stress of a life now gone for ever.

I had Sue's address in Pancras but at first could not bring myself to go. I spent most of each day with Thomas, who had found other lute players to his taste, and often they would meet in the upper room of an inn and talk and play together. I went with him there and closed my mind.

After a week I addressed a letter to Mistress Amelia Reskymer, asking if I might call. I felt this the moment for formality. Then at last I waited on Lord Henry Howard.

He received me in the same room as before. With him was another man, younger but pale and thin with a long face and narrow clever mouth turning down to meet declivities in the shaven cheeks. No page boy with a lute, but the room was again heavy with scent.

"Ah," said Lord Henry, "this is the young Killigrew I spoke of. I think I may come to employ him."

"Why?" said the other, and began to polish his nails. He wore soft Spanish leather boots and more jewels on his hands than the Queen.

"Why?" said Lord Henry, seeming a trifle nonplussed by the inquiry.

"Yes. I always believe in asking myself that question. It sharpens the reason. . . . Killigrew. We may be distantly related. My formidable but saintly mother is the sister of Sir Henry Killigrew's first wife."

"Indeed, sir." For a moment I had looked into pale hazel eyes quite like a snake's. Not unfriendly, not unlively, but slightly unhuman.

"Why may I employ him?" said Lord Henry. "Because he has a knowledge of Spanish and war and diplomacy. And he has a sharp and ready wit."

"Wit Lord Henry says you have. Is that true?"

"I don't know, sir."

"Wit, Killigrew, is like a surgeon's knife: it cuts away ill-humors, but a shade heavy handed and the patient bleeds to death."

Lord Henry chuckled and offered snuff; the other refused. "I believe," said Lord Henry, "that I took some fancy to employ this young man because I detect in him qualities I find in myself. I had your letter, Killigrew. I take it you can attend on me if need be from now on?"

"Yes, my lord. I have some business to see to but that can be adjusted to your demands."

"Well, leave your address. You have rooms?"

"I am staying with my uncle this month but I shall be seeking other accommodation as I am shortly to be married."

The younger man winced fastidiously.

Lord Henry said: "Does the word offend you, Francis?"

"Only in retrospect, my dear friend. Last year as you know, by a margin as narrow as a bootlace, I missed that El Dorado of all men's dreams. Since then regret and relief have walked constantly beside me, the first by day and the second by night. . . . *Dolor decrescit ubi quo crescat non habet.*"

Lord Henry snickered. "I had not thought you so full of sentiment."

"Well, marriage would have cured my greatest illness, which is a deep consumption of the purse." The snake eyes glanced a second time at me, not to see if I was amused but to search suddenly into my brain and thoughts. "But, then, I have resolved not to regret, for the sting and remorse of a mind accusing itself of failure doubles all adversity. Even penury has its compensations."

"My lord," I said, "I'll not intrude further. Will you give me a time to wait on you, or will you send a message to Lothbury?"

"Monday," said Lord Henry. "Next Monday there is an opportunity to write some letters for me. After that daily unless warned otherwise. Pull the cord beside you. Claude will see you out."

As I went down the stairs in the company of the insolent Claude I said: "He who was with Lord Henry. May I ask his name?"

"Mr Bacon. A member of Parliament and a lawyer." The boy gave his hair a toss in a way I have only seen women do before. "If you come to this house you will see him much. Are you coming to this house?"

"Daily I think."

"For what purpose?"

"That has to be decided."

"Oh, among the secrets, eh? There are all manner of secrets here, but one by one I split them open. It's a hobby I have."

"I wish you fortune," I said as I left.

At home was a letter.

My beloved,

I send this by your returning messenger so that no more time be lost. My sister-in-law asks me to invite you for tomorrow at ten in the morning. If we do not hear to the contrary we shall expect you. I long to see you.

All my love,

Sue.

Pancras is a hamlet about three miles from London and straddles the road to Northampton where it runs beside the Fleet Ditch. Miss Reskymer owned a farm and was a small active person unlike her brother. She greeted me and then discreetly left me alone with Sue.

Well, the desire for a woman is not altered by one's suspicions of a kind of betrayal, by discoveries about her character, by reservations as to the sort of marriage one may be going into. Desire for a particular woman is a fundamental physical sensation, born of one's animal nature, and so—the Puritans would tell us—to be despised; but it is no less potent for that, no less alluring for that. After I had kissed her I looked at her closely thinking, why these eyes?—I have seen more beautiful, though none brighter—why these lips?—Mariana's were fuller, Meg's more innocent—why this hair, lank and uncurling; the bone structure of cheek and neck?—there are better. But to me these are infinitely, carnally desirable. If men are admired for risking their lives for a woman, why should they not risk the imponderables of principle and conscience?

"You were delayed, Maugan? I expected you last week."

"Yes. There was some delay. . . ."

"You have seen Lord Henry Howard?"

"Yes. It is all arranged."

"I—with waiting so long and nothing to do I have been looking at rooms in London. There's a very pleasant apartment in Great Carter Lane by St Paul's Churchyard. It's more costly than I had thought of, but everything in London is so. It would be in the heart of things but perhaps noisy. Could we see it together?"

"Yes . . . we can do that."

"I have had the banns called two weeks in St Pancras in the Fields. Next Sunday will be the third. Did I do right?"

"Of course."

"You've the certificate from Mr Garrock? You had the banns called at Budock?"

"Yes."

"You're very quiet. Is anything amiss?"

"No, nothing at all."

"Let us sit down and talk of the arrangements, then. I shall be married from here. Amelia's cousin Robert will give me away. Do you think your brothers would escort me to the church?"

"I think they would."

"Maugan, it was you who made it a condition that the wedding should be in early February. I hope I don't hasten it unduly or seem unwomanly to you in my arrangements?"

"No. No, not at all."

So we talked on for a half hour. Gradually as this proceeded, our conversation melted the ice which for three weeks had been round my heart. I began to make plans with a new interest. Whatever else, I thought, she will be my wife. God in heaven, what more do I demand?

She was talking on, making more light conversation than I had ever known her do before. "Did you come by the Fields? Yes, then you'd cross Battle Bridge. It's where Boadicea fought the Romans. . . . The conduit runs for two thousand yards to Snow Hill. All these fields abound in springs. . . . Maugan, I think you're not listening."

"Oh, yes I am, I assure you. Sue. . . ." It had to come.

"Yes?"

"All that time you were married to Philip Reskymer—I mean before we met at the landing of the Spanish at Mousehole—it was nearly a year after I came home; did you never hear that I was alive?"

She looked at me with slightly narrowed eyes. "What makes you ask that now?"

"Well, I've often thought—when we met that day outside the burning church, you looked as if you'd seen a ghost. Yet we only lived—what?—thirty miles apart. Did you hear nothing of my return at all?"

There was a grinding grumble of cart wheels in the lane outside. "My dear, it was not necessary that I should still think you dead to act as if I'd seen a ghost. It was the first time we'd *met*. How do you suppose I felt? I'm not made of stone."

"Then when did you first know I was alive?"

"What's wrong, Maugan? Why is this important to you now?"

I looked down into the crevasse I had approached and sheered away from it. "Sometimes one wonders these things. You did not write."

"You did not write to me. And I felt that by my marriage I'd forfeited any claim on your love."

"It doesn't—happen that way."

"I'm glad. I hope you are."

"Yes. . . ."

Silence fell between us. The man outside was calling to his horses.

She said: "I heard first from my aunt. When I went to call on her about two months after my marriage she told me you'd come to see me."

"Oh . . . I thought you might have heard earlier than that. D'you remember Dick Stable?"

"No."

"He was Lord of Misrule during the twelve days of Christmas."

"Oh, yes. A tall thin boy with a big nose."

"Yes. He said he met you in Truro one day and told you about my return. He said that was soon after I got back."

"It couldn't have been. I wasn't in Truro for several months after my marriage." She leant and stirred the charcoal dying in the grate. "But what is the point of this? You haven't told me. Is it of any value to go over any of that sad time? Aren't we alive and well and in love? What else is of importance?"

"It has some importance, Sue. Do you remember meeting Dick?"

She frowned into the fire. "Yes. . . . But it was later—after Christmas. March, I think. Yes, it would be March. I went with Philip to call on the Robartes; we spent a night there. I bought some gloves one morning and Dick—what is it?—Stable was passing with another man. He recognised me and I stopped and spoke. He told me you were safely home. Perhaps I may have seemed startled to him, but—but every mention of your name at that time was like a knell in my

ears. I couldn't bear to hear you spoken of, to think what I had done."
She looked up through fringed lashes. "Does that please you? Are
you satisfied now, or have I to sit in the pillory and be stoned?"

"No, my love. No one will throw stones." As she straightened up
I put my arms under her arms and kissed her. These were the lips.

March was the month when Dick had been dangerously ill with
the wound in the head after being set on in Penryn.

One of them was wrong. Which, perhaps, I should never know.

CHAPTER 11

DURING the next two weeks I saw her only twice. Something kept
me away, and she did not press. We saw and took the apartment in
Great Carter Lane. It was a good district and the rooms were well
appointed. They were better than I would ever have expected, but
she would not say what they cost; she said the twelve months' lease
must be regarded as a wedding present.

I went a dozen times to Henry Howard's, and the work seemed
without special portent. The letters I wrote in Spanish dealt with
matters of commerce which seemed quite innocent. If they were in
a code I could not detect it.

I wondered if Lord Henry in one sentence had not summed up the
whole reason of my distaste for him. He said he had taken a fancy to
employ me because he detected in me qualities he found in himself.
Underneath ordinary reason—which vehemently rejected any similarity—the likenesses might be there. Not fortunately in any ambiva-
lence towards sex on my part, but in the old ductile qualities of the
Killigrews. The two-headed eagle again.

I had had contact with Spain; I had had contact with Catholicism;
and neither had left me as single-minded as before. Nor had the
compromises left me unchanged. Nor would the one I was going to
make in respect of Sue.

I went about town with Thomas. We sat and drank in the taverns
and ale houses, sampling the ales, the Gascoigne wines, the Malmsey,
the sack, and eating the soft saffron cakes sweetened with raisins.
Sometimes, for the first time in my life, I got drunk and Thomas had
to help me home. We went to the menagerie near the Tower and
saw the lions and the tiger, the lynx, the porcupine, the eagle. We
visited the bear pits and saw the great brown bears baited, four dogs
to a bear and the dogs often getting the worst of it. We saw a half-

dozen men hanged at Bridewell, one for rape, one for murder, one for stealing a hat valued at two shillings. They were sat each one in turn in a cart with a rope round their necks and the cart driven away; then their friends pulled on their twitching legs to help them die the quicker.

So time passed and our wedding day drew near. It was to be February 9.

We were to be married at noon. I was up at dawn, and for once Thomas was in his element. He liked dressing in fine clothes, he loved music, and he loved ceremonial when he was not the centre of the ceremony. In these weeks in London we had accorded better than ever at home where he had been overshadowed by John and Belemus, and I was touched when after breaking our fast he gave me a bunch of rosemary tied with yellow ribbons which I was to wear through the ceremony. Rosemary, representing the manly qualities, was a customary gift, but I had not thought of it.

Since I came to London I had had a wedding ring made, an enamelled hoop with small diamonds surrounding the Killigrew double-headed eagle. Sir Henry had lent me the money for these necessary expenses, but he could not be at the wedding because he was attending on the Queen who was that morning moving to Greenwich. Lady Jael was to come, and also my Uncle Simon who, to my surprise, seemed sufficiently interested to wish me well, and his son Stephen was to be my bridegroom man.

I went to take my leave of Sir Henry about eight. He smiled on seeing me and said:

"Well, Maugan, this is a happy day for you—and a fine one. All is in order?"

"All is in order, thanks to you, sir."

"I wish I could remember your bride. You say we met some years ago?"

"Yes. But now, living where we shall be living. . . ."

"Of course. . . . And how is your work for Lord Henry? Well enough?"

"Well enough."

"It could be a good attachment, Lord Henry himself being attached to the Earl of Essex, and Essex riding high. Since he was made Earl Marshal of England six weeks ago my lord of Essex is back in the best of spirits." My great-uncle frowned. "I wish I knew. . . ."

"Knew what, sir?"

"The mind of the Queen. Lord Essex is now almost in a position to dominate her. Slowly she has given ground—slowly he has won it. Often in such cases the brilliant young man seems to hold complete sway over the ageing woman. . . . And yet, *no one*, no man or woman on earth has ever dominated the Queen since she came to the throne forty years ago. She has such inborn greatness that if he is not careful he'll ride himself to ruin. . . . In that case have a care you're not involved in the fall."

"Lord Henry is also very close with Sir Robert Cecil these days. He has written a letter to him every day this week."

Sir Henry tied the points of his doublet. "On what, may I ask?"

"I think, sir, if I am employed by him I must keep his counsel."

"Yes . . . yes, that's true. I should not have asked you."

"Much is to do with Scotland. I can only tell you that."

"Affairs in Scotland?"

"Affairs in Scotland. Nothing of apparent consequence."

"What is or is not of consequence depends on the writer and the reader, Maugan. With the Queen in her sixties we all walk a rope drawn across a chasm. She is much racked with rheumatism and with headaches. Any day anything may happen."

"I pray it will not."

"All men pray it will not."

Sir Henry straightened his paned velvet hose over his thin shanks. "But it's not for you to be concerned with that now, Maugan. This is your wedding day. . . . I remember well when your father—it only seems yesterday—came first to Court as young and as eager as you. *His* father, my elder brother, brought him up, and we all thought him a handsome young man. Our Queen was then in her thirties, and some hoped he would catch her eye and be advanced, as Leicester and Ralegh and Essex have been. But it did not happen. Perhaps he lacked the stature. . . ."

I said: "Did you ever know my mother?"

"What?" Sir Henry scratched his beard. "What? Your mother? Well, yes, I did."

I stared at him. The question had been put casually, without any expectation of this answer.

He said: "I think I was the only one who met her in our family. Your father—as happens with handsome and well-bred young men new to court life—had a number of interesting affairs. None of them was serious, and your grandfather and grandmother, having regard to their great debts, were making inquiries to see what suitable heiress he might be betrothed to. Then he met your mother, and, it seemed, fell in love with her. She was a Londoner of no distinction of family but some personal charm, and I believe your father even contemplated marriage. However, this was forbidden—particularly by your grandmother, whom you will still know as a woman of forceful character—and the attachment was broken off. I really believe," Sir Henry finished dryly, "that it is the only time in his life your father was in love with somebody other than himself."

"What was her name?"

"Maugan, the same as yours. You were given her surname as your first name. The plague was rampant soon after you were born—it had lingered on as it sometimes does from the previous year—and all the Maugan family fell ill with it. Much against the wishes of his parents, your father went down to the Thames side where they lived and took you away. He hired a wet-nurse and bore you down to Cornwall. Lady Killigrew was vastly annoyed, for this was just at the time when a betrothal party had been arranged at Arwenack for the Moncks, whose daughter your father married later that year." Sir Henry smiled as he tucked a handkerchief into his pocket. "During the celebrations attending the betrothal you were kept in the kitchen and passed off as the son of Sarah Amble who was then caring for you. But I believe that Dorothy Monck, after her marriage, never took exception to your presence; indeed, you could hardly have had a more affectionate step-mother."

"I could not. What was my mother like?"

"To look at? Tall, a trifle big boned for a woman. Blue-eyed; dark-haired. You take after her somewhat. I met her only once but was impressed by her appearance."

"Do you know where she is buried?"

"No, I have no idea. She did not die then, and I suppose might still be alive—she would scarcely be forty yet."

"She didn't die? But—"

"She recovered from the fever but her father died. He was a herbalist called William Maugan who lived near Hermitage Stairs. Katherine Maugan carried on his business for some years, and became well known for her cures; then she got into trouble with one of the guilds and left London."

Sir Henry picked up his stick. "I did hear she went into the west country; but that was years ago. Women who ply that trade sometimes arouse suspicion of witchcraft and the like; I trust she came to some peaceful haven, for she was a worthy woman."

It was a good day for February, with a north-west breeze and the white clouds high in a sky of starched blue. I went by horse, and Lady Jael and Uncle Simon and Philip Killigrew followed in her coach. We left London by Ludgate and crossed the Fleet Bridge, with its pikes set into the stone and its stone lanthorns ready to be lit for travellers on winter evenings. The fields were just losing their morning frost. Sheep were pasturing in groups. Two windmills were clack-clacking beside a stream. My wedding day.

The worthy son of a worthy woman.

Sue was wearing a gown of russet, I remember that well, though I do not recall a great deal of the ceremony. I think I must have been at the church first, because I remember standing at the church door and seeing her come in from the lych gate, with Thomas on her right hand and Henry on her left, and a cousin by marriage, Dorothy Reskymer, as a bridesmaid, following with Mr Robert Reskymer, who was to give her away. Sue was wearing her hair braided, not down over her shoulders as she would have if she had not been married before. Round her head she wore a circlet of gold, and the gown was of finest home-spun silk. On the gown were stitched the usual favours, of milk white, flame colour, blue and red. Gold colours were never used because they signified avarice. Had she worn these at her first marriage? Flesh colours were also eschewed for they signified lasciviousness. I should have worn that instead of rosemary. She looked as desirable to me as the scarlet woman.

More people than I had expected. Some bystanders, but some friends. The effeminate Claude from Lord Henry Howard's, a half-dozen tavern friends of Thomas's, Mistress Amelia Reskymer, a cousin Killigrew who had come with young Henry, our faithful steward, Thomas Rosewarne.

Sue smiled at me, and I do not think I returned the smile. In spirit another woman was beside us, holding my hand, peering into my face.

The parson standing at the door said some words, and in some words I had learned I responded. He led the way into the church. A hand was in mine, gloved, fine boned, the hand of a lady. It held to mine with a discreet pressure and then we separated again. There was music in the church. We walked up it, she in advance with my two brothers and Dorothy Reskymer, I following with Philip Killigrew. "Saffron for measles; marjoram and aniseed; comfrey and liquorice. . . ."

We were kneeling then at the altar, the slim frail dark-haired scheming girl who was in process of becoming my wife. I turned my head and looked at her. I seemed to see quite clearly—and quite cynically—her cool, fine-boned body lying naked beside me in the bed at Trewoofe. I saw her pale drowned face with the lank black hair lying on the pillow like seaweed. I saw the tiny beads of sweat on her lip, felt her lashes moving on my cheek. All that was going to come again.

"Love and hate. There is always love and hate between every man and woman. You will learn that it is so."

"I require and charge you that if either of you do know of any inpediment why you may not be lawfully joined together in matrimony, that you confess it. For be you well assured that so many as be coupled together otherwise than God's word doth allow, are not joined of God, neither is their matrimony lawful."

The church smelt of mildew and dust, but sometimes a waft of scent would carry from the girl beside me. The sun was falling through a stained-glass window behind the parson, and the light, a vivid red and blue, stained the marble floor and the edge of his vestment. I had carried Victor Hardwicke bleeding down such steps. "Take care for yourself," she had said once, meeting me on the stairs. "I told you there was blood on your hands."

"Wilt thou have this man to thy wedded husband, to live together after God's ordinance in the holy estate of matrimony? Wilt thou obey him and serve him, love, honour and keep him in sickness and in health? And forsaking all other keep thee only to him so long as you both shall live?"

"I will."

Sue, I saw, was standing now. What had once been said to me about—

"Get up," whispered Philip Killigrew behind me. I stood up, feeling my hands and knees stiff and aching, as if emotion, knowing no other exit, had turned to poison and run through my body. "The ring," he said.

I fumbled and found the ring and almost dropped it. She had taken off her gloves. The hand I took was warm and calm and feminine and thin and beautiful.

"With this ring I thee wed," I said. "This gold and silver I thee give. With my body I thee worship and with all my worldly goods I thee endow." I placed the ring on her thumb. "In the name of the Father." I moved it to her first finger. "And of the Son." I looked at her now and she was looking at me, eyes glinting in the coloured light, black fringe held under the gold circlet, finely modelled nose, high cheek bones, lips, reddened with madder, slightly parted and smiling. In her eyes I seemed to see all my past. I moved the ring to the second finger. "And of the Holy Ghost." This was the moment to walk out, to dash the ring on the stone steps, to begin a life entirely of my own creating, building on what I now knew of my ancestry, my mistakes. Above all on my mistakes. Mistakes in perception of the character of the only two women for whom I would ever care.

Yet if I did that now, knowing the impossibility of retreating through time, did I not flee from the destiny of my own making? Of my own choosing?

I moved the ring to her third finger and slipped it on. "Amen."

We took communion. Then, while still at the altar steps, friends were around us, plucking at the favours from Sue's dress. Smiling she unpinned them one by one.

In a haze I was drinking muscatel from the shallow mazer bowl which she had passed me. I handed it on to Philip Killigrew and took a piece of the cake.

Everyone was talking and chattering, moving around us and wishing us well. The music began again, from the lutes which Thomas's friends had brought. By chance they were playing the tune that Victor Hardwicke had played so often in the prison in Lagos.

> *Weep not, my wanton, smile upon my knee;*
> *When thou art old there's grief enough for thee.*

THE END

POSTSCRIPT FOR PURISTS

THIS has been a novel primarily about the Killigrews, a not unimportant Cornish family whose history appears and disappears tantalisingly among the records of the time. Sometimes the bare facts of their existence are recorded, sometimes the facts are richly and revealingly clothed, sometimes there are frustrating and impenetrable silences.

Bibliographies in the historical novel are pretentious—it cannot matter to the reader, or should not, whether a novelist has read thirty or three hundred books on a subject—but perhaps I ought to say that in research for this book I have wherever possible gone back to original sources, and I have not wantonly distorted the known facts.

I have taken some small licence with the age of one or two of John Killigrew's children, though not more than a year or so. Because there were so many Elizabeths at the time I have called his eldest daughter Odelia and slipped Elizabeth in where Odelia should really be. For the same reason I have called Sir John Arundell of Tolverne Sir Anthony, and John, his eldest son, Jonathan. At this time almost every eldest son was John.

For the misdemeanours of the Killigrews I have relied on the *Lansdowne MS*, the *Salisbury MS*, the *Acts of the Privy Council*, etc., not on Hals, who was wrong as to this family in several respects, nor on the so-called *Killigrew MS*, which was not written until 1737. The only reliable modern summary of all this—except for scattered if illuminating references to them in A. L. Rowse's books—is in D. Matthew's contribution to the *English Historical Review* for July 1924.

The account of the kidnapping of John Killigrew's base son by Captain Richard Burley and a Portuguese freebooter, and his being placed as a page at the Spanish court is to be found in a report in the *Calendar of State Papers* for February 1596.

Blavet, in Brittany, frequently mentioned in these pages, was Port-Louis opposite the modern port of Lorient. Throughout the book I have used the modern calendar.

In the Spanish landing at Mousehole the only liberty I have taken is that John Tremearne was incumbent of Paul at this time; he did not come to the parish afterwards, as in this book. Otherwise I have kept to the contemporary reports in the *Salisbury MS* and elsewhere and to the almost contemporary Carew—father of Gertrude—who got it direct from Sir Francis Godolphin.

That Ralegh's sudden warm reconciliation with Essex at the end of 1595 came about through the marriage of his close friend Northumberland to Essex's sister, has not before been put forward, but it would seem to have the justification of probability.

There are a number of eye-witness reports of the raid on Cadiz, most famous, no doubt, Ralegh's own. But in the main I have relied on an unpublished manuscript in the Lambeth Palace Library, probably written by someone on Ralegh's flagship; and it is on this manuscript that I have depended for the account of Ralegh's adventure the night before the battle—an adventure which, at least in detail, seems to have escaped his numerous biographers—and also for the story of the loss of the *Peter of Anchusen*. The treasure fleet at Cadiz was in fact not burned until twenty-four hours later than stated in this book.

The extent to which John Killigrew became committed to the Spanish cause is perhaps arguable, but the evidence which exists does seem to me conclusive. Not only Facy's report on William Love's statement, mentioned in the novel, but many other reports of a like nature which filtered in at the end of 1597 and continued to do so through much of the following year. William Astell's testimony, February 22, 1598, was that it was rumoured at the Groyne (Coruña) that John Killigrew had been executed for treason. Peter Scoble reported May 5, 1598, that while a prisoner of the Spaniards he was constantly questioned as to whether John Killigrew had been put to death or was in prison. But the conclusive testimony comes from the Spanish side— hints and references in various letters—and perhaps most of all in the order issued by the Adelantado that those at Falmouth were to be well used during the landing, all others put to the sword.

I have no evidence that Ralegh spoke up for John Killigrew when he was brought to London to answer for his behaviour, but it is not out of keeping with his character that he should have done so.

For details of the Second Spanish Armada—technically it should be the third if one counts the abortive sailing of the previous year—I have gone, apart from English sources, of which perhaps the most informed is Ralegh's despatch of late October 1597, to the *Calendar of State Papers (Spanish)*, the *Calendar of State Papers (Venetian)*, the Adelantado's own despatches, letters from Father Sicilia, S.J., De Soto's letters, and the King's letters to various of his commanders at that time. I have strayed from fact in making De Soto secretary to the Adelantado as early as 1594—he was officially appointed in May 1597—but he worked behind the scenes for long enough, and this seemed a useful simplification. The profound secrecy attaching to the destination of this Armada has not been exaggerated; the only ones likely to have known anything of it before the sealed orders were opened, were the King himself, Don Juan de Idiaquez, Don Cristoval de Moura, and the two secretaries, De Ibarra and De Prada. (See the contemporary report by Vendramino; Alberi's *Relazioni degli Ambasciatori Veneti*, vol. 13; and Gregorio Leti's *Vita del Catolico Re Filippo II*, Cologne, 1679.)

As for the future of these people. John Killigrew survived until 1605, in prison—or sometimes, when the Privy Council relented, out of it, in company with a gaoler to see to his chaotic affairs. The mystery of Jane Fermor's dowry has never been cleared up, but the one reasonably well-grounded account is that the whole dowry came with her on her wedding day and was buried secretly by her two servants at Gyllyngvase—in the Arwenack grounds about a mile from the house —where she contrived to have access to it in time of need while denying it to her husband and her father-in-law. John Killigrew, her husband, in a career of many vicissitudes—including a decade-long battle to divorce his wife—obtained from James permission to found the town of Falmouth; and his brother Peter, walking a successful tight-rope between King and Parliament, procured a charter for it in 1661.

Jack Arundell of Trerice became Sir John Arundell and was governor of Pendennis Castle in 1646 when with a tiny garrison it held out against Fairfax for five months, being the last place in England to fly the royal standard for Charles. Thomas Arundell married his Bridget Mohun, sold Tolverne, and moved to London. He was knighted at Greenwich in 1603, inherited Truthall from his uncle and, after losing money in an unwise speculation, returned to Cornwall and made his new home there. Gertrude Arundell (*née* Carew) soon remarried. Her second husband was William Carey of Clovelly, brother of Jack Arundell's wife.

Lord Henry Howard was of course one of the principal movers behind Cecil in bringing King James smoothly to the throne. He was also largely responsible for poisoning James's mind against Ralegh and was a judge at Ralegh's trial in 1603. During James's lifetime undeserved honours were heaped upon this man.

Finally perhaps I should say that I have attributed to Maugan certain characteristics of one, Robert Killigrew, who became a close personal friend of Ralegh's, who was highly skilled in the mixing of medicines and herbal remedies, and who was later innocently involved in the murder of Sir Thomas Overbury. But that is—or some day may be—another story.